THE BEST SHE COULD HOPE FOR

He shook his head. "I want you to remain here."

"And what *I* want is to come with you." Marian smiled. "Men go, and men *do*," she said. "Women wait. Women wait, and worry—"

As a man he answered, "There is no need to worry."

She pointed to the moon. "Tell it not to rise."

He sighed. "Marian . . ."

"I will dress myself in the colors of the forest, and hide myself . . ."

"Do you want my attention diminished? My concentration divided? I would be but half a man facing the sheriff's Normans." His voice was soft. "You would be the death of me."

"Who suffers more then?" she asked. "The woman here, waiting, or the man there, fighting."

He reached out to her, touched her. "I know, Marian. But I refuse to risk you. Stay here at Locksley, stay where you are safe, so I may come back to you."

She had lost, and she knew it. She was her mother reborn, and every woman before and since who had lived to send a man into a danger that he would not share with her. *Not fair*, she thought bitterly. *In the name of preservation, men deny us the chance to live.*

But her hand reached out to his, fingers touching, then locking, and she knew the best she could hope for was to take what he gave her now, in the shadows beneath the moon.

JENNIFER ROBERSON

LADY OF THE FOREST

ZEBRA BOOKS
KENSINGTON PUBLISHING CORP.

ZEBRA BOOKS are published by

Kensington Publishing Corp.
475 Park Avenue South
New York, NY 10016

First Hardcover Printing: September, 1992
First Paperback Printing: September, 1993

Printed in the United States of America

For Mark

ACKNOWLEDGMENTS

Special appreciation must go to several people for a variety of functions and influences, most notably to my agent, Russell Galen, a man of patience, vision, and insight. To Betsy Wollheim, for generously and unselfishly allowing me the opportunity to stretch my wings; to Michael A. Stackpole, for research materials and conversation; to Gail Wolfenden-Steib, for information and sourcebooks on 12th-century fashions; and particular appreciation to Maryeileen McKersie, for continuity, comments, and support.

Additional thanks to Dr. Neil Kunze, history professor at Northern Arizona University, who has undoubtedly forgotten the journalism major who took his English history courses for the sheer love of it; to Ray Newton, journalist, who taught me much of what I know about writing, then encouraged me to do it *my* way; and to my editor, Ann LaFarge, for her enthusiasm and support.

Special appreciation to my grandfather, S.J. Hardy, and to my mother, Shera Hardy Roberson, whose love of books proved to be genetic; to Georgana Wolff Meiner, for being there at the beginning; also to the Thursday Morning Corgi Club, for helping to keep me sane.

Many other people contributed to this novel in ways both large and small, none so insignificant that I discount them as unimportant because, as any author can attest, even a single word dropped in passing can help shape a manuscript. To those who dropped the words, I thank you sincerely, even if I've forgotten the time, the place, the reason.

Lastly, heartfelt thanks to my husband, Mark O'Green, for help, hugs, faith—and understanding.

Then from among the dispossessed and banished arose the most famous freebooter Robin Hood, and little John with their accomplices, whom the foolish multitude are so extravagantly fond of celebrating in tragedy and comedy; and the ballads concerning whom, sung by the jesters and minstrels, delight them beyond all others.

—*entry for the year 1266 by Scottish chronicler Walter Bower, Abbot of Inchcolm, 1445*

Fethersage

Linsley Village

Sherwood

to Lincoln

Huntington Castle

Nottingham

Ravens Keep Manor

Croxden Abbey

N

danforth 92

to London

Prologue

Nottingham Castle
Late Spring—1194

Darkness. Silence. The weight of solitude: Each was a weapon meant to break her, to drive her into humiliation out of defiant self-possession; to goad her into surrender, into pleas for mercy, for compassion, for understanding.

Grimly she reflected, *But mostly into compliance, in bed and out of it.*

A sound destroyed the silence even as light banished darkness. The heavy door scraped open. "Marian."

She wanted to laugh. *Such a soft, seductive whisper—* But with the edge of a blade in the sound, issuing from a man long accustomed to being heard no matter how softly he whispered.

He brought the torch with him, unattended by liveried soldiers; what he wanted from her he wanted given—*or* taken—in the privacy of the chamber. *Capitulation?* she wondered. *Perhaps even retribution.* Or merely the opportunity to have what another man had.

The roaring of the torch swallowed the darkness and the world was alive again.

She lurched abruptly upright, squinting against the torchlight, then forced herself to relax. Her legs were tangled in heavy bedclothes, bound up by twisted skirts.

She knew what he saw: tangled black hair harboring bits of dungeon straw; a soiled, dishevelled kirtle smelling of horse and sweat and smoke; gritty blue eyes red-rimmed from tension and

11

lack of sleep. *I know very well what he sees.* What he wanted was as blatant, though he would say nothing of it. Not yet. He was a subtle man, she knew, and therefore all the more dangerous.

He held the torch aloft. Flame blazed in the darkness, setting the room alight. She stared, momentarily transfixed by fire, by the flare and gutter in the eternal dance, the courtship of air and flame. *"Marian."*

The room was bathed in shadow, courting the flame. As he walked the shadows walked, gliding across the floor, into cracks, into corners, running up the walls, quick and black and sly, like the rats she had left in the dungeon below.

Illumination glittered in the silver threading his curly dark hair, forming an eerie nimbus around his well-shaped head. An artist might choose to paint him. But *she* was disposed to believe he made a supremely unlikely angel.

He smiled, baring a blade-sharp line of square white teeth against the dark rim of his bottom lip as she rearranged her skirts to make certain her legs were covered. She refused to give him that. What he got from her would be stolen.

He carried the torch closer yet. Smoke teased the air, curling around his head. She looked through it to his eyes, brown by the light of day, now blackened by firelight.

For the third time he said her name, as if by keeping it in his mouth he possessed it, and her. But she refused to bow down before it, to show any sign of surrender or even acknowledgment. All she did was stare back steadfastly and defiantly, denying him the victory he desired so very much.

Flames transfigured hair from silvered brown to raven gold. Light overlay his face, dividing it precisely in half. One side was made flat, stark, without character, leeched of humanity; the other was cast into shadows that licked at eyes and nose, caressing his smiling mouth. Divided face. Divided soul. *Black and white,* she thought, *lacking all the grays.*

Legs now puddled in skirts and bedclothes, she sat against the wall. She was no longer in the dungeon, where she had made the acquaintanceship of rats, but in a bedchamber fully furnished and well-appointed; he was a refined man. A painted cloth hanging cut the chill of dark stone. But not enough. Not nearly enough. It did nothing to warm her blood.

"You have a choice," he told her. "You have always had a choice."

Marian wanted to laugh. Slowly, with unstudied grace, she put out her left hand to him. Palm down. And as, surprised, he reached out to touch it—thinking, she knew, that she meant him to—she snapped the wrist over and turned the palm up-right. His hand instantly retreated; she knew he regretted the motion already.

"Choice," she said softly, in her smoky, dark-toned voice. "Repent before the abbot, then take vows and become a nun—though I lack a true vocation."

He waited in silence, intent. The torch spilled smoke and flame.

She put out her other hand and snapped it over. Light bled briefly across the ragged edges of broken nails, the grime of harsh usage. "Choice," she said again. "Make vows and become your wife, though I lack a true vocation"—she smiled before he could speak—"or even a *trace* of desire."

The torch robbed his face of color. "What do I want of desire?" His tone was cool, divulging nothing. "With or without, I can have you."

"Unless the stake takes me first." She turned her hands down and let them lie across the hillocks of skirts and bedclothes. "When you are done, will the abbot come to argue his side? Or did you mean to keep this attempt at persuasion secret?"

He smiled faintly. "Truths, not persuasion. In the morning you will be tried on charges of witchcraft. We both know you are guilty, so I doubt you will survive."

She knew very well she would not, though guilt had nothing to do with it. No one, witch or not, survived being burned at the stake.

"Truth," he said quietly. "Take vows and enter a convent, and there will be no trial."

Bitterness crept in. "And my lands will go to the Church—" she paused a moment, looking for additional truths, "unless you mean to take part of them as payment for what you do now."

The tone—and confirmation—was ironic: "Suitable dowry, I think, for a bride of Jesus Christ."

Marian laughed; she knew him better, now. "But that isn't

what you want. That would deny *you*, and you couldn't counte-nance that. Not William deLacey. His pride would never per-mit it."

It banished the hint of a smile. "Take vows and marry me, and there will be no trial."

Now her own irony. "And you will have *all* my lands."

His eyes were alight with quiet laughter. "Suitable dowry, I think, for the Sheriff of Nottingham."

She looked at him steadfastly, maintaining an even tone. "And if I take no vows, perishing in the flames, neither of you shall win. My lands will go to the king."

He permitted himself a smile. "Your father was the Lion-heart's man, always. He died in Richard's cause, in Richard's holy insanity."

He knew how to goad and succeed even with her, who knew him better now; it was a particular talent. "My father would *never*—"

The sheriff cut her off. "But now it is said Richard himself will not come home from his cell in Henry's German prison—in which case his brother John, our present Count of Mortain, shall inherit the throne of England." William deLacey paused. "Do you think your father would rest easy to see his lands given over to *John?*"

No. No and no. Bitterly she said, "They are *my* lands now, in accordance with all the laws of England . . . and it might be worth giving them to John Lackland if only to thwart you and the abbot."

The sheriff stepped closer to her. She looked at the hand on the torch—his sword hand, and strong, hardened from years of experience. No longer a soldier's hand, but lacking none of the strength or skill. She thought of that hand in her hair. She thought of it at her throat. Imagined it on her breast.

Marian wanted to vomit.

He bent over her carefully and set the torch into a bracket. The shadows, sly and silent, lay thick everywhere but on the bed. She could smell him: oil of cloves, and incense. He had bathed. Had he prayed?

In the light his face was as naked to her as her own to him.

In his she saw suffering of a sort she could not fully comprehend. *Or do I dare not risk it, having learned a little of pain?*

"Marian," he rasped.

Abruptly she tore back the bedclothes, lurching out of the bed. She meant to run from him, to snatch open the door and fly down coiled stairs, to escape Nottingham Castle—

But he caught her, trapped her, sat her down upon the bed. And then took his hands from her. "Do you know what I see?"

She drew in a ragged breath. Mutely, she shook her head.

"The little girl," he answered, "astride her father's great destrier. With black hair all tangled and dusty, coming out of useless plaits."

It was not what she had expected.

"Sir Hugh FitzWalter's daughter, little Lady Marian, born and bred to Ravenskeep on the edge of Sherwood Forest, so close to Nottingham." He smiled, though bitterness wracked the corners of his firm, well-cut mouth. "I married twice, and buried them both. I loved neither of them."

"They gave you children," she said.

DeLacey's tone was bland. "Getting children on a woman has nothing at all to do with love."

She drew in a steadying breath. She was not afraid of him; she had *never* been afraid of him, but she knew enough now to be uncertain of his intentions. "You were my father's friend."

"I was. And am, Marian. He asked me to tend your welfare should misfortune befall him."

She knew that better than he. "But he did not require *this!*"

White teeth gleamed in torchlight. "You make this necessary."

"You are a fool," she told him. "A ruthless, coldhearted fool—"

"And worse," he agreed, "but I do not stoop to rape."

Marian wanted to spit. "You will get me no other way."

The sheriff merely smiled. "Do you know what I see? FitzWalter's black-haired, blue-eyed daughter, but four months of age and without a tooth in her head. Laughing and waving impotent fists in the Sheriff of Nottingham's face."

She knew then what he meant to do, how he hoped to reduce

her to helplessness in the face of shared memories of childhood, of girlhood, of when her father lived.

His smile dropped away. Now the tone hissed. "Do you know what I see?"

Resolutely she held her silence.

He answered her anyway, harshly. "A woman ripe for bedding, begging for it with her eyes."

Jaw muscles tautened. "Give me a knife," she retorted, "and I will *show* you what I am ripe for."

The sheriff raised a single eloquent eyebrow. "Did he teach you that? Did he also teach you the *sword?*"

She knew precisely what he meant, though not long ago she had known nothing at all of hardship or the harsh argot of such men. Now she knew, and spoke it, answering him in kind with cool self-possession, fully cognizant of what the admission could mean. "The fleshly sword, yes. But he also taught me what you cannot: what it is to love a man."

Dull color stained his face. Her thrust had gone home cleanly, and more deeply than she had hoped. Her matter-of-fact confirmation of his crude insinuation turned the blade back on him.

His eyes glittered in flame. "Do you know what I see?"

She knew very well what he saw. She named it before he could. "Robin Hood's whore," she answered. "And grateful for the honor."

One

Marian smiled crookedly. *This place transforms Ravenskeep into a hovel.*

It did not, quite; her beloved manor was a worthy enough residence, and far better than a serf's hovel. But Huntington Castle, in its towered and portcullised grandeur, *was* hugely imposing as well as exquisitely new, boasting the latest improvements in architecture and defenses. The keep was surrounded by a newfangled curtain-wall replete with ornate defense machicolations and murder-holes, but Marian was less overwhelmed by the size and sheer massiveness than by its master's ambition and wealth.

The great hall itself was no less impressive, if a trifle intimidating, with its fashionably massive masonry walls intermittently shielded behind painted cloth hangings. The hall was awash in candle- and lamplight, painting ochre and umber shadows in corners, cracks, and crannies. Lute-song was an underscore to the warmth of so many bodies, the odors of sweetmeats, spice, strong wine; to the animated discussions swirling throughout the hall. Marian was aware of them all, if distantly, thinking instead of the reason she and the others— even those uninvited—had attended.

He will not remember me. He could not, of course; why should he? He was an earl's son, and she a knight's daughter. That they

17

had met once, as children, would mean nothing to him. *I wish—* But she cut it off. There was no purpose in it.

Lute-song drifted to her through a break in the crowd. Marian glanced idly at its source. The handsome minstrel— some might call him pretty—she had seen upon arrival, marking him as true to type in bright-eyed, eloquent discourses designed to snare a female audience before he played a note. The rapidity of his success made her smile, but not fall victim; an answering glint in long-lashed blue eyes told her he marked *her* as something more than a simple, immediate conquest. But she had not entered the game for more than one reason: she was not disposed to play, and she had come for Robert of Locksley, Huntington's heir.

Something pinched her stomach. *This is wrong. I know it is. I shouldn't tax him with this; simply because he's from the same shire, I can't expect him to know anything more than I do.* She drew a deep breath. *But I'm here now; it's done. I'll approach him anyway. What harm in the asking?*

No harm at all in the asking . . . *if* he deigned to answer. If he even knew who she was, or what her father had been.

She knew of no one else, no one at all. Men came home from Crusade nearly every day now, but she knew none of them. *No more than I know Locksley . . . but at least I can ask*—Marian bit her lip. *No harm in asking, is there?*

She stared hard at the empty dais. Irritation flickered minutely. Marian sought and rekindled it, aware of guilty relief; it was far simpler to be annoyed than to dwell on flagging self-confidence. *No doubt he holds back merely to make an impressive entrance.*

Robert of Locksley, heir to vast wealth, an ancient title, and his father's brand-new castle, sat very quietly on the edge of the chair, holding himself perfectly still. If he didn't move, if he did not so much as twitch, the chair wouldn't break.

And neither will I.

Through the studded oak door, carefully closed and latched for privacy, noise crept into awareness: echoes muted by wood, by stone, by distance; warped by perceptions, by interpretations shaped of circumstances now lodged in the past, yet oddly still part of his present. He wondered in a detached, negligent way if the selfsame echoes would also shape his future. He heard so many, now. Even those that were not real.

Shoulders and neck were set stiffly, unyielding to quiet protests of aching muscle and tendon. He sat with meticulous precision on the edge of the heavy chair, banishing the tremors of too-taut sinews, allowing himself no slackening of knotted muscles, no tranquility of his spirit. Listening to the noise.

A lute, clear and sweet, notes interspersed with women's laughter, and girlish giggles. Lute and women, he thought distantly, were requirements of one another, if only to fulfill the fashion of Romance as dictated by a queen: Eleanor of Aquitaine, Richard's indomitable mother.

Richard. He closed his eyes. Hands, splayed slackly across bunched thighs, flexed spasmodically, then doubled into fists, scraping nails against hosen fabric. A tremor shook his rigidity, then died. He sealed his traitorous eyes with all the strength he could muster. *If I refuse to hear—*

But the lute-song and the laughter beyond the door transmuted themselves without effort. The noise now was screaming—

—the boom of stone on stone, hurled against Christendom's walls . . . the shrieks of a man dying, disembowled by the splinter from a trebuchet stone . . . the swearing and the praying, so often one and the same, making no difference at all to the Crusaders who knew only they served God as well as king, and perhaps their own ambitions—

And the Lionheart's lusty laughter, no more inhibited by decorum than his appetites by rank.

For the thousandth time, Marian let her fingers examine the seating of narrow silver fillet over the linen coif and sheer veil covering her head and hair, and the double-tied embroidered girdle binding her waist and hips. Huntington's great hall was filled with a significant portion of England's nobility, men and women of great Saxon houses, and those of the newer Norman regime who had replaced the English tongue with French, so that the earl's hall was replete with bilinguality. Marian, too, spoke both languages, as one was required; the other, older language, shaped by Norse invaders, was considered impolitic where business was conducted. Peasants spoke it primarily, while those desiring to rise resorted to English only among themselves, or when ordering villeins about.

Even the lute-player sang in French, though Marian supposed it was required. French was the language of legend and love, according to the Dowager Queen Eleanor's dictates, and troubadours who reveled in the traditions of the storied Courts of Love inevitably sang of both, relegating the more ordinary day-to-day concerns to the reality they attempted to obscure.

She was distantly aware of the music, but was no more interested in it than she was in the conversation between four old beldams clustered before her. They spoke of nothing but the earl's wealth, his influence, his unflagging support of King Richard, who would doubtless reward such loyalty, once his release from Henry was procured, and thereby render the earl yet more powerful and wealthy. Marian found such talk tedious; she was interested in the earl's *son*, not in the earl himself. She disliked even more her own consciousness that the heir to one of England's most preeminent barons would most likely find her question disrespectful and impudent.

He will brush it off like a passing impertinence, then have me dismissed before the nobility of England. Marian shut her eyes, hearing lute-song and conversation. *Give me the courage to ask. It isn't so very much.*

Locksley twitched as someone called out his name. Blind eyes snapped open. He fought his way to the surface, groping for comprehension. Surely the voice was one he knew . . . But the latch, quickly lifted, became the sound of a trebuchet crank as they readied to loft the stone—

—hurtling through the dry, dust-swathed air, crashing into the wall, pulping the flesh caught beneath—

Wood boomed on stone: a door against a wall. *Wood*, not stone on stone, or flesh, or bone, nor men to die from its force.

The voice: inflections of impatience, awkwardness, austere authority wary of preemption by concerns that could not be known, and dared not be questioned. "Robert—" More quietly now, but with no less pointed query, "will you keep my guests waiting all night?"

With effort Locksley roused and recalled himself from Holy Crusade to the war of wills now fought more subtly within the halls of his father's castle. He rose, aware of deep-seated fatigue, and back-palmed the dampness on his brow beneath a shock of pale hair. Physically he was sound. The journey home had allowed him time to recover most of his former vigor, as well as the weight he'd lost. But what his father desired was nothing he wanted to do. Better to stop it now, to refuse quietly and politely, before the travesty went forward.

He turned, summoning courtesy, intending to say it plainly, so as to offer no room for misinterpretation. His father stood poised before the door. Beyond it milled the multitudes of English nobility, of whom Richard I, called Lionheart, was sovereign.

Self-control slipped into place, schooled to expected courtesy. "Forgive me." He kept his tone very civil. "Had you asked, I would have told you not to bother. With—*that*." A hand gestured briefly, eloquently, indicating the world beyond the door. "I would sooner go to bed."

The earl nearly gaped at his unexpectedly recalcitrant heir. Then astonishment altered into autocracy, reshaping eyes, nostrils, jaw. Clearly the refusal, however politely couched, was not to be borne, nor could its understated plea be acknowledged. "By God—you will come out. At once. Everyone was invited. Everyone has come. Everyone is *expecting*—"

The residue of memories overlaying the present thinned, tore, then faded. Locksley had learned to adopt a quiet intransigence others viewed as self-confidence, though he himself knew better. Stubbornness, perhaps. Defiance, more like.

He kept his tone soft, but firm. The fleeting plea was banished. "It is none of my concern what everyone expects. You gave them leave to expect it without consulting me."

The earl closed the door with the force of damaged authority and a desire to mend it at once. "By God, Robert, I am your father. It is for me to plan what I will plan, with or without consultation." And then the thunderous expression faded. The

21

earl crossed the shadowy chamber to clap both hands on his son's arms. "Ah Robert, let this go. Why must we argue now, and about such a trivial matter? I thought you *dead*—and yet here you stand before me, full-fleshed and larger than life. . . ." Blue eyes shone; the smile was a mixture of wonder and intense pleasure. "By God, all those prayers answered at last . . ."

Locksley gritted teeth. When his jaw protested he relaxed the tension with effort. *Let him have it*, he told himself. *Let him have this moment. For all I know it* was *the strength of his prayers*.

"Come now, Robert—you must admit your return is worthy of celebration! The Earl of Huntington's only son back from Crusade with King Richard himself? I *want them to know*, Robert! By God, I want them to *know!*"

"They know," his son replied quietly. "You have seen to that."

"And do you blame me? Do you?" Bluffness dismissed, the earl now was intent, albeit underscored by parental impatience. "I believed my son dead. I was *told* my son was dead, killed at the Lionheart's side . . . and yet a year and a half later that son comes to my castle, close-mouthed and dry-eyed, saying little of such things save the stories lied. 'Not dead,' he says. 'Captured by the Saracens' . . ." The earl's blue eyes filled. "By *God*, Robert!—no father alive could resist a celebration."

Very quietly, with infinite respect no less distinct for its resoluteness, Locksley suggested, "Had you consulted me—"

"Back to that, are we?" The earl scrubbed his clean-shaven, furrowed face with both hands, mussing clipped white hair, then gripped the top of the nearest chair and shut his hands upon it, leaning toward his son to emphasize his declaration. In muted light, crease-couched blue eyes were now nearly black. "Two years on Crusade may have grown the boy to manhood, but *I* am still the father. You will do as I say."

Age had dog-eared the edges, but the tone was well-known. It was one to be obeyed, one to be feared, presaging punishment.

But that had been in boyhood. Save for the scratchiness the tone was unchanged, and so was the expectation of instant obedience, but the son who heard it was not the same individual.

Something odd and indefinable moved in the son's eyes. Had the earl been as adept at judging his own flesh and blood as he was at judging most people, he would have seen the brief interplay between duty and desire, the pale glint of desperation quickly banished and replaced by grim comprehension.

To the earl, his son was a hero returned from battle and captivity, companion to the king. Above all, his son was his son. That superseded all other knowledge, all other judgments. But Robert of Locksley now was far more than an earl's son, and, by his own lights, far less than a free man.

The earl's belligerence faded as he gazed at his silent son, and the tight-clenched line of his jaw weakened until the flesh sagged minutely. The arch of the proud nose, stripped of youthful padding, pierced the air more keenly. He was, unexpectedly, an old man. The Earl of Huntington had always been strong and vigorous. Yet now the muted tone was rough-textured and unsteady, thickened by emotion. "By God, Robert, let me be proud of you," he begged. "Let me show you off to those who will deal with you when *I* am in the tomb."

Locksley's belly clenched. He had recalled, while on Crusade, all of the earl's strength of will, his inflexibility, his autocratic authority. Never had there been softness; better yet, a soften*ing*, in memories or daydreams. Yet his father, now, was old.

I am all he has left . . . unless one counts this castle. The thought was answered by a flicker of self-reproach, that he could be cynical in the face of his father's pride. *I perhaps do him an injustice—what immortality does a father have, save for begetting sons? And I am his only son . . . I am more costly than most.*

Inwardly he surrendered, releasing the intransigence which was as newborn to himself, who had always been dutiful, as it was frustrating to his father. It was not worth the battle. He had fought too many already. Let his father win this one: In captivity Locksley had become adept at not caring. Caring too much hurt.

The son acquiesced. The earl, seeing that, smiled in relief, then triumph, then complacent satisfaction.

23

Sighing, Locksley pulled wide the door. Beyond milled the multitude, telling stories of his captivity, his heroism, his valor. Making up what they could not know, to be certain of their reception in the eyes of those who knew no more, but would not admit to less.

The son, seeing that, cursed himself for a fool.

Two

Marian pressed damp palms against her kirtle. Locksley was here at last and she was after all no different from the others despite her high-flown ideas. She was as curious and fascinated as everyone else.

It galled her, because she had desired him to be—*counted* on him to be—no more than merely a boy come home from playing at war. That sort of person she could approach without feeling so obviously self-serving.

She swallowed the lump of increasing nervousness. *Other women lost fathers. I have no more right than they have to ask this man a question.*

But no less right, either.

He stood before them all, poised upon the dais. Her instinctive, unexpected response was unspoken, but loud inside her mind: *He is much changed.* The boy, having gone to war, had returned from it a man. She wondered if anyone else saw him as she did, sensing what she felt, or if they were utterly blind. *How could they miss it? They have only to look at him!*

And they looked, even as she did, but saw what they wanted to see: the Earl of Huntington's heir returned from the dead; a live man in place of a corpse, wearing rich Norman garments instead of dull linen shroud and flesh in place of the steel of a dead Englishman's sword taken back from a Saracen thief.

He had gone on Crusade with the Lionheart as so many of them had, forsaking in the hot pride of youth his noble father's attempt to buy back his service by paying honorable scutage. It was a thing done often enough among high houses and un-remarked upon, and he was his father's only son, heir to an important title and vast fortune. Fortunately, though King Richard needed men, he needed money more, and in place of flesh he would accept shield-tax.

The earl had tried to pay. His son had other ideas.

Marian nodded. *He is much changed.*

Robert of Locksley stood on the low stone dais next to his father, beneath the heavy dark beams bedecked with green-and-gold Huntington colors. Torches from wall cressets and tripod dais stands behind both men did little to illuminate their faces, painting only heads and shoulders. From a distance, all Marian saw clearly as she looked at the earl's son was the blazing spill of white-blond hair worn much too long for fashion. He had always been fair, she recalled, pale as an Easter lily except for his hazel eyes.

I remember him from that Christmas . . . It gave her an unexpected spurt of renewed conviction. *I* will *ask him . . . surely he can't begrudge me a single, simple question.*

Sir Guy of Gisbourne stared. With effort he shut his mouth, wiped the smear of perspiration from his upper lip, and bathed the dryness of his mouth with wine, too much wine, gulping all of it down until the cup was empty. He thrust the cup toward a passing servant-girl and saw how it trembled; he stilled it as best he could, daring the girl to indicate she saw his state. She did not. She merely poured him more wine, then took herself off.

He stared again at the woman who had stolen his wits away. He could not stop looking at her. *Who—?* He did not finish the question even within his thoughts. It would serve no purpose.

He had seen her arrive, attended by an aged maidservant now asleep on a bench by a wall. He had watched her make her way into the throng, exchanging greetings with few, keeping her own counsel. He had noted the fit and color of kirtle (a lustrous rich blue silk embroidered in silver at neckline and cuffs, bound slim at her waist by a beaded Norman girdle); the elegance of her posture; the glory of coif-shrouded hair; the richness of blue eyes—and, unexpectedly, the stubborn set of her delicate jaw as she gazed at the dais.

Shaking, Gisbourne scrubbed a hand across his brow. He swallowed painfully, sucked a breath through constricted lungs, and tried to master himself. His thighs and belly bunched, aching with erection; he more than wanted the woman, he *needed* the woman.

It had been months. There was an occasional serving-girl to ease him, but he found such women lacking and therefore the act as well. He wanted more, but knew not how to find it. Emptiness and frustration had become intimates of his spirit, leaving him with nothing but his obsessive attention to detail. His was the kind of temperament men like the sheriff treasured, because *someone* had to organize the administration of castle and shire. The sheriff of Nottingham dispensed justice. Sir Guy of Gisbourne, his seneschal, carried it out.

He had never been overly ambitious, nor was he an acquisitive man. His mistress was duty; his master William deLacey. But now, he would forsake all other vows if it put *her* in his bed. *Not the knightly code . . . no chivalry, in this.*

Self-contempt flagellated him. He was, after all, *not* a knight as a knight used to be reckoned—that is, before the reign of Richard the Lionheart, whose compulsive need to go on Crusade had moved him to begin the practice of *selling* knighthoods to anyone who could afford them, along with lands and titles.

A knight is sworn to many things, among them courtesy. Gisbourne was not innately a discourteous or unkind man. He knew himself humorless, old for his age, consumed with conducting his life—and the life of Nottingham Castle—with an obsessive dedication that rendered him invaluable to deLacey, but annoying to others. They couldn't see that what he did was needful in the ordering of their lives. They saw only that he was hard and uncompromising and incapable of reducing his personal standards to suit their whims.

26

But when he looked at the woman he forgot all of that. He thought only of her body, of her beauty, and what it promised him.

For Marian, the dais ceremony did not grow tedious. She watched fixedly as Robert of Locksley without hesitation accepted the welcome of each man and woman who came to the dais for presentation. His manner was quietly gracious but oddly restrained, as if he performed the ritual solely for the sake of his father. He was taller than the earl by half a head or more, which had not been the case when Marian had last seen him, two years before. Then he had been a youth with narrow shoulders and bony wrists. The shoulders now were broader; she could not predict the wrists.

Memory warred with reality. More than a decade had passed. People changed. Children grew up. Women married and bore children, while men went to war. But she recalled the past so well she couldn't reconcile it with the present. *One night only, one kiss, one Christmas Eve.* But he would never recall it, not as she did.

From where she stood, buried in the throng, Marian could hear nothing of what was said. She saw the earl's broad smile, the movement of his mouth, the clasping of hands and arms as each man came forward to pay his respects, presenting wives and blushing daughters. But the son didn't smile. The son merely waited in watchful silence as each guest approached. He clasped arms if they insisted, murmured something back, but his mouth never curved. The eyes never lighted.

It was as if, Marian decided, the fire inside had died. Or perhaps it was merely banked.

William deLacey, the Lord High Sheriff of Nottingham, caught his youngest daughter's arm and steered her away from the knot of women clustered near the minstrel. It wasn't that he disliked music or was deaf to the minstrel's skill, but there were far more important things with which to concern himself.

"Eleanor," he said as she opened her mouth to protest.

27

She subsided quickly enough, but he was not blind to her resentment. She was plain, not pretty, with no promise of improvement as the years went by. It was no wonder she threw herself at the head of every girlish musician. They were invariably more beautiful than she, and certainly more talented.

But possibly less intelligent. What Eleanor lacked in looks, she made up for in cunning.

He drew her behind a screen and released her arm. A quick glance ascertained that she had not yet spilled wine on her dull saffron kirtle—*could she not have dressed more brightly?*—and her lank brown hair—*could she not have crimped it more?*—had not yet begun to come down from an elaborate coiffure. "You are here for a purpose," he reminded her.

She dipped briefly in a mocking curtsey, lids lowered over angry brown eyes.

"Your future depends on it."

Lids flickered. Lifted. She looked directly at him. *"Your* future depends on it."

His mouth thinned. "Yes. Certainly. You know what I want, just as I know what you want—"

"You don't know the first thing about what I want." The tone was quiet but virulent. "You never have, and you never will, because you never *listen*—"

"Enough!" It shut her mouth instantly, as he intended. "You will behave yourself, Eleanor. I will not have you demeaning me by playing the mooncalf over that minstrel, when you are here for another purpose."

Eleanor smiled calmly. "The minstrel is exquisite."

A flicker of irritation flared briefly into anger. "I don't care if he played for Henry himself at his deathbed, Eleanor! You are to conduct yourself as befits a woman of your station."

"But you are, as always, more concerned about *your* station." She showed teeth briefly, and an overbite. "If you understood music, you would know how good he is."

He caught her elbow and squeezed. "Eleanor . . ." But he bit back the impatience, channeling it into a quieter passion that would touch even his stubborn daughter. "I want what's best for you. I want a man for you who can give you what you deserve."

Eleanor nodded sagely. "So that I can share it with you."

He shook his head slowly. "Don't waste yourself, Eleanor. Look in the mirror I gave you."

She blinked. "In the—mirror?"

"In lieu of lands and dowry, a man will marry for beauty. I have no lands of my own, your dowry went to the king, and your beauty is nonexistent."

Eleanor's color vanished.

DeLacey patted her arm kindly. "I'm sure you understand that what I do is as good for *you* as it is for me."

It was expected that everyone would greet the earl's son. It was why Huntington insisted they stand on the dais, he and his heir, greeting everyone. His son was back from the dead. His son was on display. See how the son lived in defiance of the tale of his death at Richard the Lionheart's side?

Marian, too, had heard the tale, grieving for his death. For one night she had cried because her father also had died, and because she recalled a Christmas no one else would. But Robert of Locksley was home, against all odds. Her father never could be. Only his sword had been sent.

She closed her eyes as fingers curled into fists against her skirts. It wasn't fair, she knew. Locksley's survival merited prayers and gratitude, not resentment. Not jealousy.

Grimly she chided herself: *Be pleased the boy survived. Too many others did not.* She opened her eyes again. *No, not 'the boy.' There is nothing boyish about him.*

A man stopped at her side. The voice was quiet and cultured. "I have brought you wine, to cool your pretty throat."

She glanced up sharply. William deLacey pressed a goblet into her hand, smiling warmly. Condensation on the goblet very nearly caused her to drop it; she closed both hands around it and thanked him with a nod.

The sheriff's brown eyes were compassionate. "I miss him as well, Marian. And I would, given the chance, trade that boy for your father. Hugh of Ravenskeep is worth three of him."

She was surprised by his bluntness as well as his presumption. They were in the earl's hall. Anyone wanting favor might carry the words to the earl; or worse, to his son, who no doubt would find them churlish as well as humiliating. "We should give thanks God was merciful in sending *one* of them home."

DeLacey smiled. "Your kindness does you credit, but you know I speak the truth. Locksley is nothing to you. Your father was everything."

Was. Not is; *was*. Her father was of the past, while she was of the present.

What now was her future? She was Hugh FitzWalter's only heir, and on his death she had become a ward of the Crown. By English law she held the manor in trust for her future husband, and although she had had no plans to marry, certainly it would be suggested very soon, now that her mourning was done. Ravenskeep, as other manors, was a valuable source of revenue. Marian FitzWalter, ward of the Crown, was one as well. At the moment she was unencumbered because the Crown, in Richard's person, was imprisoned in Germany.

Treason, she mocked herself, *to be grateful for the time while the king is being held.* She drank, swallowing rapidly, trying to ward off the bitter taste of the future she despised. *If I were a man . . .* But she broke it off at once, knowing it served no purpose.

The hand brushed her shoulder. "You didn't have to come."

Marian summoned a smile over the rim of the goblet. "I came, like everyone else, to pay the earl honor."

"Not to impress his son?"

"To impress—?" Seeing his eyes, she laughed. "You brought Eleanor."

A rueful smile replaced the guardedness of his manner. "I am found out."

Marian matched his smile. "You must not be so anxious, my lord Sheriff. Eleanor will marry, just as her sisters did."

One corner of his mouth flattened. "Eleanor is plainer than her sisters, as well as headstrong. And older; time is running out."

It was not what she expected a father to say of his daughter, even his least favorite one. Eleanor was, she thought, too much like her father. They detested one another, while needing each other's regard.

Marian arched black brows. "So, you have brought her here in hopes of interesting Robert of Locksley."

"In hopes of interesting the *earl;* I care little enough what Locksley thinks of the girl. He has no say in the matter." Impatiently, William deLacey frowned down the line. "If Huntington is the man they say he is, he will see to it soon. There is talk of the boy already."

Marian was astonished. "He has only just come home!"

DeLacey flicked his fingers. "You know as well as I how servants carry tales. They all of them are peasants; they have no sense of decorum."

"And perhaps they are only tales." Marian looked toward the dais. "I cannot imagine there is anything anyone could say of Robert that impugns his honor. The king *knighted* him—"

"In war," the sheriff said grimly, "honor is often lacking. Survival is what matters."

"And if there is truth in these stories," she retorted, "why are you so eager to wed Eleanor to him?"

The sheriff laughed aloud. Brown eyes glinted. "You know better than that: he is still the son of an earl." Amusement faded, replaced by a quiet intensity. *"Did* you come for Locksley?"

Marian drew a constricted breath, conscious of her reddened face. How could she explain? She herself did not know all the reasons she had come. "I came . . ." She hesitated. "I came because my father would have wished it. You knew him, my lord . . . would he not have wished it?" *Neatly done,* she thought. *Let deLacey deal with it.*

He smiled, saluting her with a raised goblet. "Indeed, he would have." Before she could answer, he squeezed her shoulder briefly. "You will excuse me, I pray—I must present Eleanor now."

He left her, gliding smoothly through the throng to gather up his youngest daughter and escort her to the dais. He ignored those before him, depending on authority to take the place of rank. He was not a lord by ancient ancestral heritage, being of a minor Norman family, but the Conqueror had rewarded exemplary service in the defeat of England by distributing confiscated land and titles. Thus the sheriff had been born into the new nobility and had, with each wife, married above himself. His appetite for power was obvious to Marian, but oddly enough it did not diminish him. He was the sort of man who survived no matter the odds.

Marian looked to the dais. *Much as Robert did.*

Unlike the sheriff, she waited her turn. She drank wine, gave the empty goblet to a servant, and eventually reached the dais where she looked fully into the face that was devoid of all expression, into pale hazel eyes masked to all of those before him. Indeed, the fires were banked. There was little left save an ember.

She opened her mouth to ask him her single, simple question, but no words came out. She was utterly bereft of speech, robbed by cowardice. Who was *she* to ask him anything, and why should he know the answer?

He doesn't care. Look at him—he'd rather be somewhere else than wasting time with sycophants! Self-consciousness sealed her throat. But she was there before them both, duly presented to the earl and his son. Short of turning and fleeing, the least she could do was blurt out the words of welcome she'd practiced at Ravenskeep. She'd meant them to break the ice; now they would save face, a little.

"My lord Earl." She curtseyed. By rote she said her little piece, uninspired by the subject for whom she had invented it. She hardly heard the words herself; they contained something of gratitude and honor, a scrap of piety. She cared no more than Locksley, who stood so bored beside his father.

And then the boredom vanished. A hand was on her arm even as she turned to go. The wrist, she saw clearly, was no longer thin and bony, but sheathed in firm muscle. The fingers were taut as wire. "Marian of *Ravenskeep?*"

Baffled, she nodded—and saw rage blossom in his eyes.

Three

Locksley's clasp on her arm hurt but Marian let it go, offering yet another curtsey, briefly startled by his question as well as the contact. She looked more closely at him, baffled by the unexpected tension. The rage had dissipated, replaced with impatience; he did not require the honor everyone gave his father.

"Yes," she told him clearly, wondering what it was about her name that drove him out of silence into abrupt intensity. "Marian of Ravenskeep; Sir Hugh is—" she checked, *"was* my father."

The hand remained on her arm as if he had forgotten. Through the fabric of her clothing she felt the grip of his fingers. "It was to you I sent the letter. I trust you received it."

She turned slightly, twisting her wrist to free it. He released it at once, but made no apology. He was too intent on her answer. "I received no letter, my lord."

Clearly it was not what he expected. He frowned. Beneath a shock of white-blond hair his brows knitted together over a good, even nose without the prominence of his father's. "I sent it," he declared, leaving no room for doubt. "Months ago. I thought you should know how your father died."

The bluntness took her breath away. *How can he know that was my question?* Jerkily she shook her head. "I received no letter—"

"Robert." It was the earl himself, briskly cutting off her words. "Robert, others are waiting. If you must speak with this girl, perhaps another time—?"

Blankly, she said, "It must have gone astray—" And then a

servant was at her side, urging her away. Her time with the earl was done. His son's attention was needed elsewhere.

She acquiesced to the servant, too distracted to delay. It had not occurred to her that Locksley would readily recall her or her father. It had not occurred to her he might have met her father on Crusade. It had never occurred to her that Robert of Locksley might really know the details of her father's death. She had merely meant to ask him out of a childish need to *ask*, not really expecting an answer, expecting nothing of what he'd implied.

If he knows—if he knows. Abruptly she stopped and swung back, meaning to force her way to the dais. As abruptly, she halted. Locksley's attention was elsewhere. His face, and his eyes, were empty of all emotion save an abiding, helpless impatience.

Faces, with moving mouths. Locksley heard almost none of them. He hadn't heard the woman, either, until she said her name. The first part hadn't touched him. But the second, *FitzWalter*, had exploded in his ears like a wall besieged by sappers.

Marian of Ravenskeep. Hugh FitzWalter's daughter. *What would my father say, were I sick all over the dais?* Marian of Ravenskeep. The dead knight's daughter.

She had vanished into the crowd. With her had gone forbearance. "How many more?" he asked, as yet another guest left the dais.

His father's smile was for the hall. "As many as are here."

It was a tone from his childhood, cloaked in quiet courtesy, framed upon cold steel. He had spent too many years under its sway to withstand it easily even now, or to protest its need.

He looked out again at the hall. What he saw was a Saracen battlefield, and dead men dying. Among them Hugh FitzWalter.

Eventually, when food and tables were cleared away, there was dancing. Marian would have preferred to remain inconspicuous, but this was prevented by William deLacey, who insisted she partner him. Her year of mourning was done, he reminded her, and her father would not require such rigorous devotion when there was dancing to be done.

And so she danced, if circumspectly, with deLacey and a handful of others, and eventually Sir Guy of Gisbourne, who presented himself to her in good Norman French, betraying his origins. She knew little about him save he was deLacey's man and had been spared from the Crusade by the sheriff himself, who paid the shield-tax in order to keep his office effective in the administration of the shire.

Gisbourne was an intense, dark, compact man, short of limb and, she thought, imagination, to judge by his conversation. He danced a trifle stiffly, obviously ill at ease even in simple patterns, but undoubtedly he was more fluid in the activities of his service. He said very little of consequence, being more disposed to stare, which she found unsettling. She did her best to avoid his eyes as she glided through the pattern.

As a knight, Gisbourne was entitled to some honor. She was a knight's daughter and understood that very well. But Gisbourne was of an entirely unprepossessing merchant family who had bought him the rank, and was too young to have legitimately earned any lands in royal service. He therefore had no property, no manor, and had taken service with the sheriff of Nottingham two years prior to Richard's latest Crusade, because the sheriff required a steward to supervise his household. In time Gisbourne might earn his own holdings, but for now he was dependent upon the largesse of Nottinghamshire.

His expression was ferocious, low of brow and hairline. The features were strong and blunt, lacking refinement, and his posture was blocky. He wore good wool dyed black. "Lady," Gisbourne rasped. "Methinks you forget the pattern."

She *had* forgotten. In her reverie, she had turned the wrong way. It brought them close, *too* close; she fell back a step, hot-faced, and saw the glint in his eyes. *Boar's eyes,* she thought. *Too small, too black, too bright.*

"Lady," he repeated. "Do you wish to stop?"

There was nothing in his words save a self-conscious courtesy she did not expect from a man with the eyes of a boar. Marian felt ashamed, conscious of heat in her face.

She managed a casual tone. "I think we had better stop. I am

35

a trifle overwarm—perhaps a cup of cool wine . . . ?" She asked it deliberately, knowing he would go and she could make her escape.

It seemed Gisbourne knew it also, by the glitter in his eyes. He bowed his departure stiffly. Marian watched him go, then turned to hide herself in the revelers. She had wanted nothing to do with the dancing from the beginning, and less to do with conversation. It was rude to desert a knight who ostensibly did her bidding, but at that moment Marian wanted nothing more than to find a quiet corner.

In the distance she heard a lute and the clear voice of the minstrel soaring over the muddy music of too many people talking. She could go to him, she knew, and linger to listen. But he had gathered a loyal knot of women and girls, and joining them did not appeal to her. Perhaps her best choice would be to go find her old nurse, Matilda, and sit quietly with the woman.

She halted, brought up short by a tall man just before her, and opened her mouth to beg pardon. Then she shut it; it was Locksley. His hazel eyes were oddly intense.

"Come with me," he said. "This is not the place to talk." No, it was not, but she had not expected to. "This way," he declared, and closed her right wrist in his hand.

Gisbourne knew it the moment he returned to the place he had left her: she *was* gone. And of her own choice, seeking to escape him.

It burned within his belly. He clung to both goblets, smelling the stink of strong wine, and hated himself. He was a false man, jumped up via a corrupt preferment system, and the woman knew it.

Everyone knew it.

He gulped down the contents of one goblet, then gave it away to a servant. He clung to the other, nursing the wine, flagellating himself with the knowledge of his lack. He knew very well that had he been taken into the household of a man other than William deLacey, it would not be so painful to name himself

36

what he was: a landless knight with few prospects for advancement.

Things had changed since old Henry had died. Richard the Lionheart, had handed out knighthoods like a hengirl throwing grain. The rank once attainable only through feats of skill no longer meant quite so much. The sheriff of Nottingham, requiring an able steward, had further sealed Gisbourne's fate by buying him out of battle; therefore his only claim to knighthood was a feat of passing the purse.

He bit into his lip. *Sir* Guy; no less. But no more, either. He sincerely doubted serving William deLacey would ever result in anything more than what he had, with no land in the offing.

Sir Guy of Gisbourne.

He gritted teeth. He wasn't like the sheriff. He didn't want or need nobility. He merely desired land of his own, a manor, a name—and a woman to bear him sons.

Locksley's manner was proprietary, intent, and more than a trifle selfish. He did not ask, he told. *But then,* Marian decided in fairness, *he is the son of an earl.*

Through the throng he took her, very nearly dragging her, but the throng made way for him, noting who he was, then noting who *she* was. In wry amusement she reflected, *The sheriff will be dismayed.*

But it faded quickly, overruled by an acknowledgment that what she did—rather, what he did *to* her—was the sort of thing others would note, consider, remark upon, within the context of their natures. Even now, eyebrows arched. Skirts were pulled aside. Mouths murmured comments into attentive ears.

Her face flamed and her breasts prickled. She did not think again of the sheriff or of his unmarried daughter. She thought instead of herself, and of the man who led her so unerringly through the hall to an adjoining antechamber. They passed even the minstrel, watching over his lute. Blue eyes were brightly knowing; his smile was meant for her.

Inside the chamber Locksley boomed shut the door behind her. Marian looked past him, noting chairs, candle racks, tapestried walls. *At least,* she thought wryly, *it does not have a bed. That much he will spare me.*

He swung back, stopped short, and nearly tripped her as she moved from the door. His tone was laced with bitter defensiveness. "Do you know what it is like coming home a stranger, and finding everything changed?"

She was not certain he wanted an answer. He was not looking at her.

And then, as abruptly, he was. *"Do* you?"

She folded hands into kirtle skirts, seeking the proper demeanor, the words he might want to hear. "When I have been away, I have a ritual. I reacquaint myself, to see if things have altered. Room by room. Hall by hall." She shrugged defensively, unsettled by the unrelenting stare. "Perhaps you might do the same."

"A ritual," he echoed. "Such as a knight riding into battle, seeking victory, honor, and glory . . . and the approval of a king?"

It was not meant for her, she knew. Perhaps for himself. "I don't know, my lord. I have never gone to war."

Her forthright tone and words startled him out of whatever privacy he might have wished to retain. She saw it plainly: the sharpening of his gaze, the hardening of his mouth. "No. They do not send women to war."

She did not hesitate. "Only into marriage."

Beneath pale hair, brows arched. She could see only their movement, not their color, though she remembered it. "Is that why you came?" he asked. "To cast the lure for the lost falcon at last returned to its mews?"

The bitter vehemence startled her. She had come for no such thing, not even contemplating it in a brief, fleeting daydream. She had been consumed with her father, determined to learn what she could, and only that. She did not blame Locksley for his assumption. Not one bit. It struck the mark cleanly. But she was not the arrow, loosed to catch a man. She was not Eleanor deLacey.

Marian smiled. Her teeth were good; she showed them. "Better to ask the sheriff. Better to ask the others, trailing chains of bright-clad daughters."

The flesh by his eyes creased. She thought at first it might be amusement, but the mouth did not smile. "What of you, then?"

"What of me?" she countered. *"You* brought me here."

He sighed and turned away, scrubbing one hand through his mane of blond hair. She saw how the breadth of his shoulders stretched the fabric of his samite tunic, checkered green-and-gold. The belt clasping lean hips shone with worked gold and the meat-knife at his right hip.

He swung back. "I brought you here," he agreed. And then, yet again, he frowned. "We have met before."

Marian managed to nod. "At Ravenskeep, my lord. One Christmas Eve"—it was harder than she'd expected—"you and your lord father rode home from London, but a storm brought you up short. You came instead to my father's manor and spent the night with us." *Perhaps that will content him. Perhaps he recalls nothing more.*

"Ravenskeep . . ." The eyes were unrelenting. "You dragged me under the mistletoe and claimed the forfeit of me."

He does remember. Heat washed through her face, leaving color in its wake. It took all her courage to meet his gaze, to smile; to hide with great effort the self-consciousness his intensity engendered. She was not so certain of men's regard that she knew how to conduct the conversational conflict so many other women relished. "I was very young, as you were," she began, relying on the truth no matter how embarrassing, "and I had kissed everyone else. You were the only one left."

She thought he might laugh, but he didn't. She thought he might at least smile. But all he did was dismiss the recollection with an autocratic gesture reminiscent of his father. "I sent a letter," he told her flatly. "After your father died, I wrote."

The wave of heat and color faded. Self-conscious amusement died. Locksley's manner, relegating her own feelings and responses to those meant merely to answer his questions, annoyed her intensely.

In her own way, Marian fought back. "Why you, my lord? Surely there was someone else. Someone of lesser rank—"

He heard the quiet derision in her tone. For the moment his eyes were bright, but with anger rather than humor. "Rank had nothing to do with it," he answered curtly. "When a man saves another man's life on the battlefield, such things no longer matter."

Tightly, she reminded him, "The Lionheart made you a knight."

"I said, it does not matter." He gritted his teeth, flexing muscle in his jaws. Color stood in his face. He was so fair, it showed easily—and then she saw the scar.

It was thin, jagged, ugly, tracing its way from his right earlobe along the line of his jaw to curve upward, only briefly, at the point of his chin. There it ended as abruptly as it began. It was almost nonexistent: a seam of uneven stitching. Someone had cut him badly. Someone had sewn him up. It was not a new scar, but one she did not recall. *He has been gone two years . . . war remakes us all.* "It does not matter," she told him, tearing her eyes from the scar.

His color faded. The scar disappeared, unless she looked for it. "Forgive me," he said roughly. "I have not been with women of decency for too long . . . I have forgotten all the words." The jaw muscles flexed again.

It was hard for him to say that. Marian smiled faintly. "They will come back to you. Now, as for the letter . . . ?"

"I wrote it, because he asked it . . . and because I wanted to tell you myself. I felt it only just, that the man who saved my life was well worth my own labor." His helpless gesture was awkward. "It was all I could do for him."

Grief renewed itself. "I was told he died in battle."

"He died at Richard's feet."

Richard. Not the king. Not the Lionheart. Not even "my lord." Marian wanted to cry again but refused to do it here, where Locksley would see. Her mouth felt slow and stiff. "If it pleases a man to die, he must have known great pride. He thought very highly of his king."

"So do we all." But the tone held an odd undercurrent. "He died at Richard's feet because I was not in my place."

She stared blankly, wanting not to comprehend; afraid she did all too well. "I don't understand."

The gaze did not waver, nor did the bitterness. But he did not mean it for her. "You understand it very well; I can see it in your eyes." The line of his mouth grew taut. "But you are too well reared—you would rather not say it for the sake of courtesy."

It was true, but irrelevant. Marian swallowed heavily, making herself go slowly. Maintaining precarious control. "Are you saying, then, he died because of you?"

"No." The pale eyes, oddly, were black. "Not because of me, but because of what happened *to* me." The voice was exceedingly harsh. "He died because he took my place at Richard's side."

"Your place," she said. Then, with quiet directness, because she could not help herself, "Why were you not in it?"

Self-contempt was unmistakable. "Because a Saracen warlord had already captured me."

She saw it clearly, paraded before her mind's eye. "And so my father took your place. To protect his king. To keep the Lionheart safe." Grief briefly spasmed in her face; she suppressed it with effort, knowing instinctively this man would despise helplessness, or what he perceived as a woman's weakness. "And did he not do so, my lord? Did he not protect his king? The Lionheart yet lives."

"In prison," he said grimly. "In Henry's German fortress."

Anger blazed forth. "At least he *lives!* My father is dead a year!"

A muscle twitched in his jaw. He offered her no answer.

Marian drew breath, trying to steady her voice. She had expected something other than anger, the quiet but powerful anger: this was an earl's son. No doubt he had expected something else also, accustomed to deference. But she was already begun. "If he died at Richard's feet, with you already captured, how did you know to write?"

"He had asked me that morning. We shared a cup of wine." The scar writhed briefly. "Whether he knew, I cannot say. It is thought some men know the hour of their death . . . all I can tell you is he asked me, on my honor, to write you should he die."

The old pain was new again, exquisite in resoluteness. She could not help but murmur, "This is the worst yet."

"No," he answered tightly. "I saw him die. In *my* place, he died . . . while Saladin made me watch."

"Saladin." She stared. "The Saracen himself?"

"Salah al-Din. Salah al-Din Yusuf ibn Ayyub." The name, abruptly, was foreign, *more* foreign, with a different pronunciation; an alien phraseology she realized was, to him, proper and correct, and all too familiar. Not slurred and run together, as English tongues said it. As she herself had, not knowing any better.

Salah al-Din. Saladin himself, the Lionheart's devoted foe.

The jaw muscle twitched again, as if Locksley himself heard the difference echoing in a chamber very far from the Holy Land. He raked a hand through his hair. "Helmless, I am not easily missed. Richard kept me by his side—" He cut himself off, then continued. "The Saracens learned very quickly to look for me if they wanted Richard. Richard was the target. Richard was the goal. Once we knew it, I protested"—again the scar writhed—"but Richard would not hear of it. I was his *banner* . . ." Locksley's tone was ugly. "They took me, then killed your father as he tried to fill the hole."

It occurred to her somewhat laggardly that men in the throes of great guilt often lie about their actions. She did not doubt her father died as Locksley told her. She did not even doubt the truth of his explanation. What she doubted was that no matter what he said, the son of an earl would hardly take the time to write to a knight's daughter. Particularly if, as he said, he was taken prisoner.

Marian cleared her throat, purposefully smoothing heavy skirt folds to hide the trembling of anger in her fingers. "If you were captured just prior to my father's death, how were you able to write?"

Eyes narrowed. "I did not write at once. It had to wait, as did my ransom . . . I wrote when I was free."

"How long ago?"

He shrugged. "Eight months, perhaps nine."

"Eight months! You have been free that long, yet only now come home?"

The jagged scar whitened. "I went to the Holy Land on Crusade. I swore oaths, Lady Marian. . . . Regardless of the circumstances, I do not easily forswear myself. I stayed as long as Richard needed me—" Abruptly, he altered the sentence. "When my service was completed, I set sail for England."

She drew breath, seeking strength and self-control, and recaptured courtesy. "So," she said quietly, "now your task is done. Your letter went astray, but the messenger has not."

The scar burned whiter still. "The messenger *has*," he said. "Very much astray, and cannot find his way back."

She stared openly, startled out of her personal reverie by the nuances of his tone, by the intensity of his emotion. And was equally surprised he would show it so plainly to her. "My lord—"

"There is one more thing," he told her. "I wrote it in the letter, but the letter has gone astray. And so I will say it myself." He looked past her to the door, shut for privacy. Then the gaze returned to her. "Your father said to tell you he can think of no better man. He wanted you to marry the Sheriff of Nottingham."

Four

The knock on the door was loud. Marian did not move. *He wouldn't . . . my father? Would he?*

Locksley, turning from her, lifted the latch, then stepped aside as the door was pushed open with uncompromising force. The earl himself came through, clearly irritated. His expression was black until he saw Marian. He transformed it instantly into a bland, urbane mask. She was nothing at all to him, merely a nameless woman, but peers of the realm divulged nothing to those of lesser rank.

In view of the news from Locksley, the presumption made

her angry. But she said nothing at all. Behind the earl stood the sheriff. She would keep her emotions in check, even as Huntington did.

"Robert," the earl said mildly, "there are guests who wish to see you."

Locksley's face, too, was masked. "They saw me."

The earl's frown was fleeting. He glanced briefly at Marian, assessed her judgment of Locksley's answer, then smiled paternally at his son to make light of the matter. "I understand what it must be like to share the company of an Englishwoman again . . . but you must recall our purpose here, Robert. You can hardly hide yourself away when so many have come in your honor."

Marian looked more closely at the earl. Nothing in his face belied the intent of his words or the cordiality of his tone, but she was struck nonetheless by his lack of comprehension. Clearly he thought only of himself and his own plans for the feast, not of the guest of honor.

She glanced back at Locksley, marking the subtle tautness of jaw, the guardedness of his eyes. Surely the earl could see it. Surely the earl realized this was not what Locksley wanted; that he desired to be elsewhere, in different circumstances.

Plainly, the earl saw nothing of the kind. Merely his son alone with a woman, and not one to whom Huntington aspired to link his heir.

He is blind, Marian thought in shock. *He looks at his son and sees nothing, only the boy who went away. He does not know what he faces . . . he does not know* whom *he faces.*

"Marian." Now the sheriff spoke. "Marian, surely you cannot deny me the pleasure of another dance."

Inconsequentially, it amused her. *Surely I cannot deny your daughter the chance to catch Locksley.* Marian smiled politely. "No more dancing, I pray. Sir Robert brought me news of my father and thought it best divulged in private; he is a most discerning man, well cognizant of my grief. Now, if you will excuse me——?" *There,* she thought, smiling privately, *let them chew on that.*

But her satisfaction faded. Even as she attempted to slip out the door, commotion beyond raged. She heard shouting, some form of declaration——or was it a presentation?——and then the crowds within the great hall were falling back, bumping into one another; or standing in place, bowing and curtseying.

"What now?" the earl demanded irritably as the sheriff moved aside. "By God, what is all this noise——?" And then he halted abruptly, bowing. "Prince John!"

He had her, the minstrel knew. Or *could* have her, if he wanted her; if he so much as suggested. He had grown adept over the years at judging the moment—and the woman's willingness. This one was his.

But did he want her? Perhaps. If none better were forthcoming. That better existed, he knew; he had seen several already, but a rare few had entered the game, playing the proper parts. It left him now with this one.

"Fair Eleanor," he murmured, and saw the answering color blooming in her face, the glint in dark brown eyes. Lips broke, then parted. Her slight overbite intrigued him. "Fair Eleanor, my sweet—I shall make a song just for you."

So easy, she was. Like so many other women. Lowborn or highborn, women were all the same. Give them a smile, a song; the bedding soon would follow.

Fair Eleanor—who wasn't—met him look for look. "Alain," she murmured back, with a throaty Norman inflection learned from her father.

Alain, in Norman French; in English, unadorned Alan. One and the same, to him. He didn't care what they called him, any of them: Norman, Saxon, French. So long as the women filled his bed, and the men filled his purse.

He plucked a single note upon his English lute. "Fairest Eleanor," he murmured, letting her languish on his look. Smiling, he sang.

The earl of Huntington put one hand on Marian's arm and pushed her bodily aside, making room for the newest arrival: Prince John, Count of Mortain, brother to the king. She stumbled, but the sheriff caught her neatly and pulled her out of the way.

John, called Softsword or Lackland when not cursed roundly, came unsteadily into the room aclatter with a heavy chain of office and jeweled ornaments. He was dark-eyed, dark-haired, small, narrow of shoulder and in the space between his eyes. His color was very high and his breath stank of wine. The voice was thick and slurred. "Are you having a feast without inviting *me?*"

It was all at once obvious the Count of Mortain was deeply in his cups. The earl, a powerful peer in his own right, was clearly irritated; just as clearly he desired not to show it. He displayed a polite—and politic—smile as he shut the door. "My lord, I understood you were in London."

"Was," John declared, swaying slightly, until he hitched himself upright. "Now I am *here*. With or without an invitation." His glassy dark eyes went beyond the earl to the sheriff, at whom he raised a negligent forefinger in barest greeting— deLacey grimaced minutely—then paused on Marian's face. And brightened perceptibly, focusing abruptly. "Huntington— is this your *daughter?*"

Marian's skin tightened. She stared blankly back at John, transfixed by his expression.

The earl barely glanced at her. "No, my lord. She is not."

"But—" A royal hand waved irresolutely, seeking the proper answer. "Certainly not your *wife!* Or have you taken to robbing cradles?" His smile displayed bad teeth. "Worth robbing, in this case. Is she?"

Marian felt exposed, stripped naked before the prince. She was cold, then hot, wanting nothing more than to take herself out of the chamber, or fade inconspicuously back into the shadows. This was nothing for which she could have prepared herself, this assault by way of implication and assumption. She felt sick, unsettled, stunned, and desperate for escape. *If I ignore him—if I avoid his eyes*—Clenching teeth painfully, she stared hard at the chain of office dangling from John's shoulders.

Huntington did not smile. "No, my lord. My lady wife is deceased."

John's wavering focus sharpened. "Ah. How convenient . . . neither a wife nor a daughter—" He moved forward, smiling warmly at Marian. It did not improve his breath. "What is your name?"

Make him forget, she appealed. *Distract his attention—do something, anything . . . please don't let it go any farther . . .*

Smoothly, the sheriff interposed an answer before Marian had to. "Lady Marian," he said quietly. "Of Ravenskeep Manor, near to Nottingham."

John glared at him. "I was just there. You were here. But I could go back. It's mine, after all . . . and all the taxes, too."

So the poor complained, and many of the merchants. Again the sheriff spoke easily. "My lord, the Lady Marian is only just recovering from mourning her father's death."

John's dark eyes flickered. "Dead, is he? How did he die?"

He was close, too close. She could smell the bad teeth, sour wine, soiled clothing. She had never before met any man so closely linked to supreme royalty, and yet she could not believe, in good conscience, John was a king's son. Were they not taught better manners?

John's gaze narrowed when she did not answer at once. "How did your father die? Poaching the king's deer, was it?"

It was hideous. He provoked purposely, crudely, seeking chinks in armor so he could rend it, then mend it, reaping a woman's regard. *But to suggest such a crime* . . . Marian felt the shock vibrate through the chamber, understanding it too well. Poachers were common outlaws often purposefully maimed or executed for their crimes. To suggest an English knight was guilty of the same was too much for anyone.

Save apparently for John, who awaited an answer.

Marian cleared her throat, petitioning God for courage and patience. "On Crusade, my lord . . . with your brother the king."

John laughed, then gestured expansively, sketching an ironic and sloppy cross against forehead, abdomen, chest. "How inspiring. Surely God will reward him for piety and duty." Dark eyes did not smile, if the wine-darkened mouth did. "And just out of mourning, are we?" He took one of her hands and tucked it into his arm. "Shall we not waste time?"

"My lord—" She was helpless and apprehensive. This was the king's brother, powerful in his own right; it was entirely possible John could, beneath the earl's roof, do exactly as he desired. "My lord, if it please you, I beg you to let me go—"

"What would *please* me, lady, is to take you off to bed." The slurred tone now was steadier, fixed upon a goal. "Have you a bed, Huntington? And free of local vermin?"

Eleanor leaned closer as the minstrel sang to her. *I have him. He's mine.* She smiled, displaying overbite, promising him full pleasure. She saw no sense in playing coy or delaying what she wanted. And while her father had taken cruel pains to point out she was no beauty, she had not yet met a man who would refuse to lie with her. She was plain, perhaps, but lush, with a body made for bedsport and the temperament to want it.

Others still gathered: matronly women overcome by his blandishments; two or three young wives who had only recently discovered true romance was confined to songs and poetry; a handful of young girls much taken with Alan's Saxon beauty. He was fair, like Robert of Locksley, but with richer, deeper tones in hair, skin, eyes. Curls tangled on velvet-clad shoulders. A smile lingered in blue eyes. Long, supple fingers caressed the strings of his lute.

Eleanor's breath ran ragged. *Why must the game last so long? Why not end it now, and tend to our bodies' needs?*

The shock of John's bluntness and vulgarity overcame the knowledge of who he was, though Marian's natural inclination was to give way to a prince of England. She could withstand what he said of her, no matter how vulgar, no matter how blatant, but to so insult her father roused her to defense.

Apprehension dissipated beneath unexpectedly firm resolve. She jerked her arm free. "My lord—*no.*"

The chamber went very quiet. John stared at her from blood-shot eyes. His chancy temper was legendary. "By God—you *refuse?*"

She coaxed anger and outrage higher to maintain the new-found resolve. She did not resort to displaying either of the former, knowing it too risky, but she did bestow upon John a declaration allowing no doubt as to its intention. "My lord, if

48

it pleases you . . . I am a decent unmarried woman only just out of mourning—"

"And I am heir to the throne of England." John's tone was cold as ice. He stood firmly now, legs spread to steady himself, narrow shoulders thrown back. He had come in a drunkard and was no better now, but had assumed, in an instant, an air and poise of womb-birthed royalty. Dark eyes glittered as color stained his face. He was Angevin-born and bred; one of the Devil's Brood. Everyone in England knew he suffered fools not at all, and tolerated no refusals when his mind was made up. Rumor said he was known, when enraged, to throw himself to the floor, rolling in the rushes and foaming at the mouth.

But he did neither now. He simply waited for her to respond.

It was Robert of Locksley instead, speaking for the first time since John's entrance. "My lord, I invited the Lady Marian into this chamber to hear news of her father. I was with him when he died, and I brought her his final wishes. Surely a man of your sensitivity understands that a young woman having only just heard such distressing news might wish to spend time alone." He paused. "Unless the count is *fond* of tears . . . ?"

John stared back at her. Some of the intensity faded. He was, after all, drunk. "Will you cry? Will there be tears?"

"Yes," she answered at once, knowing how men despised tears.

He loomed close again, bestowing upon her the full effects of sour wine and bad teeth. "Then perhaps you will let me dry them."

She recoiled involuntarily, aware of the sheriff's hand in the small of her back. Men everywhere: before her, beside her, behind her.

"By God," John breathed, "you're the prettiest piece I've seen in *months.*" He reached out a ring-weighted hand and pulled free a lock of black hair, then put the other hand on a breast.

Humiliated, Marian jerked away from the sheriff. If she could get past John, the door was close at hand. She had only to get through it, and lose herself in the crowd.

John laughed and reached out to catch a hand. She pulled it away, twisted aside; her back was to the door. Before her stood four men: the earl, the sheriff, John . . . and Robert of Locksley.

They stared at her, to a man. What they saw she knew: a bodice pulled awry, face flushed from shame, coif knocked slightly askew, and a lock of black hair now freed by a questing male hand. She, who had been treated with respect and honor all of her life, now looked on the dual faces of man: one carved out of power, the other of fleshly desire.

John was the worst. What he wanted was obvious, so blatant as to strip her before them all. But he was in his cups, and a prince of England; no doubt he took a woman the moment he saw her, if such was his whim. Then the earl: cold-eyed, cold-faced man, staring at her now as something other than a woman come to greet his son, but a woman made for a bed. Not his own, never. But did she want his son's?

And the sheriff, preeminently eloquent yet now silent, gaze unwavering. She could not discern his thoughts. She could not separate her judgment of him from the knowledge that her father desired her to marry him.

Lastly, Robert of Locksley.

It was in his eyes she saw the comprehension and the brief, unexpected compassion. To the others she was game; John had made her so. His crudeness had stripped away any pretense of chivalry or decency, discarding dignity and discretion in one moment's burgeoning lust. Women, no doubt, queued up outside the bedchamber door to share Prince John's bed in hopes for a jewel or coin. But she would not. And Locksley, looking at her, surely realized it. He could see it in her eyes; she could see herself in his.

"By God," John whispered, "there's enough for *all* of us."

What little remained of Marian's self-control snapped. Shame flooded her. She turned stiffly, unhooked the latch, and jerked the door open. Even as John began to protest she fled the crowded chamber.

Faintly she heard the words couched in Locksley's quiet voice: "My lord, I was with your brother. Is there anything I can tell you?"

It was, she knew, for her sake. And she blessed him for it.

* * *

Gisbourne gulped too much wine, hiding humiliation in the resultant blurriness. The woman had run from him like a hare from the hound. Was he so bad, then? Was he not worth speaking to? He believed he had been polite, using softer words than was his wont. But he had no personal experience with ladies of high station save to act in the sheriff's stead, and then only briefly. He was to them merely an extension of the sheriff's office, acting on deLacey's behalf; this time, with this woman, he had acted on his own, spoken on his own, hoped his own hopes without recourse to his service.

And she had run from him.

Gisbourne drank wine, tasting only bitterness. Her flight did not make him hate her, nor did it cool his ardor. If anything, he knew now how much he truly desired her, having seen her so close as to smell the tang of her scent; to mark the flawlessness of her skin, the richness of her hair, the glory of Celt-blue eyes.

He sweated. *I must have done something. I must have said something.* But he could not think what. *Please God,* he begged, *let me find the way. Give me the words, bestow upon me the manner, send me the aid I need. I swear, I mean her honor.* Abruptly he broke it off. The wine in his goblet was gone. Only the dregs remained, and he had no more taste for them. What he required was air.

Gisbourne, swearing, sweating, shoved the empty goblet at a servant and hastened from the hall.

Marian made her way back through the celebrants, blinking away the hot tears of humiliation. Each pair of eyes slewed in her direction, each faint smile directed at her, every whisper spoke of *her*—and yet she knew it was untrue. Still, it was worth discussion; she had been the lone woman in a chamber full of men. Wealthy, powerful men. And all of them unmarried.

Heat bathed her flesh. She wanted nothing more than to order her mount saddled so she could return home, but that would require an explanation to her host, the earl, and she could not face him just yet. Not so soon, before so many people. Certainly not as he spoke with Prince John. So instead she would retire to the room she was meant to share with other women guests at evening's end, and make good her escape there. Where she could, God willing, rid herself of the profound distaste John had engendered.

William deLacey prevented her. On her heels he followed, and as she made her way out of the hall he stopped her in an alcove. "Marian—"

She faced him angrily. "Can't you let me go? Have I not been humiliated enough?"

"I am sorry," he said quietly. "John is—difficult."

Tears threatened again. "He is a rutting boar," she declared, overcome by a painful humiliation that gave way to anger, "and someone should castrate him!"

The sheriff squeezed her arm briefly, comfortingly. It was a gesture she would not have questioned, before. But now the subtle intimacies were no longer so subtle; they were replete with potentials she did not wish to consider. Locksley's news had altered her awareness from innocence into mistrust. "Undoubtedly someone will draw the temper from his sword, one day—although they say he has none." DeLacey smiled, striving for the joke. "Perhaps his brother the king, if he ever returns to England."

She did not wish to speak of John or his brother the king. What she wished was to leave, but as she turned to go deLacey's hand on her arm prevented her.

"Marian, wait."

She turned stiffly, irritated by his continued use of her given name. It had not bothered her before, because he was of her father's age and due the familiarity of an elder to the young, but the news from Locksley cast William deLacey into an entirely different light. He was no longer merely the sheriff, friend to Hugh FitzWalter, but also a man who might well become her husband. Marriage vows would make him privy to much more than her name.

"Marian, I beg you—share some time with me. Let us forget John and speak of pleasanter things."

She was wary. Pleasanter things . . . such as marriage? *Does he know?* she wondered bleakly. *Did he speak of me to my father? Did Locksley say anything?*

DeLacey smiled, gestured for a servant, took two goblets of

wine from the offered tray. One he handed to her without asking if she wanted it. Yet another irritation; she scowled into the goblet.

"Come," he said gently, "I know it must be difficult to hear about your father after so much grief, but there is no sense in crying. Why spoil your pretty face?"

Her tone was deliberate. "Now you sound like John."

His smile dropped away. "I merely meant to flatter you for the sake of flattery. Do not hone your tongue on me, when I used mine in your defense."

So he had. He *had* tried to turn John's attention to something other than bed. Marian drew in a deep breath and released it, mastering herself. "I thank you for your kindness and your words about my father, but I prefer another subject."

Mild surprise transformed his urbane features, but a smile banished the moment. He drank a sip or two, then looked out into the hall. "Very well," he said. Then, somewhat tightly, "There is Eleanor. Wasting her time on the minstrel."

Marian saw that indeed the sheriff's daughter lingered very near the minstrel. But so did other ladies. It was not an uncommon occurrence with handsome, eloquent minstrels so knowledgeable of the world and as knowledgeable of women. It was expected. It was part of a minstrel's function.

"It will be difficult, but not impossible. It will take time, of course . . . and a generous dowry . . ." DeLacey frowned absently. "If only I knew him better."

Her attention diverted from John's crudeness or her father's apparent wishes, Marian turned back to the sheriff. "Locksley, or the earl?"

"The earl, of course—Locksley doesn't matter. No, I speak of discovering the earl's appetites . . ." The sheriff glanced at her sidelong, assessing her expression, and smiled. "If you wonder why I speak of such things to you, it is because, in some respects, you are very like your father. He and I shared similar ideas . . . I found it easy to speak with him. And easier, with you; a man would be a fool to deny himself the company of a woman such as Marian of Ravenskeep, even for a moment."

Apprehension welled. *He does know. This isn't because of John— he knows* . . . Marian gritted teeth. *Why not simply say it?*

He shook his head patiently. "It is difficult for me, you know. Your father held Ravenskeep, and now it passes to you. But I am merely a servant . . . if I am to rise in this life, I must use what I have at hand."

Tension increased, but Marian forced an easy, guileless tone. "Such as marriages, my lord?"

He did not bite immediately. "If Eleanor marries Locksley, we are both set for life. It is attractive, I confess . . . but am I wrong to want security for my daughter? Or even for myself?"

Here it is. She gripped the goblet and waited. She knew it would come any moment, the declaration that he knew what her father wanted. Had deLacey known all along, waiting for the time he considered most suitable? Or perhaps Locksley had told him, and now he merely moved to secure her?

The sheriff's smile was pleasant. "A woman of your holdings has no need for Locksley's wealth."

It was not remotely what she expected. She very nearly laughed as tension abruptly dissipated, leaving her strangely giddy. "Lord Sheriff, I promise you, what we spoke about, Robert and I, had nothing to do with alliances. Only with my father." Smiling, she glanced out into the hall where Eleanor stood beside the minstrel. "If you are concerned that my presence might deter a betrothal between Eleanor and the earl's son, be assured I play no part in it. Do whatever you like to make the marriage come off."

DeLacey's smile was odd as he gazed at her. He shook his head slightly. "Poor Eleanor . . . I fear she would be defeated before she reached the field."

It made no sense at all. "My lord—"

Smoothly he interrupted, "I think they will make a fine couple. Do you not agree?"

Marian thought of Robert of Locksley, of whom she knew too little. And of Eleanor deLacey, of whom she knew more than she liked. "Of course," she murmured politely.

While inwardly, unexpectedly, an emptiness was born.

Five

The Earl of Huntington eyed his son in apprehension. Robert was not, the earl felt, paying proper heed to John's temper; in fact, he was not paying heed to *anything*. Certainly not to his father, who had tried and failed discreetly to signal the need for careful voyaging; nor to John himself, currently peering from beneath scowling dark brows in squinty-eyed intensity at the young man only just returned from Crusade.

"Well?" John snapped.

The earl held his breath as his son turned from the door. Locksley's face was devoid of expression. "Well?" he echoed.

Has he gone mad, to treat John this way? Huntington's lips jerked in a brief rictus as he grimaced distaste sharply, giving away his concern. Fortunately John was not looking at him, but at his son.

Not known as a patient man, or one much given to tolerance, the Count of Mortain displayed his intemperate ill-humor. "My *brother,*" he declared between clenched teeth. "You said you had been *with* him."

Locksley inclined his head. A lock of pale hair forsook his back and fell forward across his shoulder, shielding the oblique line of one cheekbone and lower jaw. "So I was, my lord. In the Holy Land."

The earl pressed a hand against his heart, which beat somewhat irregularly beneath costly cloth. Did Robert think any small favor the king had bestowed upon him thousands of miles away might render him inviolate to John's more immediate wrath? Everyone *knew* John was unpredictable, petty, vindictive . . . and completely indifferent to his eldest brother's wishes.

Be calm, he told himself. *No good is gained by assumption before its due time.* Inwardly he nodded. In charity, perhaps his son *didn't* know about John Lackland. Before departing Robert had not been much concerned with court intrigue or the growing discontent among the peers whom his father counted as friends and companions. He had always been a quiet, private boy, much given to disappearing into forgotten chambers in the old hall, or into the nearby wood. Robert had eschewed many of the interests other heirs slavishly followed—but then, Robert had never been *quite* like any of the others, ever; too much of his mother in him.

But he was not now like his mother or anyone the earl recognized, so cold-eyed and masked. *This is not the boy I knew* . . . It registered somewhat sluggishly, with slow acknowledgment. *Private, yes; secretive, often; but not this overwhelming inwardness.*

"My brother," John repeated. "When did you see him last?"

Locksley's eyes flickered minutely. "Before I sailed for England."

John's gaze narrowed unattractively; he had little flesh to spare across the thin bridge of his nose. "Before he fell into Leopold's Austrian hands, and thence into German Henry's."

"Just so, my lord."

In an idleness belied by an underlying intensity, John smiled coolly. "What did he *say,* my lord? The last time you saw him?"

For the first time the earl became aware of the scar winding the underside of his son's jaw. Not new, not old; obvious now only because Robert's color had altered, if only minutely. And then it faded, and the scar was gone, and Locksley was answering quietly. "Many things, my lord. Issuing orders, discussing strategy—"

"With *you?*"

Locksley paused a moment, then let the insinuation pass. "He spoke with many of us, my lord. I was honored to share his confidence on many occasions . . . it was his way, my lord, to gather men to his presence to see what they thought of certain situations—"

" 'Certain situations,' " John again cut in. He rubbed idly at his lower lip, weighing Locksley's expression, then smiled and paced away from the earl and his son. Eventually he swung back. The swaying, slurring vulgarian was abruptly replaced with a cunning intentness and pointed declaration. "We all know what kind of 'confidences' my brother shared, do we not? Am I then to believe *you* were one of his—especial companions?"

Sweat tickled the earl's upper lip. He rubbed at it in distracted annoyance, staring worriedly at his son. He desired very much to interrupt, but recognized the baleful light in John's eyes: he was a hound upon the scent, and nothing would turn him back.

Locksley's quiet tone was uninflected. "There were many of us he called 'friend,' my lord. Does he not call his brother such?"

John was undeterred. His voice was a whip-crack. "He has a wife, and yet no child. Certain reports say Berengaria is barren—while others say it is no fault of hers; that a woman can hardly be expected to conceive when she is yet a maiden. A *married* maiden, Locksley!"

The shout echoed in the chamber. The earl drew a careful breath and looked at his son. *Let him be circumspect. Let him remember there is no need for battlefield manners here, nor a tongue too sharp for John's unpredictable taste.*

Locksley stood very still, strangely at ease. *Collected,* the earl thought, as if he considered this dalliance with words, albeit a dangerous one, as much a battle as anything he had faced in the Holy Land. "It was his greatest regret, that there was no heir for England."

The earl caught his breath in an undetectable jolt of surprise. He was adept at reading the truths behind purposeful falsehoods and approved of Robert's shrewd, layered answer, but was nonetheless taken aback at the magnitude of the undertaking. Perhaps Robert *had* learned statecraft and intrigue—often one and the same—while on Crusade. In between killing Saracens.

"No heir?" John hissed. "Of *course* there is an heir! *I* am heir, by grace of God, two dead brothers, a harridan for a mother,

57

and a fool for a father who named Richard instead of me—"
And then he stopped, very black of face, shaking with rage, and
let the shouting die. He smiled at Locksley, color fading slowly,
abruptly calm once more. He smoothed the soiled fabric of his
costly clothing, touching the heavy chain of office. "There is an
heir, of course. He must have meant no blood of his own
blood—no *seed of his own loins* . . ." The tone thinned, sharpened,
as the topic was altered. "Has he loins, do you think?"

The earl held his breath. He had seen that look before:
probing, precariously tumescent; had heard that tone before,
elaborate provocation. Clearly, John walked the edge. A single
word could push him off, and then everyone would suffer.

Locksley did not hesitate. "Men call him a bull, my lord."

The words hung in the air. The earl began to breathe again,
shallowly, and waited for John's reaction.

Dark eyes narrowed. Then John arched a single brow.
"What do *you* call him?"

Locksley inclined his head. "King of England, my lord."

"Damn you." John's tone was malevolent. "Damn your
pretty face and prettier mouth—I want the truth from you!" He
lurched forward a step, clutching the chain of office so hard his
knuckles shone white. "Do you think I am a fool? Do you think
I have no resources? Do you think I haven't *heard?*"

"Heard, my lord?" Pale brows rose. "Forgive me, but I have
been away for two years. Perhaps you could enlighten me—"

"En*light*en you!" In three strides, John stood before Locksley.
"They say he sleeps with boys. And you were one of them!"

Sunset gilded the walls of Huntington's castle, playing hop-
rock with crenelations and coy arrow-loops. Sir Guy of Gisbourne, sweat drying in the dusk, paused outside the exterior
door leading to the inner ward and leaned against the masonry
wall. Part of him automatically calculated the cost of rebuilding
as Huntington had, marveling at the depth of the earl's coffers.
Another part of him acknowledged the reason why he had fled:
he couldn't face the truth.

He scrubbed at his blunt-featured, saturnine face, unmindful
of the severity of his attentions to vulnerable flesh. Foremost in

his mind was the sense of humiliation he'd felt as he'd discovered the woman gone, after sending him for wine.

God, but it *still* pinched!

It had occurred to him not to ask her to dance. He hadn't really meant to, because she was beautiful, and he was not; and the grace he saw in her movements was alien to himself. A poor match, physically—and yet he could not keep his eyes from her, or the hope from his heart. And when he saw the sheriff dance with her, he knew he had to try. He could not bear to let deLacey prove superior in that, also.

Gisbourne closed his eyes. *I can't* be *what they are. I was born a merchant's son* . . . It niggled at his spirit. He had never been poor, but distinctly *common* . . . and likely to remain so, if he didn't rectify it. Certainly his father had taken the first step for him, buying him the knighthood—but what was left to him? He could offer a woman nothing, save himself, and that was not so much. Not very much at all. *Unless I had more. Unless I were more—somehow.*

A footstep scraped beside him. Gisbourne opened his eyes, half fearing it might be *her,* but it was a man, a stranger, clothed in velvet and brocade.

The man arched a silvering brow as he saw Gisbourne and spoke a greeting in Norman French. Gisbourne answered in the same tongue automatically, responding as he would to his father even though the Saxons clung stubbornly to English, and realized the stranger was as Norman as he was. The accent was pure.

And so they were kindred, recognizing one another. It made them easier with one another, quietly discussing the ugliness of English, and how difficult it was to conduct affairs of business in anything but the language of their homeland and the occasional Latin.

Names and ranks were exchanged: the man was Gilbert de Pisan, seneschal to Prince John.

Gisbourne's response was instant. "But I too am seneschal! To the Sheriff of Nottingham; not so high as your lord, but there is some credit attached." He gestured deprecatingly.

De Pisan lifted a single shoulder in a slight, dismissive shrug. "The ways of the prince are not so different from anyone else's, save he is heir to the throne. And like to be king, soon, if the Lionheart remains imprisoned."

There it was: opportunity. Gisbourne knew it instinctively. He could go no higher in deLacey's service, unless deLacey attained higher office and Gisbourne was named his successor—which he believed unlikely—but there were other masters than the one he served.

Now, he told himself. *If you do nothing now, you have only yourself to blame.*

"I have some skill at stewardship," he declared bluntly, eagerly, knowing no other way; he was not adept at diplomacy. "You have only to ask, and they will tell you. Nottingham Castle thrives under my care."

De Pisan shrugged again. "I have no doubt."

Self-consciousness flickered faintly; was the man patronizing him? Gisbourne forged ahead, knowing himself committed. "Yet a man such as I would be a fool to look askance at a place with a lord such as yours."

De Pisan's smile was wintry. "Just now he has a seneschal."

Gisbourne was horrified. "No! No—I don't mean to apply for your place. I mean only to tell you, and your lord, that if there is room for me in your household . . ." It was not going well at all. He was not a clever man, but honest. And now it was too late. He steeled himself and took a deep breath. "I am accustomed to keeping secrets."

"Ah." The wintry smile altered faintly, though wry amusement still underlay it. "So are we all, we who act the steward. Surely it is a high recommendation that you know when—and when *not*—to speak."

Gisbourne nodded vigorously.

De Pisan lifted a languid hand and gestured idly. "Perhaps. I promise nothing. Be certain I shall tell the prince."

"That is all I can hope for."

Gilbert de Pisan eyed Gisbourne a moment. "Indeed."

John's clear insinuation regarding Locksley's appetites shook the earl soundly. Huntington gagged hoarsely, reaching unsteadily for a chair back. "My lord, I beg you—"

"Silence!" John snapped. "This is no idle accusation, Huntington—I am surprised you yourself have not heard it."

The earl pressed a hand against his chest, breathing noisily. "I—have heard nothing, my lord . . . nothing of the sort—"

"My lord Count." It was Locksley, with faultless courtesy. "If you will permit me to inquire as to the exact nature of your information—"

"I told you," John declared. "Do you wish me to divulge my sources? Do you think me so witless as that?"

"No, my lord. I think the information your sources have given you may be incomplete."

"How 'incomplete?' In nature? They say he sleeps with boys. Do you forget I am his brother? It wasn't kitchen *maids* he tumbled—"

In disbelief Huntington heard his son break into John's diatribe quietly, but decisively. "My lord, the information was incomplete."

"How incomplete?"

Locksley drew breath. "Did the sources mention me by name?"

John leaned forward and grabbed a lock of white-blond hair, shutting it up in a tight fist. "It was told to me, Locksley: a man of fair mien and fairer hair shared my brother's bed."

Locksley's jaw muscles bunched, then released. "Blondel."

John's eyes narrowed. "What are you mouthing now?"

"A name, my lord." Locksley made no attempt to dislodge his hair from the royal fist. "Blondel. A minstrel. A lute-player, my lord."

"And does this *lute-player*"—John made it an epithet—"also boast hair this fair?"

"Yes, my lord. It was often remarked upon that the king had raised up *two* men of such fairness—"

"Raised up?" John pulled Locksley close. He was considerably shorter, which required him to tilt his head back against padded shoulders. "How did my brother the king *raise you up?*"

"He knighted me, my lord."

John released the captured hair abruptly. "Knighted you, did he? And are we *Sir* Robert, now?"

"Yes, my lord. By the grace of God—and the King of England."

John made no answer at once. The blackness had faded from his countenance, leaving him wan, sickly, drained. Dark smudges encircled his eyes. "And Huntington's heir, to boot."

The tone was oddly hoarse, lacking vitality. It was, in a way, resignation; the earl realized, in that moment, John needed Huntington—and all the earldom represented—badly. For income, if nothing else. And influence. And power. John was not king. John was not even officially Richard's heir, not while the marriage to Berengaria of Navarre, however unproductive it might be, promised a potential true-born heir. John needed them all.

Locksley flicked a glance at his father. "Unless he declares otherwise."

The earl summoned a faint smile that masqueraded as paternal indulgence, suppressing the flutter of rising acknowledgment: *John needs us.* "Considering the king himself has knighted you, only a fool would declare otherwise—"

"And are you not a fool?" John was intent once more, summoning reserves as he still scented the hunt. "No, of course not; not our Huntington . . . they say you are the power of Nottinghamshire."

"No, my lord." The earl bowed respectfully. "That, of course, is yourself."

"So should you both recall it." John looked back at Locksley. "This Blondel—does he yet live?"

"I believe so. It was he who found the king in Germany."

"A *lute-player?*"

Privately the earl questioned the abilities of John's informants. Even *he* had heard of Blondel, if in an indirect way. Rumor said he had been raised up from penury by Berengaria herself; only later had Blondel made his way into Richard's service.

"There was a song, my lord—a campaign song. One of the king's favorites. When he was lost, Blondel took it upon himself to travel the lands, following rumors of imprisoned sovereigns—it is said Richard heard the song in his cell, answered it, and so was discovered."

John studied Locksley intently, weighing words. But when he answered he did not question the story. " 'Richard'?" he asked softly.

Locksley's mouth tightened. "The king, my lord."

"He allowed you use of his Christian name?"

"In battle, my lord, such things as rank are often superseded by the familiarity of comradeship—"

"Blondel," John said clearly. "It was a *lute-player* in his bed . . . and not a newly-knighted stripling with a tongue too smooth for his mouth?"

Locksley inclined his head. "You need only ask for the truth of Blondel's appearance—"

"I need only ask for his *presence*. Be certain I shall." John flicked an imperative hand, then turned to the earl. "What entertainments have you for this evening? We are in mind to be suitably honored—and suitably entertained."

The earl drew breath to answer as his son, duly dismissed, departed the chamber in silence.

The trembling lute note died away, sighing into silence of unrequited love. Alain, also called Alan, smiled in bittersweet appeal at the woman so close to him. Just *so*—he had smiled in precisely that manner hundreds of times before. "A sad song, lady. Perhaps a livelier one would appeal more to your taste?"

She was flushed and dark of eye, clearly aroused. Too much wine to fuel the passion, he reflected, as the tip of her tongue breeched parted lips to moisten them. He would enjoy the first tumble, before the wine caught up.

She was trembling, strung to breaking with need. He saw the nakedness of it and the weakness of her will. Easier, he knew. Easier than the others, who played the game with tighter rules, requiring infinite patience. At times, he preferred it; this time, he did not. She was the daughter of the Sheriff of Nottingham, a man of some power. Wiser by far to tumble her quickly and then look to other game.

"Songs have their places," she told him huskily. "But there is more to living than music."

"Is there?" Languidly, he stroked lute strings. Down the neck to the belly with a gentle, long-fingered hand—as he would caress a woman. "Pray, lady, I am but a poor man hoping to share his talent . . . music has *been* my life. I am unaccustomed to other entertainments and certain—civilities."

Eleanor deLacey touched a seemingly idle finger to a plump lower lip, reshaping the line of her mouth. Her eyes were black in dim light. "There are those who can offer instruction."

He smiled. "Indeed."

She removed her finger, swaying forward slightly. "Have you a room?"

He shook his head. "The hall floor shall be my bed." It was customary during overcrowded feasts. Men such as Prince John or the sheriff would have chambers, but most would put blankets in the rushes, slapping away the dogs.

Her mouth crimped in faint annoyance. "Nor have I one to myself. I must *share* . . ." But she let it go, glancing birdlike around the hall. Subterfuge was not her gift. "There are other arrangements."

"Of course."

She leaned closer yet. "Find us a room."

He affected a sigh. "I have no coin, Lady . . . I can hardly bribe a man to leave when there is nothing in it for him." Of course, if the woman were willing to accommodate them *both*, there would be no problem at all. In the past it had proved an efficacious way, but he was not so certain of Eleanor deLacey. Women who drank were unpredictable, subject to flights of fancy.

She clenched teeth. "Find a *room,*" she hissed. And then, on another note entirely: "My father. I must go."

And so she went in an unsteady sweep of skirts as the minstrel contemplated his task. Such things were not impossible. He doubted he would find it difficult to locate an appropriate room, as certainly other men would be pursuing other women, thereby leaving *someone's* chambers available for the taking.

Alan smiled furtive anticipation. As the sheriff approached, he began another song.

Six

The chamber was cool, quiet, dim, and untenanted save for one. Along each wall blanket-wrapped straw pallets butted their heads against stone, offering lumpy but adequate rest; even in the earl's sprawling castle there were too many to house comfortably with proper beds and pillows. But such was often the way even of nobility, stretching hall and castle corners to offer traditional hospitality. Ravenskeep, merely a manor, could not house even a half of the throng crowding beneath the earl's roof.

A single lamp nearby spilled dull illumination, limning the contours of concentration in the angles of Marian's face and robbing it of repose. She stretched limply atop a nubby woolen blanket, contemplating the shadows of thick rafter slabs looming far over her head. In seeming idleness she braided and rebraided a thick lock of black hair.

She recalled in childhood her father hosting friends in Ravenskeep, before her brother, then mother, died, but not so many as to put out the household, or necessitate turning the main hall into a bedchamber. A host must find places for his guests to sleep; that was customary. What was *not* customary, was the sheer multitude here tonight: The earl had invited hundreds of people to feast his son's return, and that many had arrived.

She smiled briefly. In charity, she supposed not *all* of them had arrived; surely there were those who could not attend. And yet she supposed many of them had come less out of true good wishes than expediency. Huntington was a powerful, wealthy nobleman whose holdings stretched wide, as did his influence. He and others like him ruled England in Richard's stead, albeit unofficially. No matter what Prince John believed.

Inwardly she squirmed as she gripped the braided lock. It made her hot to think of John's behavior and hotter still to recall the witnesses. Bad enough, she thought, that the sheriff had to see her treated so badly, so provocatively; worse when she knew full well he wanted to marry her, and that her father desired it.

Had desired it. Sir Hugh of Ravenskeep was no longer in any position to desire anything.

Marian clenched her teeth and threw aside the crimped braid, wedging her temples between two palms as she scowled at the rafters. "How *could* he?" she asked aloud. "How could he decide such a thing during his absence, and then send word through *Huntington's* son?"

That troubled her nearly as much. She had come of private, close-knit kin, desirous of keeping things to themselves. That her father had seen fit to send word regarding such a personal matter without consulting her beforehand was unsettling, particularly in the way he had employed, but his instrument of communication was far worse.

Marian let both arms flop down and squinched shut her eyes. "Why did he have to do it?"

Because he had had little choice. What else was a man to do as he labored in the name of Christ?

It was clear, even behind tightly shut lids. Darkness hid nothing of the harsh truth. She was the sole holder of Ravenskeep, by English law, and yet the protection of that law offered a woman little. It lasted until she married, at which time her property passed to her husband. Yet if she tried to remain *un*married, refusing frequent and persistent suitors, she became therefore a target to the Church, which would suggest to the Crown she marry Christ, so the Church could benefit from her holdings.

It was not at all unusual for a father to make provisions for his daughter's future before going on Crusade. That he had said nothing to that daughter was a cause for pain, because she believed herself privy to everything in his mind. He had said

66

so, once, after her mother had died. *But a man might change his mind on the eve of going to war.*

Now that he was dead and her official mourning finished, she was subject to pursuit. And she would be pursued. Ravenskeep was hers, until she married. It was entirely possible that within a week, a man would come to call. If not sooner.

Noise: a door unlatched and pushed open on the expulsion of impatient, unsteady breath. "Already?" Marian murmured, sitting up to face the door.

The earl turned to Prince John as Locksley left. "My lord, I must apologize for my son's behavior—"

John cut him off, waving an imperative hand. "Never mind him. Who was that *girl?*"

It took the earl a moment to recall the young woman. His mouth tightened. "Precisely that, my lord: a girl. Her father was Sir Hugh FitzWalter. He died on Crusade."

John leaned forward slightly. "She is not wed?"

"No, my lord."

Brows arched speculatively, then snapped together once more. "Then who is her protector?"

The earl kept his voice even. "Your brother the king, my lord."

For a moment only, John's expression was blank. Then the scowl returned. "No, *no,* you fool—I mean, whose mistress is she? Yours?"

It was outrageous. The earl's face tightened. "No, my lord."

One dark brow shot upward as the definitive undertone caught John's attention. He placed a hand across his heart in mock astonishment. "What? Too high for the girl?" He laughed, showing bad teeth. "A fool, then, in truth . . . she looks properly ripe for the bedding." He fingered his chain of office, chiming link against link. Lamplight glittered off rings. "Is she no one's, then?"

The earl's tone was severe. "She is in wardship to the Crown, my lord. I believe such women are required to be chaste."

"At least until the Crown decides to *relieve* them of that chastity." John's expression was speculative. "God knows Richard will never do it . . ." He chewed his bottom lip, eyes narrowed. "Has she lands?"

"Ravenskeep Manor, my lord. Near to Sherwood Forest. The lands are privately held, bequeathed to the family by the Conqueror, after Hastings."

"Then the revenues aren't mine . . ." John nodded thoughtfully. "She is valuable for her holdings, if naught else—though any man with eyes and cock would neglect to think of anything other than bedding her." He scratched through costly clothing to the itch beneath. "No wonder she's in wardship. Richard knows what's good for the treasury, if not what's good for his cock." Small eyes narrowed. "But as I myself *am* the Crown, in all but name . . ." He thought about it, sighed, plopped himself down sloppily into the nearest chair. "Money is scarce, these days. With Henry requiring ransom . . ." He slewed a look at the Earl. "But of course it will be paid."

"Of course," the earl murmured.

John's assessment was blatant. "Because all England wants her warrior-king safe, does she not?"

"Yes, my lord. All England."

The assessment was done. John's attention wandered. Then his expression darkened. "How am *I* to live if all the money goes to the ransom?"

The earl smoothed the weave of his surcoat, thinking about his castle. Thank God the rebuilding was completed, the masons all paid. All too obviously, John was fishing for money. "My lord, the Crusade has drained England badly. But she looks after her own. I'm certain you will be cared for in the manner you prefer."

John grunted. "I doubt it." Then he waved a hand. "Oh, do sit down. There is drinking to be done."

Huntington lingered a moment. *This is my home, not his.* But he did as he was bade.

Marian relaxed as the door opened fully. The intruder was a woman, and therefore no intruder.

The newcomer stopped dead in the doorway. "Who is it?

Who is there?" Her tone was strident, alarmed. She squinted through bad light. "Is there someone here?"

Marian shifted on doubled knees, moving more clearly into wan, smoky lightfall. "Marian of Ravenskeep."

"Marian of—? Oh." The tone conveyed a rush of released tension, renewed impatience, negligent acknowledgment. "I forgot you were here." The woman moved into the chamber and shut the door. "I should know better—*everyone* is here."

"Eleanor?" Marian gathered herself as the woman wavered unsteadily. "Are you well?"

Eleanor deLacey's plain face burst into exuberant, bouyant delight. She crossed both hands against her bosom, as if to still its breathless heaving, or to revel in its unalloyed presumption of passion. "Better," she whispered huskily. "*Better* than well . . ." She moved forward dreamily, into the frayed edges of the sphere of weak light. "*You* saw him. Didn't you? Didn't you see him there?"

Marian, thinking of the sheriff's matrimonial plans for his daughter, nodded. Privately she wondered how anyone could ask such a question; the earl had made such a spectacle out of his son that no one could have missed him.

Eleanor sighed noisily, high-colored and heavy-lidded. "Is he not *magnificent?*"

Marian's smile went crooked, hooking to irony, as did her amusement. Better that Eleanor at least admire her husband-to-be than despise him utterly. "He is—magnificent." If in a hard-edged, taut-wound way.

"And such *music* . . ." Eleanor stumbled over the edge of a blanket-swathed straw pallet, caught her balance with an out-flung hand, then swooped down upon the bedding. On hands and knees, skirts rumpled, she leaned forward, sharing a confidence. "I think he is the most gifted *jongleur* I have ever heard."

"The *minstrel*—" Seeing the sudden alertness in Eleanor's eyes, Marian altered her answer. "Of course! As you say, he is magnificent . . . although I'm quite certain you have been privileged to hear more musicians than I."

Eleanor relaxed minutely, eyeing her sidelong. "Probably," she agreed, then sat back upon her heels. Something blossomed in her dark eyes. After a speculative moment she began to roll slightly from side to side, shifting hips in an odd, loose-jointed rhythm. "I have heard none better," she declared, less effusively but with no less conviction. "And when the Earl is done with him, I will have my father hire him."

Marian was oddly fascinated by Eleanor's odd, repetitive rocking motion as she sat upon her heels. She saw the bloom of color in the woman's face, the slackening of her mouth. "Perhaps the minstrel would be a good addition to your household," Marian agreed, the answer being the easiest to offer. She doubted Eleanor would pay much mind to anything she heard, unless it fit within the confines of whatever momentary thought occupied her, which seemed, for the moment, to be connected to her movements.

"Magnificent," Eleanor murmured. "And if he can find us a room . . ." Dark eyes widened abruptly as she recalled her circumstances. "*Who* are you?"

"Marian," she said patiently; she smelled the wine on the woman. "Of Ravenskeep. Sir Hugh's daughter."

"Oh. He's the dead one." Eleanor stopped rocking her hips. Briefly she stretched her neck taut, clutching her skirts, then sighed gustily and focused once more on Marian. "We should be friends in this. This is of my *own* choosing, not my father's choosing for me. *You* understand." Her gaze was very intent. "Your father's dead, which means you're free—but how would *you* feel if your father had the disposing of you?"

Marian's mouth twisted.

"How would you like it?" Eleanor repeated. "Men lie with whatever woman they will, dipping their tallow ten times a day. But women? We are not supposed to like it. We are to be virtuous, and docile, spreading our legs only for a husband—or two, or three, or four. A *duty*, we are told—and no thought given to us." She grimaced. "There is nothing for us but marriage. And even *that* is not our own choosing!"

Marian stared at her. Eleanor was blunt-boned, brown of hair, brown of eyes, with skin tending to sallow. And yet now, flushed with the passion of her words, with eyes alight and mouth slack, she was something more. Something somehow *confusing*.

"No," Marian said finally. "We're not given leave to choose."

Eleanor bared her overbite briefly in a fierce, feral clenching. "He would not have this minstrel in my bed, given the choice. He would have *no* man in my bed, save the one to which he gives his leave—and I have nothing to say. Do you call this fair?"

Marian politely offered answer, merely to keep the peace. "No, it isn't fair."

"But I will *have* this minstrel—I will!—and there is nothing the Lord High Sheriff of Nottingham can do to stop me." She gazed fiercely at Marian. "Unless you tell him."

This, then, was her point. For the third time, quietly, "No."

Eleanor stared hard at her. "Promise me that. A woman to a woman. No man to meddle with us."

Marian wet her lips. She knew wine when she smelled it, drunkenness when she heard and saw it. But her heart knew an unexpected agreement with Eleanor, a desire for freedom, in choice as well as men. "I promise, woman to woman, I will say nothing of this to your father."

Eleanor weighed her words avidly, poised like a doe set to leap. One hand traced her breasts, another tucked down in the dip of skirt between her legs. "Have you been bedded yet?"

Against her will, Marian felt heat rise into her face. It was all the answer Eleanor required.

"No." The woman's dark eyes narrowed speculatively a moment, glinting renewed apprehension. Then it faded. She smiled, but there was nothing of humor in it. "Then you can't know. What I said, about not being *allowed*—it's always like that, for us. Let men do the sowing of seed . . . it is for the women to reap the harvest nine months later. But let her *enjoy* it? Let her dare admit it gives her pleasure?" She squeezed a nipple until it stood out. "They would name us whores, all of us. And stone us from our houses."

Struck dumb, Marian waited, damp palms splayed across knees. She saw something of John's avid need in Eleanor's eyes, as he had looked upon her in the chamber before the other men.

71

Eleanor bit into her lip. "Is it so bad a thing?" she whispered. "So bad a thing to want a man? Just to *want* a man?"

Silence was loud. When she could, Marian swallowed tautly. "I think . . ." Words failed. She knew nothing of bedding a man, nothing of need, save vague, inexplicable yearnings that occasionally troubled her sleep. But she *did* know there was an answer for Eleanor. "I think it isn't the—wanting. I think it's the *doing*, without the marriage vows."

Eleanor laughed. "No. Even *with* the marriage, we're not allowed to want." She was but a handful of years older than Marian, yet her tone made her aged. "You don't know, yet. And they won't let you, if they have their way. They will marry you off to an old man and you'll spend your life in his bed wondering if there should be more. And ashamed of your wondering."

Marian said nothing. She found herself empty of words, empty of comprehension, aware with painful poignancy of emotions she couldn't share.

Eleanor sighed. "Say again you will not tell my father. He wouldn't understand. He slakes *his* needs, but my own must remain unspoken, lest he send me into the streets for the others to call me whore."

It required something. "He is your *father*—"

Eleanor's teeth showed briefly. "He is a hard man."

Marian did not answer, shut out of a daughter's perception of the man who ruled her life. *Her* father was dead; her life, for the moment, her own.

"You don't know him," Eleanor declared harshly, answering a reprimand Marian had not offered. "Until you live with a man, you cannot know him. You don't know his habits, you don't know his tastes—you don't know *him*." She pressed the back of her hand against a damp brow. "I know myself. I know my tastes. I know my habits. I know what I *want*, and I know how to get it." Dark eyes gleamed in dimness as she pressed palms against flushed cheeks. "I know my father very well. He is a hard man."

And the daughter harder yet. Marian did not smile. "A man must be what he is."

"No." Flat, succinct declaration. "A man must be what he

72

wants to be, no matter the truth of it. If he acts as he truly is, he will never better himself."

Marian did not answer. She watched Eleanor drag aside her skirts as she rose, steadying herself with effort, and take herself to the farthest pallet, nearest the door, to wait for the time she deemed proper to go to the man she wanted so desperately as to risk censure—or worse—by her father. Who was a hard man.

Slowly Marian lay back down, seeking refuge in wan lamplight. She stared hard-eyed through shadows at the heavy rafters overhead, contemplating the freedom Eleanor wanted so badly and her willingness to risk discovery in her pursuit of it.

After a moment she took into both hands the small silver crucifix she wore on a chain about her neck. Softly Marian whispered, "I don't have that courage." And more firmly yet, on a note of despair, "I don't have that *strength.*"

Seven

William deLacey touched fingers to his lips as if in passing, shielding the uncontrollable twist of mirth that seized his mouth. It was gone quickly, banished into bland serenity as he transformed the touch of his fingers to his lips into an idle rubbing of his chin. Inwardly, he rejoiced. How many other men would spend half a fortune to be where he was just now, at *no* cost, absorbing information and intentions known only to those closest to the throne of England? And how many other men would be as able to profit from it?

The chamber was small and excessively private, as John had demanded, lit by a single fist-fat candle placed on the table

73

between them, and the dying light beyond the narrow window. The day diminished quickly.

They were alone, unattended by even a servant. DeLacey had, at John's impatient motion, poured wine for both of them, then settled into the chair he had dragged off the wall to sit opposite the Count of Mortain.

The sheriff glanced thoughtfully at the chamber door. Huntington, no doubt, would profit as well or better from this meeting, if such it was, though with different motive. Huntington apparently aspired to no higher rank than he already had attained, and therefore would not see the confidences in quite the same light as deLacey. No doubt he would weigh the profitability in completely different currency.

But the earl was not present. Prince John had dismissed him to tend his guests, desiring, he said, that the highest ranking official of his shire discuss with the Count of Mortain the business of administering Nottinghamshire.

And so they did discuss it, albeit briefly. John explained he had gone first to the sheriff's city because that murdering peasant bastard was due to be hanged and he wanted to witness it. After all, it was four of the prince's own men the peasant had murdered; he thought it politic he demonstrate to the people how much his men meant to him, and how deadly was such folly. It would not do to let peasants think they might kill with impunity.

DeLacey remarked that of course every man was important to John, and that indeed a public demonstration of justice was required—although initially he couldn't recall the murderer John referred to. Gisbourne attended to the carrying out of executions, although deLacey witnessed them. It was only as he talked idly about other shire matters that he remembered the man in question. A peasant indeed, some nameless English villein—*Will something, was it?*—who had murdered four Normans in John's service. Beyond that, he could not recall; it didn't matter, really.

John quickly lost interest in the shire, muttering of unnamed nobles who plotted against him, and proceeding into a wandering, slurred recitation of his intentions not for Nottinghamshire, but for England herself.

The Count of Mortain slopped loose-limbed in the earl's heavy chair. Prior to and during the meeting he had consumed countless cups of wine and now he suffered for it, though he did not appear to regret it. He propped himself up as best he could, stretching the flesh of his face out of shape as he planted a splayed palm against a reddened, puffy cheekbone. The eyes peering across the table at the sheriff were dilated, bloodshot, slitted.

"Have you bastards?" he demanded.

DeLacey hesitated only a moment. "Of course, my lord."

John nodded. "As have I. As have we *all*—except for my lord Lionheart." He snickered. "Lionheart. Capon-*balled.*"

DeLacey waited. It was best. Prompting John might elicit suspicions, or turn his attention elsewhere.

"Capon-balled," he muttered. Then, more clearly, "No bastards. No mistresses. He tumbled kitchen *boys.*"

Still deLacey held his tongue.

John pulled himself more upright, though the line of his shoulders tilted precariously slantwise. "Do you know what that means?"

This at least he could answer, and correctly. "It means the throne of England is in jeopardy, my lord."

"No." It was curt. John leaned forward, clutching chair arms. "No, it does *not*. I am heir, Sheriff—there is no jeopardy so long as I stand to inherit."

The candle flame between them smoked and danced in John's wine-drenched exhalation. *Not* the correct answer. But then deLacey doubted John would credit him with the perspicacity to comprehend the right one, as Lackland would undoubtedly prefer to point out another's shortcomings to the elevation of his own. "Of course," he murmured.

"Of course," John echoed pettishly. Then he slumped back into the chair, gnawing at a thumbnail. Dark eyes were oddly bright in guttering candlelight. "What do you want, Sheriff?"

DeLacey did not hesitate. "To serve, my lord."

One dark brow arched. *"Do* you?"

"Of course, my lord."

"And is that *all*, Sheriff? Truly all? Or merely the diplomatic answer?" But John did not wait for a response. He leaned forward intently. "All men want something. It isn't a bad trait, you know . . . wanting breeds ambition, and ambition breeds noblemen." He leaned back into the chair. "Sometimes even *kings.*"

Locksley went out of doors because there he knew he could breathe. There he might find peace and freedom, and escape from expectations, parental or otherwise.

The spring evening was cool and exceptionally clear, showing the first pale light of stars. The moon crept above the top of the massive curtain-wall, toothed by crenelations and the square-cut merlons. So much masonry, now. He recalled very clearly when the building had begun, because he had protested. And his mother had been alive.

He walked with newborn shadows, taking solace in secrecy. No one knew he was gone. No one came after him. No one came to pluck at his sleeve and drag him back inside.

No one *knew* he was gone.

As a child Locksley had prized it, his retreat from his father's world. The earl of course despised it, punishing his son many times for neglecting responsibilities, but Locksley had perservered. He made Huntington Hall his, and the forest surrounding it.

But Huntington Hall was vanquished, replaced by Huntington Castle.

He came to a wall. Stopped. Put both arms out and pressed fingers to the brickwork, touching hard, dark stone. Cold, impersonal stone, alien to his flesh. Alien to his soul.

The girl had said something of that. *"When I have been away, I have a ritual. I reacquaint myself, to see if things have altered. Room by room. Hall by hall. Perhaps you might do the same."*

But all the rooms were new. And all the halls remade.

He had prayed so many times—*let me go home again—all I want is to go home*—and eventually was heard. Eventually was answered. And now he *was* home. Other men were not.

Sir Hugh FitzWalter was not.

A tremor ran through him. Bare hands, sheathed in calluses,

spasmed against new walls. Cold, dark stone, now unexpectedly transmuted—

—*to a warmer, paler stone of sun-painted, ochre-gold in the light of a desert sun*—

He shook it off literally, tossing back his thick hair.

—*someone shouted a prayer as the scimitar flashed in sunlight, cleaving air and flesh and bone. One limb, two; the man was abruptly armless*—

"No," Locksley croaked. Sweat ran down his temples, dampening his fair hair. He tucked his face into his arm, scrubbing it free of perspiration, then sank his splayed fingers deep into his hair, scraping it back from his face, tugging against his scalp as if discomfort might replace the visions within his skull. He turned and sagged against the wall, staring blank-eyed into darkness. Before him bulked the new keep. "No more," he muttered. "I am home—what more can there be?"

More than he had expected. Less than he had hoped for.

DeLacey sat very quietly in his chair, daring no comment. He knew now John wanted something specific. He sincerely doubted John talked to men merely to pass the time. And since they had somewhat rapidly disposed of Nottinghamshire as a topic, clearly it was something else. Something John deemed currently important. *Or worth pursuing for future attention.* The Sheriff lifted his cup to stall, drinking only a little. *Does he know something about me? Or merely probe to learn possibilities?*

"Ambition is required, if a man is to be a king." It was a declaration. And then John swore viciously, battering his chair arm with a fist. "Can none of them see how much I care for the realm? How much I long to administer England as she should be administered?" He glared at deLacey. "I am *here*, do you see? Not capering about the Holy Land looking for Jerusalem!"

DeLacey held his silence. In a moment, as expected, John's fury passed.

"I care," John said forlornly. "I want to *protect* the realm. My brother absents himself and leaves her shores unguarded, stealing from her heart the men England requires to keep her people safe."

The sheriff decided against mentioning that England—and

her people—appeared to be quite safe, as Philip of France did not currently have designs upon her shores, and everyone else of any note was as drained of soldiers as England, since Richard's passion for crusading had touched so many hearts.

John's tone thinned into petulance. "Surely if my father had known Richard intended to absent himself with such rapidity and determined repetition, he'd have named *me* his heir."

It was time to give him something. "Undoubtedly, my lord."

John laughed. The candle flame curtseyed and bowed, nearly extinguishing itself. John lifted and studied the heavy chain of office slanting across his chest. When he dropped it, gold chimed. "How did you get your place, deLacey?"

A new tack. DeLacey hid his instant consternation. "I was appointed, my lord. By the king, your father."

"And?"

DeLacey wanted to echo the question, trying to anticipate John's goal. But he could not. "And so I served him, dispensing the king's justice."

John picked at a stain on his costly surcoat, but the dark gaze didn't wander. "And was there not something else? Something more?" Fingers stopped plucking. "Were you not dismissed from office?"

A coldness invaded deLacey's belly. With effort, he kept it from showing on his face. "My lord, I was."

John once again inspected the chain of office. "And yet here you are."

Damn him, does he want me to repeat what everyone knows? But yes, of course John did; it was his way. "I was reappointed upon the king's accession."

"No." John smiled. "You were not *re*appointed, Sheriff. You bought your way back to the office by paying my brother a predetermined sum."

DeLacey sat very still. "Crusades are costly, my lord. The king required money."

"And to get it, he sold off half the kingdom." The chain was dropped again with a chime of finality. "Oh, don't be so concerned, deLacey!—hundreds of *others* did it, as well. It was my brother's idea . . . as you say, crusades are costly. The warrior-king was more concerned with the state of the Infidel's soul than with the state of his own realm." John's color was high. "But he gave me Nottinghamshire, along with a few other counties—generous of him, was it not? To give the poor youngest son a pittance?"

Pittance indeed. John had married into property via Isabelle of Gloucester, and Richard had given him more: six great counties—Nottingham, Derby, Dorset, Somerset, Devon, and Cornwall—not to mention the honor of Lancaster. No more Lackland was John. Just as Henry was no longer king.

The Count of Mortain shifted in his chair. "Why did you not buy a higher office?"

DeLacey smiled thinly. "I couldn't afford it. I bought what I could with my late wife's portion."

"Ah." John laid seige to his other thumbnail. "But why *this* office? Why not another one?"

Tell him no more than you must. He knew it instinctively. "I am known here, my lord. My policies are established. It seemed the sensible thing."

"Sensible thing." John smiled, spat nail. "And are you a sensible man?"

"I believe so, my lord."

John grunted. His gaze, despite the wine he'd imbibed, was unclouded. "What do you *want*, deLacey?"

The sheriff tilted his head in quiet deference. "To serve you, and Nottinghamshire."

John's eyes lidded. The tautness of his body slackened even as the hard line of his mouth softened, hooking cynically. "Not precisely the answer I wanted. But for now, it will do." He waved a dismissive hand. "Leave me, deLacey. And send Gilbert de Pisan here."

De Pisan came and shut the door behind him. "My lord?"

John shifted in the chair. The glitter in dark eyes was unmistakable. Much wine had passed his lips, but the brain was mostly untouched. De Pisan had learned that John, whose tolerance for wine was higher than most men's, often played the drunkard as a ruse to lure careless comments out of allies and enemies. De Pisan was neither: he was the prince's seneschal.

"Well?" John invited. "What have you learned?"

De Pisan inclined his head. He was older than John, silvering, spare of frame and words. But he knew what he knew, and shared it freely with his lord. "The earl is far wealthier than even we suspected, my lord. To build this castle another man might have beggared himself, yet Huntington's coffers appear untouched."

John hitched a single shoulder. "He could have borrowed it all from the Jews."

"The Jews have suspended much of their moneylending, my lord. Just now, few men can borrow coin."

Dark brows snapped together. "I had heard no such thing."

De Pisan smoothed velvet and brocade. John allowed him luxury, so far as it did not exceed his own. "There is talk the Jews intend to raise much of the king's ransom. Instead of lending coin, they gather it for that purpose."

"*Do* they?" John slumped back in the chair, chewing absently on a fingernail. Both thumbs were barren. "What do they want of Richard? He's no friend of the Jews . . ."

It was rhetorical. De Pisan held his tongue. Others, he knew, might name John *less* of a friend, but he was not the man.

John grunted, dismissing it, and looked more intently at his steward. "What else?"

"The earl is in constant touch with others of his ilk, my lord. The barons are displeased."

"With me? Are they? Damn them." John leaned forward and scooped up the cup of wine. "Can't they see I am king in all but name? Kings need money."

"Yes, my lord."

John drank, slapped the cup down, and tugged irritably at the fit of his surcoat. "Anything else?"

De Pisan gestured deprecatingly. "There is a man, my lord—a knight, though the rank was bought. Sir Guy of Gisbourne. He is the sheriff's seneschal." De Pisan smiled slightly. "He requested most vigorously that I commend him to you."

"Did he?" John pursed his lips, gnawing absently at the bottom. "DeLacey's seneschal . . ." He slumped back in the chair. A smile curved his mouth. "Send him to me tomorrow."

Shadows lived indoors also. Locksley sought and stood in them, watching in some bemusement the celebrants come to praise him for a nonexistent valor because they wanted to please his father. They were different, all of them . . . so different from what he was. And yet once he had *been* them, each and every one of them, taking shape as his father wished, because the potter's hand was sure. The clay christened Robert, later apportioned Locksley as a mark of his heritage, had been malleable as any, mere sludge upon the wheel—until Richard took up the newmade work and broke it into pieces. Perhaps it might have been mended, once, before Saladin shattered the fragments.

Locksley shut his eyes. He wanted no part of this. He wanted no part of *them*.

"Robert?"

His eyes snapped open. Before him stood the sheriff, who was not, most emphatically, Richard Coeur de Lion.

DeLacey's manner was practiced elegance. "Forgive me if I intrude. But there is something we should discuss."

Locksley's shoulders tightened. *And so it begins.*

William deLacey smiled. "You are just home, I know, and doubtless needing time to reacquaint yourself with a way of life set aside for two years . . . but I am a man who believes in confronting a difficulty head-on."

Locksley didn't smile. "The king could have used you at Acre."

The frown was infinitely fleeting, but the brief glint in deLacey's eyes told Locksley the bolt had gone home, regardless of subtlety. Which therefore told him something of the sheriff. "Indeed, Robert—but if we *all* went on Crusade, what becomes of England?"

"Indeed, Sheriff." The edges were fraying. He could *feel* them fraying. "Pray, pose me the difficulty."

DeLacey's brown eyes glinted with something akin to rueful amusement. "Plainly put, Robert: my youngest daughter is unmarried."

He might have laughed, once, saluting the sheriff's sally. But now he did not. "And so am *I* unmarried."

The sheriff smiled urbanely. "And now it lies in the open; no more subterfuge. I doubt obscurity is what you'd choose, given a say in the matter. And I do intend to give you a say in the matter—"

"And my father."

"And your father." Another man might have faltered, might have blustered, or fidgeted, or denied it. William deLacey did not. "Others will also present themselves, their lineage, their daughters. Certainly the dowry. But they will go first to the earl. I come to you."

A stray, unbidden thought crept into Locksley's mind. *I am light. Too light. There is no weight.* "I took it off," he said aloud. "No—they took it from me. There, in front—" He stopped. He *stopped* himself. The face staring back was not the Infidel's. It belonged to an Englishman, an Anglicized Norman, or a Normanized Englishman. They all of them were so, people like deLacey, born and bred in England but adhering to Norman ways. *And I serve a Norman king.*

William deLacey, staring. Then asking him the question: "Are you all right?"

No, Locksley answered silently. Aloud, he said, "Of course," offering nothing more. If one offered little, others would then have to take. That he could live with. With giving he could not. "Of course," he repeated, for the sheriff's benefit.

DeLacey's gaze was speculative. Then he inclined his head. "If you will excuse me, Robert."

It wasn't a question. Thoughtfully, Locksley watched the sheriff go, knowing he'd given the man cause to temporarily cut off—only temporarily, Locksley anticipated a siege—his overture concerning the daughter made that clear. Not in words, perhaps. Nothing in what was said. But in what he hadn't said.

Whatever deLacey was—ambitious, opportunistic; no different from the others—clearly he wasn't a fool.

Locksley gripped and rubbed a forearm, aware of a vague disquietude because he didn't know the cause for the conviction nagging at him. *Too light. No weight.*

And then the answer arrived, cloaked in memory.

They had stripped him of his mail, there on the battlefield before his compatriots. He'd never worn it again.

Though Richard had offered him new.

Eight

At cockcrow Marian awoke. She lay very still, contemplating her state: she was abed with Matilda, her old nurse, and countless other women all tangled amidst shared covers and rustling straw-filled mattresses put down to soften the floor. A draft touched knee and elbow; she had slept at the end nearest the corner and therefore suffered more than others the whims of fickle covers.

Marian hunched, pulling knee and elbow back into scratchy warmth, and squinted somewhat resentfully into the dim, mote-filled daylight. *I should go home.*

It was as definitive as abrupt, shocking her out of lassitude into total wakefulness. Her disquiet passed into painful recollection: all too vividly she remembered John's actions and the sick humiliation that had followed. Marian gritted her teeth. She wanted nothing more to do with John, or her host, or her host's son; most certainly she wanted nothing more to do with William deLacey.

But why? her conscience asked. *Better to marry him, whom you know, than a decrepit old stranger.* Yet Marian was not at all certain. Each time she thought of the sheriff she thought also of his manner, the underlying suggestiveness and secrecy she was beginning to see too clearly. And after talking with his daughter—

Eleanor was perhaps not the most unbiased of observers. Better she judge for herself.

Should I marry him? Or, perhaps a better question, why should I not marry him? Her father clearly wished it. He had sent the message with the earl's son, which indicated he knew himself likely to die and Locksley likely to live.

Because he was Huntington's son?

It's too early to think of such things. She flung back covers and was rewarded by grumbles from Matilda, who hitched a heavy hip so it jutted roofward and yanked the covers back over a substantial shoulder.

Marian smiled briefly. Then amusement and fondness were replaced with determination. "I'm going," she muttered. "That is that; it's decided." On knees, she shook her sleeping-braid free of straw and tried valiantly to tame the escaping locks so she could tuck everything away into her linen coif. Then, having smoothed the rucked-up kirtle and undershift, she was all bound up inside *and* out, wanting to flee Huntington Castle but hating herself for cowardice.

Courtesy required she find her host and beg his leave to go, but probably the earl wouldn't miss her if she simply slipped away. *I doubt he knows I was here* . . . Marian staggered to her feet, picked a last bit of straw from her hair, turned toward the door.

Through it came Eleanor deLacey, pale, with dark-circled eyes aglitter. Lank brown hair was mussed, falling free of her stained, lopsided coif; the saffron kirtle was soiled, and a rose-hued smudge of a bruise stained the side of her neck. Briefly she touched it as she saw Marian's gaze, then drew her hand away with a grimace. A flick of fingers pulled her hair close to hide it.

Outside in the bailey someone shouted an order. A second shout answered it. Eleanor sighed deeply, thumping the door closed. "Damn him," she said evenly. "Damn him *and* his hunt!" She squinted the length of the room, marking the swaddled women still under coverlets. A few were stirring; one slurred a complaint about the inconsiderately loud talking. Eleanor merely laughed. "If you think *I'm* talking too loudly, what will you say to the hounds?"

Another woman peeled back the bedclothes, scowling

blackly. "What hounds, Eleanor? Or do you mean the men gathering at your heels?"

But the gibe went wide. Eleanor merely laughed again, unperturbed by the discourtesy or the edged tone. "And don't you wish *you* had a few, Joanna . . . or even one." She paused, tilting her head, as the shouting beyond the wall was joined by a chorus of hounds answering the winding of a horn. "There. The oliphant; what did I tell you? The count has decreed it, and now the poor earl must roust out his huntsmen without giving them proper time." Eleanor raised her voice. "Nor *us*, I might add; we're all to accompany John."

The last was met by groans, murmured prayers, noisy sighs of resignation. But no one said she would not join the hunt.

Irresolute, Marian scowled toward the door. Eleanor, lingering there, arched her eyebrows. "Did you not sleep well?"

Marian shrugged. "Well enough."

The sheriff's daughter smiled. "And I not at all."

Upon reflection, Marian wondered why Eleanor had entreated her the night before not to reveal the assignation with the jongleur. Here, before all the others, Eleanor made no secret of her behavior, nor did the other women appear to be ignorant of her habits. If anything, Eleanor appeared to *enjoy* it . . . and yet the night before Marian would have sworn Eleanor *did* care; that perhaps she cared too much.

On the other side of the wall the oliphant sounded again. The women in the chamber answered the summons with less enthusiasm than the hounds, but with no less attention to duty.

The Earl of Huntington was a wealthy man and a powerful peer who enjoyed the privileges of his rank. His family had been granted vert and venison, which gave the Earls of Huntington and subsequent heirs the right to hold and hunt private chases, portions of the forest given over by the king. The Forest Laws set out by the Conqueror and codified by Henry II did not apply unless the earl chose to apply them. He was free to hire his own wardens and foresters, and did; to hold his own forest court so as to administer the law, which he did twice a year; and to dispose of poachers and trespassers in the manner he desired.

The earl believed in leniency; he usually sentenced poachers to imprisonment lasting no longer than a year and a day.

The chases of Huntington were thickly wooded and as thickly inhabited. Prince John, aware of the reputation the earl's estate enjoyed, declared himself much taken with the idea of hunting boar. It bothered him not in the least that boar was winter sport; he professed himself weary of stag and falconry and desirous of hardier game.

The earl, weary of John, nonetheless bade his huntsmen do their work, and waited in resignation as the kennels were emptied of hounds, the stables of horses, his kitchens and larders of bread, wine, and ale.

And his castle of bleary-eyed guests.

Locksley lay abed even after the oliphant sounded, seriously considering remaining there the better part of the day. He was lethargic and unexpectedly wan-spirited, though he had done little more the day before than listen to his father discussing plans for the feast. That done, he had intended to ride to the village of Locksley and the surrounding lands. He felt it only just he pay heed at long last to his namesake holdings, which he had never visited.

He had drunk little but watered wine with the meal, taking his leave of the festivities before many of the guests. Unlike others he would suffer neither for too much wine nor too little sleep. Yet now, uncharacteristically, he lay sprawled beneath covers in his huge curtained bed and hoped against hope no servant would come to rouse him. He wanted nothing to do with the hunt, nothing to do with his father, nothing to do with Prince John, William deLacey, or deLacey's faceless daughter.

He frowned. *Was* she faceless? Nameless, no; the sheriff had seen to that. Eleanor, for the queen—except Eleanor of Aquitaine no longer was queen. That title had passed to Berengaria of Navarre, once Richard had married her—and yet Locksley knew some might argue the poor Spanish princess was no queen at all, deprived of the title even as she was deprived of husbandly attentions to the extent that she could not even be called a *wife*.

He stirred. Lethargy evaporated, replaced by frustration and a vague, annoying disquiet. He rolled over onto his belly and pressed his face into the pillow, damning Richard and John and dead King Henry—and even Berengaria, who was hardly to be blamed.

Aloud he muttered, "Faceless Eleanor . . ." He could recall no particular woman. Many of them, yes, but all now were blurred: fair-haired, dark-haired, even one or two with red, and myriad Norman kirtles and girdles belting waists both large and small, hips both sprung and tight.

Except for FitzWalter's daughter. Her he remembered if for no other reason than the knowledge of who she was: the only surviving heir of the man who'd died in his place.

Beyond his chamber, echoing off masonry walls, the oliphant sounded again, followed by a chorus of hounds. Locksley swore, covered his ears, and felt the pull of scar tissue across spine and shoulders. Because of it and other scars he slept in a fine-worked Norman bliaut. He wanted no servant to see. He wanted no questions asked.

A knock at the door, followed hard by inquiry. "My lord?"

He shut his teeth together and stared with some determination into murky day, counting motes on a shaft of newborn sunlight.

The voice was unrepentant. "My lord—your father the earl requests you attend him. Prince John has called for a hunt." It was muffled by thick wood, but clear enough for comprehension.

Locksley considered a succinct, pointed comment that as he was not deaf he knew very well there was to be a hunt. But he said nothing, knowing it would mark him churlish and ill-tempered—he was not that, usually—and it was unnecessary to chide a servant for merely doing what he was supposed to.

Locksley twisted his head across a shoulder, stirring his shock of near-white hair. He pitched his voice to carry. "Tell my lord father I will attend him directly."

It was enough to content the servant; nothing more was heard from the other side of the door.

Locksley swore again, mixing Arabic with English, then scrubbed his face with a splay-fingered hand, scratching stubble so fair as to be invisible. He abjured the oliphant to cease its winding, then absented the bed and groped for fresh clothing. Plain, unadorned clothing, less ostentatious than those he'd worn the night before.

But green again, nonetheless, the better to hide in foliage if the hunt offered an opportunity to slip away unnoticed.

Marian was adamant even as gray-haired, gray-robed Matilda remonstrated. "He won't even know," she declared. "All we have to do is go one way when the hunt goes the other."

" 'Tisn't *right*," the woman declared, putting voluminous clothing into order with short, spatulate fingers. "You're to ask the earl's leave."

It was said as forthrightly as a mother would to a daughter, rather than servant to lady. Matilda *was* a mother to her and had been for years, and she was due equal courtesy. With effort Marian held her tongue from harsh words. Matilda was aging, far too fat, and her joints ached in the morning. It was not Marian's choice that the nurse accompany her on longer journeys, but Matilda said she had sworn an oath to Sir Hugh that required her presence; it mattered little there were other, younger women who could accompany Marian. She had nursed her from a babe, and would go on until she died.

Marian forbore from reminding Matilda that one unnecessary journey could well contribute to that death. Refusing the woman would merely make Matilda feel unworthy and useless.

She wrapped the dark blue woolen mantle over her shoulder, suggesting Matilda do the same with her own. "We'll go down," she said, arranging the folds deftly. "If the earl is free, I'll ask his leave—but if he's busy with Prince John or the like, we'll simply go." Knowing he *would* be busy; it was what she counted on.

Matilda's brown eyes narrowed into rolls and creases. "And no breakfast first?"

Her charge proposed a compromise. "I'll ask for bread. We can eat on the way." Before Matilda could comment Marian bundled the old nurse into her mantle and aimed her toward the door.

* * *

Alan, in the musicians' gallery overlooking the great hall, watched the men and women of England's nobility rouse themselves from rushes and cowpats of cloth, even as others spilled into the hall from stairs, then out again through doors to the morning light beyond. He leaned his elbows against wooden balustrade, lute strapped over his back, and smiled in idle amusement; they were, he thought, less men and women than children, scrambling to keep a short-tempered father from shouting with impatience, then resorting to a buffet on this pair of ears or that.

"King of England," he murmured. "Or near to being, anyway—unless the Lionheart comes home."

Richard Coeur de Lion. The lute-player's callused fingers twitched; there was music in the name. A chord entered his head, then another and another, and a title, melody, and lyrics, tumbling over one another in the rush toward creation. Sometimes they came too fast, and were lost. Or sometimes too slow, while he despaired of pleasing his Muse. If he could catch this one . . .

He straightened, reaching to unhook the lute—then stopped, arrested. The others had all gone out, answering the horn. One now came late—no, two. But the second one didn't matter.

The coif was slightly askew, as if she hastened, baring much of a milky brow. Braided black hair spilled free of containment, falling over a shoulder to dangle below a breast. She paused at the bottom of the stair, extended a slender arm, and put out a hand to her companion—an old, fat, stiff-moving woman, not worthy of his time—then glanced quickly around the hall.

She did not look up, only around. And Alan, somewhat abruptly, *wanted* her to look up. He leaned down, gripping wood, and whistled as for a hound.

Once. A soft sound that nonetheless carried. She heard it, followed it, glanced up, mouth parting, clearly startled. He saw the pure piquancy of features and the clarity of bone, the tilted set of wide blue eyes, the slant of crow-black, upswept brows beneath the white band of coif.

Their eyes met. Color bloomed in her face. She turned

quickly, caught at the old woman, and hastened her out of the hall.

Alan clutched the balustrade. He had known the night before that she was beautiful. He had known the night before she was fodder for a song. But now, seeing her caught in midstride, swaddled in summer mantle, obviously in flight—Daphne from Apollo—he found his Muse even more demanding than before. *She was made for a song.*

"You will be late," a voice said.

Alan jerked upright and turned stiffly to face the man. What struck him first was the change from darkness to daylight: the face, the eyes, the hair . . . fair, so *very* fair, while she was blackest black . . . Knowledge flowed sluggishly in. *God, it is the earl's son.* He nearly stammered. "My lord?"

"You will be late." A clear baritone, hiding nuance with matter-of-factness.

Alan tugged at his tunic, feeling the weight of lute hung belly-heavy and somewhat haphazardly aslant his spine. "I had not intended to go."

One fair brow arched beneath pale hair. "Why not? Does the count not require music when he breaks his fast?"

Alan gestured deprecation. "Nothing was said, my lord—" And then hope surged. If he were able to go after all, doubtless there would be more reward in it. "Do *you* require it?"

Robert of Locksley, dressed in uncompromising dark green and a touch of brown—tunic, leather jerkin, hosen—shrugged negligently. But the eyes were not so compliant, nor entirely *there.* "What I require has little to do with music."

I don't follow him . . . But Alan dismissed it, summoning his notorious charm, meaning to hold Locksley until an invitation was extended. He had done it many times, with men and women alike. Men as well as women were helpless before unfettered flattery and the unmatched skill of a practiced minstrel.

First the prelude: "Ah, but there you err, my lord. I am but a poor minstrel with little skill, save for an ear of unsurpassing acuity—yet I hear the rich timbre in your tone. I'll wager you could pluck a lady's heart from her breast with your song, were you to honor her so."

90

Immune, Locksley did not so much as smile. "I leave that to you."

It was decisive, providing no room for maneuvering. Short of grasping Locksley's arm, Alan could do nothing but give way gracefully. And so he did, stepping aside as Locksley moved by him. He inclined his head briefly in tribute to the other's rank, but lifted it almost immediately to watch the earl's son go. When Locksley was out of sight, the minstrel swore softly. Nothing for it, today, but to wait for the hunt to end.

"Is he gone?" ·

Alan turned swiftly and rearranged his expression. "Fairest Eleanor!" Just the right tone, he thought; color surged into her face.

"Dearest Alain." She was dressed unremarkably, with bundled hair hidden by linen. The sallow, plain features underscored the clarity and beauty of the other coif-rimmed face he'd seen. "*Dearest* Alain—I must go on the hunt. But given the first opportunity, I will slip away and come back to you."

"Here?" And then cursed himself for his laggardness; of *course* she meant here. He smiled, took the outstretched hand, pressed a kiss upon it. "Fairest Eleanor, I shall be counting the hours as I wait."

The smile was intensely suggestive. "Don't count so many— I'll come straight back as soon as I break off. It shouldn't take too long. . . . My father will be much too busy trying to impress the earl or the count—or possibly both at once, if he can contrive it—and won't even notice when I leave." She impressed her body upon his own and reached between his legs, unmindful of the openness of the narrow, unscreened gallery stretching across the hall. "Make me a song," she whispered. "Make one just for me."

Alan, bending to kiss her parted mouth, wondered how he could transform the newly conceived song for the other woman into one for Eleanor.

But his consternation was brief. His experience was vast.

Sir Guy of Gisbourne, summoned somewhat imperiously by Gilbert de Pisan as the first oliphant sounded, relieved himself with alacrity, dressed even more hastily, and accompanied the count's steward willingly enough, though he had no idea why de Pisan might want him. He merely went as bidden because he was accustomed to doing the bidding of others; it was reflexive. Authority spoke. It was not something of which he was proud, but at least no one could fault his dedication to duty.

He knew no one would. No one cared enough.

Gisbourne was brought up short at a chamber door flanked by armed men and realized, with some surprise and more unsettlement, he was not brought to see de Pisan but de Pisan's lord. "Briefly," John's seneschal warned. "And disagree with nothing. My lord count and mornings do not often agree." Something like contempt passed through de Pisan's eyes. His smile was faintly derisive; he unlatched the door and paused with fingertips resting on wood. "You understand my lord count is the man to whom England looks while the king is imprisoned."

Gisbourne, skilled with accounting and administration, did not claim to be courtier or diplomat; words were not his skill. But he had attended the sheriff long enough to understand implication, even couched in falsehood. "Of course," he agreed stolidly, thinking ahead to the chamber housing the king's brother. He would agree with whatever de Pisan said. His experience was vast.

"I knew you were a man of sound judgment," de Pisan murmured. "I have told my lord so."

"Told—him?" Gisbourne lingered between corridor and chamber.

"Of course." The mask was bland. "Did you not ask that I commend you to him? I have done so."

Gisbourne nearly stammered his thanks. Then, as de Pisan waved him on, he crossed into the chamber and came face-to-face for the first time in his life with England's sanguine savior.

Or the man who would *like* to be.

Nine

Prince John smiled a measured welcome as body servants labored to attire him. Gisbourne counted three men, deftly adorning their slightly built lord with bliaut, chausses, tunic, padded surcoat, belt, boots, and myriad ornamentation. Through it all John stood loose-limbed and malleable, letting them beautify him.

He doesn't look discomfited by morning. Gisbourne bowed. *He looks alert as a hunting hound.*

"Ah," the count said. "I was so hoping you'd come."

Gisbourne, straightening, wondered if any man would refuse.

"Do you hunt boar?" John inquired.

Gisbourne did not answer at once. He was transfixed by the knowledge of whom he faced, by his wholly unanticipated closeness to sovereignty. He had not aspired so high; he had merely desired knighthood because it lay within the realm of possibility, as Richard sold off the chivalry of England. But this was impossible. This was preposterous. He, Guy of Gisbourne, never mind the "Sir," stood in the same chamber—to which he had been *summoned*—with Prince John of England, who might one day be king himself.

He didn't *look* like a king, Gisbourne reflected. He didn't much look like a prince, either, except for his richness of dress. He was small, dark of hair and eyes, swarthy of complexion. His nose was a trifle too long, and the negligible width of shoulders beneath the careful padding was no broader than slim hips.

He looks like a bird, beak and all. But Gisbourne shook it away.

Boar, John had said. Did he hunt boar? "My lord, yes. I have. And *will*, today, as you have invited. If there is boar, this time of year." He paused, briefly horrified. "I mean—of *course* there will be boar." Gisbourne cursed himself, wishing he had de-Lacey's unflappable temperament. *He* would know what to say, and how to say it. "There will be, of course. Boar."

"Of course." John tightened a ring on one finger as his body servants clustered around, arranging folds, tying ties, settling heavy, embroidered sleeves. "God grant we all have good luck."

Gisbourne nodded mechanically. *He is narrow between the eyes, like a horse with a small brain.* But from what he had heard, neither John's brain nor his ambitions were undersized. "Yes, my lord. God grant."

"I had you brought here because there is something I must ask. It regards your employer." John's expression was tranquil. "It is my task, you know, to administer my brother's realm while the king is imprisoned."

There was a peculiar pause. Gisbourne rushed to fill the poised, expectant waiting. "Yes, my lord."

"Therefore I must take measures to insure the welfare of all the shires—no, not *that* one, you fool . . . this one!" John snatched a ring from one of the body servants and thrust it onto a finger. He contemplated the choice, then nodded once and returned his attention to Gisbourne. "I believe you may know William deLacey best of all, Sir Guy. What say you?"

Dampness stained the sleeves of Gisbourne's undertunic. He cursed his nervousness. "My lord, it would seem so—I am his steward, and am privy to his business."

John selected another ring. The emerald glistened richly. "He is a modest man, your sheriff, as becomes a man of taste—we would have him content in his office, so he may continue to serve us as well as can be expected from a man of his talent." Gisbourne did not miss the shift to the royal "we." John admired the emerald, and the slim hand that wore it. "Therefore we are at some pains to discover the true ambition of our most loyal servants, so we may reward them accordingly." Dark eyes glittered briefly as he lifted eyelids fractionally to hold Gisbourne's gaze. "Is there something he desires above all else? Something within our power to grant?"

Gisbourne thought frantically. He knew very well deLacey wanted power and preferment, but so did everyone else. For that matter so did *he;* what could he tell Prince John that might set him apart, marking him, Gisbourne, as an attentive man, alert to his lord's desires more than other men?

Hastily Gisbourne brushed at the dampness stippling his upper lip and struck at the first option. "His daughter, my lord."

John's brows arched eloquent inquiry.

"His daughter," Gisbourne repeated, "married to Huntington's son."

"To Huntington's son? Locksley?"

"He's the only son he has. The earl, I mean." Gisbourne cleared his throat. "Eleanor, my lord. To Robert of Locksley."

"A worthy, if ambitious, alliance." John's expression was closed. "The earl is a powerful man."

"She's the only one left, my lord. He's married off all the others. He was despairing of a match, until Locksley came home." Gisbourne shrugged, affecting nonchalance; he felt far from it. "She's old for it—twenty-three, my lord—but not so bad a match."

"The earl might look higher. He is Huntington." John's smile was fleeting. "And the sheriff might look lower, to a faithful steward. Who is nonetheless a knight, and due certain respect."

It was fact. Gisbourne said nothing. It was not for him to decide. But the idea, abruptly born, altered to a possibility and a blossoming promise: a dream of something more. *If he means to give me a woman . . .*

John shrugged off the hands of his servants, waving them away. His eyes were red-rimmed but alert: "You have our gratitude," he said lightly. "There must be something we can reward your loyalty with . . ."

Gisbourne sucked in air through constricted lungs. "My lord—if I may ask—"

John waved a ring-crusted hand. "I hereby declare you may

have the first thrust today when the huntsmen have rousted the boar."

Gisbourne had wanted much more. He had hoped for more, for the one whose name he did not know, but whose face had filled his dreams. "Thank you, my lord. My lord—" But England's savior was gone. So were Gisbourne's hopes.

"Boar?" The huntsman nearly gaped. "But—it's spring!"

The earl grimaced in disgust. "Given the opportunity, I daresay our dear count would change the season to suit him."

The huntsman's tone was dry. He was not serf or servant, but a man of skill and repute, well paid by the earl. It gave him a little freedom. "Can he conjure boar?"

Huntington glanced around the bailey, marking the milling throng awaiting mounts as hostlers brought them from stables. "I believe he expects us to do it for him." The earl closed his eyes and sighed, squeezing the prominent bridge of his nose between thumb and forefinger. "Do your best, Dickon. Send out extra beaters and rob the kennels, as you see fit . . . this man may one day be our king."

"What of the untried alaunts? They are young dogs, worth bringing along properly . . ." The huntsman gestured submission even as he counseled defiance. "Your kennels are the finest in Nottinghamshire, my lord. It would be a shame to destroy the promise of years to come."

The earl's fine white hair glistened in new sunlight. "Would you have me defy him, then?"

"Let it be stag," Dickon suggested. "There is stag aplenty . . . we needn't risk the alaunts, but set lymers and brachets on him—"

The earl flicked a speck of dust from the sleeve of his embroidered surcoat. Another more attentive glance around the bailey acquainted him with its fitness to host so many. "I shall have new livery for the porters and men-at-arms . . ." His attention returned to Dickon. "He said boar."

The huntsman gave in. "Yes, my lord. Boar. But—" He gestured helplessness. "And if there *is* no boar?"

"We will of course be breaking our fast in the fields . . . I will

96

have the kitchens delay as long as possible, then do my best to make the meal last as long as possible. But if neither ploy is successful . . ." Huntington sighed heavily and cast a scowling glance across his shoulder. "Then beat out every stag you can find and send it down upon us. A veritable *flood* of stag." Without much conviction, he added, "And if we are fortunate, perhaps a well-placed hoof will rid us—and England—of our mutual trouble before it sucks us dry."

The huntsman smiled, then disguised it behind a hand. "Treason, my lord."

Huntington's answering smile was wintry. "No more than John's attempt to sever his brother from the crown."

The day promised well, if the morning was any indication. But Marian paid scant attention to the sky and the weather, thinking instead of how best to have horses brought out for them, in the midst of so much preparation, without becoming a part of the hunt. She held her chemise and mantle close, wending through guests, following directions given by one of the household servants. It might have been easy enough, were the bailey untenanted, but so many people milled and clustered, on foot and on horseback, that it was difficult to hold to a particular line.

Fat Matilda, wheezing, thrust out a pointing hand. "There. See? The earl."

Marian followed the gesture. "Busy," she said, and adroitly avoided the nearest knot of Huntington Castle's guests. "Do you expect me to simply walk up and interrupt his conversation?"

Matilda followed in her mistress's determined wake, clutching impotently at the voluminous robe. "You're a knight's daughter, my girl—not a common scullery maid."

"You forget . . ." Marian wound her way through the crowd, wishing she'd waited a little longer. "To the Earl of Huntington, I'm not much more."

Matilda was affronted. "You're Sir Hugh FitzWalter's daughter! No shame in that, my girl. He was a fine man, your father was, and worth a moment of the earl's time."

"Yes," Marian agreed. "A fine man indeed, but—" She turned sharply to face the woman. "Why is it so important? Can't I just go home? Can't I just *leave?*"

Swaddled in gray wool, Matilda was warm and flushed. She wobbled to a stop, mopped her chin, gazed at her mistress's face. Tears glittered in Marian's eyes, but did not overflow. Matilda knew she hated to cry.

The old woman blotted her brow beneath the damp coif, the folds of throat-flesh and wimple. "Your mother wanted me to see to it you grew up fine, Lady Marian. She said so before she died."

The voice, with effort, was steady. "I have grown up very well, Matilda. You have done an admirable job."

"Your father wanted me to see to it you were looked after while he was gone. And now that he's dead—" Unexpectedly, tears brimmed in Matilda's eyes also. Her voice was thick. "I want to do right by you."

"You have," Marian said. "And you will. But leaving now, without disturbing the earl, is not so important a thing to set us at odds."

"Leaving *now?* Why?" The hand slipped under an elbow. "Pray, my lady, don't desert me. My day would be quite destroyed."

William deLacey's grasp was gentle on her elbow, but Marian stepped aside, removing her arm from his fingers with a murmured comment. "All these people . . ." She sought for and found an excuse. "I have been isolated this past year, in my grief—I find myself discommoded by such great numbers."

"And so you run? The daughter of Hugh FitzWalter?" DeLacey shook his head. Morning light touched the tracery of silver in his wavy brown hair. "That is not like the brave maid I know."

"So *I* told her, my lord." Matilda ignored Marian's pointed glance. "What she needs is to be out of doors with everyone."

"Then we are in complete agreement." DeLacey's smile was easy. "If I promised to look after her, would you leave her to me? You know me, Matilda—I will be at some pains to make certain she is well."

The old nurse dipped an ungainly curtsy. "Of course, my

lord. And I don't mind admitting I'd just as soon rest my bones a while longer."

Marian gritted teeth, smiling through them with effort. "Matilda—"

But deLacey was too quick, too smooth. "But of course, Matilda. Go in to breakfast in the kitchens. I will tend her welfare myself."

Another unbalanced curtsey. "Thank you, my lord. I know you'll do your best."

"Wait—" Marian reached out, but deLacey had her arm again and was turning her away. Matilda, smiling, swung ponderously toward the keep and breasted the crowd.

Marian opened her mouth to chide deLacey. But the sheriff was deftly escorting her through the throng, murmuring greetings as they went. He made no attempt to lend her his attention until they stood near the inner curtain wall, by the gate leading into the outer ward. "Forgive me," he murmured. "I had no wish to deprive my day of your beauty."

"Stop it," Marian said.

He laughed. "Am I found out? Do you grow weary of pursuit?"

"I grow weary of manipulation."

He laughed again in honest admiration. "I should know better. Hugh was never one for prevarication, either—why should his daughter be?" He tucked her hand into his elbow. "Come now, Marian—"

She removed her hand, clasping fingers behind her back. "Stop that, also."

DeLacey's expression was suddenly wary: a hound aware of a new—and possibly hazardous—scent. "You have me at a disadvantage."

"Surely not," she retorted. "You? I think: never."

He smiled. "Very well. What would you have me say?"

"The truth." *That you know very well my father wants us to marry.* But she did not dare suggest it, in case he *didn't* know.

"The truth is difficult for a man such as I." DeLacey, clearly, was unperturbed by her expectations and no more willing to give up the game than she was to play. He simply changed the rules. "But here it is, ungarnished: I would like you to accompany me on the hunt today." He paused. "Is that so cruel a wish?"

She was forced to admit she supposed it was not.

He nodded. "Good. Here, step away—the hunt prepares to leave."

Purposefully he pulled her out of harm's way as mounted guests vacated the inner bailey for the outer, and the forested chases beyond. The noise was clamorous: leashed hounds belling and barking, horse hooves clattering, men shouting to one another, women laughing shrilly, the oliphant winding again.

DeLacey's expression changed. Marian twisted her head, searching, and found Prince John very close, looking down upon her from a restless mount. The horse pawed, scraping the cobbles, and gnawed fretfully at the bit. Foam dripped from its mouth.

John continued to assess her, much as he had the night before. Hastily she lowered her gaze and stared fixedly at the bailey cobbles. *Let him go away—let him not notice me—let him want someone else.*

Miraculously, he did. "Lord Sheriff," John said, "will you accompany me?" He flicked an impatient, imperative gesture. "Now, if you please. Some men might accord it an honor."

Most men would. Certainly those behind him, waiting on his pleasure. Certainly William deLacey. "Of course, my lord. At once." He inclined his head, flicking a glance at Marian beneath lowered lids. Softly, he promised, "This won't last all day. I will find you later."

She said nothing, acutely aware of John's perusal. She kept her head bowed, counting the endless moments as deLacey turned and moved away, calling for his horse. Nearby, the ring of hooves on stone diminished. Marian chanced an upward glance and found herself unattended.

Relief made her dizzy. Pressing one hand against the small lump that was her crucifix, she gathered the mantle with the other and stepped back into the shadows of the towering wall. *When they're gone, I'll go—and no one will be the wiser as to my direction.* A hostler came and asked if she wanted her horse, then brought it in accordance with her wishes, tugging his forelock; Marian thanked him, bade him go, and held the horse quiet as the last knot of mounted guests trailed out, hastening to catch the others. *Thank you, God.* She wrapped her hands around the pommel and prepared to mount. *I should summon Matilda, but she'll only berate me.* Someone grasped her foot and threw her up into the saddle.

Startled, Marian landed badly and scrambled to right herself as the horse sidled. She hooked her toes into the stirrups hastily, muttering words a lady should never mutter as the horse snorted and danced aside. By the time she had recovered her balance and control of the horse her coif had come off and her skirts were bunched. The thick black braid, barely contained before, tumbled free of confinement. Her head, and one leg, were bare for all to see. "You might have *warned*—" She checked herself.

Robert of Locksley held her reins and the remains of her coif. He offered neither to her.

His expression was, if briefly, an exquisite blend of perfect stillness and assessment, of compassion for her embarrassment and comprehension of the cause. Then it passed, and the mask replaced it, altering his face, his eyes, his posture.

She felt at the braid, acutely aware of its disarray. Hastily she jerked down her skirts, attempting to cover her bared leg, but the fabric was caught between her thigh and the saddle. To free it might cause more dishabille; hot-faced, she snatched at her mantle and dragged it over her leg, leaving only her foot and ankle bared. Far too much, but better than before. "I'm going," she blurted out, to fill the awkward silence.

The voice was quiet. "The boar will be much impressed."

Her response was immediate, and wholly honest. "No—I meant I'm going *home*. Who wants to go with them?"

Something flickered in hazel eyes. "Indeed."

"I'm going *home*," she repeated. "After last night—" She hadn't meant to speak of it. Neither he nor the others required reminding, yet now she had done it. Humiliation burned anew in the tight emptiness of her stomach. "I'm just . . . going."

"Going home," he said, "has its appeal. But never put faith in it, lest—" He broke off, bent, caught up the ruined coif, and put it into her lax hand. The mask was in place.

Behind them, hooves clattered. "Marian of Ravenskeep!" It

was Eleanor deLacey, harried and hasty. "I am late—much too late . . . ride out with me, will you? Before he sends back for me."

"But I was . . ." Marian let it go. Clearly Eleanor had no intention of releasing the woman companion she required for propriety's sake, and Marian's own furtive bid for escape had failed ignominiously. "Of course," she said, resigned.

"Good." Eleanor, mounted on a mettlesome gray mare, glanced down at Locksley. Her expression was one of impatience and barely concealed intent. "Had *you* better not hurry? You are the guest of honor." But she didn't wait for an answer, gazing at Marian again. Her expression stilled, then relaxed. She smiled acknowledgment, marking Marian's bunched kirtle and fallen coif. "Ah," she said. "Then I will need no excuses." But the brief comradeship fled quickly. "Hurry *up,*" she urged.

Grimly Marian leaned forward and at last caught a handful of the offending kirtle fabric. She jerked it down into place.

"Good." Eleanor leaned and slapped her hand against the rump of Marian's horse. "Let us go, if you please."

Marian scrabbled to catch the loose reins as her mount sprang forward. The coif, forgotten, fell from her hands to spill the once-pristine linen against the grimy cobblestones.

Locksley bent once more, once more caught up the coif, and rose to stare after her. Her black hair in its loosening braid was a Crusader's banner in the daylight, snapping in the freshening wind.

FitzWalter's daughter.

He looked again at the coif, crimping the linen in both hands and twisting it through his fingers.

Blood filled the cloth, spilling over onto his hands. Warm, crimson blood, running out of the cracks between fingers to splatter onto stone in a broken necklet of ruby drops.

A tremor wracked his body. Sweat bathed him briefly, then dried slowly. He stilled his breath with effort. When he looked at the cloth again it was clean and white and pure. "Let me forget," he begged, knowing he never would, knowing he never could, and he let the linen fall, calling grimly for his horse.

Ten

Breakfast was haphazard. The guests clustered in tight knots as the morning mist dispersed in the infant sunlight, laughing and talking while servants held restive horses nearby or spread linen cloths on the still-damp ground, or milled around aimlessly awaiting someone's command as to what to do while they waited for food and drink. The huntsmen, beaters, and excited hounds were conspicuously absent, combing the nearby wooded chase for the spoor of an appropriate boar.

When at last the lumbering wagons brought bread, cheese, and wine out from the castle to the meadow, appetites were well-engaged. Huntington apologized elegantly for the laggardness of his kitchen help and waited upon Prince John himself with meticulous precision as the others set to.

The Count of Mortain did not deign to sit upon the ground, cloth-draped or no; one of the wagons had also brought him plump cushions and his personal chair. Mounted, he waited until the chair was placed on the ground, steadied, and brushed clean. When told the chair was ready, John dismounted and accepted his first cup of the day, albeit it was tasted first, and sat down. Thus ensconced, he also accepted a chunk of still-warm bread, inspected it, then began picking out pieces he found unappealing and flinging them onto the ground. Crumbs and thumb-sized pieces freely littered the cloth serving as a carpet against the encroachment of grass.

John gathered to his personal cluster those servants he required, and certain other men: Gilbert de Pisan, William de-Lacey, the Earl of Huntington. Then, taking mute measure of them all, letting them wait on his pleasure, he waved away from the immediate vicinity everyone but his cupbearer, a boy with a salver of bread and cheese, and the earl.

"A stool," John said idly. After a brief delay, a stool appeared. The prince watched as Huntington seated himself. Dark eyes glittered balefully as Henry's youngest son gestured for a fresh cup. "*I* should see to it my steward punishes the lazy villeins who shirk their duties, were breakfast served me so late."

"And so shall I, my lord." The earl, now seated, waited composedly as one of John's tasters tested the freshly poured wine, then handed the gem-studded cup to the glowering prince. "But one must realize that the arrival of a personage such as yourself can occasionally cause disarray within the household staff. They want so badly to please you, my lord—but too much wanting, no matter how earnest the desire, can result in ineptitude."

The shrewd Angevin eyes narrowed appraisingly over the gem-weighted rim of the cup, measuring the comment's intent. Was the latter meant for him? Did the earl begin the game?

Huntington's expression matched his manner: an annoying and perfect tranquility.

John grunted, shrugging, and drank wine. Then he lowered the heavy cup and gazed directly at the earl. Casually he observed, "One might also find it somewhat difficult for peasants to adapt to life in a *castle.*"

Huntington didn't flinch. "Just so, my lord."

John bit off a hunk of bread, chewed, swallowed. "Why *did* you build a castle?"

The earl ate cheese, bread, drank wine. Quietly he said, "Because I could."

It was bald, and defiantly blatant: a sword, freshly honed, set on the ground between them, waiting for the hand that would dare to take it up. And yet no one need do it. One needed merely to judge its worth, the possibilities, and let it alone, knowing where it was, in case one required it.

Color rose in John's narrow face, a splotchy network of angry webbing. But it faded away almost immediately to white, leaving bruised-looking, tissue-fine flesh beneath reddened eyes.

Gemstones glittered as rigid fingers shredded bread more rapidly yet.

John's tone was peculiar. "An old name, Huntington—an old, Saxon name. Yet you build a Norman castle."

The earl smiled faintly. "I am persuaded the Normans build the best castles of all, my lord. They are well-nigh impregnable. Why should one not build the best, if one has the means to achieve it?"

John's jaw was tight. "Indeed." He picked viciously at the bread, flicked crumbs away, then smiled benignly. "Of course, the timing was perhaps unfortunate. The coin spent on the castle might better now be spent on my brother's ransom."

"No doubt, my lord. But Huntington Castle was begun in your father's lifetime."

"My father's lifetime, here, was one of abundant peace." With a fingernail, John dislodged a hard bit of cheese from between bad teeth. His tone was exquisitely dry. "That is to say, civil peace throughout England. Domestic peace within the household was quite another thing entirely."

The earl spread his hands. "Only a fool puts his faith in a parchment roof when the weather is bound to change for the worse." He paused delicately. "I prefer stone."

"Which might lead one to wonder if, in using stone, one was merely pleasing a personal conceit, or if one was peculiarly perspicacious with regard to the future." John waved a man to cut his cheese up into smaller, bite-sized pieces, then began to eat them one right after another, with little time for chewing. "Huntington is not a coastal holding, nor does it sit on the Welsh or Scottish border. Therefore one wonders why a castle at all."

The earl drank wine from a cup less ostentatious than the prince's, then set it aside. "As you suggested, my lord: a personal conceit. One man's way of leaving his stamp on the realm."

John ate cheese, lids lowered. "Some men might look to sons for that."

Huntington smiled calmly. "I look to both."

Heavy lids lifted. "He will need sons himself."

"Of course, my lord."

"And a woman to wed." The prince turned idly and flashed a glance at deLacey, sitting very close by. That the sheriff had heard, John knew; he was tight around the mouth. The prince smiled disingenuously and signaled for more wine. "Ah, but we have time. He is yet a young man, and there are women aplenty."

Eleanor viciously speared a chunk of cheese with the small meat knife. "Why must we wait so long? Why not have this benighted hunt begun?"

Marian, wishing she could sit elsewhere but trapped for the time being, labored to sound courteous as she tamed her wind-whipped braid. "The earl has sent out huntsmen and beaters. If there is no boar to be found, there is no hunt to begin."

Eleanor gulped her cheese. "I can hardly slip away as we sit here spread out across the meadow like an ocean made of bodies; my father would *see* me."

Marian, still braiding, sighed. "Yes."

"He's over there right now, hanging on to Prince John's and the earl's skirts . . ." The tone was contemptuous. "If he would for one moment stop thinking of himself, and think instead of me—of what *I* want, I mean, not of what he wants for me." She carved another chunk of cheese, married it to bread. "He could wed me to Alain, and I would be content." She paused, considering it, then shrugged lightly. "For a while. But jongleurs have need of the road, and I would stay at home." The slow smile was suggestive. "Where married women have more freedom than unmarried ones."

Marian made no answer as she tied off the braid, then carefully carved cheese and sliced bread as she thought about Eleanor's words. DeLacey's daughter was solely caught up in the minstrel, wholly ignorant of other possibilities, as if only the moment mattered.

Eleanor's tone altered. "What is he doing? There—you see? Gisbourne!" She jabbed the meat-knife into the air. "He's just standing there, staring . . ." Then she laughed, even as Marian twisted her head to look, and cut another chunk of cheese. "As well he might, our *Sir* Guy—I think this hunt is very much out

106

of his ken. His knighthood was bought, not earned—better he were back in Nottingham Castle seeing to his sums. It's the only thing he's good for." She chewed vigorously, thinking, and then her attention shifted abruptly. "Better *I* were back in Huntington Castle, seeing to my Alain."

Marian wondered what Eleanor might say if she knew her father was angling for a much larger fish. Surely Robert of Locksley was the much better catch, but he was her father's choice; possibly, Eleanor would reject whatever man the sheriff suggested—for spite if for nothing else.

I don't want—She broke off the unbidden thought, astonished by the intensity of her reaction. Where had it come from? And then she dismissed it, acknowledging only the realization, the startling conviction. *I don't want Eleanor deLacey to marry the earl's son.*

Guy of Gisbourne stood rigidly at the very edge of the groundcloth, clutching a pewter cup redolent of spiced wine. Meticulous in his placement of feet and person, he did not allow even so much as a booted toe to touch the cloth. He had drunk more than he'd eaten, but his head was amazingly clear, perhaps more clear than ever it had been. He understood for the first time in his life that a man such as he would have to take specific measures if he were to rise in the world.

There. *There* she was. With Eleanor deLacey.

He believed himself a prudent, fair-minded, assiduous man, dedicated to details. That most people found such details—and the men who tended them—tedious in the extreme, he knew; he was neither well regarded nor well liked in Nottingham Castle, because it was to him all the dirty work fell. The sheriff might well be the man who gave the order for this to be done, or that, but it was up to Guy of Gisbourne to see the orders were carried out.

Doggedly content with his place in deLàcey's household, intensely careful in his work, he had anticipated little advancement in the way of his service, until he met Gilbert de Pisan. Then he had acknowledged other potentials, including his own.

A realm was not run on the deeds of heroes alone. There

were details to attend to; offices to administer. Hadn't deLacey taken him into his service because he needed an able steward to help him run Nottinghamshire? And was it so very different from running a realm?

Gisbourne set his teeth. There was *room* for a man like him within the prince's service. Gilbert de Pisan had implied it; the prince himself had confirmed it.

He was the sheriff's man. Could he also be the prince's? Was it possible—

Oh God. Eleanor had *seen* him. Eleanor was pointing him out to her companion, who turned and looked his way.

Gisbourne froze. He lingered painfully on the threshold of retreat and holding his place, wishing he had the quickness of wit to know what to do. Should he bow? Smile? Nod? Or ignore them entirely? Should he—no, never mind. They were no longer looking at him.

Sweat ran from his armpits. Gisbourne, standing so rigidly on the precise edge of the groundcloth, shut his eyes. He was not the sort of man a mature widow of some standing would consider for an alliance; nor was he the kind of man a highborn father looked to for his daughter, desiring to link like rank to like, or to improve his family's standing.

Which left him like a pebble kicked to lodge between a crack: entirely insignificant, and likely missed by no one.

But *she* belonged to no man, because her father was dead.

From the depths of Huntington Chase, a horn wound. The pure notes carried clearly on morning air, as did the frantic belling of the hounds and shouts from beaters and huntsmen. On the heels of the noise other voices joined the tumult, as men and women jumped up from damp, crumpled linen and shouted for mounts, kicking over forgotten wine to stain the grass-soiled groundcloth.

The earl, spying his huntsman, took leave of the prince and made his way through the animated throng to stand aside of the ruined groundcloth, peering at the wood beyond. "Well?" he asked quietly, as horses were led by them. "Boar or stag?"

The huntsman presented the bell of his oliphant, displaying

droppings. "Fresh fumes," he said. "A large print, but not too heavy, and tusk marks on the trees; a young male, my lord." The huntsman's face was solemn as he lowered his voice. "Are you wanting such for *him?*"

Huntington didn't smile. "He said boar, Dickon. I think we should give him boar." He spared a glance over his shoulder to John's chair, being loaded onto the wagon, and to John himself, being assisted onto his horse. "I doubt our lord Softsword will have a firmer spear."

Eleanor sprang to her feet as the oliphant sounded. *"Now!"* she exclaimed. *"Now* I can go!"

Marian, pulling skirts out of the way as she rose, reached out a staying hand as Eleanor turned to call for her mount. "What if he asks for you later?"

The sheriff's daughter caught impatiently at the reins as the mare was brought. "He won't want me. Who am I to him? He's much too busy trying to worm his way into Prince John's good graces . . ." With little help from the horseboy she flung herself into the saddle, hooking her feet and knee into their proper places. "I can't go at once—we must ride into the wood first, and then I'll turn back." Imperiously, Eleanor waved away the horseboy as the mare stomped and tossed her head, flinging foam into the air. "He won't ask, but if he does—tell him nothing! Remember the promise you made."

A horseboy offered reins and a hand up to Marian, who lingered on the ground. "Eleanor—I think—"

Eleanor leaned down. "Come *now,* or don't, as you choose. But this is the only way I know of doing as *I* please, instead of letting him rule my life." The mare stomped and pawed, longing to run with the others heading toward the wood. Eleanor's hands were firm, very nearly rough, but their competence was undeniable.

Marian made no answer.

Contempt flared briefly and was extinguished by something instead very close to pity. "You can't, can you?" Eleanor asked. "You can't say no to the man. You haven't the spine for it."

And then she was gone, racing toward the wood, digging divots from damp turf. Marian, left behind, scraped mud blotches from her face, feeling the cool sting even after her burning face was clean.

She stared angrily after Eleanor, thinking not of the woman's father but of Huntington's son. "Haven't the spine," she murmured. "Then perhaps it's time I *grew* one!"

Prince John rode as far as the edge of the wood, where he then ordered his chair unloaded, and dismounted. Once the chair was prepared, he sat himself upon it.

The hunting party, already insinuating itself within the thickly wooded chase, devolved into mass confusion as prospective hunters fell back nearly as one, fighting once more through untamed forest, attempting to locate the man who was, in his brother's absence, likely to wear the crown.

Inured to it all, John waved the sycophants away. When the mass of horses and riders fell back but a stride or two, thus encapsulating him in moist, hot horse breath and damp, sweaty bodies, Prince John, the Count of Mortain, shouted at one and all to leave him room to *breathe*—and reminded them it was the hunt upon which they were engaged and that they couldn't very well hunt the beast if they danced the maypole around *him*.

As for himself, he said, he would wait. When the boar was found, and contained, he would advance to witness the kill; whereupon everyone, thus dismissed, deserted John for the boar—save for those few required to personally attend the prince. One of them, John decreed, was William deLacey.

The prince smiled. "For we have not concluded discussing the administration of Nottinghamshire."

DeLacey, who doubted Nottinghamshire was the issue, gave his horse over to a servant and made himself instantly available.

John smiled warmly. "The last time we met in private, I asked you a question. Do you recall it?" He waved a hand. A cup of wine, tasted, was placed in it. "It was last night, Sheriff. Or have you forgotten already?"

DeLacey had forgotten nothing. He said so, very politely.

"The question I asked was simple: 'What do you want?' And

110

now I ask it again, as you've had a night to sleep on it." John sipped appreciatively, dark brows arching over the rim of the studded cup. "Do you have a better answer?"

The sheriff smiled faintly, certain of his course. "I want whatever you see fit to give me."

"Ah." John's smile briefly matched deLacey's, then faded to a thin, retentive seam. "No one *gives* me anything. What I want, I take."

DeLacey nodded. "We inhabit considerably different worlds, my lord. I am wholly answerable to you for my actions."

"While *I* am answerable only to God—and to myself. And God is, methinks, a more merciful taskmaster than I. He *expects* less of me." John drank more wine, then thrust it into the hand of the waiting servant. His tone was excessively casual, emphasizing nothing; that in itself put deLacey on his guard. "I think God would not want a man to be king of England who cannot sire a true heir."

Ah, thought deLacey, there it was. No more subterfuge. No more implications. It lay between them both, bared for all to see on a fine spring morning beneath an English sun. Ambition, and intention. Now it was up to him to decide which course to take.

John leaned forward in his chair. "I think that is the heart of the matter, deLacey. Richard goes haring off to the Holy Land whenever he feels God is discounting him. He intends to *bribe* God. Perhaps he hopes God will provide him an heir without requiring *him* to do the work . . ." John sagged back again, chewing idly on his remaining thumbnail. "So long as he sleeps with boys, there will be no heir. So long as Berengaria does not have the wit to fill her bed with a proxy, and claim the get of him *Richard's*—did she do *that*, she had best have him murdered, of course, or I'd have him hauled here for the truth—there will be no direct heir." He tore, then spat out the ragged nail, contemplating deLacey across the brutalized thumb. Very quietly, he suggested, "And so long as German Henry does not relinquish his honored guest, there will be no direct heir. There will be no heir but *me*."

DeLacey inclined his head, praying John could not guess his thoughts. *This is not what I might have foreseen. This is not a choice any*

111

sane man would choose *to make, this alignment with a would-be king
against a man who is—but what choice have I? Neither would anyone have
predicted that Richard would get himself thrown into a German dungeon!*

Contemplatively, John remarked, "Huntington has a castle.
A *Norman* castle, no less; as he himself has put it, nearly impregnable. And a man would be a fool not to wonder why he built
it."

DeLacey said nothing.

John smiled thinly. "He also has a son. An only, and unmarried, heir. And *you* an unmarried daughter, like not to wed, at
this rate, before her teeth fall out."

The pain was very distant, because the promise loomed so
large. DeLacey felt light-headed. "My lord, yes. Eleanor."

"Eleanor." John nodded. "I have always liked the name."

"Oh, my lord—yes, it is quite a lovely name—" The sheriff
gritted his teeth, seeking and finding a modicum of control.
More quietly, he said, "I named her for your mother, the
dowager queen."

John was indifferent. "They all did."

DeLacey drew in a breath to ask the question. If John were
serious with regard to Locksley and Eleanor . . . "My lord—"

The prince gestured. "Pray, do not delay. Do not keep the
boar waiting."

It was a dismissal. DeLacey tensed. "My lord—"

Then the king's sole remaining brother laughed, changing
tack abruptly. "And what will you say in private, when I am
gone?"

The sheriff met John's avid, unwavering eyes. His own future
now was sealed. He had told John the truth: William deLacey
was wholly answerable to the Count of Mortain, within whose
control Nottinghamshire thrived or died. As did the careers of
ambitious, intelligent men, who understood very well that an
absent king, no matter how popular, was no match for a resident younger brother who lacked scruples of any kind.

DeLacey knew what John wanted. He required leverage. A
plan to force the hands of any number of men such as the Earl
of Huntington with his new Norman castle, wealthy, powerful
men who might otherwise stand against him. John required a
subtle, undetectable means of establishing, then fixing personal

112

control, in such a way as to insure no one could accuse him of trying to wrest England from beneath his brother's nose.

Especially if the nose remained in Germany.

The knot in his belly tightened. But commitment was called for. Commitment—or destruction. Quietly deLacey declared, "I would say, were I foolish enough to speak of this at all, that I believe most confidently in your ability to succeed to the throne—in the unhappy event that the king's Crusade has drained England of the very wealth she now needs to ransom her beloved sovereign."

"Ah." John smiled. "I so hoped you also would see my way is the only way to help our beloved England."

"Yes, my lord."

"Raise the taxes, Sheriff."

DeLacey sat very still. Damp fingertips rested on his knees. "My lord, I would be remiss in my duty if I failed to inform you there is already some complaint regarding the taxes."

"Of course." John waved a ring-weighted, indifferent hand. "Noted, Sheriff; I doubt you are ever remiss in anything, save when it benefits you." A glint from slitted eyes. "Raise the taxes, deLacey. I have debts. Nottinghamshire is mine. Raise the taxes, and bring them to me in Lincoln. Do you understand?" He leaned forward from his chair. "Do I make myself clear? *Raise* them, on my authority—and *bring them to me.*"

DeLacey, sensing dismissal, rose. "It will take some time, my lord."

"I think not." John smiled. "See to it those taxes go nowhere but to Lincoln, and into my coffers. Do you understand?"

The sheriff bowed. "Yes, my lord."

John slumped back in his chair and waved a hand. The audience was finished.

DeLacey turned away and motioned for his horse, which was brought instantly. He mounted, gathered rein, inclined his head to his lord, then rode away into the wood, little marking the hounds in the distance or the winding of the horn, thinking only of Prince John and the magnitude of his ambition.

A little distance away, shrouded in trees and shrubbery, the sheriff drew rein. He sat very quietly in the saddle, staring at the tree just in front of him, and laughed softly, incredulously, as he acknowledged fully John's intent.

"He'll take what's left," he murmured. "What little the Crusade has left, John will take for himself. At the cost of Richard's ransom."

DeLacey closed his eyes a moment, wiping the sheen of dampness from a chill face. Then opened his eyes once more and signaled the horse to move. His hands, on the reins, trembled.

Eleven

The world was all of green: a verdant verdigris, shaded emerald, olive, and jade. Trees eclipsed the sun, charging shadow with dominion. Here the day was cool, muted, still damp and dazzled by dew. Fine mist was beginning, like tissue, to shred. Even sound was muffled, lending each horse and hunter a passing sense of separation, a transitory isolation.

Marian beat her way through brush even as the others did. She knew very well most of the other women rode with men, or had male servants to break a trail before them, but that was a luxury she couldn't enjoy. She was left to fend for herself, contemplating Eleanor's determined and hasty departure— *likely she is halfway back to the castle, by now*—and wondering if she should not mimic it, though toward Nottingham and Ravenskeep rather than Huntington Castle.

But that would prove Eleanor correct in the matter of Marian's spine. "I'll find him first," she muttered, wincing as a leafy stem broke free of her warding hand and slapped her in the face. "I'll find him first—ask my questions—then go on."

Or go first to Huntington Castle, collect old Matilda, then venture on toward home.

The hounds belled in the distance, sound muted by dense-grown trees and acres of tangled vines. She heard the wood-damped noise of cracking brush and shredded vines on either side, muttered oaths as men hacked a way, the breathless laughter of highborn women emboldened by the hunt. For all Marian knew, another rider could be but ten paces away; the wood was so thick as to swathe everyone in a private, personal shroud of green.

"A man could hide in here for years, and no one ever find him." Grimacing, she unhooked an encroaching branch from a fold in her mantle. "And if anyone ever got lost . . ." She reined in her mare, still wrestling with branch and mantle. *"Wait—"*

A crashing very close by caused the mare to sidle sharply toward the tree even as Marian yanked cloth from the branch. Her knee collided with the trunk. She grimaced and reined the mare away, pushing one-handed against the tree to take the weight off her knee.

"Lady Marian!"

Occupied, she barely glanced up. Briefly she marked Sir Guy of Gisbourne, breasting through undergrowth, but paid him little mind as she finally persuaded the mare to move off the tree, and leaned down to rub her knee. Bruised, she thought, but whole.

"Lady Marian. I thought—" He broke it off. "Are you all right? Are you hurt?" He spurred his horse forward anxiously. "Is there anything I can—?"

Marian thrust out a hand. "Stop! Just—stop." As he reined in, white-faced, she laughed a little. "No—it's all right . . . I'm sorry. Your horse startled mine, no more . . . hold your place, and she'll be all right. As for me . . ." She shrugged, laughing a little self-consciously. "My horsemanship wants improving."

He began yet again: a litany. "Lady, if there's anything I can do—"

"No." It came out more harshly than she intended; he was embarrassingly persistent. "I am well. I promise. I think she is only a little unsettled by so many others, and the hounds, and

115

this shadowy wood. She is only a gentle mare, and quite unused to hunting."

Beyond them, from the depths, came the bright sound of the oliphant. The barking and yelping grew frantic. Marian's mare shook her head and sidled uneasily.

Gisbourne's swarthy, dark-featured face was dubious. "Lady—"

She cut him off. "There! The oliphant—do you hear it? Perhaps they've trapped the boar." Marian waved a hand. "No need to stay here for me, Sir Guy. Better you go to the boar."

He straightened in his saddle. "Prince John promised me first thrust," he declared. "But if you—if there is anything—if I can do—"

She recognized the declaration for what it was: an attempt to claim some importance. If indeed he was as ineffective a knight as Eleanor had implied, such a boon was a true honor. "Go," she said quietly, smiling encouragement. "I would not keep you from that."

Indecision warped his expression. "But I—"

The belling of the hounds grew imperative. Muffled shouts threaded more distinctly through the trees: huntsmen and hunters. "They have need of you," Marian told him. "You shouldn't keep them waiting."

Red-faced, he blurted, "There is something I must tell you—something you must hear—"

His earnestness touched her. But clearly the hunt was nearing, and if it were true John had promised the first thrust to Gisbourne—though why an untried knight better accustomed to doing the sheriff's sums would be given such an honor baffled Marian—she didn't want to be the cause of him missing his chance.

"Sir Guy, please . . . we can speak later."

"I won't have the courage," he cried. "Don't you understand? But here—*now*—"

"Sir Guy—" But her protest was cut off as the hunt arrived most spectacularly in their midst, in the guise of a foam-flecked boar.

Marian had time only to see the small, lurid eyes; the blood-stained, wicked tusks; the bristly, compact body. And then leashed hounds broke through the brush, dragging cursing handlers at the end of leather thongs, and other hunters on horseback, hoisting spears into the air; and she smelled the stink of fear and rage and wildness, from the boar, certainly, and undoubtedly from the hounds. But from the men also, she thought, gathering to kill.

They are as avid as the boar—But the observation died before she finished, lost in the porcine grunting and the high-pitched yelping of frustrated hounds.

"First thrust," someone said, and she saw Gisbourne abruptly go white.

"I—I have no spear—" he blurted, grasping impotently at his saddle. "I forgot—"

Laughter, and murmured comments. It made her abruptly angry. *What right have they*—But her mare stomped, snorting fearfully, and the panting, grunting boar abruptly took a step in Marian's direction.

"First *thrust*," someone suggested, derision thick in the tone.

White-faced, Gisbourne unsheathed his sword and flung himself from the saddle.

"No—" Marian cried, even as others shouted, but the boar charged Gisbourne.

The mare shied, nearly unseating Marian. She scrambled to regain her balance, dragging herself upright one-handed as she hauled on the reins, forcing the mare to comply. She heard the frenzied barking of hounds, the cursing of their handlers, the shouts of gathered hunters, the bellows-breathing of her mare. Already she was free of the clearing, free of danger. Marian reined the mare up short, spun her back, urged her forward again. *There's Gisbourne*—

A horse broke through beside her, nearly knocking the mare over. At first Marian thought the horse unmounted, possibly Gisbourne's, running from the boar, because she saw no rider—and then she did see him and realized he was clad in the colors of the forest, nearly invisible, almost indistinguishable against the emerald, olive, and jade. It was the shock of white-blond hair that betrayed his identity, and the grimness of his features.

"Stay back!" he shouted at her, cutting diagonally across her path to knock the mare aside. And then the bloodied boar was free of brush and vines and hard upon them both.

His horse was in the lead. Marian, frantically reining in her mare, saw the flash of bloodied tusks; heard the screaming of Locksley's mount; saw the plunging forelegs collapse as the boar sheared through them both. Blood sprayed flesh and foliage.

It came in pieces, a shredded coverlet sewn haphazardly back together:

—Locksley, free of his ruined mount—

—nothing more than a knife in his hand—

—white-haired, white-faced—

—shouting something unintelligible in a language she didn't know—

And others, breaking through: the earl, the sheriff; others. But Gisbourne wasn't with them. *Gisbourne—?* The horse thrashed its shattered forelegs, spraying blood into the air. *Oh God—not Locksley—*

Gore-clotted tusks slashing, trying to rend fragile flesh.

—and Robert of Locksley, one-handed, slashing down with a stroke of his own: a single edged-steel tusk slicing through hide and fat and muscle to peel back the substance of throat—

White hair ran red with blood. His face was a ruddy mask. *"Ya Allah!"* he shouted hoarsely. *"La ilaha il' Mohammed 'rasul Allah!"*

And then let the boar fall slack, collapsing against blood-muddied ground.

A scream filled Gisbourne's throat, but only a whimper issued. His arms trembled, and his hands; the shaking rattled his bones. But he could not stop the trembling. He could not ignore the fear. *Can't let it harm her—*

A puny, slender sword against a maddened, vicious boar. Everyone in England knew how dangerous the beasts were, even a man who had never hunted for his food, nor turned to boar for sport.

The powerful beast came on, knocked aside the trembling sword, threaded tusk into hosen and thigh-flesh and shredded both with a practiced slash. Gisbourne smelled the stink, felt the compact weight, saw the small, unblinking eye, but the pain, as he went down, was inexplicably absent.

I'm dead, he thought. Then, *no*—?

The boar hewed him down like a sapling, tipping a massive, tusk-laden head to hook vulnerable flesh and fabric, then broke over Gisbourne's shoulder to flee through deadfall and bracken.

—not dead—?

Behind him he heard the crashing, the scream of an injured horse, the shout of victory warped awry by an unknown language.

"Not dead?" Gisbourne murmured, struggling to sit up.

And then they were on him, all of them, with hands at shoulders, belly, hips, pushing him back to the ground. He was abruptly cold, and shivered; stared wide-eyed, mouth agape, as the men gathered above him, telling him to lie still; don't move; hold still; keep quiet; until he wanted to scream.

He didn't scream, but he wanted to. At them, from fear, in panic. "Not dead?" he whispered. And then, in his head: *Yet?*

Beyond, he heard the hounds, most eloquent in their yearning to answer unreasoning instinct, born and bred; the duty trained into them: to find and rend the boar. And their handlers, remonstrating, pulling the dogs away, to sate them with other flesh.

"Robert," someone said sharply. The earl, Gisbourne realized, who went pushing through vines and foliage to locate the man—*his son?*—who had shouted whatever it was he had shouted, in the moment of victory.

The beast is dead. Relieved, Gisbourne levered himself to an elbow to inspect what the boar had done.

"Sir Guy?" Marian FitzWalter, come back to see how he fared.

"*Jesu*—" he croaked. "Lady—no—" But she was there, slotted between two men, all blue-eyed, black-haired, and white-faced, perfectly still in shock as she looked upon his wound.

"Cautery," someone said.

"It'll have to come off." Someone else.

"No!" he cried. "*No*—"

A hound yelped. Someone murmured something. The crowd around him stirred, muttering, then someone said something imperatively, and everyone but the men kneeling at his side and the woman clutching a blood-splattered mantle fell back, giving precedence to the newcomer.

Prince John paced to Gisbourne and looked down upon the man. In one hand he held a cup. The wine it contained was as red as the blood spilling from Gisbourne's leg.

The dark eyes were oddly avid, strangely amused. "I gave first thrust to you," he drawled, "but it appears the boar was quicker."

Gisbourne wanted to laugh, even as others did; it was what John expected. But all he could do was whimper as they began to wrap his leg.

"A wagon," someone said.

And someone else, less charitable, "He'll be dead before we get back."

No, Gisbourne thought, as pain at last blossomed. The last things he saw were Marian's eyes gazing fixedly at his face, merciless in their pity.

The earl tore aside vines and beat back bracken fern as he made his way beyond Gisbourne and the clutch of men around him. Only dimly was he aware of the man's pain, and the fact that the sheriff's steward still might die, if he was not dead already. For the earl, Gisbourne was a casualty whose fate did not concern him. Whose fate *did* concern him was his son's.

Above the constricted wheeze of breath expelled from aged lungs, he heard the distress of the injured horse. But the horse didn't matter, either.

His mantle fouled on a bough. The earl felt it catch and slapped at it, then tore it free when the fabric remained hooked. Cloth ripped. He cursed it and went on, clawing aside the vines, cursing age and helplessness, promising God a monument if his son remained alive. "One son," he husked. "Do not rob me of that . . . I ask for so very little—"

He broke free of vines and close-grown bracken, staggering so badly he fetched up against a tree, and there, clinging, gasping, he saw his only son, wet head to foot with blood as he knelt over the boar.

"Robert—" Not much issued from his throat. A thready exhalation, relief and inquiry. And then, in shock: *"Robert—?"*

Locksley, with only a knife, methodically sawed off the boar's head. From the gaping wound in the neck he cut and hacked and sawed his way around the neck, murmuring beneath his breath, paying no heed to his father, or the dying horse behind him, or to anything at all, save the task that consumed him.

Through gristle, muscle, and flesh he cut, peeling aside the hide, until the head was completely severed from powerful, bristled shoulders. Once he scrubbed at his eyes, smearing blood across his face. And then, as methodically, he cut each leg from the boar's body.

"Robert?" the earl whispered.

Locksley at last looked up. He hunched over the dismembered carcass, one haunch clutched in his hand. His eyes, Huntington saw, were black instead of hazel.

The old voice trembled. "Is this—necessary?"

His son stared back, unmoving. And then did move, slowly, looking down at the haunch in his hand; at the remains of the boar. At the knife still gripped in the other hand, dripping blood.

He started to speak. The harsh words were unintelligible. He stopped. Frowned. Tried again. This time in English, so the earl could understand. "This is what you do," he said hoarsely. "In war."

"But—" The earl passed a trembling hand over his face. "Robert—you are home. In England. This is England. There is no war here. The beast you have killed is a boar."

A shudder wracked Locksley's hunched body. "He wasn't."

"He was." The earl drew in a deep breath, meticulously rearranging the folds of his soiled mantle because it was something he could comprehend. "Robert—he was a *boar.*"

"He wasn't," Locksley repeated stolidly. "They said he was, but he wasn't."

There is no time for this. The earl walked very carefully and deliberately around the dismembered carcass to stand at his son's side. He reached down, shut a gnarled hand on Locksley's shoulder and gripped with surprising strength. "Robert—come

121

away. At once. Do as I say. I'll send someone back to tend to the horse."

"*Ya Allah,*" Locksley murmured. And then, with a trace of desperation, "No—I mean, *God.*"

The earl's tone was definitive, the words explicit. "Do as I say."

Stiffly, Locksley rose. The once-green tunic and hosen were stained a muddy red-brown as the blood began to crust.

The earl assessed his condition. His mouth thinned a moment, hardening. "Robert . . ." But the lips loosened fractionally. There were the others to think of. "It was well done, Robert. The others will hail you a hero."

"No," Locksley rasped. "What was done was—butchery."

Huntington gave a coarse laugh. "It's what you do to boars!"

His son stared down at the carcass. "But not what you do to men."

Twelve

The hand closing firmly on Marian's shoulder snapped her out of her reverie. "Come," the sheriff said quietly, pulling her away. "There is no need for you to stay with him. The wagon will take him back to the castle."

It disturbed her that he cared so little for his own man. "Perhaps I could aid him . . . comfort him, somehow—" She felt it was important, as if she were to blame.

"How? And why? He is nothing to you." DeLacey grasped her by both shoulders and steered her easily away from the men clustered around Gisbourne. "What good can you do him?"

But Marian had fastened onto an earlier sentence. "Nothing to me? But he *is*—it was for me he confronted the boar—"

He laughed gently. "I think not. Surely not. I believe he felt challenged by the others . . . I confess to a weakness, Marian. Men will do unbelievable things if their pride is brought into it . . . and Gisbourne is not a common sort of knight."

Shock gave way to anger. *Perhaps Eleanor is right—he is harder than I thought.* Marian hitched both shoulders convulsively and shrugged off his hands, swinging to face him. "An *uncommon* knight, Sheriff? Surpassing brave, is he not?"

The disarming smile faded, replaced with a more attentive assessment of her reaction. She saw the lines in his face deepen, the brown eyes harden. "He is my steward. An able man, withal—as it concerns tending a household. But not what any man, even Gisbourne himself, would claim particularly brave. Not as knights are measured, lady. Not as your father was."

It infuriated her. "We will leave my father out of this!"

"Your father died in battle against *men*, Marian. Not against beasts."

It shocked her. "Do you count Gisbourne's act less significant because it was a *beast?* What if it had harmed me? What if I had fallen, and it had threatened me?"

"He should not have dismounted." The tone was cool, clipped; and then he once more took her arm and turned her away, ignoring her inarticulate, murmured protest. "I applaud his intent, Marian. But it was foolhardiness, no more. Now. Let us speak of something else—"

"What if he dies?"

"If God hears our prayers, he will not."

"Don't you want to return with him?"

"Of course. Even now my horse is brought, and yours. Do you think I mean to spirit you away into the forest?" The sheriff laughed. "No, Marian. I mean for us both to accompany him back to the castle. The hunt is quite completed—not what anyone anticipated, perhaps, but certainly finished. Now allow me to help you mount . . ."

Before she could speak he caught her up and pressed her into the saddle. Marian found her seat and caught up the reins the horseboy offered as the sheriff mounted his own horse. She

123

thought to protest, but didn't. He was a man, he was older, he was her father's friend, due respect and courtesy—

But what had Eleanor said? She couldn't say no to the man?

It annoyed Marian intensely that her spirit was judged so lacking by a woman who hardly knew her. *Grow a spine,* she told herself sternly. "My lord Sheriff—" She meant to tell him he was being too high-handed with her, that he had no right to order her around, to force her this way and that, as if she were wife, or servant. She meant to tell him that perhaps his youngest daughter judged him more accurately than he knew, stripping away the facade to bare the true man underneath.

But the words died away. She said nothing after all, looking beyond the sheriff entirely as he readied to mount, because Robert of Locksley, with the earl, had come into the clearing as the others labored with Gisbourne.

The front of his clothing was soaked. White-blond hair hung lankly on his shoulders, weighted by ruddy ribbons. His face, a blood-smeared mask but moments before, had been scrubbed haphazardly by a forearm. The rough ministration left him no less bloody, no less barbaric. No less than what he had been as he had cut open the boar's throat.

Grimly, as the earl spoke to someone, Locksley looked across the clearing and found her watching him. She saw him go very still. Transfixed, he stared blankly at her for a long, arrested moment—and then the face beneath the blood blanched into deathly white.

Alan frowned over his fretwork, oblivious to the servants as they worked around him, carrying out soiled rushes and replacing them with fresh. Racks were checked for spent candles. Clean linen was spread on the tables and silver polished again. He had moved twice already, muttering irritation, and now took residence on a stool near the chair reserved for the earl.

The tune was coming along well, if he could master the fingering necessary. A jammed finger the year before had rendered him less than what he had been when it came to certain chords. He had labored for months to recover strength and flexibility, but as yet hadn't recaptured it. And now, most decidedly, it interfered with his intent.

"Alain!" The hall echoed his name.

He glanced up, head still full of notes, and saw her rushing toward him, kirtle and mantle pulled awry so as not to foul her steps.

Alan rose hastily to catch her before she could harm his lute. She flung herself into his arms, albeit one was occupied, and trapped his mouth with her own.

"Fairest Eleanor," he gasped, when at last she loosed his mouth. "I—had not anticipated your return so quickly." In fact he had forgotten about her entirely in the need to capture the burgeoning song, thinking of lyrics and other things, far from Eleanor's sturdy arms. He recalled her promise to return, and his words of encouragement; both now came back to haunt him. He had believed he had more time.

Eleanor giggled huskily, working at the drawstring of his hosen. "I let nothing delay me when my appetite is so engaged."

He caught her questing hand. "Not here, I pray—"

She was impatient, which might have excited him once. "Then a chamber, and hurry. We have time, but not so much that I wish to forgo a moment."

The night before it had been of his choosing. He had tumbled her once, finding her appetite intriguing. Now the sport had palled. There was new music to discover; he knew her, now, too well. "Eleanor—"

"A *room*," she urged. "Or I will take you here and now."

It whetted his appetite, making her more attractive. But he knew better. They dared not risk so much. Not on a second bedding; the first, well, that was different. Risk during a first encounter made the bedding that much more exciting.

Not here, then. But he knew she would not give up. So Alan laughed, kissed Eleanor back, took her and his lute to the first chamber he could think of, so close to the hall's entrance. A small, private room. It lacked a bed, but that didn't matter. The floor would do just as well.

* * *

It had gone wrong, deLacey knew. He was a man who understood nuances, the shifts in the tones of mood, the fleeting expressions in face and eyes, and the posture of the body. Instinctively, he knew it: he had handled Marian badly. She was not Eleanor, to be ordered this way and that because it was the only way to control her. She was Marian, and worth far more time and care. It had been a mistake, though not entirely his fault. The meeting with Prince John had shaken him badly, and that in itself was disturbing. He was long used to meeting even unpleasant surprises with calmness and self-control; he was usually quick-witted enough to turn aside even the worst of setbacks.

But John was different. John was dangerous. And now de-Lacey had entangled himself so deeply he doubted there was an escape, short of finding it in the grave. He dared not misplay the prince, or his life was surely forfeit; by the same token, if John's bid for control of England failed, and King Richard was ransomed, the sheriff gave not a single penny for his own future. If John fell, he would fall. But if he aided John, and John became king . . . ?

A chill touched his spine. Such thoughts were treasonous. Better he think of something else.

He chanced a sidelong glance. Marian's head was bowed as she rode, her flawless profile pensive. No doubt she thought him too harsh, too autocratic, and he didn't blame her for that. He had miscalculated, allowing concern for John's intentions to override his plan for her. He wanted to woo her into his bed, not command her there; to win her regard if he could, because what she thought mattered to him. No other woman had mattered, not even his first two wives. They had briefly entertained him, even given him children—*daughters!*—and had aided his rise in the world. But they had not loved him, and he had not loved them. The marriages had been expedient, no more. And though this one would also benefit his coffers, gain was not the sole reason he wanted FitzWalter's daughter. There was the girl herself.

Inwardly, he marveled. He had watched her grow up, in a patchwork sort of way. It allowed him better judgment in the matter of her maturing. A mother or father, seeing a daughter daily, was unaware of the changes. But another man, seeing a girl but occasionally, was alert to her sudden leaps in growth.

She had been a plain, coltish, ungainly girl, all awkward limbs and tangled hair. FitzWalter had allowed her too much freedom once her mother died. He was too indulgent to guide her hoydenish habits into properly womanly ways. But that had changed in the last year, as she mourned her father. Grief had become the threshold of adulthood, and she had crossed it with colors flying.

She was exquisite. He knew of no better word. And he knew of no man better than he to give her the life she deserved.

To teach her what bodies were for.

Locksley rode Gisbourne's horse because his own was dead. He was sticky with drying blood. The smell clung to him like a shroud, filling his head with recollections he had no wish to recall.

Any more than recall the expression on Marian FitzWalter's face, when he had told her her father's message regarding William deLacey.

Or when she had seen him dismember the boar.

He had meant only to kill it. That it had attacked Sir Guy of Gisbourne, he knew; he had come upon the scene, judged the boar's line of retreat, and moved to cut it off. He hadn't counted on the girl being in the way. He had intended merely to kill it before it did more harm. An enraged boar, possibly wounded, was a highly dangerous beast.

And then she had been there, in the boar's path, leaving him with only one option.

He had not planned to hunt at all, riding out only because his father expected it, had *ordered* it, and he was not yet disposed to refuse his father's wishes. It was easiest to give in. Captivity had taught him that.

He was weary. Used up. He had been weary for months, for more than a year. In that weariness, in the exhaustion of his spirit, lay the seed of what he was; of what he had become. Of what they had made him, Saladin's men, and all the others as well. Even his own kind.

She had cried out for him to beware, when his horse had been hurt, and fallen. And again when he'd stabbed into the boar's throat. He recalled it clearly: *"Be careful!"* she had cried. *"Oh my lord, take care!"* But nothing else, past that. Because with the cries of his horse in his head, and the stench of blood in his nostrils, what he killed was no longer a boar. What he was, was no longer a man, but a body, mind, and spirit remade on the anvil of war, remixed in the terrible crucible of a holy insanity.

He pulled the horse up short, clutching the reins clutching the pommel, wracked by guilt and self-contempt. He wanted to heave it out, like a man spewing vomit. He wanted to *bleed* it out, like a surgeon releasing impurities by cutting into rotting flesh.

He wanted to tell the girl exactly *how* her father had died, so he was no longer alone.

He had used the boar to show her. But knew he could never tell her.

Eleanor clutched at the minstrel's buttocks, digging nails into bare flesh. He was not enough, not *enough*—

She swore at him, then released taut flesh to grip his hair as she arched hips up from the floor, trying to capture more of him. She heard him panting, murmuring, saying things against her throat, her breasts, but his words were unimportant. She wanted more of *him,* not the practiced jongleur's phrases.

"Where is your lance?" she gasped. "Where is your sword, *ma petite?* Where are you hiding yourself?"

Alan was incoherent.

"Hold nothing back," she commanded. "Give it all to me—"

He gave her as much as he could.

"—to *me*—" Eleanor cried.

And the door to the chamber burst open.

The earl gestured sharply as he led the way inside the hall to the door just off the entry. "That door—*there.* Take him inside and put him down . . . *you* there—open that door!" He swung to face another servant. "Have the surgeon summoned. Bring linen and water, and blankets for bedding. We'll put him here for now, until the surgeon is done with him."

The door was unlatched and shoved open, even as the men bearing Gisbourne shouldered into the chamber. Behind them came the earl, his son, the sheriff . . . and Prince John, but lately arrived, asking pettishly for more wine.

"Over there," the earl ordered, gesturing toward a corner. And then, in shock, "My *God*—"

Save for Gisbourne's moan of pain, the chamber was utterly silent.

Eleanor deLacey, clad in little save tumbled hair, burst into noisy tears. "He *forced* me!" she cried, hunching as she knelt. Then displayed a livid mark on the flesh of one hair-shrouded breast. "See what he did to me?"

Alan, bare-flanked and flaccid as he stood against the wall, opened his mouth to protest, to deny the wailed words. But as the sheriff advanced upon him, white of face and black of eyes, he knew for once in his life a nimble tongue wouldn't save him.

"Damn you," he muttered, before the blow broke his lips on his teeth.

William deLacey carried out his duties, such as they were in another's castle, then sought refuge in solitude, in the dimness of newborn twilight, the gloom of wan candlelight. Anger now was spent, the fury burned out. He was a shell of flesh over bone newly brittled by the knowledge of what she had cost him.

"Eleanor," he murmured, and collapsed onto the sole chair.

The chamber was small, very private; the earl, saying nothing, had seen fit to send him to it, to give him his time alone before he was made to face the others, to hear the first of rampant rumors to which the scene would soon give birth.

He slumped, lax of limb, gazing blindly into the gloom, then gathered himself and rose, walking quietly to the table, and poured himself wine. He was distantly pleased to see his hands shook only a little.

He raised the cup in the air, as if in tribute. "To Eleanor," he rasped, "who has taught me, only today, to discount no piece in the game, lest it prove itself more important than anyone had foreseen."

A knock sounded. He was instantly furious, outraged that anyone would dare come to him now, when he had given orders he not be disturbed. But the anger faded. He was weary, too drained.

"Lord Sheriff?" A servant's voice. "The Lady Marian to see you."

Marian. *Here? Now?* He strode to the door and unlatched it, then pulled it open into the room.

Marian, here and now, unattended by her nurse. In the dimness her eyes were enormous, black pupils ringed by blue irises. The light from corridor cressets and from candle racks behind him were merciless in their attentions, yet imputed no flaw to her. She stood quietly before him, hands folded against her skirts, locked over the embroidered girdle wound twice around her slim waist.

It was most irregular, but he did not damn her for it. She took his breath away.

DeLacey moved aside. It took effort to speak evenly, giving nothing away of his thoughts. "Will you come in?"

She shook her head. She had combed and tidied her hair, though as yet it remained uncoiffed, confined only in a single thick braid hanging across one shoulder to dangle at her waist. The creased kirtle, he marked absently, was spotted with dark-dried blood. She had taken no time to change, which meant she counted very important the thing she had come to say.

DeLacey flicked a glance at the servant, who stood with eyes averted. "Come in," he told her quietly. "If it concerned you what people thought, you would have brought your woman."

It was a telling blow. He saw the flicker of acknowledgment in her eyes, the faint tightening of her mouth. She stepped inside, and he shut the door behind her.

"Wine?"

Again she shook her head. She was clearly ill at ease, yet just as clearly determined to say what she'd come to say, no matter what he thought.

That told him a thing or two. He used it to his advantage, as he always did. "You are your father's daughter, and predictable in your heart. You've come to plead for the minstrel."

Color bloomed in her face, staining the exquisite cheekbones. Her voice was low and courteous, but he heard the spark in the tone that underlay the smoke. "What they're saying about the sentence—it isn't true, is it?"

He turned his back on her and moved away, still holding the goblet of wine. He turned back, smiling grimly. "I have the authority."

Plainly, she had disbelieved the rumor. She had not truly believed he would carry out such a sentence. It touched him, if very briefly, that she could see him for something other than the man he knew himself to be. *A pity*, he thought, *that I must disabuse her.*

Marian took a breath. "But—"

"But." He overrode her, softening it with a smile; dismissed that a moment later. "What would you have me do? I am the lord high sheriff . . . and the woman is my daughter."

He waited, giving her time, giving her truth, and the chance to comprehend it. And so she did. She gazed at him a long moment, weighing words and tone and expression. He, who knew how to judge by such things, saw she did as well, if by instinct rather than guile.

The color drained from her face. Her hands gripped the girdle, as if it might give her strength. "My lord . . ." Then words, like her color, faded. He saw the muscle jump in her jaw, the faint line across her brow, the minute squaring of her shoulders. And the lifting of her chin. Quietly she said, with eloquent clarity, what no one else would dare. "You have no cause."

"Ah." He wanted to smile, to laugh and say he knew very well what she meant, and how much it had cost her to come so close to declaring it. She was loyal and tender-hearted, hesitant to hurt even a man she now questioned, curious as to his intent. But he would not let it dissuade him. She had no conception as yet of what the world was like. "That is not what my daughter says."

She avoided it. She would not accuse Eleanor of lying. Instead, she relied on a different accusation, on arguing the method. "What you mean to do is barbaric."

He lifted one shoulder slightly. "It lies within my authority."

Passion flared, and color. "That doesn't make it *right!*"

DeLacey sipped his wine. "The minstrel is fortunate I take no more than his tongue."

"My lord—" She gritted teeth. "He loses more than your daughter did."

"Ah." His grasp on the goblet tightened. "Be candid with me, Marian—say what you came to say."

"I—" But she couldn't. "You already know the truth."

"Do I?" He smiled. "For the sake of argument, I'll agree. But do not come before me, fired with righteous indignation, and tell me she lost nothing."

"Eleanor lost nothing more than she willingly *gave*—"

He cut her off. "Not that. That she lost long ago. I speak of other things. I speak of her future." Anger flared anew. "I speak of security, and wealth, and rank and privilege."

"All of the things *you* want!"

The accusation rang in the chamber. For one brief instant it startled and intrigued him that *she* would challenge him so, and then the anger took over. She didn't understand. She *couldn't* understand. Therefore he would take pains to explain it in terms she could comprehend.

He flung the cup aside, spraying wine across the chamber. It silenced her at once. "Would you have me call her a liar before everyone in the castle?" He took a single step toward her. "Would you have me proclaim her dishonor predates what happened today?" Yet another stride. "Would you have me destroy my own daughter for the sake of a *jongleur?*"

She pressed trembling hands into the weave of her skirts, yet no less determined for all his passion had startled her. "I would have you treat him fairly, as is due an innocent man."

DeLacey laughed aloud: blatant, blinding contempt. "Innocent, is he? Alan of the Dales? That is his name, Marian . . . he is a minstrel of some repute, though little of that comes of skill. A passing fair musician . . . but better by far in bed!"

He stood just before her, trembling now with anger, with suppressed humiliation, thwarted ambitions, the knowledge he was trapped within a web of his own spinning. He had agreed to betray his king to further his daughter's future, so his own might be secured, and Prince John had accepted, for reasons of his own. *He* wouldn't care that the price he had promised deLacey was no longer possible.

The bed I must lie in is no longer to my taste. Desperation and futility took possession of his soul. And in that moment, against his will, he let Marian see what he was. He let her see that even though he knew full well what his daughter had done, he could not and would not agree to alter the minstrel's sentence.

"If this is for pride—" she began.

He caught her shoulders cruelly, startling her with his strength. "For pride, and much, much more! Do you know what she has done? She has cost me Huntington's son! Do you think he will have her now? Do you think any man of rank will take to wife a despoiled woman?"

Marian stood her ground. "Is that worth a man's tongue?"

He let her go so quickly she nearly staggered. "Other fathers might thank me. Certainly your father would."

"My father!"

"What if it had been you? What if his blandishments had won more from you than you were willing to give?"

"I would never—"

"A woman cannot say what she would never do."

It silenced her utterly.

DeLacey reached out and touched a strand of her hair. "You can't know," he said quietly. "No one can, until it happens. Until he is faced with the moment itself, with the decision he must make, no matter the truth of it. I never claimed to be kind, because there is very little room for kindness in a sheriff's duties . . . but I am a consistent man." The hand slipped down the lock of hair to gently cup her face. "I hold the power of life and death in the seal of my office," he whispered raggedly, "and all I need do is affix it to the parchment. That, Marian, is power. But power must be balanced. Power must be used. Power must be displayed so that others learn its worth."

She was very white of face. "An example, then."

"A lesson." He took his hand away, freeing her face, her hair. "You had best hope he learns it, or forfeit more than a tongue."

Desperation ravaged her face. "But you rob him of his future!"

She couldn't understand. DeLacey's mouth crimped. "As he robbed my daughter of hers."

She stared at him blindly, for longer than he could bear. Then her hand touched her mouth, fingers trembling. And the other, meeting the first, fingertip to fingertip, as if she meant to pray. "Oh," she said on a rushing breath, gusting into her palms. A second breathy, *"Oh,"* and then she was gone, tugging open the door, to leave him alone again.

DeLacey nodded stiffly as the door was shut. He understood. He knew. He was adept at reading people. He was a practical man, who knew how to judge them all, and how to use what they gave him, freely offered or no, in word and deed and posture.

Even in the eyes.

He turned stiffly and moved to the chair, then sat himself down upon it. He closed his eyes very tightly, willing himself to be still.

DeLacey understood. He only wished she could. "Forgive me," he murmured in the pallor of the room.

Thirteen

Just outside the sheriff's door, Marian stopped short. She was vaguely aware of the servant asking something, but she paid him no attention. All she could do was stand rigidly, staring blindly at the corridor wall facing her, and hug herself against the bone-deep chill of realization: *He is going to cut off that poor man's tongue, and all for a lie!*

It was to her more than unbelievable, more than barbaric, more than unfair. It was the betrayal of her faith in a man and a system she had been brought up to believe in, knowing no other way, and to whom she could turn in the face of adversity, when her father was on Crusade and later after his death.

She had known deLacey all her life, if not well; he was her father's friend, not hers, and therefore once she had reached adulthood the relationship between them was limited to normal courtesies. But there had never been a reason to think badly of the sheriff, or to question his actions. It had never occurred to her that he could be so wrong, so *ruthless,* as to make a man mute who depended on his tongue to put food into his mouth and clothing on his back.

For the sake of a wanton daughter who had, in all probability, been the pursuer, not the prey.

Marian shivered. She was sick at heart and in belly; she wanted nothing more than to go to bed, pull the covers over her head, and wake up in the morning with unpleasantness erased.

But that was the coward's way. That was the way of a woman who had no spine.

"Eleanor," she murmured, recalling who had said it. And then she knew what to do.

Prince John, bored after the botched hunt, desired a tour of the earl's new castle. It mattered little to him that the sun had set and twilight was swiftly turning to dark. Having fixed his mind on the thing, he sent a servant to the earl to order—no, *request*—that Huntington conduct the tour personally. Because, John said, the castle was in itself the earl's idea, and therefore no one else was better suited to point out its strengths.

He needed to learn its strengths. He needed to learn how they might be used against him, but mostly he wanted to bind the earl to England's prince rather than to England's king, if such a thing could be done. The barons, John knew, were not overmuch pleased by his taxation policies.

Huntington escorted John out of doors, to the inner ward, into the gatehouse, up the narrow coil of stairs to the sentry-walk along the inner curtain-wall. From there a man could look into the outer bailey, marking its organization, as well as the outer curtain-wall with its towered corners and portcullised main gate. And he could just as easily look the other way into the inner bailey, or ward, to make note of the stone keep and *its* apparent strengths.

They walked the wall slowly, talking desultorily about architecture and improvements in personal quarters with the coming of Norman castles, halls, and manors—wisely, the earl did not mention that the arrival of Norman castles was forced upon England by the man who had conquered her; John's heritage was, after all, Norman—and before long the prince felt he had lured his host into the proper frame of mind to entertain a new notion.

John paused at one of the crenelations, a notch in the wall most resembling a squared-off tooth warded on either side by the taller sections called merlons, and leaned between them, resting elbows on the crenel lip. He nodded approvingly. "A fine castle indeed. Well thought-out and built."

Huntington stood quietly next to John, surveying the outer bailey with a keen eye. The watch was lighting torches. "Thank you, my lord."

Sidelong, John assessed the man. Old, growing older, but still strong enough, still vital enough, still immensely powerful. It would not do to dismiss Huntington because of white hair and wrinkles. The man was not a fool, and not likely to fall for simple tricks in conversation. "A pity," John remarked. "So easily is a man undone by the folly of his children."

The earl stiffened minutely. "Yes, my lord. A pity."

"No doubt the sheriff had hoped for a fine match." John leaned out, peering down at massive brickwork. "It's only natural, after all—so much is achieved through wise alliances . . . though I've heard she is his last of several daughters, and therefore this will not destroy his inclinations for improvement." He scratched idly at stone with a fingernail. "Other men are not as fortunate. You, of course, have a son—but only one."

"There were others, but all died. He was the only one who survived." The earl nodded. "Yes, I am fortunate. God saw fit to return him to me whole."

"And a hero." John smiled. "No doubt my brother placed

much trust in him." He did not speak again of perversity; his goal now was different.

The earl's expression was guarded. "I believe he is worth that trust, my lord."

"But of course!" John's gesture was deprecating, dismissive of the need to state the obvious. "And now you are faced with a task similar to the sheriff's: of finding a proper match for your remaining child."

Huntington did not respond instantly. Behind the bland mask, John knew, the shrewd brain was working rapidly.

"Of course, it will not be a simple matter," John continued. "Huntington is an old name, a fine house . . . you can hardly accept the first girl offered. Unless, of course, she were as worthy as your son."

Huntington was very still. "It will be a decision worth making in its own time."

"Of course. But he is of an age . . . and you are faced with what all men face: the necessity of putting your house in order as the old enemy approaches." John turned his back on the outer bailey and folded his arms, leaning against crenel notch. "You don't strike me as a man who will allow death to catch him unaware. No doubt you have plans for your son and his future."

"In good time, my lord, I will suggest—"

Quietly, John cut him off. "I understand your plight. I, too have children, albeit they are bastards. But they *are* children of royal loins, and therefore more important than mere casual by-blows might be . . ." Dark eyes glinted in wan torchlight. "My daughter, Joanna—a fine, bright-spirited girl . . . young yet, but a delight." He let it rest a moment. "But, as you say, in good time."

There. It was done. The bait, duly dangled, would eventually be taken.

Alan was allowed to dress himself before the guards took him deep into the castle foundations and introduced him to the earl's new dungeon. He was briefly grateful for that much; a man's pride, much bruised by false accusation, is nonetheless

137

more battered when the body remains unclothed. He had pulled on hosen and shirt, but was allowed nothing more. Barefoot, lacking his fine brocaded tunic—and his lute—he was escorted from the chamber so quickly converted from intimacy to Guy of Gisbourne's hospital room, and unceremoniously urged to descend the wooden ladder into the dirt-floored cell below.

Alan sat in the dark and gingerly tested his split lip, first with a careful tongue, then with his fingertip. They had not chained him or bound him. He was simply confined in an otherwise empty pocket lying deep beneath the supports of the castle. Far over his head the trapdoor was closed and bolted. The guards had, of course, withdrawn the ladder as soon as he'd descended.

It was cool and damp, even in spring; in winter it must be very cold. Another small thing for which to be grateful.

He shut his eyes a moment, trying to quell the sudden surge of panic. It did not please him to know himself the inaugural inhabitant of Huntington Castle's dungeon. It pleased him less to know he deserved no part of the treatment. But he was wise enough to hold his tongue in front of Eleanor, in front of Eleanor's father, because accusing the sheriff's daughter of wantonness before witnesses would earn him more than the single blow deLacey had meted out.

Better he speak to the earl, were he allowed to do so. Huntington did not strike him as a fool, and it was possible he might be able to convince the earl that while indeed he and Eleanor had made the beast with two backs, it had been a willing liaison. Huntington was powerful; surely he would have some influence with the sheriff.

Unless, of course, the earl felt his courtesy had been sorely abused by a traveling minstrel, and made no move to suggest leniency.

Alan drew up his legs and hugged rigid knees, pressing his brow against them as if the pressure might chase away the seriousness of his situation. He had run the risk before, aware that were he ever caught by husband or betrothed, he might well be beaten to death on the spot. But risk was a part of the enjoyment, a fillip to the encounter; he had never seriously considered the consequences.

Now he considered them. Apprehension made him sweat.

He lifted his head and stared wide-eyed into darkness, digging fingernails through hose into the flesh of his shins. If he could speak to Eleanor . . . if he could *speak* to her, and convince her to go to her father, to tell the truth, to explain what had happened . . .

But futility swamped the thought. He doubted she'd recant. He'd never known a daughter willing to tell her father the truth about her sexual experience when a lie would improve her state.

It wouldn't be *death*, would it? Would they kill him for such a thing? Would Eleanor allow it?

He slumped against the wall as the dragon of speculation moved sluggishly in his bowels. The shudder that wracked his body had nothing to do with cold, damp stone.

"God," he begged aloud, "please don't let me die. Please don't let them *kill* me—"

It did not occur to Alan there were other punishments a musician might find worse.

Marian shut the door behind her with a definitive thump. The sleeping chamber she and others had inhabited the night before was empty of women save the one she most wanted to see. "Tell him the truth," she said. "Go to your father *now* and tell him the truth."

Eleanor's kirtle was soiled and crumpled. Her unbound brown hair hung lankly on either side of her sallow face. It did not hide the state of her mouth, swollen from Alan's attentions, or the dusty bruise staining her throat.

She had risen as Marian entered and now stood rigidly five paces away. She was clearly taken aback by the strength of Marian's determination, but her astonishment altered almost immediately to aggression, as did her posture. One hand rose to strike as Eleanor crossed over to Marian, but Marian quickly moved into the woman, catching her by both shoulders with flattened palms, and stiff-armed her back, knocking her so off balance Eleanor's feet became entangled with the nearest mattress. Eleanor sat down unceremoniously, staring up in shock and outrage. "How dare you—"

"How dare *you?*" Marian countered, cutting her off. "Do you expect me to believe the man you were so hot after forced you against your will? Do you expect me to say nothing at all when they haul him out of the dungeon and cut out his tongue?"

"You told my—"

"I told him nothing!" Marian cried. "I honored my promise to you, woman to woman—"

"You went running to him the moment my back was turned—"

"When?" Marian challenged. "You were barely gone from the hunt when Guy of Gisbourne was hurt! Do you think in the midst of that, I took time to beg your father's indulgence while I told him a little thing about his daughter's sleeping habits?"

"He wouldn't have known!" Eleanor retorted. "How could he have come back so soon? How could he have known—"

"He didn't know," Marian snapped. "Nobody knew anything at all about you, because I doubt anyone cared. Your father came back—they *all* came back!—because Gisbourne was badly hurt. Didn't you see that? Didn't you see all the blood when they carried him into the chamber?" Eleanor's expression was stolidly arrogant. Marian wanted to swear. "But no, of course not—you were too busy trying to cover up your nakedness and accusing an innocent man of rape!"

The expression altered from arrogance to anger. Hectic color clouded Eleanor's cheeks. "You told him. You helped him set a trap. You can lie to me all you want, but I know better. You're jealous of me. You've never slept with a man because you have no spine, and this is how you strike back—"

Marian's breathy laugh was of disbelief, not amusement. "My God, Eleanor—have you listened to yourself? You sit here before me and spew vile lies—"

Eleanor jumped to her feet. *"You're* the one spewing lies! You thought you'd ingratiate yourself with my father, so you went to him and told him about Alan, about *me*—"

"No." Marian shook her head. "Oh, I doubt he was surprised to find you rutting with a man in secret, but he didn't know which one it might be. My *God*, Eleanor—you heard

140

those women this morning! They knew perfectly well what you were doing. And you took no pains to dissuade them of it!"

Color stained Eleanor's face. "You're like all the rest. You lock away your virginity and accuse me of being a whore just because I have the courage to enjoy my body."

Marian shook her head. "You may sleep wherever you like— *I'll* say nothing about it!—but you can't turn your back on an innocent man. Pay the price, Eleanor. Go to your father and tell him the truth. I doubt he'll cut out *your* tongue."

Eleanor's eyes glittered. She lifted her chin. "Don't fool yourself by thinking I'll forget what you've done to me."

Marian wanted to crack a hand across the smug, self-righteous face. "I don't care what you think about me. Curse me in your prayers, if it gives you pleasure. But don't let them mutilate an innocent man."

Eleanor said nothing.

Desperation was swift-rising and painful. Marian began to realize she was no more capable of convincing the daughter than she was of convincing the father. "Eleanor—*please!*"

"He raped me."

"Eleanor—"

"He raped me."

"Think about what you're doing!"

With exquisite clarity: "He—raped—me."

When the cask was at last filled with heated water and the stool placed within it, with soap and towel nearby, Locksley dismissed the servants and stripped out of his soiled garments. He couldn't stand the smell of himself clothed and crusted in blood. Naked, itching, and bruised from his wrestling match with the boar, he climbed into the cask and sank gratefully onto the stool.

He hissed, holding his breath against the bite of heated water. When his body was sufficiently adjusted to the temperature he slid off the stool and ducked his head beneath the surface, stripping his hair of blood.

It crossed his mind that drowning might be a pleasant way to die, to rid himself of memories and unpleasantries associated with the Crusade. But his breath soon ran out, and the pleasure was less certain.

He came up spewing water and resumed his seat upon the stool, letting his knotted muscles loosen in the heat. With eyes closed, disassociated from his chamber and the trappings of his father's vanity, he could drift, forgetting himself entirely. But it was a transitory escape, because with lassitude came recollection. The heat of the water brought back the heat of the Holy Land, the acrid smells of dust and sweat, the tang of unwashed bodies, the effluvia of the marches and campsites, and the stink of rotting bodies.

Locksley tensed upon the stool, locking both hands over the rough-hewn edge of the cask that once housed wine. The peace was banished. Teeth set, he stood, taking up the soap, and began to scrub himself violently, concentrating on ridding himself of the remains of the encounter with the boar, and with his own fragility.

"My God, Robert—*what did they do to you?*"

He spun around, dropping the soap, peripherally aware that the awkward movement had driven a splinter into one foot. But he forgot that quickly enough. His father had entered. His father had seen.

The earl stopped awkwardly just inside the closing door. He gaped in undisguised shock as he gazed upon his son. Then shock became revulsion. The old face was the color of death. "Robert—my *God*—"

Locksley sat down at once, sinking his shoulders beneath the surface. It was an instinctive retreat, though now much too late.

The earl's hands clutched his surcoat, crumpling costly fabric. "Robert—*Robert*—"

Locksley shut his teeth. "You were never to know."

The old face spasmed. "Why did you say nothing?"

He recoiled. That, he had not expected. It was never contemplated, even envisioned, that he would speak a word of it to his father, *his* father, who could never understand, never even *believe*—He expelled the question abruptly, aware of an underlying hostility for the man, any man, who would dare to ask, to intrude. "What would you have me say?"

"But—Robert . . ." The earl passed a shaking hand over his

face. His pallor lessened, tinged with the first trace of returning color. "They are barbarians!"

The hostility receded. Locksley found it cynically amusing: his father was predictable in his outrage, a man born to wealth and rank and power but above meting out physical abuse save when it benefited discipline. "I think it made no difference *whose* son I was."

The earl scrubbed his face with both hands, as if cleansing himself of shock. Blue eyes glittered balefully. "Barbarians, all of them."

"Yes," Locksley agreed, and let it go at that. He knew better than to explain. "I didn't know you wanted me, my lord." A gentle reprimand, though he doubted the earl would mark it. But that he dared offer one, however subtle, was a new and tentative freedom.

The earl retreated to the bench along the wall beside the door. He sat down, clasped his hands over his knees, and studied his son thoughtfully. The shock was banished, replaced by parental assessment. White brows knitted themselves into a single line across the shelf of his brow.

Am I like him? Locksley wondered. *Is that what I will be?*

Huntington sighed. "I had not intended to speak to you of this. Not yet. But another has spoken of it to *me*, and so I bring it to you. You are a man now, as this Crusade—and its treatment of you—has proved." His elbows collapsed; he interlaced his fingertips across the pleated surcoat. "This is not something to which you must pay immediate attention. I have some comprehension of how you must feel, but newly come home . . . there is no need to discuss it in great detail, or make a decision. Not yet. In time."

"My lord—?" He found it more obscure than his own implied reprimand.

Huntington smiled wryly. "You are much admired, Robert, for many things. Most of which you will know. But foremost among them is your unmarried state."

Locksley grimaced. It had taken less time than he'd anticipated. "I see he has been at you."

White brows rose. "Has he spoken to you?"

Locksley shrugged, kicking the soap up from the bottom of

143

the cask so he might begin again to scrub. "He said something of it last night. I gave him no answer. But I thought surely now, after what has happened, there would be no chance of it."

Huntington frowned. "What happened today that might alter the possibility?"

Locksley considered the question carefully. It was unlike his father to give tacit approval to anything untoward, which certainly the supposed rape of Eleanor deLacey must be considered. "She's been publicly despoiled, has she not?"

The earl recoiled. "I've heard nothing of it!"

Is he so old as that? "You were *there*, my lord."

Huntington stared, then expelled a bark of startled laughter. "Good God, Robert! Not *deLacey's* daughter—my God, d'you think I'd consider that notorious baggage for you?"

His son nearly smiled. "I didn't know she was notorious. She wasn't, when I left."

"Most certainly notorious. We will not speak of the girl." The earl's tone was stern.

"Very well." Scrapes and scratches stung from the lather. "What of the minstrel, then?"

"The minstrel? He is none of my concern. It is a matter for the sheriff."

"Isn't William deLacey somewhat more closely involved in the matter than you might be? She is his daughter."

Huntington scowled. "Let him deal with the matter, I say. The man was a fool. He will stay the night in the dungeon, then be taken back to Nottingham Castle tomorrow. The sheriff may do with him as he likes. I have no interest in it."

"Cut out his tongue, I heard." Locksley's tone was uninflected.

The earl shrugged. "He's fortunate not to be killed."

His son scooped wet hair out of his face. "And if he's innocent?"

"Innocent! You were there, Robert . . . there was no doubt of what they were doing!"

Locksley nearly smiled. Clearly the image made the earl uncomfortable. He was affronted that such goings-on could occur under his roof; that any of his guests would so flagrantly abuse his hospitality. "No doubt of what they were doing, perhaps—but what of the matter of fault? You said yourself Eleanor deLacey is notorious."

"It doesn't matter," the earl retorted. "It isn't my concern, nor is it yours. We have something far more important to discuss."

And so the topic was altered. "Marriage," Locksley agreed. "Pray continue, my lord."

The earl nodded. "A bastard, but still acknowledged. Certainly royal by-blows have married into fine houses before."

Locksley stopped scrubbing. "Whose?"

"John's. Her name is Joanna." The earl shrugged. "It was mentioned, nothing more. The man's a consummate conniver, I'll give him that." The earl was up, striding around the cask to the far wall, where he peered out the window slot. "He discusses castles as if he has an abiding interest in the dirt and dregs of it, when it's perfectly obvious he wants to know if I intend to stand against him, now that I have the means."

Locksley himself wondered that, if in a detached way. He and his father had never discussed policy. He and his father had never discussed much at all. This was the first conversation he could ever recall having that contained fewer commands than opinions and declarations. He doubted his father would change his habits now, but at least he paid lip-service to the fact his son was grown.

Cynicism asserted itself, breaking through lethargy. *At least, while it suits him.*

Huntington swung back. "He compliments you now, when but yesterday he insulted you by implying unspeakable things. And so he dangles a daughter. A conniver, I say. He knows he's unpopular with the barons. He knows how badly he needs us. So now he comes calling, like a boy wooing a maid. Faugh! I'd as soon be quit of him before this night is through!" Huntington strode back toward the door. "But I doubt we'd be so fortunate as that. The larder is yet full." He unlatched and opened the door. "Don't trouble yourself about this, Robert. I have no doubt he's using the girl's name to every baron with an unmarried heir."

Locksley watched mutely as the earl went out and thudded the door closed behind him. "No," he said at last. "I won't trouble myself about it." He had no intention of marrying anyone.

Fourteen

Just after dawn, as the other women in the chamber began to stir sluggishly, Marian yanked her mantle into place over her clothing and met old Matilda's chiding gaze forthrightly. "We're not staying another moment," she declared. "I've done what I could to change the sheriff's mind, but he won't listen. Neither will his daughter. So, we're leaving now. We can eat something on the road."

"The sheriff's riding back to Nottingham today himself. We'd be safer—"

"We'll be safe enough," Marian said firmly, cutting her off. "The road to Nottingham is too well-traveled to afford thieves much chance of success, and I have no desire to spend one more moment in that man's company. We're going."

Matilda appealed to propriety as always. "Have you asked the earl's leave?"

Marian set her teeth. She had neither time nor patience for argument, no matter how well intended. "We're *going*, Matilda!" She turned on her heel and marched toward the door, snapping the folds in her skirts and her mantle out of her way as the old nurse, who was stiff and slow in the mornings, followed more carefully.

The door was opened before they reached it. A big-eyed servant-girl bobbed a quick curtsey. "Lady Marian?" At

Marian's nod, she went on hurriedly. "I been sent from the barber. You're to come and see Sir Guy, if you please, lady. The barber says he's asking for you."

It surprised her. "Sir Guy is asking for me?"

"My lady, yes. Will you come?"

There was no indecision, only puzzlement aplenty. Marian cast a glance at Matilda as she nodded. "Of course. Run ahead and tell him we're coming."

"Aye, my lady." The girl turned and hastened off.

"There, now," Matilda said as she joined Marian in the corridor and pulled the door closed. "You see? We're not meant to leave so quickly."

"We'll go as soon as we've seen him." Alarmed, Marian stared worriedly at the heavy-set woman. "You don't think he's in danger of dying, do you?"

"No thanks to the boar," Matilda muttered, moving in Marian's wake. "Run ahead, my girl . . . I'll come along in my own time."

Gisbourne breathed noisily through clenched teeth, clutching wadded bedding in both hands. He was very careful not to move, not to so much as twitch, but the pain was a wise beast and stalked him effortlessly, beating down his defenses until it found his thigh and sank its teeth into his flesh. The virulence of its bite reached up into his hip, and threatened the state of his belly.

He didn't want to vomit. Vomiting required movement, and movement, regardless of the cause, would bring renewed pain of a magnitude he had no wish to consider, nor most certainly to encounter.

The barber had cut the hose from his left leg and had cleaned and bandaged the angry wound as best he could. But he did so against his wishes; the wound, he explained, would certainly mortify. Gisbourne's best bet for survival was to have the leg cut off.

Gisbourne refused. Gisbourne declared he would die two-legged, if he were meant to die.

The barber called him a fool. When his patient mentioned

concern for the Lady Marian's safety, the barber spied his chance. All he need do, surely, was take the lady aside and explain the facts to her. Then she could prevail upon the man to accede to greater wisdom and let the leg be amputated.

Gisbourne knew this. He was not and had never been a dull-witted man. For this reason he refused the sleeping draughts the barber pressed upon him. By now he was dehydrated and very thirsty, but no less determined a patient than when the men had brought him in.

Marian. Would she come? He wasn't sure, and now he wasn't sure he wanted her to. Part of him had no desire for her to see him like this. Another part of him wanted badly to look on her face again, to reassure himself that the boar had not injured her. His memory of the encounter was blurred by pain and remembered panic; he could not recall what had happened after—even when he tried.

His concentration faltered. He thought back again to the day before, after the hunt, when he had been put into a chamber not meant for housing the sick. Not meant for lovemaking, either, but that had proved no deterrent.

Faintly, Gisbourne smiled. Eleanor deLacey—and a wandering minstrel! How was *that* for the downfall of a lady?

Attention snapped back at the sound of a lifted latch. The door was opened and Marian admitted, swathed in a dark blue mantle. He recalled it from the day before, blue against the green forest, and the tumbled mass of hair. She wore a white linen coif now and the glorious hair was braided into submission, dangling against her waist. But neither mantle nor headcloth hid even a whisper of her beauty. Gisbourne, abruptly self-conscious, pulled a coverlet over his legs.

The barber took her aside, speaking quietly and quickly. Gisbourne knew what he said. He prepared to answer her, albeit more politely.

And then she was there at his side, kneeling gracefully, quietly folding the voluminous mantle around skirts. The white skin, so close, was flawless, touched with healthy color. In her black-fringed eyes he saw sincere consternation.

He wondered if perhaps the wound, after all, was worth it, if it made her think of him. Better than being ignored. Better than being forgotten.

"Sir Guy?" The voice was low and smoky. He was not a passionate man, withal, being quiet in his habits, but she sounded like no other woman he had known, in bed or out of it. He could not help himself. He could not suppress the vision of Marian instead of Eleanor, bedding a man here in this room.

His face flamed instantly. He felt sick to his stomach, and cursed himself for his weakness. She was deserving of better.

She smiled tentatively, as if afraid it was inappropriate to smile at a man who might yet die. He understood her discomfort. He had watched two sisters die, and had found it unsettling. Most of all he had disliked not knowing what to say.

He swallowed painfully. His throat was dry, but he dared not quench it. He feared the water might contain something to put him to sleep, and he couldn't risk that. He might wake up—*if* he woke up—with a leg missing. "Lady," he croaked. "How do you fare?"

A true smile flowered; she was, he saw, relieved to hear him make sense. "Much better than you, I think."

He swallowed again. "I was afraid the boar might have harmed you."

"Oh, no. He was quite satisfied with you." Self-consciously she smoothed her hunt-soiled mantle. "There was no danger. Robert killed it before it could hurt anyone else."

The door opened again, admitting a fat old woman. Her attendant, he knew, so the meeting was circumspect. "Robert—of Locksley?" He thought it odd she would use his given name so intimately, but she appeared not to notice.

"Yes. It was over very quickly." Marian gestured. "I have never seen a man quite so fast, or so skilled. There was no fear in him, only determination."

Gisbourne gazed into her face, hearing the undertone of admiration. It rankled; Locksley had accomplished what he, Gisbourne, had not, and with surpassing skill. Hail the conquering hero, returned from the Holy Land . . . He drew a breath, gritting teeth, and set the thought aside. "I wanted to be certain you were well. To see for myself . . ." He gave way, hot of face. He had no skill with words. His gift was with sums, and weights

149

and measures. He could run a household, not kill a boar. Gisbourne knew very well which impressed a woman more.

Marian glanced over a shoulder at the barber, hovering in the background. Her expression was serious when she looked back. "Sir Guy, he says—"

"He says he wants to cut off my leg." He nodded tightly. "Lady—I can't allow it."

Her approach was careful. "He says it could be dangerous, if nothing is done."

"He thinks I'll die. He thinks the leg will rot." Gisbourne shook his head. "I couldn't bear it, being one-legged. And he hasn't tried, past poulticing it. There is cautery. Have him burn it closed first. If that doesn't work . . ." Gisbourne's hand twitched. "Better then that I die. But I'll die with both legs whole."

She gazed down at him mutely, weighing his words. He saw the genuine concern in her eyes, the assessment of the validity of his wishes. Then, smiling, she pressed a soft, cool hand against his burning forehead. "Then I will tell him so. It is *your* leg, after all—your wishes must be followed." She paused. "May I pour you water?"

"No," he rasped. "He will drug me, then cut it off."

She checked the beginnings of an answer and turned to the barber, gathering skirts and mantle as she rose. "Have you spoken to the sheriff? Have you told the sheriff what Sir Guy's wishes are?"

The barber bobbed quickly. "Lady, he's sore hurt. If I leave the leg on—"

"You *will* leave it on. He wishes it so. Have you spoken to the sheriff?"

The barber was unhappy. "He says I am to tend him as best I can."

"Then do so. Clean the wound and use iron. Tend him carefully, as you are bidden . . . do you understand?" Her tone was inflexible. "You will do as this man wishes. You are not to drug him insensible and then cut off the leg. Do you understand?"

"Lady, I do, but—"

"But nothing," she said firmly. "If it eases your sense of duty, *I* will go to the sheriff—"

"No need." It was deLacey himself, entering the chamber. "I am come myself; what would you say to me?"

Gisbourne saw the subtle but instantaneous change in her attitude. The solicitude vanished, replaced with physical stiffness and a taut self-control. Yet the words were quiet enough, if still inflexible. "This man insists on cutting off Sir Guy's leg. It's not what Sir Guy wishes. I've told this man to clean and cauterize the wound. The rest is in God's hands."

She doesn't like him. It was, initially, preposterous. But he was certain of it. *She doesn't like him!* Gisbourne twitched as a bolt of pain bit into his thigh, cutting through the startled realization. *What has he done to turn her against him?*

DeLacey's expression was momentarily arrested, but he moved quickly enough to counter her quiet hostility. He inclined his head to her. A brief glance in Gisbourne's direction was meant to convey sincere concern for his steward's health and condition.

Gisbourne, gritting his teeth against the pain, saw something more. *He's using my condition to sway her opinion.*

"Indeed, in God's hands," deLacey agreed easily. He looked sternly at the barber. "You will do as the lady orders."

"Aye, my lord." The barber bowed.

Gisbourne waited for the sheriff to acknowledge him now, to speak, but beyond the merest flick of a glance in his direction, deLacey looked only at Marian. "I understand you and your woman are to leave."

"Yes, my lord." Very stiffly.

"Then may I suggest you travel with my party? I am taking Eleanor back to Nottingham."

Marian's tone was icy. "And the minstrel, my lord?"

"Yes, of course. They're bringing him up now." DeLacey glanced at Matilda. "You and your woman will be most welcome. It will be company for Eleanor . . ." The tone abruptly went dry. "More *proper* company, though her reputation is quite beyond repair."

Marian was undeterred, which also surprised Gisbourne. More often than not people folded beneath deLacey's desires.

"I think not. Matilda and I have already ordered our horses. I tarried only to see how Sir Guy fared." Her glance at *him* was kind. "You must conserve your strength, Sir Guy. I will pray for your recovery."

"Lady—" He wanted to delay her, to make her stay, but she was clearly anxious to be gone from the sheriff's company. "I—" But he couldn't say it. There was so much he couldn't say, to a woman such as she. "Thank you, Lady Marian."

"Marian." DeLacey, overly free with her Christian name, Gisbourne thought, reached out to halt her even as she moved toward the door. "I insist—" But the rest of his sentence was lost in the noise of the door and the hurried words of a guard.

"Lord Sheriff? My lord—" The liveried guardsman stopped just inside the door and stood stiffly. His face was expressionless. "The man has disappeared."

DeLacey's eyes narrowed minutely. "The minstrel?"

Gisbourne, who had seen that expression before, wanted to snicker. *As if his doubt could alter the truth!*

The guard swallowed visibly. "My lord. Yes."

DeLacey's enunciation was most distinct. "Disappeared?"

"Yes, my lord."

"From the cell?"

"Yes, my lord."

DeLacey was thunderstruck. "The minstrel has escaped from the earl's *dungeon?*"

Marian's laughter filled the chamber. It was a sound unfeigned and unforced, eloquent in its delight. Astonished, Gisbourne stared at her, then looked at the sheriff, who was infinitely chagrined, and irritated by it.

"My lord." The guard, however, was grim. "My lord, the earl wishes to speak with you."

"Yes." DeLacey's tone was hard. "I imagine he does." He glanced briefly at Marian, expression masked, then looked back at the guard. "Escort the lady and her woman to the great hall. She will accompany my party. I would have her needs attended."

"My lord—*no!*" She shook her head as a wave of color blossomed in her face. But she regained self-control quickly. More quietly, she said, "We can't wait any longer."

152

"But of course you can." DeLacey spared a glance for Gisbourne, but it was quickly spent. "Wait in the great hall with the guard, if you please. I think it imperative that Eleanor have better company than I alone can provide."

"My lord." The guard inclined his head as the sheriff left the room. Then he looked at Marian. "My lady—if you please?"

Gisbourne was astonished by the venom in her voice. "No, I do *not* please. But I have no choice, have I?"

The guard looked nonplussed as Marian swept by him. The last Gisbourne saw of the party was the hem of Matilda's mantle. Then the door thudded closed.

The barber came forward. His smile was insincere. "Cautery, then. As my lord desires."

Gisbourne forced the words past tightly shut teeth. "Cut it off, and I'll kill you."

"No need, Sir Guy. You'll be dead before you can try." The barber leaned down and closed his hand around the cup. "Water, Sir Guy?"

Helplessly, Gisbourne cursed him.

The interview with the earl was of brief duration, netting no explanation for the escape. William deLacey bit his tongue on the words he longed to say. One did not say such things, make such accusations, to the Earl of Huntington. One asked what one could, with requisite courtesy, then accepted what one was told. Eventually, one was left with nothing but the thoughts in one's head.

The earl was no more content, the sheriff knew, if for different reasons. His brand-new castle, of which he was so proud, had proved to have one immense flaw that rendered it useless as a prison: a contingent of guardsmen open to bribery.

It was the only explanation, Huntington had declared at last. Certainly no man could escape a cell reached only by way of trapdoor and ladder, unless he was aided. And since three guardsmen were missing, the answer was obvious. Someone had given them money to release the prisoner.

And which of all his guests, asked the earl pointedly, had the most cause to want him released?

This left deLacey chewing his tongue, marking the implication but saying nothing of it. Instead, he concurred with the earl and took his leave, saying his duties required his immediate return to Nottingham. He would send men out after the minstrel.

The earl seemed not to care particularly *what* was done about Alan of the Dales. It hadn't been *his* daughter, after all, nor was the minstrel of his household. And his implication regarding the source of the bribe pointed yet another finger in deLacey's direction.

Better simply to leave, before one said too much.

Marian paced in a corner of the great hall, scuffling through scented rushes, kicking clumps out of the way. Matilda sat on a bench, resting sore joints and swollen ankles, from time to time suggesting that Marian sit down, but Marian had resisted. She was too annoyed to sit still, too frustrated by helplessness.

I should just go, she muttered inwardly. *Who is he to stop me? He isn't my father, nor my husband; he has no power over me.*

The guard stood near a pillar, hands folded behind his back. He wore the well-cultivated blank expression Marian had seen on the faces of other soldiers given tedious duty they didn't dare complain about, for fear of censure—or worse—yet nonetheless gave away what they thought of the duty. She didn't really blame him. Were *she* a guardsman, she wouldn't care for it, either.

She spun around on her heel and marched back to the man, stopping directly before him. "You have no right to keep us here."

Brown eyes flickered. "Lady, the sheriff asked it."

"Whose man are you? That's Huntington livery you're wearing, is it not?"

A muscle jumped in his jaw. "He is the lord high sheriff of Nottinghamshire—"

"You owe service to the earl, not to William deLacey. And we're not prisoners, are we? Not like the minstrel was." Her tone stung him; she saw the grim acknowledgment in his eyes. "You have no right to keep us here."

"Lady, for your safety—"

"And have you seen the bailey?" she asked. "Even as we speak, tens and twenties of people are riding out of the castle. They're going home from here . . . what danger in it for me? No outlaw would dare to rob us in the midst of so many people."

The taut facade cracked a little. "Lady, I can't let you go. After the minstrel's escape? Three of us are already tainted—do you think the earl would give me no more than a tongue-lashing? Lady, he would discharge me—and I have a wife and three children to feed."

He was, she thought, but a handful of years older than she was. No doubt a place in the earl's service was much sought-after among young men as yet unattached, and offered true security for a man with a wife and children.

"Did you know them?" she asked. "The three men who freed the minstrel?"

Brown eyes flickered. "Yes, lady."

"Were they married?"

"No."

She nodded briefly, seeing it. "A man with no wife or children might be more willing to take the risk." He hunched a single shoulder briefly, clearly disconcerted by her questions. Marian smiled, relenting. "Then do your duty, soldier. I have no right to task you for it." His relief was muted, but apparent. Marian smiled more widely. "If I promised to wait here, to not go without your leave, would you do a service for me?"

"Lady?" He was cautious.

She made a small gesture. "I know. After what I have just said, I don't blame you for distrust. But I promise to wait right here for the sheriff. I give you my word."

From the bench, Matilda spoke up. "She's a headstrong girl, I'll own, but she's never broken her word."

He looked at Matilda, then back at Marian. Mutely he nodded.

"Good." Relief sparked briefly, then faded away. She felt hideously self-conscious asking such a thing. "Will you take word to Robert of Locksley that I would like to speak with him?"

"Lady, I would . . . but he left the castle this morning."

The faint hope and newborn determination spilled away, leaving Marian empty. She had not thought of that. "Oh." She felt tiny, diminished. "I see. Then—never mind." Hot-faced, she turned and went directly to the bench, where she sat down somewhat stiffly next to Matilda.

The old woman arched her brow. "What plan were you hatching?"

Marian sighed, slumping back against the wall. "There was a thing I wanted to ask him."

"Ah, well." Matilda patted her knee. "Another time, my girl."

Marian barely heard her. She gazed blindly into the hall and thought about the message her father had sent with Locksley. *I have to convince him to say nothing to the sheriff. I can't have the sheriff knowing anything about it.* Vision swam back into clarity. *I have to explain that I can't marry a man who would cut off another man's tongue.*

Mutinously, Eleanor deLacey glared back at her father. That he was sincerely angry, she knew, because only rarely did he let so much of his guard down.

He scooped up her mantle and threw it at her. "Put it on now. We're going immediately."

The mantle puddled briefly over a shoulder, then slid off to land on the ground. She made no attempt to pick it up.

Her father inclined his head. "Very well." He reached out to catch her wrist. The pressure was intense as he dragged her toward him. "Did you pay them with coin? Or pay them with your body?"

She was startled by the virulence in his tone. He was a passionate man capable of high good humor as well as black moodiness, but most did not realize it. He was a consummate diplomat within the bounds of his service, cognizant of how to play man against man, and how to control the balance of emotions. For himself, he was as controlled—except when very angry.

"I don't know what—" she began.

"Don't lie to me! Not now!" His breath ruffled the fine

156

strands of hair hanging limply about her face. "Did you spread your legs for guardsmen as well as for the minstrel?"

"I did noth—"

"Don't lie to me!" He released her wrist and instead closed his hand on her throat, fingertips resting on the bruise Alan's mouth had left. "You press me, Eleanor. *This* time, you've gone too far. I have overlooked much in your past, but this time you've gone too far. I'll be lucky to find any man at all willing to take you."

"The minstrel would take me!" Even as she said it, she knew it foolhardy, born solely of defiance. It only made him go white instead of red, and the fingers on throat-flesh tighten.

"By God, I should sell you into whoredom," he rasped. "I should play procurer for you, and make a little profit. By *God*, Eleanor—have you no wits? You might have had an earl's son!"

She bared teeth at him. "And you an earl*dom?*"

He released her roughly. "It was you, wasn't it?"

Eleanor laughed at him. "I'll tell you nothing."

Slowly, he shook his head. "You try me, my girl. A saint is better prepared to deal with the likes of you."

She put up her chin. "Then send me to a nunnery. Be rid of me altogether!"

He smiled thinly, with no amusement. "Ah, no, not that. I know what nunneries are, my girl—you would have too much enjoyment of it, when the young men came to call. No, what's best for you is to take you home with me, and lock you up in the castle. Perhaps a chastity belt might cool your ardor a bit."

She blanched. "You wouldn't dare!"

"I'll dare anything, if you give me reason enough. And you very nearly have." He made a sharp gesture. "Pick up your mantle, Eleanor."

She challenged him automatically. "And if I said no?"

He caught her elbow in his hand and escorted her roughly out of the chamber into the corridor, forsaking the mantle entirely. She attempted once to twist free of his grasp, but he simply tightened it until she cried out in pain. It didn't move him in the slightest. He simply moved *her*, without the faintest hint of compunction.

She thought about what her father had said: Alan was free.

Vaguely she thought she ought to be glad for him. He was, after all, innocent, though she dared say nothing of it. And if anyone asked her, she'd swear he had raped her. What else could she do?

Except now they'd probably kill him, instead of merely cutting off his tongue. If he were foolish enough to be caught.

Alan had not struck her as a foolish man, but then neither was her father. Much as she hated him, she had to give him that.

Fifteen

DeLacey's party was more than his daughter, himself, Marian, and Matilda. As befitted his duties and office, he rode with six men armed with swords and crossbows, wearing mail and Norman helms with dehumanizing nasals. The guard was meant not only to stave off attack from outlaws, but also to imprint upon the minds of surly peasants that no matter how much they believed themselves wronged—though such an assumption was of course ludicrous—they lacked the power to do anything about it. Norman justice was powerful and ever-present, as proved by the sheriff's men.

Marian rode wrapped in a dark mantle and darker thoughts, withdrawing as best she could from the sheriff's company. He had initially tried to open a friendly conversation, but she refused to be drawn into it. Her answers were clipped and to the point, leaving no room for discussion or speculation; eventually he gave way and broke off further attempts.

Eleanor also was icily silent, although she shot Marian venomous looks. Marian briefly considered declaring yet again that she had said nothing to the sheriff regarding his daughter's dalliance with Alan, but decided against involving herself any further. It would do no good. Whatever Eleanor wanted to believe was what she *would* believe.

Morning bled into midday as warmth dried dew and dampness. The track they rode to Nottingham was wide and well-traveled, inviolate to outlaws as Marian had told the earl's man. Trees and foliage fringed the track, thick with cart and foot traffic, powdered into softness by countless thousands of hooves. Busier than usual, she thought, until the sheriff reminded them all it was the first day of Nottingham Fair. In the midst of the earl's festivities, all of them had forgotten.

"We shall have to go," deLacey remarked, slanting a warm glance and smile at Marian.

She knew the tone now, and was moved to protest. "Matilda and I must go straight on to Ravenskeep."

"Nonsense." He was irritatingly tranquil. "We are nearly to Nottingham now; you may as well see the day out. You will be my guests at the castle."

"I think not, my lord." She wished she had the courage to speak more forthrightly, instead of with the kind of meek courtesy men with stronger wills overrode easily. But it was difficult to do so in the face of civility. Only when she was angry could she speak bluntly and effectively; it was one of her weaknesses which she disliked more and more. "I think it best we go on."

DeLacey, riding a pace ahead with his silent, stiff-limbed daughter, looked beyond Marian. "I think it best you give your woman time to rest."

Marian glanced back across a shoulder to the old woman, whose mount had fallen behind. "Matilda!" She pulled up sharply, reaching out to catch a dangling rein and bring Matilda's horse close to her own. The old woman rode slack and slump-shouldered, pressing her right hand against her breast.

As Marian halted her horse, the old woman roused. "What—? Oh no, no need—"

Marian was thoroughly frightened by the grayish cast to the woman's face. "What is it? Are you ill?"

The old nurse shook her head, blotting weakly at a sweat-shiny face. "No—no . . . only a little tired. It will pass, I promise."

DeLacey came back to Marian's side. Eleanor waited beyond, sallow of face and attitude, against a backdrop of men and mail. "She's ill," Marian said tightly. "We need to stop immediately."

"No, no." Matilda waved a limp hand. "It's passing, I say— no need to wait for me."

"But of course we must." The sheriff was at his most solicitous. "As I have said, you are welcome at the castle. You will stay the night, and rest. In the morning I well send men with you to escort you safely to Ravenskeep."

Matilda looked wistful a moment, then drew herself up. "My lord, I thank you—but I am already better. 'Twas but a momentary weakness."

The decision was rapidly made, albeit against Marian's preferences. There simply was no other choice. "No, Matilda . . . listen to *me*, now, instead of giving me orders." She softened it with a smile, trying not to let the old woman know how worried she was. "We will indeed go on to the castle and stay the night." It was difficult to say it, after refusing the sheriff's invitation, but she saw no help for it.

"Here." DeLacey drew up his waterskin, unstoppered it, and leaned out to offer it. "Drink, old friend. Refresh yourself. You are my guest, now, and in my care."

Shakily, the woman took the skin and drank. Her color was improving by the moment; Marian wondered briefly if she *could* go on, but dismissed it almost at once, chiding herself for the thought. It would do no harm to stay the night with the sheriff. She would simply remain in her chamber with Matilda and avoid him entirely.

Murmuring courtesies, deLacey took the waterskin back when Matilda was done drinking. Watching him, Marian had to admit he was kindness itself when the moment required it and did not go against his wishes. But she recalled all too clearly how unwilling he had been to give an innocent man his freedom.

She gritted her teeth. *How could my father have suggested a match between us? Surely he knows*—knew—*this man, and what he is capable of!*

And yet perhaps he hadn't. Perhaps William deLacey had conducted himself with perfect fairness and decorum in Hugh FitzWalter's company.

Or perhaps it was merely the cost of holding the sheriff's office.

She shivered. The last thought suggested a man who did things he didn't want to do, in the name of rank and office. And she didn't want to acknowledge that perhaps it was the way of life itself. *But my father could never have condoned what the sheriff did. He would* never *agree to cut out an innocent man's tongue.* And yet a nagging thought remained: what if it had been she? What if, to her own father's mind, the only way of retrieving a portion of dignity for a publicly despoiled daughter was to punish an offender who had, in truth, offended nothing except propriety?

As Matilda resettled her mantle, murmuring assurances of her readiness to continue, Marian looked ahead to Eleanor deLacey. She didn't like the woman. She believed her to be entirely selfish and utterly heedless of other people's needs. But Eleanor had spoken sincerely of a woman having needs equal to a man's, with no means of expressing them. What more had she done but satisfied those needs in the arms of a man who had known such freedom lifelong?

But they would have mutilated him—And yet Alan was free. Someone had freed him.

Cold struck Marian to the bone. She sat stiffly upright in the saddle, clutching the reins spasmodically, and stared wide-eyed at William deLacey. She was painfully aware of a new and discomfiting thought.

What if it was—? No. It couldn't be. And yet the question came back again. *What if the* sheriff *did it? What if he played the part of a man concerned with duty only in public*—?

He might have told her, when she went to see him to plead for Alan's release. He might have divulged his plan. But a careful man wouldn't. A shrewd, meticulous man wouldn't tell a soul but one who *had* to know, and she wasn't one of them.

"Marian?" It was deLacey, of course, quietly curious.

Mortified, Marian looked away, gathering up the reins. She

couldn't apologize. He had told her nothing for a reason. If he had wanted her to know, he would have said something. She thought it likely he wanted his secret to *remain* a secret, even now.

It was easier simply to think of Alan's freedom without considering means and methods. Easier by far than reconciling new possibilities with older convictions.

The lute hung heavy on Alan's back. The instrument itself was no different, he knew, but the knowledge of what he risked by coming to Nottingham made him nervous. Worse, he knew very well the lute made him more conspicuous; though a fair drew more than one itinerant musician and it was ordinarily unlikely anyone would mark him out as different from any other lute player, he was no longer ordinary. Eleanor deLacey had seen to that.

He needed money; it was that simple. He had been told to go to Nottingham, to a small, quiet alehouse very far from the castle, where he would be met and given coin. When Alan questioned the necessity of going into the sheriff's own city, he had been told deLacey would not return immediately. There was Prince John to entertain and the earl to impress—William deLacey would wait a day or two before returning to Nottingham.

He knelt by the roadside, screened by foliage. The walls of Nottingham loomed up before him, fluttering colorful banners to celebrate the fair. For the past half hour he had watched the road traffic closely, marking fair-goers and city-dwellers going about their concerns. There were no soldiers on the road. He knew very well the gates were routinely manned, but the soldiers there would have no knowledge of what had occurred. His danger lay in a messenger sent from the sheriff, but instincts told him none would be forthcoming, as he doubted the sheriff would believe a wanted man would purposely go to Nottingham. That certainly was one reason he had been told to go there.

Alan scrubbed his face with both hands, stretching flesh out of shape, knowing himself grimy and soiled from the dungeon cell. His fingernails were black-rimmed, his bliaut and hosen damp and stained with grass. But at least his crimson brocaded tunic, with his lute, had been returned. That lent him a little splendor and restored his spirits.

But the *hair:* he combed it with his fingers, trying to put order to the tumbled golden ringlets so appealing to the ladies, and scratched glumly at his stubbled, bruised jaw. He needed a bath and shave, as well as food, but all that required coin, and he had none to his name. All he could do was go into Nottingham and find a suitable corner for exhibiting his talent, with his hat conveniently placed where listeners might donate a silver penny, or two—better than that, he hoped, but anything would do. He needed to leave Nottingham before the sheriff returned.

A cart rattled by, pulled by a lop-eared mule. Following it was a cluster of adolescent peasant boys giggling among themselves. Likely predicting success with the girls they might meet, Alan thought, as he did the same himself.

He tugged his tunic into place, ridding it of as many creases as possible, then stood up. The lute lay athwart his spine, reminding him of his talent. Reminding him of Eleanor and the darkness of Huntington's dungeon.

DeLacey was relieved when at last they entered the city and proceeded to Nottingham Castle. He felt somewhat battered by events of the past two days: Prince John's unexpected arrival, Eleanor's costly behavior, and Marian FitzWalter's adamant challenge to release an innocent man or, at the very least, to offer that man more humane treatment. Then of course there was Gisbourne's injury, which would deprive the sheriff of his steward, thereby causing *him* to deal with the tedious day-to-day concerns he preferred to leave to Sir Guy.

Stupid fool, he reflected. *What did he think he was about, charging a boar on foot? He's hardly a true knight. Such behavior was uncalled-for.*

Indeed, Gisbourne's absence would cause all manner of inconveniences in certain matters of household and office administration. He would have to summon Gisbourne's mousy little assistant to sort out what needed tending. There was the murderer—*something Scathlocke?*—Prince John had come to see hanged, for instance, as well as more ordinary complaints and lax enforcement of Forest Law and the like, requiring his attention.

DeLacey followed his contingent of soldiers through city streets to the castle proper, where he and his small party rode under the raised portcullis into the outer bailey. It struck him anew that the Earl of Huntington had effectively reestablished himself as a premier peer of the realm, with a brand-new castle. His was far larger and far more impressive than Nottingham Castle, which lacked some of the modern masonry techniques deLacey had seen in Huntington's defenses. Of the two, he believed Huntington's more likely to withstand a true siege. And yet he wondered if it were entirely necessary. Who would lay siege to a castle *inside* England, while the Normans—and their Plantagenet descendents—held the English Crown?

John, his conscience told him as he dismounted his horse. *God knows what John means to do in his quest to make himself king.* DeLacey gave his mount over to the horseboy and turned at once to Marian, moving to help her down as she untangled her skirts and mantle from the saddle. Then, knowing instinctively his care would impress the girl, he turned away to the fat old woman who had no business riding out when clearly her heart was weak. He helped Matilda dismount, murmuring meaningless assurances of her welcome, then solicitously shepherded her into the keep with Marian following closely. Eleanor, he knew, would fend quite well for herself.

Locksley passed unobtrusively through the crowds thronging Nottingham's narrow thoroughfares, many choked off by too many bodies, coughing up stragglers into alleys, or into tiny "squares" where dwellings, stalls, and businesses rubbed wooden elbows and shoulders. He was near Market Square, where several wider streets came together, forming an open space; it was there the heart of the crowd gathered to watch games of skill, to gossip, or to buy a trinket or two at the flimsy lath stalls and cloth booths leaning haphazardly against one another. He wanted to do none of those things, but it was there he went regardless.

He wanted to hear and smell England again, trading too-vivid memories of foreign things for those he had known all his life. It was here, in the midst of a fair, that he could begin again to understand who and what his people were.

The sky was clear of clouds and the temperature mild, promising a good day. Locksley moved slowly, impeded by others, begging pardon quietly if he stepped upon a toe or was jostled against another. He had clothed himself without ostentation in a plain brown tunic, leather belt, hosen, and aging boots; not so different, on first glance, from what a peasant might wear on a fair day in Nottingham. But cut, cloth, and workmanship was of far superior quality, as was his manner, unassuming though it was. He mistakenly believed he could fit in, thereby experiencing the fair as any peasant might.

He made his way out of the street into Market Square itself and halted by a roughly made stall where he could, if he desired, buy a lady a colorful ribbon. A brilliant array of streamers fluttered in the thin spring air, but his eyes marked something other than ribbons to braid into hair; what *he* saw, from the corner of an unsuspecting eye, was the flutter of a pennon, the snapping of a banner, the ripple of a herald's tabard in a land very far from England.

He moved away from the stall even as the merchant held out a basket overflowing with a tangled cloth rainbow.

Odors were thick. He smelled pasties, young wine, sweetmeats, spices; the effluvia of streets that were home to the four- and two-footed alike. His ears were stopped up with the nearly indecipherable accents of Nottingham's merchants, the shire's peasantry, the babble of women telling stories on their men, the wild shrieks of children, the deeper-pitched tones of husbands freed of a serf's duties to lose their cares in ale.

He closed his eyes and let the sounds wash over him.

The call of stall merchants and shills working the crowd . . . clay flutes, sweet and somber . . . the staccato patter of stick against drum . . . the chime of finger bells. Even the thread of a nimbly played lute, the sighing song of an Irish harp. But the music faded raggedly, replaced by other noise transmuted by memory.

The shrieking of children playing was the shrieking of children dying

. . . the shrill laughter of their mothers was the keening of cloth-shrouded Turkish women dragged from safety into the streets by men whose names he knew . . . the shouts of merchants hawking wares became the shouted orders of Christian soldiers liberating a Moslem city in the name of a God the Arabs knew as Allah, the most merciful and most compassionate, but who now turned a deaf ear, blind to the carnage carried out in His name.

He smelled blood and bowels and butchery in the midst of Nottingham Fair, surrounded by the people who labored to pay the costs of a war in which he could no longer believe; underwriting destruction in the guise of a warrior-king whose conviction was as sincere as it was undimmed, no matter the price paid in the blood of his own men, and the blood of the Saracen.

The blood of his own body, spilled by men of both sides.

"Richard . . ." he murmured, but banished it with movement both awkward and abrupt, passing swiftly through the people until he fetched up against the wooden frame of a raised platform. He stopped, caught support, clung. Sweat stippled lip and brow. When he could, he wiped it away with the cuff of his tunic, stirring the thick lock of pale hair shadowing his left eye. Time he saw the barber, if he were to see at all.

He looked up at the stilt-legged platform that had offered him support, and realized it was a gallows. He lurched away from the framework, needing to remove himself from yet another means for meting out death to men.

Someone banged into him from behind, then slid off his hip as if jostled by the throng. Locksley, knocked free of dark thoughts and balance, caught only a glimpse of the other: small, slight, quick. And already swallowed by the crowd.

He remembered too late a thing no man, with coin to his name, should ever forget in the midst of so many. Fingers felt the ends of the leather thong knotted around his belt. Sliced through cleanly, with nary a tug or snag. His purse was simply *gone,* as was the thief.

Thoughtfully, Locksley stared down at the cut thong. The task he had come to perform now was impossible, unless he were to turn thief as well.

He sighed, rubbing idly at his left wrist that, once broken, reminded him from time to time of its injury. It had healed cleanly enough—so had everything else of flesh and bone—but would not let itself be forgotten.

Indicative, he thought wryly, of the misuse of a man's body in the name of vanity. For what else was a Crusade but the context of a man's—no, a *king's*—wish to prove himself to God, ally, and enemy, lest he be unremarked in life as well as in death?

An old argument. Richard had not been convinced.

Locksley tugged the cut thong from his belt, studied it a moment, then dropped it to the street. Nothing left for it, then, but to find another way.

The first of deLacey's orders was for servants to see to it the Lady Marian and her woman were comfortably settled. The second was for Eleanor to take herself to her chambers, where she was to wait upon his summons. The third was for Gisbourne's assistant to appear before him at once in his personal chambers, where the sheriff promptly retired to change his clothes. He anticipated no problems with the assistant, intending only to get a sketchy idea of how things stood; he then would pay a courtesy call on the old nurse and take Marian to the fair, provided she could be pried loose from the old woman.

Gisbourne's assistant arrived in short order. He was a pasty-faced, mousy man, thin of frame and spirit, with fine colorless hair and the squint of a weak-sighted man better accustomed to entertaining sums than human company. The name was Walter, deLacey recalled, as he signaled for and drank down a cup of watered wine.

"Sir Guy will be indisposed for a matter of days, perhaps weeks." DeLacey handed the cup to the hovering servant, working his belt loose from his hips as another servant waited to divest him of his surcoat. "He met with an accident, and will remain at Huntington Castle until well enough to travel. Until then, you shall have to assume his duties."

Walter's mouth opened, then shut. He blinked, squinting a little.

The sheriff waited for a response as the servant tended the

surcoat, but none was forthcoming. "Well? May I entrust the duty to you, or shall I hire another man?"

Walter wiped his palms against the soiled front of his gray-brown robe. "No, my lord. I mean—yes, my lord."

DeLacey, wresting his arms free of sleeves, frowned impatiently. "Which is it, man?" Next the undertunic and bliaut, baring a winter-pale torso as yet unsoftened by age. Then he sat down upon a stool to facilitate the removal of his boots. "Yes or no?"

"My lord, you may entrust the duty to me."

"Good." Freed of his boots, the sheriff stripped out of hosen. "Now, what has happened while I've been gone?"

"There is the matter of the murderer, my lord. He was to be hanged this morning . . . but of course, with you gone, nothing was done." Nervously, Walter tugged at his frayed robe. "The gallows is built, my lord . . . but when shall it be used?"

DeLacey gestured his choice of fresh clothing, then shrugged dismissively. "Prince John is still at Huntington. As the men killed were in his service, it's best we leave the hanging until such a time as he pleases himself to attend." High-necked bliaut, fresh hose. "Leave the murderer below. He'll do well enough in the dungeon for a day or two more." Next came the longsleeved undertunic, a fine lightweight wool of pale saffron, embroidered at each cuff. "Anything else?"

"The new clerk is come. The one Sir Guy sent to the abbey for."

DeLacey was distracted by the appearance of a fresh surcoat and the exertions required to don it. "Sir Guy sent for a new clerk?"

"Yes, my lord. Brother Hubert died two months ago, if you recall it . . . Sir Guy said it was impossible for him to keep up with his own work as well as the correspondence. He sent for a new clerk."

"Very well." Such things lay within Gisbourne's office. DeLacey waved a hand. "Another monk, is it?"

"Yes, my lord. From Croxden Abbey."

The sheriff grunted, standing still as the servant looped and pulled taut the long leather belt that, once knotted, hung nearly to his left knee. "Anything else?"

Walter tugged again at his ink-stained robe. "There are the usual petitions for hearings on interpretations of Forest Law, my lord . . . the foresters have brought in six more poachers since you've been gone . . . and there's the matter of the last tax collection. Some of the villages are late."

DeLacey sighed. "When are they ever on time?" He bent and tugged on his freshly dusted boots. "We shall have to see to it the taxes are paid, punishments melted out. And payments increased . . . the peasants will complain, of course, but there is no choice in the matter." John had made that clear. DeLacey straightened, stamped his feet, and waved away the servant. "Another time, Walter. See to it the clerk is given those letters I wanted recopied—I don't expect Gisbourne saw to them himself?" He paused. "Or you?"

Walter blanched. "No, my lord."

"Very well, give them to—what is his name?"

"Tuck, my lord. Brother Tuck."

The sheriff nodded. "Tell him I'll expect them finished in a good hand by morning, and that I desire to see him immediately after breakfast."

"Yes, my lord." Walter paused. "Will you be wanting an order written for William Scathlocke?"

"William—?" But he recalled it: the murderer. They said he was half mad, a man empowered by demons when the battle fit was on him. DeLacey had heard of such things, but had never seen it himself. "Have this Tuck see to it." He unlatched the door, thinking ahead to Marian. "And tell him to use his best-taught English and Latin . . . this is Prince John, after all, who wants it with so much drama."

Sixteen

Marian perched on the stool next to the bed. The chamber was tiny, offering no more room than was required for a narrow bed, but it sufficed. Already Matilda seemed better, propped against feather-stuffed pillows murmuring repeated assurances that she would be well, that Marian need not worry, that her difficulty on the road was merely a dizzy spell now passed.

Marian smiled and nodded, keeping her thoughts to herself, and helped the old woman drink an herbal tea. When the mug was empty she set it on the floor next to the stool and smoothed the woolen coverlet over the mound of Matilda's body. *How many times did she do this for me?* Too many times to count. Since her mother had died, Marian's true solace and place of comfort had been with the plump nurse.

"He's a good man," Matilda murmured. "A hospitable man, to take me in like this."

"The sheriff?" Faint surprise pricked Marian's conscience; she should be more gracious in her thoughts of him. "What else could he do but have us in? Only a man with no heart or soul would have denied us shelter."

Matilda's eyes were crouched in creases more pronounced in her weakness, though her color was mostly restored. "But you would have denied it, if it weren't for me. Don't hide it from me, my girl. I've seen the look in your eye."

So easily Matilda made her feel like a child, defensive and determined. "I think he handled the matter of the minstrel poorly," Marian said finally, wondering uneasily if she had wronged deLacey again. "There are other ways of dealing with penalties."

"Fathers of daughters don't always see what's best." Matilda shifted her bulk. "They see the girl, and proprieties."

"And lost opportunities?" Marian smiled. "He wanted to betrothe her to Robert of Locksley."

"Aye, well, that's gone now." The edge of Matilda's wimple was stained with sweat and grime. "The earl will find someone better."

"What of the sheriff?" Marian reached up to unwind the soiled linen. "What does he do with a daughter so publicly ruined?"

The old nurse grunted as coif and wimple came free, baring her compressed gray hair. "Likely put her in a nunnery, or marry her off to the man least likely to protest." Blue eyes glinted briefly. "Now, as for you—"

"Me!"

"Your year is up, my girl. With your father gone now, 'tis best we look at finding a man fit for Ravenskeep."

Marian busied herself with folding the linen, setting it aside, and removing nonexistent folds and creases from the coverlet. "I am in no hurry."

"You'll be no younger tomorrow."

"And only a *bit* older." Marian grinned at the answering twinkle in Matilda's eye. "You see? You're in no hurry to lose me, are you?"

"Pah, I won't be losing you . . . unless you mean to turn me out. Who else is there to look after the babies you'll bear?"

Marian laughed. "I think it's *much* too soon to think about babies—" She broke off as the door scraped open.

"Marian." It was deLacey, clean and refreshed and smiling. But after the greeting for her, he went directly to the woman in the bed. "Matilda, how do you fare? I see you have tea—is there anything else I can have brought to you? Food, perhaps, or another coverlet?" He knelt down easily, taking her plump damp hand into both of his as he smiled warmly into her eyes. "You must not hesitate to tell me or any of my people, Matilda . . . I won't have you suffering out of a displaced idea of saving us trouble. You are my guest here as long as need be."

Color splotched the woman's face. "Oh, my lord Sheriff—"

DeLacey cut off her protest easily. "I won't have it. You and your lady are my guests." He smiled faintly, cast a sidelong glance at Marian, and looked again into Matilda's eyes. He leaned closer, lowering his voice intimately. "It is my right as lord high sheriff to command you both to stay, but I know better than that: such high-handedness would merely earn me your enmity. Certainly that of your lady, who knows her own mind." Teeth glinted briefly. "There is no cause to reproach yourself for honoring me with your company, no matter the cause . . . I am most pleased to host both of you, on whatever terms I must."

"My lord—" the old woman began.

He silenced her with a raised hand. "I'll have none of it, Matilda. The matter is settled." He chanced another glance at Marian, arched eloquent brows, looked again at the old woman. "If there is but one thing I might ask of you . . ." Deliberately, he let it fade suggestively.

Matilda rose to the bait instantly. "My lord, of course!"

He smiled. "Then convince the Lady Marian to go with me to the fair."

The object now was plain. Marian shook her head. "I can't."

"Of course you can," Matilda retorted. "It's best you go, rather than staying here all shut up. What good d'ye do me staring down on my sleeping face?"

"I couldn't go." Marian cast a chiding scowl at deLacey, undaunted by his rank. "I can't leave her alone."

"Of course not," he agreed smoothly, as if surprised by the implication that he would dare to suggest such a thing. "I intend to have two women stay with her at all times, to help her in any way. You are too good-hearted to desert, Marian . . . I mean no insult to you."

"Go," Matilda insisted. "The air will put color in your cheeks."

Marian looked accusingly from one to the other. "You conspire against me."

DeLacey exchanged a smiling glance with Matilda. "We understand each other."

"Say you'll go," Matilda told her. "You'll be back before nightfall, and we'll have supper together."

Marian shook her head firmly. "I don't think so—"

"For me," the nurse said stoutly. "Bring me back a ribbon, or a fresh spring pomander."

Marian had no desire to go, but staying behind might only add to the problem if Matilda came to believe her health was in jeopardy. Her color and breathing were much improved, but Marian recalled all too clearly the panic she'd felt on first sight of the old woman's distress.

DeLacey rose. "I'll send the women in," he told Matilda. "You can pass the time exchanging gossip."

Marian sent a glare in his direction, but softened it as she turned back to Matilda. "I can't fight both of you."

"Nor are you meant to; we both know what's good for you, even if *you* don't. Go on, my girl. An old woman needs time to herself."

"There, now." The sheriff rounded the bed to extend a hand. "Dismissed smartly, I think. She reminds me of *my* old nurse, may God bless her soul."

Marian scooped up her soiled blue mantle and rose. "My lord, I think—"

"Wait." He took the mantle from her hands. "This has seen hard days, thanks to Gisbourne's bloody courage. I'll have another brought. One of Eleanor's."

Yet another thing for Eleanor to resent. Marian opened her mouth to protest, but he had turned from her to unlatch the door. He waited for her there, eyebrows arched inquisitively.

Later, she promised herself. *Not now, not here . . . we will discuss this later.* She glanced down briefly at Matilda, then abruptly made up her mind. "Before dark," she said firmly, brooking no argument.

The sheriff's eyes glinted. "With ribbon and pomander."

It was inelegant, Alan believed, but the best he could do: he filched a wooden bucket from a stall as the merchant looked away, took it to a place around a curve, overturned it to spill out the cupful of water, and set it upside down on the ground.

Whereupon he perched his rump upon it, unhooked his lute, placed his scarlet cap upon the ground and began to play.

It was not what he had been told to do, but he seemed to have little choice. The alehouse to which he had been directed no longer existed, as he had discovered to his intense dismay. A fire a year before had destroyed a number of buildings, among them the alehouse; Alan was left to contemplate cynically whether his rescuer had known that and sent him there purposely, intending to withhold promised coin.

Not much sense in that game with me—there are ways for men like me of winning other coin. But for some time no one much noticed. Music was a staple of fairs, and Alan was hardly the sole practitioner setting up to earn some coin. But he was good, knew it, and let the confidence carry his voice. Soon enough he caught an old dame, then a younger one, then two little girls with their mother. After that came a young man or two, and then young wives with their husbands, and his audience was born.

It changed, of course. New people came, others departed. He noted expressions indicative of attentiveness, or lack of, and adapted his style to suit. Peasants were poor folk—he was more accustomed to playing for lords, earning marks in place of pennies—but before long a few silver coins littered the cloth of his hat.

A young woman came up, as he paused to work tension from grimy fingers, and offered a cup of sweet cider with a bob of her head and brief curtsey, paying tribute to his talent. She was plain, too thin, mostly shapeless, but female nonetheless, and responsive to his smile, to a warm glance from bright blue eyes.

Be careful, his conscience said as he drank. Then, as the girl smiled tremulously, *I will sing this one for her.*

He gave her back the empty cup and bent his head, letting the tangled ringlets tumble across a shoulder. Fingers found their places, pausing as he built anticipation. Then, softly, somberly, Alan began to sing.

He won them easily. He was, if nothing else, a genuinely talented minstrel and took pride in his appeal, using lute and voice to dominate the moments it took to complete the ballad. As he finished the peasant girl was crying, tears running down her face though she made no sound at all.

Alan unexpectedly was moved to shame. She was not Eleanor. She was not a rich man's wife. She was not a silly ladies' maid looking for a moment's dalliance. She was a young English peasant girl touched by a tragic story and the power of his skill.

I waste myself . . . But then two coins fell into his hat, followed by three more, and the thought passed from his mind, as did the peasant girl.

Games of skill and strength abounded, offering purses of various sizes. Locksley, who had wrestled the Lionheart himself, though unsuccessfully—Richard *always* won—briefly considered trying for a purse as a way of restoring his coin, until he saw the prospective opponent. He stopped short, shoulder to shoulder with other gaping men gathered around the lopsided roped-off ring near the center of Market Square, and stared in startled silence. Then, with exceeding—if unspoken—fervency, he gave pronounced and explicit thanks to God for bestowing upon him the wit to know when to hold his tongue.

As did so many who had seen him, Locksley measured men against King Richard when determining size. Part of the Lionheart's personal power and tremendous grasp of command was derived from his physical appearance, and his willingness to use it. Richard was a head taller than most men, particularly the smaller, slighter Saracens. His limbs were thick with muscle refined through arduous marches. Where others dwindled in the privations of Crusade—Locksley himself was one—Richard thrived. Known as a hearty trencherman, the king, being *king*, wanted for nothing in food and drink. In frame, habits, and spirit, Richard Coeur de Lion was impressively robust.

But this man was *enormous,* even as he bent over to scoop up his hapless and squawking opponent, who vociferously protested being dangled by an ankle in midair from one hand.

Locksley nodded absently. It lacked style, he reflected, but not effectiveness.

He glanced around the swelling knot of onlookers as they gawked at the giant, traded wagers among themselves, and murmured vulgar appreciation for the power of the man.

Someone called out that the victorious giant should dump Hal on his head, to teach him better manners. The unfortunate Hal, still suspended, shouted back, but his words were distorted by his precarious position.

It drew a laugh from the others. Then a red-tunicked man stepped out of the crowd, brandished a purse, and challenged the next brave soul to go a fall with the giant.

Locksley arched a brow, surveying the suddenly quiet audience. He grinned to himself. Then, not being a stupid man— and marking how the red-tunicked man's eyes roved the audience speculatively—he took himself off to find a game promising less exertion, fewer chances for defeat, and an opponent who did not resemble a man less than some red-maned tree.

DeLacey, clasping Marian's elbow, deftly steered her around a puddle of urine left by a passing horse. Coolly she said, "That was cleverly done." She eased her elbow from his grasp. "Matilda had no chance at all."

He gave in at once, knowing when to discard prevarication. "Yes, it was clever—and the device of a desperate man. Had I addressed myself to *you*, we would not now be attending the fair."

"No," she agreed. "And you know why."

He nodded as an off-duty soldier called a greeting. "Matilda was much improved, Marian. You saw that for yourself." He allowed the faintest tinge of iron to enter his tone. "You have been a year in mourning. It's time you thought of frivolity again."

She pulled the hem of the crimson mantle out of the dust. Eleanor was taller. His daughter's height, he thought, was the only thing in which she surpassed Hugh FitzWalter's magnificent daughter. Certainly not in voice; Marian's was low, and oddly—seductively—smoky. "I am more concerned, just now, with Matilda's health."

"She is old, Marian. Even rest will not replace lost youth."

The bluntness startled her, striking home with truth. "My lord—"

"Let us not argue." He took her hand and tucked it into his elbow smoothly, locking it into place. "Believe me, if I thought Matilda to be in serious jeopardy, I would summon the finest physician in Nottingham. But she is old, and weary, and journeys tax her now. She shouldn't have gone with you."

"No." Marian's expression was sober. On Eleanor's face it might have been sullen; on hers it was exquisite. "No, I thought not myself . . . but how do you say so? She has been with me all my life . . . how do I tell her I want her to stay at home?"

"The way a knight's daughter must," he told her evenly. "With gentleness, with compassion, and utter inflexibility. If you want her to live to be nurse to *your* children, she must stay home."

His words triggered something. Surprised, deLacey saw a wave of high color wash away the Celtic pallor. It lent her a vividness that took his breath away. Then, aware of his gaze, she made a pretty gesture meant to stave off a question.

The compulsion was overpowering. At that moment—*this moment!*—he wanted nothing more than to strip the mantle from her, and all the other fabrics, to lay bare the flesh he needed so much to taste. To yank the coif from her head and free the glorious hair, sinking his hands into it, losing himself in the satiation of the flesh that was, if only briefly, as intoxicating as power. *I want it all. ALL. The wealth, the power, the woman.*

"My lord?" she inquired.

Sanity rushed back, filling in the hole that desire had so unexpectedly uncovered in his soul. "William," he said harshly. "You must call me William."

For a long, too-long moment, she regarded him intently. He felt hideously exposed; that she read every nuance in him, every fleshly need, and was repelled by it.

But Marian was unawakened. Marian as yet did not understand such needs. Not as Eleanor might. "No," she said merely, in her quiet, smoky voice, and pulled her hand away.

Seventeen

Locksley stopped at a well, since he had no coin for cider, ale, or wine, and waited his turn in the midst of Nottingham's inhabitants and country peasants. He heard their desultory talk, the comments of dissatisfaction, the muttered imprecations against those who taxed them unduly, who sentenced them to starve because venison was denied them, in the name of the king's selfishness, or the earl's private holdings.

The sheriff, all agreed, was a harsh, unbending man who carried out his office with no thought to their plight. How would *he* like it, they wondered aloud aggrievedly, if the Lord High Sheriff of Nottingham were forced to toil for others, denied the forest game that could feed a thousand villages throughout the worst of winters? Was it any wonder poachers were made of farmers? And what *then* could they do, they and their women, when the men were maimed for trying to feed their children?

Mute, Locksley waited his turn, listening closely, and at last was given the dipper. He nodded his thanks and took water from the bucket that quenched the thirst of peasants; set his lips to the dipper that peasants had set their lips to; drank from the water that peasants also would drink from. Water, at least, was free, requiring no physical toil, exacting no tax or servitude, requiring no permission from the lord who ordered their lives.

Locksley lowered the dipper, staring blankly into the well as water ran down his chin. The realization was abrupt, and as unsettling. *I am they, and they are I . . . there is no difference between us. The Saracens made me their peasant, just as I make these men mine.*

"Here, now." It was the man behind him. "Here, now—d'ye mean to drink it dry?"

Locksley swung to face him. The man fell back into the man behind him, who cursed, muttering of clumsiness, and then shut his mouth abruptly as he also saw Locksley's expression. They were peasants, both of them, trained from childhood to know and acknowledge their betters. He wore plain, unadorned clothing not so different from their own, unless one studied workmanship and cloth, but the bearing and intangible power of presence set him apart from them.

Each man hastily tugged at a forelock, wondering inwardly what *he* was doing here, drinking so publicly from a well best used by the peasantry, but neither said a word save to murmur a servile greeting.

"No," Locksley said tightly, pressing the dipper into the first man's hands. "No, I'll not drink it dry. You deserve it more than I."

Marian could not look at William deLacey. He had spoken so easily of Matilda being nurse to her future children, not knowing he echoed the woman's own words. In and of themselves the words were not so startling, nor particularly uncommon, but to hear such things mentioned by the sheriff, whom her father desired her to marry—and who had, inexplicably, assumed an intensity she had never seen in a man—left her feeling oddly unsettled. He had stared at her so oddly.

She dragged the borrowed mantle more tightly around her shoulders, tucking her hands out of sight. Steadfastly she stared into the crowd, searching for a distraction, and saw it almost at once. "Ribbons!" she cried. "I must fetch Matilda a ribbon—" She moved swiftly across the street, to busy her hands and mind with the examination of color, fabric, and length.

He followed, of course, as she had expected him to. But by the time he stood again at her shoulder Marian had recovered her self-control. And so, she saw, had he; he put out a steady hand and pulled loose from the basket a single crimson length. He laid it across her shoulder, atop the bright woolen mantle. Then, sharply, he said "No," and took the ribbon away.

It was altogether puzzling. Marian turned from him again and pieced through the baskets, finding many colorful ribbons that took her fancy. In the end she chose dark wine, knowing it suited Matilda.

Before she could speak, the sheriff paid for the trifle. Marian protested, but he dismissed it easily. "Come with me," he said. "There is something I want to do."

She accommodated him, tucking the newly purchased ribbon into the purse hung beneath her mantle as he escorted her to a stall full of finely loomed wool. The quality was exquisite, the dye-lots rich and clean. No slubs in the weave, no splotches in the color.

"This," deLacey declared, and pulled up a fold of cloth. It was a rich, brilliant blue. "This," he said, "not that. Blue to match your eyes, and for the blackness of your hair."

"No," she said promptly. "No, my lord—I forbid it."

He smiled easily. "The other is ruined. And this—" He touched a fold, "—this one is Eleanor's. It does you far less credit than you deserve."

She was adamant. "I have other mantles at home."

He was as inflexible. "I will have it made up, and bring it to you myself."

In that moment Marian realized the confrontation would color the rest of their lives, if she took no pains to change it. Something had happened. Something had given him leave to pursue her. Something in his eyes, that indefinable intensity, told her very clearly he intended to do so. *How do I deal with this? How can I dissuade him without destroying the linkage with my father?* "No," she said, half pleading, protecting her memory of Hugh FitzWalter. "Please, my lord—"

"It pleases me," he agreed. "I will not be denied."

It will get worse, not better. She sought her only weapon. "I will not wear it."

His expression was very still. She could not pierce its facade. "That is your choice," he told her evenly. "But I will have this done." He had told her to be inflexible. She saw the example before her.

He is buying little pieces of me, breaking them off bit by bit. No matter what I say, no matter what I do . . . Firmly, she repeated, "I will not wear it."

DeLacey turned from her and looked at the merchant. "Have it taken to the castle. The account will be settled later."

Marian put a hand on his wrist, knowing instinctively it would hold him. "My lord, I beg you—don't put me in such a difficult position. I can't accept it."

"Indeed you can, and you shall. I insist. The matter is settled."

She jerked her hand away, knowing the ploy failed. "Have I no say?"

He smiled. "In this, no. Marian—honor me. I have seen you grow up from an awkward, coltish girl into a lovely woman. I wish only to pay tribute to what you have become. Can you deny me that?" He continued before she could answer. "Your father and I were friends. I ask no more intimacy than that, Marian . . . allow me to give you this in memory of his name."

He was smooth and eloquent. She knew him for many things, not all of them admirable, but she could not deny the effectiveness of his words. His manner was impeccable. The underlying tension she had seen but moments before was gone, banished by a courtesy no different from that he offered others.

And yet there remained a single small weapon, born of bitterness, that she should be so weak. "What are you like, I wonder, when you speak as you'd like to speak, without the requirements of office?"

The recoil was minute, but present. She knew it when she saw it, because she had waited for it. "Do you imply I am a liar?"

Marian laughed, seeing and hearing genuine astonishment. "A diplomat, my lord. A man overschooled with words, who understands phraseology far better than most, I fear. And while I understand the means, I don't comprehend the intent. Why manipulate *me?*"

She had at last effectively undercut him. "Because," he said finally, in an unfamiliar tone, "you insist upon it."

It dumbfounded her, but he offered no explanation. He offered nothing at all, save a tight, masked expression she found less than eloquent, yet strangely illuminating.

The smell of meat pasties roused Locksley's appetite, but he had no coin with which to buy any. While water cost nothing, victuals weren't free, which only renewed his determination to find a game at which he could win a purse.

He heard the sound before he saw the cause: a whining hum of displaced air, cut through by wooden shafts. He knew it instantly. Swiftly he made his way through the multitude, and stopped short at the edge of the green near Market Square. Six archers competed, shooting at a distance that would soon bespeak their skill. Locksley watched closely, marking longbows and cloth-yard arrows, fletched with ticked goose quills.

The targets were vaguely man-shaped, made of straw stuffed into sacking, then bound against movable wooden standards. On the breast of each "man" were painted multicolored rings, with a heart-shaped bull's-eye in the center.

Locksley smiled, folded his arms and spread his legs to relax his stance. He watched as the six men drew arrows, nocked, and loosed. One shaft flew wide, ending that archer's participation. Two others struck straw, naught else, which also ended the turns. One struck the outer ring, two others the center ring. But none pierced the heart. No man could continue.

Absently, he nodded. The barker was calling for new archers. He marked his man apart, and when all six failed archers stepped away from the line, Locksley moved to intercept him. "A good stout bow," he said lightly, altering his accent to something less than aristocratic, "but a bit too tall for you."

The man glowered at him. He was dark-haired, dark-eyed, sullen, with a squint to one eye. "D'ye think you could do better?"

Locksley hitched a shoulder. "But one way to see. Give me the loan of your bow and five of your arrows. You'll share in the winnings."

The man assessed him, noting quality and cut of clothing; considering possibilities. "How much?"

"A quarter," Locksley answered.

"Half," the man countered. "Without bow nor arrows, you'll win nothing at all."

Locksley paused a moment, as if thinking it over. "Bargain."

The man squinted at him. "Who be you, then?"

He hesitated. "Robin. Robin of Locksley, hard by Huntington."

"I know it." The man handed over the bow. "I'm Tom Fletcher, of Hathersage. 'Tis what I do, d'ye see: make arrows such as these. So what, I ask myself, do *you* know of bows?"

Robert, newly christened Robin, hitched a single shoulder. "Watch me shoot, Tom Fletcher, and you'll see what I know of bows."

"Hmmmph," was Tom Fletcher's comment, but he stood aside to watch as Locksley tested the bow.

It was smooth, sleek yew, measuring more than six feet. Locksley found the pull to his liking, as anticipated, and the fit of the leather-wrapped handgrip. He put out his right hand for an arrow, and Tom Fletcher gave him one.

"Clear away!" someone shouted. "Clear away for the archers!"

He stepped to the line, along with five others. The butts remained at the same distance, as no one had struck the heart. He measured it automatically, marked the play of breeze, and honed his concentration. A strange bow and a strange arrow; it would take him more than once.

Five others loosed. Locksley nocked his borrowed arrow, raised his borrowed longbow, brought back his right hand to his jaw. Tension sang through string and arms, promising sweet power. He hadn't handled a longbow for more months than he cared to recall.

He counted, then loosed. The string hummed briefly as it catapulted the feathered shaft through the light spring air. It struck into the target just outside the heart-shaped bull's-eye.

Tom Fletcher grunted. "Not so bad a first shot."

But not good enough. Locksley put out his hand for the second arrow. He loosed as the others loosed. This one pierced the heart. None of the others did.

A cheer went up. Tom Fletcher slapped his back. "Done, then! And half of the winnings mine."

"Not yet," Locksley said. "Three more arrows yet."

"But you've won! You've beaten the others, Robin. What more is left to do?"

Find out if I can still do it. But he said it to himself.

"Target!" someone called. "Back ten more paces; d'ye think you can manage that?"

Locksley nocked the arrow. When he loosed it, the heart boasted a second shaft.

"Target!" was shouted. Another ten paces added.

Tom Fletcher swore. "Boy, you'll not do it. Take your winnings and go."

Locksley's eyes glinted. "After dividing them?"

The fletcher spat. "Hit that heart but twice more, my lad, and you'll have my half as well."

Twice more Locksley shot. Twice more the heart was pierced. But when the watching crowd threatened to bruise him with celebration, the former Robert of Locksley, companion to the king, merely gave the bow back to Tom Fletcher, accepted the purse with murmured thanks, and disappeared into the throng.

Alan of the Dales finished the chord with a flourish and bent over in a cramped bow. The listeners around him applauded. Coins landed in his hat. He saw the glint of silver marks and looked up with a grin of thanks. "My lord—" But he let the false flattery die out when he saw the title was applicable. Instead he rose to his feet, dangling the lute at his side.

He was all-over brown, Alan saw: plain brown tunic and hosen, with a plain brown leather belt, and plain brown leather boots. He was unremarkable save for his stature and the set of his shoulders, for the shape of facial bones, the wide-set hazel eyes, and the near-white hair that tumbled across wide shoulders.

The tone was cool. It might have been mocking, save there was no emotion at all. What little he knew of Robert of Locksley convinced Alan the earl's son was sparing with his feelings. "I told you to go to the alehouse."

Resentment goaded him into challenge. "It burned down last year—or did you forget, my lord?"

For only a moment surprise replaced the cool implacability. Then it faded, replaced by a grim bleakness. "Last year I was on Crusade."

It was answer enough. Alan was briefly ashamed of his rudeness, but could not restrain the impulse to use the knife again. "I wasn't sure you meant it." Nobles made promises frequently. Rarely were they kept. That the earl's son had actually come surprised Alan more than a little, certainly no less so than when Locksley had opened the trapdoor to the cell and lowered the ladder.

Locksley tossed more silver into the forgotten hat. "I suggest you take your earnings and go while you still have the chance to do so." He paused. "Or do you value your tongue so little as to risk it to William deLacey?"

Alan hooked the lute over one shoulder, sliding it into place across his spine. "My lord—why? You bribed the guards, set me free . . . and now you give me silver. How may I repay you?"

"I have some acquaintanceship with captivity." Still Locksley didn't smile. "As to repayment—choose your partners more carefully, and the chambers to which you take them."

Alan's vision, caught by a splash of crimson color, focused beyond Robert of Locksley. "Oh God—it's *she*. The sheriff was sniffing around her skirts—she'll likely tell him—" Hastily Alan bent and scooped up the coin-splattered hat and tucked it inside his tunic. With a muttered word of thanks, he shouldered his way through the crowd and disappeared into an alley.

Marian pulled up the hem of Eleanor's mantle as she walked, dragging the fabric out of the dirt. She blessed it for its length, for it gave her an excuse to keep her hands busy and free of deLacey's intimacies, subtle though they were.

She had become increasingly aware of an undercurrent growing between them. There was tension in his body she had never seen before. Even his voice reflected it, in tone if not in words; as always he was eloquent, most fluent in flattery, but the compliments, though polished, had a quality about them that spoke to her of something she could not comprehend.

He was solicitous and generous, buying her cider, buying her sweetmeats, buying her anything she so much as happened to glance at, ignoring her protestations. His purse appeared bottomless, or his credit honored by all, and Marian took to staring groundward so as not to encourage his generosity. *If he thinks he can simply buy me* . . . The words were ash in her mind. If he knew what her father wanted, he need buy her nothing at all.

"A moment." He paused to turn away, to examine something she could not see at the nearest stall.

Not something else . . . Marian edged away from him, clutching the mantle more closely, wishing she might disappear into the crowd. It was possible. It would hardly be difficult to become separated, but such rudeness was inexcusable. Her mother, and later her father, had taught her better manners.

She caught the sound of a lute, the flourish of a final chord. Through the crowd she glimpsed him, in brief scattered slits between moving people, bowing over the instrument as his listeners applauded. Then a man stepped in front of the minstrel, blocking her view of him, and tumbled silver coins into the crimson hat.

Locksley? It was. The fall of pale hair, the set of wide shoulders, the posture of his body. Unmistakable. She knew him instantly. And knew, without knowing *why,* that she would always know him.

Locksley. With a minstrel.

Marian moved slightly sideways, peering through the crowd, trying to see around Locksley. Yes, it *was* the minstrel, the selfsame minstrel, Eleanor's jongleur. Alan of the Dales.

And Locksley *with* him. Putting coin into his hat. Marian twisted her head to look across her shoulder at the Sheriff of Nottingham. *It wasn't deLacey after all—it was Huntington's son who freed him.* Comprehension surged up. *He will have him taken—*

Without thinking of the consequences, Marian snugged the brilliant cloak around her body and darted through passersby, cutting diagonally across the street to the upended bucket to Locksley himself, brushing by his arm. When she arrived the minstrel was gone. "Oh good," she said on a breath of relief. "The sheriff is over there—*just* over there—do you see?" She glanced back at Locksley. "Why did he come here? Why was he such a fool?"

His expression, as always, was masked. "I told him to come."

"Here?" She nearly gaped, hiding nothing of her feelings. "Are *you* a fool, then, to send a man into danger? The sheriff would have him in a moment—no doubt he'd call up the guard and have his tongue cut out right here!"

He weighed her distress, though she did not know the result. Coolly he said, "I have no doubt of that." Before she could speak again Locksley glanced back toward the sheriff. "The minstrel saw you looking at us. He thought you would give him away."

It was astonishing. *"Why?"*

Locksley's gaze returned to her face. "He said, somewhat inelegantly, that William deLacey had been sniffing around your skirts."

The heat of humiliation took possession of her face. Marian knew of no words that could adequately express the embarrassment she felt. A strangled "No" was all she managed.

His examination of her was intense, lacking in pretension. She had told him the truth, but clearly he was unconvinced, relying instead on his own measurement of such things as honesty and honor. For that, she admired him, but wished his target were someone other than herself.

"No?"

"No." Marian hated herself for being so unworldly. A woman like Eleanor would handle this so much better. She wanted to tell him she knew precisely what he did, measuring her against a private inner criteria, but held her tongue. If she protested too much he would count her false. *"You* did it, then. Not the sheriff."

"DeLacey!" It startled him. "Why would a man so publicly humiliated *free* the man who ruined all of his plans?"

Explanations filled her head. None of them now seemed adequate for Robert of Locksley, who undoubtedly found her lacking in wit and conversation. *He will think I am a fool.* Well, perhaps she was. "I thought it was possible that he would quietly release a man he knew to be innocent."

One eyebrow arched minutely. "And did he know such a thing?"

Marian nodded mutely, refusing to incriminate Eleanor any further.

For the first time since she'd seen him standing on the dais, Robert of Locksley smiled. It was a true, unfeigned smile, unhindered by self-restraint, dazzling in its power. "It does seem as though everyone in these parts is aware of Eleanor deLacey's indiscretions. Perhaps I should be grateful to the minstrel for divulging them to *me.*" The tone was exquisitely dry, inviting a reaction other than diplomatic obscurity, or overmuch discretion. At last, he was human.

Emboldened, Marian laughed at him. "The sheriff was very plain, my lord—he wanted to match his daughter with the Earl of Huntington's son."

"And so I am yet free of encumbrances such as a wanton wife."

The smile was gone, but a glint of humor remained. *Do it now . . . there will be no better chance.* Marian drew breath. "My lord Robert—"

"Just Robert," he said. "Or—Robin."

"Robin?" It was incongruous. It did not fit a fully grown man, a former Crusader, freshly home from the king's war. Robin was a *boy,* and he clearly not.

"My father named me Robert. To my mother, I was Robin."

Marian stared at him. Such intimacy she had never anticipated, not from *him.* The tension she had seen and heard on the dais, in the chamber, was banished. Even the mask was gone. There was, in tone, in expression, an odd hesitancy. A kind of *need,* she realized, for acceptance on a level other than that offered by other people, yet wholly bestowed by his father.

Yet she had no time to pursue it, nor the courage to proceed. What she asked now was for herself, because that she understood. That she could control. "My lord—" She broke it off, seeing his eyes: fragile withdrawal. "Robin." She swallowed tautly. "There is a bargain we should make."

"Oh?"

She lifted her chin, refusing to show him the nervousness she felt. "There was a message sent from my father. The one you brought me the night before last."

Tension returned fourfold, enveloping his body. So swift it

was that she nearly gasped, astonished by his sudden stillness. The mask was back in place. The eyes, once amused, assumed a clouded darkness. Even the mouth was taut, and the scar along his jaw. *My God—what have I done?*

"I recall the message." Crisp, cold words, yielding no emotion.

This was a mistake. But it was too late to withdraw. She had opened the subject. Now she must close it. "A bargain, my lord." Formality was called for in the face of such austerity, such iron-willed self-control. "You say nothing to the sheriff of my father's message, and I for my part say nothing to the sheriff of Alan's whereabouts."

The words were clipped. "You no longer know Alan's whereabouts."

That was true, but she had no other weapon. "He shouldn't be hard to find."

"He should be impossible to find, if I took pains to make it so."

She stared at him, bargain forgotten in the face of compelling conviction. "Would you do that?"

"Yes." It was distinct.

"Good," she declared forthrightly, surprising even herself.

A hint of warmth intruded into frigidity. His eyes were speculative. "A bad bargain."

Chagrined, she sighed. "But the only one I could think of."

"Need you think of any?"

"I believe so, my lord."

"To keep me from telling the sheriff a private and personal message your father intended solely for you."

"Yes, my lord." She did not hesitate, even though she understood how such a suggestion imputed dishonor to him. She did not know the man. She did not know of what he was capable, and she was beginning to learn that no man was *in*capable of doing things she found abhorrent.

Locksley looked beyond her, toward the stall where she had slipped away from her escort. "And you have no wish to marry William deLacey."

"No, my lord." With explicit emphasis.

Robert of Locksley looked back into her face. His eyes were unreadable. "Then perhaps you should tell him so."

"I can't."

Brows arched. "Why not?"

"Not until he's asked."

"Will he?"

"Probably not. Most likely he will *tell.*"

The edge of his mouth loosened. "Yet you are here with him."

The implication stung, as no doubt he meant it to. Marian glared at him. "You are not a woman. You have no comprehension of what a woman must be, in the face of a spoiled, powerful man who knows what he wants, and who is convinced *he* is the only one who knows what is best for the woman."

"No," he agreed, after a long moment of solemn silence.

"Nor ever can," she reminded.

"No," he said again.

She gazed up at him. He was considerably taller. "I will not marry a man who believes in cutting out the tongues of innocent men." There. It was said. Clearly and forthrightly, begging no part of the question, leaving no portion unsaid or weakened by the courtesy that was all too often a crutch. *If I can say it like that when the sheriff raises the subject* . . . But courage spilled away. He *was* a spoiled man. He *was* a powerful man. And she merely a woman; what chance did she have?

"The sheriff," Locksley said.

Marian stared at him.

"The sheriff," he repeated.

This time she understood. This time she turned and looked, and saw deLacey approaching. His eyes, dark as death, were fixed on Robert of Locksley.

Eighteen

DeLacey turned at last from the stall to Marian and found her gone. At first he thought little of it, assuming she waited nearby, perhaps at an adjacent stall, but a cursory search did not discover her.

Difficult to miss, in crimson—ah, there she is. A splash of the brilliant color betrayed her location but several paces away, on the other side of the street. Speaking with someone. *Who is she—? Locksley!* He did not know precisely why, but the discovery disturbed him. And not knowing why disturbed him even more. *Why?* Then, with a flicker of irritation, *No time, just now* . . . He let it go with effort, thinking instead of Marian herself and the recapture of her company. He wanted her with *him*, not wandering off to speak with others.

For the first time he had her to himself, separated from childhood, father, and maidservant. And he needed her to himself, as he had needed nor wanted no woman before *this* woman, not even the wives he'd married. *I am become a proprietary man.* But he knew that of himself. He also knew how to use it, to gain and to keep the things he most desired.

"Locksley," he murmured intently. It was a habit of his to speak such names aloud, as if in the declaration he marked out the enemy. Locksley was Huntington's son. One day, when the earl was dead, he would inherit all. Title, wealth, power. But Robert of Locksley was not an enemy.

Unless he insists upon it. DeLacey arranged his face in a suitably pleasant expression and crossed the street to them.

* * *

Very smooth, Locksley thought. Without excess exertion, without too much insistence, William deLacey grasped Marian's arm, forced her hand from beneath the mantle, and locked it into his elbow.

"Here you are," he said. "I thought I had lost you." Then, before she could speak, he smiled warmly at Locksley. "Robert! Had I known you intended to come to the fair, I would have invited you to join us."

"Indeed." It was as much answer as Locksley could offer. His attention was diverted by Marian's face, marking the bloom of annoyance, the tautness of her jaw, the glitter in her eyes. A certain tension in her forearm told him she attempted to free her hand, but deLacey merely folded his own over hers and crooked his elbow more tightly.

"Join us *now*," Marian said, in an odd undertone of dictatorial desperation.

In it, unexpectedly, he heard the echo of her father, begging Locksley to carry a message if death were his fate that day. *Tell her*, he had said. *Tell her he will tend to her personal welfare, and the welfare of Ravenskeep. Tell her also I miss her. And please to tell her, I pray you, how very much I love her.*

He had not done the latter. Or the one before that. He had told her merely that she was to marry the sheriff, who stood before Locksley now daring him to intrude upon the thing deLacey had marked for himself.

Tell her, FitzWalter had said.

But as Locksley gazed at the dead knight's daughter, he found he could not do it.

Dismayed, Marian watched Robert of Locksley—*Robin*, he had said so—turn on his heel and walk away into the crowd. He had murmured something, something she did not hear, and simply disappeared, as if he could not bear to remain in her company. *Does he think me a hypocrite? Does he think I want this man?*

"Marian." DeLacey's hand tightened on her own.

192

"Marian—come. Forget his discourtesy . . . there are other things for your attention."

He's glad *Robert's gone.* Annoyance captured her tongue. "Then let me decide them myself." With effort, she yanked her hand from his imprisoning elbow. *Tell him. Just—tell him!* "My lord, I think there is something you should know."

He cocked an eyebrow. "Indeed?"

Impulsive courage wilted beneath the level gaze. *How do I say it, now that I've begun it?* Marian wet her dry lips, knowing she needed an inflexibility equal to his own; knowing also it was difficult to turn it back on him. He was, as she had said, a spoiled, powerful man. "I dislike assumptions," was the best she could manage. *No spine. No spine at all.*

"As do I." He smiled crookedly. "I admit it: I am jealous."

So swiftly the topic was changed. Or was it the same topic, merely turned upside down? "Jealous of Robert?" *Robin* was hers; she would not share it with him.

"Of Robert *of Locksley,* the Earl of Huntington's son." De-Lacey gestured in self-deprecation. "What am I, after all, but a man in someone's employ? He is a peer of the realm."

"And you meant him for Eleanor." It was a desperate ploy, designed to interject yet another person.

"But Eleanor is discounted." His eyes were oddly avid. "Marian—"

"No." She said it with every ounce of will she could muster. "I think—" But what she meant to say was forgotten utterly as she saw the boy next to the sheriff, a slight, slender boy with deft hands on deLacey's purse. *"Much!"* she cried, astonished. And then, "Don't hurt him!" as the sheriff shut a powerful hand around one bony wrist.

Now he had coin. Locksley went immediately to a wine-seller and bought a cup, which he drained at once. And another. It was heavy, powerful stuff, uncut by water, thickening in his belly even as it arrived.

More? No, he was not a drunkard, nor, for that matter, a drinker. He despised the weakness, the cowardice, that had driven him to it at all.

Marian FitzWalter.

He turned away abruptly from the wine stall, striding into one of the narrow, twisty alleys hedged with close-built dwellings. There he paused as abruptly, hugging himself, and fetched up against a wall, banging shoulder blade and ribs.

Set to the task, he had believed it unnecessary. They all did, Richard's men; no one envisioned defeat in the midst of Crusaders' fever. When Hugh FitzWalter, assailed by premonition—or no more than the simple fear that wracked all of them, though none admitted it—had bade him speak to his daughter, Robert of Locksley accepted the duty casually, dismissive of its intent. He had, in truth, been annoyed by the request, not because of its content, but that FitzWalter had spoken of an ending, when so many of them preferred to think only of the beginning.

Richard made it so easy. He shut his eyes and saw the woman before him. *FitzWalter never said his daughter was beautiful.*

It was inconsequential. What did it matter? A woman was a woman, a daughter a daughter.

He had not bedded a woman for nearly two years.

A shiver wracked Locksley's body. He opened his eyes and stared, transfixed, seeing nothing but the face of a man foretelling his future, in the midst of creating yet another for his only child. *Tell her to marry the Sheriff of Nottingham.* That, he had told her. The rest, he had not. *I gave her the message the wrong way round. Now, she is trapped . . . what grieving daughter will go against a dead father's wishes?*

She had declared her intentions: not to marry the man. But he had seen her eyes. He had heard her voice. He, as much as she, understood realities.

As much as her father had, on the day of his death.

A boy, nothing more. Swift, slender, agile. And very deft of fingers. He was skillful, like other pickpockets and cutpurses. But deLacey, this once, had caught him in the act.

The wrist was thin, bony, fragile, stripped of flesh and strength. But deLacey paid that no mind, shutting his own powerful fingers ever more tightly to insure the boy remained caught. He saw the warped mouth, twisting in pain, the brown eyes stretched wide in shock, the pallor of a face reflecting patent astonishment.

Surprised I caught him at it—and what is?—ah! DeLacey caught the other hand, stripped the knife from it, then dragged the captured arm up so high it made the boy stand on his toes. "Cutting purses, are we?" And as the brown eyes flickered, "How many would mine have made?"

"Don't hurt him!" Marian cried, reaching out to catch de-Lacey's sleeve. "My lord—you'll break his arm!"

"I'll do more than that," he promised, glaring at the boy. "By God, you little worm, did you think you'd never be caught? Did you think yourself immune to the lord high sheriff's justice?"

The boy hung there, shivering, rigid fingers extending claw-like beyond deLacey's hand. The patched sacking tunic had pulled free of one shoulder, baring a knobby joint.

"Answer me!" The sheriff squeezed the slender wrist, grinding bone against bone. "Did you spit behind my back, swearing you'd never be taken?"

"My lord!" Marian again, closing hands around his arm. "My lord, I beg you—"

Tender-hearted, she was. He expected nothing else. But just at this moment he found it irritating. "By God, Marian—am I to ignore this? His hand was on my purse! I am the lord high sheriff. Need I more proof? Need I the testimony of anyone else?"

Marian's face was nearly as pale as the boy's. "You're hurting him," she said.

With effort, deLacey gave her courtesy. "Perhaps it would be best you returned to the castle. This is unattractive duty."

Clearly she was alarmed. "Why? What do you mean to do?"

His patience waned. He had no time for this. First there was the minstrel, conjured out of a dungeon after destroying Elea-nor's chances; then Robert of Locksley, winning Marian's attention; and now this *boy,* a common peasant cutpurse who dared to put lowborn hands upon the sheriff's own purse.

"What do I mean to do? Why, treat him as he deserves to be treated! Boys who put hands where hands do not belong *lose* those hands."

"No!" she cried. "My lord, I beg you—don't do this! He's a *boy*—"

"He's a thief, nothing more. He'll be treated as one." Her protests were drawing attention. Even now passersby paused, gathering near to murmur among themselves. Someone said the Watch was on its way, saving him the trouble of bellowing for aid. "Marian—" He altered his tone with effort, striving for calm. "Go back to the castle, I pray you."

"No." Her hand was on the bared shoulder. "I know this boy, Sheriff. This is Much, the miller's son. We've bought flour from Wat for as long as I can recall—and I daresay you have, too!"

"I daresay." It was ground out between set teeth. Obviously she would not be easily dissuaded, but he had no intention of giving in; he had lost too much already. The boy was the final straw atop a bundle of resentments. "It makes no difference . . ." He glanced quickly around the gathering throng. "By God, Marian, have a care for what you say. Do you question my authority before all of Nottingham?"

It struck home, he saw. She too realized the crowd increased with each moment. She, too, saw the avid eyes and moving mouths. *Now she will realize the magnitude of what she does.*

Blue eyes were very bright as she looked once more at him. "No," she said quietly. "I cannot let you do this."

The Watch arrived: Norman soldiers in Norman dress, the livery of deLacey's service. He handed the boy over at once, glad to be quit of physical contact, but gestured for him to be held where he was rather than dragged off in front of so many people. He wanted nothing more than to lop off the hand himself, here and now, insisting on public punishment as was his right, but to do so in front of Marian, who had made her opinion clear before an ever-increasing crowd, would likely destroy forever any regard she might hold for him. And that regard he wanted. Force was not to his taste. When Marian came to his bed, she would of course show maidenly modesty and a natural hesitation becoming to her rank, but he refused to entertain an angry or indifferent bed-partner. He had wasted himself on two cold women; he would not do so again.

But the cost . . . What was the cost? Loss of face before the people? Eleanor's wantonness with the minstrel had already lost him too much. That story would get out no matter what he did to suppress it, and soon enough he would be the laughingstock of a peasantry who hated any man responsible for administering the law. He could not afford to be lenient with the boy, or they would construe it as weakness.

He glared at the boy. Weakness was dangerous. Weakness would destroy him.

Much stared at Marian. It was *she*. She hadn't gone away after all.

Same blue eyes. Same husky voice. Same slenderness, wrapped in a woolen mantle.

But something *wasn't* the same: something had frightened her. Something made her *scared*.

In the tangled skein of his mind, that his mother said was simple, Much recognized fear. Much understood fear.

Marian? he asked, though never once had he spoken the name.

"It's Much," Marian said. "Wat the miller's son. *You* know Much, my lord . . . you know what they call him."

Simpleton and lackwit. Much had heard the words. He recognized such things as pity, contempt, disgust.

The sheriff's mouth grew taut. "And now thief, as well."

Marian? Much asked. But Marian didn't hear. None of them ever heard.

Locksley bought a meat pasty at a stall, ate it on the spot to assuage a dull hunger, then drifted aimlessly with the flow of the crowd moving out of the street and back into Market Square. Vaguely he thought of going home, but lacked the will to leave. It was simply easier to let himself be guided by the others. Habit, if nothing else; for too long the Saracens had ordered his life, while his mandate was merely to serve.

"Insh'Allah," he murmured reflexively, in the tongue they had made him learn, in the words they had made him speak, lest they remove the tongue from his mouth.

Absently he marked someone behind him shouting above the din—"Make way for the Watch"—but he was unconcerned with the warning. It wasn't until a pike was thrust against one shoulder, knocking him roughly aside, that he realized the Watch was indeed coming through, no matter who stood in its way. The crowd, parting raggedly, muttered of high-handed Norman justice meted out all too rapidly when poor English-men were involved.

Someone steadied and set him on his feet again, patting him on the back and murmuring something unrepeatable about Norman tyrants. He watched the pike-wielders go, broad-backed Norman soldiers in the sheriff's blue livery, and for the first time wondered what England had become while he fought in the Holy Land. Two years without a king could bring about much change. He had left a different realm.

Or come home a different man. That, too, was a new thought: that he, not England, had changed so markedly. That he had *been* changed, regardless of his desires. *Richard would not be so blind to the needs of his people.*

But Richard was not in England. Nor likely to *be* in England, were his ransom not paid in full.

Locksley clutched impotently at the pouch of coin he had won as his archery prize. Little now was left. But it didn't matter, he knew. Even a purseful of silver marks would not go very far against the hundreds of thousands required.

And the people who needed Richard the most could ill afford to pay so much as a silver penny.

"It's Much," someone muttered. And another, murmuring: "—boy's simple, can't the sheriff see?" And "Only a *boy,*" said a third.

Then the most telling of all: "Better the sheriff's purse than a peasant's empty one."

Marian heard them all. She knew the sheriff did. But looking into his eyes, at the expression of conviction, she knew nothing more could be used to change his mind.

But I have to try, regardless. "Let me have him," she said. "I'll take him back to the mill."

"So he can run off again?" DeLacey shook his head. "Marian, I honor your compassion—but this boy is a *thief.*"

Desperation made her angry. "And did *you* steal nothing when you were a boy?"

"Eggs from a hen," he retorted. "Never a man's purse, and it still on his belt!"

The crowd's tongue grew louder. The mood was clearly sullen, fraught with increasing tension. Marian realized she had, by her intransigence, placed the sheriff in a highly precarious position. Better she had tried another tack, but now it was too late. He was angry enough to act. *And I am angry enough to stop him, if I can find the means.* "My lord—"

"Sheriff." A thick, deep voice. "Sheriff, let him go. He's naught but a boy. You've scared him roundly enough—near broke his arm, I think—now let him be. Let him think on his good fortune. I'll wager 'tis the last time he sets fingers to a purse."

Marian turned, as they all did. Thrusting his way through the crowd was the largest man she had ever seen. Her father in armor was huge; this man was bigger yet.

He was red of hair and bare of chest, wet with glistening sweat. Even his features were oversized, in accordance with his frame. He had pale, prominent blue eyes; a crooked, imposing nose; and a wide slash of mouth partially hidden by a ruddy beard. The loose woolen hosen he wore were knotted at his hips and cross-gartered nearly to the knees. Enough fabric, Marian reflected, to clothe two women her size.

"Wager what?" William deLacey was clearly contemptuous, she saw, and as clearly impatient. He wanted the boy taken off away from the crowd, where his sentence would not be questioned. "Will you put up *your* hand as stakes?"

The freckled giant grinned. "I doubt your swords are sharp enough to hack through one of these!" The wrist he thrust into the air was sheathed in knotted muscle. The thickness of bone was enough to silence the crowd, contemplating the picture he had painted before them all.

"An ax," the sheriff retorted. "An ax would do very well."

The giant shook his head, flinging damp hair back from his face. "I'm made of iron, my lord—I'd blunt the steel of the ax!"

It brought a laugh from the crowd. Marian, staring up at the huge man, felt the tension fade. The giant had altered the confrontation from promised violence into anticipation of what the next moment might bring.

"Who are you?" DeLacey demanded.

"John Naylor, my lord. Of Hathersage. Shepherd by trade. Wrestler at the fairs."

Marian stared at him. *He must be the largest man in the whole of England.*

"Wrestler," the sheriff muttered, as if the occupation were the lowest on the earth.

"Called Little John, my lord." The giant grinned, undeterred by the contempt. " 'Tis a jest, I'm told."

DeLacey was amused. "Indeed," he replied. "Little or large, it makes no difference to me. The boy is a thief—"

"He's a *boy*," the giant declared stolidly. "Lock him up a night or two, to let him think about it, but don't cut off a hand, my lord. He may be bound to lose it, if he learns naught of this, but let him lose it a man, when he understands it better."

DeLacey's tone was cold. "And will you stand proxy for him?"

Transfixed, Marian decided she was wrong. He wasn't the largest man in the whole of England. *More like in the whole world.* His thighs, in sagging hosen, were the size of young tree trunks.

The good-natured raillery faded from the giant's face. "Aye," he snapped, "I'll stand proxy. But not the way you'd like. My hand is my own—unless a man can win it from me." John Naylor grinned. "Have a man out, my lord. Any man; I care naught who it be. I'll give you *three* men, even . . . if any of them beat me, the hand is yours to hack off."

"Why?" DeLacey asked. "What is this boy to you?"

The giant shook his head. "Naught to me, my lord . . . but a lamb caught by a wolf."

Marian studied his hands, then his face. His conviction awed her. *He could do it . . . he could win. He could save Much's hand.* "Do it," she murmured quietly. "My lord, accept his wager."

She could see the sharpness of deLacey's glance from the corner of her eye. "Will you not argue that it is a travesty? That the loss of a hand, regardless of whose hand, renders me barbaric?"

Marian met his gaze. *Now is my chance. I can't let him win this time.* Steadily she said, "Much stands no chance. He *is* a lamb, my lord—and you, I daresay, the wolf."

She saw it in his eyes: comprehension, and recoil. It *mattered* to him, she realized, what she thought of his actions.

The realization blossomed slowly within her mind. *At last, I have a weapon.*

Nineteen

Much remembered Marian. She had been a part of his life for as long as he could recall. Where she came from he didn't know, merely that she was *there*, one day, at the mill, all wet and slimy with weeds. Young, then; younger than now. Younger than *he* was, now. His father had brought her home, once he'd pulled her out of the millpond.

Images, no more. Fleeting recollections. A soaked, soggy girl undeterred by her state, speaking compellingly of the nixies who lived in the water.

Dimly, Much recalled, his mother had muttered a prayer against bewitched children, but not against him this time. This time, against *her*. It bonded them in that moment, though she could not see it; what *he* saw, between them, he did not recognize.

Much remembered her well. Marian, she'd said. And his father knew who she was. His father had sent his brother off to find *her* father.

Now she stood beside him, one proprietary hand upon his

bony shoulder even as a soldier held his arms, while a bearded, red-haired giant and the Sheriff of Nottingham made a pact between them.

She was no longer a girl. He was no longer a child.

How had it come about?

Marian? he asked. But Marian didn't hear.

DeLacey weighed the crowd and knew it better than it knew itself. He had been sheriff too long to blind himself to hatred; to deafen himself to insults no matter how quietly muttered. No man, in his office, would be popular. It was exacting service, meting out discipline against miscreants, thieves, and poachers, but he had not bought the office to become popular with peasants. They would not be content no matter who held his office, nor what the man did in his stead.

No one could question the boy's crime. He had been caught in the act, caught gripping the knife with which he sliced purse thongs. Punishment was required. But the boy was one of *theirs;* Marian had, by protesting so vocally, given them leave to do the same, if less vehemently. Had deLacey simply dragged the boy off to the stocks and lopped off his hand on the spot, no one would have dared question him. It was well known that thieves and poachers lost offending extremities.

But Marian was neither peasant nor Norman. She was one of them, English-born and bred, the daughter of an honorable knight killed in the Crusade. And if she felt moved to protest, so could they feel moved.

He had intended, in the face of growing hostility, to have the boy taken to the castle, where discipline could be applied. But now the giant had come forward, too large to overlook, too flamboyant to ignore. The big shepherd had, deLacey realized, assumed control of the situation. If the sheriff were to salvage any portion of self-respect, any portion of control, he would have to reassume it by means that on the surface appeased the waiting crowd.

They are stupid as sheep, and as easily misled. The trick was, he knew, to give them what they wanted. Then alter the rules to win the game for himself.

The crowd was expectant. To his left, the boy—*Much?*—stood slackly with a soldier's hands upon him, brown eyes dull, dirty brown hair hanging lankly. To deLacey's right waited Marian, ablaze in borrowed crimson. The circlet binding her brow glinted in a bright spring sun.

A peregrine, he reflected, *poised to stoop and strike me down.* Fleetingly, he smiled, giving her her due. And then he turned to the giant. "One man," he declared. "Defeated, the boy goes free." The giant merely waited, wide hands sprawled on hips. "But if my man *wins,* the boy—and your hand—is mine."

The crowd stared avidly, watching both men. "One man?" the giant—John Naylor—rasped. "You'll risk it on one man?"

"More would be excessive." DeLacey smiled coolly. "I'd not have the good citizenry of Nottingham declare me dishonest or opportunistic . . . I trust you won't mind a single opponent?"

The shepherd Naylor, called Little John, grinned, leaned down, and spat. " 'Tis for you to say. One man, two, or three. Alone, or all at once."

DeLacey arched a single eloquent brow. A swift glance at the waiting crowd gave him his answer: too many had heard the discussion to question the bloody result when the giant's hand was cut off. Besides, the sheriff knew they believed his man defeated already, so certain were they of the giant. A worthwhile opponent, yes, and not to be taken lightly—but then neither was William deLacey so easily dismissed.

And yet they had dismissed him, as they dismissed his proxy man.

He glanced at the giant, assessing what others missed in their fascination with Naylor's size. His bulk was more than impressive, but William deLacey had learned many years before to judge men by other criteria than the size of their bodies. There was the weight of a man's heart, and the conviction of his soul.

A pity, the sheriff reflected. *Left whole, he would be worth giving to Prince John.* But deLacey would hold to his word. He was not a two-faced man. "Done," he said quietly, then turned to a waiting soldier. "Fetch out William Scathlocke."

* * *

In the shadows between two steep-pitched buildings, Robert of Locksley counted out the coin left in his purse. Not so very much. Even if each man in Nottingham were to donate a single penny, or so much as a silver mark, the ransom could not be met.

He knew what it was. He had heard his father speak of it. A king's ransom, the earl called it: one hundred and fifty thousand marks.

But England was impoverished. The man who needed her most had drained her of her money, spending every penny to finance a Crusade.

He stared blindly at the coins glinting against his palm. "Richard," he murmured, "do you rot in Henry's dungeon? Or does he treat you like a king?"

Beyond him, in the square, a woman selling pomanders shouted praises of her wares. To ward off sickness, she said. To chase away foul odors.

"A contingency," he said dryly, "that you did not foresee."

No. Richard would never foresee ignominious capture and chafing imprisonment, just as he had not foreseen the ramifications of his legendary temper and bombast, when he had argued with Leopold in the Holy Land. So many men lost, and not to the enemy. Philip of France, Leopold of Austria, and others. Disenchanted with the task. Overweary of Lionheart.

Locksley conjured Leopold's saturnine face before him, recalling Richard's fury upon hearing the man would leave. *Had you not insulted him, likely he would have stayed. Certainly he would not have captured you, then sold you to German Henry.*

But Richard had insulted Leopold. He had insulted many men. He, who was without doubt Christendom's greatest warrior and most transcendent king, had not the slightest understanding of how to placate other men who shared the blood of royals. To the common man in the dust, Coeur de Lion was a god. To men of equal rank, of equal pedigree, unimpressed by grandiose title, he was an egomaniacal beast intent on winning Jerusalem merely to magnify *his* name, instead of the name of God.

"A misjudgment," Locksley murmured. "And you pay dearly for it."

He shut his hand around the coin, feeling the metallic bite of poorly struck edges. His father was a wealthy man who supported his king, but also supported his personal will and conceit. The castle had cost him dear. He had, the earl said, donated to Richard's cause, but only so much as to leave Huntington unencumbered by choking debt.

"There is Locksley . . ." He chewed the inside of his cheek, scowling in deep thought. Locksley was his personal domain, *his* manor and village, bestowed by his father just before he left England to join his king. The village of Locksley, as did every village, paid taxes to its lord.

I am Locksley's lord.

For two years, the earl had collected in his stead. Perhaps it was time he saw to the coffers into which the taxes were put. Surely there would be *something* he could donate to Richard's ransom.

Better yet, he could see to doing it now, here in Nottingham. All he need do was visit one of the Jews, who could advance him monies against Locksley revenues.

Done. He poured what little remained of his archery prize into his purse, tucked now inside his tunic instead of hanging from his belt, and set off to find the street of moneylenders in Nottingham's Jewish Quarter.

William Scathlocke was neither particularly tall nor particularly heavy. Just a *man*, Marian saw in surprise, not unlike any other, and with nothing that set him apart save they had bound and gagged him, weighting wrists and ankles with iron, strapping leather across mouth and chin.

She did not know what he had done, to put himself in the sheriff's hands. "Why?" she gasped, seeing the expression in dark, fierce eyes: a brutal, naked fury that they dared to treat him as beast before others who knew the man.

"He killed four men," the sheriff told her as soldiers dragged Scathlocke across the Market Square even as spectators gave way. Chains chimed on packed dirt. "He murdered four of Prince John's men, no less; it was why John came here, to see the murderer hanged." He affected a shrug. "Two of them he stabbed. One he beat to death. The fourth man he bled to death by biting the flesh from his throat."

Marian recoiled, staring at the prisoner. No doubt deLacey intended to frighten her, or merely cause her to hold the tongue that had, with aid from the giant, brought them to this pass. And in that he succeeded. The sheriff's matter-of-fact yet vivid description sickened her.

"I don't know him," she murmured, grateful for that much.

"I believe he's from a small village near Croxden Abbey." Another indolent shrug. "Gisbourne attends to such things as names and places. Will Scathlocke is all I know, though the peasants are calling him—" he paused, frowning, "Scarlet?" He stared at the chained man as they brought him forward. "Marian, I insist—you must return to the castle. I will have one of the soldiers escort you."

Marian glanced at Much, held by a liveried Norman. The boy's expression was one of dull hopelessness. Clearly he did not understand the agreement between sheriff and giant. All he knew was his hand was to be cut off. *If he even knows that much.* "No," she said firmly. "No, I will stay. Or else send Much back with me."

DeLacey glanced down at her. "I think it best he watch. His fate will be decided—do you not think he should see?"

She gazed up at him, marking the tautness of his mouth, the network of fine lines etched into the flesh near his eyes. Silver flecked his wiry brown hair. He was twenty years and more older than she. His knowledge of people was far greater than her own, but she could not agree with him.

"My lord." One of the soldiers spoke. "The murderer, my lord."

He was close, so close, Will Scarlet. Marian could smell him. The stink of the dungeon wrapped him in its shroud. *Just a man.* Not as tall as the sheriff, who gave two or three inches to Robert of Locksley, the tallest man she knew save her father—and the giant. This man was merely a man. Peasant. Villein. Not of the ruling class. No different at all from any of the people gathering to watch. Near-black in eyes and hair, swarthy of skin—though some of that might be dirt—clad in the tattered remnants of what had been tunic and baggy hosen. His feet below the shackles were wrapped in leather and rags.

Marian stared at him as deLacey raised his voice. This man had killed four others. This man had murdered soldiers. She thought there should be something in his face and eyes that marked him for what he was, something that indicated he was beyond humanity, a man capable of killing four others, and soldiers to boot.

But she could see little enough. The leather gag across mouth and chin hid the bottom portion of his face, and distorted the rest. All she could see was a crooked nose, knobbed over the bridge; stubble-etched cheekbones, bruised and scabbed; a pair of near-black eyes, empty of all emotion save a vicious hatred and an incandescent fury.

"Behold!" the sheriff shouted. "William Scathlocke, murderer, known to you as Scarlet. He has been sentenced to hang for the deaths of four men, their lives torn from them in a brutality known only to beasts."

William Scathlocke could say nothing for the gag, make neither protest nor comment, but his eyes were free of restraint. Marian, in that moment, saw the man who had killed four others. Reflected in grief and rage, Scathlocke's guilt was plain.

The sheriff, unheeding, went on. "But let it be also known that this day he is afforded an opportunity to resurrect his future . . . all he need do, to live, is defeat the giant."

Scathlocke made noise against the leather bound over mouth and chin. The sound of that noise was transmuted by gag into the bleat of an animal.

"John Naylor, of Hathersage, called 'Little' John—" the sheriff smiled faintly and allowed them the snickers, "has agreed to stand proxy for the boy, Much, a cutpurse, who dared lay hands on my own purse. Let it be known that the giant assumes the boy's guilt, discharged only by victory."

Little John, the giant, bobbed his head in agreement. Spectators murmured.

"Let it be known also that should the giant be defeated; his right hand will be cut off. But should the giant win, the boy shall go free."

It was a popular ruling, by the murmuring of the crowd. A

fair chance, it said, bobbing heads in agreement. The boy would be spared. No one, Marian knew, believed the giant could be defeated. And what did it matter? The opponent was a murderer. His loss would be as nothing.

Marian chanced a glance at Will Scarlet. Dark eyes glared balefully, full of frustration and futility, and a wild, kindling anger. He stared directly at her. "What of him?" she blurted. "What is promised this man?"

DeLacey turned. "You heard me," he rasped. "His life."

"But—if he has been sentenced . . ." Marian looked from the murderer to the sheriff. *He wouldn't. He would not promise this man release, then deny it. Would he?* "You said he had been sentenced."

DeLacey smiled faintly. "You pleaded for the minstrel. You pleaded for the boy. Leniency, you begged; well, is this not leniency? Have I not heard your arguments, and acceded to your wishes?" He flicked a glance at Scarlet. "But let this man be victorious, and I will spare his life."

Marian was neither convinced nor placated. *I know him better, now. There is something in this he wants . . . something in this he gains.* But she could not discern what it was, unless it was meant to salvage a thing he believed lost. "A bone to dogs," she murmured, frowning. *A bone, perhaps, for me?*

His name was Abraham, and he was a Jew. Robert of Locksley, looking down on the small, wizened man, could see nothing about him that marked him different. And yet people did. *Englishmen* did, naming him and other Jews perfidious usurers who robbed good Christians of their coin in an attempt to destroy them.

Locksley, who had just returned from two years spent in the lands from which Abraham and his family had come, no longer understood the distinction between good Christian men who murdered in the name of their God, and devoutly peaceful Jews who worshipped the same God. Their ways were different, yes, but the results markedly less contentious, lacking in violence. The Crusaders leveled cities, killed Saracens, raped women, and murdered children. As if, somehow, God desired such atrocities to be certain of their souls.

In England, Jews had been killed. Boarded up in a tower and burned to death, in York. And in London, at Richard's coronation, hundreds of others had died. Simply because they were Jews. A part of the earl's son wanted to say he was sorry. But how did one man apologize for the hostility of a nation?

The old Jew nodded welcome and gestured for Locksley to seat himself on a stool by a table. He himself was already seated at the same table, a deference due, he said, to age and infirmity. England's dampness sat ill upon his joints, though spring and summer were easier seasons.

Locksley sat down. He was not a man for inanities in prelude to conversation. Richard valued his bluntness, but Richard, though a king, was himself no courtier. "I need money."

Abraham nodded. The sagging flesh by the dark eyes creased. It was not an unexpected request. "And how much do you need?"

He had no idea, but Abraham might. "I am Locksley," he said diffidently. "Robert of Locksley. My father is the Earl of Huntington."

Abraham's face lighted. "Ah, of course! You are the hero-son!"

It made him intensely uncomfortable. "If you require proof, there is this." He extended his right hand on the table, displaying the signet ring upon his forefinger. "There are other proofs at Huntington, if you require them."

"No, no. It is enough, my young lord." Abraham smiled warmly. "I am acquainted with your father."

No more than that, but it told Locksley something, even in subtlety: a moneylender would not divulge a customer's name. Yet clearly the earl had borrowed. "The castle."

"And a fine, large castle." Dark eyes glinted. "Do you wish one for yourself?"

"No!" It was expelled instantly, framed in vehemence. "No, not for me . . . I need money for a man. Money for—a king."

The old man's expectant expression faded. Gnarled hands smoothed the embroidered border at his robe's neckline. "You want money for King Richard's ransom?"

"Yes." Locksley touched his ring, turning it on his finger. "There is this. A few more things left to me by my mother.

And—Locksley." He looked at Abraham. "Can you give me money against the revenues?"

Abraham's expression was troubled. "I cannot, my lord. Forgive me. But you see—they mean to raise the taxes. We have already given what we can to the king's cause . . . across England, we have raised thousands of marks—but what is left we must hold back. The taxes, you see." Hands gestured futility. "We dare not be late, we Jews—they will use any excuse."

But Locksley's attention was fixed on something other than tardy payments. "The taxes are being *raised?*"

"There are rumors . . ." The tone was delicate. "With the king held prisoner, his brother governs the realm. And Prince John is . . . well . . ." Abraham sighed. "He is not his brother."

"Nor is he king," Locksley declared. "He is a wealthy man since marrying the Gloucester heiress . . . and Nottinghamshire is his. The rest is Richard's money. And as he is in Germany, he can't authorize increases."

"Perhaps not." Abraham's expression was oddly sanguine, as if serenity could mask his true opinion. "Nonetheless, my sources are impeccable. Within a matter of days, the sheriff will send out tax collectors."

Still Locksley protested. "It isn't the proper season."

"My lord . . ." Abraham diffidently touched Locksley's hand for an instant, then withdrew it. "You have been long out of England, my lord. There have been—changes."

"John," he said flatly.

"In lieu of sons by the king, the Count of Mortain is heir," the old man said. "If the king is not returned, his brother will rule in his stead."

Locksley considered it, looking for alternatives. He did not want to believe so much corruption had entered England's breast. "These additional taxes may well be intended for the king's ransom."

"Indeed, my lord, and a worthwhile reason, if it be true—but there is no money left to give. In the last two years, taxes have been raised three times. Twice, to finance the Holy War. We gave, my lord. Then word of the ransom came. We gave, my lord. And now, again, the king's safety is the excuse . . ." Abraham sighed wearily. "There are those who say the money will be diverted elsewhere. That the king will not benefit while his brother is in debt."

"John is in debt?"

Abraham smoothed his robe. "Even the highest are known to live beyond their means."

The face before him blurred. Locksley, deep in thought, did not see the old man's expression. He stared transfixed at Abraham while he worked through the repercussions. "He would not—" He broke it off, frowning. "I know him, Abraham. The king. For a war, for a Crusade, he would persuade an old woman to give up the last tooth in her head—but for himself, he would not. He would not impoverish his realm."

"The people know, my lord. That is why they have given freely."

"But this is *John's* doing."

"They know that, also. But knowing the truth of the matter does not lessen the penalty should one refuse to pay."

"But if you *can't*—if there is no money . . ." Locksley shook his head. "He will say it's for his brother."

"Yes, my lord."

"And keep it for himself."

In Abraham's silence the answer was implicit.

Twenty

Marian frowned, watching as the soldiers cut the leather gag from Will Scarlet's mouth. The flesh beneath was pale and compressed, baring a long-set network of creases in the midst of grime-smudged stubble. She knew it must be painful, but he made no move to rub his face. He was, withal, filthy, and no doubt lice-ridden as well. Her body answered at once, setting up a chorus of nonexistent itches she longed to scratch vigorously, but didn't because she felt it would give a murderer victory, when he deserved nothing more than contempt for such base brutality. *Four men,* she reflected. *Out of spite, or out of temper?*

"I want to know," deLacey said, "if you understand."

Will Scarlet stared at him from dark eyes aglitter with abiding malignancy.

The sheriff was patient. "Do you understand?"

Still the man was silent. The crowd began to murmur.

And yet a third time, with additional explanation. "If you win the match you will not be hanged. I say this before witnesses: half of Nottingham."

Scarlet's fixed stare did not waver. He merely thrust out his manacled wrists in a jangle of chiming iron.

The sheriff looked to his guard contingent. "I charge you with the keeping of this man. If he attempts to escape, you will kill him at once." He looked at the crowd, raising his voice, pitching it to carry. "Is that not fair? That if a murderer escape, he be killed immediately so as not to risk innocent souls?"

Marian looked at the faces. Everyone was nodding. *He plays them with words. He plays them all like fish. They know the giant will win. All they want is entertainment.* Iron chimed again as Will Scarlet altered his stance. The sheriff motioned a soldier to unlock the shackles. *Why?* Marian wondered. *What does he gain from this?*

She was a blaze of crimson before Will Scathlocke, all swaddled in brilliant wool. It made it easy to find her. It made it easy to see her. It made it a simple thing to mark out the sheriff's woman, who believed he should be hanged.

Had she not proclaimed it? *You said he had been sentenced.* Telling him, very plainly, she thought he should be denied a chance to save himself.

Wife, daughter, mistress. The title didn't matter. She thought he should hang. Even without her words she damned him with her eyes, with the stiffness of expression, sickened by his crime.

No crime at all, killing those men. Had he to do it again, he

212

would do much more than kill them. He would rend each limb from limb and laugh while doing it.

She was beautiful, he saw, in the Celtic way: dark and bright at once, with a fey, compelling glamour set to snare a man's attention even in repose, when she put no thought to it. Not so very different from the woman he had loved.

Noise around him rose. Vision flickered faintly. Even the smell had changed: prelude to the madness. He tingled in his groin and armpits, felt the tightening of genitals. Saliva filled his mouth.

They asked: would he fight the giant?

He'd fight any man; often, he had no choice, when the madness came upon him.

And a second ludicrous question: would he not attempt escape?

In that also, there was no choice. What fool would stay behind, to suffer for Norman justice? To be hanged for Norman lies?

But William Scathlocke nodded.

DeLacey motioned for the iron to be removed and watched dispassionately as a soldier bent to unlock the ankles, then rose again to tend the wrists. Weight fell from imprisoned limbs, clamoring of freedom. DeLacey heard the murmuring spread: Nottingham was astonished that he would treat one of them so fairly as to give a second chance to a man, a brutal murderer, already tried and sentenced to hang.

It would do, he knew. The fight and its fury would command their attention, and then, very quietly, in the midst of so much turmoil—he knew Scathlocke's history would ensure a violent battle—the sheriff could at last tend his office. The boy would surreptitiously be taken away to the castle, to receive proper punishment as prescribed by law. The giant, Little John, would eventually prevail, because no single man, regardless of battle madness, could win against such power.

And William Scathlocke, who would of course attempt escape—only a fool would not, and Scarlet, regardless of birth, was no fool, they said—could be cut down in the streets like the brutal beast he was. *And all my problems solved with nary a word of protest.*

With everything settled so neatly before all of Nottingham, even Marian couldn't protest that the sheriff had been unjust. A woman's weapon, the tongue; but he would blunt it, for now.

John Naylor, Little John, Hathersage Giant and shepherd, stared down in some consternation at the man who was meant to fight him. He did not know him personally, but knew a little *about* him; William Scathlocke, called Scarlet, had become notorious. Everyone in Nottinghamshire knew well what he had done. And none, so far as Little John knew, blamed him for any of it.

But murder was murder, even in Norman England. And that a lowborn English peasant had dared to lay his dirty villein's hands on four Normans in Prince John's personal service, let alone *kill* them . . . well, no man guilty of such could hope for an attempt at understanding, nor even a chance to explain, save from his own people. People such as dared speak no word in Scathlocke's defense, lest the Normans look to them.

Scathlocke, he decided, did not *look* like a murderer. He looked very much like every other Englishman trying to make a living in an age of brutal indifference, ruled by ruthless, selfish men. Little John knew nothing of nobility, save names and royal castles, and how to offer servility when such behavior was required. His entire life experience was limited to shepherding and peasanthood, to ignorance and hardship, to unending labor performed to pay killing taxes to Norman overlords. He knew what was fair, and what wasn't; he knew the grinding poverty so many others shared. He knew a little of anger, something of resentment; had more than a passing acquaintanceship with frustration and helplessness.

Madness he didn't know. But William Scathlocke did.

Little John was not afraid of the man, whom he couldn't understand, whom rumor claimed went mad when the heat of battle was on him. Little John's fear of physical abuse at the hands of others had died in early adolescence, when he stood head and shoulders above even the tallest of men. Of course, such tremendous size did not ward him from other abuses. He had grown up with a raft of names meant to cut him to the heart, if not harm the body. Some had managed to do it.

He discovered the only true escape, the only true chance at making a life for himself, was to turn from humans entirely and take solace in animals. They loved unconditionally. And if they couldn't speak, not as men and women spoke, at least the language they used offered comfort and release.

Shepherding suited him. He expected no better life, content to tend, to lamb, to shear. But when a sweating, belligerent man at a North Country fair had challenged him to a wrestling match—he'd beaten everyone else—Little John discovered he could do more than tend his sheep; he could win by sheer power if not by technique. But making a living from the fairs was not fulfilling enough. There they gawked at his size, murmuring comments behind his back, muttering of the monster, resurrecting the old names, though with less virulence than simple astonishment underscored by a trace of distaste. Always, it was the sheep to which he went for personal peace.

He was not a violent man. He was not a difficult man. He was not a man who desired to irritate his betters, yet irritate one he had. Little John knew it instinctively, as well as who the man was: the lord high sheriff himself. But the giant could not stand silently by and do nothing for the boy, who was like to lose his hand without a protest in his behalf.

No—the woman had protested. She had spoken her mind, voicing the concerns that Little John felt as well, but she was a woman, with no more influence in matters of decision than a serf. She couldn't win without someone to help her, without a man large enough to propose a way to alter the "justice" that would deprive a boy of his hand.

And now here he stood, staring down at the man called Will Scarlet, murderer, whom everyone said was mad. A man but half the giant's size but who, in his madness, could kill four armed Norman soldiers.

Scathlocke had, rumor said, beaten one man to death. The fourth and final soldier he had relieved of his throat.

Little John was not afraid, but neither was he such a fool as to assume there was no danger in a man with nothing to lose.

Much stood very still, offering no protest. He was quick and deft and agile, but he knew when he was caught. He knew also, instinctively, when it was best simply to wait, because trying to escape when the time wasn't right merely resulted in additional pain.

The soldier was big, sheathed in mail shirt, blue tabard, and the conical Norman helm with its ugly metal nasal that distorted a man's face even as it protected it. The Norman's hands were big also, and very strong; Much felt the weight of them around his wrists, crossed snuggly behind his back.

He breathed noisily through his mouth, letting it hang slack. It was easier to breathe that way, because a backhanded blow in childhood—he didn't remember from whom; not his father, was it?—had collapsed the bridge of his nose. Things were better now that he had grown, but spring and fall were difficult seasons because his head was always stuffed.

The giant he found astonishing. Never had he seen a man so tall, nor with such an incandescent bushiness of red hair and beard. He wore only baggy hosen so his freckled torso was bared, giving Much—and everyone else—an unobstructed view of a massive chest.

Blue eyes, Much saw, tilting back his head to look. And pale, reddish lashes. *Giant,* he said in silence, thinking of the world he had created for himself, where imaginary beings treated him like a king.

He added someone to it. A friendly, red-haired giant, who protected him against harm.

Marian, and the giant. Princess and protector.

Much smiled happily. His world was getting better.

Cold, Marian thought. *Cold—and very angry.* The near-black eyes were unsettling, so fixed and oddly compelling. She would not have characterized them as the eyes of a madman, because she had never seen a madman before; if Will Scathlocke-Scarlet really *were* one, he was her first. She hoped he was her last.

DeLacey stirred beside her. "Get on with it," he commanded.

She glanced at him sharply, hearing the undertone of anticipation; of an odd, unstated pleasure, as if he knew perfectly well what would come of the bout. She found it both interesting and dismaying at once, that a man could predict a thing so accurately as to display not even the slightest concern over men he did not control.

Or did he? He was, she had come to believe, a consummate manipulator of people and things around him. She had seen it in the past two days; she had been a victim of it herself. She understood there existed such things as subterfuge and intrigue—she was not an ignorant woman, and her father was plainspoken—but never had she seen the practice of gamesmanship applied before her eyes, when she had the vision to see it.

For example, the game of matchmaking: he had intended to make a match between Eleanor and Locksley and had worked toward that aim with concerted diligence. That the ploy had failed was hardly his fault—Eleanor herself had destroyed the chance of a marriage—but for all Marian knew the earl himself might have withheld his permission once it got that far. And, of course, there was Locksley—

Robin. She conjured his face, hearing in his tone the thing that had made him someone else, someone other than what *they* claimed; not so much a hero-knight as a vulnerable young man, come home to things unknown. *Robin.* She was cognizant of new confusion; of victory and pleasure in the name no others used.

"Marian." The sheriff put a hand upon her arm to move her out of danger.

The ring was abruptly a battlefield. Marian knew nothing of wrestling, and very little of fighting. This was, plainly, mayhem, the focused, obsessed intent of one man to defeat another so he could escape execution.

She did not know what the giant expected. Perhaps it was a time spent in introduction, in the courtesies of discovery while they tested one another. But what Scarlet answered with superseded courtesies, being nothing more than a brutal display of raw, unfettered need, and physical expiation for sins only he understood.

Will Scarlet spun on his heels and charged at the giant, aiming for his shins. Hands clutched at knees, thumbs dug into muscle. Little John growled a startled protest, then grabbed doubled handfuls of Scarlet's ragged tunic and shoved down across bunched shoulders even as he himself stumbled back, struggling to hold his balance.

A simple shove, no more, yet the giant's unthinking reaction hurled Scarlet to the street, smashing his chest into packed dirt. Onlookers shouted, elbowing one another and raising myriad wagers.

Scarlet coughed, swore, then scrambled up, wiping at a split lip. The tunic was filthier than ever, stained now by manure and blood. Lank, dirty dark hair hung into his face and eyes. He hunched, twitching fingers and rolled his head against taut shoulders, cracking the bones in his neck. Marian saw the same cold, wary look in eyes and expression as he moved around the circle, measuring the giant. This time when he dove, Little John was ready.

The giant snatched Scarlet out of the air like an insect caught in midflight and slammed him down again, driving the air from laboring lungs in a blurted, garbled bleat. This time he knelt over Scarlet, leaning on splayed hands. Legs were spread and braced.

As Scarlet, gasping, pressed himself up from the dirt, Little John slid an arm between his opponent's wrist and the ground and neatly hooked away the braced limb that held up Scarlet's weight. The murderer fell. Again. And again, as the giant alternated arms. The maneuver, repeated four times, deprived the smaller man utterly of mobility and dropped him easily every time he tried to rise.

"D'ye give in, then?" Little John asked. "D'ye yield to the better man?"

Scarlet lay prone, panting in the dirt, and the giant hovered over him, waiting for him to move.

A trick, Marian saw. *Wrestling tricks a body when the man least expects it . . . the winner uses weight, and balance, and power—*

Spectators were shouting encouragement to both men. It

didn't seem to matter to them which man won. Amazed, Marian stared around the throng closing in on the ring. The faces were avid, the eyes oddly vacant of sense or comprehension. To them it was enough merely to shout aloud, for one man or the other, before the hated sheriff.

Little John was laughing. He sprawled on knees and hands across Scarlet's body, then slapped him on one shoulder, murmuring something Marian couldn't hear. Another call for surrender, she guessed, which still wasn't answered. The giant turned his head to look at Much, whose hand would remain attached now that victory was assured.

Scarlet moved then, kicking out at Little John's ankles even as he snatched a thick wrist and jerked it from the ground. As the giant wavered, shouting unintelligibly, Will Scarlet carried the big hand to his mouth and bit deeply into flesh. Little John howled as blood began to flow.

"Cheating!" someone shouted.

"Forfeit the match!" cried another.

"You've doomed yourself!" came a third. "They'll have to hang you, churl!"

The giant slammed a fist into the side of Will Scarlet's head, hurling him across the ring. People continued to shout that Scarlet had cheated; that the giant was the winner.

Marian glanced at deLacey for a ruling. "What becomes of him now?"

DeLacey's expression was grim. "There are rules to a match, albeit unspoken ones." He looked down at her. "This cannot be tolerated."

"Then you'll hang him anyway." She looked past him to the boy. "What about Much?"

In the ring, Scarlet charged Little John, who caught him by the shoulders and hurled him away once more.

"The boy will—" DeLacey's hand reached for her arm. "Marian—*beware*—"

And then a body fetched up hard against her legs and feet, nearly knocking her down. Marian cried out, staggering, flailing her arms awkwardly as she attempted to regain balance.

The body came up clawing, rolling upward from the dirt, snatching at mantle and kirtle, dragging cloth aside as it fouled his route. Hands dug through fabric, gouging into tender flesh. She smelled the stench of the man. *"What do you—?"*

But one arm went around her ribs, squeezing the breath from her body. Another clamped down on her throat. She felt a man's rigid body pressed hard the length of her spine, crushing her buttocks into his thighs, smashing her head against his heaving chest.

"I'll kill her," Will Scarlet promised. "And don't think I can't. I like the taste of throats, especially Norman ones."

Twenty-One

Locksley heard the muffled tumult as he stepped out of Abraham's dwelling, mentally counting coin he had counted three times over, thinking bleak, dark thoughts about ransoms left unpaid and taxes unfairly diverted to greedy, treacherous princes desirous of being king.

The narrowness of the twisting alleyway funneled and distorted the sound, making it difficult to determine from which direction the shouting and cheering came. He paused, listening, wondering at its cause. Market Square, he guessed . . . and then it stopped, cut off like a stewing hen's head. The uncanny absence of sound was as eerily absolute as the moment after a thunderclap so loud as to still a heart.

He heard through the funnel William deLacey's voice, raised in fury and fear: *"Kill me this villein!"*

And then a second voice, bellowing another order in low-born, deep-toned speech: *"Let the woman go!"*

Marian FitzWalter had been with the sheriff. Locksley touched his meat-knife, then broke into a run.

* * *

Marian could smell the stink of the dungeon on Scathlocke, the tang of filth and physical exertion mixed with tension and fear. She thrashed once, flailing violently, trying to kick free of her mantle and the man who imprisoned her. Half throttled, she gasped, "But—I'm not—"

Dirty, bloodied fingers locked into her veil and braid, jerking her head into stillness. The arm across her throat cut off the rest of her protest. "D'ye think I care? D'ye think it matters to me? You're meat for eating, lady . . . sheriff's leman, are you?"

It was harder to speak now, but she gritted it between her teeth. "No—I'm n—" And then vision darkened perceptibly as the pressure on her throat increased. She choked, wailing mutely, trying to claw at the arm.

His breath stirred her veil, gusting across her cheek. "Best come with me, little whore. You'll buy Will Scarlet his freedom."

Even as he spoke he backed away from the others, pulling her off her feet. Marian scrambled for purchase, digging in her heels, trying to right herself even as he moved, but Scarlet was taller, stronger, heavier, more determined even than she. Half dragging, half carrying, he worked his way through the murmuring crowd as deLacey and soldiers followed.

The sheriff's eyes were wild. His mouth, as he gave terse orders, was warped into ugly grimness. Marian, seeing that, felt a measure of relief. Surely deLacey would stop him.

She stumbled, hissing in startled fright. Scarlet held her elbows pinned against her sides by one thick arm, immobilizing her head with the other even as he dragged her. All she could do was kick, hoping to hook an ankle. But slippered feet fouled on heavy folds of crimson wool, thwarting her attempt.

He can't mean to carry me off . . . Acknowledgment blossomed: indeed, he *could* carry her off, even through Nottingham. And probably would, using her as his parole. *Someone has to stop him.* Marian grimaced, baring teeth, wishing she could bite. Wishing she could *breathe*.

"Kill me this villein!" the sheriff shouted in fury.

And then the giant, bellowing, blood smeared on his face: "Let the woman go!"

Scarlet stumbled, cursing, and caught her up more closely than ever, near to cracking ribs. Above her own choked gasp Marian could hear his ragged breathing. He wasn't certain, she realized. He wasn't completely convinced that she would be enough.

Inconsequential thoughts fed her frenzied mind inanities she didn't want to consider. *He killed four men.* He had called her little whore. He had called her the sheriff's leman. He had even called her a Norman. *I'm not!* she railed futilely. As if it might make a difference.

Much gaped as hands fell free. He was *loose*. The soldier let go of his wrists as the murderer grabbed the woman.

Grabbed *Marian*.

Transfixed, Much stared. He wouldn't kill her, would he? Not Marian. Not her.

The sheriff, enraged, was shouting. Even the giant was.

Should he shout, too? But wouldn't they catch him again?

Much laughed: he was *free*.

He spun on his heel and ran, darting through the crowd, ducking arms and elbows. Keeping in the tail of one eye the blood-bright woolen mantle.

A woman, the giant raged. How could he threaten a woman? It was one thing to attack a man twice your size, even unfairly; another entirely to offer harm to a woman.

Little John strode through the crowd rapidly, thrusting aside human impediments with huge, practiced hands. Sheep were more amenable, and certainly considerably smaller, but they were similar in habits to Nottingham citizens, who followed a single man as the flock followed the bellwether.

But this bellwether, he knew, was no castrated ram with a bell around his neck. This bellwether intended to desert the flock, taking the finest ewe with him.

He did not know her. He had never seen her before. It didn't matter to him that she was the sheriff's daughter, or wife, or mistress. What mattered to Little John was that she was being treated unfairly, much too roughly, and had no recourse at all.

The giant recalled what that was like. When he was small, and powerless; when he was bigger, and shy. He also remembered the day he had put a stop to it, using for the first time sheer physical strength—and the anger of too many years—to stop the verbal abuse that hurt worse, in many ways, than the beatings he'd undergone.

No more beatings. No more verbal abuse. No one dared, now.

Yet Will Scarlet dared. And he dared it with a *woman*.

Not fair, Little John muttered inwardly. *One thing to bite a man . . . but to carry off a woman—*

If no one else could get the woman back, Little John would see to it *he* did.

DeLacey was cold, very cold, in mind as well as body. A part of him wanted very much to lose control absolutely and bellow to the heavens of this incredible outrage, screaming furious epithets at the outlaw who had so confounded him. But to do so risked Marian; it also risked his precarious governance of Nottingham itself.

He had felt it clearly but moments before. They questioned him, the people. They dared to question him, even within their minds; even if they didn't realize what they did, he knew they questioned him. Marian had caused it initially, but that had passed. He had won back control with the introduction of the murderer into the contest for Much's hand, intending to maintain that control with the outcome of the match.

But now the murderer had gained control for himself by abducting Marian. And everyone in Nottingham—including Marian herself—expected the sheriff to resolve the situation. With an abundant expediency. *I will have her back,* he declared. *Alive, unharmed, untouched.*

Or he would, in his authority, order Will Scathlocke hanged, quartered, decapitated. With all of Nottingham made to watch.

"—*mistake!*" Marian gasped. "I'm not—" She swallowed convulsively, gritting her teeth against the pain of her throat. "I'm not who you think—" But the voice was weak and thready, distorted by compression even as it died out. She doubted he heard her over the rasp of his own breathing, or the muffled hum of onlookers. *Can't someone—? Anyone—?*

No, they could not. Or would not. He had killed four men. And who was she to them? Most of them didn't know her, even if they knew *of* her. Why would anyone risk himself in an attempt to stop Will Scarlet?

One of her slippers was lost, baring stocking and foot. Marian scrabbled awkwardly, trying to regain purchase, but Scarlet merely tightened his grasp and dragged her more quickly yet. She could barely breathe through the constriction around her ribs. If he loosened only a *little*—

"Be still!" he snapped.

Marian gritted her teeth. *If he wants so much to drag me, why not let him* carry *me?* She sagged, going briefly limp. As Scarlet cursed, paused, hitched her up again, Marian doubled up both legs and kicked out backward. She wanted to land both feet in the most vulnerable place she could reach, be it belly, groin, or knees. Anything would do, so long as it obstructed him.

He was spread-legged, which defeated her attempt. One of her feet grazed the inside of a thigh and went through, doing no damage. The other, bare of slipper, caught a knee briefly, then fouled on baggy hose.

One of her arms was free. Marian reached up behind her head, clawing, and caught an ear. With what strength remained, tapping also into anger, she attempted in all violence to rip the ear from his head.

Cursing, Scarlet clamped a hand closed on her wrist. "Let it go—Let it *go*—"

She wanted to curse back, but the pain in her wrist demanded all her attention. He didn't twist it. Didn't even try to pull her hand away. He just *squeezed*.

Fingers sprang free of the ear. Scarlet forced the arm back down to the other, caught at her midsection, and thrust the aching wrist into his other hand. There he held her just long enough to catch a handful of mantle and sweep the folds of summerweight wool up over her head. He swaddled her in the mantle, blocking light, vision, air, then lifted and dumped her facedown across one shoulder.

She tried once to struggle. The arm slackened briefly, showing her without words the danger she risked. If she struggled, he'd let her fall. Headfirst to the street, where she'd likely break her neck.

Marian's thoughts worked swiftly, purging her of pain and humiliation, the overwhelming fear. There was more here at stake than being carried off like a sack of flour. There were plans to be considered. *Patience*— She damped her bitterness. An opportunity would present itself no matter what she did.

Eventually, he would stop. Eventually he would take her down from his shoulder. Eventually he would unwrap her. And then she would do whatever it took to win herself free of him.

Locksley thrust his way into the crowd, shoving others aside. He saw the red-haired giant doing much the same, working his way through the throng. The streets were almost impassable, clogged with hundreds of people now all oddly intent upon a single thing: to follow the giant, who followed the sheriff, who followed someone else.

He caught an arm, stopping one man in his tracks. "Who is it? What has happened?"

The man scowled back. "Fight's over." He shrugged. His face was pocked with the scars of a childhood disease. "Scarlet's got himself loose."

Locksley frowned. "Scarlet?"

"Will Scarlet, they call him. Man what killed four Normans. Sheriff let him fight the giant for the boy's hand, but he snatched the woman with the sheriff instead." The pockmarked man shrugged again. "I never seen her before."

He was curt in urgency. "Was she wearing red?"

The man lacked three teeth. He displayed his lack in a grin. "Bright as day, she was. Made her an easy target."

Locksley stared at the man. "He killed four men, you say."

"Four Norman soldiers. Due to hang, he is—if the sheriff doesn't kill him barehand for this."

Locksley stood very still in the midst of constant motion. The man stared at him a moment, then shrugged and edged away. Locksley was aware of movement around him, the comments of the people as they eddied around the obstruction, then passed on by him. But none of it was important. None of it mattered.

Marian FitzWalter, in the hands of a murderer.

Once, he might have assumed a man would never harm a woman, but war had changed that assumption. War changed men; it had certainly changed him. And though he had protested, though he had tried to stop them in the name of God, the king, and chivalry, not a single Christian soldier had listened. They had done whatever they pleased, shouting then of conquest; later, of education: the dead were Saracens, they said, heretics and faithless dogs God wanted destroyed.

He knew better. He had seen too many women sundered by Christian swords to trust to gender to save her. He had seen too many women raped by groups of Christian men to trust to manners to save her.

Stripped of the weapons to stop it, of the freedom to do it, of the will to even attempt it, Locksley had been forced to watch the father die.

This time was different. He had weapons and freedom and will. He would not stand idly by and let the *daughter* die.

Twenty-Two

Will Scarlet was a stranger to Nottingham, hailing from a village near Croxden Abbey. He knew nothing of the alleys, the streets, the winding passageways between buildings that nearly touched one another, so closely were they built. He knew only that if he gave way, if he let the soldiers take him, the sheriff would see to it he died in a way much more lengthy and painful than hanging. And so he carried the woman down every winding alley that gave onto another, hoping to foil the men that surely would follow, to gain back the sheriff's woman.

After putting up a fight that had taxed his patience and temper, she'd quieted. She hung now across one shoulder, slack as a sack of flour, not even so much as moaning. He heard no crying, either, nor the stifled sobs of a woman in fear trying not to let him know. He knew that sound very well. It woke him every night, in the darkness of his dreams.

She was still, and very quiet. Not even so much as a twitch. *Not dead, is she?* Abruptly he wanted to stop, to let her down, and lay her gently in the street, and strip the mantle back. To see if she breathed. *Don't let her be dead.*

But he didn't dare stop running. If they caught him, *he* was dead. Dead for four killings, not counting the sheriff's woman. They'd hang him anyway, even if she lived.

No choice, then. Just run . . . and run some more, until he was free of the city, safe in the shadows of close-grown woods, where he could *be* a shadow and hide himself in foliage and see if the woman lived.

Panting, he went on, ignoring the trembling in his legs, the gnawing weakness of an exhaustion that threatened to bring him down. No decent food, very little water, beatings twice and three times a day—there was little of him left, save what he manufactured out of hatred and anger and pain.

Don't let her be dead.

That, he couldn't bear. It would drive him mad again. And he would kill again, lost in grief and pain. Kill and kill and kill, until someone killed *him*.

Maybe it was best. Maybe he deserved it. Maybe letting them kill him would stop the sounds he heard, in the darkness of his dreams.

Let her be alive, he thought. But he said nothing aloud. If she was dead, she couldn't hear him. Alive, she wouldn't believe him. No more than the sheriff himself, when Scarlet had told him the truth of the killings.

Alan of the Dales reached out and caught the boy, pulling him up short. The object of his attentions twisted in his grasp, but Alan's hands were strong. "Wait," he said only, using the tone of voice he'd heard used by men of power, when they wanted a thing done.

The boy froze stiffly, one arm trapped in Alan's grasp. He made no protest, made no sound, merely waited, as he'd been bidden. Lank brown hair straggled into eyes the color of ale, dark with a tinge of russet when the light hit right.

Alan redistributed the weight of his lute. "Do you know what happened?" It was important that *he* know; a minstrel needed fodder for his music, if he were to continue.

The boy stared back at him, big-eyed and pale of face.

Alan shook his arm. "A question, boy. Do you know what happened?"

The boy shivered. He was thin, and slight, and fragile. His face was made of hollows, cut through with oblique angles. The nose was misshapen, flattened across the bridge by something other than nature. Circles like smudgy bruises lay beneath his lackluster eyes.

Alan had seen such faces on the beggars in every city. He had thanked God often that his music saved him from the life, when there were no other prospects save scrabbling in the streets. He was fortunate his mother had lived long enough to buy him lessons from the duke's old lute-player. His pretty face would have bought him a living, if he'd stayed at the keep with the duke, but his tastes lay in other directions . . . ah, but that was long ago. His life was different, now.

He loosened his grip on the arm. "I don't mean to hurt you, boy. I'm only asking a question." It got him nothing. The boy stood perfectly still, watching out of eyes slewed sideways in his head, like a dog about to be whipped. Alan let him go. "Never mind. I'll ask someone else."

The boy didn't run at once. "Marian," he said softly, in a muffled, slurry tone. Then darted into the throng and was gone almost instantly.

Marian. Marian FitzWalter? The woman from Huntington Castle?

No. Surely not. And even if it were, what did it matter to him? She was dangerous. She could tell the sheriff he was in Nottingham. He wanted nothing to do with her.

Alan shrugged a little. Not worth the wondering. What concerned him now was the temper of the crowd, moving onward through the streets like a herd of the king's deer being worked by huntsmen and hounds.

Worth following, the boy. If he could be seen again.

Alan hugged his lute. No sense risking it. He would move, like everyone else, toward the edges of the city. Hoping for the sort of thing he could put into a song.

The right sort of song could make him his fortune, but he hadn't found it yet. There was no one in England worth making music about. Certainly Prince John wasn't. The only one who *was* worth the effort was imprisoned in a dungeon in a foreign king's castle.

They said a minstrel had discovered the Lionheart. Blondel, they called him. King Richard's personal lute-player, who'd been with him on Crusade.

No doubt *Blondel* had plenty of inspiration, while Alan was left with none. "Give me a hero," he begged, speaking to his Muse. They were on personal terms. "Give me a man—and a woman?" He considered. "There should be a woman, so love can play a part . . ." He nodded. "Give me a man and woman about whom legends can be made." He paused again, thinking seriously, then added a final request, because it wouldn't do to present himself to his Muse as a man with no humility, though some might argue that he had none anyway. Alan shrugged, dismissing that. "And give me the talent to make those legends live."

William deLacey was furious. The guard contingent summoned from the castle faced him in the center of the street, every man a fool, protesting the sheriff's orders without saying a word.

"You have crossbows," he said flatly. "If swords can't stop him, a crossbow quarrel will."

"But—" One of the blue-tabarded soldiers shifted from foot to foot. "My lord Sheriff, he's *carrying* the woman. There is a danger that we might strike her instead."

DeLacey shut his teeth on the fury he longed to display. "I sent for the eight of you because you are reputed to be the best archers in the castle." He waited for comprehension. When none came, he lashed out. "He has legs, has he not? Aim for his *legs*, you fools!" He stared angrily at each man, noting reticence and resentment on the dark Norman faces. "Or is it you fear your reputed competence is lacking? That no matter how careful you are, your *in*competence will harm the woman instead of the man?"

The soldiers exchanged glances. Their expressions did not improve.

DeLacey wanted to strike each and every one of them. "While we stand here debating your merits," he said venomously, "that villein is escaping. Go after him and stop him. *Now.* All I ask is that you do your jobs." Even as they shifted, he stilled them once more with the virulence in his voice. "If you can't accomplish *this* much at my asking, perhaps you would do better to give up your present positions and become Norman villeins." He paused, contempt inserted delicately like a blade between two ribs. "And wouldn't the *Saxon* villeins love to teach you your place?"

It had the anticipated effect. The soldiers moved hastily away to obey his orders in precisely the way he suggested.

"Legs," deLacey muttered. "Are they blind as well as stupid?"

Locksley retrieved his horse from the stables and mounted, thinking rapidly ahead to Will Scarlet's intended destination. A few careful questions at the stables had told him Scarlet was a stranger to the city and its immediate environs, which meant it very likely the man would head for the closest shelter he could find. Locksley doubted he would choose any of the dwellings, for fear the sheriff would institute a house-to-house—or hovel-to-hovel—search, as was his right. DeLacey had the authority and manpower to carry through with any kind of search, even if it meant burning down half of Nottingham. It made it more likely the man would leave off looking for conventional shelter and search for something else.

A fox going to ground . . . Locksley set his mount to a noisy long-trot through the streets and stood in the stirrups, letting his legs absorb the pounding rather than buttocks and torso. *He will look for ground well sheltered on all sides, obstructing a proper search.* He left behind the tattered edges of the poorer district, guiding the horse away from the city. *A man of the country, accustomed to close-grown forests, would seek out familiar ground.*

Sherwood Forest. It cradled much of Nottingham, and the High Road as well. Remnants of Sherwood even encroached on Huntington lands. It was an old, well-grown forest, known throughout the shire as a haven for poachers and outlaws. Soldiers who went in very often did not come out.

But the same could be said of certain outlaws who sought refuge. Sherwood kept its secrets, along with many lives.

He will look for the shortest route. Undoubtedly he already had, since Locksley was certain Scarlet and his prisoner had preceded him out of the city. It was possible both were already gone, swallowed by the forest, in which case his task was to track them somehow through dense foliage, tangled trees, and the detritus of ancient deadfall.

He sought the most direct route from Nottingham to Sherwood, and dismounted at the forest's edge. He tied the horse to a tree, draped his dark green cloak across the saddle, and melted into the shadows.

Marian was muffled in layers of wool, arms trapped by constricting folds, face pressed against the weave. There was air, but little. She found herself short of breath, light of head, and very cramped of will. *Patience,* she counseled herself again. *Let him think you are utterly helpless.* She reflected with more than a little irony that it should be easy enough. She *was* helpless.

He was weary, she knew. He staggered, cursed, growled breathless exhortations to himself as he made his way onward. They must be out of the city, because the sound and smells had changed. She did not feel so compressed as she had before, weighed down by close-built dwellings. The day was brighter.

Out of Nottingham, bound for—where? Her ignorance alarmed her. She could understand using her as a shield while in the city, but why now? Why do it once he was free? Why not simply dump her where she was, so he could move faster? Of what use was she to him, save to slow him down?

The answer seemed obvious. Why would any man keep a woman?

The sound of the day altered again. She heard the crackle of twigs beneath him, the rustling of displaced grass and leaves, the harsh alarmed croak of a nearby crow. Sunlight, once tinted crimson, was changed to bloodied purple.

Trees. She frowned. *A forest?* The answer was implicit as the first bough snagged on her mantle, digging into her back.

Marian bit her tongue to keep from protesting, to keep from shifting her weight in an attempt to avoid the bough. There was no sense in letting him know she was awake and alert. Let him believe she was unconscious. That way she would have the benefit of surprise when he finally put her down.

His grasp on her slackened. Marian held her breath. *Don't move—not a twitch.* He stopped. She felt his grasp shift, looking for new purchase. And then he pulled her down, levering her off his shoulder.

She inhaled a soundless breath. *Don't rush—lure him into care-*

lessness. She was down. She felt the ground beneath her. He had put her on her side, trapping one arm. Marian squeezed her eyes tightly shut. *Wait until there is room.*

It was difficult to lie so still. A part of her mind screamed at her to tear wildly at the mantle, to strip herself from its folds, but she knew better than to give in. If she moved too soon, she gave herself away. Best to wait. When he relaxed, his vigilance would decrease—and she could attempt escape.

He knelt over her, digging his hands into her mantle. She felt the fabric tighten, then slide. A shaft of muted light found the opening. The air was sweet and cool.

She waited. His hands were on her, grasping new folds. He tugged one free of her face. *Not enough—not enough yet.* God, the waiting would kill her.

He caught hold again of the mantle and yanked it free of her. Tumbled onto her face, Marian gritted teeth. *Not yet.* Let him think her dead.

He closed a hand on one arm and pulled her over onto her back. Her head lolled to one side. Marian held her breath. *If he'll only give me up as dead and move aside.* He knelt beside her. She could hear his breathing, harsh and raspy; she could smell the stink of him. *Can't you see I'm dead?*

He touched a strand of her hair, peeling it back from her face with hands that shook. "Don't be dead," he begged.

Marian clawed for his eyes even as she lunged, scrambling up, trying to knock him back as she thrust herself up from the ground. She heard his blurt of surprise, felt him fall back a little, saw the astonishment on his face harden into a new and ferocious resolve. If she took time to look for a weapon, he'd be on her again.

Marian yanked at kirtle, undertunic, and mantle, cursing her missing slipper, and dug in her toes as she leaped away from Scarlet.

Two strides, and he had her by the cloak. So easily, *too* easily; Marian cried out incoherently as the cloak-band tightened abruptly, snugged up against her throat. She tore at it, trying to rip it over her head before he could use it to pull her in like a fish. The tine of cloak brooch bent. Fabric stretched and tore.

Let it go. She bolted, worrying at the cloak, trying to keep her footing against the hardships of too much fabric, too much foliage, too little knowledge of where to go. Branches slapped her face, snagged her arms, rapped her on stocking-clad ankles.

He jerked her off-stride easily, using the cloak, then was on her in a leap. Arms locked around her hips. She fell, as did he, twisting as she went down, trying to snag bough or rock with two clawing, grasping hands. "No—" A stick. She hammered at him with it and saw it break up like pottery. *"No—"* She clawed now at the hands that caught gouts of kirtle.

"Let be!" he snapped. "Let *be—*"

She caught up handfuls of crumbled leaves and damp soil, scooping up clots of mold and mud, and hurled it all at his face. "Let me *go—*"

"Let be!" he shouted.

His hands were on her waist, all tangled in kirtle folds. He was sprawled across her legs, imprisoning her lower body with nothing more than superior weight. Marian dug elbows into the ground and tried to lever herself up, twisting against his grasp.

A rock. A small rock. Not enough to batter him senseless, but *something* . . . She shut it up in one hand, twisted to gain more room, hurled it hard as she could at his exposed face. *An eye,* she begged. *Let it be an eye—*

It struck cheekbone, leaving behind a clot of mud. She saw his shock, his warped mouth as he swore; the bristled pallor of his face. She scooped up more dirt and debris and threw it into his eyes and mouth. One knee was partially free: she hooked it upward as hard as she could, hoping to hit something vital.

"Little whore—" he spat.

"I'm not *anybody's* whore—"

"Let be!" he hissed. "D'ye want me to kill you?" He ducked the hurled stone, then lunged forward toward her face, coming down atop her hips. His weight nearly crushed her. "Let be, little whore, or I'll show you what I can do—"

She battered at him with fists, aware of rage, both cold and hot, the wild anger that lent her strength in the place of fear. She acknowledged it and drew upon it, using its power in place of her own.

The flesh beneath her fists was stubbled, dirty, slack. She saw the lips moving, mouthing curses and complaints, but she lis-

234

tened to none of them. The only thing she thought about was breaking free from him, no matter what it took.

His hands now were in her hair. Marian twisted her head and tried to close her teeth in his flesh.

He caught her by her braid and the fabric of her clothing, handfuls of it, dragging her up from the ground as he lurched to his feet. He stood her there, like a rag doll, staring at her in grim fury. A trickle of blood dribbled down his face from the cut on his cheekbone.

Marian kicked and caught a shinbone, bruising bare toes in the process. He caught her up instantly, jerking her into the air completely off her feet, and slammed her full length into the nearest tree trunk. Her head thumped dully on wood.

Marian sucked noisily at the air, wishing her vision would settle.

"Listen here——" he said. "Best do as I say, little whore——" But he didn't wait for the protest she couldn't make, still breathless against the tree. He simply yanked her free and dumped her down again, hard, sending arms and legs awry as she landed flat on her back, then sat fully upon her as she sprawled across the ground. His weight was oppressive. "Now," he said, "I'll do what I should have done first. . . ."

She thrashed once, weakly. "I'm not who you think I am——"

"Doesn't matter, does it? You'll do." Grimly he jerked the meat-knife from her girdle, then cut strips of wool from her mantle.

"I'm Marian FitzWalt——"

"Doesn't matter, I said." One strip for her mouth, tied so tightly it cut into the corners of her mouth even as she tried to tongue it away. Then he lifted from her, flipped her over and sat again, grinding her facedown into the damp, moldy earth. Another length of wool bound her wrists behind her.

Marian thrashed again, wriggling against the ground. He tied off the knots, stood and pulled her up, then spun her to face him, locking one hand into the hip-length weave of her braid.

"I've two strong hands," he rasped. "Don't make me use them."

Through gag and nose she wheezed. *Don't let him see you're afraid.* But she was. Reaction made her tremble violently, much as she hated it. She breathed heavily against the gag, trying to fill her heaving lungs, and stared back at the man.

She wanted to scream at him, to shout that he was wrong, he was a fool; couldn't he listen to her? Couldn't he believe her? She wasn't the sheriff's woman. She wasn't a *Norman* woman. She was of good, sound English stock, just like his own.

He tore the mantle from her, snapping the band at last. "Too bright," he muttered.

If I could break free and run—

Dark eyes were malignant. "Walk," he said only, and began to beat his way through the forest, dragging her by the braid like a balky cow on a rope.

Twenty-Three

Nottingham's keep was far older than the modern one at Huntington, without ostentation or amenities to soften its angled, sharp-edged harshness. It was utilitarian both in nature and presentation; William deLacey, its latest tenant, wasted neither effort nor expense at making it anything else. It was, he had said, to be a castle boasting strength, impregnability, and something that suggested a powerful, brooding malevolence, so as to remind its visitors—honestly met or captured—exactly what it stood for: justice and retribution.

The hall therefore was nothing more than that: a high-beamed masonry cavern, lacking wall hangings, painted plaster, or tapestries, as well as adequate light. One end was screened to provide a walkway between the adjoining kitchens, pantry, and buttery. The other end boasted a low dais with a massive fixed table and one equally massive chair, meant to

inspire awe as the sheriff made decisions and issued pronounce-
ments.

The hall was always a trifle dark, with an overriding chilly
dankness that helped to crush the spirits of those fools stupid
enough to fall foul of the law. That it was no more hospitable
to its inhabitants, including the sheriff himself, was something
no one mentioned. Sir Guy of Gisbourne, in his zeal to save
money, had decreed a cutting back of household expenditures,
a measure which included candles, torches, and lamps.

Eleanor deLacey glanced up as her father entered the main
hall, striding through one of the doorways into wan candlelight.
She had ensconced herself in *his* chair in *his* hall behind *his*
table. She didn't move as he entered. She simply sat back and
waited for his protest. He was a proprietary man who guarded
his possessions as well as his pride and his office.

But he made no protest. Grim-faced, he merely shouted for
wine at the first servant who appeared, and tore his cloak free
of brooches without unpinning them as he strode the length of
the trench.

He is out of temper. Eleanor's smile reflected an odd contentment. "Let me guess," she said lightly. "Someone called you a
bad name."

The malignant glance deLacey shot her, which displayed his
mood, also informed him that she had usurped his place in the
hall. Yet he said nothing. He merely flung the cloak across the
table and began to pace before the dais, kicking aside rushes
and the remains of an earlier meal. The Sheriff of Nottingham
did not countenance dogs, so the rushes were worse than most.

The wine came. DeLacey drank down the goblet's contents,
thrust it out for more, then waved off the hovering servant. The
pacing began once more. This time he drank in less haste.

Eleanor smiled more widely, aware of an intense, almost
sexual pleasure, and sat back in the massive chair. Quietly she
tapped bitten fingernails against the scarred wooden tabletop.
It was amusing *and* intriguing to see her father so discomposed;
generally he kept such black moods to himself altogether, or
contained them in the privacy of family quarters rather than the
hall.

Something has set him off . . . "Someone spat upon you," she suggested. "Or dumped a nightpot on top of your head."

He spun, slopping blood-colored wine over the rim of the goblet. His sibilants were harsh in the shadowed hall. "I sent you to your chambers."

She lifted a single eloquent shoulder, a premeditated gesture she'd learned from him. "You were gone. I came out." Eleanor displayed a triumphant smile, along with her overbite. "Would you expect anything else?"

He glowered at her, creases deepening around his eyes. The fleshy pouches beneath, she saw, were heavier than they had been the year before. "Do you realize that between your wantonness and the actions of a murderer, my plans are well-nigh ruined?"

Too bad. Eleanor arched eyebrows plucked thin. "Is someone dead?"

"No. Why?"

"You mentioned a murderer."

"He was due to hang this morning, but the task couldn't be done because I was at Huntington Castle." He scowled and drank more wine. His tone was thick. "And now he's escaped, taking Marian with him."

"Marian . . ." Eleanor's attention sharpened. She sat rigidly upright in the chair, rapping out her question in thinly disguised alertness. "Do you mean that little black-haired bitch from Ravenskeep?"

DeLacey spoke through his teeth. "That 'little black-haired bitch,' as you call her, has more beauty and grace in her smallest toe than you in your whole body."

It hurt, as he meant it to, but the pain faded because she made it fade. It was a test, a purposeful provocation, and therefore unimportant; they had spent years gibing at one another. No. What *was* important was the other implications of his remark.

Eleanor lurched to her feet. "And you want her for yourself. Is that it? You want her in *your* bed, and he's stolen her for his."

"More than that," he growled.

"More than that?" she echoed, faintly alarmed. "There *is* no

238

more than that. You want her for your whore, and someone's taken her from you."

"I want her for my wife."

Eleanor gaped. It was worse, far worse than she had anticipated. Shock left her breathless.

"Yes," he said quietly, seeing her expression, "you may well hold your tongue. But it is what I intended."

"To marry—*her?*"

"Yes. You for Robert of Locksley, Marian for me. A fitting dual pairing, wouldn't you say?—except now you're ruined." His glare was baleful. "Not much is left to you, now."

But for the first time in her life, Eleanor didn't care about herself. "You wanted FitzWalter's daughter?"

DeLacey drank wine. The silence between them was loud.

He couldn't mean it . . . this is sheerest folly, designed merely to annoy me . . .

It had to be. There had been no mention of a third wife for as long as she could remember, certainly since she was old enough to understand what a wife was. One by one her sisters had married, leaving only her. Eleanor had long played the part of chatelaine, more recently coexisting intemperately with Sir Guy, and had accustomed herself to doing much as she wished in spite of her unmarried state, even to the point of deciding a husband was unnecessary; that in fact one might prove more than a little difficult in the face of her vigorous and fickle physical tastes.

A new wife would require things, because new wives always did. New wives *changed* things, to make the old place new. To put their mark upon a man, his hall, his holdings. A new wife would usurp a daughter's role and much of her freedom, even as the daughter usurped her father's chair.

Eleanor collapsed into that chair, clutching the edge of the table. "But—she's ruined, too. Don't you see? You can't have her. You *can't have her*—"

"Enough," he said.

"Don't you see?" Eleanor laughed out loud. "If some man's carried her off, she's as ruined as I am!"

DeLacey's tone was deadly. "You forget yourself," he said softly. "A man may accept whatever affronts to his pride, honor, and name he decides to accept. In your case, neither the earl nor Locksley would have you . . . but I would have *her*. By *God*, I'd still have her . . . so long as she'll have me." His expression was grim. "*If* she will have me, in spite of what has happened."

Desperation made her strident. "But if he's raped her—"

"As the minstrel raped you?" DeLacey arched one brow. "Ah, but I forget myself . . . it was the other way around, was it not? You were the aggressor, not Alan of the Dales."

Heat stung her face. "I told you what happened—"

"You told me what you wanted to tell me, before all those others, to save whatever shred of dignity still clings to your name." His contempt was plain. "I should send you to a nunnery. Or marry you off to a wild Welshman, to teach you humility."

Eleanor bared her overbite. "I hope he rapes her so many times she'll not let a man touch her—"

"Be silent!" he roared. "By God, I wonder if you're mine! I wonder if your mother didn't lie beneath the sheets with a common, lowborn herdsman . . . your manners are no better."

Eleanor glared back, hating herself for the film of tears in her eyes. "I am what you have made me."

"But your mother had no taste for bedding at all, be it human or animal." He slammed the goblet down on the table, splashing wine. "I will have her," he declared. "Be certain of that, Eleanor. Jab at me all you like, but I will have the woman."

She swallowed painfully. "What will *I* have, then? What is left to me?"

He eyed her with undisguised disgust. "Nothing of virginity. To that I will attest."

It was easier to be angry than to show him vulnerability. "Neither will she!" she spat. "Neither will *she* have any!"

DeLacey laughed. "Ah, but you forget. Provided she survives, by the time he is done with her—or if we rescue her beforehand—she will be properly grateful. Her disgrace will be mitigated by my willingness to marry a woman who's lost her virginity. She will be widely pitied, and I as widely admired."

Eleanor gritted her teeth. "If she doesn't kill herself from shame."

Her father smiled faintly. "Not Marian. Too much of her father in her for that. As for you, well . . ." He shrugged. "One can always hope."

The mantle was a puddle of blood on the ground: bright, brilliant, new blood, welling up through leaves and deadfall. Frowning consternation, Little John knelt and touched it almost hesitantly, marking shredded cloak-band and a hole torn in the weaving. Something glittery fell as he pulled a crimson fold from the ground. He scooped it up and cradled it in his palm: a round, elaborate silver brooch in the knotted Celtic pattern.

For a long moment he stared at it, transfixed not so much by the brooch as by what it suggested of its wearer's fate. Less than an hour before she had been watching the wrestling match with everyone else. And now, but a short time later, she was being dragged into Sherwood Forest by a killer already sentenced to hang.

Little John's generous mouth became a grim, flat line in the midst of his fiery beard.

He shut his hand over the brooch, warming the raised pattern of elaborate knotwork against his palm. Wiry russet hairs bristled from beneath the sleeve of his soiled tunic to the big knuckles on his massive hands. They were very soft, his hands, from dealing with the wool. It made them sensitive to textures, in fabric and in metal.

"She'll be wanting this," he murmured, and tucked the brooch into the pouch that swung from his hosen drawstring.

He heard it then, in the distance, moving away from him. Going deeper into the trees. The sound of grass, leaves, and foliage, as well as deadfall and detritus, all being disturbed by the hasty passing of two people.

Once, it had been easy to ignore the plight of others, turning his face away from the abuses heaped upon serfs and lowborn wretches like himself. But now his sheer size could make a difference. All he had to do was summon the courage to do it, then stand by his convictions. As he had before the sheriff.

He knelt there listening, puzzling out their direction. When he was very certain, he set off in soft pursuit. He took great pains to be quiet. For a man his size, he was very quiet indeed.

Scarlet broke a passage as best he could through the foliage. The task was difficult. Sherwood was no park tamed by verderers, but a forest in full glory, deep and dark and tangled about with fern and vines and creepers. The thick-boled, spreading trees themselves were no friendlier, closing ranks against interlopers.

He slapped aside branches, broke through limbs that threatened to snag his clothing, or worse, to snag hers. He at least wore tunic and hosen, while she was wholly encumbered by layers of kirtle and undertunic.

The thick braid gripped in one hand proved a superior rope, exerting control with the faintest snap of a wrist. It forced her to walk with her head at an awkward angle, but he found it appropriate. That she made no protest as he jerked her this way and that, pulling her through the forest, was a function of the gag. He knew very well that if he took it off, she would curdle his blood with her screams.

Though she hadn't screamed before. All she'd done was call him names, hurl dirt and rocks, and try to batter him blue.

Like Meggie did with them—He cut the thought off abruptly.

Not that he blamed this woman for it. She wanted free of him as much as he wanted free of *them;* the difference was, he intended no real harm to her. They would hang him.

If they didn't do worse first.

It was enough to harden his resolve, no matter how sorry her state. She was the sheriff's woman; she was, therefore, valuable. He could use her to buy his way free, be it from the sheriff's men, the sheriff himself, or even Sherwood Forest. They said outlaws lived here, hidden among the trees, footpads and brigands who worked the forest tracks stealing goods—and lives.

She tripped often, stumbling over rocks and logs and deadfall, because she couldn't hold up her skirts. It was obvious that she was weary, exhausted by her labor to go where he bid her to go, but he dared not cut her hands free. She'd proven her mettle already. *Likely she'd look for the first full-blown limb to batter my head to bits.*

Scarlet stopped short, breaking through high bracken onto the grassy bank of a fast-running stream. Spring rains had thickened it, giving weight to its usual presence, so that it splashed out of its course onto the rags and strips of leather masquerading as his shoes.

The woman stopped next to him as he guided her by the braid, and tottered briefly a moment, on the verge of falling in. He jerked her back with a curse, which made her stagger against him, then lurch away awkwardly.

He glared at her. She glared back from angry eyes between strands of raven hair. Meggie's had been fair.

No. No more Meggie.

"Time to get your pretty skirts wet," he growled at her, and stepped out into the stream as the woman slipped and slid behind him.

His thoughts went back to the sheriff. Fair trial, indeed. Scarlet had known from the start, from the instant he'd been captured, they'd no more treat him fairly than give him the Lionheart's crown.

Or Richard's brother's throat, that he would crush in his bare hands.

The woman went down behind him, crying out against the gag. He tottered himself a moment on stream-worn, unseen rocks, then steadied himself. Somehow he'd dropped the braid.

She realized it even as he did, and she scrambled up clumsily in clothing drenched to her waist. She staggered, braced legs awkwardly against the current, then lurched away from him.

Cursing, Scarlet lunged. The footing was poor, and painful; rocks rolled beneath his feet even as he snagged her braid. He jerked her back with a snarl, wrapping her soaked hair around his fist.

She was down again, sprawling in the stream. She spat against the gag, furious and desperate words he couldn't understand. Calling him names, again.

Scarlet grinned. "Mite bedraggled, are you? Not so fine anymore . . ." He dragged her up, steadied her, then took the final three strides to the other side of the stream. Sopping wet,

243

she was, and her skirts ran heavy with water, like Meggie's in the rain.

Not now, he raged.

It wasn't fair. He tried very hard not to think of her, not to remember what she said, or how she'd meant to be brave, trying so desperately not to cry from the pain and the shame. But they'd damaged her too much, in mind as well as body. There'd been little left to do save dig her a shallow grave.

And make her a promise to kill the Norman beasts who had, in their sport, killed Margaret Scathlocke.

Locksley followed the track. It was narrow and barely discernable, little more than an animal trail. It was unlikely that Scarlet would use even this primitive track, preferring to hide himself, but for his pursuer this was a faster, quieter way.

He was aware of a rising urgency. Sherwood was legendary as an impassible tract of sprawling woodland, save for one or two roads and a handful of forester tracks. That other tracks existed, he and others knew, but those they left to the brigands who lived among the foliage no better than field warren. It was possible that in the vast woodland he could lose Will Scathlocke, and Marian as well. If he went the wrong way, or if they turned back on him . . .

Desperation pricked his conscience. He wanted it not to happen. He wanted very much not to lose FitzWalter's daughter as he had lost FitzWalter himself.

I will do what I can do . . . But what if it wasn't enough? Locksley clenched his teeth. *Have I been so wretched a man that God would punish me more?*

It was entirely possible. God could be capricious.

"Insh'Allah," Locksley muttered, forgetting his English again.

It was worse. Not better. *Worse.*

What have I done, Marian wondered, *for God to punish me so?*

Her mouth was cut and bleeding. Her bloodless hands were numb. The remaining slipper was in the stream, and her stockings had worn through. Bare and bruised of feet, battered in body and spirit, she wanted nothing more than to simply *stop moving* so that she could recover her breath. So that she could wring out her skirts, before their sodden, clinging weight tripped her and broke her neck.

The anger had died. It had come back, briefly, at the stream, when she had believed she might escape. But he had caught her, and the anger died away, replaced with a deliberate calmness she recognized from before, when she'd been carried over his shoulder all swaddled in Eleanor deLacey's crimson mantle.

The foliage beside them rustled. A huge body crashed through, shredding vines and flowered creepers. From the tangle of broken foliage a tousled red head appeared, followed by a hand that clamped down on Scarlet's shoulder.

"Let her go!" a deep voice boomed. "You've no cause to hurt a woman!"

Twenty-Four

Much knelt by the edge of the swollen stream in the shadows of Sherwood Forest, staring fixedly at the footprints. One set was smudged with every step, almost indistinguishable as human, but Much looked very closely and saw the faint but regularly spaced impressions of poorly woven cloth pressed into mud, indicative of the rags a man might wrap around decaying shoes. Will Scarlet, he knew: the man all set to hang, till he'd stolen Marian.

Marian.

Much extended one long finger and touched another print tentatively, gently exploring the shape. Hers, he knew, mixed helter-skelter amidst Scarlet's rag-blotted prints. Her passing fixed in mud, like an insect in hardening sap.

Much shaped her name mutely. She wore no shoes, nor boots, and her stockings now were nonexistent. The prints she left behind were clearly those of bare feet: small, rounded heels; the fan-spread of the balls; five graduated indentations representative of toes.

His Marian wore no shoes.

Much looked at his own feet, shod in clumsily made but serviceable shoes tied on at the ankles with leather strips.

A princess did not go barefoot.

Marian's footprints disappeared into the water, as did Will Scarlet's. Deftly, Much undid the leather knots, tucked the thongs into the shoes, then slid them beneath his tunic. The toes he thrust beneath the drawstring of his hosen. Then he picked his way across the stream, undeterred by its coldness or treacherous footing, and found as he had expected the telltale prints of bare feet on the other bank.

Much nodded. He patted the bulge of unseen shoes hidden beneath his tunic.

He would find her yet. And he would give her his shoes.

Scarlet nearly swallowed his tongue when the giant grabbed him. Then anger replaced astonishment. "Give over!" he cried indignantly, trying unsuccessfully to wrench his shoulder free. "What's she to you, this whore?"

The giant's bearded face loomed through leaves and boughs. "A woman," he growled. "Worth better than you've shown her, whore or no." One hand closed over Scarlet's wrist and clamped down hard until his fingers spasmed in protest. The braid fell free of his grasp. "I told you to let her go."

"You fool—" Scarlet writhed in the grip, straining to twist toward the woman. "She's the sheriff's whore—or maybe the sheriff's daughter . . . she's worth our freedom, you fool!"

"Not a fool, now, am I?" The giant bared big teeth. "Smart enough to track you. D'ye think the sheriff won't be?"

But Scarlet ignored the question. Frantically he tried to catch the retreating woman with his other hand. "You don't understand—"

The giant's laugh rumbled. "I understand well enough."

Scarlet swore as the woman lurched and stumbled away, well out of his reach, her wrists still tied, her mouth still gagged. Breathing noisily through the wool, she backed hastily away from them both, then turned and bolted into the shadows, ducking the dense foliage.

"No!" Scarlet shouted, his tone throttled by frustration. "By God, you fool, d'ye know what you've done?"

The giant grabbed a huge handful of soiled tunic and yanked Scarlet up onto his toes. The beard loomed close. "Who's the bigger fool—a man who murders others? Or the man who saves a life?"

The tunic, near to throttling him entirely, also cut into Scarlet's armpits. He thrashed, trying to regain control. "I won't hurt her—"

The huge man shook him: terrier with a rat. "By God, *I* say you won't!"

No help for it. He'll choke the life from me. Concentrating what little power remained, Will Scarlet brought his free arm up and battered the giant beneath the nose with a doubled fist. Blood broke and spilled freely as the big man roared in outrage.

Scarlet's captor did not drop his victim to tend his battered nose; instead, he clasped Scarlet more tightly yet, lifted him off his feet entirely, and slammed him into the nearest tree, much as Will himself had tamed the woman before him, but with greater force.

He hung there rigidly, held fast by massive hands. "Wait—"

Blood painted the giant's mouth, but he paid it no mind. "Your quarrel is with the sheriff. Not with his woman."

Scarlet tried to breathe through an aching chest. Had the benighted fool cracked any ribs? Or maybe even his spine? "Listen . . ." he gasped hoarsely. *"Listen* to me—"

"You'll leave the woman be."

The shout was desperate. "They'll hang us both, you fool!" Pressure increased. Scarlet clawed ineffectually, aware of the ache spreading down to touch his kidneys. "No—no . . . *not* a fool. But listen—" He drew in an unsteady breath and tried to

247

sound as reasonable as a man could while pinned against a tree. "They'll hang us both."

The giant spat blood from his mouth. Teeth were smeared pinkish red. "I've done nothing to warrant hanging."

"They won't see it that way."

"They will when I tell them."

"You're a *peasant*," Scarlet hissed. "That's all the excuse they'll need."

The grip slackened, but only slightly. "The sheriff knows who I am. John Naylor, called Little John. Shepherd, not woman-stealer!"

"John Naylor . . ." Scarlet gasped. "Listen to me, now. I don't want to harm the woman. I just want to *sell* the woman."

"Sell her!"

"For my freedom. For *our* freedom." Scarlet twitched in the grasp. "Put me down, and I'll tell you how it will be."

"Tell me now. As you are." Pale blue eyes were steady. "I like to hear a liar dance his way around the truth."

The woman was gone, Scarlet knew. If he didn't find her soon . . . "She'll die," he said flatly. "Outlaws live in Sherwood. They'll find her, and they'll kill her."

Pale eyes flickered.

"She'll die," Scarlet repeated. "I only wanted to sell her. They'll want to do worse than that."

Free. Marian crashed through dense foliage, cursing inwardly the helplessness of a woman bound and gagged, thrashing her way clumsily past soaked, heavy skirts that fouled every step.

Free. Her bare feet kicked at shift and kirtle, scraping bruised toes against wet fabric, then digging beyond the ashy scattering of dead leaves to the cool soil beneath.

Free. Her weight fell more heavily into her shoulders and breasts because her hands were tied behind her back. She tripped, staggered, stubbed a toe against a stone, caught the slackening weave of her braid on one twisted bough, and nearly put out an eye on another. Angrily she ducked, tearing her hair free, and stumbled into another tree, banging her shoulder against the trunk before she stopped short and leaned, breathing noisily through the gag.

Marian sagged slightly, winded and exhausted. One knee ached abominably whenever she put weight on it. The soles of her feet hurt, and one ankle bone twinged as she rolled the foot to test for damage.

But she was *free.*

Free, was she? To do what? To go where? The wool at wrists and mouth made it impossible even to call for help, if there were help to be had.

The cut corners of her mouth hurt. Marian tucked her chin toward her chest, trying to take the pressure off the strip of wool tied so tightly around her head. She thought briefly of attempting to snag the back of the gag on a tree limb, then working it off, but dismissed it as unfeasible. Likely she'd catch naught but hair, and yank it free of her scalp.

She peered into the shadows. *Where am I?*

The hems of her shift and kirtle, water- and mud-weighted, had come loose from stitches set in by a maidservant's skilled hand. A step forward now would result in a foot planted on fabric, rooting her to the spot; annoyed, Marian kicked out violently and felt the cold wet slither of shift against her ankle, clinging stickily. She shook the foot free and twisted back the way she had come.

What do I do now? She hadn't gone far. She could hear voices, male voices, muffled and indistinct, but harsh with tension. It was the murderer, she knew, and the giant who had freed her.

Marian frowned. Why would the giant take pains to set her free, then enter into conversation with the man who'd stolen her? Why not simply bind him, gag him, and call out that she could approach without fear of recapture?

Marian cast a sharp glance around the immediate area, then quietly edged her way to a vine and bracken-choked fallen tree. Awkwardly she hunkered down behind the massive trunk, kicking aside her wet skirts.

Stay here, for now . . . don't assume anything, yet. She craned her head back and peered up through towering trees to the limb-scraped sky overhead. *How long—?* The sky was blue, for the moment, and full of brilliant sunlight. But within a few hours the world would be swallowed by night.

Marian painfully gulped an unsteady breath through the gag, then blew it out noisily. She tried to ignore the twinge of fear in her belly. *I'll find my own tracks, and follow them back out. It shouldn't be difficult.*

But the fear inside increased.

Much breathed through his mouth as he paused in the midst of a step, listening raptly. When the seasons changed his head felt stuffed with rags most of the time, sometimes making the inside of his forehead ache dully, and he couldn't breathe as well through his nose as he could at other times.

He shut one hand over the bulge of shoes, clutching them tightly through the threadbare warding of his tunic. They were still there.

His breathing stilled. He waited, stricken into immobility.

Sound.

Where was—? Ah. Ahead. To the side, a little. Men's voices. Quarreling. A deep, rumbling voice and a lighter, more urgent tone. He heard none of the words, merely the sound and the nuances: urgency, desperation. The fraying of self-control. Much knew all of those things.

Marian. And shoes.

Mutely, with a meticulous wariness, Much crept toward the voices.

Little John tightened his doubled-up fistfuls of Will Scarlet's tunic beneath the man's jaw as he pressed him against the tree. "No more of such nonsense, now. I've not heard such blather ever in my life."

Scarlet hung there slackly. Steadily, he said, "It's true. All of it. Every bit of it."

Little John shook his head. Blood still flowed sluggishly from the nose Scarlet had battered, but he ignored it for the moment. "No."

Bleak, dark eyes stared back. The flesh beneath one twitched.

"I may be a murderer, but why would I lie to you? You could choke me to death right now."

Little John allowed more of his weight to threaten tunic and throat. "Aye, so I could."

Scarlet's eyes were steady, curiously opaque. His tone was empty of passion. "Do it, then. Save *them* the pleasure."

Little John glared. Doubt niggled at him mercilessly, even as he tried to push it away.

"They won't thank you for it," Scarlet told him. "You're a Saxon dog. I'm a Saxon dog. No pleasure in it for Normans if the Saxons kill each other."

Little John bared gritted teeth, then with an exclamation of disgust mixed with frustration, he unknotted his hands from the tunic and let Scarlet go. Pressing the sleeve of his soiled tunic against his bleeding nose, he spoke through the fabric. "Doesn't matter now, does it? She's gone."

Scarlet slowly unpinned himself from the tree, watching Little John closely. "She wouldn't be hard to catch." He pulled at the rucked-up tunic, tugging it back into place. "You know them, John Naylor. All of them. Meet a single man, and you know them all. Norman pigs, every one."

Little John offered no answer.

The murderer was relentless. "How many times have they mocked you? How many times have they used you? Beat you? Made you kneel in filth and slime, bowing your head and pulling at your forelock?" Scarlet yanked at his own hair, mocking the subservient gesture. "How many times has any Norman pig allowed you even to speak? To say a single word of protest, or offer explanation, or stand up to them as a man?" The saturnine face twisted malignantly. "To them, *we're* the pigs! We're naught but beasts, to be used at pleasure, to work the land until it's barren, like an old woman, then give over the last bit of grain to them so *our* families starve in the winter!"

Little John stared balefully at the blood-spotted sleeve, avoiding the man's eyes. *He's twisting me all around.*

"Think about it!" Scarlet snapped. "Aye, I killed four Normans . . . four Norman beasts who saw a Saxon woman and—" He stopped short, convulsed, rubbing one grimy hand across an even grimier face. For a moment Little John thought he would break. He was mad, they said. But Scarlet did not break. And when he spoke again, he had mastered self-control. "What are *you* to them but a brute to be collared and yoked, naught but an English ox, to be set to the Norman plow?"

Little John gritted his teeth, fastening upon the overriding thing that had driven him to interfere in the first place. *"She's* naught but a woman——"

Scarlet spat the single word as if it were an epithet. "Norman."

Little John lost his temper. "And what is the difference? You speak of Norman beasts and a Saxon woman—what is *this,* then?"

Scarlet allowed the bellow to subside, then answered quietly. "She's the coin to buy our way free." The tone thickened almost imperceptibly. "No matter what they tell you, I'm not a madman. I had a woman, a good woman . . . I'd not harm even a Norman one, but to save myself."

Slowly, Little John shook his head. "I'm a shepherd. Not an outlaw."

Dull color mottled Will Scarlet's face. Something simmered near the surface, lending a tightness to his tone. "He'll have us killed for this. If we let her go, they'll hunt us down and kill us."

The giant slapped a massive hand against his chest. The sound was audible. "I've done nothing——"

"You have!" Scarlet shouted. "You've put hands on a Norman woman, *defiled* a Norman woman—d'ye think he'll not use that? D'ye think he'll thank you for this, and invite you in to supper?" Bitterly, Scarlet shook his head. "You're a fool, John Naylor, to expect good of the man. He's Norman. He's the sheriff. She's his daughter, or his wife, or his woman—does it matter? D'ye think he'll let you go when he can make an example of you?"

"If she told him the truth——"

"She won't. She's a Norman." Again Scarlet shook his head. "She'll tell him we both abused her, just to see us hang."

Desperation was painful. "She's naught but a *woman.*"

Scarlet's tone was deadly. "So was my wife. They killed her anyway."

Little John scraped rigid hands through the fiery bush of his hair, tugging at trapped locks as if the violence might ease his mind. He turned away, staring blindly into the forest as he paced away from the man, trying to ward off the words Will Scarlet had used. It was much easier to ignore them. He had learned to ignore so many, from Normans and Saxon alike.

He shut his eyes tightly. *I should have stayed in Nottingham—I shouldn't have come out here* . . . But his conscience told him he'd had to. The look on the woman's face as Scarlet had captured her—

Little John swung back, glaring balefully. "I'm naught but a shepherd. I wrestle at the fairs."

Will Scarlet shook his head. "Not anymore."

"I can tell them the truth. I came here to help the woman."

"We'll sell her back to them in exchange for our freedom."

"Then I *will* be an outlaw!"

"And what will you say when accused of helping me escape?"

Little John nearly gaped. "I had naught to do with that!"

"They'll think you did. They'll think we planned it; that even now we conspire in the forest." Will Scarlet's mouth was hard. "They'll say what it pleases them to say."

The blood had stopped. Little John felt his sore nose gingerly. "Why d'ye tell me this? So there will be two of us hunted?" He leaned and spat, clearing his mouth of blood. "Seems to me you've more to lose than I."

"I can't stop you," Scarlet said. "Go back, then, and tell them. Say to them you took the woman back from me. Take *me* back, if you can, along with the woman. Give the Normans what they want."

The realization came swift and sharp. "You'll tell them, won't you?" Little John challenged. "That *we* planned it, you and me. You'll see to it I suffer the same fate as you."

Will Scarlet did not so much as flick an eyelash. "No man wants to die alone."

Futility seized him. Big hands curled into fists. "I came here for the woman, not for you!"

Scarlet hitched one shoulder. "Too late, now. I'm here, and she isn't. I'm as good as hanged."

Little John wanted to smash his fist through Will Scarlet's

grimy face. But that would do nothing to change the truth Scarlet himself had stated so plainly.

Or the falsehood to which he would swear.

This is wrong. This is wrong. But doubt waxed like the moon. He knew what Normans were. He knew what Normans did. Little John fixed Scarlet with a scowl. "I'll not have her harmed."

Will Scarlet folded his arms. "Then bring her back yourself. I'll wait here for you."

Little John eyed him. "And what if I find her, and take her back to them after all?"

He shrugged. "I'll be a free man, safe in Sherwood Forest. You'll be an honest one, rewarded with Norman justice." Scarlet's voice was steady. "Which of those fates offers a Saxon peasant a chance?"

The arguing had ceased. Marian sat rigidly behind the felled tree, listening intently. But there was nothing more. Whatever they had argued about no longer was in contention.

She'd heard no outcry, no blurted exclamation. She supposed a man could die in silence, but it seemed unlikely. Surely a man, nearing death, would fight with all his strength, even if he lost.

Her doubled-up legs were nearly asleep, numbed by dampness and tension. Marian rolled onto one hip, slowly straightening out her limbs. Everything ached. *In the morning, it will be worse—* But she cut off the thought. She didn't like the idea of not knowing where she might be, when night gave way to dawn.

She wiggled her fingers. They felt thick, swollen, useless. The wool cut into her wrists even as it cut into her mouth, chafing the tender skin. Her braid, already littered with debris, picked up more as it dragged the ground, and something had found its way into her left eye. Marian closed it, trying to work the irritant away, but the discomfort worsened. She sat helplessly, letting the tears fill that eye, wondering angrily if she would succumb to womanish weakness. She did not cry easily. She saw no good in it. Swooning would earn her nothing, nor would crying. The only thing that might save her was her own determination.

The eye teared. Marian sniffed, blinking rapidly, trying to see clearly again. She longed to rub her eye, but had no hands with which to do it.

Sound. The faintest hiss and rustle of a body sliding by leaves.

Marian spun, tumbling backward, hitching herself against the bulwark of a fallen tree. A muted wail of fear combined with denial ended at the gag.

The body stepped out of the shadows. Marian blurted a name, but the gag made it indistinguishable.

Much. The relief was overwhelming. She scrabbled up, lurching forward on her knees, angling her shoulders away from him so he could see her bound wrists.

Much came forward slowly, wary as field warren. Marian waggled her hands and encouraged him with emphatic noises warped by her woolen gag.

His touch was light and hesitant. She felt him work at the knots. His fingers were long, slender, deft, the hands of a talented cutpurse, but the wool was wet and snugged taut. It would take time.

Marian tried to remain still, but she felt herself trembling. *Hurry.* His hands stopped moving. She expected them to fall away, as would the binding. She expected herself to be freed. She intended to rip the gag from her mouth, spitting its foulness away. But her wrists were still tied.

She made a sound of urgent appeal, but Much, transfixed, waited. When the giant came noisily out of the shadows the boy scrambled up and ran.

The giant's fiery hair stood up in a wild halo around his head. Blood marred his freckled face, as well as his tunic. His nose, already prominent, appeared to be swollen.

His astonishment was plain. "Boy!" he shouted. "No, boy— come back!"

There was nothing to mark Much's passing save the twitch of a sapling tree.

"Boy—" the giant rasped, reaching out a huge hand. Anguish twisted big features as he looked at Marian.

She stared, transfixed. *He killed Will Scarlet after all* . . . And now he wanted Much.

"He'll tell," the giant whispered. "D'ye see? I've no more choice, do I? No choice at all, now." He bared teeth, flexing his massive hands. "That boy will tell them 'twas me, and what Will Scarlet said will come true!"

Marian scrambled up. Something in his eyes was wild with grief and anguish.

The giant looked at her. "I meant to let you go. I did mean to. But now there's the boy, and what Scarlet said—" He shook his head in a slow, desperate sorrow. "Now I've no choice at all but to do as *he* wants to do."

It was all she needed to hear. Marian spun on bare heels and lunged toward the shadows where Much had disappeared. He was huge, the giant . . . if she could get through, get ahead of him, surely she would be swifter.

But in one stride he had her. Her left shoulder disappeared into the massive hand. Marian tried to wrench free, but he merely hooked a hand under one arm and swung her around.

"I'm sorry." He touched her briefly with his free hand, tentatively, as if afraid she could burn him. "I'm sorry, lass, I am." Pale blue eyes were sad as he studied her face. "Poorly used, I know—" And then he cut it off, as if he'd given too much away. The grasp on her arm tightened. "Best come with me," he told her. " 'Twas naught of my idea, but there's no going back, now. We'll trade you to the sheriff to buy our way free."

He was too big, too strong.

The hand tightened again, its tentativeness gone now. "Come along now, lass."

Marian glared at him, very close to tears. She was wet, weary, bruised, and battered, aching in every bone. *I was so close.* Her fear was abruptly replaced by a furious, desperate anger. With all the strength she could summon, she lowered her head and butted it hard into his belly.

It rocked him but briefly, and that from astonishment alone. Marian meant to twist free as he staggered back, but the giant didn't stagger. He merely scooped her up easily and hung her over his shoulder.

Marian wanted to scream. *A sack of flour. Again.*

Twenty-Five

Much squatted behind the tree in an agony of indecision. He clutched the shoes in both hands, his traitorous fingers knotting themselves into the flaccid leather.

The opportunity was gone now, and Marian still tied. Still gagged like a common peasant poacher hauled away to forfeit a hand.

He squeezed his eyes shut, biting his lip so hard he felt the teeth cut through and the blood welling into his mouth—punishment for failure.

He leaned toward the tree, pressed his brow into the bark, and he beat his head against it, grunting in despair, battering at skin until the flesh was raw and damp.

His giant had stolen his princess.

What next, then? He was too small to stop him. He was a simpleton: everybody said so. The very best *he* could hope for was to find someone to help. Someone bigger. Someone friendly. Someone who understood.

Should he tell? Should he tell?

But who *was* there to tell?

Not the sheriff. Or his Normans.

Who, then, was left?

His giant had stolen his princess. The fragile perfection of his self-built world was broken.

Much hugged the tree, like a baby clutching a breast discovered unaccountably empty.

He hugged, and rocked, and whimpered.

He'd forgotten to give her the shoes.

Will Scarlet, once called Scathlocke, hunched upon the stump. The ringlike, spiked corrugations of what once had been a tree but now was merely a pediment did not dispel the tension, did nor serve in any way to distract him from the acknowledgment of the events he'd set into motion.

"Meggie," he whispered tightly, then ground the heels of his hands into burning, dust-scoured eyes, red-rimmed and gritty from lack of sleep; from lack of tears, as well.

But Meggie couldn't help him. Meggie was the *reason*. He had only to think of Meggie, to see her again before him, sprawled upon the ground like a rag doll with shredded limbs, all slack and empty and lifeless.

Trouble was, she'd lived. For a night, and half a day.

Pretty Meggie Scathlocke.

"Mad," he muttered aloud. "—'s what they say I am. And maybe I *am* mad, to wish I could do it again . . . over again, all of it . . . again and again—and *again*—"

It trailed into nothingness, a futile plea for understanding; for a regeneration of his spirit, shrunk down from good Will Scathlocke into murder-mad Will Scarlet: to a tiny, hardened pellet of an irredeemable rage.

Elbows dug into bunched thighs, his legs spread to lend him balance. He leaned his weight upon them, and scoured his face, stretching it out of shape with callused and blood-smeared hands.

Giant's blood, he knew. Not Norman blood, this time, but that of an Englishman. Spilled in the woman's defense.

"No." He said it aloud. Then, viciously, to ward off even the suggestion of guilt, "Little Norman *whore*." Nothing like his Meggie, reaping naught from rape but death.

Scarlet shut his eyes. Fingers curled around the weapon thrust into the drawstring of his hosen: the Norman whore's little meat-knife, barely big enough for his hand.

Meggie. Meggie. *Meggie*.

He jerked the knife free of hosen, staring at its blade. With infinite, exquisite precision, he set it against his forearm midway to the elbow, where dark hair, blood, and dungeon filth showed through the rent of his sleeve.

"What color is mine?" he rasped, and cut into the flesh of his arm.

Little John frowned fiercely as he carried the sheriff's woman through the dense tangle of undergrowth. She was an exquisitely tiny thing, and as exquisitely fragile. He was absolutely convinced that if he held her too firmly, or bumped her against a tree, she would break into little bits.

It wasn't right, he knew, but the boy would tell the sheriff.

She was tiny, fragile, and vulnerable, like the smallest of twin-born lambs. *I'm sorry,* he said inside. *I'm sorry, little Norman.* He stumbled, cursing in sudden, jolting panic that he might drop and break her, and she cried out against the gag as he clamped his arm more tightly around kirtle- and shift-bundled thighs.

She was rigid and stiff as wood, bent like a greenwood sapling across his massive shoulder. Her breathing was ragged and noisy, constricted by the wool, but he dared not take it from her. He couldn't bear to hear the names she would call him, the threats she would hurl, the promises she would make of death by hanging, or worse; of the hands they would chop off, of the tongue they would cut out, of the cautery they would use to keep him from bleeding to death and robbing them of their sport.

He recalled her expression just as he'd scooped her up. Her eyes were alive in her face, reflecting his own fear as it was magnified in the mirror of a transfixed, weary gaze abruptly empty of hope.

It had made his spirit quail, the expression in her eyes. Not hatred, though he'd expect it; but an opaque, futile acknowledgment that nothing she had done, and nothing she could do, would win her the slightest freedom.

Little John strode on again, shredding foliage in his haste. *I'm sorry, little Norman.*

But she offered no answer, hearing nothing of his thoughts,

and he was glad. He knew how words could cut. He knew how hatred could harm. He knew he deserved it all.

Little John walked on, feeling the beat of her braid as it slapped the back of his knee with every step he took.

The track was narrow and winding, a skein of umber-brown wool tangled upon the floor. Trees crowded either side in haphazard communion. It was dark in the depths of Sherwood, musty with shadowed dampness. Here spring did not exist, save for the budding and blossoming of flowers scattered through grasses and fern. It was olive and ash and charcoal, and a sullen yellow gone rusty where the sun could not creep through.

Locksley walked easily, boot soles cushioned from dirt by layers of skeletal leaves and decaying ferns left over from winter, soft in place of brittle, crushed quietly into death with no crackle of protest.

The air was heavy and damp. He was alone among the shadows, human interloper within the secretive depths. This was *England*, the heart and blood of the land, so distinctly different from the sand and heat of the Holy Land, where the sun baked a man's armor so that a new fashion was invented: the brilliantly colored surcoat blazoned with England's—and Richard's—folly, borne forth into senseless battle in the name of Jerusalem.

Then sound, where there had been none. Unexpected intrusion. Locksley halted abruptly, stiffly, swinging gracelessly to face it.

—the thunder of mounted Saracens riding out to battle the English. The rumble of massive seige engines rolled up to the walls of a city Richard decided would be his—

Locksley's breath ran ragged. He felt the pang in his belly, the clenching of his bowels. A glint of sun on mail sent a shudder through his body. *Not here . . . this is England.*

And then memory was gone, banished by comprehension. He stepped aside hastily, relinquishing the track to the horsemen riding by, except instead of continuing on they chose to rein in abruptly, setting horses onto haunches, powerful hocks digging into track as iron-shod hooves plowed barren furrows, spraying dirt, debris, and dampness.

Six men. All Normans. Blue-clad sheriff's men, boasting Norman livery, Norman equipage, and Norman arrogance.

He was the son of an earl. His pedigree was impeccable, if anyone cared to inquire. But he was very, very English, Anglo-Saxon to the bone. The Conqueror had altered nearly everything in England, including courtesy, and Locksley was not of the proper blood, Earl's son though he was.

He moved aside, forsaking the track, not because he was English, nor that they were Norman, nor sheriff's men who believed themselves superior to a common English peasant, but because the six rode *horses;* and any man not a fool gave way were he on foot.

One of the soldiers rode forward, reining his mount close to Locksley, who stood his ground a moment, then moved aside yet again. It was a game he recognized, having seen it played before. He lost nothing at all by giving way easily; if anything, he won much more in the safekeeping of his feet. The Norman's horse was large, snorting wetly as he stomped. Locksley offered the horse respect, if not the man who rode him.

The Norman gazed down at him from beneath the curving shelf of his conical helm, his eyes shaded by the nasal vertically bisecting the center of his face. In bad English, he said: "A man, and a woman in red."

Locksley shook his head.

The Norman moved his horse closer yet. "It is necessary to tell the truth."

Locksley smiled politely, offering no cause for comment, then said in good Norman French, "I have seen no one since I left Nottingham, neither the man they call Scarlet, nor the woman wearing it."

"But you know them!" Only the tiniest flicker of his eyes betrayed the soldier's surprise at hearing his own language, and fluently, in the mouth of a man so obviously English, and therefore inferior. "How do you know them? Who are you?"

He hesitated a moment. Then, "Robin," he said merely.

A rook flew squawking from the foliage beyond. The Norman scowled. The eyes were not dark after all, but gray, shadowed by the nasal. "You have a pretty tongue, for a peasant."

The insult was not lost upon Locksley, who smiled faintly. "It was necessary to learn the language of the Conquest, lest we *be* mistaken for peasants among those born to the tongue."

"But you *are* . . ." The Norman frowned again. The five behind him spoke quietly, murmuring among themselves.

"I am English," Locksley said, still speaking in Norman French. "You need know no more than that."

"I know you require education," the soldier snapped. "We are of the sheriff's personal garrison, out of Nottingham Castle. We pursue a man wanted for murdering four of Prince John's men. He has stolen a woman."

"Prince John?"

"The murderer, you fool!" The Norman edged his mount closer yet, imperiling Locksley's toes. "She is an *English* woman. Would you have one of your own harmed?"

Locksley kept his tone pitched low, to make the man work to listen. "I would have no English woman harmed, nor an English man. Nor would I harm a Norman, save to keep him from harming me or mine. Perhaps that is what the murderer did, in killing Prince John's men."

The Norman's face was stiff. He examined Locksley closely, weighing accent, language, and manner against the clothing he wore, which, being simply made, unadorned garb, marked him as a man of no consequence—save for the other things, which marked him as something else.

"Who are you?" the soldier repeated. "Robin who? Of what village?"

"Locksley," he answered easily. "Hard by Huntington Castle."

"The earl's domain." The tone was less hostile now; the mention of Huntington and its earl changed matters significantly.

Locksley, who knew it, and why, smiled. "Yes."

The Norman glanced briefly back at his five compatriots. Very slightly he shook his head, as if admonishing them to say nothing before a man who understood their language—or a man who lived within the protection of the earl. Then he turned back to Locksley, mail glinting in sunlight.

The earl's son squinted; in the shadows it was blinding. *Norman mail, not Saracen.*

"It should mean something to you that he has stolen an English woman," the soldier declared. "One might believe that you wish some harm to her, were you to hide what you know."

"I know no more than I have told you."

The Norman gritted teeth, muttering to himself. "Then we'll waste no more time with you. Be on about your business."

Six horses thundered away, throwing damp sod into his face. Methodically Locksley wiped his face clean, then pulled damp grass for his hands, and looked across the track at the foliage beyond. "You may come out now."

Much froze. He clutched at fern and grass. Should he run? Should he flee?

The blond man spoke again. "You have no taste for Normans, or you would have joined us. And since you listened to us, you know I have no more fondness for them than you yourself do."

Much waited, wishing he could turn invisible and sneak away without the man knowing a thing. But it was too late. He could run, but so could the man. He thought it most unwise to risk yet another beating.

Much rubbed at his flattened bridge, wishing he could breathe. Then crept out from the foliage and stepped onto the track.

Eyebrows arched beneath pale hair, expressing mild surprise. Then the man smiled. "One can hardly see you in the shadows. I know the Normans didn't. I only knew you were there because of the rook."

Much stared at him. He knew him. He *knew* the man, from somewhere. The same brown clothing, the same spill of pale hair.

He stiffened, remembering. He knew him now.

The man saw it and crossed the track to catch him by the arm before Much could flee. "Wait."

Much struggled, trying to break free. But the man didn't let him go.

"I said, wait. I won't hurt you. If I meant to, I would have

263

given you to the Normans." The grip increased. "I won't hurt you, boy. I promise."

Much ducked his head, expecting a blow. He hunched one shoulder to protect his left ear. If he said nothing, the man would never know. He'd beat him anyway, but he'd never know for sure.

"Why are you here?" the man asked.

He was so fair that he lit the shadows around them. The wash of pale hair, the arch of blond brows, the equally pale lashes. And yet the flesh, for his fairness, was weathered by a sun much harsher than the one looking down upon them now. And the eyes were not so pale, but a clear, perfect hazel: sometimes green, sometimes brown, changeable as summer weather.

The grim mouth tightened faintly. "Why are you hiding from Normans?"

Much said nothing. He waited for the blow.

"Do you live here in Sherwood Forest?"

Still Much held his silence. He noticed the pinkish scar winding its way along the man's jawline, like a serpent bound for his mouth to steal the breath from his lungs.

"I'm looking for someone," the stranger-who-wasn't-a-stranger said. "The same two people the Normans seek. A man, and a woman. She was wearing a crimson mantle, though any man with a bit of sense would have stripped it from her by now." The grip loosened slightly as Much did not answer. "The woman is in some difficulty. I want to find her so I can take her back to Nottingham."

Startled, Much lowered his shoulder and stared at the man. Then, as abruptly, he realized what he'd done. Only a blind man would miss his reaction.

The man wasn't blind. After a moment's hesitation, he knelt down on one knee. "My name is Robin. I mean you no harm. I know you've seen her, or you know her. Which is it?"

Much held his tongue.

"She deserves better," Robin told him quietly. "She was taken against her will."

Much breathed through his mouth, determinedly saying nothing.

Eventually Robin released him, rising. "All right. Go on. Tend your own business." He turned, heading down the track in the same direction as the Normans. The threat was abruptly banished.

He went, taking the light with him, and Much watched him. He thought about Marian. He thought about the giant. He thought about the madman, and the Normans who wanted to find them; Normans who would cut off his hand, given the chance again. For trying to steal the sheriff's purse.

He stared hard at the back of the man, who walked steadily down the track, not even looking back. The shadows now had deepened. In brown, he was hard to see.

Robin, Much said inside. And then, "Marian," loud enough to be heard.

Robin turned. His expression was obscured by distance, but the tone of his voice was distinct. "Yes. Marian."

He wasn't Norman, the man who called himself Robin. He disliked Normans, as had been proved by his behavior on the road when accosted by the sheriff's men. He wanted to find Marian, to rescue her from the madman, and the giant of Hathersage.

Much gestured him to come near. Robin answered it, pausing in poised silence. Much pointed. "There."

"Why now?" Robin asked. "Why not before?"

Much lowered his gaze. Then he reached out with nimble fingers and touched the belt from which the man's purse had depended.

"Ah," Robin said, on a note of discovery and comprehension.

"Marian," Much said.

Robin smiled faintly. "Show me the way."

Twenty-Six

Marian felt sick to her stomach. Her position athwart the giant's shoulder pressed her belly against her backbone, and the continued jouncing as he strode through the forest, beating vines and creepers aside, merely added to her discomfort. Her blood had all rushed to her head, putting pressure on eyes and ears. And with no hands free to balance herself, she was absolutely helpless.

If I were sick upon his boots, he might put me down. But she didn't feel like seeing if it worked.

The giant thrashed his way through one more veil of vines and halted. "Here," he said harshly. "I've brought the girl. But you'd best not harm her. I'll break you in two, if you try."

Marian could see little but the giant's back. Even when she craned her head around, the effort added nothing to her vision but her own braid and the forest.

Then the giant clasped her roughly and hoisted her down, swinging her to her feet and turning her deftly so that she stood with her back to his chest. One huge hand imprisoned her shoulder.

It was the murderer, Will Scarlet. He wasn't dead at all, not even injured. He stood just before her, staring mutely out of near-black, lifeless eyes, with a jaw hard as stone and an alertness in his posture that put her in mind of an animal just before it bolts.

A knife was in his hand. Her own knife, Marian saw. And one of his arms was bloody. *He means to kill me.* She thought instantly of flight, but felt the giant's hand close more firmly yet. She could not help the throttled moan of protest cut off by the gag.

"You'll not harm her," the giant declared.

Marian heard the challenge implicit in his tone. For all his roughness, he *had* treated her kindly enough; she saw now the threat came not so much from the giant as from the man who faced her, in decaying shoes and shabby clothing, with blood upon one arm.

Scarlet moved away from the stump, stopped rigidly, and pointed. "Put her there. I'll not touch her."

The giant took her to the stump, urging her to sit as she moved stiffly, awkwardly, uncertain of their intent. She sat, wincing inwardly as the wooden "teeth" of the shattered trunk pierced shift and kirtle, biting into flesh. She shifted slightly, not letting the pain show on her face. She'd give nothing to them save whatever calmness she could summon.

Scarlet, still staring, nodded. The fixity of his gaze unnerved her. Marian looked away briefly; like a submissive dog, she wouldn't challenge him. But it made her angry not to. When he moved, she found she could not keep from looking at him, to see what he might do.

What he did do was approach. She smelled him: extremity, ordure, the dungeon. He showed her the knife. "This was yours." Marian did not so much as nod. "Yours," he repeated.

"Here, now," the giant said uneasily. "I'll not have you tormenting her."

"No," Scarlet said grimly, then tucked the knife away into the drawstring of his hosen. "You don't know me at all. No one does, now. What I've done is done; what I *will* do is yet to be done. But don't judge me by what I've done. Judge me by what I do."

Marian's breath scraped against the wool. She could not discern his intent in such a rambling discourse. He was obscure, unintelligible, and very, very dangerous.

"Here." The giant again. "What do you want of us?"

Will Scarlet stood before Marian. The clearing was small, hedged by vine- and creeper-choked trees, with fern lacing the ground. "We're outlaws," he said. "D'ye know what that is?"

She said nothing, because she couldn't.

"Outlaws are men who live outside the law," he continued,

"because either they're men who want to do that, or men who *have* to do that." He stared at her fixedly, then dropped down to squat before her. "Do you know aught of that? How men are made to live as beasts in the forest, because it's their only chance of freedom? Beasts, in the forest—but 'tis better than living as beasts under the yoke of the Norman pigs like you!"

Marian shut her eyes, cursing his mistake, until his hand on her chin brought her stiffly to awkward attention, heart banging in her chest.

"Here, now," the giant growled. "You say you want to trade her to the sheriff for our freedom. If you harm her, he'll never trade any such thing."

Scarlet stared only at Marian, dirty fingertips on her chin. "You don't know me," he whispered. "You don't know me at all. I'd never harm a woman."

Liar, she longed to say, spitting it into the stubbled face so very near her own.

Scarlet rose, taking his hand from her flesh. He looked now at the giant. "The track to Nottingham lies that way." He pointed. "They'll be coming there. You'd best go set a watch, then come back to me when you've seen them. We'll decide what to do then."

Don't. Marian tried to catch the giant's eyes. *Don't leave me here with him.*

"No," the giant said. *"You* go and watch."

Will Scarlet smiled faintly. "Me, they'll kill on the spot. You, they'll listen to. You said so yourself."

Marian stared hard at the giant, trying to make him see that he put her in danger if he left her with Will Scarlet. *Make him see.* But the giant nodded agreement despite her silent pleading.

Scarlet's voice was steady. "Tell them if they follow, I'll kill her. Leave them there on the track, then come back to me."

The giant moved close to the madman. "You'll not harm her, Will Scarlet."

For a long moment they faced one another, one huge, red-maned man, and a smaller, darker, more desperate man. Then Scarlet took Marian's meat-knife from his hosen and gave it to the giant.

It was enough. The man nodded, cast a last glance at her,

then strode off through the forest in the direction Scarlet had indicated when pointing out Nottingham's track.

Will Scarlet stared at her, malignancy in his eyes. "I'm going to tell you what they did. I want you to know. Every part of it. I want you to *know.*"

She stared back, uncomprehending, wary of the tone that promised to tell her something he wanted her to hear; that he *meant* for her to hear, because he knew it was a weapon against which she had no defense. Her plea to God was explicit: *Don't let this man touch me.*

Will Scarlet smiled slowly in a feral anticipation. "Little Norman whore."

Robert of Locksley—Robin—stopped as the boy motioned him to. He waited, watching the dirty, sharp-boned face as he listened intently to the boy's halting explanation that Marian and the giant were very near. That Much was a simpleton, he knew; it had become very clear shortly after they set off after Marian. The boy said very little, and then only in single-word sentences, or half-framed, inarticulate phrases. He had been poorly treated through much of his childhood, and poorly fed to boot; he was small and slight for his age, hollow of belly and face, with the staring, hopeless eyes of a soul needing care and nourishment in a land that could give him nothing.

This is how poachers are made. Locksley was aware of a growing dislike for the customs of his country, as well as his countenance of them. *The Normans run roughshod over every Englishman, save those with the coin to buy their courtesy or interest, and then maim and kill the peasants who have no choice but to steal to eat.*

In the Holy Land, he had seen the same: the faces of starving Saracens before they were killed by Christians. War did that to people, stripping them of food so that soldiers could be fed, but England, *this* England, was not at war at home. Yet her people, from child to adult, suffered a fate like the enemy Richard fought.

He would stop this. He would. But Richard was not in England, nor like to be any time soon.

Much waited mutely. Locksley came back to himself, realizing he'd withdrawn so far from the present that the boy now was confused, staring at him in perplexity. Briefly he put a hand on Much's thin shoulder, then nodded. "Find me what you can find, then come back quickly and tell me. I will have to make a plan."

The miller's son nodded and left him, slipping into the deepening shadows as the day slid downward toward dusk.

Locksley watched him go. Then, frowning thoughtfully, he examined the nearest cluster of saplings for one best suited to him. He had only a meat-knife, neither sword nor bow. His best bet then was to make himself a crude weapon from materials at hand. "Quarterstaff," he murmured. "Length for leverage and distance, to ward off a giant who wrestles, or a man they say is mad."

He didn't stop to consider what he would do if he faced *both* men. If it came, it came; by then, he hoped, Marian would be free, thanks to Much's intervention.

Shadows lengthened. The sun edged down the sky to dip below the canopied screen of overlapping treetops, filtered now through boughs and branches in a counterpoint of dark and light, a leafy chiaroscuro. Shadows lay long on the ground, reaching out importunately to touch the crumpled hem of the woman's soiled kirtle.

Scarlet stood before her, staring at the intercourse of shadow and woolen fabric. He saw the tips of bare toes whisked away beneath the kirtle. The stitches had all come loose; the hem was ragged and torn.

It shocked him. He stared more fixedly yet, seeing things he had not seen, blinded to the world save for what he needed from it. Now he looked at the ruined kirtle and ragged shift, still damp and weighted by mud; the tattered remnants of a braid, ratted and snagged and tangled; the defilement of her face, bruised and scratched and dirtied—and bloodied on her chin where he had dared to touch her.

It shook him. He felt it all over again, the pain, the fear, the futility, and the wild, killing, helpless rage that prior to that day had never touched his soul. Since then, it had lived there. Since then, it had shaped him.

Will Scarlet knelt down. He crept forward mutely. He hunched at the despoiled skirts, reaching out to touch the fabric, to put the tips of his trembling fingers against the ruined wool.

"No," he breathed. She stiffened. But when she made to retreat, he caught a great handful of still-soaked kirtle. "No," he told her hoarsely, and then looked up very slowly to find her staring at him white-faced out of blue eyes dilated black, with smudges beneath lower lashes and a welt at the corner of one, where the dusky birth of a bruise stained a flawless cheekbone dark.

The gag had cut her mouth.

"Don't you see?" he cried. "There was nothing left to do!"

But she was gagged, and mute. He saw the faintest of twitches in her face, in her lashes, as she recoiled from his outcry. Her body was perfectly stiff, but she did not move again.

Scarlet knotted gouts of wool in both hands, kneeling before the woman like a supplicant before a priest. "She was young," he whispered. "She was beautiful. Any man would want her, even a highborn man. But it was Will Scathlocke she wanted— it was *Will Scathlocke* she took. Though others wanted her—men better than him . . . it was Will Scathlocke she married. Because—she loved him, she said . . . because she *loved* him. Because—she loved . . . *him.*"

The woman's face was bloodless.

His own contorted. "I am not—a man women love. I expected nothing of it. She could have had any man in the village, any lord in the castle—she was that beautiful. Like you . . . like—you . . ." He gazed up at her, seeing beyond the dirt and bruises to the bones and flesh beneath. "Pretty Meggie Scathlocke."

She didn't so much as blink.

"She carried my child in her body before the winter was out."

She swallowed heavily, trying to breathe through the gag.

His pallor matched her own, beneath the stubble and filth. "And then—the Normans came. Six of them, d'ye see? Prince

John's men, aglitter with Norman mail, awash in bright silk surcoats bearing Norman arms . . ." Dark eyes searched her own avidly. "D'ye see how it was? Can you *know* how it was? Pretty Meggie Scathlocke—alone in the hovel we had made into a home."

Her chest lifted raggedly as she drew in an uneven breath through the weave of the wool.

He tugged at her skirts, crumpling the stained fabric in his rigid, trembling hands. "My Meggie, all alone—and six Norman soldiers—"

Will Scarlet broke off, choking on his words. Abruptly he unclamped his hands, dropped the crumpled wool, lurched to his feet and three steps away, where he stopped, and stared, white-faced, with near-black eyes aglitter with something akin to madness.

"Pretty Meggie Scathlocke, made to serve the Normans. *Saxon* Meggie Scathlocke, made again and again to whore for the Normans, until she could do naught for any of them, because they were all used up, and so they turned to things no decent man would think of, to continue their sport, their use of the Saxon whore." His entire body trembled. "Do you know what a sword hilt can do to a woman's body?"

She twitched a single time. He saw the tears in her eyes spill over onto her lashes, then trickle down her face, making runnels in the grime.

"Aye," he hissed, "put yourself in her place. Be pretty Meggie Scathlocke with a baby in her womb, made to do such things for six Norman beasts." He balled up his fists before her, banging his own chest. "Put yourself in *my* place, coming home to find her so, all sprawled out across the dooryard of the hovel that was our home, bleeding from what they'd done—*dying* from what they'd done, those foul godless animals who serve the devil himself, and him in a royal mask."

Her tears dampened the gag.

Three strides and he was to her, reaching down to catch her arms. He dragged her to her feet, his face but inches from hers. Spittle struck her cheek. "Put yourself in my place, little Norman whore, and ask yourself why I murdered four of your own kind. Put yourself in my place, little Norman whore—and ask yourself why I shouldn't do to you what they did to her!"

Little John walked the turf-rumpled edge of the swollen stream, each long stride crushing grasses and ferns and flowers into the marshy bank. Here the trees were sparse, no longer shoulder-to-shoulder, breaking up into ragged clusters, then giving way to a clearing cut almost precisely in half by the fast-running stream. The rush of water over slick, rounded stones did nothing to ease his mind. He was not a happy man.

"I'm a shepherd," he muttered morosely. "I should be home in Hathersage tending my sheep, not out in the woods with a murderer setting traps for bloody Normans."

But he made no effort to leave. Outlaw, Scarlet had called him, though he had protested it strongly, yet outlaw he possibly was, or would be, once the thing was done.

I shouldn't be here, by God! Little John swore violently and kicked out a loosely seated rock, rolling it aside with a single thrust of his boot toes. He'd intended to take the woman back to the sheriff and return her safely, not try to buy a freedom he already had. But that *boy* had seen him with the woman, and by now the sheriff knew who else was involved with Will Scarlet. No man, seeing Little John, could mistake him for anyone else. Thanks to the boy, he was now counted as an enemy.

"Easy as that, then," he declared bitterly. "One day a shepherd, the next a wrestler, the third day a man meaning only to help, and the *fourth* day an outlaw!"

He stopped short, glaring out into the water. Six paces upstream the water was bridged by a fallen log wedged into place with stones, mud, and kindling to afford steadier footing, linked on one side by a narrow trail leading deeper into Sherwood, on the other to the Nottingham track.

Little John scowled at the rude bridge. His freckled hands knotted into his tunic, threatening the haphazard stitches. With a boot toe he dug repeatedly at a clump of turf until he broke it free, then kicked it flying into the rushing water. It sank immediately, weighted down with soil.

His voice was a thick shout. "No help for it, is there? Now you've done your part."

The water gave him no answers.

He heaved a huge sigh that lifted his massive shoulders and dumped them down again. He felt helpless as a babe.

"Helpless as that woman . . ." Working his mouth around the absence of a molar, he scowled bleakly across the water to the still-invisible track.

Movement caught his eye. He squinted fiercely, trying to pinpoint the cause. Near twilight things often blurred, indistinct and transitory. But he saw it clearly enough. A man he didn't know came quietly out of the trees into the clearing on the Nottingham side of the water, thick fall of blond hair made luminous by the setting sun. In one hand he carried a quarter-staff, though crudely cut and barely trimmed.

Here it is, isn't it? Little John drew in a breath to fill his massive chest. "You!" he challenged. "Have you come for the woman, then?"

The fair-haired man stopped, inspected him, then leaned upon the staff. His expression was indistinct, though his words were clear. "So I have."

Little John bellowed again. "Are you of the sheriff?"

"I am of myself." The stranger spoke quietly enough, but pitched his voice to carry above the rushing of the water. "You have the advantage of me . . . you know where she is."

Little John smiled. *It won't be so hard, after all.*

The blond man raised one brow. "Will you take me to her, then?"

Little John folded thick arms. *Better and better.*

"I don't suppose you'd bring her to *me?*"

This time Little John grinned.

"I thought not." The other took his weight off the staff and hefted it in the air. "Shall we fight for her, then? I win, you take me to her. I lose, I go away."

Little John's eyebrows arched. *No wasted words, with this one.* "Normans send you, then?"

"I came myself, upon my own business."

That Little John contemplated, along with the man himself. His clothing was drab and plainly cut, but he wore it like a lord.

His accent was not of the highborn, but oddly heavy-handed, as if he worked at it. There were Saxons, Little John knew, who tried hard to please the Normans so as to reap the benefits.

Accordingly he bent and spat, then bared big teeth in an unfriendly grin. "I'll wrestle you for her."

The other appeared neither taken aback nor dismayed by the invitation. He smiled faintly. "I think not. I am not so immodest a man as to believe I can beat the Hathersage Giant."

Little John frowned. "But you'll match me in quarterstaffs?"

"I am but a fair wrestler. At the staff, I am better." He looked beyond Little John's head. "The sun begins to set. If this is to be decided while there is yet light to see by, I suggest we begin."

Little John barked a laugh. "You've a staff cut already!"

The other tossed his across the stream and nodded as Little John caught it. "There. I'll cut another."

"Oh no." Little John flung it back. "I'm not so daft as that. I'll find me my own staff, thank you."

The other planted his and leaned upon it again. "I'm waiting," he said mildly.

Much crept through the forest carefully, making little sound. He knew he was close, very close, because he had heard the murderer, Will Scarlet, shouting something. He could not make out the words, merely the tone, which spoke to him of grief and rage and decaying self-control.

Marian's in danger.

It was a fully complete thought, unlike many of his. He was a creature of instinct, reacting to others rather than initiating action, save for his thievery. And that had come about merely because he had seen another do it once, and badly; the man had been caught, given over to the Watch, was sentenced by the sheriff, and had lost his right hand in a public display of punishment. Much had seen it all, but was dissuaded by none of it. The man had been slow, and clumsy; Much itched to try it himself. He knew instinctively that he was faster, and his fingers were defter. His father and mother had said so, when he lived with them at the mill.

Times had changed. It was easier cutting purses from unsuspecting souls in Nottingham than working at the mill. But he didn't do it often, not being a greedy boy, and he did it only then for the actual doing of it, not because of the money. Most of it he gave away when he had enough for food. There were those whose lives were crippled by physical misfortune. From them Much learned he had value after all, for they never laughed at him, or called him simpleton. They just took the coin he gave them, and bought enough food to live.

But Marian was special. She was unlike any of them. They shared a childhood bond, though she recalled none of it. Much recalled it all. "Nixies," he murmured, and crept slowly through the trees until he saw movement, and heard the voice. The murderer, Will Scarlet, standing before Marian.

Much hunkered down, settling quietly into the squatting position he had learned to hold for a long time. Robin had told him clearly to be certain of himself before he attempted the task, and to wait for a distraction. The distraction was to be provided by Robin himself, should the plan work properly; Much knew he was to wait, to give Robin time, or his part might not work.

Marian, he murmured inwardly, peering through bracken and foliage to the stump on which she sat. His princess was all bedraggled. And she still lacked shoes.

Locksley watched as the giant acquired a length of wood approximating a quarterstaff similar to his own. He kept his expression fixed, betraying nothing of his thoughts, but was vastly impressed by the sheer strength of the man. Using no knife or other implement, the Hathersage Giant strode over to the nearest stand of saplings, selected one he liked, and jerked it out of the ground.

Locksley sighed inwardly.

With his meat-knife the red-maned man pruned his tree judiciously, hefted it to test its weight and balance, then grinned balefully. "You're sure you want to do this?"

I'm sure I don't *want to do this . . . but I think it's the only way.* Locksley hitched a shoulder. "Something to pass the time."

"Come on, then, let's not waste any of it." The giant strode directly to the log bridge, stationed himself on his side of the stream, and waggled imperative fingers. "Come across—if you can."

This could hurt . . . Locksley paced more deliberately to the crude bridge, judging his footing carefully, and the length of the giant's staff. *Were it a test of archery skill, I'd be a happy man.* He paused, set one booted foot on the end of the log, tested it for solidity.

"Come now, will ye take all night?" the giant chided. "Or d'ye think to lull me to sleep with all this, then sneak across in the dark?"

Locksley continued to test the bridge, ignoring the baiting. His body had changed in the two years since he'd left England to join the Lionheart's cause, and then again while on campaign, and yet twice more in captivity and restoration. Weight had come and gone, dependent on nourishment, while muscle lengthened, increased, and gained power. He had grown up in Richard's army, trading youth for hardened manhood in the deprivations of crusading. No more was he the whip-slender youth his father knew, but an experienced fighting man. He knew himself much better than ever before, in mind and body. He had beaten bigger men than himself in many things, but none so big as *this* man in anything so purely physical—or painful—as quarterstaffs.

"Come on, then," the giant said. "D'ye want the girl, or not?"

I want her. Locksley rolled the staff in his hands, seeking the most comfortable grip. *But not in the way you think, nor for the same reasons.*

The giant shook his head. "She'll be old before this ends."

Locksley walked out on the bridge, assessing steadiness, footing, and balance. "And you'll be exceedingly wet."

Twenty-Seven

With the sun nearly set and only a token number of candles lighted, Nottingham Castle's hall resembled a shadowy cavern. William deLacey, seated on the dais, rose from his chair and set both hands upon the table, leaning on braced arms. "Where *are* they?" he roared.

The castellan was a tall, heavy man, thick through the shoulders and chest, and thicker yet through the middle, where an ever-expanding belly pressed uncomfortably against unforgiving mail. He was a dark-haired man, with a face naturally saturnine; now, before the sheriff's unadulterated anger, it took on an uncompromising hue of new bronze. "My lord—"

"Where are they?" deLacey repeated, very softly now. "Six of your best, Archaumbault . . . a reflection of you, perhaps?"

Archaumbault shifted self-consciously, chafed by his tight mail and shame. "My lord, it may be that the forest hinders them. It is Sherwood, after all . . . once off the tracks, it's difficult to follow anyone conversant with the forest—"

"He isn't a fox," deLacey ground out. "He's a man, who is dragging a woman with him. Will Scathlocke isn't from Nottingham, he's from a village *east* of here; do you think him conversant with Sherwood?" He glared at Archaumbault. "He is on foot; they are mounted. He is unarmed; they have crossbows. They should have caught him before he *got* to Sherwood."

"Yes, my lord."

"Well, then." DeLacey straightened and folded his arms. "What do you propose to do?"

"Assign more men to the task, my lord. More *capable* men, my lord—obviously those already searching are not up to the task. I will see to it personally that only the best will be given the duty."

"Do." DeLacey smiled. "Lead them yourself, Archaumbault."

The man didn't so much as twitch. "Yes, my lord."

The sheriff flicked his fingers. "Go."

"My lord." The castellan turned smartly on his heels and strode out of the hall.

"Fool," deLacey muttered wearily, collapsing into his chair. "The incompetence appalls me . . ." But he let it go, breaking off, because Gisbourne's mousy assistant, Walter, had come into the hall. "What is it?"

Walter, squinting, bobbed a hasty bow. "The clerk, my lord. Brother Tuck. He has a letter for you regarding his employment here. From the abbot of Croxden, my lord."

"Very well." DeLacey sat back, sighing. "Have him bring it in."

Walter nodded and hastened back out. The sheriff, not much interested in what the abbot had to say, idly contemplated the dimness of the hall as he waited for the new clerk. "Gisbourne will have us all blind," he muttered crossly. "How is a man to see if there is no light at all?" Mentally he told himself to have more candles put out.

"My lord Sheriff?"

DeLacey motioned the man forward. "Brother Tuck, is it?"

"Yes, my lord."

"Come closer, into the light—though God knows there's little of that."

"Yes, my lord." Brother Tuck came forward. "I have a letter, my lord—"

"From Abbot Martin, I know. Bring it here." DeLacey put out one hand.

The monk acceded, wheezing very slightly as he stepped up to the dais and handed over the sealed parchment. He retreated quickly enough, folding his hands into the deep sleeves of his black cassock.

DeLacey broke the seal and scanned the letter. Eventually he

279

looked at the monk: a young man of great girth and humble demeanor, with a cow's-cap of curly brown hair surrounding a freshly shaven tonsure. Even his eyes were cowlike: large, brown, and placid. "It says here you've been sent from the abbey because you're a discipline problem."

The quiet voice was steady. "Yes, my lord."

DeLacey's tone bordered on disbelief. "*You* are a discipline problem?"

The young friar blotted at his upper lip nervously. "Lord sheriff, I confess to a great sin I have as yet been unable to conquer." His smile was sad. "I eat too much."

"Indeed." It was obvious.

"Far too much, my lord." One plump hand splayed across the belly swelling the unadorned cassock.

"Abbot Martin says you are to be on half-rations while here."

Brother Tuck sighed. "I've prayed and prayed, my lord . . . so far, nothing has worked."

DeLacey angled a single brow upward. "And *I* am believed able to provide the discipline your faith cannot?"

Tuck's wide, fleshy face was oddly bland, putting deLacey once again in mind of a cow. "Abbot Martin believes you are capable of eliciting any kind of behavior you desire."

"Does he?" DeLacey's smile was thin. He appreciated the two-edged content of the statement. "As well he should. Your Abbot Martin and I have crossed swords before—in a manner of speaking."

"I admit my weakness," Tuck declared earnestly. "I would be very grateful if there's anything you can do to aid me in this. Until I conquer my sin, I won't be able to return to the abbey and take full orders."

"And that's what you want?"

Tuck's face took on an almost unearthly light. "Oh my lord—*yes!* More than anything!"

"Very well." DeLacey rattled the parchment. "Serve me well in all things—and accept my discipline—and I'll send you back to Abbot Martin with a recommendation he wouldn't dare ignore."

Tuck gulped heavily, clasping his thick-fingered hands. "My lord, I would be most grateful."

"Meanwhile . . ." The sheriff fingered his chin. "Meanwhile, I would have you draw up an execution order for William Scathlocke. Leave the date open. The final fate of the man rests upon Prince John's pleasure." *Provided Archaumbault's six expert archers haven't killed him yet—or Archaumbault himself, once he gets to it.*

"Yes, my lord." Tuck bobbed a bow and turned away.

"Brother Tuck."

He swung back, cassock billowing. "Yes, my lord?"

"You are unable to preside at a wedding, then?"

"Yes, my lord. Until I take orders."

"Yes. So I thought." DeLacey waved a hand. "Go along, Brother Tuck. I'll have the order in the morning."

"Yes, my lord. Thank you, my lord."

The sheriff watched the corpulent priest make his way out of the hall. When again he sat in dimness, gazing thoughtfully into the distance, he folded the parchment into a precise, palm-sized square. "Abbot Martin," he murmured. "For this, I thank you truly: you've sent me an idealistic fool who puts his trust in God, yet aspires to very little while believing in Him too much. This man will be easy to use."

Little John laughed aloud. "Wet, will I be? No, I think not—only if I'm thirsty, and I spill a bit down my front."

The stranger offered no answer as he stepped out onto the log bridge. His expression was masked, but his eyes were fiercely alert as his deliberate, precisely measured steps brought him closer. Whatever else he was, he wasn't a bully-braggart, but a man who understood winning took more than words.

"My name is Robin," he said gravely. "Of Locksley. My mother taught me I should know a man's name before fighting him."

Little John grinned toothily. "Did she, now? Well, Robin Redbreast, my name is John Naylor, though the jest is 'Little' John. But you may call me 'my lord' when this awkward dance is over."

Robin nodded. "And what will you call *me* when the dance is over?"

"You? A wet bird, that's what!" Little John shifted his substantial weight, spreading booted feet and legs. "Come on, then," he murmured, mostly to himself as he assessed his opponent.

Robin halted halfway across the bridge. He stood calmly with one foot in front of the other, balancing with ease, knees slightly flexed. He gripped the staff firmly but not too tightly, and kept his elbows tucked to his sides so as not to diffuse the power to the ends of the staff, or too far from the center of his body. He could not rely on footing to offer an advantage, so it fell to his arms and shoulders to do the required damage.

Little John nodded. *A man who understands.*

Robin hunched, then flattened the line of his shoulders, working them loose, and raised his chin. "Will you come?" he invited.

"Ah, 'tis for *you* to come across."

Robin shook back loose hair from his face. "It seems unfair that we begin with you on solid ground, and I on a bridge likely to roll at a single misstep."

I know what you do, friend Robin. Little John grinned as he moved out onto the log. "Having tested it, like I do now, you know as well as I do the log won't roll. As for fairness or unfairness, 'tis *you* who wants something. Buy the ground, if you will, by making your way across."

The younger man shrugged. "I'll make it as I can—" And struck his first blow.

A feint. Little John knew it even as his body reacted, moving to block the blow that wouldn't come. Only brute strength allowed him to stop his own momentum and anticipate the second blow, which was not a feint, and which would have opened up his scalp had it landed. It didn't only because Little John stopped and turned it.

"Hah!" he cried, then snapped massive wrists and flipped his own staff around, only to have an equally heavy blow turned back as he had done.

Blond Robin grinned. "It will be dark before we are done."

"Aye, so it will." Little John laid on again. And again was turned back.

Within a matter of moments each had taken the other's measure and found nothing wanting. Where Little John excelled in sheer power, Robin used finesse to dart a blow at thighs or ribs, to snap a quick slap toward the staff, or to feint once again at the head. In turn he warded as many similar sallies from Little John, until each man slowed his pace and thought very carefully about what strategy might work before attempting it.

'Twill take all night, Little John thought sourly. He was accustomed to winning quickly through sheer intimidation.

Robin swiped at ankles, then knees, then head, but was turned back each time. Like Little John, he panted, fair hair dampening at the line of temple and jaw.

Quarterstaffs locked. "A pretty boy," Little John jeered, "but the staff takes a *man.*"

Robin grimaced against the immensity of the pressure applied by Little John. "Then why do *you* have one?"

"I earned my right to the staff when you were still in the cradle."

Robin grunted with the effort of holding his place on the log. "Better a cradle than a cow-byre."

"Sheep." Little John grinned. "I'm a shepherd, not a cowherd."

"No doubt the sheep are sorry."

"Are they?" Little John jerked back his staff, spun it quickly, then tried a slashing maneuver that would have broken a bone. But Robin caught it and turned it back, fair hair flying, then swung a flat blow that scraped Little John's staff and slipped beneath his guard to smack him stoutly on the ribs.

Little John grunted. *No damage, but a warning.* Staffs clacked and meshed. "No doubt your mother was sorry when she whelped you—she must have wanted a son, instead of a pretty daughter."

Robin laughed, adjusting his footing deftly as Little John leaned. "Since you tend sheep, no doubt you can't tell the difference between a boy and a girl."

Little John, who had heard that old joke a hundred times, did not rise to the bait. But he admired the boy for trying. "Here, then . . . we'll give the girl a taste—" He feinted, ducked the response, feinted a second time, aiming low, then straightened to his full height and snapped the staff at head height. *That's got it.* The end of the quarterstaff, poorly deflected, banged off Robin's and caught him above the right ear, precisely where Little John had aimed. "There, my pretty girl—the bath'll do you good!"

Blood broke from the abused scalp immediately. Knocked off balance, Robin dropped the staff, clutched futilely at Little John, then pushed off from the log bridge as physical control deserted. He landed flat on his back, full-length, arms and legs awry. The accompanying splash was shallow, but most satisfactory.

Little John nodded, leaning on his staff. "Clean that pretty face before your mother sees it."

Robin came up almost at once, spewing water and flinging his hair from his eyes, then floated a moment, arms outstretched, face screwed up against the ache in his head. Wet, the pale hair was darker, and slicked back from a face, Little John reflected in some surprise, that really *was* pretty—in an austere, masculine way. And there was a scar bared by the ducking— no, two. One underneath the chin, and another on the forehead, just at the hairline. A pinkish-purplish slash stretching from midway across the brow to the left temple, where it cut into wet hair, then disappeared.

"Who's the wet one, then?" But Little John asked it with less conviction than he might have. "Was that a quarterstaff?"

Robin frowned faintly as he slowly lifted his head. "Was *what*—oh. No." He gingerly touched the right side above the ear of his head, bleeding pinkly into his hair. "*This* was the quarterstaff."

"I did warn you, Robin Redbreast."

"So you did." Robin stood up, still gently fingering the lump. The water lapped at his thighs.

Stouter than I thought. Little John squinted; the dusk was deepening. "So. You'll be off to the sheriff to tell him where you met me, so he can set his Normans on me."

"No." The bantering fled Robin's tone, altering his expression. The mask was in place again, but the eyes betrayed an almost feral attentiveness. "I told you I came for myself, not the sheriff. I owe the woman something."

"Do you, now?" Little John grinned. "All but Norman, are

you, to take a Norman leman? Or is she your wife, consorting with the sheriff to gain you a little favor?"

Blood trailed down to mix with the water soaking Robin's tunic. He did not appear to notice. "She is none of those things," he said flatly. "Her name is Marian of Ravenskeep. Her father was a knight with the Lionheart on Crusade, before he—died."

Little John lost his smile. "Then what was she doing with the sheriff?"

"Sharing his company, albeit reluctantly, because he gave her no choice." Arms hung slackly from wide shoulders; wider than Little John had noticed before when half hidden in pale hair. More than ever was plainer now, in the honesty of wet wool glued to a powerful body braced against moving water. "He would marry her, if he could. But the lady is a Saxon, and will have none of him."

The accent had changed. Little John heard it, recognized it, felt the dull spring of dread in the hollow beneath his breastbone. The "pretty" boy was much more than he appeared.

And the woman—? "Saxon . . ." he echoed.

"Born and bred," Robin declared. "Like you. Like me."

Little John threw down his quarterstaff. "Will Scarlet has her."

"I know. It's why I came."

"He calls her—" Little John swallowed harshly. "He calls her a Norman whore."

Fair brows rose. "And she allows him to?"

Little John felt sick. "She's gagged."

Robin cupped hands to his temples and slid fingers through, slicking water from dribbling hair. "I came to bring her back. If you want to fight me again, we'd best get at it."

"No. No need." Troubled, Little John shook his head. "He said I'd be named an outlaw."

Robin's gaze was steady. "Is that what you are?"

"No! I told him so. But the boy saw me with her, and he'll go back to the Normans." He hitched his big shoulders awkwardly. "By now he's there already."

"Much." Robin nodded. "He's not gone to the Normans. They'd cut off his hand for thievery." He waded toward the bank. "He said you saved it, earlier today. Do you believe him so ungrateful as to carry tales to the Normans?"

Little John reached down a hand, clasped Robin's, and pulled him from the water. "*That* boy . . ." He frowned. "D'ye mean 'twas him all along?"

"Much saw you with Marian. He thought you might hurt him, so he ran. But it wasn't to the sheriff."

The enormity of the truth stunned Little John. "*That* boy," he whispered. "By God, if I'd known, I'd have—" But he broke off, distracted by something else. "He went to you. You were waiting."

"We met upon the road." Robin grimaced, fingering the lump on the side of his head. "We should have had this conversation *before* you pitched me into the water. It might have saved me a headache."

"Aye," Little John agreed glumly. "Come along, then, I'll take you to the woman. Though I can't say what Will Scarlet will do about it—he's wanting to sell her to the sheriff in exchange for his freedom."

"William deLacey would never allow that. He might agree because it's politic, but he'd never stand for it. He'd merely find another way to have him taken and killed." Robin bent slowly and caught up Little John's forgotten quarterstaff. "Before it gets dark, if you don't mind."

Little John looked down at him. "Not a Norman. Nor a peasant."

"No." Robin's grim smile hooked crookedly. "A 'pretty girl,' you said."

Little John grunted. "I've been wrong before."

Much froze into poised watchfulness. Was it time? Was it now?

No. Surely not. Where was Robin?

Now?

He could see Will Scarlet standing before Marian, stubbled face twisted into an expression Much had seen on other faces before now. It was helplessness, futility, and an unalloyed need to do something, *something*, anything at all, to relieve the painful emptiness that filled a peasant's soul.

Marian's back was to him. He could see her hands from where he squatted. Her wrists were still tied, her hands still slack. The knots, he didn't doubt, were no less taut than they'd been before, and he still lacked a knife.

He might have taken Robin's, but he'd said he could do it with naught but nimble fingers.

Then Scarlet abruptly grabbed Marian and snatched her off the stump. His strident shout was clear to Much. "Put yourself in my place, little Norman whore, and ask yourself why I murdered four of your own kind. Put yourself in my place, little Norman whore—and ask yourself why I shouldn't do to you what they did to her!"

Much's mouth dropped open. He lingered on the border between flight and some kind of protest. Did Scarlet mean to harm her?

But Marian said nothing, nor did she make any attempt to move. She just hung there in Scarlet's hands. Much rubbed distractedly at his stuffy nose. This was for *him* to do, to set the princess free.

He fixed his gaze on the strip of wool binding her wrists. If he were a magician, like Merlin, he could *conjure* the knots undone. But he wasn't. He was Much. He'd have to do it himself just the way he always did.

Marian refused to shut her eyes. *He'll do whatever he wants—but I won't let him make me cower.* Part of her wanted to cower. Part of her wanted to cry. But a greater part of her was angry, very angry, that she would be violated not because he was a man who believed in abusing women, but because of a *mistake*.

His eyes were nearly black. His hands clasped her arms, fingers digging in. She could smell the stink of him, hear the hiss of his breath, see the malignant grief and helplessness that drove him so mercilessly. "Meggie," he whispered.

The cracking of a twig heralded an approach. Even as Scarlet stiffened, fingers digging more deeply, a crude quarterstaff was inserted almost leisurely between his body and hers.

"You *will* let her go." Robert of Locksley, moving abreast of the red-maned giant, stepped out of deepwood shadow into the gilt-clad glamour of sunset.

Twenty-Eight

Will Scarlet released Marian so rapidly she lost her balance, staggering back a single step to ram one bare heel painfully into the tree stump. Brought up short, she sat down awkwardly. Splinters bit through fabric into flesh, but Marian didn't care. What mattered this instant was that Robert of Locksley—somehow wetter even than she—must be able to hold off Scarlet before he could grab her again.

With that, I can help. And she did so, jumping up hastily to edge around the stump, putting its solid presence between her and the murderer. Her breath hissed raggedly past the painful gag.

"Back," Locksley suggested mildly, tapping the staff very gently against Scarlet's ribs.

He backed, fingers splayed stiffly on the end of rigid arms. Marian wanted very much to warn Locksley—*no*, she recalled, *Robin*—of the man's reputation for violence, of his acknowledged madness, but the gag prevented her.

"Down," Robin said.

Scarlet sat down. The butt end of the quarterstaff hovered at his throat. He glared at the giant. "How much did he pay you? How much did he promise you?"

The shepherd shook his head. "Not for money, Will Scarlet. For the *truth*."

"Truth? There is no truth. The Normans are lying pigs—"

"So they are," Robin agreed in clear Saxon English, "when it suits them to be so. But there are also Saxon liars, and Saxon pigs . . . which one, I wonder, are you?"

Marian stared at him. He was different, somehow, in a way she could not define. He was more alive, more *intense* than the man she had seen on the dais of Huntington Castle. And somehow less vulnerable than the man who had killed the boar, mouthing prayers—or curses—in a language she didn't know.

"Take her, then!" Scarlet rasped. "Take the whore and go."

"And leave you here?" Robin's thin smile was edged.

Will Scarlet twisted his head and spat a clot of saliva to the dirt at Robin's feet. "Will the sheriff buy me from you, then? Is that why you came?"

Robin set the staff against Scarlet's throat and prodded very gently. For an interminably long moment the murderer didn't move, glowering blackly at Robin despite the pressure at his throat. But in the end he gave in, sinking stiffly to the dirt. He lay flat, limbs rigid.

The quarterstaff lingered. "Why I came," Robin said, "is none of your concern."

"It is!" Scarlet cried hoarsely. "By God, Saxon or Norman, you're all the same! You treat us like dogs, to creep about your ankles hoping for scraps of meat, belly-down in the dirt with our tails between our legs—"

"Enough," Robin said.

"—and all because you were born to a name with money, while the rest of us grovel in dirt from the day we take a first breath to the day we take a last one—"

"Enough."

"—and you don't even *care*. None of you cares. You just expect us to *do,* so you don't have to—"

Robin raised the quarterstaff. One blow would crush a throat.

"No—" the giant blurted, even as Marian tried to protest.

"No," Robin agreed. "It's what he wants me to do, to prove his point."

Will Scarlet's face turned red, then faded to bleached white. "You're like all the others—"

"I'm like *none* of the others." Robin planted the butt end of the staff in the dirt next to Scarlet's head, and leaned. "What you did to four of Prince John's pet Normans troubles me not at all. It was—and is—your concern. But what you did with this woman—"

"I didn't hurt her!" Scarlet snapped. "Ask the giant. I promised."

Robin smiled grimly. "And what is your promise worth?"

Dull color suffused Scarlet's face. Dark eyes glittered balefully. "I'd do it again, if I had to."

"That, at least, is truthful." Robin flicked a glance at Marian. "This woman—"

But Scarlet kicked out, knocking the staff away, then swung his legs and hooked Robin's right ankle, jerking him to the ground. *"Now* we'll see—" he hissed.

William deLacey leaned forward in his massive chair and fixed the man with a cold stare. "Say that again," he commanded.

Abraham the Jew clasped his hands quietly before him. "My lord Sheriff, we have contributed more than enough to the cause. We can do no more."

"This is for *your king.*"

Abraham shrugged slightly, "My lord, we have already given so much for the king's ransom . . . to do more now would destroy us—"

"Then let it." DeLacey sat back. "It is treason to refuse a king's command."

The old man nodded. "But this isn't a king's command. This is a prince's greed."

DeLacey was thunderstruck by the Jew's audacity. It was true, of course, but one did not *say* so—certainly not a Jew who survived on the sufferance of others; not Abraham, who made money off Normans and Saxons, and who most certainly had more coin to spare than he admitted.

They're all like this, these Jews . . . they think God loves them more. DeLacey smoothed a wrinkle in his tunic. "You will of course carry word to the Jewish Quarter that the tax collectors will be circulating in two weeks' time. If the taxes are not met, penalties will result."

"My lord . . ." Abraham spread his hands. "You may levy all the penalties you like, but it will avail you nothing. We have given three times the normal amount. There is no more."

DeLacey bit back an angry retort. "King Richard has been most generous toward the Jews. That you would so sorely disappoint him now—"

"We disappoint only his brother, the Count of Mortain. Surely the king would admit defeat when he has drained a people dry of everything save the coin they require to live by."

This was getting him nowhere. DeLacey suppressed a scowl. It was important to put forth the impression that such intransigence meant nothing to him other than a brief inconvenience. If Prince John knew how difficult it was dealing with the Jews, he very well could appoint a new man in deLacey's place to attempt other methods. The Jews, in the end, would pay, but deLacey would not be there to enjoy it.

"Harsh times require harsh methods," he said quietly. "Perhaps if you charged a higher interest rate, the excess could be put toward the king's ransom."

"And give those who borrow even more reason to hate us." Abraham's tone was limpid. "If we could be *assured* that the taxes would be put toward the king's ransom—"

Self-control was obliterated. "Damn you for an impertinent fool!" deLacey roared, thrusting himself to his feet. "This is a royal command, not a passing whim! You will do as I say."

Abraham inclined his head. "My lord, be assured I will tell my people of the requirement. But as to their ability to pay the additional tax, I cannot say."

The sheriff leaned forward on braced arms, using the table as support in lieu of self-control. "Do not place yourself so high, Jew. You and your people are not the only ones in England being commanded in this manner. Your money is no better than anyone else's."

Abraham kept his eyes downcast. "And yet it is to us the nobility turns so very often. Coin to build castles, buy jewels, ransom kings—"

"Just *do* it!" deLacey shouted. "I'll have the money by the end of the month, or you'll surrender your silver plate!"

"My lord." Abraham bowed.

"Go," deLacey rasped. "I'm sick of the sight of you."

The Jew removed himself at once from the hall and the sheriff's offended vision.

Damn him—damn them all. . . . DeLacey plopped himself back down in his chair, rubbing wearily at burning eyes. He was tired and needed to sleep, but this business of Marian and Will Scathlocke would keep him awake until it was resolved one way or another.

"My lord?"

DeLacey squinted into the gloom. "Yes, Walter?"

Walter dipped his head briefly. "My lord, the old woman is asking for a priest."

I have no time for this—"What old woman?"

"The woman attending the Lady Marian, my lord."

Impatience was arrested. "Matilda." DeLacey nodded recognition. "We haven't got a priest."

"There is Brother Tuck—"

"He's a clerk, not a priest. He can't hear confession, or celebrate any other offices." He leaned upon an elbow braced on the arm of the chair. "Is she dying?"

Walter shrugged. "Perhaps, my lord. The women say she worsens."

DeLacey waved a dismissive hand. "Then send along Brother Tuck. If she's near to death, she'll never know the difference. We'll let him worry about it." He tapped a fingernail against the chair. "And Walter . . . have more candles put out."

"But—"

DeLacey glared, daring him to bring up Gisbourne's ridiculous edict against the profligate use of expensive and unnecessary items such as beeswax candles, which gave much cleaner light than cheaper tallow candles. Some things, he thought, were worth paying for.

Walter did not bring it up. He bowed himself out of the hall.

* * *

Will Scarlet walked the edge of the blade, very close to falling off. Distantly he heard the flutter in his ears, tasted the flat metallic tang, smelled the familiar odor he couldn't describe properly, because he didn't understand it. He knew only that the madness teased at his mind, begging to be let in, promising him victory if he gave himself up to it. He had done it before. When he'd attacked the six Normans.

Two had run away, seeing what he was. The other four had died before they realized it.

And now this man—?

He didn't know this man. A Saxon, by language and accent, certainly by color. But one of *them*, withal, by bent and temperament, forcing him to obey, to sacrifice his dignity.

—*s'what all of them want*—Flesh lay in Scarlet's hands. He caught it, gripped it, twisted his fingers in it. He heard the raspy inhalations of a constricted throat, the grunt of extremity, the hissing invectives of a man hard-pressed to live when another wanted to kill him.

He made the same noises, swore the same curses, mouthed identical threats. The effort expended matched the other's, as did the intent. Only the accent differed.

Die, Scarlet thought, thrusting a thumb toward an eye.

The old woman was dying. Brother Tuck knew it at once.

It frightened him. His place was not at the side of a dying woman in grave need of a priest, because he could not fulfill that need. His place was at the abbey, learning self-control and the responsibilities of the offices a priest was required to know, so he could *become* a priest. He wasn't prepared for this.

But there was no one else. And the woman had seen him enter the tiny chamber.

He approached hesitantly, hands folded tightly into the sleeves of his black cassock. His palms were damp and cold, not fit to touch the flesh of a woman such as this one, who deserved much better. But there was no one else, and she had so little time.

Drawing in a huge breath, Tuck moved to the side of the bed and halted there, looking down upon her face. It was eerily naked with neither wimple nor coif to hide forehead and neck, gray and glazed with sweat. Hair too was gray, trailing to her shoulders in limp disarray.

Her eyes fluttered closed. Tuck bent, pulled the stool close, then settled his bulk upon it more gracefully than one might expect. But he was accustomed to kneeling; squatting upon a stool was little different.

He withdrew his hands from his sleeves and made the sign of the cross. Softly, he chanted, *"In nomine Patris, Fili, et Spiritus Sancti—"*

Her eyes snapped open. Her voice was barely a sound. "You must hear my confession—"

Tuck broke off, lowering his hand. Indecision warred with honesty. "I am sorry, but—"

"You—must hear—" The old woman coughed painfully, clutching at her breast. "Hear me—I beg you—" She was gray, and plainly fading. In moments she would be dead, lacking the comfort of confession or last rites.

He could offer neither relief. He should tell her so at once. But.

What harm? Tuck fretted. *What harm in comforting her?*

It was a lie. It was a disservice. It was a sin.

The old woman was fat, like him. Her breathing was noisy and uneven. "My lady . . ." she gasped. "Who will see to her now? No mother, no brother, no father—" Time ran out so swiftly. "Hear my confession, I beg you—" Hands groped for his. "Please—hear me—"

Tuck caught and held her hands in his own. They were strangely dry, almost chalky, as if her skin turned to ash even as she spoke. "We will pray together," he offered; it was all he had.

Her eyes gazed blankly. "Will you hear my confession?"

Tuck bit at his lip. *What harm in it?*

"Hear me—please—"

I cannot. But Tuck squeezed her hands. What harm, indeed? If it would ease her passing . . . Wasn't it more important that a devout woman be made to feel at ease? Didn't God want people on the verge of joining Him in heaven to look toward that reward with joy? Surely He would not want the faithful to die in fear of unworthiness.

Surely God would understand.

Even if the abbot doesn't. Tuck managed to smile kindly. "Of course I will hear you." God would understand.

The old woman did. She smiled tremulously. "Forgive me——" she began.

Tuck listened in silence to her list of sins so insignificant that only a good and devout woman would consider them worthy of confession. And his sin was only half a sin, because his part in the absolution was not required. What God wanted as penance would be tended now in heaven. "Forgive *me*," he murmured, folding her lifeless hands on the coverlet.

Locksley felt the breath fade from his chest. Nothing replaced it. Hands were on his throat, shutting off air entirely.

He lay sprawled across Will Scarlet, legs twisted awry to gain balance and leverage. He had intended to drag Scarlet up from the ground so he could batter at him again, but something had gone wrong. Scarlet had caught his throat and was squeezing it dry of air, digging avid fingers and ragged nails into his flesh.

The edges of his vision turned a bloody, opaque crimson, red as Scarlet's name.

One hand clawed at Scarlet's fingers, trying to pry them free. The other bunched and struck his nose, adding blood to stubble and grime.

Scarlet roared. The hands slackened minutely. Locksley jabbed an elbow just below the ribs, then jammed a knee between splayed legs. Scarlet's bellow of pain at the offense against his nose altered instantly to outrage as something else was threatened.

Not hard enough—But enough to break the grasp on his throat. Locksley twisted, lunged aside, came up even as Scarlet did. And the dance began again, albeit bloodier than before and with less civility. Locksley staggered to his knees, then his feet, twisting his fists into Scarlet's tunic. Blood from the broken nose streamed down the stubbled chin.

Scarlet sagged, throwing his dead weight into Locksley's

arms, then he stabbed one foot against the ground as he hooked an ankle again. Locksley staggered and nearly went down, but regained his balance long enough to try the trick on Scarlet. Two stumbling, sideways steps sent them both into a bush, which gave way immediately and spilled them to the ground.

Locksley banged his opponent's head against the cushioning layers of disintegrating leaves padding the harder earth. Will Scarlet retaliated by scrabbling for a stick, which he smashed against Locksley's face. The old wood, half rotted, broke up instantly, showering bits of bark and dried-out pith.

Locksley shook it off, considering a similar action. *A rock would accomplish much*. But he didn't want to kill the man, just over-power him.

Will Scarlet reached up from the ground and caught double handfuls of wet hair. *What——?* Shouting incoherently, the murderer jerked Locksley's head toward his own, using his forehead as a weapon. The dull smack was audible.

Senses faded. Locksley was only dimly aware of Scarlet's wriggling body twisting out from under his own, tipping him over onto his side even as he attempted to move. His limbs felt heavy and awkward.

Scarlet was coughing on blood as he crawled out from under Locksley. He spat, spat again, then bent toward the ground and scooped up a rock. *"This* will do," he rasped.

The chapel at Nottingham Castle was tiny, dim, and damp. It smelled of mildew and rotting cloth, with the barest trace of stale incense and greasy tallow candles; a commingling of odors the sheriff somewhat ironically equated with sanctity. Clearly no one had cared for the chapel since the previous monk—*Hubert, wasn't it?*—had died. DeLacey seriously doubted anyone had even been in it since then, a fact a priest undoubtedly would find abhorrent.

DeLacey did not care. He was not a devout man, considering a man's faith mostly unnecessary, but most certainly his personal domain and therefore subject to no prescribed public requirements—except, of course, when religion became a tool for acquiring—or using—power.

Abbot Martin, for example—he knows a thing or two about using God for secular power. DeLacey smiled grimly, stepping just inside the chapel door. He was there not for his soul, which he considered safe enough because he paid to make certain it was, but for the newest member of his household, the monk called Tuck.

The Benedictine knelt before the sadly denuded altar in an attitude of prayer, murmuring quietly. DeLacey assumed he addressed himself to God, as well he might considering what he'd done.

The sheriff's smile lost its grimness. *All to the better, for what I'll need from him.* "Brother Tuck."

The monk's thick shoulders stiffened minutely, but he didn't break off his murmuring. As deLacey waited impatiently Tuck finished what he'd begun, then eased himself to his feet and turned to face him.

My God, the man's been crying—! DeLacey was astonished, though he maintained a bland expression. The plump, placid face with its brown bovine eyes was warped by genuine grief. *For Matilda?* She'd had her uses, certainly, with regard to Marian's welfare, but Tuck had never known her. *Unless he grieves for the loss of his innocence, a not uncommon thing for a man lacking imagination, and the wit and ambition to use it.* The sheriff smiled kindly, divulging nothing, exuding quiet admiration. "Surely God treasures a man such as you."

Tuck blotted briefly at his damp cheeks, then sighed heavily. "I am—unworthy."

"Why? Because you eat too much?"

"No." His tone was dolorous. "Because I allowed the woman to believe I was a priest. I—heard her confession."

"Ah." The sheriff nodded, commiserating mutely.

Tuck pulled at the folds of his rough-spun cassock, shoulders drooping disconsolately. "I was sent here because of my gluttony, and now I have compounded that sin with another."

"You comforted a dying woman."

Tuck nodded glumly. "So I told myself. It seemed the thing to do. She needed it so badly."

DeLacey folded his hands behind his back, relaxed and circumspect, offering compassion. "I daresay God understands.

You are a good and faithful man. You placed the comfort of a woman before yourself. That can't be a bad thing."

Tuck thrust his hands inside the heavy sleeves of his cassock. "Abbot Martin will say it is."

DeLacey permitted himself a small smile. "Abbot Martin— or martinet, as he is called—is an ascetic. Men such as he are best left to themselves, rather than the disposition of other men's futures." He spoke quietly, reasonably, without excess emotion. He judged Tuck impressionable, but sensitive; he would know when words rang false.

The young monk's fleshy face was genuinely anguished. "He will see to it I never complete my orders. As perhaps I should not—you see what I have done already."

DeLacey spoke gently, discarding even a hint of rebuke. "Punishment, if deserved, is best left to God."

Tuck's expression was troubled. "Abbot Martin believes in earthly punishment."

What Abbot Martin believes in is pleasuring himself through excess scourging of others. DeLacey shook his head. "You saw a need and served it. In good conscience, you assuaged the fear of a dying woman. Imagine the state of her soul had she died with sins unconfessed."

"So I told myself." But Tuck was patently unconvinced, trying very hard to reconcile beliefs he had been taught with those of his conscience.

DeLacey's brows rose. "Then you have the wit to understand that occasionally we must make the best of a bad situation, regardless of what may be expected, or required." The sheriff smiled warmly. "You eased an old woman's passing. No doubt there will come another time when you can assist someone in great need, even if part of you believes it should not be done."

"Yes, Lord Sheriff."

The lord sheriff laughed gently. "Ah, Brother Tuck, be not so discontent. This will pass, I promise . . . but if it comforts you, know that even Abbot Martin has been required to perform certain—duties—in answer to a greater call than the one he might prefer."

Tuck blinked. "Abbot Martin?"

"Oh yes. Even Abbot Martin. Even myself." DeLacey spread

his hands. "Life *requires* things. We do the best we can, then make our peace with God."

Sighing, Tuck nodded. "Yes, my lord—no doubt you are right."

The sheriff smiled, pleased with his work. "I am, Brother Tuck. Be assured of that."

Marian was cold, covered with gooseflesh. The fight between Robert of Locksley and Will Scarlet was abrupt, brutal, and vicious, more violent than anything she had ever seen. One man had given her no cause to anticipate humanity from him; the other had offered no reason to expect anything else. Yet both were stripped of the barest remnant, scrabbling in the leaf-powdered dirt in a primitive, visceral rite utterly alien to Marian.

Two steps back, and she stopped. She wanted to turn away, to walk away, to shut her eyes to the violence, to stop up her ears, but something wouldn't let her. She realized subconsciously she was not the prize, nor was she the cause, but merely an excuse for the battle. It would have come anyway. It *had* come anyway, in guises she recalled only as sullen mutterings, or silent but eloquent glances exchanged as the lord passed by.

This isn't over me. This is in spite of me. She chanced a glance at the giant. He gazed at the two men, the skin of his freckled face taut and shiny above the beard. The flesh near the eyes crimped as if he were in pain. Marian expected to see approval, or encouragement for Will Scarlet; the giant was, like Scarlet, peasant to Locksley's nobleman. But what she saw surprised her. The giant understood better than she what the fight was about, but he did not approve.

Then why doesn't he stop— Something touched her wrist. Marian whipped her head on her neck to gaze in panic behind her. What she saw flooded her with such powerful relief she felt her knees wobble: Much, scowling diligence, working deftly at the woolen knots.

She heard a man blurt an outcry. *Robin?* She couldn't tell at all, which frightened her very badly. *Hurry—*

They were going to kill each other.

Hurry, Much—

Slim fingers scrabbled.

Wait for him . . . don't rush— She saw little but a flurry of arms and legs, and bodies flipping over. First one man was on top, then the other was. She could not tell who was who. *Much— please—*

A pinch, a scrape, brief tautness. Then the wool was pulled away, and Marian's hands were free.

She tore at the gag, rolling it over her bottom lip, then yanked it past her chin. Instinctively she realized nothing she told the giant, nothing she screamed at Locksley or Scarlet, would have any effect at all.

Two steps to the quarterstaff, the only weapon she saw, then three to the men on the ground. The faces were indistinguishable, contorted by effort and intensity.

Shock rooted her. *He has a rock.* In a moment, he would use it to batter Locksley's face, reducing it to mush. *No time.*

She focused on the hair: Scarlet's was brown, nearly black; Locksley's was darkened by water, but not so dark as all that.

Marian knew very well what to do. *He's going to kill Robin.*

"Lass—" The giant had seen her.

I have to stop him. Marian lifted the staff.

"Lass, *no*—"

Don't think—just DO— She smashed the quarterstaff into the back of Scarlet's head.

"My God—" the giant blurted.

Marian looked down at the limp body lying sprawled across Robin's. Her words were precise. "I'm not a whore," she declared, "and I am not *Norman!*"

Twenty-Nine

Unable to move, Locksley simply *breathed,* and was grateful for the chance.

I am not dead.

Relief replaced surprise. Ragged in- and exhalations were loud in the silence, shattering the abrupt quietude. There were no further attempts by Will Scarlet to shred his flesh, to gouge out his eyes, or to batter his skull to bits. The respite was distinctly welcome, but also unexpected.

Much of him was trapped by Scarlet's unmoving bulk. The man's face was near his own, slack chin pressing limply into Locksley's tensed shoulder. He could see the closed eyes, the newly broken nose—*my doing*—the stubbled dungeon pallor vividly scribed by runnels of blood.

What did I—? But no. Nothing. That he knew. Someone else, then. *Little John—?*

No again; he recalled very clearly the giant had merely watched, letting them settle it.

Something else stirred. He knew its name: pain, the old companion of undesired familiarity. Locksley grunted breathily, trying to detach himself from unwanted acknowledgment of discomfort. Pinned, he had little recourse to movement, even to turning or raising his head. And his head ached, with no little thanks to Little John's ministrations; squinting, he peered over the mound of drab-tunicked shoulder and saw Marian standing near, quarterstaff clutched in both hands.

She was pale as Will Scarlet, and no less disreputable. Her face was mud-smeared, scratched, viciously welted, and the corners of her mouth were cut. The faint smudge of a newborn bruise stained an elegant cheekbone. A damp but drying rat's nest of black hair, yanked awry of its once-neat plait, formed a tangled tapestry on either side of her face. And the kirtle was a travesty: sodden, mud-freighted, shredded. Bare toes showed themselves in the rents of a ragged hem.

Out of blue eyes dilated black, she stared at him mutely even as he stared at her.

Recognition was abrupt, and exquisitely painful. *Oh—God—* She was, in that moment, very like her father, who had met adversity with the same determination, the same intensity, save for one blatant fact: Marian FitzWalter was unequivocally *alive.*

With limbs and head attached.

Even the expression—

"Is he dead?" she asked.

It shook him, that they could be so alike.

"Is he *dead?*" she repeated.

He wanted to shout at her, to say yes, of course he was dead; how could he *not* be dead, cut apart the way he had been? But he shouted nothing. He *said* nothing. He just looked at her, at Hugh FitzWalter's daughter, knowing she meant Will Scarlet, not her father—and realized the task was done.

Done at her own convenience . . . And Robert of Locksley laughed. It was a quiet, breathy sound, barely discernable, but laughter nonetheless, that intentions could go so awry that in the end Marian FitzWalter had the saving of him. *Expiation?* he wondered. *I fail to save the father, so the daughter saves me?*

"*Is* he?" she demanded, and he realized finally she was wholly consumed by the fear that her blow might have killed Will Scarlet.

He owed her an answer. Locksley stopped laughing. "No."

Her tone was precise. "Are you sure?"

She meant it. He heard the undertone of fear. "Yes," he told her clearly.

She relaxed minutely. He saw it in the slackening of her grip upon the staff, in the softening rigidity of her posture, in the loosening of her expression. "Thank God," she breathed.

Locksley's teeth shut tightly. *So very like her father.*

It did no good to remain pinned to the ground by the body

of his attacker, but even as he tried to heave Scarlet's body from his own, finding it difficult, Little John came forward to tend the task himself. Locksley somewhat breathlessly levered himself up to his elbows as the unconscious man was pulled aside and dropped onto his back. Scarlet's head rolled slackly.

"Alive," the giant murmured, "whether intended or no."

Marian heard him. Color rushed into her face, then ebbed again. "What do you expect?" she snapped. "After what—" But she broke it off, saying merely, "You would have done the same."

Little John, kneeling next to Scarlet, twisted his head to look at her. He said nothing a moment, then nodded slightly. His tone was subdued. "Aye, lass. So I would."

She nodded back once decisively, then looked at Locksley. A brief, odd expression crossed her face and was lost as she moved. She knelt to drop the quarterstaff, then came to stand at his side. "You're hurt."

He was, but forbore to agree. Instead, he pulled himself into a squatting position preparatory to rising, caught his breath between clamped teeth, and completed the motion. Once standing he wished he had not chanced it, wishing instead he'd stayed where he was, but it was done, and he preferred not to have her playing hen to his chick. It reminded him of his mother, and of childhood memories best left unrecalled.

Marian fruitlessly tried to put into order the tattered ruins of her kirtle. "Have you horses?"

Her hesitancy was at odds with the decisive way she had disposed of Will Scarlet but moments before. It underscored a vulnerability he had not marked until now.

Laggardly he admitted it, because she deserved the truth: she was not her father.

He stared at Marian. She was the same, exactly the same, standing before him with swollen hands working at wool, saying nothing, not even repeating her question, merely gazing back at him mutely, her face all scratched and filthy, her hair a tangled mass, her kirtle torn and muddied. *Not—her father.*

She was exactly the same. She was entirely different.

The recognition was painful. It altered his view of her. It peeled back the layers he had applied of his own volition, of his own need, so as to look upon the woman without losing control. Such things were precarious. Such things were dangerous. *She* was dangerous.

He knew it instinctively, reacting as beast, not man. Intellect failed him. Logic was nonexistent. The first trebuchet stone had smashed against the wall he had so painstakingly constructed around heart and soul to escape captivity, shattering the first layer into thousands of powdered fragments. *I—can't.*

He gestured sharply, recalling her question of horses. It was best they leave at once, if for no other reason than to occupy his thoughts. "We'll go now."

Nodding, Marian began self-consciously to loosen the tangles in her hair. "Where is—?" She turned, searched intently, then wearily peeled a strand of hair from her eyes. "Gone," she murmured, sighing. "I should have expected it."

Locksley mimicked her search. "The boy," he said, comprehending.

"He untied me . . . and now he's gone." Marian smiled fleetingly, rubbing at her left wrist. "Much is—different."

He was, but Locksley had no time to discuss it. He glanced at Little John. "I'm taking her back. Have you an objection?"

The giant rose. His hands hung slack at his sides. His expression was a mixture of futility and bleak acknowledgment. "Go," he said roughly. "I'll tend him; he did what he thought he had to, be it wrong or right."

Locksley held himself stiffly so as not to disturb his head. "You need not stay here. I will tell the sheriff the truth." He felt more than saw Marian's twitch of surprise as she looked at him.

Little John's hands rose, then dropped to his side. " 'Tis done."

"Is it?"

The giant nodded. "Tell the lord high sheriff whatever you will. If he listens, I'll be grateful. If not—well . . ." He shrugged. "I'm a peasant, after all."

Locksley smiled faintly. "I'll see to it he knows the truth. My word as—" He checked.

"As what?" Little John asked roughly. "A nobleman?"

"As victim," Locksley told him finally, fingering the lump on his head.

The Hathersage Giant laughed, then flapped a wide hand at them both. "Go on, then. Take the lass with you. Will Scarlet will be thinking of other things when he rouses from the tap she gave him." And then, more seriously, to Marian: " 'Tisn't worth much, I know—but he didn't know you were Saxon." Color flared in his bearded face. "Neither did I."

In place of expected bitterness, Locksley heard self-possession. "I would have told you," she answered evenly. "Had either of you asked."

Shrouded by foliage, Much knelt in silence. He watched and listened. It was done. It was right. His world was a world again, with the princess free of danger. The bad man was overcome, the giant penitent, and the heroic prince had shown himself at last.

The prince's name was *Robin*.

Much nodded mutely; his part in the work was done. He turned quietly, intending to go, and felt again the stiff bundle of leather tucked into his hosen. He pulled it free of his tunic, turning it over in his hands.

Shoes.

She still lacked shoes.

Troubled, Much rubbed at his face. She *had* to have shoes.

He turned back, squatting again, to peer through the shielding leaves. If she were there— But she wasn't. The prince had taken the princess with him, leaving the giant behind with the bad man.

Scowling, Much chewed a lip. She *had* to have shoes.

His work wasn't done after all.

Robin was, Marian saw, wetter even than she. She wanted to ask him how that had come to be, but forbore. Something about him, a tight-wound privacy, kept her from it. That he was hurt, she knew, though not how badly, because he took care to carry himself as normally as possible. His throat was abraded and beginning to discolor, and his face bore the marks of

305

fisticuffs and fingernails, along with other affronts. *Men*, she reflected, thinking of her father, *put pride before pain too often.*

He led her through the forest, bending aside limbs and greenery so she could pass unmolested. She found it vaguely amusing in view of the circumstances: her clothing was muddy, wet, and torn; her hair was disheveled; and, from the sting of scratches and welts, her face little better. She was altogether a mess, yet he treated her as if she wore the finest of imported silk.

"Hurry," he said curtly.

It rankled. *Does he think I mean to delay us?* Scowling, she dragged up her kirtle, baring bruised, filthy ankles. She wanted to protest aloud, if with more decorum than her thoughts expressed; to suggest they go more slowly merely so she could catch her breath, but something about his urgent intensity kept her from it.

Brambles caught at her kirtle, snagging the damp cloth. Roots tangled her feet, bruising her toes. Trailing creepers and branches insinuated themselves into her hair. Her right knee twinged with every step she took. Exertion was a flame in her chest. She needed to sit down somewhere and rest, to be still of her own volition, with hands unbound and mouth ungagged; just to sit and be quiet, savoring freedom—

"Hurry," he said again, three paces ahead.

Self-control snapped. "I *am* hurry—" But it was cut off as she tripped awkwardly, landing hard on her hands and knees. Her hair straggled in the dirt as she inhaled raggedly, tasting blood in her mouth. *If he will just give me a moment—*

"Here." He reached down and caught an arm. "There is no time." He hauled her up like a butchered hog, steadied her impatiently, then released her. Marian, disgruntled, scraped the hair back from her face determinedly and tried not to show how exhausted she was. "You said the horses were close."

"Horse," he said precisely.

Then she understood. *"One* horse?"

"One."

Suspicion bloomed. "And? Is there something else?"

Guilt flickered briefly. "As to closeness . . ."

"Yes?"

"I—lied."

She nearly gaped like a lackwit. "Lied?" It was incomprehensible.

He was grim, almost rude, evoking the man she had met on the dais of Huntington Castle. "We have a single horse, not two . . . and at some distance from here."

"But . . ." She knew even as she spoke there was no sense in protesting, or questioning his methods. The look in his eye forbade it. "Well," she said finally, resolving with effort to hold her peace no matter what the cost, "we should not tarry here."

The faintest trace of a smile softened his mouth a moment, then faded instantly. "No. But there is some question as to your ability."

"Is there?" She arched both brows. "As much to mine as there is to yours? We both of us battled Will Scarlet."

The smile returned briefly. Something kindled in his eyes, burning unexpectedly bright. "FitzWalter blood," he murmured.

It took her breath away, the intensity of his gaze. She had seen it before, just prior to their departure. It sowed confusion and reaped a strange restlessness. But she would not let him see it. "Indeed," she managed ironically, lifting a hand to touch her face. "But I assure you, it washes off."

It stilled him. "I didn't mean . . ." But he let it go, as if to finish what he'd begun would divulge too much. "We have to go on."

"I know," she agreed, "but it's nearly dark now. How far *is* it to the horse?"

He glanced into the shadows. "Too far," he said grimly. "We risk losing the track—"

The answer was obvious, but Marian knew he wouldn't propose it. He wouldn't speak of it at all, or even imply what she knew to be the issue. Such things lay within the purview of women, and within the wardship of the men reared up to protect them. *So, it falls to me.* It was not insignificant. But she saw no other resolution. "Then we had best stay here."

He turned back to her sharply. "What?"

She held her tone steady. "We had best stay here."

A damp lock of hair fell beside an eyebrow. "Through the night." Not so much a question as tactful disbelief.

"Till dawn," Marian said. "When there is light to see by, we'll find the track, and the horse."

His face was battered as her own, though with new bruises in place of welts, but she saw past the transitory mask to the more permanent one he had constructed himself. The edges of it were fraying like brittle, decaying parchment. "I can't let you—"

"You can, and you will," she said firmly. "My behavior and decisions are no more governed by you than by the sheriff."

The mask remained impenetrable. Then it slipped minutely, displaying perhaps more than he wished to, even as eyes glinted in faint amusement. Dryly he suggested, "William deLacey will be somewhat discomfited to hear of your reasoning."

She dared it finally, in the context of the issue, because it gave her the chance to address the other issue, the thing she felt beginning. "Are you?"

"I am—surprised." He side-stepped it entirely, circumventing the dance. "A woman is so careful of proprieties."

"I think such things are not as important as the preservation of our lives."

He was quietly skeptical. "Few women would agree."

Eleanor deLacey might. "Few women have been hauled off into the depths of Sherwood Forest by a condemned murderer," she retorted. "It gives me some measure of perspective."

His frown was nearly imperceptible as he evaluated her conviction. "I think perhaps you underestimate the repercussions—"

"I underestimate nothing." The light of sunset dimmed, casting wan amber light across one scraped cheekbone stained dark by the Holy Land's sun. He was aging gold and tarnished silver in the day's fading luminescence. "What you so gallantly refuse to speak of, relying on assumption, is the state of my reputation."

Above the scraped cheek, a tiny muscle twitched.

I am become like Eleanor, though not by my design. Marian drew in a breath. "I thank you for your concern, but I believe there is no place left, *now,* in my life for such things as reputation. They will think what they like to think. They will believe as they wish to believe. It is what people *do.*" She shrugged, aware of regret

308

even as she condemned those who would condemn her. "Nothing I say will change it."

His tone was rusty. "There is no need to bury yourself just yet."

It was a bone, which she accepted because to ignore it or dismiss it was discourteous. He meant only to help, to offer a shred of decency, though all now was banished. "Of course not. You will take me back to Ravenskeep—"

He interrupted. "I meant to take you to Nottingham."

It was completely unexpected. "To the sheriff? After what I told you?" She didn't know why, but it hurt. "I beg you, take me instead to Ravenskeep."

A drop of water from still-wet hair trickled down his temple. "He will expect me to bring you to him."

Marian's teeth clenched. "He may expect whatever he likes. I am neither his wife, nor his ward, nor his daughter." She swallowed heavily, aware of newborn pain where she had expected none. "That misconception has already cost me dearly . . . would you have me pay more yet?"

His face was white and taut, donning the favored mask. For a moment only the eyes were alive, burning in the angles and hollows of a face thrown into relief by the play of light and shadow. She thought he would withdraw, saying nothing, making no effort at all. But she was wrong.

He reached out his hand. In disbelief she saw the fingers tremble, if minutely, and then still. He waited.

She thought of her father's hand, so often outstretched to her. *But he is not my father.*

"This way," he said, as her fingers touched his own. "The track is not much farther, if I recall it right. We will go at least that far—"

"There is no need." She offered escape because she knew without knowing why that she needed it herself. "I told you, it doesn't matter—"

The grip on her hand tightened, banishing retreat as much as misunderstanding. "There *is* need," he declared harshly, fervent as a zealot.

It struck her dumb. She stared at him, marking the starkness in expression; the bleakness in his hazel eyes. Comprehension was abrupt. *It isn't for me he does this. He does this for—himself?*

"This way," he said.

Marian let him lead her.

Thirty

Little John squatted beside Will Scarlet's unconscious body. Fading daylight no longer was softly suggestive. Sherwood Forest assumed the lurid guise of a full-blown seductress promising darkness soon, thick and damp and impenetrable, with no taste for subtlety. The warmth of a spring day was usurped by evening's chill.

He felt poor in spirit and sick at heart. Only a matter of hours before he had stood in the wrestling ring at Nottingham Fair taking on all comers, luring would-be opponents, jesting with passersby, simply going about the business of upholding his reputation as the undefeated Hathersage Giant. Once the fair was over he'd intended, as always, to return to his sheep, leaving behind the encumbrances of less satisfying toil.

"Doesn't have to be different," he murmured, digging thick fingers into his ruddy beard to tame an annoying itch. "If Robin goes to the sheriff and speaks for me—"

But Will Scarlet's words came back, shaped in the fires of hatred, saying Little John was an outlaw now, a man with no future. He owned only his name, if Scarlet were right, and he was fair game for any who caught him for the price upon his head. That there was as yet no price upon that head did not matter; it would take but a moment for the sheriff to learn the red-haired giant had aided Will Scarlet, and to declare his capture worth the same as a wolf's bounty: he would become, summarily, another Saxon "wolf's-head," a proscribed man without recourse to the protection of English—or Norman— laws.

He looked harshly on Will Scarlet. The man lay slackly against the ground, ankles tipped outward. His feet were partially bare, wrapped in leather scraps and woolen bindings. He was altogether filthy, stinking of the dungeon, with ropes of sinew corroding the skin in place of well-fed flesh. His face was the worst of all, forming sinkholes at cheeks and eye-sockets, with a crusted coverlet of blood, stubble, and grime.

"Wolf's-head," Little John muttered. "What becomes of *you* now?"

The voice came from nearby foliage. "Depending on disposition, he may be joining *us.*"

Startled half out of his head, Little John reached to snatch up the quarterstaff Marian had let fall and lurched upright hastily, dropping into readiness. "Come out!" he roared, using sheer volume to compensate for the regrettable fright to which he would rather not admit. "I'll not be fighting shadows when there's a man behind it all."

Silence. Then, "Peace," the voice urged, sounding amused. "You'll be fighting no one. I've archers with me—can you ward off an arrow with naught but a quarterstaff?"

Little John could not, but did not relax his vigilance. "Come out of there and prove it."

Again, silence. Then three men stepped out of the shadows. Two of them indeed held bows at the ready, cloth-yard arrows nocked. They wore dark, unremarkable clothing fit for a proper peasant: tunics bound with leather belts, hosen upon their legs, crude leather boots. Entirely unremarkable in attire as well as expression, lowborn Englishmen very far from a proper village, and therefore tending to business likely other than lawful.

The man who wore a meat-knife at his belt also had a longbow hooked over his back, and a quiver. He crossed wool-clad arms nonchalantly and grinned at Little John. "What brings you into our home?"

Little John adjusted grip and stance, wary of a rearguard attack. "Your home?"

"Sherwood Forest. 'Twasn't our first choice—we had true homes, once, till the Normans hounded us from them—but it serves us well enough now." He glanced briefly at Will Scarlet. "You called him a wolf's-head. Why?"

" 'Tis what he is." Little John tried in vain to hear if anyone approached from behind without leaving his front vulnerable. "Meant to hang at the sheriff's word."

The expression on the man's face did not alter. "Then why didn't he?"

I need a diversion. Little John wet his lips. "A long story," he declared. "Worth telling over ale."

"Ah, but we have none here." The unarmed man was dark as a Welshman, slight, and quietly alert. His light brown eyes and quick movements put Little John in mind of a fox. "What we have here is ourselves, and a yearning to know the truth. You've come to *our* home . . . why have you left yours?"

Maybe later, not now . . . Little John sighed. He told them as much as he knew of himself; as little of Will Scarlet, whom he knew not at all save by reputation.

It was enough for the others. The dark man nodded. "Not so different a story from others we've heard." He made a slight gesture and bow strings were slackened. "My two friends are Clym of the Clough, and William of Cloudisley. My name is Adam Bell."

Little John started. "Adam Bell—? But—*I've* heard of you. You're outlaws. Wanted men."

The archers traded glances. "Wolf's-heads," Adam Bell said lightly. "Once we were naught but peasants. Now we're kings in Sherwood Forest, feasting on the Lionheart's deer."

Little John looked at the other two: sandy-haired Clym of the Clough, with a squint in one blue eye and a small finger missing; and dark-maned William of Cloudisley, much younger than the others, smiling sweetly as a girl.

From the ground Will Scarlet stirred, coughing and spitting. "Kings, are you?" he rasped. "I see no jewels or coin."

Two bows rose, two arrows were nocked. Adam Bell merely shrugged. "We're not fools, are we, to weigh ourselves down while hunting?"

"Hunting what?" Scarlet asked. "Me for the price on my head?"

Adam Bell grinned. "You but newly outlawed? Don't flatter yourself. I'm a sight older than you, and worth more than that. Oh, I don't say we haven't sold men before, but only if they prove unwilling."

It made Little John wary. "Unwilling?"

"Aye." Bell hitched a shoulder. "It costs to cross our land."

Little John nodded once, understanding all too well. "And if we have no coin?"

"Better men than you have tried that gambit." Bell glanced briefly at his companions. "We don't ask much. Pittance, no more. Enough to buy Cloudisley's wife a pretty trinket."

Sweet-smiling William of Cloudisley nodded. "I'm bound for Carlisle in two days. A ribbon'll do her fine."

Scarlet sat up slowly, gingerly feeling his nose. "I've naught," he said flatly. "I had naught *before* the sheriff; d'ye think he gave me a penny for guesting in his dungeon?"

Adam Bell merely shrugged. "Then you'll be stealing it."

Marian stood in the clearing, head tipped back onto sore shoulders as she watched the moon climb above treetops. Better than half a moon, but not yet full. Its light glowed silver-gilt, painting trunks and branches and leaves, creeping steadily lower to trespass across the ground. *I wish*—But she broke it off, refusing to speak it even in her mind.

Marian hugged herself hard, hands clasping elbows, aware of a brittle, unwanted fragility usurping the resolution she had relied on throughout the day. She had not, in her time with Will Scarlet, foreseen what might happen, nor had she allowed herself even to contemplate it, to waste her will on too-vivid imaginings that had plagued her since childhood. She had been wholly consumed by the acknowledgment of captivity and the need for escape. She had forbidden her thoughts to go further.

Now she stood beneath a moon-washed sky, duly rescued from crazed Will Scarlet, whose wife had been raped to death, and thought instead of the moment in which she lived and of the night that lay before her.

313

A single night, no more, and yet it reeked of one hundred endings, in spirit if not in life; in the future, if not the present. One night only—spent unattended by a woman while in the company of a man—would forever destroy her chance for a normal, circumspect life ignorant of disasters such as Scarlet's impetuous act.

This must be what it was to William deLacey, knowing his careful plans for Eleanor utterly destroyed in but a moment's feckless pleasure . . . I could not see it, could not begin to understand it. She did not condone his methods; they had nearly maimed a man innocent of the crime. But now she could comprehend.

Marian bit into her bottom lip. *I would rather not comprehend.* But it was done, and she did. All too well. Innocence was banished, vanquished by the new reality Will Scarlet had created.

She had no choice, of course. To go farther was to risk getting lost or worse, falling prey to the human beasts who stalked others in Sherwood's shadows. They halted now because they had to.

Marian recalled Locksley's earlier concern for proprieties. She had told him the truth as she saw it: the preservation of her life *was* more important than the preservation of her reputation. But her life, now, was changed, its path to lifelong security obliterated by Will Scarlet's bid for freedom.

Nonetheless, for all her blithe dismissal of his concern, the considerations he had raised were real. Then, she had dismissed them. Now she could not. They had stopped for the night. Now it stood before her, freed by a heartless darkness, like a beast born of childhood nightmare.

I wish my father were here. There. It was said.

She would not complain; there was no room for complaint. She would not speak of it, either, even in passing; Locksley—*Robin*—would undoubtedly blame himself for failing to find her sooner, in the daylight, when the sun diminished taint, and the whisper of dishonor. For his sake, not her own, because instinct told her it mattered, she would keep her mouth closed on anguish, on apprehension, and deal with it privately.

Marian shut her eyes. *Let me be strong enough.*

Sound intruded. Robin, with only a meat-knife, cut tender, leafy branches, intending to make her a bed.

Marian sighed carefully, so he would not hear. She was damp, aching, hungry, and weary to the bone. Her eyes burned. *I'll never sleep tonight, no matter how good the bedding. I'm wet and cold, and my head is too full of things. . . .* But she did not tell him that. It would be rude and tactless in the midst of his work, and she very much desired not to task him with anything more.

"It's done," he said at last.

She turned, suppressing a wince of pain as her bruised knee protested. He stood next to the pitiful mound of decaying and newborn leaves heaped to form a bed and lashed together with green sapling boughs. Moonlight was kind to his battered face, leeching it of bruises, gilding the marvelous symmetry in the clean architecture of bone: cheeks, nose, and chin, in striking chiaroscuro. The wash of hair, now dry, was bleached nearly white. She could see little of his eyes beneath the smooth arched bone of brow.

I made him kiss me, once, beneath the mistletoe.

It was a thought she banished at once, abruptly hot with shame. Saying nothing, she went to the bed he had devised and lay down upon it stiffly, settling a hip carefully as she turned onto her side. Leaves compressed. Twigs crackled. She lay very still, eyes squinched closed, jaws clenched, trying to breathe normally and hoping shadow shielded her face.

Silence.

"Well?" he asked at last. "It would be better with a cloak thrown over it, but we have none. I left it with the horse."

She smelled dampness, sap, and earth. She would not tell him the truth: even a cloak over the bedding would offer her little comfort. "It will do," she said quietly, tucking a leaf down from her mouth.

He nodded. "Get up."

"But I only just—"

"Please."

She got up, as requested, picking leaves and twigs from her hair and kirtle. Mutely she watched as he lay down in her place, testing the bed.

He was silent. Then, with infinite irony, "You are polite."

She clasped hands in her kirtle demurely. "My father taught me to be so."

"Did your father also teach you to lie?"

Surprised, she made no immediate answer. Then she grinned slowly, delighted by the tone. Urgency was banished, as was the mask. It pleased her immeasurably. "I learned that for myself."

He did not move, and yet twigs cracked. "This is the most uncomfortable bed I have ever set head upon."

"Yes," she agreed, laughing.

"And that includes the hard ground of the Holy Land, where the sand comes alive at night to creep between toes and eyelids." He sat up, shaking back hair made lucent by the moon. "A poor night, I fear, with neither of us sleeping."

Now she could tell him the truth. "I am too weary to sleep. My head is—too busy."

Locksley nodded, irony gone. "It makes the nights very long." He rose, saying nothing more, but she wondered what kind of nights they had been, so far and so different from England.

She wanted to say something. Anything. She wanted to hear him speak. So she asked a simple question she thought most appropriate. "Did you see Jerusalem?"

Utter immobility. Robert of Locksley was stone.

"Forgive me," she blurted, alarmed. "If I said something wrong . . . I didn't mean . . . I'm sorry—" She made it worse by repeated protestations, so she cut them off abruptly. Humiliated, she fell into awkward silence.

The mask replaced the face. Marian saw nothing in the flesh, nothing at all in the eyes, that told her he was alive. Even his voice was dead. "I did not see Jerusalem."

Hands linked behind his back, William deLacey paced the length of the hall with an eye toward finding fault. There was none. Walter had done precisely as he asked. Candles of good quality filled even the corners with light.

He paused near the screen dividing the kitchens from the hall and turned to look at the dais beyond the fire trench. "Better," he murmured. "Much better."

A man came to stand nearby, mail glinting dully. "My lord." It was Archambault, the castellan, garbed in the sheriff's blue livery.

DeLacey spared him a brief glance, continuing his meticulous assessment of the hall. He nodded thoughtfully, then began the slow walk back to the dais. A slight gesture indicated Archaumbault was to follow.

The sheriff said nothing as he walked, paying no attention to the soldier who paced abreast. He waited until he had reached the dais, climbed it, then sat down in his great chair. Like a cat, deLacey stretched, then gestured briefly with a single finger.

"My lord." The veteran soldier inclined his head slightly. "I am resolved once morning comes that we shall locate this Scarlet very soon—"

"Morning?" deLacey inquired, cutting off the preamble with delicate precision. "Then you have not found them."

Archaumbault hesitated only an instant, then continued steadfastly. "Not as yet, my lord, but—"

"Evening has fallen, yet Will Scarlet still roams free with the Lady Marian?"

Archaumbault, comprehending his lord's mood at last, had the grace to blanch. Then he fell silent.

"Ah." DeLacey nodded. "I see you understand."

Archaumbault tried again. "In the morning we will return again to the forest—"

"And discover—what?" The sheriff leaned forward intently. "Do tell me, Archaumbault . . . what exactly will you discover?"

"My lord, the outlaw—"

"And the Lady Marian?"

"—and the lady, yes, of course . . . the Lady Marian—"

DeLacey's voice whip-cracked. "In what *state*, Archaumbault?"

Archaumbault drew in a deep breath. "As to the lady's state, we will of course take every precaution to protect her—"

DeLacey clutched the arms of the chair. "From what, Archaumbault? What is there *left* to protect the lady from? By morning, every outlaw in Sherwood may well have been beneath her skirts!"

It echoed in the hall. Archaumbault opened his mouth, shut it, then made the attempt. "Lord Sheriff, if our prayers are answered—"

"I've never known a man yet who was held from pleasure by *prayers.*"

Archaumbault's voice was low. "No, my lord."

I doubt Archaumbault himself was ever held from pleasure by a woman's prayers. DeLacey sat back again. He assessed his castellan. *He has no imagination, which makes him a poor conniver, but a better soldier, withal. And I still need him.* "She is special to me, Archaumbault. Her father, Sir Hugh, and I were very good friends." He arched one brow. "Do you know what it is like to live with the knowledge that because you failed your duty, a beautiful young woman's life has been destroyed?"

The skin of Archaumbault's face was pulled taut over bones. "If they don't kill her—"

"She will likely kill herself."

Archaumbault crossed himself. "God forbid such a sin, my lord—"

"Yes, yes." DeLacey waved a dismissive hand. "God forbid, indeed . . . nonetheless, there is an alternative."

Archaumbault considered it, then nodded. "The Church, my lord."

"Indeed. But if she turns to the Church . . ." He chewed thoughtfully at his lip, letting the sentence die. *If she turns to the Church, her lands go with her.* DeLacey smiled grimly. "If she turned to the Church, she gives up that which is most precious to a woman like Lady Marian. Freedom, Archaumbault." He exuded sincerity. "No. That would be travesty. I think it is for me to care for the daughter of my dearest friend in the moment of greatest need." He smiled warmly. "Find her, Archaumbault, and bring her here to me. No matter what she may say, bring her here to me."

"My lord, she may wish first—"

"She will be understandably devastated, Archaumbault, as a lady of gentle birth has every right to be. Certainly my daughter has suffered from a similar happenstance." DeLacey smiled sadly. "I have had some experience with this unfortunate circumstance. Bring her here, Archaumbault . . . I will tend her welfare as her father would desire it."

"Yes, my lord."

The sheriff waved his hand. The soldier bowed briefly, then turned and departed the hall, mail glittering.

DeLacey slumped back again. *"Here,"* he repeated softly, "where I can impress upon her the magnitude of disgrace that befalls a despoiled woman." He rubbed thoughtfully at his lip. "And then comfort her most tenderly in the nadir of her pain."

Marian had, by the simple act of asking an innocent question, conjured memory again. Locksley found himself unexpectedly vulnerable, trapped in recollection.

"Forgive me," she blurted, clearly alarmed by his withdrawal, the rigidity of the features he had trained to ward his soul. "If I said something wrong . . . I didn't mean . . . I'm sorry—" She broke it off at last, letting the silence be loud between them.

She had not meant it. She was sorry. And he knew it. But it was fresh all over again, reawakened here in England: the sun, the heat, the sand; and the stink of newly spilled blood undiscerning of its origins in Saracen flesh or Christian.

Or even in his own.

The shame and guilt were renewed. It was all he could do not to shout. "I did not see Jerusalem."

Her face was pale beneath dirt and welts and bruises. "It is private," she managed tightly.

"Yes." It was all *he* could manage.

Marian nodded stiffly, eyes fixed hard on the ground, and made her way in silence two steps past him to the rude bed he had fashioned from leaves and boughs. It was horribly uncomfortable, even for all his effort, but he sensed she would lie on it to punish herself for her tactlessness.

She had every right to ask, and he every right not to answer.

Marian lay down once again, making no effort to be comfortable. He watched her a moment, knowing he had hurt her without knowing why; knowing also she deserved more than to see his private pain, but he had nothing else to give, save the truth of experience, and that was most painful of all.

She lay on her back, very still, eyes closed. He doubted she would sleep. He knew he would not.

He turned away and sought his own place nearby, sitting down at the base of a tree with his back against the trunk. Two paces separated their bodies. Much more than that their minds.

She should know. But he could not tell her.

Above all *she* should know, yet to tell her the whole of it would give her unbearable pain. *Tell her only a part.* But he shied away from that, aware of his own pain, that he himself could not bear. *Who do you protect? Marian—or yourself?*

Conscience spoke again. *Someone should be told.*

Someone *had* been told. But Richard now lay in a dungeon— or did they treat him better than that, knowing him for a king?

He looked again at FitzWalter's daughter lying stiffly on the ground, ill-cushioned by his attempt to make her comfortable. The father's voice was loud in the battered chamber of his skull. *And please to tell her, I pray you, how very much I love her.*

"Robin." Her voice was soft. "I have a right to know."

Robin. Like his mother. But Marian FitzWalter was not and never could be anything like his mother.

Nor was it his mother he wanted, looking across the two short paces to the woman in the darkness with moonlight's wealth upon her face.

Arousal, unknown so long, locked away where it could not invite abuse, was painfully abrupt. The intensity made him breathless. "No—" She would misunderstand, of course, thinking he denied her; and he did, in his own way, though for a far different reason from the refusal to tell her the truth of her father's death. He denied her on both counts, in speech and in carnal congress, or even the contemplation, because to allow himself the freedom to consider the repercussions of either would result in complete loss of self-control: emotionally, physically, spiritually.

No, he told himself, and beat at desire with words, though none of them aloud. Self-contempt warred with self-hatred, conquering a traitorous body too long denied release, too weak to insist upon it when faced with determination honed by the enemy.

Locksley gritted his teeth. What would the father say to know the man in whose place he died desired to lie with his daughter?

What would Richard say?

Thirty-One

Will Scarlet lay flat on his back, staring up at the leaf-screened night sky. Through the latticework of limbs he saw the stars, the moon, and his future. *Meggie,* he mourned, *'tisn't what we wanted. 'Tisn't what we planned.*

But there was nothing for it. Too much had simply *happened* to change his life forever. He was what he had been made by those who thought themselves better, but the time for change had come, albeit harshly and painfully. No more was he compliant. No more was he respectful in the face of unfair treatment. It was *his* turn now to shape what he would be.

Thief, he said in silence, seeing how it felt.

Emptiness answered him.

Not what he had wanted. Not what he had planned. The worm of shame was painful, eating its way into his spirit.

He drew in a heavy breath and blew it out again, hearing it hiss through swollen lips. His head felt packed and thick, his front teeth loose, and his offended nose enormous.

Sudden tears at the back of his throat made it hard to swallow. *I wish you were here, my Meggie. By God, I wish you were.*

But Meggie was gone forever.

* * *

Marian drew in a trembling breath, suppressing the desire to shout at Robert of Locksley. He was not the only one who grieved, who knew the pain and confusion of loss and sudden change. *I shouldn't be angry with him.* Yet another part asked, *Why not?*

Evenly, she repeated, "I have the right to know."

"He's dead," Locksley said roughly. "Is that not enough?"

It was, but she continued anyway because she had to know. Because she wanted to make him speak, to share with her the knowledge that drove him so mercilessly. "You said he died in your place."

Colorlessly, "Yes."

"That the Saracens had caught you."

"Yes. So I said."

Marian shut her eyes tightly, aware she walked the precipice of her own design. "Men say things . . . *people* say things, dependent upon their own vision of what is right. Even if what they recall is different from the truth." She hoped it was enough, without being too much.

His first words divulged he understood her completely, even her intent. Even the suggestion, couched in subtlety. "I failed him. He died."

No more than that. No extended excuses, no pleas for understanding, no cry for forgiveness from the dead man's daughter.

Five simple words. Because of the first three, her father was dead.

She expected the pain to renew itself, the intensity of grief to overpower her.

Quietly, she said, "Men die in war. My father knew that very well; he said it often enough, when I asked him if he'd come back." She did not look at him but lay very still, staring dry-eyed at the sky. "He was a knight all my life. Each time he rode away—when I was old enough—I asked him to come back. He said if he could, he would."

Locksley was mute.

"Men die," she repeated. "I miss him, I mourn him—I would give anything to have him back again—but how can I blame myself because *I* wasn't enough to make him stay behind?" She paused. "How can you blame yourself for being

322

more fortunate than he? You lived, he died. Short of dealing the deathblow yourself, what can you blame yourself *for?*"

His voice was rusty. "You are not a priest."

"And therefore I cannot perform a formal absolution?" Were it not so poignant, Marian would have laughed. "But that is why you came. The sheriff didn't send you—he wouldn't; you're a threat, and he's embarrassed and humiliated by Eleanor's behavior, which he believes cost him a match with the Earl of Huntington's son." It was obvious to her, every bit of it; it occurred to her, but only in passing, to wonder why it mattered, and why she cared so *much* that he be freed of self-contempt. "No, you came for another reason. You came to expunge your guilt, and to petition a different source, a far more appropriate source, for the absolution you require." She drew in a steadying breath. "Were I not FitzWalter's daughter, you would still be in Nottingham."

A noisy silence. Then, "Don't," he said, by way of admission.

I have to make him see. Marian was unrelenting. "I forgive you, Robert of Locksley. I absolve you of it. And I, not a priest, am the only one who can."

When he made no answer, she looked at him. His face divulged nothing because it was hidden from her, pressed against upraised knees with hands splayed across his bowed head.

It hurt very badly to see it. "Don't," she whispered raggedly, echoing his own plea.

At last, he lifted his head. The mask had shattered utterly, betraying the inner turmoil, the boy behind the man, so vulnerable in his pain. "It—was bearable," he said. "Bearable, because it had to be, because a man grows *accustomed*—he must, if he is to live." His face was ravaged. "Death is death, no more; a body is nothing but that, meat rotting on the ground. Because if you think about it—if you allow it into your sleep . . ." He drew in a deep breath. "It was bearable. It was *forgotten,* in the first days after my capture . . . I spared no thought for him, because all I could think of was *me,* the white-haired pet of the Lionheart—" he broke it off stiffly, thumping his head against the tree as shoulders slackened. "When I thought of it again, I could not *stop* thinking of it. He was more than a dead man.

More than a body. More than a piece of meat rotting on the ground. He had given me a *task*—he had told me of his daughter, and his hopes for that daughter, and his plans for that daughter . . . don't you see? He made me see the man, not the knight. He made me see the *father*. . . ." He shivered once, in the cold, still damp from his fight with the giant. "And I came back at last, came *home*—and there she was. Sir Hugh FitzWalter's daughter, standing there before me, *breathing* there before me, not dead, but so *alive* . . . the last remnant of the man who died at Richard's side, because I wasn't in my place. Because *I* had failed my duty."

Tears ran down her face as she bit into her lip.

"You are very like your father. You don't know—you *can't* know—what it was like . . . to see you standing before me, all ignorant of the message—to see you, and *not* see you, but to see him instead, that moment before they killed him."

Marian shut her eyes.

It was entirely unexpected. "He said to tell you he loved you."

Now she stared, uncomprehending.

"I couldn't say it," he declared. "I was meant to—I was charged to . . . but—" He scraped his rigid hands through his hair. His spirit seemed very weary. "There has been much of late I have been unable to say. To my father, to the others—" He sighed. "To anyone at all."

"But mostly to yourself."

He looked at her. His face was stark in the moonlight, white where it touched, black where it did not. Then he turned his head, shutting himself away, and she knew, without knowing why, he was building his wall again, bit by desperate bit, trying to ward away the accuracy of her vision.

Marian stared up at the stars, very certain of herself. *Then I'll have to tear it down.*

"It's not right," Little John's disembodied voice announced from out of the darkness. Unlike Scarlet he did not feign sleep, but sat against a tree a pace or two away. Even in dim light, his huddled form loomed hugely.

Scarlet didn't answer. *What else am I to do? Let Adam Bell and the others shoot me full of arrows?*

"Not right," Little John repeated. "I'm a shepherd, not a thief."

Shame renewed itself. The knowledge made Scarlet angry, because while he tried to come to terms with a new and unlawful future fraught with hardship and danger, the giant remained stolidly convinced *he* was not involved. Peasant he might be, but as certain of his place as the sheriff was of his.

It was frustrating. Adam Bell and his two men were only paces away themselves, talking quietly in the darkness, but undoubtedly aware of the giant's intransigence, which might, Scarlet felt, reflect poorly on his own intentions. Therefore he spoke for their benefit as much as for his own. "What is it to you, if you take for yourself what another has gained unfairly?"

Little John's contempt was plain. "And if it was me, then? Would you steal the coin from me?"

Scarlet laughed mutely, ignoring the pain of his nose and battered face. "What man alive would dare to steal from you?"

Little John's tone was sharp. "I'm not meaning that. What I mean is, what if the man you mean to steal from is no richer than you are? What if he's a peasant owing taxes to the sheriff—"

"Doesn't matter," Scarlet cut in, disliking the giant's direction. It made him think. It made him aware that although he had suffered, others might suffer yet from what he would do.

"It should," Little John growled. " 'Tis hard enough to scrape together the coin to pay the taxes, and then you want to be stealing it from us. Better to steal from the sheriff."

Will Scarlet scoffed. "Who could manage that? You? Even *you'd* stand no chance against a crossbow."

Little John broke in two the stick he held. "Then steal it from Norman lords."

Adam Bell's voice came clearly through the darkness. "Merchants are easier."

"And Jews," Cloudisley added.

Clym of the Clough laughed. "There are the priests, too."

Little John sounded horrified. "You rob priests?"

"Why not?" Bell asked. "They steal from us, don't they? They make themselves rich off of us."

Scarlet felt at his nose. "Doesn't matter, does it? We'll be robbing no one tonight."

The giant scrubbed his bearded face with two huge hands. "I'm a shepherd. I'll go home to Hathersage. I'll not be stealing a penny, come morning or no."

"*I* will," Scarlet snapped, angry at himself for wishing he, like Little John, still had a life to lead. "Go home to your sheep. Go home to Hathersage. Prove yourself a better man, till the sheriff comes to fetch you. Then *you'll* be the piece of meat hanging at the end of Nottingham's rope instead of Will Scathlocke!"

The giant's voice was low. "He said he'd speak for me."

"Who—that peasant?" Scarlet laughed thickly. "D'ye think the high sheriff of Nottingham would listen to a peasant about *another* peasant—"

"He isn't a peasant," Little John declared. "If you'd taken the time to look and listen, you'd have seen it for yourself."

"What, then . . . a lord? A *lord* will speak for you?"

"He's not a Norman," Little John said. "He's English, like all of us . . . who's to say what he will or won't do?"

"What he *won't* do is speak for you," Scarlet declared. "Why would he? English he may be, but if it's true he's a lord, then he's in the lap of the Normans."

The giant shook his head. "I'll bide my time."

How could he be so blindly trusting? "Stubborn fool," Scarlet muttered. "Can't you see the truth? Don't you see what our lives are, now?"

"Better than this," Little John declared. "By God, better than this. Maybe there's nothing left for you, but there is yet for me."

"*Sheep.*" Scarlet freighted it with contempt, because he had to. He was aware of envy and emptiness, that Little John could yet be so secure in his future when his own had been destroyed.

"Sheep," Little John agreed, unoffended by the contempt. " 'Tis a safer lot than yours."

Scarlet waved a hand, staving off desperation. "Agh, go to sleep. I weary of your chatter."

The giant's laughter rumbled. "Think I'm a fool, do you?

Can't see it, can you?" He laughed again, almost gleefully. "No one knows I've come. No one knows I'm here." He looked pointedly at Scarlet. "No one's hunting *me.*"

"Until tomorrow," Scarlet retorted, grasping at rejoinders. "Tomorrow I'm going home."

"Are you, then?" Adam Bell's tone was soft. "*After* you pay your fee."

Little John was belligerent. "I'll pay no 'fee' gotten off an honest man."

Scarlet barked a laugh. "Then rob a dishonest one."

The giant was unamused. "I go where I will and *do* as I will—"

"Aye," Scarlet agreed. "Until the sheriff says differently."

"Two days," Adam Bell said. "In two days, we'll know."

"Know what?" Little John asked suspiciously.

"Whether you'll be going home to your sheep, or staying here with us."

"Staying with *you*—"

"Or with some other merry band of men living outside the law." Bell's tone was quiet, dry, but very sure. "I have means of finding out what's on the sheriff's mind. In two days, we'll know."

"And me?" Scarlet asked roughly. "What about me?"

Bell didn't answer at once. When he did, the tone was negligent, as if the answer were implicit and not worth putting into words. "A man like you is welcome to do as we do, and to do it among our number. We can always use a man who likes to kill Normans."

Scarlet grunted assent, not knowing how else to answer. But even as he agreed, the worm of shame writhed.

'Tisn't what we wanted. 'Tisn't what we planned.

But his Meggie didn't answer, to chide him or say him nay.

William deLacey sat in a private chamber, sprawled slackly in a chair. That he had not yet gone to bed was attributable to Prince John, who had ordered him most specifically to gather additional taxes and take them to Lincoln, where John intended to personally see to it the money was sent to Germany as ransom to free King Richard.

John, of course, would do no such thing, because it served two purposes not to: it filled his own coffers, and kept Richard out of England.

John in power meant, eventually, John as *king;* the people wouldn't stand for a proxy regent any longer than they had to, and besides, there was William Longchamp, the Bishop of Ely, whom Richard had left in charge. Longchamp was chancellor, but had managed to do much of John's more unpopular work for him without intending to, simply by levying the taxes needed to raise Richard's ransom. Now the people hated Longchamp and wanted him removed, which benefited John for the moment; but would they tolerate John himself any better? At least Longchamp worked honestly if too zealously in the king's interest, no matter how imperious he was. John would work merely to further his own place, to seal forever his grip upon England's throne.

John as king. William deLacey laughed bitterly. *He'll bankrupt the realm.*

And what of himself? Would there be improved rank, as John promised? Would he rise in John's service, leaving behind Nottingham to rise ever higher, one of John's handpicked men, trusted to serve the new king?

Not likely. If John were smart, he would trust no one.

As I trust no one. DeLacey drank wine from a silver goblet. *If Richard comes home, I must work for my living; I've bought all I can buy. But if John becomes king, he'll have to offer a reward for good and faithful service . . . for seeing to it, almost singlehandedly, that part of Richard's ransom goes nowhere near Germany.*

A knock on the door interrupted his reverie. "Lord Sheriff?"

DeLacey sighed. "I've gone to bed."

"My lord, I have news. It has to do with the man you ordered taken."

"William Scathlocke?" DeLacey thrust himself out of the chair and strode across to the door, unlatching and jerking it open. "Have you found him after all? And the Lady Marian?"

Archaumbault stood in the corridor. "My lord, no—not *that* man, my lord. The other one you wanted."

DeLacey scowled. "What other one?"

"The minstrel, my lord. You gave orders for him to be taken."

DeLacey was displeased, though he didn't show it to Archaumbault. It wouldn't do to inform the garrison commander he was no longer particularly interested in the man accused of despoiling his already-despoiled daughter. He saw no sense in wasting extra effort, although now he'd have to give the matter some attention for the sake of propriety. "Very well. What news have you?"

"He was seen in an alehouse, my lord. The Watch was sent after him. I cannot say yet if they have been successful."

"Very well. Apprise me when—and if—they are." DeLacey paused. *"In the morning,* Archaumbault."

"Yes, my lord." The man bowed, then swung on his heel to stride down the corridor.

The sheriff shut the door and lingered, tapping fingertips against it. "The minstrel," he murmured. "Alan of the Dales . . . a fitting wedding gift, perhaps, for the woman who argued most eloquently that I preserve his tongue." He nodded. "And just in time. Tomorrow, perhaps—or the next day." He walked to the table and picked up the shining goblet, lifting it high into the air. "To Marian FitzWalter—soon to be deLacey." He smiled with anticipation. "Very, *very* soon."

Thirty-Two

The forest was cool, damp, dark, filled with the sounds of night. Much knelt in silence, shrouded by foliage, and stared fixedly at the woman who was his princess. She lay on the heaped pile of woven boughs, leaves, and deadfall, hands folded into her kirtle, much like a corpse laid out for burial. Corpselike, she lay mutely, tensely, as if afraid to breathe.

Was she asleep? He thought not. No more than Robin was, sitting against a tree. His posture was stiff, incredibly rigid, as if he expected to break.

But why would the prince break? And why would the princess not sleep?

Much clutched his shoes. He had never understood such things. He knew only what he felt, and he sensed what others felt by attending their voices, postures, and expressions. He had come too late to hear them speak at any length. He had heard nothing more from either of them than their last few sentences, and he could understand nothing of the content save the underlying emotions that blazed so brilliantly, illuminating the dullness that fogged much of his brain.

Fighting? No. Not as his mother and father. Not as Norman and Saxon. Not as peasant and peasant.

Was it because they were prince and princess?

Much rubbed at his flattened nose. His body as yet only fitfully gave way to vague yearnings, urges he didn't speak of, because there was no one to whom he could speak and no words to describe what he felt.

Did they feel yearnings, too, his prince and his princess? Or were they above such things, set apart from his world, made of different flesh?

Much stared at them. People were alien. Animals he knew, because their needs were simple, very much like his own.

Much clutched the shoes. He wanted to give them to her, to make his way quietly to her and *give* them to her, so her feet would no longer be bare. But courage failed him. The king's fool was too low to speak to the princess.

Eventually, they would sleep. Then he would creep to her side and put the shoes there, where she would find them when she woke.

The Earl of Huntington was sound asleep when the servant woke him. Blearily the earl clawed his way into awareness, intending to vilify the servant for daring to awaken him in the midst of a good night's sleep, but one look at Ralph's expression drove all thought of chastisement away.

He sat up, reaching for the robe cast across the foot of his bed. "What is it?"

"My lord." Ralph's face was pinched and colorless. "My lord, Alnwick is here."

Robe sleeve hooked over a stiffened elbow. "Alnwick . . . Eustace de Vesci is here? *Now?*"

"Yes, my lord. What should I tell him?"

"My God," the earl breathed. He finished tugging on the robe, but only because he had begun, not because he gave it any thought. Indeed, his thoughts were far away from such mundane things as apparel. "Tell him?" The earl scraped a gnarled hand through thinning hair. "Tell him I will join him presently. At once!"

"My lord." Ralph bowed and hastened toward the door.

"And Ralph . . ." The earl climbed out of bed. "By God, Ralph, tell him the *Count of Mortain* is here!"

Ralph nodded once. "My lord, I will."

He was gone, thumping the door closed. The earl slowly sat down on the edge of his bed, trying to put order to his robe. "De

Vesci," he breathed, "here. With John here as well." He felt old, weak, apprehensive. "This is a nightmare come true."

The alehouse was lighted only with smudgy candlelight that stank of poor rendering. The walls were wattle-and-daub, the roof thatching brittle and balding like an old man's head. Alan of the Dales was used to considerably better, but he felt under the circumstances this alehouse would do as well as another, since it was unlikely the sheriff or his men would frequent such a place.

He had finished half his ale when the hand came down on the mug and smacked it back to the table. "Friend," the man declared, "you'd best be on your way."

Belligerence was alien to Alan, who had perfected diplomacy and a delicate way with an insult, but this was too much. "No," he said flatly, and tried to pick up his mug again.

The man once more slammed it down, slopping ale over the rim. "Friend," he said more tightly, "I do this for your life. The Watch has been called on you."

It sent a frisson of fear through Alan. "How do you know? Who are you? Why should I believe you?" Belatedly, he considered the sort of things he should have considered before.

The man smiled humorlessly. He was dark, slight, one-handed. "I know because I know; because I'm paid to know. Who I am doesn't matter. As to why you should believe me— don't, then, friend minstrel . . . but you'll pay the price, I promise."

Alan could not avoid looking at the half-healed stump of the man's right arm, which was thrust under his nose. He was meant *not* to avoid it; a telling argument for trusting the stranger's warning.

But as much an argument for believing it might be a trap. Alan was no fool. He knew very well there were tricks meant to trap the unwary individual, especially pretty ones very like himself. His golden curls and languid ways attracted men as well as women. And men, he had learned early, were often more dangerous than women when rebuffed, because so much more was at stake.

"I've paid my price," he said coolly. "Take your dungeon stink somewhere else."

"You know the smell of it, then?" The one-handed man grinned. "Well then, you have only the sheriff to blame—d'ye think I cut off this hand myself?"

"It really isn't my concern *who* cut off your hand. No doubt you deserved it." Alan wrested the mug away and deliberately raised it to his mouth.

The man shrugged. "As you like, my pretty lad. But you'll be singing no songs at all when the sheriff is through with you, nor will you play that lute with only a stump for a hand."

Alan smiled thinly. "Scare the stranger out of the alehouse, then steal all his coin."

The one-handed man nodded. "But it only works when the stranger's wanted . . . and you're *very* wanted, my lad. The sheriff treasures his daughter."

No one knew about that. No one in Nottingham, save the sheriff and Eleanor—and Robert of Locksley, as well as the FitzWalter girl. He doubted the sheriff or Eleanor would say a word about it, and Locksley had done too much for Alan to begin the rumors himself, which left Marian. And she was in danger herself, if the rumors of *her* were true.

Alan shrugged, wagering all he had. "The sheriff has more to concern himself with than a simple minstrel."

"Not so simple, my lad. You've wounded him in his pride and brought down all his plans. It's true he wants Will Scarlet, but he wants you, too."

Alan's awareness sharpened. He put down the mug. "How do you know all this? And why tell me? What am I to you?"

"One of us," the man declared. "Even if you don't know it." He prodded the air with his stump. "And now *I'm* gone, before the Watch catches me and takes my other hand."

Brother Tuck lay very quietly in an agony of guilt. The pallet was narrow and thinly stuffed, hardly enough for a man of his size, but he knew he deserved no better. Had he not betrayed his calling? Had he not betrayed his Lord?

The sheriff said he hadn't. The sheriff spoke of things of the spirit, of a sick old woman in need. Tuck wanted to believe him, to believe *in* him, trusting to God to understand what he had done. But Abbot Martin, even now, wielded a heavier authority than the sheriff could comprehend.

If the abbot ever found out—Tuck scrunched shut his eyes, feeling folds of fat glue themselves together. He feared Abbot Martin. He feared his punishment. *He wouldn't ever know, unless I told him. Unless the sheriff told him. And he said he wouldn't.*

It was wrong. It was *wrong*. He should confess himself. He should go at once to Croxden Abbey and confess himself to the abbot, no matter how harsh the punishment. For what was he but a man who had failed his calling?

Tuck longed to pray. But he was frightened even of that. To admit what he had done—to put it into words . . . God knew already, of course, but it was so very private, still hidden from everyone else . . . if he spoke of it aloud, even to God Himself, it took on a greater aspect of sin. All would know his failure. All would know his weakness.

She was old, and dying, and helpless, in need of any comfort.

But he was not a priest. What he had done was wrong.

Sweat ran down his temples, mingling with his tears. *Who can forgive me for this?*

Surely not Abbot Martin.

Prince John woke badly out of habit, pettishly slapping aside the girl who shared his bed. She was nothing to him now but female flesh. He had done with her hours before, but she had stayed, snuggling against him as he slept. He could not abide a woman who expected to spend the night with his royal personage.

"Get *out!*" he snapped, as Gilbert de Pisan came close with a candle. "By God, Gilbert, did no one tell her?"

"Apparently not, my lord," the seneschal answered smoothly. "I would have, of course, but I have been occupied on your business."

"Have you?" John slapped at her again, smacking her ample rump as she hastily withdrew from the bed. She was fair-haired and plumply pretty, but with a certain vapidity that repelled him now. "Get you gone, get you *gone* . . . Gilbert, send her away!"

"Go," de Pisan said, even as the girl clutched at sheets.

"My clothes," she stammered.

De Pisan pointed at the door. "Surely you have others."

She bit her lip, undecided, then relinquished the sheet. Red-faced, she absented herself without benefit of clothing.

"God," John muttered. "Is there nothing better than *that?*" He sat up, yanking bedclothes over his loins. "What is it, Gilbert?"

"A late night visitor, my lord. Eustace de Vesci, the lord of Alnwick."

"Alnwick is *here?*" John stared at de Pisan. "You are certain."

"Quite certain, my lord. Even now, the earl is being awakened."

"By God, he entertains that traitor . . ." Alnwick had not yet been charged and probably wouldn't be, but such niceties meant nothing to John. "What about the others? Is Robert FitzWalter here? What about Geoffrey de Mandeville?"

"FitzWalter is not here, nor is the Earl of Essex. Only Alnwick, my lord."

"Merely the *first,*" John bit out. "By God, I didn't think it of Huntington. All those lies about this castle . . ." He scowled at de Pisan. "They want the throne for themselves."

"My lord, none of them have said so."

"They don't need to," John snapped. "Why else would they come here, but to plot my death?" He chewed angrily at a thumb already devoid of much of its nail. "De Vesci and FitzWalter alone——" He broke off, startled. Then he looked at his seneschal. "That girl. Was she not a FitzWalter?"

"The one just dismissed, my lord?"

"No, no, not *that* one—good God, Gilbert, do you think me a fool?" John expected and received no answer; de Pisan knew better. "The other girl. Sir *Hugh* FitzWalter's daughter."

"Perhaps a relative, my lord."

"And perhaps part of the plot."

De Pisan arched an elegant brow. "A woman, my lord?"

"Yes, a woman, de Pisan . . . who better to catch my fancy?" John picked at the coverlet. "Find out what you can about her,

Gilbert. If she is closely allied with my Lord of Dunmow . . ." He scowled mightily. "She will regret it, Gilbert."

"Most certainly, my lord."

John stared hard at his man. "Then go about it, Gilbert. Find out why de Vesci is here. Find out what Huntington knows. Find out what Marian FitzWalter has to do with *Robert* FitzWalter, Lord of Dunmow."

"My lord." Gilbert de Pisan bowed deeply.

"Plots," John muttered. "Do they never weary of plots?"

Sir Guy of Gisbourne lay sweating in the bed so magnanimously loaned by the Earl of Huntington, beneath the earl's brand-new roof. It pleased him little.

His thigh was afire, which surprised him not at all. The barber who doubled as surgeon had a heavy hand, and his resentment of having to sew instead of chop off showed in every stitch he took. The thigh resembled a particularly ugly piece of fabric, with the meaty cloth too thick for delicacy and the weave distorted by muscle.

The boar haunted his dreams, along with humiliation. He recalled very clearly the moment before the nightmare, when he had broken through foliage to come face-to-face with the woman he wanted so badly. He had handled it poorly, of course, as was his wont, but in the end Marian FitzWalter would never remember his declaration. She would recall only the boar, and his foolish attempt to kill it.

"For her," he muttered thickly. As indeed it had been.

He squirmed in the bed, then wished he had not done it. Movement sent fresh pain shooting to hip and ankle, reminding him of his folly. *For her, and her alone.* So she would take notice of him. So she would *respect* him, which was more than he'd earned before, in his limited dealings with women.

So little accomplished, too, save to get his thigh sliced open. In the end it had required someone else, another man entirely, to kill the maddened boar. While *he* lay writhing helplessly, fearing his leg cut off and his blood all spilling out, Sir Robert of Locksley had managed to kill the beast.

The hero-knight himself, the *real* Crusader knight, home from glorious battle, compatriot of kings.

Gisbourne lay in bed and sweated, thinking of Marian.

He was pressed belly-down on the sand, burning alive in his armor. Sand was ground into mouth, into nose, into eyes, even as he spat. He inhaled, trying for air, and inhaled sand instead because he had no other choice, squashed flat as he was, coughing and choking and hiccoughing, made to swallow more sand because to do so suited them.

Then a hand locked into his hair and jerked his head from the ground, nearly cracking his neck. Someone stood on his spine to keep the torso in place, while the head was bent back.

They were going to slice open his throat.

He flailed convulsively, hearing the bestial grunt escaping his constricted throat. Lips drew back in a rictus of effort, baring gritted teeth now caked with sand.

A foot slid beneath his hip and prodded his genitals. He flailed again, struggling, thinking they might cut there as well, spilling blood and manhood both beneath the Saracen sun.

He saw him then, Sir Hugh FitzWalter, cut away from Richard's side even as other men replaced him. As Locksley himself had been cut away, felled by a blow to the head, so was Hugh FitzWalter. The English swarmed their king and dragged him out of danger, while Robert of Locksley and Hugh FitzWalter were borne down by Saracens.

He was Richard's pet, and so they valued him. FitzWalter was merely a soldier: they tore the armor from him and carved him into bits, dismembering the body before the man was properly dead.

They threw the head at him, calling out in Arabic. It landed close enough to splatter him with blood, to look into his eyes with its own widened in shock, turning flat and opaque and dead, but staring in spite of it.

He lay belly-down in the sand with a dead man staring at him, and the blood flooding his face. He inhaled it as he breathed—

Locksley came awake with a start, exhaling a garbled protest muted by the dream. Sweat poured from him as he shivered. It was happening *again*.

He saw the figure then, close by Marian's side. Locksley thrust himself to his feet, crackling twigs . . . the crouched figure swung jerkily, then was up and running, darting into the trees even as Marian awoke. "What—?" she began.

But Locksley was gone, moving by her, aware of deadly calm and a deadlier resolve. *"Insh'Allah,"* he murmured, as the vestiges of the dream became his reality.

Thirty-Three

Eustace de Vesci was a bull of a man, big of bone and spirit. Men had likened him to the king, if of a different color; de Vesci, lord of Alnwick, was dark instead of ruddy, in skin as well as hair.

But his face was not flushed now, as the Earl of Huntington entered the chamber quietly. His face in fact was pale, with a sickly hue underneath. Only his eyes were alive: deepset, dark and glittering, sharp as a newly ground awl. "He is *here?*" he said only.

The earl shut the door firmly, surveying the chamber as he turned. All was well. Only de Vesci was present. Ralph had left them wine, and his absence. They did not have long, Huntington knew; the castle was full of John's household, and he trusted none of them.

The panic on first waking had gone. There had been time enough to think, as he dressed himself, and time enough to consider all the alternatives. Huntington was calm now, his breathing controlled, exuding competence. He was a man of iron will who did not suffer weakness in any measure, of the spirit or of the body. "There was no warning," he said quietly. "Do you think I would send no word?"

De Vesci swore, swinging to pace across the chamber, then

back again. Massive shoulders stretched his dark gray surcoat, very plain for his station, but appropriate to evening travel. "By God, this is the worst of all possibilities. One would think he knew—"

"He does not." The earl gestured. "Wine?"

"No." De Vesci glowered, reminding the earl of his father, the former earl, dead for several decades, though the Lord of Alnwick was younger than himself. It was the air of impatience and physical power that Huntington knew was absent in himself. His particular personal strength lay in a self-control de Vesci needed to temper his own more passionate nature. "We shall have to turn the others back."

"How?" The earl poured himself wine, then retired to a chair. He saw no reason to act overhastily. "I cannot very well send men out at dawn to every road, seeking to cut off the others. It would look highly suspicious to John."

"Nor can we meet while he is *here,*" de Vesci snapped. "It would mean our deaths."

The earl put out a staying hand. "Perhaps not. You were invited ostensibly to celebrate my son's return from the Holy Land—who is to say that is not the actual reason for your presence? John will suspect us, but John suspects *everyone*—we need only stand firm, and he will find himself without cause or justification to suspect us of anything."

"John Softsword requires neither," de Vesci declared. "Do you think he would hesitate to arrest all of us?"

"All of us? Yes. He needs us as yet."

" 'As yet,' " de Vesci echoed. "When will he *not* need us?"

The earl maintained a reasonable tone. With de Vesci, it was necessary; the man was undeniably courageous, but often too quick to act. "There is no law saying we cannot meet among friends to discuss the state of the realm—"

"He will call it treason. You know that."

Huntington sighed. "Yes, I believe he will. But he is not king just yet, and Richard left Longchamp in charge of the Seal, which is required for such an arrest." He set down the cup of wine, rose, crossed to the door and opened it.

De Vesci frowned. "What is it?"

"A moment." Huntington gestured his servant into the doorway. "Ralph," he said quietly, "will you go and fetch my son? At once, if you please." He shut the door and turned. "We will give John no grounds for suspicion. We will create truth out of falsehood."

"Your son." De Vesci's dark eyes narrowed. "What does your son know of us?"

"As yet, nothing. But if we are to present the play for John, we had best have all the players."

De Vesci's jaw was tense. "Then he will learn everything."

The earl folded his hands into the sleeves of his robe. "My son has returned from the Holy Land a hero and a knight, having escaped brutal captivity to once more stand at his king's right hand. Do you suggest to me he is anything but trust-worthy?"

De Vesci knew better. "No."

"Good." The earl went again to his chair and took up his wine. "When the others arrive—"

"My lord Earl? My lord!" It was Gilbert de Pisan's annoy-ingly imperious voice on the other side of the door. "My lord Earl, may I present the Count of Mortain!"

"God!" De Vesci went white. "He will have our heads for this!"

The earl fixed him with a level, unruffled stare. "Not unless you plan to serve it to him yourself. And if you do . . ." He smiled coolly. "Allow me, if you will, to have Ralph bring the silver platter."

Alan's taste for ale palled as the one-handed man slipped out of the alehouse. Abruptly he set down the mug, gathered up his lute and followed the man into a narrow alleyway as quietly as he could. It stank of refuse and ordure, damp and slick under-foot, treacherous to a man more accustomed to stone floors beneath a lord's high roof than a ceiling of stars overhead.

He meant to follow in secrecy, to see if indeed the one-handed man had intended to set a trap. But Alan's skill lay in verbal subterfuge, not physical activities past those to be found in bed. It did not take long for him to trip over a bolting cat and curse the mistake aloud, instead of within his head. A lute string twanged discordantly as he hugged the instrument.

Dim moonlight glinted on steel as the one-handed man stepped out of shadow. "Well then, has he thought twice about my warning?"

Alan was disgusted. "Twice *and* thrice," he agreed sourly, warding his lute against harm. "There is no need for a knife."

"Unless I mean to use it to part you from your money." The knife disappeared, as did the bantering tone. "You'd best be on your way. You don't fit in here, with your fine clothes and pretty ways . . . even if the Watch doesn't find you, someone will sell you to them."

"Why did you warn me? Who are you?"

The one-handed man grinned as he turned away. "I'm the eyes and the ears, my lad."

Darkness closed over him. So quickly he disappeared. "Wait—" Alan began, and then broke off as he heard the familiar call:

"Make way for the Watch!"

Alan fell back against the wall, slamming shoulders and spine into wattle-and-daub. He hugged the lute to his chest, breathing rapidly. He swallowed convulsively, thinking he should have heeded the man's warning, should have left immediately, should not have come at all.

"Make way for the Watch!"

"Foolish lad," the voice said. "D'ye plan to wait for them?"

"No—*no*—" Alan felt unexpected relief as the one-handed man showed himself again. "But—I'm a stranger to Nottingham—"

"Should have thought of that." The man put out his hand. "Give me the lute."

Alan hugged it more tightly. "Why?"

"By God, lad, they're just around the corner . . . they'll *know* you by it, you fool, that and your pretty tunic." He motioned impatiently. "I'll see to it your lute's kept safe."

"But—" They *were* just around the corner. Alan swore and handed over the lute, hastily pulling the brocaded tunic over his head. "Wait for me—" He jerked his head free of his tunic, words muffled by fabric. "Where will I find you?"

"In Sherwood," the man answered, fading into the shadows, "and I'll find *you*."

"In *Sherwood*—" But the Watch was there, *just* there, rounding the corner even as he began, moonlight glinting on pikes and swords. Breathing noisily, Alan quickly stuffed his telltale tunic into a hole in the crumbling wall of the alehouse. Now all he wore were hosen, shoes, and crumpled sherte, soiled by his stay in the dungeon. He thought about slipping back inside the alehouse and pretending he was a peasant. It wasn't a bad idea—but he recalled the one-handed man's warning that someone would sell him to the Watch. He dared trust no one.

Perhaps not even the man himself. "Sherwood," Alan muttered, hastening after the stranger. "My God—there are *outlaws* in Sherwood!"

And soon his lute as well.

The crackle of brush but paces away broke apart Marian's fitful doze and threw her headlong into wakefulness. *Someone is here*—

Someone *close*, creeping carefully to her bedding.

She lurched back frenziedly, scrabbling in the leaves and branches. "What?—" But the night-muffled stranger fled quickly into the darkness even as Locksley pursued him, shedding leaf mold as he ran.

Not Will Scarlet— Panic and anger commingled. Scrambling to her feet, Marian clawed for and found the quarterstaff Locksley had brought with them. *This time I'll hit him so hard I'll knock his ears off his head.* She kicked free of branches that could foul her movements and gripped the staff tightly, trying to ignore the sickness in her stomach born of shock, sudden fright, and a much too-abrupt awakening.

Then Locksley was unexpectedly *back*, casually ducking a low-hanging limb as he stepped out of the shadows into the moonlight. He did not appear particularly winded or concerned, raking a hand through his pale hair, but decidedly relaxed, picking leaf mold from his damp tunic.

"Well?" she demanded.

Locksley stopped short. His face was bruised and battered,

distinctly the worse for wear, but as he stared at her she saw a change in it, a pronounced alteration that took her breath away, so complete was the transformation.

Robert of Locksley grinned. And then he began to laugh.

"What?" Marian asked.

Laughter softened his face. It lasted but a moment, then faded into an amusement more gentle in its expression, lighting his hazel eyes and curving the corners of his mouth. "You," he declared. "I need not have come at all."

"I don't—" And then she did understand. Marian's face burned as she put up her chin, clutching the staff more tightly. "There is no sense in doing *nothing* in your own defense, simply because you are a woman."

"No sense at all," he agreed gravely. "I was merely thinking there was no need for my intervention in any of this. You appear more equipped for battle than I . . . after all, it was you who stunned Will Scarlet, not me." He shrugged. "I might have remained in Nottingham and saved myself some trouble."

"So might I," she retorted dryly, "but Will Scarlet desired otherwise." She jerked her head in the direction of the trees, wanting to turn the topic. "Since you are back so soon, I must assume you did not catch him."

"I did catch him. I let him go." He returned to his tree and sat down once more, leaning against the trunk. "He seemed to prefer it. It was the boy."

"Much?" It surprised her. "Why did he run?"

"You frightened him."

"He frightened *me*." Immeasurably relieved, Marian leaned and set down the quarterstaff, then knelt upon the bedding. She trembled slightly in the aftermath, chiding Locksley more tartly than she intended. "You might have told him he could join us."

"I did. He simply ducked away and disappeared, much like a rabbit."

Marian nodded, sighing. "Much trusts no one."

"He seems to trust you."

She shrugged, working again at tangled hair. "I spoke to him whenever I went to the mill. I think they gave him little time there, save to send him out of the way. He was always quiet, always odd, quick to dart away. One day he wasn't there. I never saw him again, until today." She stopped untangling her hair. "It was only—this morning!" She stared at him in shock. "First Much, then the giant—and then Will Scarlet. But—it feels like *seven* days!"

Locksley stared over her head, setting his own against the tree. He shivered once, then rubbed a splay-fingered hand over his face, then through his hair, as if his skin hurt. "Captivity alters one's understanding of time."

Marian sat very still, wary of stepping off but wanting to very much. "Did it alter it for you?"

The mask was back in place but the facade seemed thinner, less substantial, oddly attenuated. He was markedly different from the man she had seen on the dais, still reserved, still intensely private, but more approachable. *Or is it that I desire to approach?*

His voice was subdued. "At first I counted the days. Then the weeks. After two months, nothing mattered anymore but that I survive the hour." After a moment of noisy silence, he looked directly at her. His gaze did not waver, nor did his tone. "Your father would be proud."

"Of—" She swallowed painfully, surprised by the magnitude of the unexpected uprush of anguish, "me?"

"As you should be proud of him." A muscle twitched in one cheek. "He died defending his king. He died defending his God."

Marian locked hands into her kirtle. "Was it very—bad?"

He did not hesitate. "No. It was over immediately."

The mask was sealed again, like wax over parchment. Marian knew he lied.

The Earl of Huntington composed himself as the chamber door was flung open. He hoped de Vesci had done the same.

Gilbert de Pisan stepped aside. Prince John, fully clothed, swept into the chamber. "Alnwick!" he cried. "To think I would have missed you had you not come in tonight!"

"My lord Count." De Vesci bowed elegantly. His composure lacked for nothing, even on short notice. The earl smiled privately; had he been practicing? "I am sorry, my lord, I don't take your meaning—had I not come in tonight?"

"Yes." John nodded. "I intend to depart at midday tomorrow. Unless, of course, the earl desires me to stay?" He cast Huntington a pointed stare.

"My lord—of course. You are welcome to stay at Huntington as long as you like." Mentally the earl began to count his larders. If John did stay, he would have to arrange for additional victuals and supplies. "May I tell my steward?"

But John did not answer. He was staring at de Vesci. "You missed the feast."

"Yes, my lord. It is my misfortune—I had intended to present my best wishes to Sir Robert."

John's eyes narrowed. "Odd that you would not make better plans to assure your arrival on time."

De Vesci's mouth crimped tight, hindering a smile. "We were set upon by thieves, and delayed."

"Thieves." John nodded sagely, dark eyes narrowing. "The forests are choked with them—I shall have the sheriff see to it something is done immediately."

"My lord?" Ralph came into the chamber, paused as he saw Prince John and his seneschal, then bowed hastily. Only the barest flicker in his eyes betrayed his concern. "My lord, I am sorry—your son pleads illness."

"Illness?" Huntington frowned. "What manner of illness?"

Ralph's face was pasty. "An overindulgence of wine."

John laughed. "No head for wine, has he? Or is it a woman instead?"

"No, my lord." Ralph flicked a glance at Huntington. "In captivity he was not allowed wine, my lord. He drank too much in celebration of his homecoming."

De Vesci forced a laugh. "Then we shall have to teach him what it is to drink properly again!"

"How droll," John declared. He glanced around the chamber, assessing appointments, then cast a tight smile at the earl. "A fine castle indeed, my lord. Very strong, very safe. Quite remarkable."

"And expensive." The earl inclined his head. "I owe the Jews a fortune."

"What? Have you impoverished yourself?" John's eyes glittered. "Naturally you have donated to my brother's ransom."

"Indeed, my lord. Generously. Several times, in fact."

"Mmmm." John was abruptly disinterested. "And are you expecting any more guests, my lord?"

"Indeed, yes. Two more, in fact—Geoffrey de Mandeville, and Henry Bohun."

"Essex and Hereford." John's color was livid. "Anyone else, my lord? Robert FitzWalter, perhaps? Or Robert de Vere?" His nostrils were pinched. "So many great houses, my lord—and all in one place."

The earl permitted himself a proud smile. "A father's poor attempt at welcoming home his only son and heir."

"Indeed." John cast de Vesci a black scowl, then swept toward the door once more. "De Pisan. I retire. Until the morrow, my lord."

The earl bowed deeply as John marched out.

"My God!" de Vesci gasped as the door thumped closed. "He knows all of us. *All* of us!"

"He suspects," the earl said. "Come now, Eustace—the man is not a fool. He has informants, as we do. We simply must take care to see that no one learns how many of us are involved, and what we plan to do."

"You needn't have mentioned de Mandeville and Bohun." De Vesci poured wine with a trembling hand and quaffed several gulps. "Why tell him what he may only suspect?"

"Because if any of the others *do* arrive tonight, I want them expected." Huntington sat down. "It would not be in our best interests to make John any more suspicious."

"No." De Vesci squeezed the cup in one massive hand. "Right here before me—I could have cut his throat."

"And died for it." Huntington turned to Ralph. "Where is my son?"

"Not in the castle, my lord. He rode out this morning. No one has seen him since."

"Does it matter?" de Vesci asked in exasperation. "He need know nothing. It is better that he does not."

The earl glanced at him coldly. "He is heir to all I have. If he is to succeed me, he must know what we do. And besides—"

he laughed softly, "the Count of Mortain has suggested my son might be a worthy husband for his daughter."

"He hasn't a daughter," de Vesci said blankly. And then, in growing alarm, "You mean the bastard girl?"

"Joanna."

"She's but a child, yet!"

"I doubt John cares how young she is. If John considers it advantageous, he'll marry her off at the time he deems appropriate."

"My God." De Vesci collapsed into the nearest chair. "Do you know what this means?"

"It means if we overthrow John, my son may stand to benefit."

"*And* you."

The earl smiled. "And us *all*, my Lord of Alnwick."

"My God," de Vesci whispered.

Thirty-Four

Locksley awoke very stiff, equally sore, and disinclined to move even so much as an eyelid. He had not expected to sleep, but at some point near dawn the enemy Exhaustion had wielded the sword of a Saracen and defeated his attempt to remain awake. He woke slumped and disoriented at the foot of his tree like a discarded pile of soiled clothing, head crooked awkwardly against an exposed root.

This is—England. For a moment, only a moment, he feared it was not. Relief left him weak.

He heard the hiss and rustle of dead leaves and twigs and the quiet, alert voice—*too alert for this morning*—underscored by a trace of dryness. "You cannot possibly be comfortable."

He wasn't, of course, but forbore to tell her so. Already she had accounted for knocking Will Scarlet unconscious, and he did not doubt she would have tried much the same the night before with the selfsame quarterstaff, had she found it necessary. She did not know about his battle with Little John, nor did she need to; he had lost that one, also.

She moved into his line of vision. He saw dirty bare toes, a ragged hem, kirtle stiff with dried mud. "I've collected some nuts. Not many, I'm afraid—the squirrels got most of them."

He moved then, trying to shift his head into a more natural position. Every joint ached. Even his eyes ached. He redistributed his weight and pushed himself up into a sitting position, cracking knots in his spine, and gazed in wan consternation at the cluster of nuts in her hand.

"No," he said at once.

Smudges underlay her eyes, but he hardly saw them for the lash-fringed color above: deep and blue and impossibly bright for a gently reared knight's daughter but freshly awakened from a long night on damp ground. "There is nothing else, until we reach Ravenskeep."

"No," he repeated more tightly, aware of increasing discomfort. He felt shivery and listless, though his clothing and hair had dried. He felt altogether *squashed*—and then realized all at once, with more than a little dismay, what the matter was.

He shut his eyes, scrubbed haphazardly at his stubbled, sore face, and felt the first tentative shiver of the expected bone-deep shudder that would soon wrack his body into knots. With great effort, he suppressed it.

"Are you sure?" she asked.

"Quite sure." He had expected the bruises to hurt. He had expected his lumps to ache. But the recurring fever so many acquired on Crusade had settled quietly into joints and brain overnight and now threatened to overpower the ordinary discomfort earned in honest battle with its sly, pervasive ill will. "We had better go."

"Yes, but—"

He thrust himself to his feet, turning his back to her so she wouldn't see his face and the grimace of pain as his head protested movement. "The horse is some distance away. We had best go at once."

"The nuts are *something*—"

"Then eat them," he snapped, and set off through the brush.

"At least let me put on the shoes!"

He stopped and turned back, pulling aside foliage. Her feet were bare. He was sure of it. "I thought you lost your shoes."

"I did. Before we left Nottingham." She sat down, struggling with the ancient leather. "They were set beside me when I awoke this morning."

"*Shoes?*"

"I think Much left them. It would explain why he followed us." Her tone was odd. "He has left me things before."

It amused him faintly. "Like a cat with a dead bird."

"Not like *that*." A fleeting frown departed swiftly. She laced on the first shoe, then pulled the second on. "They do not fit very well, but are decidedly better than nothing."

So they were. It displeased him to know someone, even the boy, had been able to come so close as to leave shoes beside Marian no more than paces away from him. But it hurt his head to think about it. Even his eyelids ached, and he squinted, wishing the infant sun did not stab his eyes quite so sharply.

Marian finished lacing on the second shoe and stood up, shaking debris from her kirtle. Her hair was as tangled as it had been the night before, her clothing as tattered and muddied. The delicate, flawless face was mottled with ugly bruises and livid welts, and the cuts at the corners of her mouth were puffed and pink. They looked exceedingly painful.

And yet she says nothing. He wondered if he knew of another living woman who would not protest in such a state. He wondered if he knew of another living woman who would put on a peasant's shoes.

The sweep of black brows rose inquiringly. "What is it?"

Nothing, he answered in silence. *Nothing.* But that was a blatant lie . . . in truth it was *everything*—everything just to look at her, to see what a day with Will Scarlet had done to tarnish the beauty, while somehow it polished the spirit. *I am delirious.* And yet he knew he wasn't. That would come later. "This way." But he said it less impatiently than before.

Prince John smacked one of the body servants on top of the head. "Faster, buffoon! Am I to stay here all day?" Before the man could answer, John transferred his attention to the Norman seneschal standing silently by the door. "Treachery, Gilbert. I can smell its perfidious odor like an Irishman left to rot."

Gilbert de Pisan gestured for one of the other hovering servants to attend to his master's feet, setting shoes on over hosen.

"I can *smell* it, Gilbert! I tell you, Eustace de Vesci is here for more than good wishes . . . and Essex and Hereford, too, when they arrive, as I know they will! Does Huntington think I'm a fool? Does he think I'm blind?" He tore a sleeve free of a servant. "*I'll* do that—"

"It may be just as he says, my lord." De Pisan, as always, played devil's advocate, because it helped John to think.

"I've no doubt Oxford will come, too—and Mowbray? Of course, Mowbray . . ." Dark eyes glittered. "What will they say, I wonder, when *I* am king?"

De Pisan's voice was exquisitely dry. "No doubt they will express their perfect love and utmost fealty."

"No doubt." John scowled blackly. "I should stay, Gilbert. I should stay here, and disrupt their plans . . . do you think they can accomplish anything with me in residence?"

"No, my lord."

"But there is the money," John muttered. "I must go to Lincoln and await the sheriff . . . I have ordered another collection." His expression was sublimely sanguine. "For the ransom, you see."

De Pisan's expression was guileless. "Indeed, my lord."

"Of course, now that his daughter is ruined, there is no possibility of marrying her to Huntington's son, which leaves our brave hero-knight free for Joanna . . . but no bait to dangle before deLacey . . ." John chewed a fingernail. "I like to know they are mine . . . I will have to promise something else. Surely he would prefer advancement than to remain *here* forever."

"Surely he would, my lord."

Musingly, the prince said, "And if I *do* offer Joanna to the earl's son, it serves to keep Huntington quiet."

"One would think so, my lord."

John's gaze sharpened. "Is that man still here? That clumsy fool who botched the boar hunt?"

De Pisan did not so much as blink in response to the change in subject; he was well accustomed to things more demanding than that. Besides, he knew the answer, because he took pains to know everything he could, so as to satisfy his master. One did not merely *hope* to please John. One did so, and effortlessly, or his place was lost instantly. "Yes, my lord."

John waved an imperious hand. "Then go find out, Gilbert. He'll know."

De Pisan nodded patiently. "What is it you wish him to know?"

"The sheriff's price." The Count of Mortain smiled. "Every man has more than one."

De Pisan bowed deeply. "At once."

"Gilbert—" John broke off, motioning the servants out of the chamber. When the door was shut, he fixed de Pisan with a malevolent stare. "I want this stopped. I want this stopped now. I want this to go no farther than this castle, this day. I will not have men who profess to being loyal subjects believing they can plot treachery beneath my very nose." John swore viciously. "By *God*—this sort of thing could lay the groundwork for a much more serious threat."

"They are powerful men, my lord."

"Then it is time we clipped their wings." John flicked a finger. "Go."

Gilbert de Pisan went.

Little John squatted in leaf mold, scraping hair out of his face. He was in a foul, belligerent mood, worsened by the fact he had not slept well, and was disposed to argue no matter what was said. Accordingly, he glared back at Adam Bell. "I told you I wouldn't. I won't. I'll have none of this."

Bell, arms folded, shrugged narrow shoulders. "Your

choice," he said, "but 'tis hard to be a shepherd when your belly's full of arrows."

"You'll not kill me over this!" Little John was peripherally aware of Clym of the Clough and Cloudisley restringing their bows and counting their arrows. *Would they?* Desperation grew. "You've enough men to steal for you—you don't need my help."

William of Cloudisley laughed, warm brown eyes alight. He was a sweet-faced boy, the kind the girls would sigh for, but for all his innocent looks he had killed men before. " 'Tisn't your help we want—we're wanting your *coin*. But if there's naught to give us, you'll borrow from someone else."

"Borrow," Little John spat. "D'ye mean me to give it back, then, once I've loaned it to you?"

Will Scarlet was on his feet, gingerly testing his battered ribs. "Who's to know you've stolen it?" he asked sourly. "D'ye think *we'll* say aught?"

"The man whose coin I steal might! He might go straight to the sheriff, who'll know at once who did it—"

Scarlet flapped an arm. "He'll know what you did with his woman. D'ye think a man's purse will matter?"

Little John thrust a hand against the ground and rose to his full height. "I did nothing to the woman. Nothing at all, d'ye hear? I meant to take her back—" He broke it off abruptly, recalling the promise he'd made to fetch the girl back to Scarlet.

Scarlet's dark eyes narrowed. "Aye," he said roughly, "I thought it might be that. A trustworthy soul, you are."

"Never mind that," Adam Bell interposed. "We've other business to tend to." His look was no longer amused. "Which one of you goes first?"

Scarlet spat, wincing slightly. "I will," he growled. "Let him see how 'tis done, so he'll know what's expected of him."

Bell nodded. "You'd best make it worth our while."

Little John shook his head. "You'd not kill me for this."

Clym of the Clough laughed. It had an ugly sound. "I've killed men for less. With you, I'd just use more arrows."

* * *

Alan dreamed of plump breasts and plumper bottom, and the taste of a clove-scented mouth hovering near his own—

Someone kicked his foot. "Here, you. I'll not have a peasant sleeping in my stall. You'll spoil all the wares."

Breasts and bottom dissipated into the wan sun of a misty, malodorous morning. Nottingham stank. Alan cursed the merchant looming over him, fists planted on wide hips; in elaborate French the displaced minstrel muttered a comment about the man's ancestry, then slowly unwound himself. The merchant was a thick, contentious sort, ill-disposed to hear anything Alan might have to say, no matter how politely couched, which was just as well, he decided, since he felt no urge to use politeness anyway.

"Get out of my stall!" the man ordered, rolling back a tunic sleeve from a meaty forearm.

Alan eyed the forearm, the wrist, and the fist, and decided to acquiesce. It was a stroke of brilliance, he thought, that he had tucked under his tunic the purse of silver marks Robert of Locksley had given him, or else the merchant would surely have robbed him before sending him on his way.

He departed the stall amid additional threats to smash in his pretty face, then stepped into a narrow alley to relieve himself. He recalled his brocaded tunic was in the other direction. Worse, his lute was in Sherwood Forest, in the hands—no, *hand*—of a man who would not know how gently to treat a lovely instrument.

Alan glumly rubbed at stubble. Little about him gave away his employment. No one, looking at him, would claim him a minstrel well placed with nobility—well, he *had* been, before Eleanor had seen to it his new placement was somewhere no man would choose to be.

Eleanor. God rot her. *And* Eleanor's father.

Alan sighed, scratching vigorously at the flea that had taken up residence in the hair furring his abdomen. There was nothing for it but to go into Sherwood and look for the one-handed man. He had money enough to buy a new lute, but instruments of quality were hard to come by, and there was no certainty Nottingham boasted a luthier at all, let alone a good one. Also, it would be foolish to buy one in Nottingham even if there *were* a luthier, because the sheriff had undoubtedly warned his men to look for a man with a lute, and his salvation, for the moment, lay in *not* having one.

So he would go to Sherwood and get back his own lute, of which he was exceedingly fond, as it was of excellent tone and quality and, beside that, had won him more women than anything else might—excepting his tongue, of course, and the sheen of his golden curls.

Alan snorted derisively. He was at present too dirty to be golden. "Fool's errand," he muttered. "But some would say it fits." Food and drink first, he decided. Then Sherwood Forest.

The horse was a fine one, Much knew. From a distance he watched it, waiting for someone to step out of the trees and claim it, but no one did, and after a while Much decided no one was near enough to prevent him from stealing it. And so he made his way very quietly out of the bushes, approached the horse from the front, and put his small, deft hands upon the reins. The horse did not protest.

Much stroked its nose, liking the warmth of the breath whuffing against his arm. It was a fine, tall horse; a deep-chested, unmarked bay. Much petted the horse, slicking the long, sloping shoulder where it joined the heavy neck. The leather trappings were of excellent quality, and the brown cloak hooked across the saddle bespoke an expert's hand at the loom. He smiled, content with his prize, and untied the reins. He would lead him down the track, then into the backside of Nottingham Castle, where he knew a man who would pay silver for such a horse.

Gisbourne heard the door open. Inwardly he cursed; it was the barber, he knew, come to goad him into protest, to complain of discomfort, so the barber could respond that the leg was rotting off.

God, but he hated the man!

"Sir Guy." It was not the barber. He did not speak with such a cool, mellifluous voice in the accents of Gisbourne's childhood.

Am I dead? He opened his eyes. No, he wasn't dead. The voice belonged to Gilbert de Pisan, elegantly attired in a rich blue surcoat of Oriental cut left open to show off the embroidered tunic beneath. Obviously the prince's service paid better than the sheriff's.

Gisbourne struggled to right himself, to pull himself straight against the bolsters, even as de Pisan made a gesture meant to stay him. Damply, Gisbourne smiled, wishing he had a cloth to wipe his burning face.

"Sir Guy. I am commanded to express my lord's deepest sympathies for your wound."

Gisbourne was feverish and flustered, knowing he looked his worst. "I thank him for that. And you," he added hastily, "for bringing word to me."

De Pisan's smile was cool. "Of course." He eyed the bloody bandage with some distaste. "You will recover, Sir Guy? There is no threat to your leg?"

"No threat," Gisbourne declared. "I will be fully recovered very soon."

"I am most pleased to hear it," de Pisan said tranquilly, "as will my lord be pleased. There is a service you can do him, but of course we must wait until—"

"A service?" Gisbourne scrubbed his damp face with a sweat-stained tunic sleeve. "What service may I do the prince?"

De Pisan frowned faintly, stroking his upper lip with a slender finger. "You recall you spoke with him before with regard to rewarding the sheriff's most diligent service."

"Of course." Gisbourne momentarily wondered how de Pisan knew the nature of the conversation, as he had not been present; he realized, belatedly, the seneschal had been informed after the fact. As to who had done the informing . . . Gisbourne swallowed tightly. "I told him the sheriff would be particularly pleased to have his daughter wed to the Earl of Huntington's son."

"Yes. A good match—until two days ago." The tone was oblique.

"Two days—?" It confused Gisbourne, who recalled little of

two days before save the confrontation with the boar. "I don't remember . . ."

De Pisan's brows arched. "The lady was despoiled. Do you not recall? The culprit was discovered even as you were brought into the chamber."

Gisbourne remembered none of it.

De Pisan waved a dismissive hand. "It is no longer important, save to alter the reward my lord had planned to bestow upon the sheriff. It seems now we require more information. And as you know him so well, undoubtedly you are well informed as to what else might please the sheriff."

Gisbourne wanted to tell the seneschal to ask the sheriff himself. "I fear I do not know him *that* well—"

"Surely you are aware of something, Sir Guy."

Gisbourne stared at de Pisan a long moment. His innocence had ended most decidedly, with the death knell sounded during the sheriff's visit the day before. He had actually come to visit Marian; Gisbourne understood that now. He understood quite a lot. If he did not make shift for himself and his future, no one would do it for him.

Gisbourne cleared his throat. "I have served the sheriff—"

"My lord is aware of that."

Gisbourne gritted his teeth. "May I have water?" he temporized.

A flash of impatience showed briefly in de Pisan's eyes, but was banished instantly. Murmuring apologies for his oversight, he poured a cup of water and handed it to Gisbourne.

Gisbourne waited, watching *him* wait. He understood all too well that Prince John had not been interested in his abilities, but had only sought information that might be used to manipulate the sheriff. Gisbourne had most willingly told him what he knew. And he would tell de Pisan now, but he would have more in return than the privilege of being ravaged by a wild boar. It was time Sir Guy of Gisbourne laid the groundwork for something better than service in Nottingham.

He held out the empty cup expectantly, staring fixedly at the seneschal. He had seen agreements reached in perfect silence between the sheriff and other men. De Pisan served Prince

John; surely he would understand the complexities of such things.

A muscle ticked in de Pisan's cheek, and then he reached for the cup and set it on the table next to the pitcher. He turned back to Gisbourne and folded his slender hands into the wide, banded sleeves of his Oriental surcoat.

"Yes," he said clearly, his gaze unwavering.

Gisbourne smiled. He was beginning to understand how to manipulate a person. "I am a knight," he said, "of respectable name and family. But there are sons before me—there will be no portion save what I make for myself."

"Yes," de Pisan said; clearly he understood the opening gambit and what would follow.

"To advance myself, I need to marry well. And there is a woman . . ."

De Pisan's tone was uninflected. "Yes, Sir Guy. There usually is."

Gisbourne told him about her. He told him her name. He told him her holdings. He told him he wanted her. And then he told de Pisan what would most please the sheriff.

De Pisan nodded. "I will inform my lord."

"Soon," Gisbourne suggested, then closed his eyes and slumped back against the bolster.

"Soon," de Pisan said dryly, and the door thumped closed behind him.

Thirty-Five

Just after dawn, William deLacey strode out of the castle keep into the inner bailey. Mist still lingered along the top of the curtain-wall, shrouding the castle in transient isolation. Beyond lay Nottingham, only beginning to stir, noise muted by the wall and the dampness. In the east a brassy sphere of light, tarnished by the mist, marked the sun's new birth.

Archaumbault and five men prepared to mount as horses were brought to them. The castellan was grim and terse, snapping out curt replies to brief questions from the others. DeLacey stopped behind him and said with deliberate softness, "You will fetch her back, Archaumbault."

The man started, bit his lip on a protest, and turned smartly. His eyes searched the sheriff's face a moment, and then the merest trace of comprehension altered his own expression from military rectitude into human understanding: more than his position was at stake. "Yes, my lord. As soon as possible."

The sheriff nodded, satisfied. He could go on to another subject. "What of the minstrel? I received no report on rising."

"No, my lord." Archaumbault's eyes were bloodshot. "The Watch was unable to catch him, my lord."

DeLacey arched a brow. "I believed it as good as done."

"As did I, my lord . . . but someone must have warned him. He was gone by the time the Watch reached the alehouse—they recovered only his tunic."

"His tunic." The sheriff allowed a trace of contempt to lace his tone for the benefit of the others, whom he did not desire to grow lax in attentiveness merely because he did not shout. He preferred a quieter approach, with no less attention to detail. "I am not interested in tunics."

"My lord." A quick twitch of Archaumbault's head had the others mounting with alacrity, gathering reins taut. "They are still searching for him."

"Good. I want him recovered." *Though not as much as I want Marian recovered.* DeLacey flicked a hand. "I expect success in both endeavors."

"We will do our best, my lord."

It was time the others saw no man was inviolable to the sheriff's displeasure, even Archaumbault. Such knowledge would make them aware that Archaumbault could be replaced if he failed—perhaps by one of them.

DeLacey raked the castellan with a contemptuous glance. "I have yet to see your best in either matter." Archaumbault's mouth tightened. The others exchanged glances. "Go," de-Lacey said.

He watched them do so, then swung on his heel and came face-to-face with his daughter. Brought up short, he frowned. "I told you to stay in your chamber."

Eleanor shrugged slightly. "That was yesterday. Today is—today."

He eyed her with disfavor, having less reason than ever to countenance her attitude. She had made a fool of him publicly and had destroyed his plans, and she showed absolutely no remorse. "You will return to your chamber at once."

"Why?" Her chin rose. She wore yellowed green, which was not her color; the hue deepened the sallowness of her complexion. "I'll be walled up soon enough, won't I, once the FitzWalter girl arrives." Eleanor arched dark brows. "That is—*if* she arrives . . . and if you'll have the stomach for her once the truth is known." She smiled slyly. "A night in the forest with out-laws—"

"Enough!" he snapped.

Eleanor laughed in delight. She had stirred true passion in him. "Why, my lord, one would think you really do care for her—"

Will she never shut her mouth? He reached out, closed his hand around her elbow, swung her around smartly and marched her back into the castle. "I am of half a mind to marry you to a Welshman inside of a week and let *him* have the taming of your tongue . . . if he lets you keep it." He walked her steadily down the corridor. "I care little enough what you think of me—you've made your opinion plain enough this past year—but I won't have you undermining Marian before she even arrives."

"*If* she arrives." Eleanor tried to jerk free of his grasp, but he held her arm too tightly. "Will you have *two* despoiled women living in your castle?"

"One," he answered grimly. "I'll pack you up, so help me, and send you out of it."

Eleanor scoffed. "No one will have me, now!"

"On the contrary," he said silkily, "I think *everyone* will have you—if they haven't done it yet!"

A wave of color came and went in her face, leaving it pale and waxen. Her lips trembled with anger even as he manhandled her up the stairs. "If you would stop thinking of yourself and think of me—"

"I have thought of you many times, Eleanor—too many times; if fact, I *weary* of thinking of you . . . I believe it is time I stopped. I believe it is time I gave up trying to match you advantageously and simply married you off to the first man willing to take you, well used as you are—"

She was a banshee echoing stridently in the corridors of the castle, where no secrets were wholly secret even when whispered quietly. "I only want to make my own decisions! About my body, about my future—"

Here, at last. He yanked open the door to her chamber and pushed her into it. Each word was deliberate and distinct. "No woman has enough sense and the wherewithal to make such decisions, Eleanor. Certainly you haven't." DeLacey shut the door between them before she could finish.

Marian walked a step or two behind Locksley only by virtue of shorter legs. His pace was not fast, nor was it particularly deliberate in deference to her gender, but it appeared to be determined wholly by the moment, and by which way seemed easiest. He bent back threatening boughs when he could, but an increasing number escaped his grasping hand as he miscalculated distance and density. Marian warded off the fugitive branches, but one or two slapped her in face and neck, scraping across welts and bruises. It left her a trifle disgruntled, wishing he would or he wouldn't; halfway measures netted her increasing discomfort.

Ahead, Locksley stumbled over a creeper, caught his balance awkwardly, almost tentatively, then paused to turn back toward her, as if to warn her of treacherous footing. But by the time he turned Marian was well past the tangling foliage, staring in some consternation at his face.

Something was wrong. His color was bad, his flesh had a pinched look, and he carried his head gingerly, as if it hurt to move. *The fight with Will Scarlet.* Marian's mouth tightened. He would say nothing of it, of course, just as her father would not, and *had* not, often enough, following a particularly painful weapons practice session. So she said nothing of it also, raising another topic. "How much farther?"

He shivered, then rubbed an arm as if to ward off a chill. "Not far. The track lies a little that way"—he pointed—"and the forest proper ends just ahead. We are not so far from Nottingham—"

"Ravenskeep," she said firmly.

A faint smile hooked one corner of his mouth. "Ravenskeep." Dampness stuck together the finer strands of hair at his temples. "I have only one horse."

"Yes, so you told me." Marian smiled. "One of us shall have to ride pillion."

He arched a single brow. "They will remark it an intimacy."

"*I* will remark it a necessity." She grinned. "Besides, who will see us? And if anyone does, who will recognize us? Your face is near to purple, and mine no better, I fear."

"No," he agreed judiciously.

"Well then, we shall be free of idle gossip—surely an uncommon occurrence, and therefore to be treasured." She caught up her kirtle once more, dragging the torn hem out of the way. "In our dishabille, we will be fortunate if we are not taken for peasants riding a stolen horse. We would be hanged on the spot."

His tone was odd. "Your father did not sire a peasant."

She opened her mouth to retort, but something in his eyes stopped her before she could answer. His expression was strangely intent, almost fixed, with a burning, feral intensity, as if there were more to the statement than a simple rejoinder.

Why does he——? But she let it go, because she was afraid of the answer, afraid it would be the one she did not desire to know, because she wanted more of him, more and more of him, without understanding why.

Marian swallowed tightly. "Neither did yours."

It broke the moment. "Mine? No. And he would be at some pains to make certain you knew it." Now the tone was dry and a little ragged, fraying at worn edges, like a length of threadbare cloth. "This way. Through here."

She went on even as he did, thankful for Much's shoes as fallen tree limbs cracked beneath her. "Why did you not leave the horse closer?"

He peeled back a bough. "Sherwood houses outlaws other than Will Scarlet. One need only ride a track, and your coin is taken—if not your life, or your horse. I did not want to make myself so obvious to men more conversant with Sherwood than I."

Marian ducked the branch, feeling the caress of a leaf across her scalp. "But you *are* conversant."

He let go of the bough, moving ahead. "A little. I roamed the fringes when I was young. The village of Locksley is on its edges, close to Huntington."

"What is it like?"

The silence between them stretched, filled with the crackle of their passage. "I have never been there."

"But—your name . . ." She let it go then, because she feared to intrude.

"My father bestowed Locksley upon me before I left on Crusade, so I would be more than Huntington's son, but a lord in my own right. I should have gone, but . . ." He shrugged. "I was too impatient to be away. A village and small manor in the English countryside did not interest me, when Jerusalem—and glory—beckoned."

Her kirtle snagged, bringing her up short. Impatiently, Marian jerked it free. "And you are sorry for it."

He glanced briefly back, saw her level gaze on him, and turned away quickly, as if he could not bear the simplicity of her comment. "I should have valued the people, if not the revenues."

"You have the chance now."

"Yes." He pulled aside a creeper. "Here. My horse is—" He stopped short, clinging to creeper, *"gone."*

"Your horse?" Marian came up beside him, picking at a sticky substance in her hair that proved to be a cobweb. Making a moue of distaste, she wiped the residue from her hands on the nearest tree trunk. "Are you sure this is—"

"Yes. Completely sure." He gestured. "Right *there;* see how the grass has been uprooted?"

She looked, seeing the telltale signs of an iron-shod horse and the damage done by its hunger. The horse was decidedly absent. "Yes."

He sighed heavily, murmuring something she couldn't quite catch as he scraped both hands through his hair distractedly. "And I said the *track* was hazardous . . ."

He sounded so disgusted, so ineffably dismayed that Marian smiled. She was footsore, aching, and tired, but short of conjuring a horse there was little they could do.

She moved two paces and sat down on a moss-clad stump, settling her skirts around her. "We'll rest, then go on."

He pressed his spine against a tree and leaned heavily, then slowly slid down, scraping bark, until he sat on the ground. He appeared altogether exhausted, scrubbing his face all out of shape like a toddler in need of a nap. The pinched look of the flesh around his eyes and mouth deepened almost imperceptibly, but Marian saw it.

"Are you hurt?" she blurted. "I mean—worse than the obvious?"

Eyebrows lowered into a knitted shelf no less forbidding for its pale hue. The scowl was eloquent.

Marian put up a staying hand. "Oh, I know—men are never to say what does or does not hurt them . . . I learned that from my father. But from my *mother* I learned that men generally lie, because they feel it unmans them to admit they feel pain." She picked a long-stemmed flower and put the end between her teeth. Around it, she said, "How badly did he hurt you?"

A ghost of a crooked smile softened the austerity of his expression. "Not so badly as you just have."

"It is the truth, and you know it."

"Then if I tell you I am not hurt so badly, you will accuse me of lying."

"If it *is* a lie—though it usually is." She grinned around the stem. "Fairly caught, Robin. The truth, if you please."

He stared at her a long moment, saying nothing, so intent she felt her peculiarly high spirits wane. And then the mask slipped, and the faint smile returned. He scrubbed again at his face. "It isn't so much what Will Scarlet did—"

"You see?"

"—as what the Holy Land did," he finished stolidly, ignoring her comment.

"The—oh." She took the stem out of her mouth. "I did not mean to pry."

"Yes, you did. Why else would you ask?" He lessened it with irony, which surprised her; he had displayed very little of amusement before. "Men born of England do not fare well in heat and sun. There are fevers—" He shrugged. "I, like many others, brought one home with me."

She sat very straight. "Then you're not just hurt, you're *ill*—"

"But it will pass. It always does."

"Always does . . ." she echoed. "Then this has happened more than once?" She had believed it of no consequence; clearly, this was different.

"At least three times. Richard had it twice—" Abruptly, the mask was back in place. "It isn't worth discussing."

Which means, he won't discuss it. Marian sighed, tossing aside the long-stemmed flower. "Then perhaps you should remain here, while I—"

"No."

She took offense, albeit mild. "You don't even know what I intended to say."

"Oh yes. I have taken your measure, Marian"—which both

astonished and intrigued her—"and I know very well what you intended to say, and what you would like to do." He stood up, scraping bark bits from his tunic. "I am not so ill or infirm that I will allow a woman to strike out through Sherwood Forest with no one to escort her."

It called for something, if only to lessen some of her concern. She saw him shiver again. "As if *you* could do anything," she declared archly. "Who was it stunned Will Scarlet?"

Clearly, the audacity astonished him. He was rigidly, perfectly still.

Her spirit wilted. *I've gone too—*

For the second time in two days, she heard Robert of Locksley laugh. She found it intensely pleasing.

Alan of the Dales tripped over a half-buried tree root and fell sprawling into bracken, flinging out hands to catch himself, then twisting onto a shoulder because his hands were too valuable to risk on unseen hazards. He landed awkwardly and painfully on his left shoulder, then his left hip; lastly—and most annoyingly—he banged his head on an accompanying root.

He lay there a moment, swearing inventively in French, then switched to English, which he found cruder and therefore more satisfying. French was for music and women.

Alan sat up in the midst of hip-high fern, peeling a frond away from his mouth, and glared sourly at the offending root. It did not please him to realize he had undertaken a foolish and impossible task. It did not please him to admit he had been even more foolish to leave the track. But he had heard hoofbeats—or *believed* he heard them—and now he found himself dirtier than before, with green stains soiling his clothing and mud on his elbows.

I am thoroughly disreputable . . . And so he was. Before, it had been through his exploits in bed, which merely added to his allure. Now it was solely because of his appearance, which did not please him at all.

He stood up, muttering in English, and brushed as much dirt and debris from his clothing as possible. He took a single step toward the track, heard hoofbeats again, and ducked down into bracken.

This time it *was* hoofbeats.

Alan squatted very still, daring only to breathe. With the FitzWalter girl missing he had no doubt the sheriff's men were searching for her in Sherwood, where rumor said Scarlet had taken her, but even if *he* were not the target of the search he dared take no chances. They would snap him up readily enough for the sake of Eleanor's lie; only the night before the Watch had been set on him.

He waited. Morning sunlight glimmered through the spring foliage. He saw a flash of steel and blue livery as the hoofbeats grew louder.

Normans. As expected, deLacey's men, armed with swords and crossbows. He recognized none of them, except to know their livery and the arrogance of their faces.

Alan watched them go by. He lacked his lute and tunic—and much of his minstrel's demeanor, as well as a razor—but he had no doubt they would at least draw rein to question him, if only to ask about the girl. Better to hide himself than to risk recognition.

The Normans were gone. He waited a little longer, then slowly made his way out of the foliage onto the edge of the track, massaging his left shoulder. He set out once more, heading deeper into Sherwood, assuming at some point the one-handed man would appear. He was after all an outlaw acquainted with the forest, which meant he likely knew it well and who belonged in it. And as he had extended an invitation—

The faint jingle of bit and bridle intruded. It came from behind, from the direction the Normans had ridden . . . Alan froze, then lunged off the track once more. This time he chose his bolt-hole more carefully than before.

He dropped to his knees, ducking beneath the surface of the tall bracken, and peered through gaps as best he could. But ten paces up the track came a boy with a horse—a boy *leading* a horse, with no apparent intention of mounting the horse even though it wasn't lame and showed no other infirmities.

Alan frowned, chewing a lip. The horse was very fine. The

boy was not. They did not belong together. *If I could impress upon him my need to borrow the horse—*

But Alan's need went unmet. Even as he considered stepping out onto the track, inventing an explanation, someone else did so first—a dark-haired, dark-eyed man with bruises on his face, and the pinched, pale, desperate look of a man hard-pressed to survive.

His explanation was much simpler than Alan's. "Here," he said roughly, "this horse is mine, now."

Gilbert de Pisan, overseeing the packing of Prince John's retinue and baggage train in the bailey, gave a series of commands in a quiet, unhurried tone, saw to it those receiving the commands began to follow them properly, then took himself inside the earl's remarkable new castle and found his master alone in denuded chambers, chewing his fingernails.

John lowered his hand as de Pisan entered. "Well?"

"Things commence as they should, my lord. We shall be able to leave for Lincoln the moment you desire it."

John perched a portion of his weight upon the corner of a slab of English oak set upon trestles. One braced, booted leg propped him up. The other was hooked across the corner, swinging in small arcs of restless energy and poorly suppressed impatience. His crimson traveling cloak, much finer than any worn by others on the most elaborate of occasions, drooped from jeweled brooches pinned at padded shoulders.

The prince's expression was feral. "What I desire is information."

De Pisan inclined his head, folding hands inside wide sleeves. "The girl is a relative of Robert FitzWalter, Lord of Dunmow. Sir Hugh FitzWalter, her father, was a distant cousin. There is no indication they have had any dealings together, to hatch plots or for any other purpose.

"Her father's dead. What of his holdings?"

"They are hers, according to law; she is a ward of the Crown."

"Then my brother administers her dowry."

"Yes, my lord."

John mused silently, working at another nail. "She is wealthy?"

"Not incredibly so, my lord . . . Ravenskeep is a modest manor with moderate income. But she is the only remaining issue of the marriage, and both her parents are dead."

John nodded. "Find out what you can about the current state of her coffers. My brother has been somewhat occupied this past year himself . . . and if this manor is as modest as you claim, it may well have been overlooked during the ransom collections." He spat out a sliver of nail. "If so, we shall have to see to it she donates to *this* collection."

"Yes, my lord."

John's gaze was level. "What of the sheriff's price?"

De Pisan smiled faintly. "I was put on notice that Sir Guy of Gisbourne will not be so malleable as he once was."

Angevin brows rose. "Oh?"

"Indeed, it was made most clear to me that Sir Guy expects to be as well-rewarded as the sheriff. In fact, I found it most fascinating to learn of *Gisbourne's* desired reward." Briefly, de Pisan's amusement displayed good teeth. "He told me explicitly what he wanted. He then told me what the sheriff wants."

"And?"

"They are one and the same, my lord. He did not say so—in fact, he said otherwise; something about a rich old North Country woman—but it was obvious to me. He lied about the sheriff, because he knows very well a simple knight of no reknown will stand little chance against a man like William deLacey."

John sat very still. The leg no longer swung. "Yes?"

"The selfsame FitzWalter girl."

"For knight *and* sheriff?"

"It would seem so."

John's dark eyes narrowed.

De Pisan smoothed his surcoat. "My lord, if you would entertain a suggestion from your seneschal, it might behoove you to look to the FitzWalter girl yourself, with an eye toward administering her disposal upon the proper man. They say she is beautiful—that even a man of high station would care little enough for her holdings so long as the lady comes to his bed."

John made no answer.

De Pisan drew a breath. "Men such as Alnwick, Hereford, and Oxford are wealthy already . . . I believe flesh would mean more than yet another tedious manor."

The king's brother said nothing.

"Ravenskeep lies on the other side of Nottingham, my lord. In fact, a man who held lands on either side of the city—such as Huntington, and Ravenskeep—would be in position to dictate Nottingham's strength."

"Yes," John said at last. "Oh yes, I do see . . ." He looked at de Pisan. "It would be most unfortunate to waste a woman held in such high regard—and with such valuable holdings—on a mere sheriff."

"Yes, my lord. My thoughts exactly."

"In fact . . ." John smiled. "The Earl of Huntington himself, with his brand-new castle, has no wife to house in it."

Thirty-Six

Much gaped at the outlaw. He knew him: Will Scarlet, who'd fought the Hathersage Giant, then stolen Marian.

"Here," Scarlet repeated. "Save yourself a hand and let me have the horse."

Much fell back, dragging at a rein; the horse, protesting, yanked its head upward. Much did not relinquish his grasp upon the leather, which stretched his arm taut and nearly unhinged his elbow.

"Let *go*—" Scarlet grabbed his own share of rein. "By God, boy, don't make me hurt you—"

Much kicked one of Scarlet's shins, then bent and scooped up a handful of dirt and flung it at his face, jerking the horse his way. *"Mine!"* Much cried.

Scarlet swiped dirt out of his eyes, then lunged toward Much. Frightened, the bay stallion set back, digging up track, even as Scarlet's grasping hand came down on Much's shoulder, grabbing a handful of tunic. "You little—"

Much bared teeth, jerking the rein again. The bay squealed and plunged backward, dragging Much and Scarlet in tow like fish on a willow stringer.

"Mine—" Much hissed.

"You little whelp—" Scarlet attempted to halt the horse by sheer force of will, but he was no match for a frightened horse.

A body darted out of the trees and leaped for the saddle, flinging a leg across cloak and leather. Toes dug for stirrups. "I'll settle this," the man offered breathlessly. *"I'll* take the horse—"

"By God, you *won't*—" Scarlet caught at a hosen-clad leg. "Get down from there—"

"Mine!" Much shouted.

The mounted man jammed heels into the bay's flanks, grasping one loose rein even as the other remained well-claimed. He pulled the horse's head around toward his knee, trying to turn him, to deprive them of leverage, so he could break the horse free.

Scarlet jumped for an arm. "I'll have you down—"

Much kicked at Scarlet even as the golden-haired man laughed and said, "A horse requires a rider, not an oxen-driver!"

"Oxen-driver, am I?—By God, boy, stop your kicking . . ." And yet again to the rider, *"I'll* have you down—"

Much clung to the rein, making furious, inarticulate noises. The bay squealed and set back again, pawing clots of track, snapping his head skyward in a bid to break free.

The rider pulled the reins taut. The horse, steered so cruelly, swung his hindquarters and nearly trampled Much. Will Scarlet jerked the stranger's right foot out of the stirrup, then grasped handfuls of hosen, hauling him bodily down from the saddle even as the rider grasped at mane and rein.

"Mine!" Much shrieked.

The horse backed up quickly, shedding its rider over a shoulder as Scarlet dragged him free. Much, still clinging to rein, was jerked off his feet, but refused to release his find. He was dragged several paces before the terrified animal stopped, quivering and snorting.

"Hold!" a voice shouted.

Much, spitting dirt, craned his head around.

Four men stepped out of the trees. Three of them had bows; one did not. He was the Hathersage Giant.

Will Scarlet, tangled on the track with the golden-haired stranger, let go of the man. "The horse is *mine*," he snapped. "My portion of the fee."

"Is it?" Little John retorted. He strode forward, caught the stranger by tunic and shoulder—and a handful of hair—and dragged him to his feet, swinging him to face the three men. "Then this one's mine! His coin is *my* fee!"

"Wait—" the man protested, but Little John shook him sharply. "No noise out of you. This doesn't concern you."

"But it *does*—"

"No noise, I said!"

Much got up on hands and knees, watching closely, and slowly backed toward the horse. If he could get up without them noticing, then mount the animal—

One of the nocked bows was lifted in his direction. Much stopped moving. "Here," the outlaw ordered. "And bring the horse with you."

The Earl of Huntington waited in the bailey as both men dismounted, handing their mounts to the horseboys. They were similar in appearance: both tall, both slender, and both powerful barons of ancient families and established titles: Geoffrey de Mandeville, the Earl of Essex, and Henry Bohun, Earl of Hereford.

Mandeville was the eldest, a spare, gray, dignified man. Bohun was younger, darker, more fluid in movement. Each man came forward, offering outstretched hands to the earl and his companion, Eustace de Vesci.

"Well timed," de Vesci said. "Prince John has only just left."

"Yes," de Mandeville said. He was terse and austere of feature. "We met him on the road."

De Vesci's arm dropped away from the handclasp. "Did he say anything?"

De Mandeville's tone was frosty. "To me he says little, as if fearing he will condemn himself to his brother's man."

Bohun's expression was sober, but less severe. "He fears Essex, as is to be expected. But to me he was more forthcoming. He suggested we make haste, if we were to wish well to Huntington's son." His tone was dry. "He left no doubt as to his suspicions."

"He would not," Huntington agreed. "That is John's way, to sow discord as he can. Now. Come in. There is much to talk about."

The others followed him, murmuring comments about the castle. De Vesci was gloomier than de Mandeville and Bohun, remarking on his fears that John would contrive a way to learn of their discussion. Huntington signed him into silence, then led them all into a private chamber.

"Ralph will bring wine," he said. Then, to de Vesci, with dry deliberation, "If you *desire* John to know, do say so in the hallways."

The gentle chiding found its mark. Red-faced, de Vesci scowled back. "Do you not trust your household?"

"As much as you trust yours."

Bohun laughed harshly. "John disunites us even in his absence."

De Mandeville's gray eyes flicked from man to man as he stripped off his gloves and moved to unpin his cloak. "I think it important we waste no time here. John moves quickly—"

"Softsword," de Vesci remarked in contempt.

"But not his wits," de Mandeville retorted. "He is the Old King's son in many ways, and Henry was not a fool."

Huntington's smile was cool. "He would not thank us for this."

"He would not have brought us to this." De Mandeville dropped cloak and gloves into a chair. "Nor would Geoffrey; he was less stubborn than John."

Bohun scoffed politely. "But a vain fool, withal. To die in a tournament—"

"An accident," Huntington said.

"One wonders. He was older than John, and would have been named Richard's heir . . ." Bohun turned, found a chair, seated himself. "But we are not here to speak of dead men—"

De Vesci's voice was harsh. "Geoffrey had a son. Arthur of Brittany may well be our best hope."

"Richard is our best hope." De Mandeville's voice was crisp. "Do we forget ourselves? Our loyalty is to the king, not to destroying John merely for our own sakes."

Huntington turned as Ralph came through the door with a tray bearing a flagon and silver goblets. "Thank you, Ralph. There, on the table. I will pour for my guests." Ralph set the tray down and turned to leave. Huntington delayed him with a gesture. "My son?"

The servant shook his head. "No, my lord. Not yet."

Huntington's mouth crimped briefly. "Send him here at once when he arrives."

"Yes, my lord." Ralph pulled the door shut behind him.

Huntington moved to the table and began to fill the goblets. "Now. I am informed that John has sent a message to Philip of France, suggesting their mutual interests are best served by the Lionheart's continued captivity. I am also informed he has written to Germany, offering Henry money to *keep* Richard there."

"But—" de Vesci frowned. "So long as the king lives, John cannot rule. Everyone knows Richard is held prisoner."

De Mandeville shrugged. "All Henry need do is raise the ransom demand. The realm is near bankrupt now—when the people realize they cannot afford to meet Henry's demands, they may well give it up as a bad risk."

Bohun nodded. "And if Richard should meet with an accident—"

De Vesci shook his head. "No one would believe that."

"No. But dead is *dead*—and England would require a king. Since Berengaria has not conceived . . ." Bohun gestured. "John is the obvious choice."

"There is Arthur," de Vesci insisted. "Geoffrey was the oldest, after Richard—his son would take precedence. Richard himself is said to favor Arthur. That is why John was given the Gloucester heiress and all the honors with her, to take what his brother chose to give him and be silent the rest of his life."

Huntington shook his head as he handed out the goblets. "Arthur is eight years old. A boy would stand no chance in a fight for the throne of England."

"And he's in Brittany," Bohun added. "His mother is sister to the Scots king—she knows too much is at stake. And the Bretons prize him too much to risk him now. Later, perhaps, when he is older—"

"When John holds the throne?" De Vesci drank, then glared at them all. "You know what he will do. He will have the boy killed."

De Mandeville sipped his wine more deliberately, then lowered the goblet. "Not if he poses no threat. And he won't, for a time . . . and if we succeed in this, we'll have no need of Arthur. For Richard will be home, and England safe."

De Vesci was openly skeptical. "You are so secure in that. You wear the king as your banner."

De Mandeville's temper flared. "By God, I should! He made me Justiciar of England—it is your folly to forget it!"

Huntington spoke quietly in the sudden silence. "Old friend," he said to the Earl of Essex who, with the Bishop of Durham, personally administered England in the king's absence, "no one forgets it. You risk more than us all."

The older man sat down suddenly, clutching at a chair arm. "This foolish Crusade—it strips England of her king when she needs him most."

"The Crusade is ended," Bohun said. "Already our soldiers return home—as Huntington's son does." He flicked a glance at the earl. "Do you intend to inform him of what we do?"

"He must know. And you must allow him to know. He was close to the king himself." Huntington's face was masklike. "After all, it was the Lionheart who personally ransomed him back from Saladin." His slight smile was stiff. "Not his father."

* * *

Locksley was hungry, sick, and out of sorts, but he said nothing of it, because Marian faced the circumstances with a fortitude and spirit he had not expected to find in a gently bred young woman.

She stepped over tree roots, picking her way with care. "I imagine this is not what you are accustomed to."

He smiled faintly, thinking she negotiated treacherous footing easily enough in borrowed shoes, with an unaffected, coltish grace he found peculiarly engaging. In no way did she resemble the decorous and subdued young woman who had come to the dais to give him a colorless if circumspect welcome home. Then she had been very like the others, watching him sideways, as if weighing him with an eye toward a future relationship.

Or was it she judged me against other soldiers? Perhaps even her father.

"Walking," she elaborated. "That was a fine horse . . ."

It pinched. "Yes."

She scraped tangled hair out of her face, tucking a lock behind her ear. "Perhaps he will make his way home."

She meant to be kind. He was less so. "Perhaps. I rather think he will find his way to someone else's stable."

"If they know he is yours, perhaps they will bring him back."

He looked at her levelly. "Do you really think so?"

She gazed back a long moment, then sighed. "No. I wanted to lift your spirits."

He smiled crookedly. "My spirits will do well enough without discussion."

Her expression was skeptical, but she did not address the issue, choosing instead another tack. "What of your fever?"

"It also requires no discussion."

Marian was clearly undaunted, no longer intimidated by his tone or expression, which he found both curious and puzzling. "You sound like my father." The hem of her kirtle caught. She jerked it free. "Then what *would* you prefer to talk about?"

He bent a limb back to keep it from her face. "We need talk about nothing."

She thrust out an arm to steady herself. "There is no sense in punishing ourselves because someone stole your horse . . . we may as well make the best of it."

Leaf mold hissed beneath his boots. "I have not found talking to be the best of anything."

She slanted him a look under lowered lids. "No. I recall that about you—you said very little that Christmas Eve."

It took him a moment to recall the one she meant. When he did he was moved to smile, but forbore to let her see it. "Perhaps because I was somewhat taken aback by the forwardness of a knight's daughter who took it upon herself to trick me under the mistletoe."

Marian's face flared red.

"Well?" he prodded. "You did trick me."

"I told you," she muttered self-consciously, "I had kissed everyone else."

"There was no need to kiss *me*, merely to count me as a conquest."

"It wasn't—you weren't—" She shrugged awkwardly. "Never mind."

He scrubbed briefly at his forehead, faintly amused he had managed to discomfit her. She had a ready tongue and a readier wit and was quick to defend others, but now, when she required it for herself, she offered nothing in her own defense save a self-conscious silence. "And I thought it was for the man to seek out the woman."

She cast him a sideways glance. The tangle of her hair framed an exquisite face, even bruised as it was. "You wouldn't have. You barely spoke to anyone. You stood in the shadows and *watched* everyone . . ." And then, as if realizing she might yet offend, she let it trail off as if inconsequential. "I just thought . . ."

Oddly it intrigued him, to discover what she had thought. "Yes?"

"I thought you needed it," she murmured, mostly to herself.

"Needed it." *A strange observation.*

Marian's tone was level. "You looked very lonely. Very— solitary."

He broke dried limbs beneath his boots. "Solitariness is not so bad a thing. There is some security to be gained in relying on oneself."

"But you weren't," she said quietly.

He looked at her sharply, aware of an undertone. "You recall the evening more clearly than I."

Her face was red again. "You were not relying on yourself. You were there in the midst of many people celebrating Christmas, a happy time for all, yet you hung back and stood in the shadows. Even when my mother attempted to draw you out." Marian's expression warped very briefly. "It was her last Christmas."

His tongue lay dead in his mouth, stilled by the simplicity of her statement and the knowledge of what it meant. *Both parents dead. And no brothers or sisters. No more family holidays.*

He wanted to apologize. He wanted to tell her he could not recall why he had been so reluctant to join the festivities, save he was not a boy who showed much of himself to others. He wanted also to express condolences, that her mother had not lived to see another Christmas.

Mostly, looking at her, he wanted to tell her very plainly he wished for mistletoe *now*, so he could be the one to ask the forfeit of her.

Alan hitched a shoulder, trying to jerk it free of the massive paw that held him still. "Since when did the Hathersage Giant take to outlawry?"

The grip slackened only a moment, then clamped down again. "You see?" the giant asked. "Even *he* knows the truth!"

Will Scarlet laughed harshly. "Aye! He called you outlaw."

The Hathersage Giant swung Alan around. "Have you coin?" he barked. "Have you anything of value with which I can pay my fee?"

As if I would tell him. Alan shook his head, glancing at the others. He knew none of them.

The sandy-haired one beckoned to the boy. Only three fingers were wrapped around the longbow. The fourth was missing. "Here. Bring that horse *here.*"

The boy approached. Alan was faintly surprised to discover he recognized him: the cutpurse he'd caught in Nottingham, who'd told him Marian FitzWalter was taken. What was *he* doing with a fine mount?—unless he'd taken to stealing horses as well as men's purses.

The other archer lowered his bow, slackening the string. He was young, younger than Alan and nearly as pretty, though dark instead of golden. He grinned at the giant. "Little John," he said, "in Sherwood we *take* coin, we don't ask if a man has it!"

Will Scarlet was truculent. "Have I paid my fee, then? The horse is enough, I'll warrant."

The boy clutched reins. *"Mine."*

The slight, dark man gestured slightly. "Clym."

The arrow was loosed. It sped the brief distance, then drove into the earth between the boy's bare feet.

Alan jerked briefly. "He's a *boy*—"

The archer, Clym, didn't smile. "So was I, once."

Little John released Alan's shoulder. "By God, Adam Bell, I'll not have you harming the boy! D'ye hear me? He's done nothing. What threat is he to you?"

Alan stared hard at the slight man. Adam Bell? Adam *Bell?* "Wait," he breathed.

"D'ye hear me?" Little John repeated.

"Is it enough?" Scarlet asked.

"Mine," the boy declared.

A soft hoot came from nearby. Adam Bell and the two archers turned sharply toward the sound. In a moment a man stepped out of the trees.

"You!" Alan said. Then, more urgently, "Have you damaged my lute?"

The one-handed man grinned, hoisting the instrument up to display it. "Buy it back, and find out!"

"Wat." Adam Bell glanced back briefly to the archer called Clym. "Take the horse. Cloudisley will relieve our new friend of his purse."

Adam Bell. Clym—of the Clough? And Cloudisley. Alan stared. *My God—I've stumbled across the most notorious outlaws in England!*

William of Cloudisley came forward, arching suggestive brows at Alan. He waggled beckoning fingers. "You can give it to me—or I can take it myself."

"He's not gentle," Clym declared. "Though pretty as you are, I might do it myself."

Alan fell back a step, but the giant's body prevented him from further retreat. "This isn't fair," he said. "I'm not a wealthy man. I'm not a lord. I'm not a Norman. You're robbing an Englishman."

"Lute-player!" Clym's tone was contemptuous. "You live off Norman bounty." He looked at Much, lingering much too slowly with the horse. "Boy, what did I say?"

The boy reached down and plucked the arrow from the track. He threw it back at Clym in a mute but rebellious gesture.

"Leave him alone," Little John rumbled.

"That horse is my fee," Scarlet declared.

Adam Bell still looked at the one-handed man. "Did you bring the lute-player here?"

"I relieved him of his lute because it would have given him away to the Watch." The man named Wat came further onto the track, gripping the instrument's neck. "He's one of us, Adam—though only just come to the life. He's the fool who tupped the sheriff's daughter."

Clym laughed harshly. "Fool to tup her? Or fool to be caught?"

"Both," Alan said glumly. "Though she is an *active* woman."

Adam Bell nodded. "Worth hanging for?"

"He wasn't going to hang me. He meant to cut out my tongue." Alan's gaze lingered briefly on Wat's stump. "At least you can still steal . . . I'd lose my living."

Wat grinned. "Aye, but I'm a thief *because* of this. . . ." He looked beyond Alan to Little John. "So, you've come, too? Aye, well ye might—the sheriff's asking for you."

The giant's face drained. It left him wan and sickly, splotched with copper freckles.

Will Scarlet grunted. "Warned you, didn't I?"

"The news," Adam Bell said. "What have you learned of the sheriff?"

"He's set his Watch on the pretty lad what raped his daughter"—Wat flashed a grin at Alan—"and wants the Hathersage Giant as well as the man called Scarlet. Has to do with a woman—*another* woman—"

"Sheriff's leman," Scarlet scoffed.

"No." One-handed Wat shook his head. "No, she's the daughter of a knight. Marian FitzWalter. She's nothing to do with the sheriff."

"You see?" Little John's tone was aggrieved. "Not a Norman at all, nor the sheriff's woman—"

Cloudisley nodded thoughtfully. " 'Tis why the Normans are out, then."

"Boy," Clym growled at recalcitrant Much, "d'ye want an arrow between your eyes instead of between your feet?"

"Anyway, she's safe now," Little John said. "Halfway home by now."

Alan put out his hand to Wat. "May I have my lute?"

"Your money first," Cloudisley said, putting out *his* hand.

"Marian," Much whispered. Then his eyes grew large. "Horse," he expelled.

"Aye, horse," Clym agreed, striding forward at last to grab the reins from Much.

Much didn't seem to notice. *"Robin's."*

"Mine now, boy."

"No!" Much shrieked it. *"Robin's—"* And he jerked the reins away, sending the horse lunging sideways.

Cloudisley's bow jammed Little John's belly. "Hold," he said softly.

"He's a *boy*—"

"My lute?" Alan repeated, looking back at Wat.

The one-handed man glanced at Adam Bell. "I did say he could fetch it."

"He can buy it," Bell answered. And then, tersely, "Riders—hear?"

Cloudisley swung at the muted drumming of hooves. "Normans?—aye, what else—?"

"Clym!" It was Bell, twisting to look back at the other outlaw. "Clym—leave the boy—"

Wat was gone, disappearing into the foliage with Alan's lute. Cloudisley and Clym fell in beside one another at the center of the track, nocking arrows and raising bows even as Bell stepped to the side. Sunlight flashed on steel.

"Normans—?" But Alan didn't wait to see, he simply leaped for the trees.

Little John grabbed for Much. "Let him go—let the horse go—"

"Mine," Much declared.

"Normans, boy—leave *them* to chase the horse!"

"Away!" Adam Bell hissed.

William of Cloudisley and Clym of the Clough loosed two arrows as the riders broke into sight: six blue-cloaked Nottingham men in conical Norman helms. Two fell instantly, plucked off their mounts by arrows.

"All of them," Bell said curtly. "Let none of them live."

Much tried to mount the bay, but its fright sent it scrabbling sideways. Little John clung to the boy's arm, pulling him away. "Let him *go*—"

"A miss!" Cloudisley shouted, twisting aside as he reached for another arrow. "One coming through—*Clym*—"

Norman sword was unsheathed, scything through the air in a flash of steel. It drove both archers aside, breaking their opportunity. Both men dropped, rolled, and came up, scrabbling for new arrows.

Little John squeezed the boy's thin wrist, breaking the grip on the reins. Freed, the horse retreated; Little John swung the boy around, ducked as the blade whistled by, then shoved Much toward the trees. "Run, boy—" He swung back, doubled a fist, brought it up swiftly to chop the Norman rider's horse in the nose.

Alan, sprawled face down in bracken, gaped as the blow sent the horse staggering backward, tossing its head violently, so that the rider, caught off-guard, had to put his mind to horsemanship instead of to killing outlaws.

"Two more!" Adam Bell shouted. "And another coming through!"

Cloudisley and Clym, falling in behind the Normans, loosed two more arrows.

Will Scarlet dodged a horse and a crossbow bolt, then leaped up to catch rein. He hung on leather, letting the horse take his weight as its rider attempted futilely to control his mount while loading another bolt. The bolt fell free, and then the crossbow itself, as the Norman reached for his sword.

"Scarlet!" Cloudisley shouted, and let fly with another arrow.

"One more!" Bell shouted. "By God, giant—take *care!*"

Little John threw himself to the track as the sword whistled down again in a glittering, deadly arc. He swore as a hoof struck his leg, rolled away, scrambled up and lurched for the trees.

"Clym," Bell said intently.

"Mine," the archer agreed, but the arrow did not fly true. It lodged itself high in the Norman's back, near his left shoulder. Clym swore.

The Norman wheeled his horse heavily, looking back at the outlaws. An older man, they saw, a coldly furious veteran whom they could not afford to let live.

"Cloudisley!" Bell shouted.

But the Norman jammed spurs into his mount, swung the horse again, and sent him down the track toward Nottingham. Robin's bay, free of impediment, followed at a gallop.

"No!" Scarlet shouted. "By God—not the *horse*—"

Alan rose cautiously as Little John broke through bracken. "Well done—" he began.

The giant clamped his shoulder tightly to hold him in place. The other hand grasped at and caught the purse tied beneath the tunic, now exposed by a rent in the cloth. "Had I a choice," the giant said hoarsely, "I'd leave your coin to you." He tore the purse free of belt. "But I haven't got a choice."

"Wait—" Alan cried. And then, as Wat reappeared, "Give me back my lute!"

Little John turned and flung Alan's purse at Adam Bell. "There! My fee. Now am I free to go?"

Bell caught the purse, hefted it and nodded satisfaction. But the look he sent to the giant was one of an odd compassion. "Why go?" he asked. "What's left to you now, but to live in Sherwood?"

"I've paid your fee!" Little John snarled. "I've robbed an innocent man, and I've given the purse to you."

Bell's gaze was level. "And you aided well-known outlaws in full view of a Norman soldier, who lived to tell about it."

Horrified, Little John stared.

Cloudisley hooked an arm through his bow, settling it across his back. "You are not a man another man forgets, especially a Norman soldier undone by peasantry."

The giant lowered his gaze from Adam Bell to the bodies sprawled on the track: five Norman soldiers in the sheriff of Nottingham's livery.

Will Scarlet laughed. "Go home to your sheep," he jeered. "Go home to Hathersage, so they can hang you there!"

One-handed Wat slapped the belly of the lute into Alan's grasp. "And *you*," he said cheerfully, "are already wanted."

Much came onto the track, wiping a wrist across his nose. He said nothing, staring sulkily at them all.

Scarlet laughed again, filling the trees with sound. "Wolf's-heads, all of us—to a boy and a pretty minstrel!"

"No," Alan said, even as Little John did.

One-handed Wat grinned. "Welcome to Sherwood Forest, where the king's law fails and *our* law prevails!"

Marian pulled aside foliage. "There," she said. "The road." It lay just ahead of them through the last fringes of forest, a rutted stretch of road leading west to Nottingham, east to Ravenskeep. She cast him a relieved smile. "Not so far, now."

"Do you—" But he stopped, turning even as she did toward the forest track but paces away from them, to the sound of galloping horses. "Charlemagne!"

She saw the riderless horse as it rounded a curve in the track. With it came another, bearing a blue-liveried man bent low in the saddle. The shaft of an arrow protruded from one shoulder. "Robin—"

"I see," he said tersely, moving hastily toward the track. "He's Norman—Wait . . . *Charlemagne*—"

But the wounded soldier rode on, as if he dared not stop, and the bay ran with him.

Marian watched him go. Then she sat down and methodically began to untie the laces binding the shoes to her ankles.

Locksley, deeply disappointed, turned back to her. "What are you doing?"

"Taking them off."

He glanced down the road again, muttering under his breath. "He was trained better, once . . . but I've been gone too long."

"At least he's free of outlaws." Marian stripped off one shoe and began on the other. "Surely the sheriff will see to it he's sent home."

There was a curious note in his voice. "Why are you—"

"Blisters," she supplied crisply. "If we're to walk to Ravenskeep, I'll have to do it barefoot." She got up, bundling the shoes together. "I just won't tell Much."

Thirty-Seven

The mews at Nottingham Castle were filled with perches of differing sizes as well as differing heights, servicing a variety of hawks and falcons: the long-winged gyrfalcons, peregrines, sakers, and the lanners, as well as the smaller merlins, for use in unobstructed hunting; and the short-winged goshawks and sparrow hawks, for hunting in wooded country. The building, built specifically for the tending and training of fine hunting birds, was purposely kept dim, illuminated only by a single window. Its door was just wide enough to allow a man carrying hawk or falcon on his wrist to pass through.

William deLacey was justly proud of his mews, for he had spent much time and money on hiring expert falconers. He deeply enjoyed the communion with fierce raptors, deriving great satisfaction from the taking of eyases—nestlings, from tree or cliff—and the juvenile branchers, carefully caught in nets or socks.

When the soldier came with undue haste into the mews,

knocking a shoulder against the narrow door, deLacey was furious. But to speak loudly and sharply in the presence of the birds would upset them unduly and do great harm to their training. He took the soldier by one arm and firmly ushered him out again.

DeLacey swung the door shut. A swift glance told him there were no falcons tied for weathering on the outdoor blocks. "Never come to me here. You will wait outside until such a time as I exit the mews. Do you understand?"

The soldier nodded hastily. He was young, russet-haired, clearly worried. "It's the castellan, my lord. He's come back wounded. We've put him in the guardhouse and called for the surgeon . . . a horse came with him. There—the bay."

DeLacey looked where the soldier indicated as they crossed the bailey toward the guardhouse. The bay was a fine animal, but one he did not recognize. "See to it the horse is tended. We'll have its presence cried later in the market." He moved past the soldier to the guardhouse door, shouldering aside the group of men gathering there. Archaumbault was popular.

He found the older man stretched out on a pallet, breathing heavily. He lay belly-down, his head turned to the side. Already they had stripped him of cloak and surcoat, but the mail hauberk remained. An arrow shaft stood up from his shoulder.

"By God," deLacey said tightly, "have the shaft cut. Then take the mail *off*."

Archaumbault's tone was harsh. "I said no. I sent for you first."

DeLacey knelt. Archaumbault's color was bad and he sweated, but nothing indicated that it was a fatal wound. "What of the others with you?"

"Dead." Archaumbault coughed, and swore. "Outlaws—with longbows—"

Contempt flickered. "Your men had crossbows."

The castellan coughed again, grinding his teeth. "All of them, my lord . . . the boy, the giant—Will Scarlet—"

He found it astonishing. "*They* were there?"

"Yes." Gloved fingers twitched. "Adam Bell, and others—but the red-haired giant was with them, and the boy—"

Grimly, "—and Scarlet—"

385

"—and the lute-player." Archaumbault held his breath. "There's more—"

"More than *that?*"

"On the road—on the way . . . I did not dare stop—it was the woman, my lord . . . the FitzWalter girl . . ."

Marian— He was poised as a fox to bolt, no longer concerned with Archaumbault, who would live. "With the others?"

"No. Not there. The road to Ravenskeep—"

"Ah." Relief was overwhelming, combined with jubilation. "Free of Scarlet, then—"

"With another man."

"Another . . . who?"

A man came into the guardhouse. He was tall, very thin, gray-haired. He carried a leather bag. "My lord Sheriff, if I may—"

The surgeon. DeLacey barely spared him a glance, fixing his attention on the castellan. "Who was the man, Archaumbault?"

The surgeon was diffidently insistent. "My lord—if you please—"

DeLacey waved a silencing hand. *"Who?"*

Archaumbault breathed tightly. "Tall—very fair . . . hair nearly white—"

DeLacey's blood chilled. "Robert of Locksley." *What has he to do with this?*

"My lord—" Archaumbault gritted. "May I have water?"

DeLacey gestured imperatively to the surgeon. "Get about your business. I have other concerns." As the surgeon bent to his work the sheriff pushed his way back through the men and out into the bailey. He went directly to the stables, where he ordered the bay horse brought to him. When it was, he studied it closely.

"My lord?" A boy came forward, bearing a bundle of cloth. "My lord—'twas hooked on the saddle."

DeLacey took it, shaking out folds. A man's mantle, no more, of good weight and weave, but no elaboration.

Something fell into straw. The boy bent, retrieved it, handed it over.

DeLacey held it in his palm. A plain silver cloak-brooch, a simple heraldic device.

He shut his hand over it. "Huntington," he murmured. He stared blindly at his fist. "Robert of Locksley." Naming the enemy.

"My lord?"

The sheriff glared at the boy, thrusting the bay's reins back into small hands. "Here. Take it. Put it with the others. Then have my horse readied and brought out into the bailey." He nearly cuffed the boy for slowness. "Immediately!"

The morning mist dispersed and the sky was clear of cloudiness, leaving the day bright with promise. But Locksley was in no mood to appreciate the weather. He wanted to stop, to sit down, to *lie* down, so long as it meant he could shut his eyes and rest, ridding himself of weakness, aches, and chills, and the vague disorientation that accompanied the fever that had wracked Richard's army. Some men had died of it, but they had been weak to begin with, deprived of proper food and rest, cooked in their mail by the unblinking eye of a harsher sun, stripped of dignity and strength by the illness that ravaged their bowels. When the fever found them, too, there was little hope for survival.

Locksley had survived. He had survived worse than that. He would survive this.

Meanwhile, he walked with increasing stiffness next to FitzWalter's daughter, who had in undimmed cheerfulness hiked up her kirtle and shift, tucked the folds beneath her girdle, and strode on barefoot.

"Not so far," Marian said, avoiding a puddle of urine.

He shivered, wondering if she could hear his bones rattle. He offered her no answer; what she had said did not require one.

"What is he like?" She strode along the road with no pretense to maidenly distaste. She did, in fact, appear to relish the freedom; he began to wonder if, as a child, she had proved difficult to discipline out of hoydenish ways.

But the question was a proper question, with an answer expected. Instead, he countered it with a question of his own. "Who?"

"The king," Marian said.

Of course. They all asked. Even those who considered the question unimportant, because its answer might divulge the sort of information they required to make decisions. Or those who asked it with a sly wink, or a smirk, or a blatant vulgarity.

None of them knew Richard. They only thought they did, basing their conclusions on rumor and innuendo. Those who *did* know Richard knew better than to ask.

Marian had asked the question. Her reason was innocent: what was the man like whom her father had died serving?

"Worth dying for," he answered.

She paused only an instant, a hare before it bolts, then strode on again. He knew then his answer hadn't been the one for which she had fished. But now that it was said, she contemplated it closely.

"He would have to be, wouldn't he?" Her tone was odd, a bit hurried, a trifle strained, with a hint of diffidence. "Kings who lead men in war *ought* to be worth dying for, since so many men do it."

Yes. Kings ought to be. Few of them were. He believed Richard was.

"My father said he was a brilliant campaigner. That a man would be a fool to place his trust in someone else."

The sun, for England, was bright, unfettered with cloud or haze. Everything sounded unnaturally loud. "Yes," he said. "That was one of the things Leopold despised."

"Leopold of Austria?"

"And Philip of France." It helped a little, to talk. "Philip was a weak man in all respects, save his opinion of himself. It was natural that men would revere Richard more—he is every inch a warrior-king, best equipped to inspire and lead men into battle. Philip was best equipped to stay at home and connive, which he eventually decided to do. Richard begged him to stay, but Philip was adamant. He packed up and left."

"And Leopold? What did the king do to him to make *him* go home?"

Locksley smiled wryly, recalling the harsh words traded by the angry men. "Leopold was not a weak man. He believed himself as good or better a soldier and leader as the famous Lionheart, with some grounds for such a belief. But no one else believed it—Richard has a way of *dominating* anything, be it conversation, games, or brute physical tests—and Leopold was insulted. He also packed up and went home."

"But there must be more to it than that. Being unable to match King Richard—or better him—in all respects is not grounds for kidnapping him and throwing him into a dungeon, then selling him to the German king."

A part of him wanted to argue that Leopold had been a petty, spiteful man who had done as he'd done out of sheer maliciousness. But another part of him acknowledged that Richard had done much to provoke and encourage Leopold's hatred without foreseeing the consequences. "It was Leopold's way of regaining what had been lost."

"Pride?" Marian laughed briefly. "Men do so many things in the name of pride."

It stung, a little; he had his own share of pride, which even now prevented him from admitting he felt too ill to go much farther. "And would you call it a bad thing?"

She cast him a sideways glance, as if startled by the question. "No. I only wonder if there are times when something other than pride might solve a difficulty."

The implied reproof made him cool. "For a woman, perhaps."

The trace of condescension did not appear to discomfit her, if indeed she noticed it at all as she challenged him. "Ah, but a woman who has pride is said to be vain."

"Because a woman's pride is often misplaced."

"How so?" Her tone was sharper now.

"A woman's pride is in her beauty—"

She interrupted. "Beauty is often equated with value. A woman must think in terms of her value, since there is so little else she is good for."

He was not prepared to argue that. "A man is most proud of his ability to protect his family and serve his king."

"Of course." She borrowed his condescension. "He takes pride in his ownership of a woman, his ability to sire children, and his placement with the king, who might reward his persistence with preferment, such as a knighthood." She cast him a bright glance.

389

She meant to provoke him, of course, who had been knighted on the battlefield by the King of England. He didn't feel it worth pursuing, except he *was* interested in the contents of her comments. "Is this what you believe? That a man takes pride in *ownership?*"

"A man does own a woman. A man *buys* a woman—"

"It is the woman who brings the dowry, not the man who pays for her. It might better be charged the woman buys the man."

She was undaunted, continuing unabated. "—or he offers certain things, certain assurances of protection or preferment, in exchange for relieving her father of her."

"An uncharitable view. Is it yours?"

Marian frowned. "I'm not sure. But neither am I certain it has no merit." She chewed briefly at her lip. "Eleanor deLacey said many things that have made me think."

He snorted. "Eleanor deLacey is one of the vainest women I have ever met—and with little cause."

Marian laughed. "You say that out of injured pride."

"How so?"

"Because she is the only woman who came to the feast who did not set her cap for you. In fact, she made it clear she preferred the minstrel to you."

He grinned crookedly. "I would say I am grateful for that, if it wouldn't be churlish of me."

"You have already proven yourself churlish by remarking upon her vanity, and the lack of need for it," Marian observed archly, then the humor faded into consideration. "But she did make sense. I had not thought of it before, until she addressed it, but Eleanor is right: women have no say in the matter of their disposal. Fathers marry us off where they will. Our chastity is well-guarded so our value is increased."

"Eleanor deLacey's was not."

Marian laughed. "But she made it *her* choice, did she not? She did what she wanted to do, bestowing her affection on the man she preferred, instead of letting her father marry her off to the first foul-smelling old reprobate who had the price—and the title—for her."

Locksley digested that. "I am neither old nor a reprobate, and I bathed only yesterday."

"What do you—? *Oh!*" She laughed again. "Forgive me—it *was* you, wasn't it?"

"And I would have said *two* women came to the feast who did not set their caps for me." He cast her an exaggeratedly austere glance. "Unless you lied to me when I accused you of it."

"No." Marian smiled. "No, I didn't lie. Nor did I set my cap. I only came because I wanted to know if you had seen my father."

Much more than that. But she knew that, now.

He swerved from the topic. "Eleanor deLacey has lost whatever freedom she knew because of her preference for the minstrel. Do you believe it was worth it?"

"I'm sure she believed she would never be caught."

"And therefore did not consider the consequences of her folly?" He nodded. "Men do that, as well. I have no doubt the minstrel gave little thought to the consequences." He considered it further. "Or, if he did, it added spice to the liaison."

"Do *I* believe it was worth it?" Marian sighed. "Had you asked it of me yesterday, *before* Will Scarlet, I would have said it depended on how much she cared for the man. But now I can no longer judge. I am myself as publicly despoiled as Eleanor. It doesn't matter that Will Scarlet never attempted intimacy . . . they will condemn me anyway. They will whisper about me, spread rumors about me, take delight in exaggerating the stories, until they will have it given out that every outlaw in Sherwood Forest had the chance to lift my skirts." She looked at him unflinchingly. "That *is* what they will say. I must be prepared for it."

She was fierce, and proud, even in the tattered dishabille that underscored the brutal truth of what she said. And in that fierceness, that pride, that dishabille, he considered her more beautiful than the woman he had met upon the dais of Huntington Castle.

His head ached. His eyes felt hot. "What will you do?" he asked. "Have you other family?"

She shrugged. "There are other FitzWalters, but only distantly related. My father's brothers died without issue. And *my* brother when he was sixteen . . . my father leaves no one to carry on the name." Her face was in stark, brittle profile as she watched the rutted road. "I am in wardship to the Crown. Before this, I have no doubt the king might have wed me to whomever asked for me. Now, I have no value." Her lopsided smile was bittersweet. "Eleanor made her choice, and now she suffers for it. I made no choice at all, but the result is the same." Marian raised her head and looked directly at him. The challenge was implicit. "Tell me again, Sir Robert, that a woman need not concern herself with such masculine things as pride."

He did not tell her so. She deserved the truth.

William deLacey. The name was inside his head. He wondered somewhat erratically if delirium had overtaken him at last, that he would think of the sheriff apropos of nothing.

And then he realized it was apropos of *something:* Locksley knew with perfect conviction that the sheriff would still take her, regardless of the stories.

Men had done less for despoiled women before. A man such as deLacey, looking at this woman, would do much more.

Thirty-Eight

William deLacey swept the amber-dyed mantle around his shoulders and pinned it impatiently with a massive brooch of Celtic knotwork set with golden cairngorm. Though different in weight and style from the Huntington heraldic brooch, it served to remind him even more forcefully of Robert of Locksley's unanticipated and wholly undesirable aid in rescuing Marian. That Archaumbault had failed made deLacey all the angrier;

he had fully expected to be credited with the rescue in his guise as Sheriff of Nottingham. It was, after all, his job.

He stabbed the tang through wool, then strode purposefully out of the chamber into a smudgy corridor, glowering at the woman ineffectively sweeping the floor just outside his door. Another time he might have chastised her for poor work; just now, he had other things on his mind.

DeLacey had counted on the rescue. More than anything the rescue of a woman by a man made that man more attractive to the woman, and he had anticipated Marian's gratitude in full measure, expecting it to aid his quest to secure her hand. But now it was Robert of Locksley she would thank for winning her back from Scarlet. The knowledge made deLacey grit his teeth so hard his jaw ached.

The overly familiar voice was strident, cutting through his surly thoughts like a scythe. "Where are you going?"

He swung around, coldly furious. "I told you to remain in your chambers. I put you there myself."

Eleanor glared back as she came down the corridor. "You can hardly expect me to remain mewed up for days on end."

"Of course not," he returned silkily. "I value my hawks more highly than you, and would not discompose them with your company in the mews."

It stopped her dead in her tracks, gaping at him most unattractively. Little helped her expression, he felt, but this one assuredly worsened it. Color suffused her sallow face. "Where are you going?"

"It is no concern of yours, Eleanor."

"It is that FitzWalter girl?"

He arched one brow consideringly. "Perhaps I should have the surgeon examine your ears."

Now her face was chalky. "She's no better than I am, now—yet you treat me like a scullery wench!"

"You conduct yourself as someone akin to that station."

Her hands clutched impotently at her kirtle, wadding up the wool until her knuckles shone white. "I came to ask you if you intended to bring her here at once."

He eyed her. "I fail to see why that is any concern of yours. You have made your place—now bide in it!"

"And how many times have *you* done it?" Eleanor cried. "You and every other man, tumbling a woman whenever you feel like it! Why is it acceptable for you, but not for me?"

"A woman's value resides in her chastity, and her ability to produce legitimate heirs," he returned coldly. "One illicit bedding destroys that chastity—*and* her value—and a man prefers to know with complete certainty if the child she carries is his. It is somewhat disconcerting to learn the required heir was got by another man."

"Ah," she returned, in a tone akin to his own, "that must be why you never sired a son—you were afraid it might not be yours."

He took one great stride toward her, lifting a hand to strike, but a call from behind prevented him from following through.

"My lord?" It was Walter, Gisbourne's assistant. "There is some commotion in the bailey."

DeLacey turned on him. "Of course there is," he snarled, "I've had my horse ordered readied at once."

"No, my lord—I mean, yes, my lord . . . but this is more."

"More? What is 'more,' Walter?"

The mousy little man twisted his hands together. "I don't know."

"And so I am duly enlightened," deLacey said with acid irony. "Never mind. I'll see to it myself." He paused a moment, arrested by a new thought. "Walter," he said more cordially, but with precisely modulated words, "do investigate the offers we have had for my remaining daughter's hand. Pay particular attention to any that have come from men who live *very* far away."

"You can't!" she cried.

"My lord?" Walter asked.

"If there *are* any," deLacey snapped. "At this juncture, any fool will do."

"You *can't!*" Eleanor shouted.

The sheriff ignored her, as was his habit. He had been doing it a very long time. If he could indeed find an accommodating man, he wouldn't be required to do it ever again. That knowledge comforted him greatly.

* * *

Marian did not like the look of Robin. He was wan and haggard, with a pinched tightness around his eyes. He moved with the careful stiffness she had seen in old men.

Should I ask him again how he fares? She knew the answer too well. *No. He will lie. Or speak of something else.*

She watched him sparingly, relying on sidelong glances. She had known men like him before, if not to this extreme, who would not at all appreciate the scrutiny of a woman concerned with his welfare. She had done what she could on their journey out of Sherwood, asking to rest so often he undoubtedly believed her a weak woman. Or maybe only footsore; and she was, a little, so that was not a false assumption. But she didn't feel weak. She was hungry and thirsty and stiff from the aftermath of the capture, but decidedly not weak. The walk along the road, toes digging into cool earth, she found exhilarating. It made her feel free as she had not felt in a year.

But she said nothing of the freedom, because he undoubtedly shared none of it. She had been ill herself. The glitter in his hazel eyes told her the truth of it: the fever had settled in. It would have to run its course.

Marian skirted a pile of manure left by a passing horse. *He will be a fool, of course, and say he must go back once Ravenskeep is reached. He will say his task is done, and he would have no more dishonor brought to me by staying. And if I let him go he will likely fall down five paces from my door, and someone will come back to fetch me, and he will have to be brought inside to sleep in the bed I would have given him anyway.* Marian sighed. *Why are men so stubborn?*

The silence between them was heavy. Then Robin broke it by asking a question she had not been asked for years. "I don't recall your brother. What happened to him?"

There was no reason he should recall her brother. Though Sir Hugh FitzWalter was a knight with all accompanying honor, his class—and his children—ranked considerably lower than an earl and his son. "It was more than ten years ago, so most people have forgotten." Her kirtle had fallen from the girdle. Marian hiked up folds again, tucking them away so she might walk freely once more. The question from him struck her as odd. She had not expected him to care much about her family, nor to initiate a pointless conversation designed merely to pass the time. That was her habit, especially when self-conscious. "He drowned in the millpond." She stepped on a stone and winced. "It was only three weeks after our mother died. Losing both so close together nearly killed my father. He swore then he would go on Crusade to win back God's favor."

Robin glanced at her sharply. "What of you? There was a daughter to look after."

Marian sobered, remembering. She had been trapped for days on end in anguish with no one to turn to, because her father had shut himself away in private quarters to mourn his wife and son, but she couldn't tell Robin that. "I had Matilda, my nursemaid—" She broke off abruptly. "I'd nearly forgotten! She is still at Nottingham—I'll have to send an escort to bring her home."

He waited patiently, then turned to the topic again. "You were telling me about your brother's death, and the aftermath."

She nodded after a moment, recalling the emotions. "My father spent as much time with me as he could, afterwards. I had always been a solitary child . . . I missed them both, of course, but Hugh had reached the age where a small sister was an encumbrance, so it was not so difficult to accustom myself to being alone."

That was mostly the truth; eventually, as in everything, she had adjusted, finding her own way through grief. She still missed them both, but the pain was now indistinct, nothing more than a remnant of the anguish that had swallowed a ten-year-old's world.

He walked in silence a moment. "I was a solitary child, also."

"I know that." She smiled at him impishly. "It became quite clear one Christmas Eve."

He colored, which surprised her. He did not seem the kind of man to be embarrassed or caught off-guard. "Will you judge me by that forever?"

"If you give me no reason to alter my opinion, undoubtedly I will." Marian was astonished by her own temerity; two days before she had hardly been able to speak to the man, so sensitive was she to his privacy and rank. It was easier now to speak because what she had experienced in Sherwood Forest altered the rules of behavior. She was no longer governed by them. That gave her an uncommon freedom of speech and released her from constraint. "But I believe you have given me reason to alter my opinion. What you did to win me free of Will Scarlet is much appreciated, though that means little enough."

He grimaced. "I did very little. It was you—"

"Does that matter?" she interrupted. "You don't strike me as a man much shaped by what others think of you, least of all a woman. I know there are men who would be at some pains to concoct a story more favorable to themselves, but you aren't one of them."

"Am I not?" he asked mildly.

"No."

"Then perhaps you might tell my father that I am not now and never have been a hero. I was a soldier, nothing more . . . I did as my king required. I saved no lives—I *took* them." His gaze was unflinching as he turned his head to her. "That does not make a man a hero. It makes a man a killer."

As William deLacey swung on his heel and strode rapidly down the corridor, his daughter went back into her chamber. It was a small, square masonry room of little warmth or comfort, boasting no more than a bed and two chests, and a single candle rack. Eleanor didn't like it there.

She thudded the studded door closed and walked to her bed, where she sat down and stared hard into the distance, thinking rapidly.

Since Eleanor could remember, she and her father had baited one another like a pair of mongrel dogs circling a prized bone, preferring the ritual to actual consumption, but the tenor of the game now had changed significantly. There were times he had been thoughtlessly cruel, or specifically brutal in response to deliberate provocation—she knew how to provoke, because she had learned it from him—but she could not recall a time when he had sounded so serious.

Eleanor understood the threat. He *would* marry her off. And no doubt he would purposely seek out the most unpresentable man in a significantly inhospitable portion of England—if he was generous it would be England, rather than backward Scotland or barbaric Wales—just to punish her.

"She's the reason," Eleanor murmured. "She is the root of it."

Thus the enemy was identified: Marian FitzWalter.

The horrible rage quieted; intellect prevailed. The game would not be won if she gave in to sheer emotion, because her father would view it as weakness. To defeat her father she would have to *be* her father, depending on wit and insight to overcome his decision; to shape her immediate future so she could shape that which would follow upon its heels.

Women had no power. Women had no *value;* he had made that clear. Therefore she would have to think as a man, plan as a man, and execute as a man.

She needed a man to do it.

"Who?" Eleanor asked, unheeding of the silence.

Surely there was someone. Someone she could buy. She had little coin to spare, no jewels to speak of, and until this was settled her physical charms were suspect because of public discovery; the rape claim might remove the taint of wantonness, but it wouldn't erase the fact. Now everyone knew what most may have suspected: the Sheriff of Nottingham's daughter was no longer a virgin.

"My choice," she said through clenched teeth, thinking of the men. "They all have been my choice."

Now the choice had been taken from her.

"Who?" she repeated. "Where is there a man as hungry as I for revenge, who will accept satisfaction in place of coin or gem?"

No one she could think of. Men hated her father, but few if any would be willing to cross him.

Eleanor sighed and pressed both hands against her face, massaging her skin, her fingertips searching for the telltale first hint of lines in the flesh near her eyes, her bony nose, her downturned, sullen mouth. She was getting older. Soon it would show.

How much—? Eleanor slid off the bed and moved purposefully to one of the chests. Deftly she unlatched the hasp and flipped it back, then lifted the lid. Her groping hand found the mirror her father had mentioned.

She knelt there on the floor, cradling the mirror in both hands as she raised it high enough. The light in the chamber was wan, casting sallow illumination. It yellowed her face, dulled her hair, threw shadows beneath her eyes.

Hastily she slapped at her cheeks, attempting to bring the blush of roses to flesh that proved reluctant. She needed paint, but her father forbade it; only rarely did she test him by smudging precious kohl onto her eyelids, or rubbing carmine on her lips.

She was not and never had been a beautiful woman. Nor would she ever be.

Eleanor bit into her lip as her face crumpled into despair. Tears swelled, spilled, rolled down her cheeks, dripping to stain the dull gray fabric of her kirtle. She hugged the mirror to her breast and wished it could lie; or that she could believe the men who praised her as beautiful, when all they wanted was for her to spread her legs. " 'Fairest Eleanor,' " she choked, recalling the minstrel's practiced flattery.

She gripped the mirror more tightly, pressing the rim into her palms. *Marian is fair.*

Eleanor had denied it, taking solace in pettiness, but she had no more time now for self-deception. Better to acknowledge that the enemy was fairer, for it would fan the kindling fires. She needed to feel the fires. When the flame ate at her soul, it was easier to hate.

DeLacey strode outside into the bailey with every intention of dealing with the interruption as quickly and curtly as possible, or of handing it off to someone else, anyone else, so he could be on his way. He had no time to waste; every moment Marian spent with Robert of Locksley reduced *his* chances. He would not tolerate that.

He located his horse, nearly lost in the morass of other mounts, milling horseboys scampering to follow shouted orders, and a baggage train of significant size.

Forebodying pinched his belly. He stopped short, caught the

tunic sleeve of a passing horseboy, and dragged him close as the boy struggled to keep the tunic on his shoulder. "What is this?" he hissed.

The boy gaped at him, one shoulder bared. "My lord—?"

"What *is*—" But he discontinued the question; he had an answer. He released the horseboy, then calmly and politely welcomed the man who parted the confusion like Moses the Red Sea.

"My lord Sheriff." Elegant Gilbert de Pisan greeted him coolly in the quietly arrogant manner deLacey detested; but then, he detested the man himself, no matter what he said. "As you see, Prince John has arrived after all."

DeLacey managed not to show his consternation. "I believed him bound for Lincoln."

"Indeed, and so we will be." As always, de Pisan phrased his words in such a way as to suggest royalty. "There was a hanging he desired to see."

The sheriff wanted to spit at the man or, better yet, send him sprawling onto the cobbles—*before* the bricks were swept free of urine and manure—so as to destroy his supercilious elegance. *This will delay me significantly . . . oh God, could you not see fit to spare me this royal lackwit?* DeLacey inclined his head. "And so he shall. If it pleases Prince John, I will see to it the murderer hangs at dawn tomorrow."

The seneschal's eyes narrowed minutely. "Not dawn," he suggested. "My lord finds it a gruesome way to begin the day. No—" de Pisan frowned thoughtfully, "perhaps during breakfast. He enjoys entertainment at meals."

"During—" DeLacey cut off the question. "Of course. As Prince John desires."

De Pisan waved an all-encompassing hand. "As you can see, there is some confusion here. We shall require your assistance in sorting everything out."

"Yes, of course." Inwardly deLacey cursed de Pisan and his lord, royal-born or not. "But if you will excuse me briefly, I must see to it that my steward has the execution order properly drawn up."

De Pisan inclined his head. "Of course, Sheriff. But my lord cannot abide a disorganized castle . . . you will return immediately to put order to this mess? He is but a mile away."

"I will return immediately." *Damn him for a fool—does he really think it falls within my purview to oversee the bailey? What does he think I have servants for?* DeLacey turned smartly and marched back into the keep, whereupon he shouted for Walter. When the small man appeared, robe askew and hair flying, deLacey fixed him with a baleful glare. "Who have we in the dungeon?"

Walter blinked bafflement, then ventured an answer. "Criminals, my lord."

"Which *ones,* blast you?" It took all of the sheriff's control not to snatch Walter up short by the collar of his tunic and shake him till he bled from nose and ears. "I need to hang a man in the morning, during *breakfast.* Find a suitable one."

"A suitable one," Walter echoed, clearly undone by the task.

Gisbourne, for all his faults, understands how to arrange such things. DeLacey cleared his throat, controlling his fury. "Pick a man, any man, and hang him during breakfast. And make sure the order says his name is William Scathlocke."

"Scathlocke?"

"Do it," deLacey ordered, seeing the horror in Walter's eyes, "or I shall use you in his place."

Walter understood that well enough. "At *once,*" he blurted.

"Good." William deLacey swung about, marched yet again into the bailey, cursing the feckless prince who didn't care a fig how he upset the lives of those around him. "We'll hang him here," he muttered, casting a swift glance around the bailey, "not in the city proper—or someone will know it isn't really Will Scarlet." He couldn't afford that. "And I'll order his tongue cut out so he can't say the wrong thing at the wrong time."

Thirty-Nine

Brother Tuck sat at the wobbly table in the tiny solar tucked into a corner of the castle, trying to hold the surface steady so he wouldn't smear his work and have to begin again, thereby wasting ink, vellum, and the time and effort which would be better spent on moving ahead instead of redoing. He wished the light were better so he could see the work more clearly, but Walter had made it clear that Sir Guy of Gisbourne would not tolerate additional candles. Tuck *had* noticed the sheriff's hall knew no shortage, but that was not his concern.

Ordinarily the conditions would not have bothered him so much, for monks were accustomed to long hours of physical toil and hardship, but the light was beginning to die out of the day. Soon he would be required to rely only on candles, and there simply were not enough.

He sighed and straightened, arching back to stretch his spine. His vision blurred briefly as he readjusted focus from close work to far, massaging with one hand the spongy flesh of a shoulder stiff from hours of concentration.

In the abbey, conditions had been better. There he had sat in a spacious room with many of the brothers, enjoying the generous daylight admitted by twenty windows. No one spoke as he worked—Abbot Martin said that to speak was to dilute the concentration—but all were content to know others labored with them to glorify God in the illumination of manuscripts requested by kings and queens.

William deLacey would request no such thing. What he wanted done were ordinary *letters;* ah, but what could Tuck protest? It was work. There was a private place for him to sleep just off the musty chapel, and as much food as he could eat, though he knew better than to ask for additional helpings. Word would get back to Abbot Martin.

The door scraped open. "Brother Tuck?" It was Walter, sliding through with little fuss.

Tuck was glad enough of an excuse to rest his fingers and eyes, and gladder still of the company. He knew no one in the castle save Walter and a few of the kitchen servants, unless one counted the sheriff, whom he did not; they could never be anything other than lord and servant.

He set down the quill and turned on the creaking bench unused to his bulk, rubbing absently at the naked skin of the tonsure carved in the midst of his curly brown hair. It itched from recent shaving. "Is it supper already?"

"No." Walter's expression was serious as he shut the door behind him. "Not yet, and not like to be any time soon. Didn't you hear the commotion?"

Tuck had, but he'd paid it no mind. When he lost himself in writing he was aware of very little. The formation of clear, elegant letters required every bit of his attention. "I'm nearly done with the recopying," he said, indicating the stack of sanded vellum.

Walter waved that away, coming to stand next to Tuck. He peered critically at the lettering, then sighed and pointed at a fresh sheet of vellum. "There is one more thing. An order for an execution."

Tuck blinked in surprise. "I'm not sure—"

"You have to," Walter declared a trifle desperately, as if he believed Tuck might indeed have grounds for protest. "Brother Hubert did it all the time."

"I hadn't thought that would be part of my duties."

"Your duties are to write whatever the sheriff tells you." But Walter's bleak expression softened the curtness of his words. "You'll have to do such things, or he'll have no use for you. He'll send you back to the abbey."

Tuck's brows knitted over his blob of a nose. That would undoubtedly result in his dismissal from the abbey or, failing that, would surely diminish any opportunity to become a priest.

"You don't have to witness it," Walter said quickly, "just write up the order. In Latin, if you can."

"Of course I write Latin. I'm a monk."

"Then write it *up,*" Walter hissed. "There is one in here somewhere for you to copy, just change the date, the offense, and the name. He wants it for the morning."

Tuck nodded slowly. "What is the man's offense?"

"He killed four soldiers."

Automatically Tuck scribed a cross in the air between them. "May God have mercy on their souls."

"Norman souls," Walter said dryly. "If such as soldiers have them."

Tuck looked more closely at the unkempt little man. Walter was officious in a lackluster sort of way, but Tuck had believed him devoted to the sheriff. Now he was not so certain. "Then I will pray for God to forgive the man who killed them."

"Why not?" Walter asked. "He's not hanging, anyway."

"I don't understand—"

"You don't need to. Just do as the sheriff wants." Walter sighed, picking at a loose thread hanging from a fraying sleeve. "Write up the order, Brother Tuck. He murdered four Normans. That's all they count as important."

Tuck was undeterred. "You just said he *wasn't* hanging."

"*He's* not," Walter agreed. "Some other poor fool will, because the sheriff's lost Will Scarlet. But he daren't tell Prince John, who's just come for supper."

"But—" Tuck's comprehension was abrupt, as was his astonishment. "I can't *do* that! Write in another man's name? D'ye mean they'll hang him as Will Scarlet, even if he isn't?"

"He'll hang," Walter explained, "no matter what his name. What's the difference, then?"

"I can't *do* that," Tuck repeated.

Walter sighed wearily. "Then go tell it to the sheriff. I'll ask Abbot Martin to send us another clerk."

"The sheriff will hang an innocent man?"

"There's innocent, and innocent." Walter opened the door. "Any man in the dungeon is bound for hell one day. This one will go there sooner."

"I *won't,*" Tuck declared. But Walter was already gone.

Locksley's world was small now, bounded by two things only: the immediate portion of track but one pace ahead of each stride, and the woman at his side. His focus had narrowed as the fever burned in his brain; he dared not even look up for fear he would lose his precarious grip on what remained of the world and disgrace himself utterly by swooning in her dooryard.

If he got that far.

"Nearly there," she said.

Did she know? No. She couldn't. He had taken great care to hide the truth of his condition so Marian need not concern herself with caring for the man who had set out to rescue her.

"Here's the postern gate." She did something with a latch. "Through here, then across the courtyard . . . it's not a grand castle, only a modest hall." Wood creaked. Hinges rasped. "Oil," she murmured absently. Then, with more urgency, "Take care—the cobbles have come loose. One good storm, and most will wash out of their beds."

He stumbled almost immediately, tripping over a lopsided brick. It jarred him, leaving him weak and sweaty. "Ravenskeep?"

"Ravenskeep," she agreed, taking her hand from his arm. "Will you come in? It is past time for supper, but something will be left. You can stay the night, then borrow one of our horses. I'll send word to your father—"

"No, not my father—" He didn't intend to sound so curt. "Send no word. I'll ride back now."

Marian shut and latched the gate. "There is no need to hasten back."

"I would prefer it." He had no desire for her to discern how ill he felt. "If you like, you can send out bread and water, but there is no need to trouble yourself."

Marian sighed. "Very well. Wait here, then . . . I'll order the horse saddled, and have bread and water sent out." She pointed. "There is a bench."

He waited until she was gone, then sat down stiffly upon it. He slumped against the wall, feeling wan and weak and dull-witted. The stones of the wall bit into his flesh, threatening his spine. Every joint ached, and the light hurt his eyes.

Locksley could see little of Ravenskeep. It was to his blurred vision an indistinct blocky shape circled by a wall well-covered with ivy, which obscured the clean lines and angles of properly mortared brickwork. The bench beneath him was weathered wood much scored by age, grayed and gouged and splintery.

Ravenskeep. He knew it not at all, though she said once he'd been there on a certain Christmas Eve many years ago.

How many, he wondered? Just now he could not recall it, merely that she said he had kissed her beneath the mistletoe.

No. She had kissed *him.*

Somehow, it mattered. It meant he owed her a kiss, initiated by him—*No.* He shut his eyes. It was the fever. Nothing more.

"Robin?"

Robin. She called him that, just as his mother had. Just as Richard had.

"Robin?" He looked up at her and saw the bundle and mug in her hands. An odd glint lighted her eyes. "Sim is bringing the horse."

He could hear shod hoofs ringing on cobbles.

She held out the mug. "Water."

He took it and drank deeply, not knowing how thirsty he was until the water slid down his throat, and then he swallowed and swallowed and swallowed until the water was gone, but it had done its work. He felt vaguely alive again.

Sim arrived with the horse. Robin paid it little mind, save to note it was bay, bridled, and saddled.

Marian tucked the bundle of food into the saddle wallet. Then she swung back smartly, standing very straight. The tangled mass of her hair hung nearly to the girdle binding her waist and hips Norman-fashion. "Simple gratitude is not enough, but I know it is all you'll accept. Therefore I say it: 'thank you.' " Her hands were linked together in the folds of her ruined kirtle. "If there is ever a service I may do you—"

He laughed, cutting her off. He hadn't meant to—he knew it sounded rude—but he couldn't help himself. "Lady Marian, you have done it."

She was confused. *"What* have I done?"

"Allowed me to recall that there are women . . . and there are women." It made perfect sense to him, though she still seemed baffled. He stood up stiffly and put the mug back into her hands. "Such a thing is easy to forget when men gather for war."

"I don't understand."

"There is no explanation." He took the reins from Sim and pulled them across the horse's neck, then hoisted a leg and hooked a boot toe into the stirrup. With an upward lurch more awkward than usual—and considerably more painful—he pulled himself into the saddle, glad the horse was quiet. "What I did was not enough . . . no more than it was enough for your father that day. But there is no help for it . . . at least you are alive."

"Robin . . ." But she let it go, merely clutching the mug and nodding as he turned the horse toward the main gate.

He left her standing there in the courtyard of Ravenskeep, thinking as he rode of mistletoe and Christmas, and a blue-eyed, black-haired girl.

The sheriff undid the latch and swung the door open, one hand on the jamb as he leaned into the chamber. His daughter was on her bed, slumped against the wall, staring vacantly into space as she sucked on a strand of hair. "You'll have to sleep somewhere else tonight."

Startled, Eleanor twitched, then sat stiffly upright. "Why? What right—"

He cut off her challenge. "I need your bed."

She scowled. "What is wrong with yours?"

"Prince John shall be in mine . . . I'll be in yours." He arched one brow. "Without you in it, preferably—although your wanton behavior could lead one to suspect you might enjoy even that."

A wave of color swamped her face. "How dare you—"

"Get out," he said succinctly.

"Where am *I* supposed—"

"With the servants, if you like—just make certain they're

kitchen *wenches.*" He shut the door and latched it, Eleanor forgotten, as he thought ahead to John's arrival.

"My lord? My lord Sheriff?"

DeLacey halted, sighing. "What now?" he muttered, turning to face yet another crisis. He blinked in mild surprise. "Brother Tuck?"

"My lord." The fat monk loomed in the dim corridor like a wool-swathed thing of the dark. "My lord, there is something troubling me deeply. You'll send me back to the abbey, I know, but I must ask you." Tuck came closer, hands clasping one another in pious rigidity. "It has to do with the execution order, my lord."

For a moment deLacey did not know what Tuck was talking about. Then he recalled his command to Walter. "Yes?"

The monk hove to a stop, filling much of the narrow corridor with an expanse of heavy shoulders. Without the fat, deLacey thought, the young man might make a respectable fighter, although that also required a certain wit, too, and he was not at all certain Tuck possessed the proper sort. "Lord Sheriff," he began nervously, "Walter said I was to write in Will Scarlet's name in place of the man's *real* name. But—you see—I don't think I can do such a thing. I mean—to write in another man's name? My lord . . ." Tuck gestured helplessly. "Surely he didn't mean it."

DeLacey maintained his bland expression. "Walter said— *what?*" Delicate inquiry.

Tuck repeated what Walter had said.

"My God!" the sheriff exploded. Then, contritely, "Forgive me, Brother Tuck—it is only I am shocked. I cannot believe a man in my service would suggest such a heinous thing. To write in another man's name? Are you quite certain that is what he said?"

Tuck's jowled face was ashen. His voice sounded squeezed. "Yes, my lord."

DeLacey scrubbed at his face. "I cannot believe it . . . Brother Tuck, I assure you, no such thing was ordered. I am the lord high sheriff—would I do such a thing? Would I ask a devout monk to abet me in such a crime?" He shook his head, expression hardening. "I'll have him dismissed at once."

"My lord, *no!*" Tuck cried. "That is—I mean—" His anguish was obvious. "Perhaps Walter merely made a mistake. Perhaps he misunderstood."

"I find it highly unlikely a man could *misunderstand* such a heinous thing, Brother Tuck." DeLacey shook his head. "No. I'll dismiss him myself." He gestured preemptorily. "Come with me. We'll see to it now."

"My lord—" Tuck appeared mortified. "My lord, I beg you—don't dismiss him. He'll have nowhere to go."

"That is no concern of mine in the face of such infamy."

Tears shone in Tuck's brown eyes. "I'm sure it was only a misunderstanding. I knew it had to be a mistake—I mean, Will Scarlet escaped—even *I* have heard the tale." He tugged ineffectually at his voluminous cassock. "Now that I know, I will of course correct the execution order."

DeLacey's attention sharpened. "You've already written it?"

"Yes, my lord . . . but as soon as I finished I knew I couldn't leave it there, I had to know the truth."

"Of course you did." Smiling, deLacey nodded. "I commend you for your foresight, Brother Tuck—imagine what might have happened if the wrong man had been hauled up from the dungeon and executed in Scarlet's place!"

The monk's face was damp and shiny. "I prayed about it, my lord. I was afraid of that very thing."

DeLacey nodded, reaching out to clasp Tuck's shoulder in a familiar, confident grasp. "Well done, Brother. I assure you, I'll see to it personally that this mistake is corrected. But if you don't mind, leave the execution order to me. If I am to ask Walter about it, I must have proof."

"Yes, my lord." Tuck smiled tremulously. "I'm sure it was all a mistake."

DeLacey shook his head, guiding Tuck down the corridor. "It might have been very costly, Brother. Very costly indeed. You were right to come to me. You must always bring such things to my attention." The corridor opened into the hall, well-filled with John's noisy retinue. "Now, I must attend the prince. I beg you, bring me this execution order so that I may see it. I'll speak to Walter later."

"Yes, my lord." Tuck licked at a damp upper lip. "I'm sure he will be more careful in the future."

"I'm sure he will be, too." DeLacey clapped a meaty shoulder in dismissal, sending Tuck on his way.

As the monk picked his way through the confusion of John's retinue, deLacey at last let the mask slip. "Walter," he murmured, "you disappoint me greatly. But until Gisbourne's back, you're all I have." His gaze found Gilbert de Pisan in the middle of the hall, ordering servants this way and that. It reminded deLacey that he would be sleeping in Eleanor's bed, while John would be in his. "May there be mice," he murmured, and smiled with perfect serenity as de Pisan signaled to him.

Marian watched as Robin rode through the main gate of Ravenskeep. One portion of her mind marked that the aged gate was beginning to sag worse, which meant the hinges needed to be rehung, but that was a fleeting thought. What occupied most of her thoughts was the way Robin held himself, very stiffly atop the horse with his head not moving at all.

He fears he will break. She nearly winced in sympathy. She had felt that way herself.

The gate was closed behind him, creaking fearfully on weakened hinges. More than oil was needed there.

Men and their pride. Sighing, Marian turned to Sim. "Fetch Hal," she told him, "and follow *quietly*. He will not get so far as the road, I am sure." Her mouth hooked wryly. "We shall have to hope that when—*if*—he falls, he does not crack his head and spill out all his wits."

Forty

Eleanor waited until it was dark and the royal retinue was settled in the hall where its members would sleep, clustered around the fire trench or coupled off in corners. It might well be *her* sleeping place as well, if she did not succeed in finding a more pleasant, private chamber.

She shut the door behind her quietly, then moved smoothly down the corridor to her father's chamber. There she halted, wiped her damp hands on her kirtle, and drew in a deep breath. Eleanor knocked on the door, then murmured a brief fervent prayer.

After a moment the latch was lifted. A face appeared in the crack between door and jamb. Not Prince John, she knew: the set of the mouth was too supercilious, the arched nose held too high in the air. Gilbert de Pisan, then; she had heard her father describe him.

"My lord? My lord Prince?" It wouldn't hurt to flatter the seneschal by 'mistaking' him for royalty.

"No," he said. "My lord is within; what do you want?"

"Oh, I am so sorry . . ." Eleanor fluttered a hand helplessly and allowed it to settle across a generous bosom. "I am Eleanor deLacey, the high sheriff's daughter. I—" She bit her lip, smiled in demure dismay, and lowered her eyes. "Would it be possible to see Prince John?"

An elegant silvering eyebrow arched. "Now?"

"If it is possible," she said softly. "It has to do with my father—I am afraid, you see, that he has not been entirely truthful with Prince John."

De Pisan's tone was cool. "And you are prepared to betray him?"

Eleanor put up her chin. Her voice rang out; who was de Pisan to turn her away? Let John himself do it if he would. "Is it betrayal to inform a prince of England about treachery in his midst?"

De Pisan's mouth flattened. "Certainly not," he declared frigidly. "Do come in at once."

Eleanor waited, hands clasped in her kirtle. De Pisan stepped aside and pulled the door open, allowing her to slip inside. He shut and latched it, then signed for her to wait as he approached the tapestry-curtained bed.

"My lord, there is a woman here to see you. Eleanor de-Lacey."

The voice behind the curtains was muffled. "Did I send for her?"

"No, my lord. She says it concerns treachery—and her father."

A hand reached through the gap of curtains and jerked them apart. "Here!" John barked.

De Pisan beckoned and Eleanor hastened forward, casting him a sidelong glance of disdain. Would he listen to what was said?

"My lord." She curtseyed briefly. "My lord, I am deeply sorry to tax you at such an hour, but I believe it is most important."

"Treachery usually is." John wore a high-necked cambric bliaut embroidered at collar and cuffs with gold thread and tiny pearls. His dark eyes glittered. "Say what you've come to say."

She cast de Pisan another glance. "My lord—surely you will understand if I wish not to speak of my father's guilt in front of another man."

John flapped a hand at his seneschal. "Outside, if you please. We must honor the lady's sensibilities."

"My lord." A brief bow, and the man was gone.

Eleanor then smiled warmly at John. "My lord—"

He interrupted. "If this is seduction, I find it tedious. I *choose* my women; they don't choose me."

For only a moment it took her off-stride. Then she recovered herself. "No indeed, my lord! Oh, my lord—" She applied a hand to her face, as if to hide confusion. "I thought only to tell you—"

"Yes, yes." John was clearly impatient. "Treachery, wasn't it? Your father's?"

She lowered her hand. "I am desolate, my lord—"

"Among other things, I am sure." Without the padding of tunics and surcoat, the royal shoulders were very narrow. It made his head look larger. "What treachery, then?"

Eleanor took a deep breath. "He killed my mother, my lord."

John's gaze was unrelenting. "I am a man of infinite patience and understanding where personal slights and insults are involved . . . surely you must believe you may meet with compassion here." Unsmiling, he assessed her. "What is it he wants to do? Marry you off to a man you find repulsive?"

"No, my lord." Stiffly. "At least—not yet."

His expression lightened. "Ah. I believe I know. *He* intends to marry—Marian FitzWalter, is it not? And it does not meet with your approval?"

Eleanor tried to swallow down the tightness in her throat. The waters were deeper here than she had ever known them to be. "No," she answered briefly. "He could do better than that."

John smiled. "Do not lie, I beg you. Liars have a bad habit of falling out of favor."

The tightness increased. "She is a whore, my lord."

"Indeed? Coming from you, that is basest slander." John smiled and leaned back against the borrowed bolsters. "I was there, lady, when you accused that unfortunate—and well-endowed—minstrel of violating you. But speaking as a man who has done his share of violating, I can only say that you appeared, at that instant, to be enjoying it most distinctly." One eyebrow arched. "Or is it merely that you *like* to have men butchered in your name?"

"No!" It burst out of her mouth. "No—I swear—"

"On what?" John asked. "On your virginity?"

She wanted to run, but her feet were rooted. De Pisan stood just outside the door; if she fled, he would noise it around the hall, and she would become a laughingstock. Her reputation was already tattered enough. *I have to see it through.*

413

Eleanor raised her head. "Very well. I want the marriage stopped."

John laughed softly. "Jealousy does not improve a woman's looks."

She gritted her teeth. "Surely *you* understand how I feel! You were a last son, and I a last daughter . . . they leave us nothing, my lord, but scraps from the table, throwing them on the floor for us to grovel after, fighting off the dogs!" She went on before he could speak, before he could shout at her, before he could have de Pisan throw her bodily from the room. "My lord, this woman—"

"—is in wardship to the Crown." John eyed her from under lowered lids. "Therefore it is the king's decision whether she weds or not, and who the man might be."

"Yes, my l—"

"As to the rest," he said silkily, "we do not believe our circumstances are even the least alike. Our lady mother is a queen; our father was a king." He leaned forward slightly. "Do you understand us, lady?"

She did. She had overstepped. Eleanor shut her eyes. "Forgive me, my lord."

"Tomorrow, perhaps. Look at me."

Eleanor did.

"I know very well your father intends to wed the FitzWalter girl. I know many things, not the least of which is that you are desperate. But it has been my experience that desperate people are willing to do many things to ensure their place in the world. Is this not correct?"

"Yes, my lord."

"Therefore I desire you to continue what appears to be a natural bent for you: spying on your father. Because he, like everyone, is indeed capable of treachery should the means present itself, and the time prove opportune. Do you understand?"

"Yes," she whispered.

John's eyes glittered in the wan candlelight. "And if you are good at it, I will consider granting your wish."

Eleanor bowed her head, wanting only to be dismissed.

John laughed sharply. "Just make certain the information

you send is the *truth,* Lady Wanton, and not female exaggeration." He waved a hand. "Begone."

She curtseyed again briefly and turned, moving stiffly toward the door.

As she lifted the latch, he spoke again. "This is your father's chamber?"

She nodded without turning around.

"And he is in your bed?"

Again Eleanor nodded.

"Leaving you with none."

She swung, hopes rising. If *John* bedded her—

"Gilbert might serve you," he said, and yanked the curtain closed.

He lay sprawled on his back in the sand, with the sun searing his face and piercing his fragile eyelids, so that heat and light ate his eyes. Vision was blood-red, then white, then black, as heat cooked away his eyes. He felt the flesh of his body dry, then burn, then crisp, peeling off to burn again, layer by layer, until nothing was left of him but muscle and sinew, and then that, too, was burned away, leaving only bone. The skeleton called Locksley lay baking in the heat, grinning into the sky where the god of hell resided.

"Ya Allah," he murmured. *"La ilaha il' Mohammed rasul Allah."*

God held his silence.

"Insh'Allah," he whispered. "Isn't that what you want?"

The Saracen answered in good Saxon English. "I want you to get well."

It was wrong, all wrong. There were Saracens who spoke English, but none of them were women. In English he inquired, "Did I not say it right?"

"Rest," the woman told him. "There is no need to speak."

He stirred restlessly. The sun had eaten his eyes, or surely he would see her. *"Ya Allah,"* he murmured again.

"Hush," she said softly. "If you sleep through the night, you'll feel much better in the morning."

English, again. Where was the Arabic? He had labored so long to learn it, so they wouldn't cut out the Infidel tongue that blasphemed their God.

He exerted himself, attempting to speak clearly, so they

would see how well he'd learned. *"La ilaha—il' Mohammed rasul . . . Allah."*

"Sleep," the woman murmured. Her cool hand was on his brow, taking the heat from his face.

He was accustomed to following orders, lest he be punished for disobedience. He released his tenuous grasp on consciousness and did as the woman commanded.

The Earl of Huntington sat up late over his wine, although he drank little. The chamber was very private, very quiet, a small nook of a room built into a corner of his new castle, appointed to his taste: nothing excessive, because the earl detested ostentation, but the quality was outstanding. White-painted wooden wainscoting—plain, no ornate carvings for him—reflected light from two tripod candle stands; a thick Persian carpet of peacock blue and green glowed against plain gray stone; a painted linen hanging of a hunt with fox fleeing hounds bejeweled a third of the wall space; a large chair of oak with a cushion for aging buttocks; a simple trestle table bearing wine, fruit, bread.

Eustace de Vesci, Geoffrey de Mandeville, and Henry Bohun had retired for the evening, leaving him alone to consider the potential repercussions of what they had discussed regarding John's current plans for England. That something needed to be done, they all knew; it remained for them to determine what it was, and in what way it might be engaged.

But just now something else occupied his thoughts. He plucked a grape from its stem, tucked it into his mouth and chewed meditatively. He plucked another and yet another, quite methodically, until the stem was nearly denuded.

A quiet knock sounded at the door. Ralph, undoubtedly; he had sent for the servant just before withdrawing. "Enter."

The latch was lifted. Ralph came into the chamber. "My lord."

The earl plucked the last two grapes and rolled them in aged fingers that found the motion painful. "My son," he said only.

Ralph's expression was properly neutral. "No, my lord. Not yet."

The earl nodded once. "Then I must assume he has chosen to spend his night elsewhere."

"It would seem so, my lord."

Huntington looked at the quiet, capable, graying man who had served his household for more than twenty years. "What do you see in him?"

Ralph was a medium man of no outstanding features and no discernable ambition, save to serve his lord, and was therefore ideally suited to his position. He performed his duties quietly even amidst high turmoil, then withdrew without earning notice. He was often invisible to those so accustomed to servants and excellent service they only noticed when things went wrong.

Ralph smiled a little. "I see his mother in him."

The earl's mouth hardened. "Then you would agree he lacks a certain maturity of character."

The servant's answer was framed carefully. "No, my lord. If you will permit me, I would say the opposite is true."

"Would you?" Huntington's brows arched. "He has always seemed soft to me. And you must concur, if you see his mother in him. She was a well-meaning woman, but decidedly too soft, too frail of spirit—she dwelt entirely too often in daydreams. There were times I despaired for her sanity—" He broke it off. Such things were not discussed even with longtime, loyal servants. "You see otherwise, in my son?"

"My lord, he was always a fanciful boy. How many times were we servants dispatched to hunt for him, when all the while he had made a snug place somewhere in the old hall, or wandered in the woods?" Ralph smiled. "He was very like his lady mother . . . but there is you in him, also."

"Me?"

"Yes, my lord. He has come home—different. Harder."

"Has he?" The earl consumed a grape, thinking his way through Ralph's observation. "I suppose that is true, if one considers his unwillingness to receive guests properly . . . and his discourtesy in riding out of this castle without a word to me." He spat the pips into a silver bowl. "But that is to be expected, is it not?—he has been to war, and I doubt not there are things he will do that I cannot understand." He ate the last grape

thoughtfully. "Nonetheless, he must see that I have requirements of him, now that he is home. He is my heir—and I am
no longer young. It is time he was married with sons of his own,
so I may go to my grave satisfied I have done the proper thing
by my descendents." He cast a satisfied glance around the
room. "He will inherit a great castle, far greater than most in
England. I will expect him to administer it properly."

Ralph's tone was deferential. "My lord, he has always been
mindful of duty."

The earl made a distinctly skeptical sound. "Once he is made
to see I insist upon it, yes. His mother coddled him, encouraging
him to waste time on bootless dreams. Had any of the girls
lived, she would have had *them* on which to practice such
ridiculous things, but there was only Robert. He spent far too
much time with her in idle pursuits, and not enough in learning
his role . . ." He frowned, remembering. "Although I do believe
the beatings helped. Eventually he forbore to speak of such
useless imaginings, so I must assume he outgrew them—or
perhaps he merely saw the necessity of my strictness, and began
to honor me for it." He sighed, thinking back on the past. "Five
children dead, and two proper sons in the ground . . . well,
Robert will have to be made to understand that his responsibilities as heir to Huntington require specific things, even sacrifices,
which I believe strengthen a soul." Huntington looked at
Ralph. "He must put behind him the follies of youth and recall
it is time he conducted himself as a man worthy of my name."

"My lord." Ralph's tone was exquisitely neutral. "I believe
he has more than proved himself on Crusade."

Pride surged through Huntington's breast, replacing doubt.
He gripped the arms of his chair. "You are right, Ralph. I
should not suspect him of being what he once was. He has come
home a new man, and I should respect that." He laughed
breathily, an unfamiliar sound. "I can hardly order him beaten
now . . . if he spends an evening with a woman, I should not
chide him for it—so long as he recalls there is better in the
offing." He sank back into the chair once again, stroking his
jaw. "John's daughter," he mused. "How high may we aspire?"

*　*　*

Marian sat on the three-legged stool next to the bed, working at knots in her hair. For a long time she had sat idle, willing him to get well, but eventually she gave in to common sense and admitted that the fever would not break because she wished it to, and the best thing for it was to do whatever she could to make him comfortable and simply wait out the illness. Meanwhile, she might as well comb her hair.

She needed a bath desperately, but she would not leave Robin's bedside. He was restless and delirious; who knew what sort of nonsense he might mouth? It would not do for the servants to hear of private things.

The knots in her hair were stubborn. Marian feared she would have to cut most of them out. But as she split the tangles first with her fingers, then worked each matted lock until the comb ran freely, she began to think she might keep her hair after all.

What I want is to comb his *hair*—Marian broke it off, astonished that she would dare to think such a thing . . . and then she thought, oddly, of Eleanor deLacey, who said women had the same sort of urges men did and deserved to act on them, too; and Marian berated herself for refusing to acknowledge the truth of that, when she knew precisely how she felt, and had felt since she had seen him standing on the torchlighted dais.

I do want to comb his hair. I want to comb it, to put my hands in it, to feel the texture and smell the smell, to brush it against my lips—Marian dropped the comb. Humiliated by her forwardness, she hunched on the stool and covered her face with both hands, trying to will herself to forget the impulses and the wishes, the hunger in her spirit that made her want to touch him, and go on touching him until he awoke so he could touch *her*.

Forty-One

It was hot, so horribly hot, but the Lionheart did not appear to notice. While other mail-clad men wilted beneath the fierce sun, Richard, King of the English, did not so much as sweat.

"Hah! Robin, do you see? The walls of Acre before us, just waiting for my kisses . . . what do you think, my Robin? Shall we bring the walls down with horns as Joshua did Jericho? Or use wits and might instead?" The king was a bluff, vulgar, roistering man whose manners were his to mind, and who did not give leave to anyone to suggest he lower his voice. "Well, what say you, my Robin?"

His Robin stood on the barren, scoured plain, staring up at the creamy brick that defied usurpation. Behind it lay a city that was a key to Jerusalem, for if Acre ever fell the Crusade was sure to succeed.

"Well? What say you?" The king slung a thickly muscled arm around Robin's neck. "Do you say they will fall, or no?"

Robin smiled. "The walls will fall, my lord. As to Joshua—why not order horns blown as we set seige so the Saracens will believe our God is on our side?"

Richard grinned. His russet hair burned molten gold in the brilliant sun. "Well said, my Robin! We'll have the cursed Infidels tearing down the walls themselves!" He unhooked his arm and turned back toward his field pavilion, striding purposefully. Richard went nowhere slowly, nor wasted time on deliberation. "Now—come. There are plans to be laid and wine to be drunk . . . where is Blondel? Blondel!"

Robin watched idly as the minstrel appeared from around the colorful pavilion marked as Richard's by the pennon hung atop it and the shield beside the door-flap: three English lions on a field of scarlet. Blondel looked sleepy, scrubbing absently at his mouth with the sleeve of a once-fine tunic.

He was slender, elegant, well-spoken, with the hands and hair of a woman, pale and very fine. Blondel was very much his own man in everything save when it came to the king, whom he worshipped. Few in the army liked the minstrel because the king liked him so well.

"Blondel! We'll have music with supper. Bring your lute, boy . . . or have you lost it again?"

Blondel duly smiled the sweet, boyish smile that lighted up his blue eyes. "No, Sire. It lives in your tent now, so it has no mind to wander."

It was a joke in the army that Blondel's idle dreaming had cost him his lute; it was restored only when the king commanded it to be. Robin knew from camp gossip that the lute had been purposely stolen merely to tax the minstrel, but no one told the king that. No one breathed a word of Blondel's reputation, nor the army's determination to part the king from king's favorite.

A chill touched Robin, cooling the day briefly. Will they say the same of me? Some do already—if they succeed in turning the king from his beloved lute-player, will they then look to me?

"Robin!" Richard shouted. "You will broil your brains in the sun—come in and sup with me! I'll have my matched boys, if you please."

They were not so alike as that, but it was Richard's conceit that they balance one another in every respect. Robin was taller and heavier, but no one noticed that. They saw a wealth of fair hair bleached whiter by the sun; that and royal favor marked them forever inseparable in the cynical eyes of the army.

"Robin!"

Men would kill to sup with the human heart of the Crusade. Robin went into the tent as Blondel tuned his lute.

Sir Guy of Gisbourne levered himself against the bolsters, trying to inch himself upward without setting his leg to complaining. Then with great care he stretched out his arm, grasped the empty mug, and hurled it against the door. A moment later the empty bowl with the damp cloth followed it. *"Here!"* Gisbourne shouted. *"Where is that cursed barber?"*

Through the door he heard voices raised and a scuffle of feet. Then the latch was lifted and the cursed barber entered hastily. "Stop your *noise!*" he hissed. "Would you wake the earl himself?"

Gisbourne gritted his teeth. "I'd wake the *king* himself if it got me what I wanted."

The barber glared. "What do you want?"

"Fresh linens," Gisbourne grated. " 'Tis past time you changed the bandages. And water, too, damn you. Am I a prisoner or a guest?"

The barber sniffed. "What you are is a clumsy fool who got himself stuck by the boar. Don't you know you're supposed to stick *it?*"

Gisbourne regretted mightily there was nothing left to throw. Sweat broke out on his face as he labored to pull himself upright yet again. "Damn your eyes," he said weakly. "Just because I saw fit not to let you hack off my leg—"

"I *meant* to save your life," the barber declared. "But now you'll die of the rot, and all I'll have for my trouble is the body to dispose of."

"I'm not going to die. I'm going to live, damn you, so I can marry the Lady Marian."

"Ah, sits the wind in *that* quarter!" The barber grinned. "Then you'll be fighting the sheriff for her."

Gisbourne went very still. The room was abruptly cold.

"It's all over the castle," the barber continued. "They say he's settled on her, but there's the lady to ask first."

"Indeed," Gisbourne remarked.

"Indeed, yes. Since he can't wed his daughter to Sir Robert—which I doubt would have happened anyway, knowing the earl—" the barber smirked; he counted himself higher because of his lord's rank, "now he looks to himself."

"*Does* he?" Gisbourne said grimly.

"Indeed, yes." The barber flapped a hand. "Sit still, then, will you?—I'll fetch clean linen and water, so you won't wake up the earl with your yammering. As to the lady, I wish you joy of her. She's a sharp tongue in her head." He pulled the door behind him.

Drenched in sweat, Gisbourne breathed audibly through clenched teeth. His wound ached abominably, but he managed a sickly smile. "Fight the sheriff?" he asked. "No, I think not—not if Prince John pays my price." He even laughed a little.

"Meanwhile the sheriff will be wed to that fat old North Country beldame!"

Robin spoke of walls, and horns, and many other things Marian could not decipher. She understood little of his speech, wracked as it was by weakness and delirium, but what stood out most distinctly was that he didn't always speak English. She heard again the tangled sentences she had heard during the boar hunt, when he'd brought the beast down. She understood them no better now, knowing only that he twitched restlessly with some inner need, and sweated against the pillows. His hair was wet with it, and his face deeply flushed.

Marian did not doubt for a moment that the Crusade had touched them all with its harshness, regardless of its bounty in the glorification of God. She had heard stories of men coming home with one leg, or no legs at all, or arms; she'd heard of sicknesses that reduced grown men to children who lapped weakly at spooned gruel. It was possible he was very ill indeed, but Robin himself had said he'd had the fever more than once, that the king had also, and did not seem concerned for the fact that he would fall ill, other than to wish it to happen out of her company.

She dipped a soft cloth into the bowl of cool water and carefully sponged his face, wiping it clean of sweat only to have it bead up again until it ran from brow to temples, wetting hair and staining pillows. He was hot to the touch, yet he shivered.

"Insh'Allah," he muttered, twisting against the mattress. And then a spate of foreign words.

He subsided, and his jaw muscles clenched briefly, then slackened. The tilt of his chin displayed the jagged scar twining like a serpent along the bone. There was another scar also, an ugly gouge at his hairline that she had not seen before.

How many more? she wondered. *Or should I merely be thankful you have all your limbs in place and not ask what else was done to you?*

Marian swabbed his face again and blotted the sweat from his neck where it soaked into his tunic. Dry lips moved briefly, but issued no sound. "Hush," she said gently. "Don't waste yourself on words. Sleep will do you more good."

Pale lashes stirred, then the eyelids cracked open. She saw the feverish glint in his hazel eyes, dilated dark. "My lord . . ." he murmured.

She grinned, suppressing laughter. "No. Lady will do. Or, perhaps better: *Marian.*"

"My lord," he said plainly, staring glassy-eyed at her, "without you, the Crusade will fail . . . let Leopold go if you must, but you cannot lose heart—"

"Shhhh," she said, wondering how ill he was if he mistook her for a lord. "You are in England, Robin. *England.* You are home. You are safe. You are *home.*"

Brows knitted briefly. "Richard . . ." Tentatively, then with more conviction, as if getting used to the name, *"Richard*—I'm sorry . . ." His eyes closed as he swallowed convulsively. "—sorry . . ."

He meant the king, of course: Richard Coeur de Lion. She had heard him say the Christian name before, as if it were his to use freely in whatever way he wished, when everyone else knew titles. What puzzled her were the nuances she heard in his tone: desperation, affection, admiration, the faintest suggestion of regret.

He stirred, twitching restlessly. She blotted his face again, murmuring inanities meant only to quiet him. The sound of his breathing altered, and she knew he slept deeply once more.

Marian stared fixedly at him for so long a time her vision blurred. And then she shut her eyes and clenched her teeth together until she thought they might shatter. She wadded the cloth tightly in both hands, sinking her nails into the weave. "It just isn't *fair.*"

The chamber was silent save for the even breathing of the man in the bed.

Marian shook her head slowly, deliberately, aware of a slow-rising desperation tempered with resentment. It wasn't fair, any of it; she wanted to shout it at him.

She lurched to her feet and strode toward the door, intending to vacate the chamber and send a serving woman to nurse him. But as her fingers touched the latch, she stopped. She muttered a curse she had heard her father use once in extremity. It had been forbidden to her, but just now the circumstances warranted such words.

Marian swung around, her spine against the door. "It *isn't* fair," she declared, challenging the man.

Robert of Locksley offered her no answer.

Doubt flickered a moment. *I should go . . . leave him to Joan. She won't think of such things.*

No. Joan wouldn't. She couldn't. She did not recall, as her lady did quite clearly, the first time Robert of Locksley had entered Marian's life, nor each time thereafter: in the hall of Ravenskeep, beneath the mistletoe; on the dais in Huntington Castle; in the streets of Nottingham; in the shadows of Sherwood Forest.

And now. Marian laughed very softly. She thought it was time she told him.

"I was a girl." Purposely she employed the conversational tone of a grandmother telling a child a story, so as to keep emotions out of it; what was required was a simple, concise, straightforward recitation. "And you not so much older . . . but very aware of yourself. Very cool, distinctly aloof, keeping well clear of the games until even my mother noticed, and tried to draw you in. But you withstood her; you withstood my *mother* . . . who understood you in that moment far better than anyone else."

She folded her arms beneath her breasts. "I saw a quiet, watchful boy whose hair caught the candlelight and made him look like an angel . . . or so I fancied him, just for a moment—I *was* ten years old." Her smile faded. "Then I decided you were not a Christmas angel because you never smiled, nor looked with any favor on anything we did . . . and so I decided to *make* you smile, no matter what it took."

Marian paused for a moment, then went on. "So—I went to you and caught your hands, and dragged you beneath the mistletoe, trying to make you smile. Every man smiled when he kissed a lady beneath the mistletoe. And so I kissed *you*." She laughed and shook her head. "But you never once smiled." She watched the rise and fall of his chest, making certain he breathed. "I told my mother the next day, when you and your father had gone. She said your mother was dead but six months

425

and your father very strict—that you were a lonely young man who needed to be loved. So—I decided to love you."

His eyes remained closed, his breathing even. He had heard none of it, but then she had not really intended him to. She had intended only to say it out loud for the first time in her life, every bit of it, as much to explain it to herself as to anyone else.

Marian laughed again, very softly. She tilted her head against the door, then rolled it against the wood in futile, resigned denial. "It isn't fair," she said, "that after so much time I have to love you again."

The scimitar was truly beautiful in its deadliness, a shining silver wafer of seductive and lethal curve, made of Damascus steel. He saw it silhouetted against the sun, blotting out the brilliance while it stood, however briefly, paramount in that moment, a cynosure held above the battlefield in homage to God, whom he would come to know as Allah. Then the Saracen hand turned the blade only slightly, and it glittered, and he knew it would come flashing through the air to sever the head and limbs from a man he knew and respected.

"No!" he screamed, ripping the flesh of his throat, but the Saracens merely held him very still upon the sand with his head jerked back so he could see, and then the scimitar sliced the man to bits, as if he were beef or goat meant to serve the king's table. The head was thrown to land at his face, where it gushed blood into a living mouth opened to scream again, and into wide eyes that could not shut out the sight, because in his shock and rage all he could think of was the daughter the dead man loved so well, who was to be told her father loved her.

"Marian." He said it very clearly, because now it was more than a name. Then, it had been nothing; it had meant nothing. He had not thought of it again, until he heard it said to him on the dais at Huntington Castle, where he saw the dead man living in the woman's eloquent face.

William deLacey lay awake in the darkness. The night was warm, even for spring; he was hot and his brain overtaxed, attempting to sort out various responsibilities, dealing with them before the fact, so that he could stop thinking and go to

426

sleep. He spent many nights this way, and cursed every one of them.

Annoyed, he contemplated the mess his daughter's behavior had created. Prior to word of Robert of Locksley's return, he had not decided on any particular man to whom he would like to wed her. Her sisters had married conservatively—one to a wool merchant, another to a goldsmith who practiced his trade in London—with unspectacular returns for a father who wanted to rise. Eleanor was his last hope, and she had just devalued herself so badly he could anticipate nothing now. All he could do was marry her off as quickly as possible, in case she ended up bearing the minstrel's child.

DeLacey turned onto one side, hooking an elbow beneath his ear. *I ought to marry her to the lute-player . . . if she were forced to wed a man with whom she merely wanted to dally, the lesson might be learned.*

He turned over yet again, trying the other side.

He had ordered Walter to investigate the possibility of marrying Eleanor off to a man at some distance from Nottingham, but that had only been to make her fret. DeLacey knew of no offers that he hadn't already turned down in his zeal to land Robert of Locksley.

"Hens coming home," he muttered. *I'll need to find someone soon. Someone of enough rank to be respectable, ambitious enough to consider it an honor—and a chance to rise in the world—and malleable enough to overlook her reputation.*

He flopped over onto his back, scowling at the curtains swathing the lumpy bed. Aggravation swelled. Aggrievedly, he demanded, "Why couldn't it have been *Eleanor* whom Will Scarlet kidnapped?"

But it hadn't been. Eleanor was safe, but ruined . . . and Marian FitzWalter by now was probably safe as well, and probably ruined, too; worst of all, in deLacey's view, it was Robert of Locksley's doing.

Forty-Two

The oil lamp cast a wan, ocherous glow, painting the royal pavilion in a chiaroscuro of saffron and cinnibar, underscored with umber shadows. Richard, King of the English, contemplated his fate as he sat upon a camp chair nursing a cup of wine. He was thirty-six years old, but the russet-gold of his hair showed the first threads of silver, won in the name of Crusade.

"Malik Ric," he said. "That is what the Turks call me."

Robin, who had played the part of a body servant at the king's request and stripped him of mail, dropped the heavy hauberk across the foot of Richard's bed. It left the king in quilted gambeson, linen sherte, and leather-gartered hosen, but Robin made no effort to divest the king of anything more. "So they do," he agreed quietly as he poured himself wine and resumed his seat on a camp stool. "Thanks to Saladin, your legend will live on."

"Not if I don't take Jerusalem." Richard gulped wine, then blotted his mouth on the back of his wrist. His blue eyes were rimmed in red and luridly bloodshot, dried out from a day of heat and sand. He had washed, but the fine dust was pervasive; a faint trace dulled the gleam of his ruddy hair. They were days out of Acre, bound first for Arsuf, then Jaffa, and on to Jerusalem.

"You took Acre in one month," Robin said. "Guy of Lusignan had two years, and couldn't win the city. That should offer some consolation."

"And the cost?" Richard's eyes bored into Robin's. "At what cost—what will the chroniclers say of me, for killing the Saracens?"

It seemed to Robin that the king was much taken with concern about how his actions would be viewed; but then his black mood was not out of the ordinary for a warrior who had been, but days before, exulting over a victory everyone claimed miraculous. And it had been, in a way: Richard's siege

*of a city that had withstood other attempts for two years had proved wildly
successful. Sappers had undermined the walls, and the trebuchets launching
stones had done the rest.*

*But that exultation was over; the king had time now to reflect upon the
uglier side of the victory, when he had ordered the beheading of more than
2,600 captive Saracens.*

What would *the chroniclers say?*

*Robin drew in a breath. "They will very likely remind those reading their
accounts that Saladin broke his word."*

*Richard grunted. "Perhaps. But a costly revenge, was it not?" He
swallowed wine. "I think the accounts will be dependent on who writes
them."*

*"Probably, my lord. Chroniclers are not known to be unbiased in the
matter of royalty."*

*The king bared his teeth. "They will most certainly write of Philip's
cowardice, and Leopold's withdrawal."*

"And how you continued undeterred."

Richard snorted. "I should declare you *my chronicler. You will see to
it I am treated fairly, no matter what it may cost you." His eyes were very
bright. "A fair friend, my Robin—they are few when one is a king."*

*"Kings cannot afford friends." Robin looked at the massive Norman
sword leaning sheathed against the king's bed. It had killed uncounted men
in the taking of Acre. "Kings must rely on such things as might and wit and
cunning."*

*"But when they lack their own, they look for it in others." Richard sighed
heavily and rubbed at his face. He was thinner now than when he had
arrived from Cyprus, and his face less round, showing the shape of his jaw.
"You did well at Acre, my Robin. The knighthood was deserved."*

*He smiled crookedly. "Some might argue it was too hastily declared, and
the* colée *not hard enough."*

*"Hard enough to knock you down," the king retorted mildly, "but then,
you're slender as a reed."*

"Bad food."

"No. You've grown taller. There's but a finger's width between us."

Robin demurred; the king was well known for his size.

*"Stand up!" Richard cried, scenting a challenge. "God's Rump, but I'll
have this settled!"*

"My lord—"

"Stand up!" The king himself jumped to his feet and grasped double

handfuls of Robin's tunic and yanked him to his feet. The cup was dropped. Wine spilled in a puddle the color of old blood. "Here, now—we'll stand back to back . . ." But Richard made no move to shift his stance, and his hands did not release Robin's tunic. The blue eyes, bright with challenge, faded into softness. The firm mouth loosened.

Robin stiffened. "I'm not—" But he bit it off.

The softness faded, replaced with a hard glitter. "Say it," Richard said harshly.

"My lord—"

"Say it! In French, in English, in Latin—I'll hear what you meant to say!"

Robin breathed shallowly, very conscious of the powerful grip upon his tunic. His answer was in English for the ears of the Angevin king. "I am not Blondel."

Marian jerked awake as the latch was lifted. It took her an extra moment to recall her whereabouts: in Ravenskeep at last, slumped on a stool next to the bed in which Robin slept deeply, twitching in fever dreams. She had not thought to sleep at all, but obviously had dozed off.

Now the door was opened enough to admit a woman's head and shoulder. "My lady? Lady Marian—please . . . will you go to bed? I'll sit with him."

Marian blinked. Her head felt curiously light; words came sluggishly, from different parts of her brain. "No—no, Joan . . . I'll stay."

Joan was an older woman, brown of hair and eyes, with a kind set to her round face and a perpetually smiling mouth. The smile dimmed only a little as she came into the chamber. "Lady, please . . . you're all set to fall off that stool and crack your head, and don't tell me you won't. D'ye want *two* invalids, then?"

Marian didn't, but neither did she want the servants privy to Robin's words. He could well say things in delirium he would want no one to know.

She sighed and stroked her hair out of her eyes. "I'll stay, Joan."

The woman left the door ajar and came to stand but a pace

away from Marian. "You've a tongue in your head and you know how to use it, but we've *eyes* in our heads. Sim came to me after bringing Sir Robert up and said I was to see you to bed as well, that you'd likely catch his fever if you sat up all night with him. And don't say me nay—you've only to look at your poor face to know how you must be feeling. You need a hot soak, and then a warm bed."

Marian blinked several times in rapid succession, aware that she was very near fainting from sheer exhaustion. She had eaten a little earlier, and drunk watered wine; now her body demanded more than simple assuagement of hunger and thirst.

Squinting to keep her eyes open, she looked at Robin. He slept deeply, lids twitching. His color remained high and sweat still soaked his hair, but his breathing was normal. She put a hand on his brow and felt the expected heat, but it did not strike her as dangerously high. If anything, he felt a bit cooler.

"Lady—" Joan again.

"All right." Marian gestured surrender, then gathered her ragged kirtle skirts as she rose unsteadily. "No—I'm only weary. I promise, I have no fever."

"Will you have a bath drawn?"

"Only to fall asleep in it and drown?" Marian smiled faintly. "No. Just point me to bed before I fall and crack my head."

Joan nodded and guided her out of the door. "D'ye want me to take you there?"

The words sounded muffled and distant; her ears were already asleep. "No," Marian managed. "I can get that far, thank you." She paused in the corridor, turning back again. "He's been on Crusade," she said with elaborate precision. "He may say things in his fever that make no sense to you."

Joan's eyes were kind. "Go to bed, Lady Marian. From what little you said of events, I'd say you had your own Crusade."

Marian touched a fingertip to her battered face. She had said little about her ordeal, and none of it the truth: her horse had, she'd explained, been frightened by a boar and, in bolting, had carried her through the deepest part of the forest, then dumped her into a stream.

As for Sir Robert of Locksley, he'd come to rescue her, but had been felled by a fever while escorting her home. That was true enough. It would all suffice, she felt; no need to say any more.

Joan was plainly exasperated as Marian lingered unsteadily to look at Robin a final time. "Lady—go to *bed*. I'll see he's kept safe."

Instinct told her Joan was not a fool. *I'm giving too much away* . . . With effort, Marian nodded and turned away from Robin.

The tiny alcove was dark, very close, and redolent of mice, dampness, and something Tuck equated with sanctity: the odor of unwashed wool and the nervous perspiration born of intense, powerful prayer and the certainty of unworthiness.

He awoke with a start and stared blindly into the darkness as his heart resumed its rhythm, wondering what sound had broken his sleep, then realized with a familiar sinking feeling that what invaded his rest was guilt and a sense of doom. This had happened many times before, but always after overindulging in foodstuffs against his genuine intentions and the personal expectations of Abbot Martin.

This time the guilt had nothing to do with food. It had to do with the certainty he had done a terrible thing; no—*two* terrible things.

Tuck lay slack on his pallet with his face upturned to heaven, and knew he was a sinner.

His breathing, always audible because of his weight, grew louder, intensifying the closeness of the alcove. He lifted both hands to his face and covered it, pressing the features out of shape, wishing he might erase his face so no one knew it was he. If he could only start over, he would be a better man; undoubtedly he would make a much better monk.

But he was a sinner. He had known it was wrong to mislead the dying old woman, just as he had known that going to the sheriff entailed betraying Walter.

He dealt with the last sin first, which he thought *might* be excusable; had it not saved an innocent man from being hanged in place of another? What if he *hadn't* brought it to the sheriff's attention, and the innocent man had died? What then would be Tuck's fate?

He shuddered, pressing his fingertips into his closed eyes. It made his blackened vision flash multicolored light and odd images. "Father," he murmured wretchedly, "oh Father, forgive me . . . tell me what I must do . . . show me the way—"

He needed a priest, of course, so he could confess and do penance and receive absolution. But short of going back to the abbey, there was no priest—or was there?

Tuck lifted his hands from his face. Nottingham was not a small village. There was bound to be a priest. He could go *there*. He frowned into the darkness. *If there is a priest in Nottingham, why didn't the sheriff send for him when the old woman worsened? Surely he suspected she might be near to dying.*

Perhaps he hadn't suspected. The sheriff was a busy man; what if no one had told him until it was too late? And so he had turned to his clerk, prevailing upon him to play the part of a priest to give the old woman peace.

It was too complex to consider. The fact remained the same: he had committed a sin on both counts. He would inquire as to the Nottingham priest's location, so as to confess. Until then, all he could do was pray.

Tuck heaved himself off the pallet and knelt on the stone floor, unmindful of the painful hardness, the dampness, the chill beneath his knees, because Abbot Martin believed punishment of the body brought glorification to the soul.

A thumping on the door woke William deLacey. In the first moment of coherence he was incensed; he had trained his household staff to refrain from awakening him except in the direst of emergencies. Then he recalled that Nottingham Castle currently hosted Prince John, whose whims were legendary, and who had more right than any man alive, other than the king, to awaken whomever he chose at whatever time he decided to do it.

Accordingly deLacey sat up in bed, saw the bedside candle had nearly burned out, and called for the person to enter. He had no intention of relinquishing his bed—no, *Eleanor's* bed—unless absolutely necessary.

The latch was lifted. A guttering hand-held lamp shed fragile illumination. "My lord Sheriff." Gilbert de Pisan's austere face, lighted by the lamp, appeared beside the door, perched atop clean tunic and robe. He appeared to consider morning welcome, and deLacey despised him for it. "My lord, the prince requires the man to be hanged at once."

DeLacey squinted, rubbed briefly at his left eye, then looked again at the fat candle beside the bed. It was marked for each hour; currently, it showed the time as near dawn.

He scowled balefully. He was in no mood to dance the dance of diplomacy. "I was led to believe Prince John required the man hanged at breakfast. In fact, I specifically recall it, de Pisan; *you* said so."

"Indeed." De Pisan's calm expression did not alter. "The prince has changed his mind."

DeLacey sighed. Clearly there was no room for argument. "Very well. If you would be so kind, please to tell the Count of Mortain I shall be with him presently. There are arrangements to be made."

"Of course." De Pisan withdrew and pulled the door closed once more.

The sheriff sat upright in the bed for several moments longer, weighing options. Then he sighed, muttered an oath, dragged himself from bed, and opened the door, shouting for a servant to attend him at once. When the yawning servant arrived deLacey chastised him for tardiness and a certain disreputable dishabille—his tunic was not on straight—then dispatched him to Walter with a definitive order to prepare the murderer, William Scathlocke, for execution, to be carried out immediately in the castle bailey.

He then washed and dressed himself and went out to do his duty as Sheriff of Nottingham, for who was he to quibble with the dictates of royalty? Nottinghamshire was John's. If he wanted to hang every peasant in the shire, he could, and William deLacey would dutifully order the service rendered.

In a more philosophic frame of mind, the sheriff strode toward the packed hall. *Well, at least he won't require me to chase after the real Will Scarlet in the depths of Sherwood Forest. If we can't catch or keep the villeins, I'd just as soon hang them all by proxy. It does make the job easier.*

* * *

Awake now and lucid, Robin lay in bed and stared fixedly at the ceiling of the chamber in Ravenskeep, Sir Hugh FitzWalter's home. The dreams had come again, reacquainting him with things he would rather forget, among them FitzWalter's death and his own captivity.

He swallowed heavily, aware of dryness and sticky pain. It would pass, he knew, along with the dull headache and the last of the fever. For now it made him weak as a boy.

He stirred, anticipating the stiffness in his spine and limbs. As always, he ached, feeling wan and dull and weary, but the worst of it had passed. He was yet among the living, and bound to remain that way. The Crusade was finished. His captivity was ended. He breathed the air of England with the smell of a damp spring morning, in place of the dust and heat and sweat-stink of the march through the Holy Land.

"My lord?" A woman's voice. "My lord, may I give you water?"

His eyes were dry and gritty. He turned his head to look at her, and found the woman a stranger.

"Here." She poured a mug full, then came to his bedside. "Drink your fill, my lord. The well is deep and full."

On one sore elbow he raised himself slightly, and was ashamed to see how his hand shook on the mug. She had to steady it, or spill the water out. He drank, nodded thanks, fell back against the pillows. The water was cool and sweet, not tepid or fouled with acrid dust. The clarity of his memories was replaced with reality, and the knowledge of where he was.

"Marian."

The woman smiled. "It's to be hoped she's asleep. She needs it as much as you."

Undoubtedly she did, but he discovered himself disappointed.

"I'll bring you broth." The woman set the mug upon the floor beside the pitcher, then folded her hands into her skirts. "We're all grateful," she declared forthrightly, "for what you did to save her. She's all we've left, the lady . . . and she's well loved by us all."

Robin's brow arched; it was all the strength he had. His voice was tired, but serviceable. "What *I* did?"

"Aye. She told us about the boar, and how her horse bolted, and how you came along to rescue her after it threw her into the stream." She opened the door, smiling. "God bless you, Sir Robert."

She was gone before he could answer, to tell her she was wrong, that Marian had seen to her own rescue; and his too, if he counted—and he did—having someone pick him up out of the dirt.

Robin's eyes drifted closed. As he faded back into sleep he resolved to tell the serving-woman the truth when she came back with his broth. He was not a man for living off the lies of a woman told to prop up his pride. There was, after all, so very little left. And no reason at all to mourn it.

Forty-Three

The hanging of the man known in death as Will Scarlet but in life as Edward Carter required little fanfare and less time. Before his legs stopped kicking—the bailey gibbet was makeshift and therefore his neck was not broken—Lincoln-bound Prince John and his retinue wound its way out through the gates into the city proper, and William deLacey was at last able to summon his horse and ride out for Ravenskeep.

He made short shrift of the road between the city and the manor, but slowed his mount to a dignified walk as he turned off the main road onto the manor track, desiring no one to consider his haste as significant; he fostered an opinion of himself as calm and deliberate, so as to convince potential enemies there was nothing they could do that might affect his judgment. It was his belief that fast thinkers were not necessarily fast movers, and that impatience marked a man as lacking a true understanding of complex issues.

Most of all, he did not want to suggest by any actions that he wanted Marian quite so badly as he did.

The track curved up through a lush meadow fringed by an oak wood. From a distance the manor appeared prosperous and attractive, as it always had, but as he rode closer deLacey saw the first signs of neglect. It wasn't significant, but it told him many things.

The manor residence itself was a large unadorned rectangular hall of plain undressed fieldstone, pierced at regular intervals by tall, narrow windows which were shielded at night by shutters; by day, if temperate, the shutters were left open. The roof was timber, and ivy swarmed the walls to round the sharp-edged corners into clouds of jade and olive. The courtyard wall also was cloaked in ivy, and the shrub roses Sir Hugh's wife had tended so assiduously had grown completely out of control, draping intrusive thorn-bedecked canes over walls and onto benches, as well as along the path. Other flowers and herbs choked the infrequently tended gardens: lavender, rosemary, violets, and tansy, along with basil, pennyroyal, cammomile and sweet fennel. The shrubbery was in full bloom and quite magnificent, but deLacey was an orderly man and found the unchecked growth unappealing.

He halted his horse at the main gate, somewhat surprised to find it shut. Before Sir Hugh went on Crusade the gate was always open during the daytime. He dismounted, frowning slightly; the gate hung askew, sagging precariously.

A rapping eventually caused the wicket to be opened, and a pair of eyes peered out. DeLacey knew those eyes. "Sim," he said, "I've come to see your lady."

The faded blue eyes blinked. "Now, my lord?"

He hesitated only a moment. "Yesterday, no doubt." But the irony was lost on the man, as he expected. "Sim, open the gate. I have business with the Lady Marian."

"She's resting, my lord."

"As well she should be, after her experience. But surely she

437

can spare time to see me; I bring her news of her old nurse."

"Matilda? Aye, my lord—she was meaning to send someone to Nottingham." The wicket was shut. Sim unlatched the gate, then dragged it open. The bottom corner dug a ditch in the dirt, unseating the border of courtyard cobblestones. "Come in, my lord. I'll be taking your horse."

DeLacey scowled at the loosened cobbles. "This is a travesty, Sim. Does no one care for the place?" He led his horse through and cast a glance around the courtyard. "Sir Hugh would never have allowed his home to become so dilapidated."

"No, sir." Sim dragged the gate closed and latched it. "And we didn't mean for it to, my lord. But with Sir Hugh gone now—"

He cut him off sternly. "You can't mean to say Marian permits this to happen."

"No, my lord—but the lady is hard-pressed to see to the running of the place. It was her father who did it, my lord—when he went on Crusade some of the villeins ran off, and the freeholders are seeing to their own first before their lady, my lord."

It was preposterous. "She has said nothing to *me* of this."

"No, my lord—she wouldn't. But she's softhearted, my lord—when a freeholder says to her he can't pay his rent because the taxes have been raised, she absolves him of it. And so when she pays *her* share of the taxes, there's little left over, my lord." Sim shrugged. "She does the best she can. She's a good lady, my lord."

"Better than you deserve." He ignored Sim's wince and cast another critical glance around the courtyard. "She should have come to me. I'd have seen to it those runaway serfs were caught and punished, and I'll have a personal word with each and every freeholder. By God, what she needs is a man . . . a woman isn't capable of enforcing discipline."

Sim scratched his chest. "No, my lord."

"Here, then; my horse." He handed the reins over. "You will tell the other servants I'll have a word with them before I go." DeLacey turned on his heel and strode toward the door, resolving to settle the matter of marriage before he left the manor. It was time Marian was made to see she could not go on alone.

* * *

Marian stood outside the door to the room in which Robin slept. She wanted very much to go in and see how he fared, but found herself subject to an almost paralyzing self-consciousness. In Sherwood they had shared much in words and adventure, but here she was among people who knew her, and amidst the memories of expectations held by mother and father. One had been dead for a decade, the other for a year, but she was the only one left to carry on the name and attendant responsibilities. They would expect her to conduct herself with decorum and competence, treating the heir to Huntington with the respect due his rank.

But I don't feel decorous. I don't feel competent. I feel giddy and nervous and foolish. She drew in a deep breath and blew it out noisily. There was more to it than that. She was afraid she would show too much of herself to a man who didn't care. *He said as much before, when he made that comment about fathers parading their daughters before him at Huntington Castle—he needs no more women casting covetous eyes upon him.*

Marian made up her mind in a rush to treat him as she would any other man, in spite of his rank and her foolishness, and opened the door before she could change her mind.

He slept. She saw at once he was much improved over the night before. His color was less hectic, he no longer perspired, and he slept without restlessness. Even his breathing was better, lacking the heavy thickness she had disliked so much.

She released the breath she didn't realize she had been holding, immeasurably relieved to find him so recovered. The tenseness was gone from his features, softening sharp angles and loosening the mouth. He looked younger, much less hard, almost vulnerable.

Joan nodded welcome. "Much better," she whispered. "I brought him broth, but he was asleep." She indicated the bowl on the floor beside the mug and pitcher.

Marian did not look at Joan or the bowl of broth. She looked instead at Robin. "I'll see he eats it. You may go."

"Aye, lady." Joan gave up the stool and left as Marian moved to the bedside.

439

Almost at once Robin opened his eyes. They were bright but not overly so, and perfectly clear. "I do not much care for broth."

Startled, Marian touched a hand to her chest, then pulled it away. *What do I say? How do I act? . . . He will think I am a fool, which I am, but*—And then, somewhat contemptuously, *You henwit— you withstood Will Scarlet! Grow a spine, you silly girl!*

He lay there looking at her, waiting for her to speak. Marian scowled, ashamed of her hesitancy, and adopted an imperious tone. "How long have you been awake? And what does it matter how much you care for broth? Our aim is to make certain you keep it where it belongs, not how it tastes on your tongue."

Robin smiled faintly. "A night's rest has refined *yours.*"

Marian sniffed elaborately, though inwardly she was pleased to hear him sound so normal, so at ease. "It is a habit of men to hide how bad they feel both before they fall ill, and immediately after. How am I to know you aren't near to death?"

"Because I am not. I have had this fever before, which is more than you can say." His tone acquired a dryness. "A gift of the Crusade."

She nodded gravely. "And will it now conquer England?"

"I pray not," he said fervently, then hitched himself upward to slump against piled pillows. "Is it cold?"

"What—the broth? I thought you wanted none of it."

"I said I do not much care for it. I did not say I wouldn't take it. As it is the only thing I have been offered since I arrived—"

Marian relaxed; he was making it easy for her. "And *that* with excess clumsiness," she chided pointedly. "You might have cracked your skull."

"Did I fall off, then?" He considered it. "Perhaps that is why my shoulder hurts." He massaged the joint in question.

"Yes, you fell off . . . Sim and Hal brought you back here to bed." She sat down on the stool, delighted by the lightness of his tone. The cynicism and moodiness had vanished with the fever, leaving behind another man. She had seen flashes of him before, but now the mask and walls were discarded. "You should be grateful to us, rather than insulting our hospitality."

"And the bed is lumpy, too . . . or is that my spine?" He shifted slightly, frowning. "No—it is the bed."

"Not so bad as the bed you made *me,*" she retorted. "Even you admitted that."

Robin smiled ruefully. "Then we've suffered equally."

Marian raised her chin in challenge, working hard to suppress the joyous laughter that filled up her spirit. *This is not so hard after all.* "It seems—"

A rap at the door interrupted. Joan put her head in. "Lady Marian? I'm sorry to disturb you—but the sheriff is here to see you."

She was stunned. All the high good humor dissipated instantly. *"Now?"*

Joan nodded.

"He wastes no time," Robin murmured.

Inwardly Marian agreed, but would not say so to Robin as her jubilance drained away. She rose, shaking out the folds in her kirtle as Joan departed; she had put on her second best of bright blue linen, bound with a Norman girdle, and washed and combed out her hair. Rebraided for propriety's sake, the thick, still-damp plait hung to her hips.

"I will come back later to see how you fare." At the door she stopped and turned back briefly, indicating the reviled broth. "With food I trust will be far more appropriate to your exalted station, *my lord.*" But the amusement dissolved instantly as she thought about William deLacey.

Tuck was laboring over the last of the sheriff's letters when Walter came into the chamber. He glanced up briefly to acknowledge the man, then raised a delaying finger as he carefully added the final flourish. Deftly he sanded the vellum, then moved it aside to dry. He was satisfied; the work was good.

Tuck turned to Walter with a smile, and found the man's face ashen. "What *is* it?" he asked on a rush.

"That man . . ." Walter swallowed heavily, collapsing against the door. "I know I said he would do it, but—somehow . . . I just didn't *believe* he would."

Tuck frowned. "Would what?"

"Hang that man."

All the breath left Tuck's lungs as horror possessed his soul. He wanted to ask what hanging, what man, what did Walter *mean?*—but he knew. He *knew.* The Sheriff of Nottingham, to whom he personally had given the execution order, had hanged the man after all.

"No," Tuck whispered.

"Yes," Walter countered. "Just after dawn."

"But—he couldn't—he said he *wouldn't*—when I went to him—when I told him . . ." Tuck felt a witless fool, unable to form complete sentences or thoughts. "The man is dead?"

Walter nodded. "It took him more time than I care to count, but he died. And then Prince John and the rest of his people rode out toward Lincoln. The sheriff rode out, too, leaving me to see to it the man was taken down."

Tuck's staring eyes burned. "An innocent man . . ."

Walter scrubbed at his face. His tone was more normal now, as if sharing the horror with Tuck had helped him recover. "Not innocent, not *truly* innocent—why else d'ye suppose he was in the dungeon?" He didn't wait for an answer. "But not Will Scarlet, either."

Trembling, Tuck sketched the sign of the cross. "God forgive him . . ."

Walter cocked an eyebrow. "Which one? The dead man, or the sheriff?"

Tuck folded his hands and bent his neck, rocking in an unconscious bid for comfort. "Oh Father, oh my gentle Lord—"

Walter sighed. "Never mind. I'll leave you to your prayers." He lifted the latch noisily and slipped back out the door.

Unsteadily, Tuck got up from his bench. He trembled all over. In a daze of shock and horror he followed Walter out of the chamber, then made his way shakily down the corridor to the tiny alcove housing his pallet.

The chamber was dim, unlighted, to save the candle for emergencies. Tuck felt around with his foot, found the chamber pot, then was thoroughly and painfully sick.

* * *

DeLacey found, to his relief, the interior of Ravenskeep's hall not so unruly as the courtyard and its surrounding wall. The earthen floor was still beaten hard, with clean rushes mixed with sweet herbs spread overall; the plastered walls remained in good order, except where smoke stained the lime-whitened plaster as smoke always did; and the familiar twin lines of timber posts still marched from front to back, dividing the hall into three separate sections, though only one was screened off to provide housing for the household servants. One shadowed staircase gave entry to the second floor where the family lived: only Marian, now.

Because Sir Hugh had been a knight, not lord or sheriff, there was no chair or table upon the dais. In fact, there was nothing upon the dais except a single bench, and that pushed back against the wall. A screened passageway led off from one side to the adjoining kitchen, with additional assorted outbuildings housing pantry, buttery, and other necessities.

He was left alone to wait, which actually he preferred; it gave him time to prepare the proper approach. Marian had proved increasingly subject to fits of independence as well as forthright speech; it was time he regained control and took her in hand.

Her voice was clear and cool, divulging nothing more than simple politeness. "My lord Sheriff—forgive me. I did not mean to keep you waiting."

He turned hastily, startled into a genuine smile as Marian came down the final two steps into the hall. And then the smile died as he saw her face, so scratched and bruised and welted.

My God—"Marian." DeLacey lurched forward and grasped her hands, pulling them out of her skirts. He meant to say many things, all of them offering comfort and protection, but he was struck speechless by the magnitude of his realization: another man had put his hands upon the woman *he* wanted. *"Marian*—"

She jerked loose and moved a step away, color spilling out of her face. Her eyes took on a hard glitter he found unattractive. "My lord—"

"My God—what do you expect me to do—?" He followed, ignoring the flash of trepidation in her eyes, to catch and cup her jaw. *"My God*—" In anger was incoherence and a helpless

443

determination: he wanted to find Will Scarlet himself and crush the peasant's throat. "What that man *did*—"

Marian clasped his wrists and stripped his hands away. Deliberately, she said, "Please don't touch me."

It fanned the flame higher, searing away the shock to bare a hotter, more brilliant fury. Scarlet had done this. Scarlet would pay for this. "I will kill him myself."

Something glinted in Marian's eyes: icy self-possession with a hint of contempt. "*If* you can catch him."

The thrust was purposeful as a knife slicing into vitals with a deft, cold-blooded twist. *My God—she blames ME—*

As well she should.

The pain was shattering. In that moment all his plans fell into ruin, undone by nothing so effective as a simple tone of voice and a coldness in the eyes.

His mouth would hardly obey. "Marian—I beg you—"

"For what?" The contempt was plainer now. "For my forgiveness? But you can hardly be blamed, Lord Sheriff. How could you have foreseen that a man sentenced to hang might be desperate enough to kidnap a woman so as to use her to buy his freedom?"

For the first time in many years, he spoke from the heart. "Don't hate me, I beg you . . . my God—*Marian*—"

She was so cold, so controlled; in that moment, she was as he *had* been. "I am well," she said plainly. "The cuts and bruises will heal."

"Not that," he said. "Not *that*—"

"Oh?" She arched eloquent brows. "Then you inquire, without using words, as to the status of my virginity."

It was agony. "Marian, *please*—"

Her face was very white. "I am as I was, my lord. Is that not answer enough?"

DeLacey felt himself shaking. With effort, he reached for a measure of fragile self-control, trying to explain in a way she could comprehend; in a way *he* could. "You don't understand—"

"I think I do. You want to know what everyone else wants to know. The only difference is, you believe you can ask it."

Some of the rage came back, kindled by her coldness. He

struck out viciously. "I was your father's friend! Allow me, if you will, to grieve for *him* a moment; to see what has become of his beloved little girl."

Marian recoiled. It was her turn to be shocked by the weapon in his tone. "You throw *that* in my face—"

"I throw nothing. I throw *nothing.*" Impatiently he swiped at the moisture dotting his upper lip. "My God, Marian, do you blame me?" he rasped. "Any man would feel as I do, seeing what has happened. As for *me*—" His smile was ghastly. "I have known you since you were born. Allow me a moment—nothing more, a moment *only*, I swear"—delicate irony—"to reconcile my guilt."

Marian gazed at him transfixed, then swallowed heavily. "Guilt?"

Painfully, he said, "You were in my charge."

It blunted her contempt. She spoke with less vehemence now, and much less challenge. "And I told you, my lord—you cannot be blamed—"

"I can." He cut her off curtly, not yet prepared to surrender the emotions, then turned away to stare blindly at the door but paces away. "To allow that to happen . . ." He shut his eyes, trying to master himself. "You have too good a heart to lay blame at my door, even when I deserve it."

She made no answer. He swung back, expecting contempt; he found unshed tears instead. "I have nothing of the sort," she said unevenly. "I am not a saint, my lord—and yes, I do blame you . . . but don't make me over into something I am not."

She had surrendered the advantage that had won her, however briefly, a measure of concern that she would prove difficult. This he understood. She was no longer warded against him, but was clay within his grasp. "Marian." He drew in a deep breath, recalling the delicate plans he had made on the ride to Ravenskeep. She had seen a side of him he had not wished to display, but it was an honest portion, and he did not regret it at all. She might now better understand the true depth of his feelings . . . but it was time to exert control again, to cause her to act as he desired her to act. He could not lose self-control again. "This is painful for us both . . . let us dispense with discussion of it and move to something else." He cast a quick glance across the hall. "May we sit?"

After a moment she nodded. He followed her to the bench and sat down as she motioned him to. "And you." He mimicked her gesture.

Marian shook her head, keeping distance between them. "I think I would rather stand."

"No," he said sadly. "In a moment, you will not. It is bad news I bear about someone dear to you."

"But who—" Her eyes widened in shock. "Oh God—not *Matilda* . . ."

DeLacey merely nodded. It was her turn for exhibition; he was done with his.

After a frozen moment Marian sat down awkwardly, staring blindly into the hall. Her voice was oddly empty. "For a while I forgot, in the midst of everything else . . . and then I intended to send someone for her—" She closed her eyes. "I should have gone myself. I should have gone sooner."

He offered her nothing at all, neither sympathy nor kindness. Marian stared mutely into the shadowed hall. He watched her mercilessly, permitting himself no tactful words or gestures to dilute the moment. He wanted to see her, to judge her state of mind, so he could adapt to the moment. His anger now was cooled, infinitely controlled; this was too important to be diminished by excess emotion.

He waited. Eventually Marian brushed away tears, speaking in a tight, strangled tone. "Will you bring her back?"

"She has already been buried."

"There?" She was anguished. *"This* was her home!"

"No one could anticipate when you might—return." He was deliberately oblique. "I felt it best to see the woman buried as soon as possible."

A spasm warped her battered face. "I should have gone straight back to Nottingham."

He didn't care to waste any more time on Matilda. "Marian." He waited until she looked at him. "This is not why I came"—although it was—"but now, however indelicate it may seem, I must discuss it with you. Because there is a solution."

446

She stared at him in silence, eyes dulled by grief. She did not much care what else he had to say.

DeLacey approached it carefully. "You see, I have sorrow of my own, and some small understanding . . . a father's rage and helplessness, much as I feel for you." He smiled sadly. "My daughter has been publicly despoiled. I know the truth of the matter, as I was at some pains to tell you, but regardless of that truth I must offer my daughter the protection of a father, and the love and the care . . ." DeLacey sighed heavily. "Arrangements must be made in case there is a child."

For the moment her grief was banished. Marian's gaze sharpened. "My lord—"

But he overrode her. "I have decided to marry Eleanor to my steward, Sir Guy of Gisbourne."

She said nothing at once, staring at him fixedly. Then, with a breathless laugh of bitter acknowledgment, "And who for *me*, my lord? Is that not what you came for?"

"Yes," he answered gently, curtailing a satisfied smile. "You shall marry me."

Forty-Four

The bed was narrow and gave in the middle, so that Robin lay in a ditch. With effort, he levered himself into a sitting position, wincing in response to the stiffness of his spine and joints, then slowly swung both legs over the edge of the bed. He counted it a victory.

For a long moment he contemplated life from that position, reaccustoming himself to the expected residual soreness, then leaned down and picked up the bowl. Somewhat forlornly he studied its contents, cooled and scummy on top, but that was his own fault; he didn't *really* mind broth all that much, but it had been something with which to provoke Marian, which had proved intensely enjoyable. He'd put off eating it too long.

He sighed and picked up the spoon, stirring the clouded top layer into the rest of the broth. He ate most of it with grave deliberation, thinking about the times in the Holy Land when there had been nothing at all; then washed the taste down with water and set all on the floor again.

He gazed at the door. "William deLacey," he muttered, "you are becoming a nuisance."

He scowled, wiggling his bare toes. Someone had stripped him of his boots and leather wrappings, leaving him in his tunic and baggy hosen. The boots stood beside the bed, but he lacked the inclination to struggle with pulling them on.

Robin stood up slowly, swore in English and Arabic as he twisted this way and that to break free the knots in his spine, then made his way to the door. The fever had broken as it always did by morning; he was much recovered, but stiff and sore. By midday he would be better, by evening better than that; for now, however, he hurt.

He met no servants on the way down. As he reached the lower portion of the screened staircase, he heard the echo of voices bouncing off the walls and high timber ceiling: deLacey's and Marian's.

He stopped short, lingering off balance between one rough step and the next. *I should not be doing this.*

Undoubtedly he should not, but he was not persuaded to make his way back up the stairs now that he was down them. Instead he let momentum carry the day and descended a few more steps. Near the bottom he paused, leaned against the pebbly wall, and listened unabashedly to the remains of a private conversation.

The sheriff's voice was dolorous. "Arrangements must be made in case there is a child."

Robin's eyes narrowed. *He wastes little time—*

"My lord—" Marian began.

"I have decided to marry Eleanor to my steward, Sir Guy of Gisbourne."

Robin blinked surprise—he had believed the sheriff to be speaking of Marian—and then cynical relief was followed by true relief: first, that he himself was no longer a target for Eleanor deLacey; secondly, that Marian was not the subject.

But then he heard the sound she expelled: a breathy, bitter laugh that banished his relief; he had not heard the whole conversation. "And who for *me*, my lord? Is that not what you came for?"

"Yes," the sheriff answered. "You shall marry me."

So—it is that. Robin's teeth shut. He stared fixedly into nothingness for a tense moment, vision unfocused, listening very hard as he waited for her answer. Marian made none, which he disliked; he interpreted her silence as consideration. Grimly he shook his head, slumping against the wall. His skull thumped stone.

He gazed into the dimness above his head. What else was she to do? A woman in her situation had no choice: she went into a nunnery, or she married a man willing to give his name to a bastard, if one resulted. He himself had lacked the courage to ask Marian if Will Scarlet had violated her, thinking it indecent and not for him to bring up; William deLacey had asked, because it was important. For all Robin was beginning to detest the man, the sheriff was correct. Uncommonly blunt, perhaps, but candor revealed the truth. Tact too often obscured it.

He shut his eyes and mouthed an expletive learned from the Christian army. He wanted very much to descend the last two steps and stride across the hall into the conversation, discomforting the sheriff severely, but it wasn't his place. It did not concern him. He should go back up to bed, where he need not worry about Marian FitzWalter's future despite what her father preferred; where he need only think about riding away in the morning on his borrowed horse, so he could once again go home to a castle he didn't know.

The knowledge pinched. *Go*, he told himself. But he lingered anyway, because he had to know.

Marian answered at last in a clear, precise tone. "I am a ward of the king."

"The king is currently imprisoned."

"That does not remove me from his protection, my lord. He

is not *dead*, after all—and not like to be while he is worth money."

"Perhaps not," deLacey agreed, with no hint of impatience, "but you can hardly afford to wait until the king is released, *if* he is released. That might take years with the poor state of England's coffers—and you, I fear, have but a week or two to waste."

"Waste them on what, my lord?" she asked pointedly. "The contemplation of ways to avoid marrying you?"

Plainly it displeased him. His voice was a whip-crack. "Marian—"

She cut him off smoothly, all meek decorum, but with an edge to her words. "Forgive me, my lord . . . I am desolated by the news of Matilda's death. I am not fit company. Please—permit me to walk you to the door."

"Marian—"

"I beg you, my lord—give me time to grieve—"

His words were crisp, ending her attempts at polite prevarication. Steel showed through the silk. "You have grieved quite enough. It is time to think of yourself."

With exquisite dryness, she said, "My lord, I do assure you I am thinking of myself."

Robin laughed mutely, stifling it with effort.

"Marian." DeLacey's tone altered. It was cold, deadly, certain. "You know very well this is what your father wanted."

Silence filled the hall. *And so the battle is won.* Robin shut his eyes, aware of a brief, intense moment of sharp regret. *I should never have told her.*

"My lord," Marian said eventually, "I will give you my answer as soon as I am able."

"Come to Nottingham. Now."

"No." Nothing more than that.

"Then come tomorrow."

"No. Not yet."

"Marian—"

"Give me time!" she cried. It echoed throughout the hall.

Robin shook his head. *She will do it because of that . . . because her father wished it. And it was I who told her.*

"Very well," deLacey agreed. Then, in silky suggestion, "Do see me to my horse."

Marian said nothing. After a long moment Robin heard the door thump closed.

He stood there against the wall. He did not climb back to his borrowed room. Instead he went down the remaining two steps into the hall itself, staring into the emptiness filled with rush motes, dust, and ash. His spirit felt no cleaner.

Marian stood outside in the courtyard, watching as William deLacey at last rode away from the manor. Without moving she waited until Sim shut and latched the gate, settling the bar into place; then with grave meticulousness she bent and picked up the loose cobble by her foot. With all her might she heaved the dense brick at the gate.

As it cracked against the wood, spraying dust and chips, Marian gritted her teeth. "I hope your horse *bolts.*"

Sim was astonished. "Lady Marian!"

"I do," she insisted. Then, as venomously, "No, perhaps I don't—or surely he will be injured and brought here for me to tend."

The servant inspected the gouge left in the gate. "Lady—he's the sheriff."

"I don't care if he is Prince John himself—I will not be made to do what I do not *wish* to do." Wind teased her hair, blowing it free of the braid. Marian caught loose strands back from her eyes and peered into the sky. "Don't storm," she begged fervently. "At least not until he is closer to Nottingham."

"Poor gate," Sim murmured, rubbing the abused wood. "Yet another scar."

In her black mood, Marian found it surpassing strange that a man could be concerned with the appearance of a gate, but she supposed Sim was welcome to care for whatever pleased him. Some men liked dogs, some women cats; for now, *she* was too angry to think past the outrage she felt. Clutching her damp hair against the breeze, she spun on her heel and marched back into the hall.

She thumped the door closed behind her, fighting tears of

humiliation and grief. Matilda dead, and William deLacey using her father's wishes to force her hand. He hadn't even the decency to allow her time to grieve.

And Will Scarlet—A shudder passed through her body, so intense it clicked her teeth together. Tears threatened again on a wave of revulsion so powerful it nearly made her sick to her stomach. She had not allowed herself to think of Scarlet in anything but terms of anger and a cold certainty that she had suffered nothing at his hands but dishevelment and discomfort.

He had not violated her physically, but he had defiled her sense of safety. Just as the sheriff had taken pains to remind her.

DeLacey. Marian knew him much better now. She understood him now. He would use whatever there was—if he didn't make it himself—to please his own ambitions.

I will tell him—She stopped dead, brought up short. "What are you doing?"

Robin sat casually on the rush-strewn floor, leaning against one of the massive timber posts holding up the roof. He looked uncommonly at ease with his knees crooked up, feet buried in rushes. His hazel eyes were steady as he hooked his elbows over his knees. "Waiting for you," he said. "I as much as the sheriff would like to know what you plan to do."

Marian pointed at the stairs. "Go back to bed."

"I think not."

She simply hadn't the strength, in view of the turmoil in her spirit. She lowered her arm limply, seeing an odd set to his mouth. It wasn't a smile, precisely, but a cool, subtle challenge, as if he lay in wait. When coupled with deLacey's behavior, it made her angry. "I'll have the servants in to drag you back up the stairs!"

"They will refuse," he said. "The son of the Earl of Huntington somewhat outranks their lady."

So easily he disarms me. She wanted to cry, but did not; she would not before him. "Matilda's dead," she choked. "She was ill, and I left her . . . and now she's dead."

"Your old nurse?"

"I left her at Nottingham Castle when he dragged me out to the fair, and then Will Scarlet took me—" Marian gritted her teeth as anger overtook grief. "I wish I were a man. I wish I could fight like a man. I wish I could hit someone. I wish—oh, I don't know *what* I wish . . . that I were a different person, able to deal with situations not of my own making."

He studied her gravely, as if expecting more.

Marian took a single wavering step to the nearest post. It was opposite Robin's; she slid down the length to the floor and puddled herself upon it, staring blindly at him. "It's all coming undone. My father, my nurse . . . now *this*." She crooked her knees, as he did, knowing skirts guarded her modesty; it was a comfortable posture and put something between them: two sets of knees and three long paces. She rested her head against the post, feeling weary and worn and helpless. "Why can't he let it be? I did not ask for his interest. Why can't he let it *be*?"

He offered no answer at first. She did not look at him, but her senses screamed of his presence. Three paces away—yet they felt more like three miles, then again only three inches; whatever the distance was, she lacked the courage to walk it, to even initiate the motion.

His tone was odd, a mixture of restraint and subtle conviction. He did not make light of the question, nor did he attempt to couch his words in chivalrous courtesy. "He wants you, Marian."

She sighed. "So he says, when it is the lands he wants—"

"No." He cut her off. "DeLacey wants *you*."

She grimaced. "Because of what I have—"

"Because of what you are."

She scowled at him. "What *am* I, then? Sir Hugh FitzWalter's daughter, ward to King Richard—"

"Marian." His face was stripped free of the mask. What she saw now was blazing, naked emotion. "What you *are* is a woman he wants very badly in bed. And I think he would do anything to make sure he gets you there."

Her shocked denial was instantaneous. "Oh no—"

"Oh *yes*."

She stared at him, undone by his conviction. This was nothing she had anticipated, this brutal, male truth. "I—don't understand . . ." And she didn't, not really, not fully. She was only beginning to, and it frightened her very badly.

His smile was wintry. "I am not the one to explain in elaborate detail why a man, any man, might feel as deLacey does."

"Why not?"

Robin sighed. "Helen of Troy."

It baffled her utterly. "What?"

"Helen of Troy. Have you no knowledge of the classics?"

"Of course I do; I was told all the stories. Helen was married to Menelaus of Sparta, until Paris of Troy cast his eyes upon her and fell in love with her at once. He stole her and took her to Troy. Agamemnon and Menelaus followed to get her back, and Troy was destroyed."

Robin nodded. "For the love of a beautiful woman."

"Yes, but—" She stopped. "Oh *no*—"

"Yes."

"But—I'm *not*—"

"Ask any man," he said.

Her heart beat very hard. She could barely breathe around it. "I am not Helen . . . and William deLacey is *not* Menelaus."

"Given leave, he will be. He most certainly plans to be."

Marian felt cold. She shivered. "This is too much. Matilda— now this—" She touched a trembling fingertip to a welt on her cheek. Softly, she said, "I could never be Helen."

"And I would rather not be Cassandra, crying doom throughout the land." Robin rolled his head against the post. "What will you tell him, then?"

Marian smiled grimly. "That I will not be his Helen."

"There may be no choice."

"I am the king's ward, not his. Not Prince John's. There is no one to tell me what I must do."

"Propriety," he said. "Society, as well. Eleanor marries Gisbourne. DeLacey will marry you."

"You listened," she accused.

He did not deny it.

Marian scraped the hair back from her face. "But there is no *need*—Will Scarlet did nothing!"

"It will be his excuse. That—and your father's wishes."

Marian shut her eyes. "You should never have told me."

Robin did not answer.

She looked at him. His face was stark and pale. Bleakness

crowded his eyes. "You're ill," she said suddenly, thrusting to her feet. "I'll have Sim and Hal—"

"No." He did not move. "I am not ill."

"Men will often say—"

"Let it be," he told her. "I am not ill."

Marian looked at his unshod feet and found it incongruous. "Where are your boots?"

"Where you—or someone—put them."

Irresolute, she wavered. "I can't leave you here."

He quirked a single eyebrow. "Why not? I am comfortable."

"You are the Earl of Huntington's son—one day you will *be* the earl . . . and you are sitting in a dusty hall amidst rushes that need changing." Inconsequentially she added, "And wearing no shoes."

He smiled. "I am comfortable."

Rushes littered her kirtle. She knew she had to go, to leave him here, or anywhere, just to regain her composure, to consider the things he had told her. But she lingered a moment more, stiff and awkward and wretched, thinking of repercussions. Unlike Paris, or Helen of Troy. "You said—any man."

The light died out of his eyes. "I am not any man."

She was suddenly ashamed she had asked, that she had *implied*. She had not meant him precisely, but men in general; she was only awed by the idea that he believed her akin to Helen.

"I didn't mean—" she began, but broke it off raggedly. *No—perhaps I did.* And perhaps he recognized it.

Marian turned gracelessly and walked toward the stairs.

William deLacey did not like the look of the sky, or the feel of the air. He sensed an understated *power*, as if lightning threatened to strike. A cool wind blew out of the oak wood and across the open meadow to buffet the track, gathering dirt and debris as a child gathers a handful of pebbles to throw at the first unwitting soul who crosses his path.

He disliked the taste of the day, but he disliked more the taste in his mouth: bitter gall. Marian had begun to mimic Eleanor to an alarming degree; clearly she expected her own desires to play a role in the decision of her marriage. It was utter nonsense that a woman would be allowed to say him yea or nay; he was a good match for her, and his able administration would soon set the manor to rights. Ravenskeep had fallen into disrepair because she had no husband; serfs had run away, freeholders denied her the rents, those who remained to help were a lazy, unskilled lot who could not even manage to hang a gate properly.

And a year without a father had eroded her self-discipline. She required a firm hand if she were to be the kind of wife he deserved.

DeLacey's mount shied sideways as a cluster of leaves blew by. The wind grew stronger, snatching at his cloak. He steadied the horse, squinted to study the sky, and considered perhaps it might be best if he went back to Ravenskeep to wait out the storm.

He discarded the idea at once. Marian needed time to see he intended only the best for her. If he returned to her now, he would only be adding fuel to the fire. Better to let her calm down. He had other plans to put into motion.

DeLacey sighed wearily. "Grant me patience to deal with women."

Sir Guy of Gisbourne was nonplussed to learn he could not have the loan of a cart and driver to return to Nottingham just yet—a storm, he was told; wait until morning. It left him considerably out of sorts. He wanted very badly to return to Nottingham. Aside from his normal duties, to which Walter would not attend quite so assiduously as he, Gisbourne desired very much to place himself back in deLacey's confidence. He needed to know what the sheriff intended to do, so *he* could be in position to tell Prince John what he needed to know about the state of the sheriff's conscience and the limits of his ambition.

"There are no limits," Gisbourne muttered. "He'd want the throne, were there a chance to take it."

There was not, of course. Unless the Lionheart proved also a lion in bed and got a son on Berengaria, John would inherit; precisely as John intended . . . although Gisbourne believed the

456

Count of Mortain might do whatever was required to expedite the succession. And if *John* were not named heir—he and his brother did not always agree—there was always dead Geoffrey's son, Arthur of Brittany.

Gisbourne slumped against the pillows. Such thoughts were new to him, who had never wasted his time on intrigue past that which the sheriff employed in the day-to-day administration of his office. Gisbourne was not an innocent; he fully understood that intrigue was required. He simply had avoided it himself.

That time now was finished. He had involved himself. He would involve himself further. The reward would be worth it.

William of Cloudisley had gone to the fringe of the forest, where sparse skirts met meadow and track. Sherwood Forest thinned near Ravenskeep, offering considerably less cover, but Adam Bell had brought Clym of the Clough and Cloudisley— as well as his newfound followers—to try better prey.

"They won't expect us here," he'd said, "and it's not near Nottingham."

Little John, very glum, sat against a tree trunk. "It's madness," he muttered.

Will Scarlet turned on him. "When will you understand? This is our sort of life, now. You can't go back to your sheep. You can't go back to your fairs."

Much, squatting mutely, watched the giant with avid eyes, as if waiting for Little John to say what he should do.

Clym of the Clough laughed harshly. "Give it up, Scarlet— he's a boy in a man's body. The simpleton is more of a man than him—I saw how he defended that horse."

"*My* horse," Scarlet muttered.

Alan of the Dales, perched upon a stump, merely shook his head. "And none of you a horseman."

"And you are?" Scarlet challenged. "I don't see you on horseback."

"Because you stole my mount." Alan struck a muted chord on his lute. "You see—"

"Quiet," Bell snapped. "Hold your noise, minstrel."

One-handed Wat laughed softly. "I'll break it, if you like."

Bell shook his head as Alan thrust his lute behind his back. "We've no need for a musician . . . he can go on his way."

"I'm as wanted as you are," Alan retorted. "None of *you* lay with the sheriff's daughter."

Will Scarlet grunted. "Was she worth being outlawed over?"

"Hush," Bell said as a bird call sounded. "It's Cloudisley."

It was. The handsome young man made his way back through the trees and squatted down before them to drink from a waterskin. He shook his head as they waited, wiping his mouth on his sleeve. "A rich man, I'll wager, but not for the likes of us."

"One man—" Clym began.

Bell lifted a silencing hand. "We've bows. We outnumber him. Why do you say so, William?"

Cloudisley smiled crookedly. "He's the Sheriff of Nottingham."

Scarlet swore even as Little John shut his eyes. "Let *me* have him, then."

"No." Bell's tone was level. "He may be one man, and easy enough to kill—but it would bring down Prince John upon us. Killing his personal sheriff would make us too dangerous—they'd want us taken at once."

"We're wanted *now,*" Scarlet said.

Little John shook his head. "Fools, all of you."

The others ignored him. Clym rubbed his jaw. "We could just rob him—leave him alive—"

"And make him angry," Wat said. "Angrier than he is. He'll set all his pet Normans on us. He'd just as soon take us now, but if we did *that*—" He shook his head. "They'd never stop looking. Why make it harder?"

Adam Bell nodded. "We've learned not to press our lord high sheriff . . . he can't stop all thievery, but if he took it into his head to concentrate on us, he'd catch us for sure. No—we'll let him be. Sometimes the largest fish can pull in the unwary fisherman. And I'm not a man who can swim."

Alan's expression was serious. "He's not a man who tolerates slights and insults. Bell's right—we'd do best to let him go."

Scarlet laughed harshly. "Speaks a man born to the life!"

"Were you?" Alan countered. "They're hanging you for murder, not banditry."

"Enough," Bell said. "It's decided, then: we let the man ride on."

"I'd do it," Scarlet muttered.

Clym set the end of his bow against Scarlet's shoulder. "We might just as well kill you."

Bell stood up and gestured for Cloudisley to gather the waterskins. "We go on. There will be others to rob."

Much jumped up and melted into the trees before anyone could speak. Bell stared after him.

Little John, rising, nodded at the man. "You'll not tell the boy what to do. He's wiser than the rest of us—he comes and goes with no one knowing."

"*He* could kill the sheriff," Scarlet muttered.

"But he won't," Little John said.

"Off with you," Bell suggested. "We've other fish to catch."

Robin sat against the post as Marian left the hall. He felt no inclination to rise and follow her, or to rise and go out of the door, or to do anything save sit there while he battled the demon again. It reared up before him, then struck low and hard into his loins, as if to castrate him.

They had done that to him already.

He drew his legs in tightly, warding loins and belly, then locked his arms around knees and pressed his brow very hard into the weave of the hosen.

He was whole in body. No knife had been used on him because the threat had been enough: how would Malik Ric like to receive as a gift the manhood parts of his most beloved companion? And so he had shut off everything, building walls and masks and facades, castrating himself in his mind until he was dead and empty and neuter, unable to look at a woman, unable to think of a woman, unable to *see* a woman when she stood directly before him.

For nearly two years he had not lain with a woman. He had not even dreamed of it.

Until the night in Sherwood Forest he had not believed it

possible he could ever respond again. He had done his work too well.

He lifted his head, sweating. The pain was exquisite. Harshly, he repeated, "I am not any man."

Forty-Five

Tuck knelt before the altar in Nottingham Castle's damp chapel, trying to muster the courage to face the sheriff and tell him what he felt. He was not a priest and could hardly consider himself anyone's conscience; nevertheless he was quite convinced that William deLacey had seriously miscarried his duties in the hanging of a man who wasn't Will Scarlet.

That his own execution order had been the instrument by which the deed was done troubled Tuck deeply, but that sin was for him to confess before God and a real priest. Right now he wanted to stand before deLacey and find out precisely what had occurred, but that took courage, and Tuck knew he lacked the kind of confidence required to brace a man as strong-willed and authoritarian as the sheriff.

Behind him, the narrow wooden door scraped open. A shaft of corridor torchlight crept into the chapel. "He's back," Walter said, "and he's asking for you."

Tuck's belly clenched. He heaved himself up from his knees and turned to face Walter. "Where am I to go?"

"His solar," Walter told him. "He wants this kept private, which means you might need to spend even more time on your knees. He doesn't do things in private unless the servants aren't to know about them, and *that* means—"

"I know," Tuck said hollowly. "Like letting the wrong man hang."

Walter sighed. "You'll have to decide how important this is to your future, Brother Tuck. There is no man in the sheriff's service who hasn't had to examine his conscience more than once—unless it's Sir Guy, and *he* has no imagination at all. He just carries out his duties and thinks only of saving coin." Walter stepped aside and held the door open wider. "Come, Brother Tuck—you'll know what you must do when he tells you what he wants. You'll do it, or you won't—and that's between you and your God."

"And Abbot Martin," Tuck murmured glumly.

Walter smiled a little. "Church politics, I've heard, are far worse than administrative ones."

"I ignored them." Tuck squeezed between Walter and the doorjamb. "But I can't ignore this."

Briefly Walter touched his shoulder. "You're a good man, Brother. You'll do what's right."

Will I? Tuck wondered. *Or don't I just do what everyone else tells me to do, because it's easier?*

Ravenskeep was a plain manor house, not a castle. Its second storey was little more than a shell: timber framing mixed with plaster and some brickwork, providing walls considerably less permanent than the thick masonry in castles such as Nottingham and Huntington. But it did allow the members of the FitzWalter household a measure of privacy, for instead of relying on thin screen partitions to delineate specific areas such as one end of the hall for Sir Hugh's family and the other end for the servants with little more than habit dividing the two areas, as was the case in other households, the upper storey provided proper rooms.

Marian retreated to her own room as she fled the brutal intensity in Robin's eyes, and stayed there for some while trying to sort out her thoughts. There was a myriad of emotions to deal with, each deserving of its own time: grief over Matilda's death; the anger and trepidation caused by William deLacey; the residue of Scarlet's actions, which she time and again pushed to the back of her mind because her vulnerability frightened her; and lastly Robin himself, who had managed without apparent intention to plunge her into a vast, abiding confusion.

The king's continuing absence placed her in a precarious position, because it would be simple enough for a man of deLacey's authority and willingness to circumvent the constraints of her wardship. With her reputation in shreds, regardless of the truth, society would demand she do something to repair it. Two possibilities therefore presented themselves: she could marry a man willing to claim the bastard she knew could not exist, or she could give up her worldly holdings and retreat to a nunnery.

Neither alternative appealed to Marian, who sat upon her bed with her spine against the wall and hugged her knees. "There is a *third*," she muttered. "I wait for the king to be released, and plead my case to him."

But she placed little hope in that. She sincerely doubted that Richard, upon his return to England after a year of imprisonment and a year on Crusade, would be much interested in the plight of a simple knight's daughter.

It is unfortunate I am not wealthy, she thought. *The king sold off enough titles and knighthoods to pay for his Crusade, so I doubt he would cavil at money offered to buy a woman's freedom.*

Once, she *had* been wealthy, at least her family had; but on the heels of Richard's coronation in 1189, the new king had declared himself eager to recapture Jerusalem from the hands of the Infidel Turks, and had called for donations—as well as instituting new taxation policies and the sale of titles and knighthoods—to support the Third Crusade. Sir Hugh FitzWalter had sworn on the deaths of his wife and only son to go on Crusade if one was ever undertaken, and he had robbed his own coffers to provide his new king with the wherewithal to go.

His generosity had subsequently robbed his only remaining child of father *and* coin; save for the Ravenskeep lands and rents, Marian had little of the former FitzWalter wealth. With the king out of the country and Prince John instituting his own taxation policies, coupled with ransom demands, England herself was not much better off. Marian could see no advantage to bleeding her villeins and freeholders dry, so she had curtailed demands for regular rents. It reduced her circumstances, but she was willing to live under strict economies. It meant little to her that the main gate sagged, or the cobbles were coming up. Things would improve when England's king returned.

"*If,*" she murmured.

Meanwhile, there was Robin.

"Oh God . . ." Marian shut her eyes tightly. Helen of Troy, was she? With William deLacey desiring to act the part of Helen's husband, Menelaus of Sparta. Who then was Paris, the Trojan hero who seduced Helen away to the fabled city that later fell?

The answer seemed implicit. Marian tried to banish the vision, but the only prospect she saw had a fall of sun-whitened hair and wore the face of Robert of Locksley.

Her smile was bitter. "He would *laugh,*" she declared.

William deLacey received Brother Tuck in his private solar, a small second-storey chamber on the west side of Nottingham Castle. It boasted two splayed windows cut deeply into the walls so that the room was illuminated much of the time by natural sunlight; just now, with the storm coming on, the light was a sickly gray that appeared to match the monk's mood.

The sheriff himself admitted Tuck, personally offered to pour him wine, which was politely declined, and gestured for Tuck to seat himself upon a padded bench.

As he pulled out his own chair, the sheriff assessed Tuck's demeanor. It was obvious to deLacey the fat young man was exceedingly nervous, and he believed it had to do with something more than being invited to the lord high sheriff of Nottingham's solar.

He sat down, distributing his weight so as to appear relaxed and unthreatening. There was no need to put Tuck on guard before it was necessary. It might not be required at all. Tuck was a timid man.

DeLacey smiled warmly. "It gives me the greatest of pleasures to share some good news with you, Brother Tuck. Do you know of the Lady Marian FitzWalter, Sir Hugh FitzWalter's daughter?"

Tuck's cowlike eyes expressed puzzlement. "My lord—I am not of Nottingham. My village is in the south of England."

DeLacey nodded. "Permit me, then, to describe her to you as a pious, lovely lady, as kind of heart and sweet of temperament as a young woman could be."

Tuck nodded baffled approval.

DeLacey smiled widely, exuding appropriate pride and pleasure. "She has consented to become my wife."

The monk's thick brown eyebrows shot up. "My lord—my congratulations. If she is as you say, surely you are a fortunate man."

"Most fortunate," deLacey agreed. "I was good friends with her father, Sir Hugh, and have watched the little girl become a woman. It pleases me a great deal to know I shall be the one to care for her well-being."

"Indeed, my lord."

DeLacey was pleased. Things proceeded as planned. "Particularly in view of the circumstances."

"My—lord?"

The sheriff allowed an expression of sorrow tempered with anger to touch his features. "The Lady Marian was the victim of unfortunate circumstances, Brother Tuck—it was she whom the murderer, Will Scarlet, abducted. He took her to Sherwood Forest and kept her there overnight. She is now safely back at her home—I have just come from there—but is of course understandably upset by what has happened. She is quite concerned with what people will say—people gossip so much, you know—and so it was decided she might best be served if she married me sooner than anticipated."

Tuck was, if possible, looking more confused than ever. "Of course, my lord. It must have been a terrible thing." He paled a little and took a deep breath. "About this Will Scarlet—"

The sheriff cut him off smoothly. "Naturally, it is my desire to put the lady's mind at ease, and to silence those overbusy tongues. Therefore I have offered to wed the lady immediately." DeLacey leaned forward before Tuck could begin again. "This is why I require your service, Brother Tuck. We have a delicate situation made worse by an unforeseen absence, and an illness."

"My lord?"

"You see, Nottingham has two priests . . . but one is on pilgrimage, and the other is quite ill. In fact, he might die." The sheriff shook his head. "Pray God he recovers."

Tuck crossed himself.

DeLacey sat back. "You see the difficulty, do you not? Here is a lady whose honor has been besmirched and can only be regained through honest, if hasty, marriage . . . you understand, of course, there might be—*issue*—from this unfortunate misadventure." He sighed deeply and shook his head. "The poor lady . . . she is understandably distressed, of course—can you blame her for desiring to put to rights whatever she can?"

"N-no. My lord. But—"

"Therefore it falls to you." He leaned forward again, clasping his hands between his knees. "Of course you must understand, Brother Tuck . . . this would not be a real marriage, but simply a proxy ceremony. Naturally there would be no consummation, for neither of us wishes to commit adultery." Consternation crossed his face. "I'm sorry, Brother—I know this must be distressing for you—but think how the lady feels. All she desires right now is to marry at once. Since that cannot be done, I offer a temporary solution: let her *believe* herself married—and everyone else believe it as well—so that her mind will be at rest. Then once the furor has died down and she feels more comfortable, a proper wedding presided over by a true priest will bind us in the sight of God."

Tuck wrung his hands. Dampness sheened his fleshy face. "But—my lord . . . will she not question my presence?"

DeLacey smiled faintly. "Not if we tell her you are a priest."

"That would be a *lie.*"

The sheriff nodded regretfully. "I realize how distasteful that would be to you, Brother—you are a devout and good-hearted man—but what of the lady? She is in an agony of faith, Brother, believing herself defiled. I would save her that distress."

Tuck nodded absently. "But—if you didn't . . . if there were no . . ." He reddened. "My lord Sheriff—"

DeLacey rescued him. "Many a bridegroom has drunk too much at his wedding feast. Either that—or I will fall conveniently ill. I have no wish to compromise the lady, Brother

465

Tuck—although that has already been done, of course. I want only to relieve her of her great distress. I believed this might be the most painless way, but if you feel it is asking too much of you—"

"My lord—"

"—or perhaps of *God* . . ." DeLacey sighed heavily and shook his head. "Surely God would not blame us for a small lie, provided nothing more was done." He appealed to Tuck. "Do you think?"

Tuck was trembling. "My lord—already I have lied before God by allowing that poor old woman to believe I was a priest—"

"Precisely," deLacey agreed. "What more harm in this?"

"My *lord*—"

"The old woman is dead and beyond harm—this poor lady is very young with many years before her in which to castigate herself for being so defiled . . . would you have her suffer so long for that?"

Tuck was breathing hard. "But she wouldn't really be *married*—"

"Of course not." DeLacey paused. "But if she believed it, and she proved to be with child, would it not mitigate the sin of bearing a bastard child?"

"But it *would* be a bastard!"

"Only until a real priest could perform the ceremony. And I assure you, that shall be done in time."

Tuck wiped at his sweating face, shutting his eyes tightly. Beneath his breath he murmured a prayer.

DeLacey waited. He knew better than to press too hard for an answer; the fat monk was the sort of naive innocent who would need to be made to believe the decision was his own.

"My lord . . ." Tuck sighed, his massive shoulders drooping. "My lord, this is wrong—"

"I would not ask such a thing for myself," deLacey said softly. "This is for the lady, a true and gentle soul who deserves far better than what she has received."

Tuck seemed almost to shrink. "Very well," he whispered. "But I pray you find a priest before the week is out."

"I do assure you, Brother, I will write at once to Abbot

Martin." He rose, extending his arm toward the door. "I know you will wish to go to your devotions. Please pray for the lady, Brother Tuck. I know this sits ill with you, but when you ask God for forgiveness mention the lady's name. I'm sure he will understand."

Tuck rose as deLacey opened the door. Much diminished in spirit and posture, he made his way to the door and into the corridor.

DeLacey dropped a comforting hand on his shoulder. "Light a candle for me." He watched the monk depart, then shut the door decisively and crossed back to his wine. He drank the cup dry, then contemplated the wan daylight outside the solar. Absently he said, "Easier than I thought. Praise God for fools such as he." And sketched a cross in the air.

Robin toiled his way back up the stairs to the upper floor, lingered irresolutely at the open door leading into his borrowed room, then went in search of Marian. He meant to take his leave, though he felt little like it because of the aftereffects of the fever, but he saw no sense in staying on. It was difficult for both of them now, because he had made it that way with his candor.

He had not intended to be so frank, to tell her, even obliquely, what she could do to a man. But it was the simple truth: she was a Celtic Helen with every bit of the beauty and power the tales ascribed to the Queen of Sparta. That she was unaware of her effect merely made it more compelling. He did not know how he could have ignored it on the dais at Huntington Castle, so attuned to her was he now, except to acknowledge two things: then, he had been a willing victim of his own defiance of nature, his personal rejection of desire in mind and body; now, he was most assuredly an unwilling victim of his longing to be free of that same rejection, to express both physically and emotionally his need of a woman.

Richard would laugh. Richard would offer—himself. Deep in Robin's belly self-contempt writhed.

He found Marian in a small chamber not far from his own, digging through a chest. The door was ajar; he stood in the opening and watched as she dragged clothing forth. A tunic and hosen, dull and faded with time. She held up the tunic, shook it free of dust, then sat back onto her heels and crumpled it in her lap.

"No," she said softly. "Hugh was younger, and smaller."

He knew then what she did. "There is no need," he told her. "What I am wearing will do."

Startled, she twitched, then stared at him wide-eyed. Lost in the past, he saw; was he so like her dead brother?

Marian smiled faintly and shook her head. "I thought nothing of it, until only moments ago. But I know how I felt when I was free of the dirt and mud . . . I thought perhaps you might like to bathe, and put on fresh clothing." She held up the faded tunic. "You are taller than Hugh. Unless—" Her face brightened. "Yes! There are my father's things . . ." She bundled the tunic and hosen back into the trunk, then rose and shook out her skirts. "He was taller and broader, but better too large than too small. Here—come this way."

"Marian—" But she was by him, closer than she had ever been, if only briefly. "Marian—" He turned and followed, meaning merely to say her nay, then ask for a horse instead. But she was ahead of him already and opening a door that screeched on rusted hinges. Marian went in and left him in the corridor.

He followed. The chamber was larger than his own, taking up a corner of the hall. The bed was enormous, curtained by blue-dyed fabric; three chests sat against walls. "Here," she said. "He would never begrudge you this."

He stopped just inside. "What of you? If these are all you have of him—"

"I have memories," she said firmly. "Those you cannot take—but clothing does not do well when packed away in the dark." She knelt, undid the hasp, pushed open the lid. "Finest chainsil," she said, pulling forth the creamy linen sherte, "and tunic, and hosen. You have boots and wrappings."

"Yes," he answered gravely. "Marian—I only want a horse."

It was blunter than he intended. She gripped the edge of the trunk, a pile of cloth in her lap, and stared at him fiercely. Her expression he found infinitely appealing: desperately proud, with an underlying hint of exasperation. "If you please, I have been chatelaine of Ravenskeep since my mother died. My brother and father are dead—will you at least allow me to carry out the duties of a host as they are meant to be?"

Robin sighed. "I only meant—"

"I know." She nodded. "I know."

She did not, he knew. She couldn't.

She rose, shutting the trunk lid. In her hands were sherte, tunic, and hosen. "This is not Huntington Castle."

It nearly struck him dumb. "By God, Marian—I was a prisoner of the Turks!" For him, it was enough; he hoped it was for her. He had not meant to show so much of himself.

Color ebbed in her face. "I'm sorry."

"*I* am." He took the things from her hands. "Have the bath drawn, then," he told her, "but no servant to wash my back. I'll do it myself."

Mutely she nodded and went by him into the corridor, calling quietly for Joan.

Robin stood there wondering how he could find the words to say a proper farewell. He had no gift with soft language, for he spoke too little; most of the women he had known hadn't wanted him to speak at all save with his body, which had done its duty by them with eloquence enough. The ladies of his rank he had addressed sparingly, preferring his own company to the exuberance of feasts and celebratory dances, knowing what they portended for an unwed man of his station. He had never been a lecher or a man for dallying; what little charm he might once have possessed was burned out in the Holy Land, and its cinder drowned in blood.

The day was dying, muted by the wind. "*Insh'Allah,*" he murmured, thinking it nearly time for the muezzin to call evening prayer.

Then, "No—this is *England*—" and realized with a start he was still a prisoner; that Richard's ransoming of him may have bought his body free, but only part of his mind.

Trembling, he gripped the clothing tightly, wanting to rend it to shreds. "Let me be free of it—let me be *free* of it!" And in English, very plainly, "There is no God but God—"

469

Forty-Six

Wind was a wolf in Ravenskeep, howling across the hills with a shrill, keening fury. Sim and Hal came into the hall littered with straw and leaves, eyes teary from gritty dust, and told Marian they had seen to securing the horses and the stable buildings, the chicken house, and the rest of the livestock, though the sheep were out on the meadow: Tam and Stephen, they said, were seeing to the sheep. It was a bad storm coming; couldn't she hear its noise?

Indeed she could. It whined about the timber roof and lunged through open shutters to flour the hall with rush motes and pungent dust. Marian sighed and nodded, then gathered up the household servants and set them to closing and latching the shutters. Even shut up, the hall was hardly wind-tight, but there were things they could do to prevent accidents and damage. She doled out extra candles to ward off the early, unnatural dark, and cautioned the servants against leaving them lighted in places the wind might reach. With a timber and plaster upper storey, they dared not risk fire.

"Lady Marian?" It was Joan, come to speak of their guest. "He's asleep after his bath—all wrung out from the fever—but his shutter's undone. Even if he sleeps through the storm, he'll have half of Nottinghamshire in his room before dawn. Shall I go in and close it?"

"No." Marian cast a glance around the hall to see that all was in order. "No—I'll go. See to the kitchen, Joan." She gathered up her skirts and climbed the stairs to the second storey, fighting down once again the familiar nervousness when she thought of

470

facing Robin. *This must stop,* she told herself. *You are behaving as a lackwit.*

And it had gotten worse, not better, since he had confused her with his candor, making her think of things she had never thought of at all, save when a drunken, vulgar Prince John had made lewd comments at Huntington. Initially she had been hesitant merely because of Robin's rank: In Sherwood things had been much different, allowing her to see him in a new light, until he had alarmed her with his unexpected frankness.

Marian paused outside his door, listened for sound that would mark him awake, then slowly and quietly opened it. She found him as Joan had said: sleeping very soundly, with the wind blowing into the room. It snagged and threw off the coverlet tossed across his legs and stripped the hair from his face.

She crossed the chamber at once, peeled the shutters off the wall, and set the bar into place. The wind rattled it stubbornly, trying to break the seal.

Marian meant to leave . . . but she stopped to look at him, to mark the slackness of his face that but an hour or so before had been tight and pale and old, far older than his years.

Any man, he had said, would want her in his bed. But he was not any man.

Humiliation stung her; not that he wouldn't want her, but that she could think of it. Quickly Marian left the room, shut the door behind her, and went down the stairs to the hall with a word to Joan that she desired privacy; she would go to the oratory to spend time alone with her prayers.

"In this storm?" Joan asked, amazed.

Marian smiled a little. "You know I've always liked storms."

He winced as the hurled stone slammed into Acre's walls, smashing creamy brickwork. The sappers had tunneled carefully to undermine the walls, so that as the trebuchet hurled stones the foundation fell out from beneath. Christians now charged the weakened portions, climbing over fallen stones and smashed bodies in their quest to enter the city.

And then Robin was charging as well, crying out for God, Richard, and England, spurring his mount forward to leap the rubble and dust. His sword was unsheathed, raised high into the air as the Christian horns sounded. Joshua at Jericho, blowing down the walls.

He was over a pile of brick and rubble, then through, his horse floundering for footing amidst the fallen bodies. Already Christians engaged Saracens, shouting of God or Allah, hacking through flesh and bone while all around them men died.

Caught up in the knowledge of the warrior-king he served and the glory they did God, Robert of Locksley felt the rush of pride and desire that filled him near to bursting. He hardly noticed that his horse crushed living bodies beneath shod hooves, or that women ran screaming through streets. He rode on, thinking of his vow to help free Jerusalem; to see the Holy Sepulchre.

Warm sticky blood sprayed across Robin's face. He felt a tug at his boot, a grasp at cross-gartered leg; he brought down his blade and felt it bite into an arm. All around him men shouted and screamed.

Acre's walls continued to fall, pounded to bits by hurled stones. He could hear the sound of it: stone after stone after stone smashing into the weakened wall, filling his head with noise—

—and he was up, scrambling from bed, reaching for the sword that was no longer at his side, as stone after stone slammed into the wall. *"Insh'Allah,"* he blurted, then heard his breathing halt.

He stood in a gloomy chamber with the wind blowing in his face, and the crack of an unlatched shutter banging repeatedly against the wall.

Ravenskeep.

Relief dispersed his strength. Shaking, he collapsed onto the edge of the bed and sat there slumped and wracked, wiping the sweat from his face as his heart regained its rhythm. The shutter banged and banged, but he let it make its noise even as dust and debris blew into his chamber.

No blood on his hands—no severed limbs at his feet. Robin sighed heavily and scrubbed his face with both hands, trying to vanquish the sluggish aftereffects of a too-vivid dream. Slowly he got up and took the two paces that put him at the window; as the wind beat against his face, he stared out into the storm, tasting the metallic tang of lightning, the turgid dampness in the air.

"England," he muttered, nodding, then closed and latched the shutters. He lurched back to the bed and collapsed across it again, knowing the bath had banished much of his soreness but as much of his strength.

He rolled over onto his back, staring fixedly at the roof. He meant to get up, to go out and down the stairs, to take his leave of the woman who so unsettled his soul. She would protest, of course, because of the storm, but it reflected his turmoil more eloquently than any words could do, and he saw no reason for wind to hinder his flight.

He shut his eyes. *I need to go*—But sleep had no more mercy than the Saracens did.

The hall at Ravenskeep had not originally contained the oratory, for it was older than Marian's parents and had housed generations of FitzWalters, not all of them particularly desirous of a personal relationship with God. But Sir Hugh's pious wife *was* desirous of such, and had asked for a private room to which she might retire for prayer and contemplation. Her husband had caused one to be built, placing it off the side of the hall nearest a small walled garden. It wasn't a proper chapel, for it lacked an altar and a piscina for rinsing the chalice after Mass, but it was quiet and out of the way, offering peace to the individual who sought communion with God—or even with herself.

Sir Hugh had, for reasons of economy and haste, built the oratory adjoining the hall, but had not had a door put through. Therefore the only entrance to the oratory was the low wooden door from the walled garden, much like a postern gate; anyone desiring to use the chamber was required to go out of doors, into the garden, then into the oratory. In winter it had proved most inconvenient; Sir Hugh had promised to have a door knocked through to the hall, but his lady had died before it was accomplished and he had never been near the oratory again.

Marian had always liked the oratory. The small cozy nook of a chamber appealed to her desire for a place of her own. As a child she had imagined it a miniature hall where she presided as chatelaine. As she grew older she played less and less in the oratory, but occasionally found it a peaceful retreat, much as her mother did. When Lady Margaret died, followed closely by her son, Marian used the oratory for its intended purpose: a private place to pray. In the weeks immediately after their deaths, she had gone there many times to vent her grief and rage where only God could hear.

She left Joan, gathered cloak and shuttered lamp and went out into the storm, defying the insolent wind. Storms had never frightened her. Carefully she made her way around the corner of the hall, opened the gate to the walled garden, then unlatched and opened the low door into the chamber itself. The hinges were shrill in protest; like the main gate, they needed oiling.

Wind whipped down through the budded trees into the garden, stripping flowers of petals and leaves. Damp air issued forth from the oratory, snatched away by its angrier brother. Marian thrust the lamp inside, then ducked down into the room.

Lamplight whitened pale fieldstone, illuminating the dimness. Marian stripped off the cloak and draped it over a bench, then carried the lamp to the candle stubs set in chiseled hollows in the walls. Deftly she lighted each candle, then set the lamp on the floor near the wall separating the hall from the oratory. She breathed in rain-weighted air. There were no windows, splayed or otherwise; crude notches knocked into the rough fieldstone walls admitted air into the room. The stone was damp and cool, colored gray and cream and chalk.

Two benches for the knights, a woven mat for the Round Table, the throne a rickety chair tied with rope to keep it together. Here she had been queen in the days of her childhood: Guinevere, Arthur's lady, or Eleanor of Aquitaine, whom her father had met; later a proper chatelaine, much as her mother was, wed to the most chivalrous and handsome lord in all of England.

Marian smiled sadly. "So many lies," she said. "Is that what childhood is?"

What then was adulthood but the perpetuation of a life built on bitter reality: childhood dreams were unreachable things that wasted a woman's time.

She walked through the tiny chamber, trailing fingers along the rough stone. The last time she had come had been but a handful of days after receiving word her father was dead. She had been grief-stricken, enraged, bereft, trying to conjure the man in the place her mother believed was best for talking to God. Marian had cried and screamed and pleaded that the message be a lie, a mistake, that her father yet lived. But not long after that the sword of Sir Hugh FitzWalter—and a casket containing the dried remains of his heart—had been brought to Ravenskeep. Her dreams were abruptly ended.

She stopped walking. She sat down in the chair, holding her breath as old rope protested. But it held, and she sat very still while the creaking subsided. The keening of the windstorm was mournful as the *bean sidhe* which according to Irish folklore presages a death.

Marian drew up a knee and hooked her heel into the chair seat, hugging her leg. She pressed her chin upon her knee and stared into the wan candlelight.

She remembered very clearly when they had brought her brother home. They had tried to keep her apart from him, to make sure she saw nothing, but she *had* seen, all of it: the blanket-wrapped form that still dripped water, the pallid, dead flesh, the livid bruises on his face. From rocks, someone said; from the millwheel, said another. Sir Hugh FitzWalter's son had drowned in the millpond, not found for three full days.

It was Much who had discovered him, the miller's halfwit son who spoke but infrequently and with little sense to his words. No one questioned him. No one said anything. They just put Hugh into the mausoleum with his three weeks' dead mother—and all the other deceased FitzWalters—and Marian never saw her brother again.

Outside there came a banging followed by a clatter. Marian, roused, left the rickety chair and went to the nearest notch that looked out into the courtyard. All she saw was premature night: an ash-gray, indigo darkness.

More clattering yet: shod hooves ringing on cobbles.

Loose horse? "—*no*—" she blurted sharply, turning toward the door, "—not in this—" She went out into the wailing, fighting imperious wind as it snatched the oratory door and slammed it against the wall. Marian struggled to shut it, but the pressure was too strong. She left it then, and shoved open the garden gate.

The storm was full upon her, buffeting her senses as she tried to remain upright. Hair whipped free of her hands, blotting out her view; she caught it again, twirled it deftly into a rope, then stuffed it down the back of her kirtle.

Debris rolled through the courtyard. She saw leaves, branches, a tree limb; a stool left out from milking; a starling caught in the pressure and slammed against the wall. Feathers shredded at once, spun away into the maelstrom.

Marian shielded her eyes with both hands. She was a fool to be outside, but she was sure she'd heard a horse. Sim had said they'd secured the stables, but if the storm had broken the gate there would be more than one mount loose.

There—it loomed ahead: the bay gelding loaned to Robin . . . with Robin in the saddle. Pale hair whipped in the wind: a beacon in the darkness.

He woke up with a cry, dripping sweat. All around him the bodies cavorted, grinning maniacally. At the forefront was Hugh FitzWalter's, keening its wild grief over Robin's failure to keep him alive; his failure to carry the message to Marian.

"But I did!" he shouted. "I *did*—"

The bodies fell together in an obscene intercourse, Saracen and Christian, man and woman, Richard and Blondel, who was Richard and himself—

"No," Robin whispered.

The *bean sidhe's* howling filled up the entire room, rattling the shutter latch. More bodies yet were fighting to enter the room, to join in the morris dance, the macabre dance of death.

FitzWalter fell to pieces. His head flew across the room and landed in Robin's lap, spraying blood in a tumbling arc.

"God—" he choked, and snatched at boots and cloak, then unlatched and yanked open the door. The *bean sidhe* followed, hooking nails into his shoulder and tearing the tunic away, the linen sherte beneath, the flesh beneath that. Blood ran from his back. Behind him, FitzWalter howled.

He tugged on boots and fled, sweeping the cloak around his

shoulders. Faces swam before him as he made his way through the hall, as he clawed for the latch, as he tugged open the door; and then he was in the storm where the bodies screamed and cavorted, and he knew his only escape lay in leaving Ravenskeep.

He fought the wind across the courtyard, tripping over loose cobbles, and at last found the stable block. It was securely latched, but he undid everything and let the wind throw open the door. Deftly he caught up bridle, pad, saddle; quickly he caught the bay; in taut silence he readied the horse, then swung up into the saddle and rode him out of the stable into the howling wind.

Eyes teared from grit: he was on the road to Arsuf, spitting and swearing and fighting to keep his seat on the horse. Debris rolled by: a tree limb torn off from its trunk like a man's arm from his shoulder, a shutter from the hall, a mass of russet feathers still attached to a one-legged chicken.

"Robin!" Marian shouted.

The bay danced across the cobbles, shedding sparks from iron-shod hooves.

"Robin—" she cried.

He glanced back as she ran toward him, buffeted by the wind. He saw the shroud of hair wrapped around her and the pallor of her face: a skull like Hugh FitzWalter's grinning into the storm. From the blackness of her mouth the *bean sidhe* shrieked his name.

"No—" he mouthed. Then, in desperate fury: *"There is no God but God—"*

Marian couldn't see his face, just the pallor of hair and hands. He wore her father's clothing. The dark cloak snapped in the wind, winding around his body.

*Like Hugh's and Mother's shroud—*And then the pain was renewed. *Not another death—*

She saw his expression as she reached the horse. He was white-faced, white-lipped, with eyes gone wide and black. If he saw her at all he did not appear to know her, for he reined the horse toward the gate. *"There is no God but God—"* And then something more, more raggedly, in a language she didn't know.

"Wait!" she said. "Robin—*wait*—" She reached for and caught rein, dragging the horse around. "—not in this storm—"

The main gate's bar gave way with a muted crack. Wood crashed open. Rusted hinges broke, freeing the gate completely.

The boom of wood striking cobbles frightened the horse into a frenzy. He reared, striking out, as Robin fought to control him. Marian, blinded by her hair, put out a warding hand. She fell back a single step, caught her heel on a cobble, then blurted an outcry as the hoof slashed by her head and snagged a tangle of whipping hair.

It jerked her to the ground. Marian sprawled there, gasping, as the horse reared again. She thrust up a rigid hand. "Robin—*NO*—"

The horse fell out of the sky.

Forty-Seven

Robin fought the horse as the bay rose up and up beneath him, flailing iron-shod forehooves like a war-trained destrier. He saw Marian fall, saw the white flash of her hand, heard her garbled outcry snatched away by wind. *Acre all over again—another woman crushed—*

With effort he battled the horse as it slung its head from side to side, mouth gaping open. He dared not let him down in the same position . . . he hauled on rein, digging in with his left heel once, twice, thrice, banging boot into flesh, fighting to move the bay a step, or two, or three . . . cursing wind and screech and equine strength. In midair he jerked the horse offstride, abusing the gaping mouth, kicked free of stirrups and jumped, sliding down across saddle and rump as first the cloak snagged, then tore free as he bent over FitzWalter's daughter.

His hands closed on her slender wrists, clamping flesh to flesh as cloak billowed and black hair whipped, obscuring her face. Robin jerked her from the ground, stood her there, peeled back her hair even as she staggered, stripping hair away from her face, expecting to see blood and a matted, splintered hole like the ones he had seen before, in Acre and here, in his room.

"No—" she said, "I tripped—"

No blood at all, only hair, and a pale face gleaming like a peeled skull, like the faces in the room, grinning with clattering jaws.

He recoiled. *"No—"*

"Robin—*Robin* . . ." She clutched at him. "I promise—I tripped over a cobble—"

He clung to her shoulders as black hair was flung at his face to mingle with his own. "No more—" he gasped. "I can't—"

"Robin—" She shook back hair, but the wind caught it again. He could see nothing of her face but white rents between whipping strands, and the flash of a Celt-blue eye. "Come in out of the storm."

"I can't—" he said again, "can't *stay* here—"

She pulled hair from her mouth. "You won't get ten paces in the wind . . . here, this way—" She slipped from his hands and caught a wrist, tugging adamantly.

The nightmare would not diminish. "Richard—" he said. Then, in anguish, *"La ilaha—la ilaha il' Mohammed—"*

She pulled him to a walled garden, through its gate, then into a tiny chamber full of lamplight and pallid stone, a milky luminescence in the darkness of the storm. "Here," she said breathlessly, and yanked shut the flimsy door that rattled in its place as the wind clutched at it again.

He breathed noisily. *"Bean sidhe,"* he murmured.

Marian smiled. "That's what *I* thought, too—" But then she lost her smile. "Robin—?"

One step and he caught her, clasping her arms, hanging on to his only salvation: the price of his survival on the bloodied plains of Arsuf, because he knew he had to tell her; he had been *charged* to tell her. But it wasn't enough, not now; there was too much in his soul. It swelled like a putrid canker, then burst through inflamed flesh to release the pressure at last.

"Why can't he understand? Why can't he let it be? I told you what he wanted—I carried the message to you . . ." His face was stark, sharp bone beneath taut flesh. His mouth felt rigid and warped. "I did what he asked me to—I did what *Richard* asked me to, save the one thing . . . I couldn't—I *couldn't* . . . and all those people dead—all those people butchered . . . Saracen women and children, the girls raped to death, the mothers spitted on swords—breasts hacked off . . . stripped naked to die in the streets . . ." He shuddered from head to toe. "Acre was *heinous*—it wasn't a victory, it was a massacre—a disgrace . . . he ordered all of them killed, all of them beheaded—more than twenty-six hundred Turks . . . because Saladin broke his word—" He gritted his teeth. "An excuse, nothing more—he'd have done it anyway . . . he could be hard and cruel and brutal, dangerous to anger—" He had to make her see, and he was doing it all wrong; Richard wasn't a monster, he was a *man*. "And yet he was never cruel to me . . . even when I said no, that I couldn't—that I was not a man for that—not for bedding men, nor kings, nor even *Richard*—" He bared his teeth. "I failed my liege in that—all I could do for him was butcher Saracen souls, not ease the needs of his body—" He broke it off then, gazing blindly into her face. "The needs of his body—*Ya Allah!*—the needs of my *own*—" Breath hissed through his teeth. "And I can't—I *can't* . . ." He laughed, then chopped it off. "What would Richard say? What would a woman say?" Fingers found her hair, threaded their way through, touched the curve of her cheek. "What would *Helen* say, to a Paris who cannot love her?"

Tears stood in her eyes, bright in candlelight, then one broke over a bottom lid and spilled down a bruised cheek to dampen his fingertip.

"Marian—" he rasped. "Oh God—*Marian*—"

"I am not—" She swallowed heavily. "I am not who I need to be, for you . . . I am not what *you* need—"

It hurt his throat. "No one is. No one can be . . . not even—Richard—" Robin shut his eyes.

"I would—like to be—" she said jerkily. "But—I don't know how."

One of the candles died, its wick spent at last. His soul felt as barren, as wasted. He was ashamed of what he had done, of what he had said, because no one not a soldier could begin to understand, and even then he might ridicule him for thinking so much about it, for permitting it to rule him; for allowing dreams to shape his life when there was duty to do it for him. *Just as my father said before he ordered me beaten.*

Robin gazed down into Marian's face, recalling where he was; better yet, where he *wasn't:* not in Acre, Arsuf, or Jaffa, nor in Huntington Hall. With effort, he took his hands from her. "You'd better go."

"Robin—"

He moved aside because he had to. He turned his back on her. "This is a chapel?—no." He answered his own question as he glanced around. "An oratory . . . good. I am in need of prayer . . . and more than that, I think . . ." He turned to her after all, risking it, risking himself, watching the play of light on her pale bruised flesh. Desperation engulfed him. "Marian— *go.*"

Her chin rose. "Will you? Run away again?"

It hurt more deeply than anticipated. He shook his head. "No."

"Then—I leave you to God." She turned away and unlatched the door. He saw the shine of tears in her eyes, but she was gone before he could speak.

Tuck knelt before the altar in Nottingham Castle's tiny chapel. He was filled with an awful certainty that whatever he did now—confession, penance, prayer—would never be enough.

He sweated in the alcove, clenching trembling hands. He had not been able to eat and his belly protested noisily, but his spirit was hungry for something much more substantial than food. He required understanding. He needed sincere compassion. He desired a measure of acknowledgment from the God who ruled his life.

"In nomine Patris, et Fili, et Spiritus Sancti," he murmured. "In the name of the Father, the Son, and the Holy Spirit—"

But he could not. He was wracked with doubt and guilt. He was not worthy even of prayer, to pay his addresses to God, who knew very well what he'd done.

He rocked there on fleshy knees: a child in need of comfort. A son in need of his Father.

"Forgive me," he murmured wretchedly. Tuck squeezed his eyes shut. "Make me strong," he whispered. "Father—make me *strong.*"

In the bailey outside the keep the wolf-wind howled an answer.

Much hunched in the dark. He was shielded from the worst of the wind by burrowing into a hollow dug by an animal between the exposed roots of a giant oak not far from Ravenskeep's gate.

He had left the other outlaws because he tasted storm. It filled his head with ringing and a vague stuffiness, setting his ears to aching. He knew what it promised, but he saw no sense in telling the others; they were men, all of them, considerably older than he. Surely they knew by the taste and the smell and the sound that the storm would be worse than most.

His world was threatened, and the woman he called his princess.

Much rubbed at his nose. Pressure was in his head, nagging mercilessly; the storm would grow worse before it blew itself out. He recalled it had happened before when he was just a boy: a fierce, angry windstorm had driven ships out of the North Sea into the Wash at Kings Lynn, where later they had sunk. It ravaged villages, blowing down daub-and-wattle; it shattered his father's millwheel; it flattened the stable at Ravenskeep— driving out all the horses—and tore down every shutter. People had died in the storm, crushed by falling trees, or flattened beneath collapsed dwellings.

Much didn't want Ravenskeep to blow down. It was the princess's castle.

He hunkered closer to ground, squinting against flying debris. He would stay the night if he had to, to make sure the princess was safe.

Marian went out into the storm and latched the oratory door behind her with hands that shook very badly. She stared at them fixedly, then shut them into fists and pressed them against her breasts. She was hot and cold at once, all bound up in emotions so raw she ached with it. There was grief and anguish and pain, that Robin could be so tortured; shock and denial and sickness, that war could be so brutal; lastly, an understanding, a harrowing comprehension of what had been done to him, or what he had done to himself, or what Richard had *caused* to be done by the insanity of—desire.

He had said: *"—not ease the needs of his body—"*

Nor even of his own.

Marian shut her eyes. She knew now what it was, the vague disquieting tension; the unacknowledged hunger; the appetite for his touch. She was as much a victim as the king, or Eleanor deLacey, who had told her what it was and that a woman could need it also, promising pleasure of it.

She had lied to him: *"I am not what you need,"* she had said, meaning not good enough, too innocent, not able to ease his needs. But she was wrong. She *was* what he needed; a woman to ease his pain, ease his needs, give him back what he had lost. She knew it instinctively.

A wave of panic swamped her. *I can't*—Will Scarlet's face hung before her, its near-black eyes staring into her own; his mouth telling her ugly truths of what the Normans had done to his wife, and his desire to do it to her.

But it was *Robin* inside. Not Will Scarlet.

Panic surged again. *I can't*—But she was no more immune to the needs of a body than *he* was, or the king.

That is Robin inside, not Will Scarlet . . . and Robin needs me.

Wind twisted the tree limb and bent it nearly in two, scouring Little John's face with damp leaves and prickly twigs. He swore, bent almost double to avoid branches clambering for flesh and clothing. The others fared better because they were not so tall; his face burned with welts and scratches.

Just ahead, Will Scarlet's hunched form was a blob against the greenish darkness. His question was shouted to reach above the wind. "Where?" Scarlet shouted. "Where are we going?"

Little John swore again. *I should be home with my sheep.* But that life seemed banished, now. The sheriff wanted him. He had been seen in the company of outlaws who had killed Norman soldiers.

"Where?" Scarlet shouted again, pitching his voice to carry to the men ahead of him.

One of them swung back. Little John saw Cloudisley's pretty face twisted against the storm. His dark hair ran wet with rain, tangling at his mouth. "A cave!" Cloudisley shouted; Little John mostly read his lips. "Not far—it will provide some cover!"

"Sheep," Little John muttered, "and good fleece for warmth—"

But that was in his past. His present was his future.

Marian swung around and snatched open the oratory door, blowing in on a gust of wind. The other candle blew out. Only the lamp was left, casting eerie illumination into the hardness of Robin's face. He sat there rigidly in the rope-bound, ancient throne: Arthur before his knights as they accused the queen of adultery, all bleak and wasted and angry, afraid to hear the truth because it destroyed the childhood dream.

"Lies," she said roughly, "all the dreams are lies. We *make* whatever we are . . . the magic isn't in dreams, but in what we take for ourselves."

He was used up, bruised and battered. He said only, "Let it be."

"No." Marian closed the door, shutting out wolves and *bean sidhe.*

He knew why she had come and what she meant to do. His eyes were black in the shadows. "I have no chivalry. Let it be the truth, then: what I would do to you should be done to no maid. It has been—too long."

She did not know enough of men to fully understand, but her

experience with Will Scarlet—and snatches of stories she had heard—persuaded her the communion between men and women could be violent. Obviously Robin knew, if he feared to harm her.

But she had gone too far. Fear was secondary. Now she meant to provoke, to lift the pain from him. "Will Scarlet took me."

His face spasmed. "Don't lie."

She could think of nothing but him. "Then let it be *you*. Let it be Robin of Locksley."

His expression was a travesty as he shook his head. "Too much of him is dead. Too much blood was spilled—too much flesh was *stilled*—"

No longer content to soothe, Marian cut him off. "You are alive," she said. *"My father* is the dead man."

He recoiled, as she intended, for she wanted to shatter the wall for good. "Is this my penance?" he cried. "Will you grant me absolution?"

Now she stood before him. She put out a hand and touched him: fingertips that trembled on the rigid line of his mouth. *I am not afraid of him.*

He came up from the chair, leaving Arthur's throne behind. He was Paris to her Helen, stripping away the useless courtesies of gentleness and compassion, cracking the veneers, shattering the facades. He was Acre to her Richard: the mask of his own construction, the wall he had labored to build, was undone by the human trebuchet who hurled the stone at his soul.

He wound his hands in her hair, drawing her hard against his body. "I want—" But he couldn't finish.

"I know," Marian whispered.

Forty-Eight

Marian awoke with a start and realized the wind had died, driving away the wolf and silencing the *bean sidhe*. All was perfectly still, save for the sound of Robin's breathing.

A simple yet complex noise: in- and exhalation, a steady continuation that stirred in her a response of which she had believed herself incapable, not knowing what it was to desire a man, not knowing what it was to give of her deepest self, receiving his in return.

Her own breath ran ragged a moment, then renewed itself. She lay on her side on the woven mat with two cloaks thrown over her, one corner tangled amidst their legs. He lay heavily against her spine, soundly asleep; she had given him that, at least.

The absence of wind was eerie, the air thick and sodden. It was cool in the oratory, hoary with traceries of morning mist that crept through the window notches. The oil lamp burned low, fretting at its shutters; it washed the fieldstone chamber in oyster and ivory and gold.

She was sore, stiff, and weary from a night on the floor. She lay quietly on the mat so as not to disturb Robin, and considered the look of the world that according to the coy rumors she had heard all her life, was supposed to look very different the morning after a night like the one she'd just experienced.

He had said it plainly: *What I would do to you should be done to no maid.* And she supposed it should not be, but it had been; it was finished. Maidenhood was fleeting, surrendered easily in the brief painful instant between virginity and carnal knowledge; she was now a woman, and if he was too rough and overhasty she could blame it, if she chose, on the brutalities of war, on the horrors of captivity, not on the man himself.

She knew him better than that. Marian did choose. And later, a little later, he had shown her a different side; he had shown her a different man, this one able to rouse her as she had roused him, proving haste was not required, nor roughness, nor possession, but the avid tenderness and slow consummation of bodies but newly awakened: hers for the first time, his after nearly two years.

His nearness was comforting. She found it also daunting, fraught with new adversities she had not fully considered in the peril of the storm and the clamor of her body. Reality intruded: she had bedded a man in the oratory and still lay with him there, absent from her chamber where Joan would go to rouse her; too obviously used by the look of hair and kirtle.

He stirred briefly, murmuring into her hair, then fell once again into silence. Emotion overwhelmed her, flushing her with a hunger not at all of belly or spirit. She wanted—*needed*—to turn over, to look into his face, to reach out and touch him so he would awaken and touch her. She wanted badly to linger and dismiss the dawn entirely, and the day to follow; to invite yet again—or initiate herself—the incredibly complex intimacy that made two people one.

But there were chores to be tended, servants to be faced, a front gate to have mended, and God only knew how many animals to be nursed, found, or butchered.

Life doesn't stop, she thought. *Not for pain—or for pleasure.*

The perils of yesterday were as present today: the sheriff of Nottingham had asked her to marry him. No—he had *told* her.

Marian frowned, listening. The cock had not yet crowed, which meant it wasn't quite dawn—or the rooster was dead.

It *felt* like dawn.

Her mother had had a saying: *Linger, and you may lose; hasten, and you may win all.*

It was time to make sure she won.

Marian sat up carefully, edging away from the mat so as not to disturb Robin. She cocooned him in swathing wool, leaving only face and boots uncovered, and a single curled hand.

She hoped the rooster was dead, so Robin could sleep a while.

The pounding on his door awakened William deLacey, with no word of explanation called out by a nervous servant. The sheriff hovered a moment between fury and astonishment; Prince John had departed, which meant there was no further need for such thoughtlessness.

He yanked back the linens and coverlet, thrust himself out of bed—his own once again, while Eleanor had hers—threw a robe haphazardly over his bliaut, and strode stiff-legged across the cool stone floor to the door, which he unlatched and jerked open. "What *is*—" He stopped in midspate. "Brother Tuck?"

The monk's eyes were red-rimmed and bloodshot. "My lord, forgive me. I must speak with you."

It was a declaration no less preposterous than unexpected. DeLacey was in no mood for discussion aired by a gluttonous monk who had yet to prove himself capable of a single independent thought. It was a trait deLacey found useful often enough, but his preferences for willing, dullard servants did not in any way convince him to welcome Tuck at such an hour. He opened his mouth to say so, but the monk cut him off.

"My lord. I can't do it." Tuck's color was bad, as was his breathing. He filled up the doorway with voluminous cassock and heavy shoulders. His face was filmed with perspiration, and he smelled of a nervous, powerful sanctity.

"Can't do what?" the sheriff inquired, hard-pressed not to slam the heavy door shut just to make a point. "Brother Tuck, I believe there may be a more opportune time for this—"

But Tuck was not dissuaded; in fact, he seemed quite determined to block the only escape route so that deLacey *had* to listen—that, or go back to bed and pull the covers over his head, which he had learned as a child solved absolutely nothing. "My lord, I did not sleep last night. I prayed all night long. My spirit is in turmoil . . ." He took a deep breath. "My lord, I *can't* pretend to be a priest."

DeLacey reached out and settled a rigid hand on Tuck's shoulder, dug into black wool, then dragged the monk inside.

It would not do to raise the topic where servants might hear. He shut the door decisively. "We discussed this yesterday—"

"Yes, my lord—and I agreed." Tuck showed no signs of surrendering the battle despite his nervousness. "That young woman is indeed in need of comfort, but to imperil my soul—*and* hers!—by commiting a sin such as this is unthinkable." The double chin was amazingly firm. "My lord, I beg you, there must be another way."

DeLacey wondered what it would feel like to sink a fist into the mound of Tuck's belly. "We discussed this *in detail* yesterday. For the Lady Marian's sake—"

"For her *soul's* sake, I dare not do it." Tuck squared his shoulders. "I understand you may well dismiss me, my lord, but I am convinced there is another way. You see—"

"What I *see*," deLacey began dangerously, "is a man in danger of being dismissed not only from my service, but from his abbey as well." The time for prevarication was done. Tuck obviously needed to be reminded of whom he served, in what capacity, and just how exacting the duties were. DeLacey therefore resorted to blunt brevity. "You misled that old woman into believing you were a priest, did you not? And you prepared an execution order for the wrong man. *Knowingly* prepared it."

Tuck's wheezing increased. "My lord, I beg you—"

"What do you think Abbot Martin would say?" The sheriff leaned closer, lowering his voice. "What do you think Abbot Martin would *do?*"

Tuck's folded hands trembled. The determination slipped, as deLacey intended. The aberration was minor, then; Tuck was salvageable. "My lord . . . there would be punishment, of course—"

"Punishment!" DeLacey allowed the word to crack through the chamber. "My God, man—forgive me, Brother—but I know perfectly well what Abbot Martin will do. There is no secret of his vice—"

Tuck's wide jaw dropped. "Vice!"

"Indeed." DeLacey now was coolly urbane, intimidating easily with a casual negligence. "The Church harbors many men whose appetites are—*unique*—Brother Tuck . . . often such appetites may be used for training other men to celebrate the

489

glory of God in many alternative ways. You are young, I know, and innocent"—his tone hardened—"but there is no substitute for truth. Abbot Martin will see to it the skin is removed from your back . . . the question remains whether he will do it himself, or bid *you* to do it."

It shocked him utterly. "Oh—my lord—"

DeLacey offered compassion. "Brother, I do know this without question . . . one of your brethren served here for years. He died but months ago. He told me all about it just before he expired."

Tuck was agonized. "He is the *abbot*—"

Silkily, he explained, "Appetite is not governed by closeness to God, Brother Tuck—if anything, wielding authority is a fillip to the taste." DeLacey smiled kindly. "Now, Brother Tuck, what say you to the wedding?"

Sunrise gilded mist, so that shafts of mote-filled saffron light penetrated the window notches and illuminated the little chamber. Fieldstone glistened damply. Robin, newly awakened in an unfamiliar place, wondered for an instant if he had died during the night and no longer walked the earth.

Then he recognized the oratory, and remembered the night before.

He sat upright instantly, jerking cloaks aside; *two* cloaks, not one, and none of them housing Marian. She had left him entirely alone without waking him, which was odd of itself; he had not slept well since Acre and small noises and movement usually disturbed him.

England . . . Slack-limbed in relief, Robin slumped back to the matting and gazed fixedly at the low timber roof looming overhead. He lay on his back with his legs propped up, his hands splayed limply across his abdomen, trying to sort out the welter of emotions surging up in place of aching emptiness, and the newly recalled responses of a body too long locked up in mind as well as in truth.

The acknowledgment was tentative and explorative, so as not to chase away the fragile, much-needed belief: that he was a man after all, despite the attempts of others to strip him, in the most elemental way, of the ability to prove it; despite also his own more successful attempts to mute his natural desires out of a sense of degradation in captivity, and also a personal shame that a man, even a king, might desire him in place of a woman.

Such desires, though named perversion in the sight of God, were not unheard of in an army, where men trusted other men implicitly, or died. In need of women but with none in attendance save those they caught and raped, some men sought release by private means, while others looked to companions. There were those, he supposed, who preferred it anyway; he had begun to think it might be so with Richard, for who but the king would have first claim on any woman, willing or no, and yet took none to his bed?

But as to *his* bed, and the woman in it . . .

He laughed joyously, in an uprush of jubilant well-being. He was whole again, or nearly so; a man again without question. It only remained for him to make certain his father realized it, so the Earl of Huntington's heir need not ever fear him again.

"Ya Allah." He grinned up at the roof. In Arabic or English, God was merciful.

Forty-Nine

William deLacey supposed Nottingham citizens might speak well of his touring of the city in the aftermath of the storm. What they did not know—and did not *need* to know—was that he didn't really care what damage had been done to the city or her people. His attention was wholly consumed by his current task, which had less to do with storm damage than with the devastation Prince John might wreak if his wishes were not obeyed.

He negotiated the twisty, narrow streets with distaste, disliking the mud that splattered his cloak and the stink of refuse and waste carried throughout the city, distributed in a most haphazard manner by the wind and rain. He noted with mild surprise, as he crossed the invisible border between the Jewish Quarter and the rest of Nottingham, that the odor was somewhat improved. Here people labored most assiduously to clean up waste and refuse, carting it away.

Two things, then, Jews were good for: lending money, and cleaning the streets.

He dismounted in front of the low-roofed, square building that was home and business to Abraham the Jew. He summoned one of the boys helping to sweep the cobbles in front of the door and bade him announce the sheriff's presence to Abraham, then come out and hold the horse. The boy was thin, dark-eyed and dark-haired, with eloquent, mobile features less offensive than those boasted by many of the Jews, deLacey decided.

Accordingly the boy went in, returned after a moment, and took the horse's reins. In accented English he told the sheriff his grandfather would receive him.

"As well he should," deLacey agreed, and unlatched the door.

The old man sat, as he usually did, for his wracked joints allowed him little latitude for movement. He inclined his head in greeting, then gestured stiffly for the sheriff to seat himself.

"No, I think not. My business will not require much time." DeLacey swept a glance around the tiny room, very plain and unadorned, as if Abraham had no desire to show off the wealth he had acquired through usury. The Jews cheated everyone. Abraham merely seemed to be cleverer than others. "You will recall our conversation with regard to the additional tax."

Abraham's mouth tightened minutely. "Indeed, my lord—"

"I have come to reiterate that no tardiness will be tolerated." The place stank of Jewishness; deLacey saw that the cloth covering the table was stitched with the cabalistic signs the Jews claimed as their written language. "It is vital that the sum be raised to ransom the king."

"Indeed, my lord, we would like to think—"

But the sheriff did not permit him to finish. "You will recall that I asked you to speak to the other Jews."

Abraham inclined his head.

"And that you were to tell them I would expect delivery of the taxes by the end of the month."

"Yes, my lord, but now—"

"Now *what?*" deLacey snapped. "Is this the beginning of a ceaseless refrain encompassing refusal?"

Abraham sighed very faintly. "The storm has done much damage, my lord. Please to allow us a little more time to discuss the matter—"

"He is your *king*, Jew! Your liege lord. There can be no excuses to take precedence over the release of our sovereign."

"My lord Sheriff." Abraham's twisted hands did not twitch upon the table. "It is as important to us that the king be released as it is to you. We have given generously—"

"And are more generous in taking," deLacey retorted. "If anything, this storm will prompt others to come to you for money to hire repairs. Will you say to them you cannot lend it to them? No, of course not, because to do so would be bad business—a Jew who smells a profit never refuses custom." He permitted himself a cold smile. "But when it comes to ransoming the king, which would not return a profit on money freely given, you refuse to consider it."

Abraham was patient. "My lord, we have refused the king nothing. We have given more than most. All I ask—"

"It is refused," deLacey stated. "You will speak to the others at once, gather the money, then bring it personally to me. I shall expect it within three days."

"My lord!" Abraham's expression was anguished. "My lord, I beg you—grant us time. This storm—"

DeLacey's hand was on the latch. "The storm was indeed a bad one, and much damage was done. So much, in fact, it will be difficult to keep whole those possessions that escaped damage—surely you know how it is with poor people who lose what little they have. Too often they riot, and steal from those whom

493

they consider less deserving than they themselves." He opened the door. "Jews are always such easy targets."

Outside, deLacey briefly considered flipping a penny to the boy who brought his horse, then thought better of it. If he were to expect the Jews to bring him the money, it had best be *Jewish* money and not coin of his own coffers. That would defeat the purpose.

Marian stood in the hall and tried to make sense of a world half destroyed by wind and rain. While she and Robin had remained oblivious to the storm save the one of their own making, Ravenskeep had suffered. Shutters had been torn off walls, so that blowing rain soaked bedding and rushes, which meant the wet bedding had to be dried on a day none too promising for steady sunlight, while old rushes needed to be hauled out by hand and replaced with fresh. The beaten earth beneath was too hard to be called mud, but was slick and treacherous.

The kitchen and pantry also had suffered losses, for water had come in beneath the doors and ruined sacks of flour, as well as other necessities; the cookfires had all been extinguished and the coals turned into black soup, which had to be disposed of before a new fire was laid. The roof had leaked badly in three places, less seriously in four others.

The hall was bad enough, but the exterior worse. Sim had come in and explained in detail how the chicken house had collapsed, scattering dead and living fowl throughout the walled courtyard. Somehow the stable door had unlocked itself, freeing the bay gelding—Marian did not explain how the lock had been opened on purpose, or the reasons for it—and letting in so much wind and rain that grain sacks were sodden and spoiled, and the bedding straw blown all over until hardly a wisp remained inside the stable, while the rest, he said, was likely halfway to Nottingham. The main gate had blown down and needed replacing, which Marian already knew, and most of the loose cobbles had been washed free of their beds, leaving muddy holes pocking the courtyard like an old woman shedding teeth.

That was the beginning. Marian listened to most of it and delegated duties by importance: she gave Sim silver pennies and sent him with the cart to the mill for more flour, because they needed bread; Hal she set to collecting and stacking cobbles to one side in the courtyard until the mud dried out and they could replace and reseat them; Joan she dispatched to supervising the airing out of soaked bedding and the cleaning of the kitchen.

Stephen and Tam reported the sheep were scattered all over the meadow and it would take some doing to gather them again; there were ewes dead, they said, and drowned lambs, and the bellwether was half-mad, which risked the rest of the flock, but they could tend them well enough. Marian set them to that task, knowing both men cared so much about the sheep they would be useless seeing to anything else until the flock was safe. So she called in Roger, who was her least favorite of all because he was lazy and sullen—he had run away twice from her father, but was brought back both times by Sim, who counseled a third chance—and asked him to see how many shingles they had stored away; if there were none, he would have to make them, as well as new shutters.

She then set three of the kitchen-girls to raking soaked rushes out of the hall, which would likely take all day, but told them not to replace the rushes because if it rained again before Roger finished the shutters and shingles, there would be all of it to do yet again.

In all the mess Marian was comforted by one thought: Robin was in the oratory. She wondered what he would say when he came in, or what *she* would say, and when he did at last come in the open door to blot out the tentative morning sun she found no words at all for a greeting, just an imbecilic smile. His own mirrored hers.

"Lady," he said then, "will you walk out with me?"

And she went, because she had to, because they could say nothing to one another where others could hear them save mouth the courtesies of rank.

Her heart was full of an unforeseen shy hesitance and an equally surprising anticipation. Was this what love was? To want and not want, to need and not need, to relish the physical power while frightened by it as well?

She drew in a breath as they stepped outside the hall. "The oratory?"

He was circumspect, taking care not to compromise her outside her very door. But his smile slid crooked as he cast her a sidelong glance. The timbre in his voice was altered, lacking its cool self-possession. He sounded wholly natural and somehow very young, unguarded by wariness. "I would forget what I have to say."

She grinned. "What *have* you to say?"

"That I must go."

She had not expected that. Not so soon.

He was quietly insistent. "I must, Marian—if I am to settle things with my father, I cannot put them off."

She believed it worth the attempt. "I offered to send him a message. You refused. And then there was the storm." It was most of it inconsequential. Marian wanted to tell him how much she desired him to stay, but words failed her. All she could do was what she had done, and hope it was enough. "I could send Sim with a message *now.*"

His expression was bleak. "You don't know my father—he is not a man of much patience when he has made up his mind about something . . . the last word I had from him was Prince John had dangled his daughter as bait to catch Huntington's heir. If I wait, it may be settled before I can speak against it."

Her joy was abruptly extinguished. "John's daughter," she said hollowly.

"Yes." He was serious now. "I had no interest in the match when it was first mentioned, and even less interest now. I promise you that."

She could think of no single phrase that would express what she was feeling. Too many words tumbled about in her head, like a fortune-teller's knucklebones. And she had no right to chide him—they had no claims on each other past what they wanted to make.

She drew in a constricted breath. "You will go to Huntington, then—"

"And come back." Most definitive; the smile in his eyes was warm. "It may take a day or two—or *three,* knowing my father!—but I will come back to you. I promise, Marian." He glanced briefly at the courtyard, where Hal gathered cobbles. His mouth tightened minutely. "I can do nothing now—"

"Here." She gestured. "The gate is open, my lord—shall I walk you out of it?"

The glint in his eyes was pronounced. "Do, Lady Marian."

She turned. "Hal—will you bring a horse for Sir Robert? He leaves for Huntington."

"Aye, Lady Marian."

"We'll wait," she said. Then, feeling jubilant again, because he was not deserting her utterly, "It would not do for him to bring the horse when we least expected it."

"No," he agreed gravely. "Marian—I will come back. He is not an easy man to deal with, but I will insist he understand."

She felt the first touch of alarm. "Would he forbid you to see me?"

His face was very still. "He may forbid all manner of things— it was always his way. But I am no longer a boy. It is for me to shape my life."

"You are his heir. What if he chose to disinherit you?"

"I am his only son—his only *child*." Dryly, he added, "And there is no one else to inherit that monstrosity he has caused to be built."

Marian laughed. "It is a most impressive castle."

His tone was scornful. "A tribute to vanity . . . worse than that, it is as much a beacon as the Beltane fire—he will use it to his own ends, because it gives him power. Power attracts others." Robin shook his head. "His fine Norman castle speaks well of his wealth, but says nothing of his intentions save he can withstand any siege. It is a promise, Marian—'do as I say,' it says, 'or beware how I can be used to withstand that which I do not approve.' "

"A message," she declared. "He sends a message to John!"

"And to anyone else who dares to disagree with him." Robin sighed, scraping a hand through shining hair. "Pray God they ransom Richard, or this realm could fall to John. And if John rules England, it will be because France permits it; he is in league with Philip. The king told me before he sailed for home."

It was astonishing. "If the king *knows*—"

Robin shook his head. "What can he do from Germany?"

She understood that well enough. "But surely the ransom will be raised. England adores the Lionheart."

"England can only contribute what money she has left. Richard drained her coffers to fuel the Crusade—I doubt there is enough to pay German Henry's ransom." His expression was grim. "Had my father looked to the king's release rather than his own vanity . . ." But he let it go as Hal approached with the horse. "I thank you." He took the reins. Somberly, he said, "I will promise the horse better treatment this time."

Marian had not asked what had driven him out into the storm, and did not now. She did not see that spending a night in a man's bed—and in his arms—gave her the right to know all his secrets, or his private thoughts. "Come out," she said quietly, and led the way through the gate.

It was a mistake, Sir Guy of Gisbourne decided as the cart journey jarred his wound. He should have stayed at Huntington another day at least, allowing his leg time to heal before banging it about in a rude cart driven by a carter who searched out every rut and pothole just to keep his passenger alert. But a part of his mind reminded him most distinctly he dared not let another day go by without supervising Nottingham Castle, or all his diligent work would be undone in a few days by the ineptitude of Walter and his ilk; nor could he allow the sheriff too much freedom from observation. It was necessary that he return to Nottingham, but he was not enjoying the painful journey.

Gisbourne managed a smile. Prince John had promised. Surely a promise from the future King of England was money in his purse.

The Earl of Huntington sat down at table and applied himself to the first meal of the day as Ralph served it. "Who?"

Ralph repeated himself. "Sir Hugh FitzWalter's daughter, Lady Marian, of Ravenskeep. He died a year ago, on Crusade;

she attended the feast in Sir Robert's honor. It was she whom your son rescued from the boar."

That woman; he recalled her well. The earl grunted acknowledgment. "And you say she has been kidnapped?"

"She was abducted during the fair by a man who was to be hanged for murdering four of Prince John's men, my lord. Somehow he escaped, and abducted the lady as his parole. He took her with him into Sherwood Forest."

Huntington's mouth pinched tightly. It was most distressing that such behavior was allowed to occur, but the earl was convinced it was encouraged by a pervasive permissiveness he abhorred. It spoke poorly of Nottingham's sheriff as well as the attitude of women in general.

"What is become of a woman's chastity?" he asked. "First deLacey's daughter, and now this dead knight's girl. They should have more regard for their families." The earl selected an apple and bit into it carefully, mindful of missing teeth. "It is just as well her father is dead, I suppose—she is quite despoiled, of course."

"Undoubtedly, my lord. But she was seen on the Nottingham road with your son."

"My son!" His attention sharpened. "What was my son doing with her?"

"There is talk he rescued her."

"Again, eh?" Eyebrows arched. "A helpful man, my son—or is there more to it than that?" He set down the apple and leaned back in his chair, tapping his fingers against the chair. "Has he appointed himself her guardian, I wonder?—or does he merely desire to follow more easily that furrow which another man has plowed?" His distaste showed briefly. "Let the young man waste his seed where he will, but he might have chosen a more discreet woman. This one is carried off like the merest trifle at the whim of a lowborn peasant, and used accordingly . . ." He sighed, tapping fingers. "Let him confine himself to women of his station—and quality!—if he must play hound to the vixen . . . this FitzWalter girl is nothing but an impediment."

"She is of good family, my lord. Sir Hugh was knighted by King Henry himself."

"Did he make no provision for her care?"

"None I have learned, my lord. Her mother is also dead; Lady Marian is said to be a ward of the king."

Huntington shook his head. "It is no wonder the girl is easy prey . . . she should be married off at once before anyone else spies her frailties and tries to make use of them. She has some value, after all; Ravenskeep is a decent enough holding for the right sort of man." He sat forward again, retrieving his apple. "Ah well, it is no concern of mine. But send Robert to me as soon as he returns. There are matters to discuss with him before de Vesci and the others leave."

"Yes, my lord." Ralph offered watered wine.

Much huddled damply in his muddy hollow, staring fixedly at the princess who was, most unexpectedly, being kissed by the prince. And kissing back, to boot. The boy, who had witnessed many a carnal coupling between his mother and father, between his mother and other men, between his father and other women, understood very well that kissing quite often led to something more. He waited, eyes stretched wide, but all his prince and princess did was kiss, then part. The prince mounted the horse and the princess went immediately back inside the wall, as if afraid to watch the prince leave.

Odd, Much decided. When were they to couple?

Apparently another time; the prince turned the horse and proceeded, somewhat leisurely, to aim the bay gelding toward the Nottingham Road.

Much emerged. He darted from the tree to stand at the side of the track expectantly, hands tucked behind him and elbows stuck out from his sides. As intended, Robin saw him and reined in at once.

He wore sherte, tunic, and hosen that did not quite fit, and a dark gray mantle thrown loosely over his shoulders. Pale hair gleamed dully in wan sunlight. "Much," he said in surprise. "I thought you had gone back to Nottingham."

Much shook his head. "Marian."

A smile of wholly unexpected proportions altered Robin's features. The austerity was banished, as was a certain coolness

500

Much had marked before. "Marian," he agreed. "Safe at last, Much."

Much nodded, grinned shyly, then slanted a speaking glance down the track.

Robin kicked free of the left stirrup. "Come up?" he invited. "It's a long walk to Nottingham. I should know, too—I walked half of it yesterday."

Much eyed the empty stirrup. To ride behind his Robin was incomprehensible; they inhabited different worlds.

Robin smiled warmly. "Come up," he repeated. "I'll stop whenever you like."

The decision was made. Much darted to the horse, swarmed up the saddle nimbly with no need of Robin's arm, and settled himself behind on the broad bay rump.

"Robin's horse," he murmured. Then, in one of the few full sentences the boy had used in a long time, "Scarlet wanted it."

"Did he?" Robin tucked his booted foot back into the stirrup and guided the horse onward. "Well, the last time I saw Charlemagne, he was bound for Nottingham with a wounded Norman. Will Scarlet might well be sporting a knock on the nose; Charlemagne is not much tolerant of roughness."

Much thought back to his own portion of roughness, employed when Will Scarlet, the minstrel, and Clym of the Clough all wanted the bay horse that rightfully was his, because he meant to return him to Robin.

"Charl-mane," he slurred.

"A great leader," Robin said. "King of the Franks, and Emperor of the Romans. He lived a long time ago—almost four hundred years."

Much nodded.

"I admire kings," Robin said. "I always did, especially at your age, when I would pretend I was one. The second Henry was king then, so I've known two of them in my lifetime. They always seemed so heroic to me. Now that I know King Richard personally, I find it perfectly true."

It was impossible that Robin might actually *know* the king. Much supposed men did, but he had never met one on speaking terms with a king. "Lionheart?"

"Richard Plantagenet; Duke of Aquitaine; King of the English; Coeur de Lion; Malik Ric," Robin agreed, as if reciting an incantation. "If England is fortunate, she'll have him back again. But only if we manage to raise enough ransom."

"Money," Much said.

"More money than *I* have."

Much thought about it. Then he dug down into his hosen, pulled free the leather pouch, deftly undid the knots. He reached around Robin and held out the pouch.

Robin took it. "What is—? Much!" He halted the horse and twisted in the saddle. "This is my own purse."

Much nodded decisively. "Lionheart."

Robin's expression was thoughtful. After a moment he tucked it away into a boot. "Lionheart," he agreed, as if chastened by the thought, and gave rein to the bay again.

Much was satisfied. He knew how to get money; nothing was easier. If it would buy the Lionheart back, whom Robin knew personally, he would steal every penny he could.

Fifty

Sherwood retained moisture far longer than fields and meadows because of its shadowed denseness. Water ran through prickly-edged holly, stuck on spikes all over thistle, beat down the climbing honeysuckle and the foxgloves with purple bells. Booted steps were muffled by damp, slick leaf mold piled up upon the black soil that was buried by multiple layers and seasons beneath the more recent deadfall.

Little John perched atop a damp, lichen-clad rock and stared gloomily into the thicket of young birch saplings, scratching at his unkept aureole of bright red hair. Three or four paces away, screened by bracken and vines, the others gathered: Adam Bell, William of Cloudisley, Clym of the Clough, Will Scarlet, and Alan of the Dales. Wat One-Hand had been sent to watch the Nottingham Road, to signal if a likely looking victim appeared. This plan did not particularly please Little John, who was increasingly aware of a painful futility taking the place of mere frustration.

He wanted nothing to do with this life, and yet he understood all too well there might be no alternative. Because of his remarkable height and vivid coloring, he was not a man who fit in easily anywhere. The wounded Norman who had survived the encounter to ride back to Nottingham simply *could not* forget to mention the huge red-haired man in the midst of the killings. Will Scarlet was right: neither the sheriff nor anyone else—any other *Norman* that is—would spare the time to ask Little John for his side of the story. All they needed to know was that the Hathersage Giant was present as Normans were killed.

He heard the threshing of a man coming through bracken. A moment later the minstrel appeared, lute hooked over his shoulder and tucked safely between elbow and hip. Little was left of his finery. His plain sherte was soiled and torn, golden curls hung in damp disarray, and his pretty features were roughened by stubble and harsh usage, which dissipated the girlish look and lent him a measure of masculinity.

But for all his dishabille, Alan's crooked, engaging smile was as always present. "Thinking about leaving?"

Little John grunted. "Why do *you* stay? You've more chance than the rest of us to go on your way."

The minstrel laughed, cradling his lute. "I am somewhat fond of my tongue."

"You could go to another part of England."

Alan hitched a shoulder. "I have a taste for the elegant life. I could go to the North Country, 'tis true, and lose myself there, but those lords are harsh and lacking in refinement. Their women are cold, I hear. No, I much prefer the warmth of great lords and ladies such as the Earl of Huntington—"

Little John grunted skepticism. "Sherwood is harsher than the North Country."

Alan nodded. "A fair observation, giant—but think again. Where do you suppose my music comes from?"

Little John shrugged indifferently.

Alan laughed. "So answers a man with little imagination and no curiosity." He set his spine against a tree and leaned indolently, fingering fretwork quietly as he caressed the strings. "Music does not spring forth from a well, my friend. Music must be *inspired* to truly touch the soul. The greatest of the troubadors understood this, and sought out inspiration." He cast a quick glance around the closeness of trees and foliage. "Sherwood Forest is a magical place offering much for a minstrel in need of atmosphere. As for inspiration, well, I need only look to the three men yonder . . . Adam Bell and the others are the stuff of legend. Did you not know of them before you met them?"

Little John admitted he did.

"There. You see? The peasants tell stories about them. They have *fame*, Little John . . . and that is the root of my magic." Very quietly, he raised music from the lute.

Little John squinted disbelief. "And you'd stay here for *that?*"

Alan shrugged. His expression was pensive as he pressed the strings into silence. "I fear I have little choice. The sheriff will see to it all the fine lords—and some of the lesser ones—know of my 'crime.' There will be no welcome for me."

It struck home in Little John, who recognized a similar fate for himself. He had known no welcome from lords, but he had a measure of fame as the Hathersage Giant. The sheriff need only put out word the giant was wanted, with a bounty on his head, and the fairs would prove deadly. He might give that up entirely and go back to shepherding, but how would he sell his wool? He was too obvious.

He leaned and spat, then looked at Alan. "So—what becomes of a minstrel who can't practice his trade?"

Alan sighed, smiling faintly. "There is another audience. 'Tis not one I am accustomed to, preferring silk to wool, but beggars can't be choosers. I can ply my trade in taverns and alehouses . . . I'll sing songs of Adam Bell, and live off the takings."

Little John grunted. "Not so much coin in that."

"No. It will have to be supplemented." Alan grinned. "I can

entertain our victims as they are relieved of their coin, and make a profit that way."

Little John stared in disbelief. "I like that!" he said. "Singing to our victims . . ."

Alan shrugged. "Better than *being* a victim."

A birdcall sounded. A moment later Adam Bell and the others came through to Little John and Alan. "Now," Bell said tersely. "We've work to do."

Little John slowly stood up and followed the others as they made their way toward the road.

At Ravenskeep, the storm had torn down much of the ivy, climbing honeysuckle, and the shrub roses Marian's mother had tended for so many years. Canes were broken and twisted, or lay tumbled across the cobbles. Marian braided back her hair, found her scissors, and set about taming the mess.

Hal had stacked his cobbles against the wall and now labored resetting the hinges on the splintered jamb of the front gate. Sim was back from the mill with flour, and Joan oversaw the replenishment of the kitchen and pantry. The hall floor was raked free of sodden rushes and now dried slowly in the damp; Roger's progress with shutters and shingles was excruciatingly slow, so Marian set Sim to helping. Frequent glances at the sky confirmed her apprehension that it might rain again in the night; she did not relish having her hall soaked all over again.

As she worked, she counted over what she knew of the losses the manor had suffered. Three-quarters of the hens were dead or in hiding, most of the chicks had been blown into sodden, shapeless little heaps of fluff, and the rooster, too, had been found dead. The hens who remained might not lay for days, which meant Ravenskeep's inhabitants would have to buy or trade for the eggs they wanted, in the unlikely event anyone else had eggs to spare. The milk cows were safe, as were the horses and pigs, but the sheep still were scattered. Tam and Stephen had not come in yet and wouldn't, Marian knew, until every last lamb was accounted for, be it alive or dead.

"We need deer," she muttered, working a flopping cane back into its place. "Were I an archer, I'd go into the forest and take

505

a roe." But she knew she wouldn't. Killing the king's deer cost a person a hand, or worse. Poaching was a high crime. "So, the king would rather see his people starve than lose a deer or two . . ." Marian cut down a twisted cane and set it aside carefully, avoiding thorns. The few remaining rose petals were limp and ragged. "The Conqueror has much to answer for—first he takes England, then strips her people of the right to eat." But Forest Law was unassailable; many had discovered, to their grief, that no lord tolerated an abuse of the king's privilege. "Surely the sheriff has more to do than enforce the poaching laws against people who are starving." She and her people were not close to starving, but many peasants were. And if their rude huts had been lost to the storm, they'd have less than ever. Poaching royal deer would become a necessity.

And the sheriff would then catch those he could and lop off hands, or put out eyes, or toss them into the dungeon at Nottingham Castle, where none of them could work at all to feed their starving families.

Marian stopped working. "They'll send out *boys.*"

She thought of Much, who had nearly lost his hand. She thought of other boys, maimed before they were grown, embittered by the crippling and turning to banditry because there was nothing else.

She thought of the sheriff, who wanted to marry her. And then she thought of Robin.

I don't want to be doing this. I want to be with him. Then, more urgently, *I don't want to be here at all.*

Marian clutched at broken canes. Thorns pricked, but she did not notice. She noticed nothing at all save the certainty in her mind, blazing like a pyre. "I must go to Nottingham."

There was no other choice, clearly; what had taken her so long to see it? *I will go now, and be back before Robin returns. We both of us have business to settle.*

Yet part of it was settled already; she had, in that moment, ceased to be the woman William deLacey knew. She was now someone else. Someone she much preferred.

Marian laughed aloud. *Eleanor said women have no right to choose . . . but I have made my choice.*

Now it remained for her to declare it. The sheriff would be

displeased, she knew, but Marian did not care. What mattered now—*who* mattered now—was the man she knew as Robin.

Robin felt an odd affinity for the boy who rode pillion on the borrowed bay. That Much was simple, he knew, but it did not disturb or unsettle him, as it did so many people to be faced with someone different. Much said little enough, but then he himself had been a quiet boy, sharing little of himself with others. His father had made him less inclined than ever to talk of things that meant very much, for the earl had been a cold, rigid man who saw no use in boys who dreamed of kings and knights, and magical bowers where the faeries of old held court.

So he had banished them to his inward self and locked Robin away, portraying himself as *Robert* once his mother was dead. She had understood the hunger in his soul and abetted his interests, but she had sickened and died, leaving him with no one but a father whose idea of shaping a boy lay in beating him free of dreams.

Much was, therefore, eminently understandable; the boy was practical and quick, governing himself by the needs of the moment. That many of those needs concerned cutting purses from unsuspecting victims did not overly concern Robin; he had himself made shift where he could in trying circumstances.

The bay horse borrowed from Ravenskeep was not as fine as those mounts to which Robin was accustomed, but considerably better than walking. Allah knew—*God* knew—he had walked more than his share in captivity, for he was given no mount, and the journey from Sherwood while fever beat in his brain had leeched him of even the smallest willingness.

"Charl-mane," Much murmured.

"Char-*le*-mane," Robin corrected. Then, more properly, "Char-le-*man*-ya—but Charlemagne will do. We English corrupt the tongues . . . it is Salah al-Din, Salah al-Din Yusuf ibn Ayyub, not Saladin." How many times had he been required to say it properly?

"Sal-din," Much echoed.

"Salah al-Din—"

The boy took it up immediately, mimicking what he'd heard. "Salah al-Din Yusuf ibn Ayyub."

"Ya Allah!" Robin laughed. "We'll make a Saracen of you yet—" But he broke off abruptly as the horse snorted alarm, for a group of men filed quietly out of the forest's skirts to block the road.

Will Scarlet bared bad teeth in an anticipatory grin. "We'll have the horse," he said. *"This* time, we'll keep it."

Inwardly, Robin sighed. Scarlet's face was bruised as his own was, and probably just as sore—especially the swollen nose— but the man showed no signs of reluctance to repeat the fight they'd begun once before.

He cast a glance over the cluster of men. Two of them he knew: Little John, and Alan of the Dales, both of whom had the grace to look, respectively, reluctant and chagrined. Two of the other men held longbows with arrows nocked. Their companion stared back, arms folded across his chest.

"No horse," Robin told them. "You had your chance at mine, and lost it; he went off to Nottingham with that Norman you wounded."

"Too bad," Scarlet jeered. "We'll take it anyway."

Little John frowned. "Is that the boy behind you?"

"Much," Robin confirmed, as the boy leaned around him to glower at the others.

Alan of the Dales wore a peculiar expression. "This is Adam Bell, my lord—" He winced as the title slipped. "Adam Bell, and Clym of the Clough, and William of Cloudisley."

It made no sense to Robin, who was aware of a peculiar impatience rising in his spirit. He was tired of giving way merely to keep the peace. Very tired indeed. "I have been out of England for two years," he declared lightly enough, prelude to anger. Then, purposefully provocative, "Have they crowned a new king in my absence, that I should surrender a horse without protest?"

Faces darkened, although Alan looked wryly amused and Little John discontented. "Aye," Clym said harshly. "King of *Sherwood,* villein—"

"No." Adam Bell's quiet voice cut him off. "Not villein

508

. . . he speaks too well"—his clear-eyed gaze, on Robin, was direct and discomfiting—"and the minstrel said 'my lord.' "

A moment of silence, only. Then Will Scarlet scowled and muttered an oath even as Cloudisley and Clym, stilled into wary alertness, fixed Robin with speculative stares.

Accustomed to judging mens' actions in battle, Robin marked how they held their bows, their stances and readiness. He flicked a quick glance at Alan, then at Little John, assessing; they were poised for nothing that offered violence. It was something.

Quietly he said, "My name, as I told the giant, is Robin. Robin of Locksley."

Clym grunted. "Locksley's hard by Huntington."

"Robin." Alan's mouth shaped it oddly, as if he felt more comfortable with titles and ranks of honor. "Robin—Robert." He avoided Robin's gaze even as he colored. "He'll have coin."

Grinning, Wat waggled the fingers of his only remaining hand. "Toss it down, then."

"And get off the horse," Scarlet growled.

"No!" Much cried.

"Agh God—not the *boy* again—" Scarlet strode forward and grasped the bay's reins. "This time I'll break your neck—"

"No," Robin said.

"By God, you'll not tell *me* what to do!" Scarlet flushed angrily, so that the smudged purplish bruises showed darker yet in the stubbled ruin of his face. "It'll be me who does the telling—"

Little John laughed harshly. "As you did when you fought him? Aye, *that* was impressive!"

Adam Bell looked at Robin. "Was it you, then?"

Clym leaned and spat. "Lapdog to the Normans."

Robin smiled faintly. "I've very sharp teeth."

"Come *down* from there!" Scarlet snapped. "By God—"

"Wait." Robin cut him off with a sharp, imperative command that stilled all of them by instinct. He had learned the tone in war; they had in servitude. Robin looked at Cloudisley and Clym. "I've an idea to settle this."

Clym swore beneath his breath, muttering epithets.

Robin shrugged. "Less painful, I will warrant, than shooting me full of arrows—or suffering your own hurts." Before they could protest, he said, "I will match you for the horse."

Cloudisley laughed. "Match us how?"

He offered them terms they would approve. "Choose your best archer."

Cloudisley and Clym exchanged startled glances that faded quickly into a private amusement; they did not consider another might have the skill. But it was Adam Bell who answered. "It'll be me who shoots." To Cloudisley he said, crisply, "Go cut us a target." And lastly to Robin, in deceptive quietude, "I'll know your name before."

Robin hitched a casual shoulder. "Robin of Locksley."

"I'll have your *real* name—" But Bell broke it off, grinning. "As you say, then, *Robin*—we'll shoot for that, too." He turned as Cloudisley, who had carved a heart in the trunk of a tree, called that it was ready.

"Cloudisley's bow," Bell told him. "You'll have no disadvantage."

Robin caught the bow and the quiver of arrows as Cloudisley tossed them. He shook back his hair and nodded acceptance. "The rules?"

Bell smiled. "Three arrows in the heart, or you lose." He pointed stiff-armed. "See that white gouge there in the center of the heart? Closest to that, wins."

"I keep the horse," Robin said, not bothering to look. "I keep my coin."

"And your life," Bell quipped. "Forfeit all if you lose."

Robin glanced back at Much, whose face was strained. He smiled at the boy, then licked and blew upon the thumb and fingers of his right hand, which he displayed to Much. "Magic," he said.

Much's thin face lighted.

Fifty-One

The sheriff, satisfied that his visit to Abraham the Jew would result in the expected—and much-needed—payment, which in turn would be sent to Prince John at Lincoln, returned to Nottingham Castle in good spirits, fixing his mind upon the approaching "marriage" to Marian. That it would be a sham ceremony did not in any way disturb him; it would get Marian into his bed. He understood very well she would not surrender readily; in fact, after their recent meeting, he had come to believe she would not agree at all, and that trickery was the only alternative.

He rode through the barbican gate beneath the portcullis. *I will lure her,* he thought contentedly. *Lure her into a false wedding in spite of her protests.* He smiled in anticipation. *With dear Brother Tuck involved, I have the upper hand.* The fat monk would do anything to avoid being dismissed from the abbey now that he understood the risks of refusing. *Marian may protest all she likes, but to no avail—she will believe herself truly married when the ceremony is over.* The genuine ceremony would come later, when Marian was so compromised as to see no other way out. *After all, what choice will she have? Will Scarlet destroyed any public pretense to chastity.*

A horseboy came running as deLacey swung off his mount. He handed the reins over, marking the cart and carthorse waiting in the bailey. He knew neither cart nor horse, and somewhat testily called over the nearest soldier to explain matters.

"Sir Guy's come back," the soldier told him. "The Earl of

511

Huntington sent him in the cart; the carter's helping him inside. My lord—"

DeLacey, on the point of leaving, paused. "Yes?"

"Will you call on Captain Archaumbault?"

"Is he dying?"

The soldier crossed himself. "No, my lord, but—"

"Then he'll do better without my presence." The sheriff turned on his heel and went into the castle, thinking about Gisbourne. *He'll complain about the candles* . . . Then, smiling faintly, *Unless he'll be too busy thinking about his approaching nuptials.*

On one side of the Nottingham Road lay the outermost fringe of Sherwood Forest, sparse and sparing with trees, and only partially clad in a tattered finery of low shrubbery and thinning vines. On the other side stretched slightly undulant fields lush with grass, divided one from another by hedgerows and low fieldstone walls.

It was on the more level side that Adam Bell gathered his men, indicating the tree Cloudisley had marked. He told Little John to walk off thirty paces from the marked tree to where they stood between road and fields because, he said, the giant's longer strides would improve the challenge; also, Little John had less reason to cheat than anyone else. Robin smiled, conceded that was true, and leaned casually on Cloudisley's borrowed longbow as the red-haired giant carefully walked off the distance from tree to gathering. Then Bell drew a line in the dirt with the worn heel of one boot.

"We'll stand behind this." He gestured. "Your target, '*my lord.*'"

Robin's impatience now was gone, replaced by the cool carelessness he had learned to wear as a mask against the stifling rigidity of his father. He raised an eloquent eyebrow. "'Twould be churlish of me to precede the King of Sherwood."

"Here, now—" Clym began.

Robin hitched a shoulder, purposefully mild. "You did say so."

"So you did," Bell agreed, casting a quelling glance at Clym. "Right, then—we'll have us a match." He stepped to the line, took his stance, nocked and lifted the bow. "Three in the heart," he said, and let fly one after another.

Cloudisley, standing off to one side of the marked tree, lifted a fist in the air when the last of the arrows struck wood and quivered into stillness. "Three in the heart!" he called. "Three in the gouge!"

Unsurprised, Robin nodded slightly. He expected superior marksmanship from the smaller man, who handled his bow with the understated expertise of a talented, confident archer. Bell employed no boasting, no goading, no flamboyance that marked him more interested in appearance than in results.

"Clear it," Bell called, then moved away from the line with a brief gesture to his opponent.

Robin waited until Cloudisley pulled the shafts, then stepped to the crude line and mimicked Bell's relaxed stance. One by one he nocked each arrow, pulled the bowstring back to his ear, released smoothly. Like Bell, he employed no flourishes that might alter the tension and detract from his aim; he had been taught too well to succumb to showing off. He lowered the bow as the last arrow was loosed and waited for the call.

Cloudisley didn't hesitate. "Ten more paces, giant! The match is tied!"

Bell nodded agreement as he glanced sidelong at Little John. "Ten more."

Little John supplied them, and another line was drawn. Robin glanced briefly at Much, whose expression was rapt, then smiled and waggled his fingers, blowing on them again.

"Enough of that," Clym growled.

Robin grinned. "Afraid the magic is real?"

"Hush," Bell said, stepping to the line. Once again he nocked three arrows with swift skill and loosed them as fast.

"Three in the heart!" came the call. "And three more in the gouge!"

"Clear!" Bell shouted as Robin nodded and moved to the line.

He shot three times. The result was the same: three shafts buried in the white flash of the gouge. Robin looked at Little John. "Ten more paces?"

Alan eyed the distance, then shook his head. "Difficult to see from here."

Adam Bell smiled. "My arrows have eyes." And he appeared to prove it when Cloudisley called the result: at fifty of Little John's paces, all three shafts buried themselves in the gouge.

Robin nodded, sincere in his admiration. "Fine shooting." But he had no more time to waste. He raised his voice to Cloudisley. "Don't clear the heart. Leave the arrows there."

"*Leave* them!" Even Bell frowned. "You'll spoil your shots."

Scarlet hooted. "Let him, then, Adam."

"Leave them," Robin repeated, stepping to the line. He glanced sidelong at Bell. "I think it should be decisive."

Bell grunted. "As you will."

Robin nodded absently, glanced briefly once more at Much, then lifted the nocked bow. "Each one," he said quietly, and with grave deliberation let fly three more arrows.

Cloudisley moved to look, then turned an astonished face to them. "By God," he blurted, "he *split* them! Each of Adam's arrows!"

A twinge of relief pinched Robin's belly; he had not been certain he could, after so long away from the butts. He had a gift, no more; an incredibly keen eye, which he had honed through years of painstaking practice. Many of the hours he had stolen from his father, slipping away into the forest, had been spent at his makeshift target.

The others were disbelieving. "No," Scarlet growled, even as Clym spat out an oath. Adam Bell's mouth was tight as he walked toward the tree.

No time to tarry—Robin tossed bow and quiver to Little John, who caught them awkwardly, then beckoned Much over with the horse. He grasped the boy beneath his arms and threw him up on the broad bay rump, then climbed up himself, hooking his right leg across the neck as he eased himself into the saddle.

Alan looked up at him shrewdly. "I've never witnessed marksmanship like that before, and I've seen my share of matches at tournaments and fairs."

It was challenge and question. From the minstrel, both were fair; Alan knew precisely who he was. "My father believed it beneath his heir's dignity to shoot against common yeomen."

514

A shout went up from Adam Bell. "By God—the arrows *are* split!"

"You'd have won," Alan declared.

Robin nodded. "It would have made my father angrier, that I dared to *win* money when he could give me all I wanted."

Alan's eyes narrowed. "But you don't want it, do you?"

Robin shrugged, lifting reins. "What I want can't be bought."

"You went on Crusade." The minstrel began to smile, nodding slightly as inspiration was born. "Fame and glory, then . . . and the knighthood you won."

"No." Robin, who considered himself unlikely ballad fodder, cast a glance at the outlaws clustered around the marked tree, in which dwelled six arrows: three of them split in half. "Freedom is what I wanted."

Alan's mouth dropped open in astonishment. *"You?"*

Robin angled the horse toward Nottingham. "You never knew my father."

"Here, now!" It was Clym, harsh and belligerent, striding toward the road to cut the horse off. "Here now, where'd you learn to shoot like that?"

A sense of urgency lent curtness to Robin's tone. He did not like this man, and he wanted very much to be on his way. "Does it matter?"

"Aye." The man put a hand on the reins. "Aye, it does—Adam Bell's the best!"

"Was," Robin countered with inoffensive succinctness. "But he is still King of Sherwood."

Cloudisley came up and retrieved bow and quiver from Little John. "And what are *you* king of?"

"Myself." Robin saw the glitter in Clym's hard eyes and the unrepentant set of his mouth, which told him a thing or two—mostly that it was doubtful he could leave without forcing the issue. And that made him angry. For too many years of his life, in childhood and adulthood, others had spent too much time telling him what to do. *I am weary of it.* He might have tried to ride through the outlaw, forcing him aside with the sheer bulk of the horse, but Robin was very conscious of Much sitting close behind him. Quietly, he said, "Take your hand from my horse."

Clym of the Clough grinned. "Come down from there and make me."

The others had departed the target also, striding toward the confrontation. Now Little John glowered. "Let him go, Clym. He's won the right to go."

"No one said *I* had to let him go." Clym joggled the reins, glaring belligerent invitation. "Come down from there, boy— let's see how you fare with me."

Let us end this travesty. Robin looked at Adam Bell. "Have you swords?"

"Swords? No." Bell frowned. "I was a yeoman, before I was outlawed . . . but I never touched a sword. Neither has any of us."

"Then the match is forfeit." Robin gazed down at Clym. "Find yourself a sword, and I'll meet you wherever you like. For now, you'll let me by."

"Let him go," Alan said quietly. "Don't test him, Clym." Then, as Clym moved closer as if to grasp at a leg, "Clym— don't be a fool! He's a *knight*—"

A heavy silence descended. Adam Bell's fox eyes narrowed. "A knight, now, is it?"

"*Sir* Robin?" asked Cloudisley, giving up no quarter. "You don't look old enough."

Alan cast Robin an eloquent glance, then grinned at the others. "They knight them young in battle."

Scarlet's barked laugh was ugly. "Battle! *What* battle—" But he broke it off. His color waned a little. "Crusader?"

"Knighted," Bell murmured.

Alan smiled brilliantly. "By the Lionheart himself."

Fifty·Two

Sir Guy of Gisbourne was barely settled in his own bed when William deLacey entered the small, low-roofed chamber and dismissed the Earl of Huntington's carter. Gisbourne, sweating from pain and twitching with exhaustion, was in no mood to give the sheriff the sort of obsequiousness ordinarily required; besides, he no longer felt quite so dutiful as before. Now he had his own ambitions to fulfill.

As deLacey mentioned something about pleasant surprises, Gisbourne tried to display a bland expression. He felt as if his betrayal of the sheriff's interests was emblazoned on his brow for deLacey to read, to realize what had been done to destroy his chances with Marian. Gisbourne felt guilty and intensely self-conscious, wishing he had deLacey's skill at prevarication.

"Welcome back," the sheriff said, casting a glance around the small chamber with its pitifully few appointments: a bed, one clothing trunk, a single candle stand bearing the stub of a tallow candle. The slit of a narrow splayed window let in a vertical bar of wan light from a dimmer day. "We have missed you, Gisbourne," deLacey announced magnanimously. "Very much so, in fact. I see we have underestimated your value to Nottingham Castle."

He's here to say something specific . . . Gisbourne nodded, thinking back to Gilbert de Pisan and his unexpected success at manipulating the man. *If I could do that here, now, with the sheriff—* He managed a self-deprecating smile. "I am the seneschal, my lord—it is my duty to see to it your needs are properly looked after."

DeLacey raised a finger. "Ah, but you do it with surpassing skill. I doubt not you could hold your own with Gilbert de Pisan."

Gisbourne's heart stopped, then resumed with a hollow cramping thump. He had said nothing of de Pisan, merely thought it. *What does he know? Anything? Or is he just talking?*

The sheriff continued smoothly. "In fact, I believe it is time I seriously considered rewarding you with something significant, Sir Guy—something that will be remarked upon by others as a sign of my favor, which of course would help you rise."

Gisbourne felt out of his depth. Once he might have been pleased by the unexpected observations and a promised reward, but now all he could do was try to knit his shredded wits back together again.

DeLacey nodded, linking hands behind his back. "It is unfortunate your father could not provide more for you than second-hand armor and mount, Sir Guy—but if he had, perhaps I would be missing my most valued servant. So, to show my appreciation, I have decided to bestow upon you an increase in your yearly income, and the hand of my daughter."

Gisbourne's tongue felt thick. "Your daughter?"

DeLacey nodded, smiling. "You will become my son, Sir Guy, in the sight of God and the law . . . any benefits accruing to me in the future shall also accrue to you, so long as you remain in my service." He laughed briefly. "Of course, we know the service shall be long, and your position secure. I have no intention of dismissing the man who tends my business so well."

Gisbourne's smile was a frozen rictus. *Why doesn't he just bury me now?*

DeLacey assessed his expression, his own assuming a more benevolent cast. "But you would do best to rest. I won't tire you with conversation now. If you are feeling better tomorrow, I'll have Eleanor visit. I know she will be quite pleased to talk of future plans."

Gisbourne nodded stiffly as deLacey turned and went out of

the chamber, pulling the door closed. As it thumped shut, Gisbourne heard the lid of his coffin being pegged down.

He dragged the pillow out from beneath his head and dropped it over his face. *I wish I had the wherewithal to smother myself.*

Will Scarlet's face assumed a peculiar ashen hue. "Is it true?" he rasped. "The *king* knighted you?"

"At Acre." Robin left it at that.

Alan nodded, smiling. "Where the Lionheart broke down the Saracen walls along with Saracen hearts."

"You," Clym said; as much a challenge as a comment. "A pretty boy like you?"

"Leave it," Adam Bell said, though his gaze was fixed on Robin. "If 'tis true—"

"It is," Alan interposed.

Heedless, Bell went on. "—and you *are* a knight, what were you doing in the depths of Sherwood Forest?"

"The woman," Scarlet growled. "You came for her, didn't you?"

Robin smiled. "I believed it a proper response for a knight to make: to rescue the maiden in distress."

Much stirred. "Marian."

Scarlet looked at Robin sidelong: a dog who has met his match, yet still wary of surrender. "I only took her to get away. I thought she was a Norman. I thought she was the sheriff's leman."

"I told you she wasn't!" Little John grated. "And even if she was, she wasn't deserving of *that*—"

"Normans," Scarlet declared, "deserve whatever we can give them—"

"So you kill them!" The giant was angry. "Four of them, they said—'twas why they meant to hang you."

"Aye," Scarlet snapped. "It's in the Bible, the priests say: an eye for an eye. They killed my Meggie, giant! *Four* of the bloody Normans killed my wife!"

No one answered that. Robin was aware of an odd thrumming tension, like a bowstring strung too tight. Clym was red-faced, with a glitter in his eyes; William of Cloudisley merely looked thoughtful; Adam Bell was chewing absently at a thumbnail. Robin wondered if each of them recalled the crimes for which they'd been outlawed.

He looked at Cloudisley, likely no older than he. *Poacher?* Perhaps. Wat One-Hand, yes. *He paid the price for it.* And possibly Bell as well, though he'd been a yeoman, and probably in service to a wealthy lord. *A man that skilled with a longbow is worth keeping on.* Then again, maybe not poaching. "Who did you kill?" Robin asked.

Bell's eyes narrowed. Then he hitched a shoulder. "Alehouse brawl," he answered. "A man in my company. No loss; he was a *Saxon.* They meant to maim me, like Wat, but a friend set me free. I've been free ever since, living among the shadows."

Robin nodded. "The Normans have only themselves to blame for the men of Sherwood Forest." He looked then at Clym, who glared balefully. *He still wants to fight.* Robin leaned forward. Without heat, he said, "If you will come to Huntington, I will see to it you're given a sword."

"Into the earl's clutches?" Clym bared yellowed teeth. "I'm not that much a fool."

"Into the earl's clutches?—no." Robin relaxed, gathering reins; Clym was no longer an issue. "He'd never foul his hands. As for *me,* well—" He shrugged. "A man soaked in the blood of Saracens is already dirty enough."

Something flickered in Clym's hard eyes. "I'll not kill the king's own knight." He released the reins. Grudgingly, he muttered, "I'd have gone on Crusade myself, but I was already outlawed."

Robin shook his head. "The king could have used you. He could have used all of you." He looked at each man in the group. "There are ways of buying pardons."

Scarlet laughed bitterly. "What good does *that* do, then? The king's in Germany!"

Robin pressed bootheels into the horse's flanks. "There are ways of buying kings."

He didn't bother to gallop. Clym, Cloudisley, or Bell, regardless of speed, could stop his departure with a single well-placed arrow.

"Nottingham?" he asked.

Much shifted closer. "Nott-ham."

Called before her father so he could explain his plans for her future, Eleanor managed first to close her mouth, which took an extra effort, only to open it again immediately and snap out a succinct refusal. "Marry that fool? You must be mad."

He drank again. "I've told Gisbourne. He was delighted, of course; how better to secure a place with an employer on the verge of rising much higher than even *he* anticipated?"

That caught her attention. He was plotting something again. Undoubtedly Prince John would want to be told of it.

Eleanor curbed her anger. She softened her tone. "How *much* higher?"

"Very high indeed." Her father smiled. "I thought it might interest you."

"It does." She smiled guilelessly. "What do you mean to do?"

Blandly, he said, "Serve my king."

Which one? Eleanor's eyes narrowed. *The present king, or the man who wants to be king?* Inwardly, she chafed. *Why can't he speak more plainly? I dare not ask him—he will tumble to my game.* "So," she prevaricated, "you are in line for something better than the office you hold now."

"I never planned to be sheriff forever," he told her. "You know me well enough, Eleanor . . . in my position, you would be no more satisfied with Nottinghamshire than I, when there is better in the offing."

"Indeed," she agreed.

"But naturally there are family responsibilities I must tend to first, such as arranging the marriage of my last daughter." He sipped again. "I had hoped for better, of course, but your folly with the minstrel has changed my plans. You will marry Gisbourne. It should suit you both, I think."

Eleanor managed to keep her tone light. "I do not *wish* to marry Gisbourne." *And I won't. I'll find some way to stop it.*

"Your wishes are no longer my concern. Leave me, Eleanor. I have things to consider."

"Gisbourne," she muttered, in direst contempt.

Her father, amused, had the last word as she tugged open the door. *"So* well suited."

She thumped it shut behind her.

The streets of Nottingham were muddy and clogged with refuse, redolent of waste. Robin reined in the horse at Market Square amidst the normal bustle. People slipped and slid, skirts and hosen stiff with mud.

Much scrambled down nimbly from the horse. There was no doubt in Robin's mind the boy could disappear easily enough, but it still concerned him that Much might be caught by the sheriff's men. "Be wary of Normans."

Much gazed up at him. *"Lion*heart."

Robin smiled, reaching to pat the boot where he'd tucked his recovered purse. "Lionheart," he agreed.

Much grinned gloriously, then darted away. He was lost to sight instantly.

Robin stared after him. He understood Much well enough: the boy wanted him to use the returned coin toward the Lionheart's ransom, something he was willing to do. But there was more in the boy's words, more in the boy's eyes. What else did Much expect him to do?

Steal? he wondered. Robin smiled wryly. *Ransom Richard with coin stolen from others . . . wouldn't* that *amuse the king!*

It would also buy him back.

Robin's smile disappeared. Scowling fiercely, he reined the horse around and headed out of Nottingham toward his father's lands.

Tuck sweated nervously, shifting from foot to foot as Walter knocked on the door before them. The sheriff had upset him with scurrilous talk and innuendo, but he wasn't certain telling Sir Guy of Gisbourne all about it was the best thing to do. Perhaps if nothing were said, it would simply go away.

A testy voice called to them to enter. Walter, nodding satisfaction, undid the latch and pushed the door open. The monk followed hesitantly, moving aside as Walter waited impatiently to close the door. Privacy was necessary, but it made Tuck feel more guilty than ever before. He stuck his hands into his sleeves and waited mutely.

Sir Guy of Gisbourne, in bliaut and soiled hosen—one fabric leg was entirely cut off—was slumped against pillows, scowling at them both. He was a dark-hued man gone pale, face drawn and stubbled, with one bare, bandaged leg propped up on a bolster. "What is it?" he asked wearily.

"This is Brother Tuck." Walter's gesture was quick and perfunctory. "Do you remember? We wrote Abbot Martin when Brother Hubert died . . . this is his replacement."

Gisbourne grunted. "So I see." He shifted slightly, wincing.

Walter looked expectantly at Tuck. "Tell him, Brother. Tell him everything."

"But—I—"

"Everything."

Tuck told Gisbourne everything.

Eleanor halted outside the door. It was a distasteful and wildly inappropriate thing she proposed to do, but she was past being disposed to conduct her affairs with regard to propriety. The issue was serious. If she did not take pains to settle it, her entire life could be ruined.

She drew in a deep breath, arranged her expression into a suitably pleasant one, then rapped on the door. After a moment it was opened. "Sir Guy—" she began, then broke it off in surprise. The face staring back at her was not Gisbourne's. "Walter," she said, "what are *you* doing here?"

Almost at once she regretted the question, since it reflected poorly on her good sense; Walter was, after all, Gisbourne's assistant, and had more reason to be in his chamber than anyone else, most particularly herself.

But Walter seemed disinclined to remark upon it. "Lady Eleanor?"

"I've come to see Sir Guy."

Walter nodded. "Aye, he's here. And Brother Tuck."

"Who?"

"Brother Tuck." Walter swung the door open more widely. "Brother Hubert's replacement."

The monk was immensely fat, brown of hair and eyes, and obviously deeply concerned about something. He appeared to be on the verge of tears. Eleanor scowled at him briefly; her business was much more important, and she resented his presence.

She transferred her gaze from monk to seneschal. "Sir Guy. There is something we must address."

Eleanor had never so much as approached him in the hall. That she approached him now in his *chamber* was unusual in the extreme; it put her at a decided disadvantage. She saw the bafflement, then comprehension. She had never considered Gisbourne capable of much thought beyond plaguing castle inhabitants with countless economies designed, she was quite certain, for the sole purpose of inconveniencing them. She distrusted his expression. She distrusted the glint in his eyes.

"Lady Eleanor," he said. "Pray, do come in."

She drew herself up rigidly. "This is a private matter."

"I know." He seemed to savor the moment. "Walter, I thank you for bringing Brother Tuck. I assure you, I'll think upon your words."

Eleanor stood aside as Walter and the fat monk departed, then moved into the room. She considered leaving the door open, then shrugged inwardly—what did it really matter?—and swung the door shut.

Gisbourne lay propped against pillows with his bandaged leg raised. She spared it an uninterested glance, then concentrated on the matter at hand. "Has my father approached you with regard to me?"

His dark face was wan, but the light in his eyes was bright. "Indeed he has."

Eleanor folded her hands primly. "We would not be well matched."

Gisbourne startled her by smiling widely. "No, we would not."

It took her off stride. She dropped courtesy entirely, speaking bluntly. "I think it's a perfectly despicable idea."

"So do I."

She frowned. This attitude was not at all what she had anticipated from him. "Why?"

"Because we do not suit."

"No," she agreed uncertainly. "I have told my father so—"

"You can tell your father nothing." He shifted slightly, grimacing, then smiled faintly at her. "He would no more listen to me than listen to you. He has *decided;* therefore, it shall be so."

She nodded. "We must see that it's stopped."

"I intend to."

Suspicion bloomed. "How?"

"I have just come into some information that may prove valuable."

"What did Walter tell you?" And then, more sharply, "What has that fat monk to do with anything?"

Gisbourne folded his hands across his belly. Save for the propped up leg and his disarray, he exuded the attitude of a man well contented with his lot—and his special knowledge. It infuriated her. "Your father," he began simply, "has seen to it a man was hanged."

She allowed her contempt to show. "He hangs men all the time, Gisbourne. He's the sheriff."

His stubbled face flushed dully. "He hanged the *wrong* man. Purposely. Merely to suit Prince John, so the prince would not learn that Scarlet had escaped."

Eleanor laughed. "Wise man, my father—the prince could relieve him of his office for losing a man who killed four of his men." Amusement died. "So, you're suggesting you'll inform Prince John of this?"

"No. I'm suggesting *we* inform your father we know all about it. There is no need to bring the prince into it. That might result in further difficulties."

Eleanor nodded slowly. *Your own, no doubt.* "I see." She spoke with clear preciseness. "You are willing to do this—you share all of this with me—simply because you want so badly *not* to marry me."

He went very still. She was secretly amused to see his realization of how the truth might sound to her, whom he did not desire to marry. It was a damning admission to a woman who had the wit to use it to her advantage. He had destroyed himself, if she chose to pursue it.

Eleanor laughed. "It doesn't matter," she said. "I want you

even less than you want me." She eyed him pointedly, under-scoring her distaste. "But there is something more. We must also prevent my father from marrying the FitzWalter girl."

Color suffused his face. His dark eyes glittered. "Indeed," he said quietly.

Abruptly, Eleanor knew. It filled her with helpless rage and envy—did every man alive want to take that woman to bed?—but she did not show it to him. "I won't have it," she said curtly. "I won't have her here."

"You won't have to have her here." Gisbourne resettled his leg. "I've spoken to the monk."

Eleanor frowned. "What has the *monk* to do with this?"

Gisbourne laughed. "Everything."

DeLacey lifted his goblet in tribute as his furious daughter departed. The solution was ideal. He should have thought of it before, except then he'd hoped for better in the Earl of Hunt-ington's son. Now that hope was gone, but she was here, and *Gisbourne* was here; the perfect solution was to give them to one another.

He grinned. He drank wine. Then his reverie was interrupted by a knock upon the door.

DeLacey swore frightfully—would they never leave him alone?—then waved a hand at the door that no one on the other side could see. "Come," he called.

The door creaked. A hesitant voice told him he had a visitor.

DeLacey sighed. "I have visitors all the time. I'm the sheriff." He turned his head. "Who is it this time?"

"Lady Marian FitzWalter."

"Marian . . ." He slammed down the goblet, heedless of spilled wine. "Send the monk to me at once."

The servant was baffled. "My lord?"

"The monk, the *monk*—the fat man, Brother Tuck!"

"Aye, my lord." The servant bowed himself out and tugged the door shut.

DeLacey stared fixedly into the distance. Then he pulled himself from the chair to thrust a victorious arm into the air. "Marian!" he exulted.

Fifty-Three

Thunderheads massed in the distance. The air tasted thick and cool: a mantle of steel and slate draped over the battlements of Huntington Castle.

The earl himself walked the walls proudly with Eustace de Vesci, Henry Bohun, and Geoffrey de Mandeville, pointing out certain modern refinements worked upon older fashions in parados and parapets in addition to machicolations, when Ralph brought him good news: the man who had just ridden so noisily into the inner bailey was his absent son, home at last.

The earl, who had maintained a calm facade regarding his son's absence, thanked Ralph politely, sent him to direct his son to them, then turned quietly to the others. "Our plans may now proceed."

De Vesci grunted. "So. Will he throw in his lot with us?"

The earl's wispy white hair was ruffled in the breeze pregnant with incipient rain. "He is my son."

"Sons do not always accede to their father's wishes." De Mandeville's tone was dry. He stood at the square crenel notch between two upright merlons and surveyed the bailey below as Huntington's heir dismounted. "The Old King might have lost his crown because of his sons . . . can you afford to be so certain yours will cooperate?"

"Henry's sons fought among themselves because of overweening ambition and Angevin bad temper," the earl retorted. "They were the Devil's Brood, after all; each one feared the other might supplant him in matters of precedence—*this* situation is quite different."

Henry Bohun, arms crossed, leaned idly against a merlon with the sky a glaucous tapestry behind him. "It would seem more realistic to expect your son to cooperate . . . after all, there is no telling how high he might rise as son-in-law to John."

De Vesci swore. "Especially if John becomes king."

"He will not," de Mandeville declared. "Do you think the barons will accept him? Do you think the *people* will?"

Bohun shook his head. "The people will do as they're told. They are sheep, nothing more . . . if John makes himself the bellwether, they'll follow quickly enough."

"But *we* will not," de Vesci said. "By God, we will not."

The earl smoothed his robe. "Ralph will bring him to us."

Marian dismounted and handed off her mount in the bailey of Nottingham Castle, waiting impatiently as Joan did the same. The serving-woman was swathed in folds of wool, her older face concerned. She had spoken of rain repeatedly on the road from Ravenskeep, but Marian—convinced if she did not confront the sheriff now she would never find the courage to do it again—refused to consider turning back.

Wind curled into the bailey, snatching at her draped hood. Marian caught at the fabric, slid it back into place over hair brushed and braided, then ran over again in her mind the things she wanted to say, and how she intended to say them.

Marian led the way inside the hall, digging rigid fingers into the weave of her woolen mantle. She felt oddly hollow and fragile, like a bubble made of glass, tense with nerves and imaginings: she would prove weak, and give in; she would be unable to explain how she felt; she would play into his hands. But then she thought of how he had attempted to assume control of her future, and cold anger replenished her conviction.

Marian halted just inside and slipped her hood, telling a servant they desired to see the sheriff. "This won't take long," she told Joan firmly as the servant left, to convince herself as much as the woman, who understood none of it.

DeLacey came swiftly into the hall, holding out both hands in warm, disarming welcome. "Marian!" He came forward smoothly, glancing briefly at Joan, then back to Marian. His tone was perfectly normal. "I cannot tell you what a great pleasure this gives me. When I left Ravenskeep, I expected you to take much more time before arriving at your decision."

He believes he's won. Astonished, Marian gazed at him; she thought she'd been clear at Ravenskeep. *He does—he simply assumes he's won, because he always wins.* The knowledge appalled her. The audacity of William deLacey shattered her fear completely, leaving anger in its place. It pleased her to be angry. She could rely upon it.

"My lord, I fear you misunderstand." She decided to say it all at once instead of dancing around it. "This is not intended as a social call, nor to bring you the answer you appear to believe was a foregone conclusion."

"Marian." His hands dropped. He glanced again at Joan. "Welcome to Nottingham Castle," he said. "The kitchens lie there, behind the screen—I will send for you when your lady and I are done with our business."

It was an abrupt dismissal. Marian opened her mouth to protest, but Joan merely nodded and turned away. *Don't let him begin first.* "My lord—"

"Now." DeLacey caught her hand and hooked it over his elbow, turning her toward the dais on which his chair and table sat. "You are out of temper, I see . . . forgive me, then, for being abrupt. Our meeting yesterday was upsetting, of course, and for that I am sorry. It has not been much beyond a year since your father died—"

Marian stopped short and jerked her arm free. *Don't let him see you angry . . . he'll use it as a weapon.* She knew him well now, well enough to seek out her own weapons in his eyes and posture. "This call has nothing to do with that."

He swung toward her, cutting her off as he did so often, standing very close, too close, as if his nearness might intimidate her. "But of course it does. You know very well your father would have wanted us to marry—it merely upsets you that you appear to have no say in the matter." He linked hands behind his back in an easy, unperturbed manner that did not fool her one bit. She was beginning to learn the signs of consternation:

a tension in spine and shoulders, an intensity in his eyes, the faint, cool smile that betokened displeasure.

Don't delay—"My lord—"

He turned as if to walk away in idle reflection, then arrested the motion and swung back. "But Marian, when *does* a woman have say in the matter? And I say, why should she?" He gestured to dilute the brutal words. "I don't mean to distress you, but women are fanciful creatures much given to unrealistic dreams . . . it is part of what makes men desire to protect them." He was ineffably gentle. "I beg you, look at my daughter, if you will. Eleanor is well-nigh ungovernable, a spoiled, undisciplined woman who seeks only to gratify the dictates of her body." He lifted his shoulders in a slight dismissive shrug; he had given up on shielding his daughter against the onslaughts of loose tongues. "Look what it has brought her," he said evenly. "She is disgraced. Despoiled. No decent man will have her to wife."

Marian wanted to laugh. It rang so false; for how long had she been deaf? With subtle derision, she suggested, "Except Gisbourne, of course."

She saw a flicker of displeasure in his gaze. "Gisbourne does as I tell him."

"Then he has no more freedom than Eleanor, or I." She wet dry lips, feeling more certain of her course. He had given her the arrows; now she had only to aim and loose. "I think you depend too much upon your own designs, my lord. I think you dismiss even the idea that a woman might have her own feelings and preferences about such things as marriage—"

"Undoubtedly she *does*," he interrupted, "but that is beside the point. The issue at hand is whether a woman can possibly understand that other things influence the decision to marry than merely the tender heart." He gestured briefly, indicating a door leading out of the open hall. "Come with me. We will adjourn to my solar. This is best discussed in private."

Marian did not move. "We will discuss it here."

He turned back after a slight hesitation, lowering his arm. His displeasure intensified, but it did not touch his manner in obvious ways, only in the small ones she had learned to recognize. "Very well. Then let me be quite frank." His smile was cool, his gaze intense. "For the moment we will make it a given: you may consider yourself a fair judge of whom you should marry."

"Generous." She wished she could swear like a man.

"Your situation echoes Eleanor's to an alarming degree," he told her bluntly. "Forgive my candor, but what man in England would choose to marry a despoiled daughter of a dead knight whose manor has fallen into disarray?"

He did not attack her personally. She had expected that, prepared to let his insinuation do no damage. But he had aimed at another target, and his skill at placing the arrow stung her sharply. "Ravenskeep has nothing to do with this!"

The passion of her response pleased him, which infuriated her. "But it does. You see?" He laughed softly. "Already you dismiss, womanlike, a very important aspect of marriage." The laughter dropped away. His tone now was icy, promising no quarter in the battle for which she had begged. "Men of rank concern themselves with everything, Lady Marian. With a woman's name, her rank, her family, her person, her holdings, her dowry. What have you to offer?"

She had lost ground by replying with heat to his mention of Ravenskeep. *Give him nothing—be a mirror—Reflect what* he *offers.* Marian smiled as coolly, displaying what she had learned. "What little I have to offer—despoiled as I am, shabby as Ravenskeep is—still appears to be more than enough to interest *you.*"

She saw the blow go home, but did not rejoice. She would be a good mirror: glass, not polished steel, with chipped and ragged edges so as to trap an unwary hand.

He marshaled his offense swiftly, attempting another direction. "I cared very much for your father—"

"Oh, *don't!*" she snapped, annoyed with herself that she had ever been such a fool as to believe in anything he said; equally annoyed with the man himself, who believed her so malleable. "This has nothing whatsoever to do with my father. This has to do with me." Marian no longer cared who might hear. "And *you,* my lord."

"Marian—"

It was her turn to cut him off. "Despoiled, am I? Very well, my lord—let me put it plainly: a despoiled woman may have lost her virtue, but she loses none of her sense. I am not a fool, despite your conviction otherwise, and you do not convince me to surrender my will to you. I know what you want. I know also it has very little to do with Ravenskeep, or my name." Decisively, Marian shook her head. "I was ignorant for too long, blinded by innocence—did you count on that, my lord?—but no longer. I know what you want—I know *precisely* what you want"—she weighted her words with care—"and I refuse absolutely to give you any of it."

Finally she had reached him. DeLacey's face took flame. "By God—"

"No," she said, "by me. This is *my* decision, not yours. I base it not on rank and name and holdings, but on one simple fact"—she leaned close, as he had, speaking with careful clarity so there would be no misunderstanding—"I have no desire— nor even the slightest intention—to bed with you."

Marian waited unflinchingly, expecting perhaps to be struck, or shouted at, or otherwise abused. But the sheriff did none of those things. He turned slightly and raised his voice. "Walter!"

A man appeared hastily. "My lord?"

"Fetch Tuck," deLacey commanded crisply. "Fetch my daughter. Fetch six men for guard duty."

Walter was clearly baffled. "My lord—where?"

"Here," deLacey declared. "At once, if you please. The Lady Marian and I have an issue to be settled."

"Aye. Aye, my lord." Walter disappeared.

"What issue?" she asked suspiciously. "I have settled my issue. And why men for guard duty?"

The sheriff sighed. "There are outlaws in Sherwood Forest. I would be a poor friend of your father if I did not see you safely home again."

"See me *home*—" It was not at all what she expected.

"Of course," he said quietly. "I am not a monster, Marian, no matter what you may believe. I leave the decision to you—" he smiled sadly, "—to prove my faith in you. You may stay the night, if you like, so you and your woman are not caught in the rain . . . or leave as soon as the guard arrives."

Marian stared at him. "Did what I said mean nothing to you?"

"Indeed, *yes*. It meant everything." His expression was oddly tranquil. "As you will see in a moment."

Robin clattered into Huntington's bailey, swung off the horse, then handed the reins over as a horseboy came running. "He's warm," Robin warned him. "Walk him first, then put him in deep bedding. I'll not have him going home sore."

The boy bobbed his head. "Aye, my lord."

Robin briefly pressed the boy's shoulder, then strode beyond him toward the keep. His mind was full of Marian and what he would say to his father.

"My lord." It was Ralph, coming out of the shadowed door. "My lord, your father desires to see you."

Robin stopped. "I imagine he does." He smiled at the quiet man he'd known for all of his life. "I imagine he intends to chide me for disappearing as I did."

Ralph reproached him gently. "My lord, you must admit you left him with no word."

"I am not a boy anymore."

"He knows that."

"Does he?" Robin's faint smile was dry. "Are you very certain, Ralph? Methinks he considers me not much older than six or seven."

"Ten or twelve, my lord." Ralph was unsmiling. "He places great faith in you."

"Indeed." Robin sighed. "Very well—where is he?"

Ralph indicated the earl's direction. "There, on the wall."

Robin looked. He squinted slightly: his father and three others were silhouetted against the ashen sky. "Who are those men with him?"

"I believe he would wish to tell you himself."

"Ah. Of course." Irritated, Robin was tempted to ignore the summons. He was full of Marian still, wanting nothing more than to tell his father about her. But to anger his father now would win him nothing. "Ralph—" He turned back, aware of rising tension and bitterness. "How do I get up there?" It was galling to admit he did not know.

Ralph pointed. "The steps are there, my lord."

He looked. So they were: a diagonal slash rising from cobbles to sentry-walk set obliquely from the gate. Grimly he nodded, then crossed the bailey to the steps.

He reached the sentry-walk and paused a moment, reassembling wits and courtesy, for to confront his father in anger in front of witnesses would shatter his intentions—and destroy the possibility of their success—before he had the chance to explain anything to the earl.

In war, it was easier. There was neither the time nor inclination for so much diplomacy—one killed, or one was killed.

He walked to the four men quietly, trying to assess the earl's temper. He knew the other men slightly. He knew their proper titles. He knew without a doubt that none of them had come merely to bid him welcome home.

Robin halted as he reached them and inclined his head. "My lords." And lastly to his father, with a cool correctness that did not in any way reflect what he was thinking, "My lord Earl."

"Robert!" It was de Vesci, very bluff, striding forward to clasp his shoulder. "What great news it was, that you had escaped the clutches of the Saracen to come home again to England!"

"Indeed," de Mandeville agreed more quietly, "and a hero to boot."

"Our liege honored me greatly." They were all Richard's men, he knew. De Mandeville, the Earl of Essex and Justiciar of England, had taken part in Richard's coronation. "My lord father, perhaps I would do well to excuse myself. Obviously this meeting is of great significance, and would do better with my absence."

"No, no." De Vesci again. "It involves you, Robert."

Bohun nodded. "And the Count of Mortain."

Robin looked at each of them a very long moment. Rising wind ruffled their hair and lifted the corners of the mantles thrown over their shoulders. Four men: four extremely wealthy and influential lords. They could plot the course of England.

Which no doubt is what they do. He saw no reason to prevaricate; he had spent too much of his life doing so. Robin turned to his father. "Is this treason, my lord?"

Rather than being appalled by the audacity, the earl smiled.

"The man we seek to displace is not the king, Robert . . . but the man who *wants* to be king. There is something of a difference."

"So." It was worse than he'd feared. Robin drew in a slow breath, then released it. "And you want me to join you." He nodded. "Perhaps Ralph was right. Perhaps you do consider me a man at last—or else still merely a boy who can be pushed this way and that."

"Robert!" The earl's color deepened.

Robin glanced briefly at the others and noted their consternation. Had they counted him in already? Did they fear he might betray them? "Forgive me, my lords," he said smoothly. "War does hone a tongue into curtness. If I speak too plainly, it is because the king desired it." He evoked Richard purposely; it would make these men think. "Did my father promise me to you? Did he swear to my willingness?" Their silence and exchanged glances was confirmation. Robin nodded, glancing sidelong at his father. "So. What is it I am to be? A figurehead hero? The king's sworn knight? A man to hail to others whose allegiance may flag?"

The earl was coldly furious. "Don't you see? We do this for England! Look at Geoffrey de Mandeville, of one of the oldest and finest families in all of Britain—do you think *he* would countenance this if there were no reason for it?"

"Perhaps not," Robin conceded. "Perhaps I misjudge the cause; I have been too long away." He swept each of them with a glance, then turned to his father. "What do you want me for?"

The earl's tone was inflexible. "To misdirect John."

"How?"

"By marrying his daughter."

Oddly, Robin felt no anger. It was very clear to him: this was the easiest and most effective of ways. It was done all the time, regardless of the ages of those deemed marriageable, regardless of their wishes. They were simply chattel to be used to the benefit of whatever design the parents deemed most valuable.

He was in that moment completely detached, looking at the problem as his father undoubtedly did, weighing possibilities and other repercussions. *There is no other way. This solves everything.*

Robin smiled grimly, though he offered no reply. The words

on his tongue were neither proper nor flattering, but packed with the passion of a man who saw his future reshaped by the hands of another who did not understand him.

De Vesci stirred, reaching up to pull back into place a wind-tangled mantle. "She has been offered, has she not? Joanna?"

The breeze lifted hair away from Robin's face, baring the scar at his hairline. He saw their eyes upon it; saw them consider it, recalling where he had been, what he had done, and with whom he had been as he did it. To them he was, unexpectedly, Sir Robert of Locksley, knighted by the king.

Robin's detachment abruptly shattered. He felt cold, *too* cold; his jaw moved stiffly. He realized that what he felt was anger, a deep abiding anger that could, if it took flame, blister all of them. "Forgive me. This is a new thought." He found the mask within and slipped it on again. It was easy. It was familiar. It was immensely comfortable.

"Of course it is," de Vesci said, laughing. "It is not every day a man is faced with the possibility of marrying into royalty!"

Robin favored him with a steadfast gaze. "Indeed."

"Misdirection," the earl said tightly. "If you wed his daughter, John will think us fairly caught, victims of his plotting."

"But you will take care to insure that he is a victim of *yours*."

Geoffrey de Mandeville's eyes narrowed. He was not a fool, Robin knew; de Vesci might be too quick to assume Huntington's heir was on their side, but the Earl of Essex was not.

Henry Bohun stirred, leaning one hip against a merlon. "England is in a sorry state," he said. "John is systematically raping our economy—"

"The king did much the same," Robin interrupted. "Its cause was the Crusade, not personal greed, but the result is as much his responsibility as John's."

De Vesci glowered. "Do you support Softsword? After riding with his brother?"

"I do not support John." He spoke with careful conciseness so they would not misunderstand. "I swore to serve the king, and I do wholeheartedly. What I question is the motivation."

"You *have* been gone too long." Robin knew that tone: his father was highly displeased. His son had dared to criticize him in front of his peers. "So long, in fact, you have absolutely no understanding of how things stand in England."

That was true, but he could give them nothing. "I understand that England is indeed very poor. I also understand that she must be made poorer, if we are to buy back her king."

"*Damn* you!" The earl trembled with anger. "Do you question your father? Do you question your betters?"

"No," he answered coolly. "Only your plans for me."

De Vesci swore. "By God, you were quick enough to take the Crusader's oath and ride off to the Holy Land! But now that we ask a simple thing of you—"

"Simple? To marry John's daughter?" Robin shook his head. "It's his ploy, my lords . . . why make it yours?"

"Because the only way you can beat John is to use his methods," the earl snapped. "He is not a fool, Robert; don't assume he has no resources. But if we appear to do as he wishes, we can use it for our own good."

Robin shrugged. "If marrying one of your people to John's bastard girl will help save England, then by all means do it. All I would ask is that you look to someone else for your sacrificial lamb."

"Robert!" Huntington was nearly purple. "By God, boy—"

"My lords." He turned to them. "My lords, I do apologize, but I have no doubt there are alternative plans. Until twelve days ago you could not even be certain I was alive; until *four* days ago no one even knew John planned to dangle this girl as bait." He bowed with careful grace. "If you will excuse me . . . I was ill overnight." Before his father could mouth another protest, Robin turned on his heel and strode back down the sentry-walk to the stairs.

He is the same man he was when I left England . . . the same man he was when my mother died— He shut it off abruptly as he descended stiffly. What had he expected? That his return from the dead would alter his father's character? Only a fool would think so. Only a dreamer could. The Earl of Huntington had been shaped decades ago, long before he married a fey, ethereal woman utterly alien to his ken, before any of his children were born, before any of them died. *Save the last one: me.* He sighed heavily as his boot struck the cobbles of the bailey. *It will be more difficult than I thought.*

Tuck was in the chapel praying when Walter opened the door. He heard the scrape of wood on stone and swung painfully on his knees, fearful of the message.

Walter's face was taut. "He wants you," he said. "It's come, Brother Tuck."

Tuck hung there a moment, unable even to breathe. And then the breath started again, filling up his chest, and he knew he could not give it all to God. He had been weak, and a fool, succumbing to a will much firmer than his own, as he always did. As he always had.

Tuck sighed heavily, admitting a thing he had no desire to acknowledge: that there were times when a man, with only the *assistance* of God, had to make his own decisions.

He nodded at Walter, wiping a trembling hand over his damp, fleshy face. Then he turned back briefly to the altar, crossed himself with crisp, deliberate precision, and climbed ponderously to his feet.

He wants you, Walter had said. *It's come, Brother Tuck.*

He walked slowly and mechanically toward the narrow door.

Fifty-Four

Robin walked into the great hall of Huntington Castle and stopped deliberately in the center. Gravely he studied the immensity of masonry, the timber floor covered with rushes, the architectural advancement his father said were trusses, which

538

held up the roof through the use of elaborate arched vaults instead of relying on columns; and indeed, the roof *did* stay up, rising above his head in seductive symmetry. Painted silks hung over walls, and the ornate musician's gallery stretched from side to side like a walkway to heaven itself.

Lastly he looked at the dais, upon which he had stood with the earl to receive much of England in celebration of his return.

Robin smiled. *And Marian.*

He recalled it very vividly: the moment she'd stopped before him to make her little speech. She had been to him then as all the others, merely a woman, until he allowed her beauty to register so strongly as to deny it absolutely, because he dared not let close a woman to a man as defiled as he; and then her name had trapped him utterly: Marian FitzWalter, the daughter to whom Sir Hugh had charged him to carry a special message.

His slow smile stretched his bruised face, then altered into a grin of quiet satisfaction. He nodded, thinking of Marian, and turned to make his way out of the hall to the chamber serving as his own. He was brought up short by an unexpected discomfort in his left boot: his newly returned purse had worked its way too low, rubbing annoyingly against his ankle.

Robin bent and dug fingers deep between leather and hosen, working until he caught the severed thongs and dragged the pouch free. He hefted it assessively. From the weight, Much had spent none of it.

Lionheart, the boy had said. And why not? German Henry desired to be paid for his hospitality before he would consider releasing his honored guest. What England had raised so far simply was not enough. Perhaps it was time everyone contributed their purses.

He raked the hall with a glance of contempt. *My father might well have made his castle smaller and given the balance to the ransom—* And then he checked the thought. He had little money of his own, and Abraham the Jew said the Locksley rents were already depleted; what then was left? What resources *did* he have to donate to the cause?

Laggardly, he remembered. "My mother . . ." he murmured. *"Ya Allah,* I'd forgotten—"

He had resources yet: the casket of jewels she had willed upon her death to her only surviving child. She had meant it for his wife, but Robin had the feeling Marian wouldn't mind.

He strode out of the hall at last. His mother's jewels would do nicely. No doubt Abraham would give him a good price for them, and know how to send on the money.

DeLacey stood at an angle to Marian, shoulder turned obliquely. He glanced about casually as if to assess the ordering of his hall. In no way did he indicate the intensity of his anticipation as the moment drew nearer. He wanted to shout aloud exultantly, crying his jubilation, because to him it was as gratifying as carnal congress to witness a plan come together.

The sound of footsteps echoed sibilantly as the six-man guard came into the hall. From the corner of his eye he saw Marian turn her head to mark them, to watch in polite disinterest, believing them present merely to escort her home if she declared that her desire.

Tuck entered then, coming into candleglow out of dimness. His face was pale, but his gaze was clear and steady.

Good. He is prepared. DeLacey gestured slightly, indicating where Tuck was to stand. He drew in a deep breath, released it very slowly. *Now.* He savored the slight turn, the idleness of his gaze, the controlled approach. He felt much like one of his falcons, preparing to fold his wings and stoop upon the prey.

DeLacey smiled disarmingly, watching the play of emotions in Marian's face: curiosity, wariness, a subtle involuntary recoil. The bruises and scratches marring her beauty were still visible, but such disfigurements would fade. He would tend them himself.

He paused before her, deepened the warmth of his smile, then reached out smoothly and caught both her hands in his own. He did not permit her to withdraw them. "Marian," he said tenderly, "you know very well your father would approve."

In that instant, she understood. Vivid color stained her face. A flash in her eyes took him aback; not anger, as one might expect, but guilt. It was gone quickly, replaced fourfold by intense displeasure, but clearly there was more here than even he had anticipated.

Comprehension was abrupt. "By God—" he blurted, "he *did* want this—"

"No." She tried again unsuccessfully to pull her hands free. "If he knew what you truly were, he would never countenance friendship, let alone a marriage." She tugged ineffectually. "Let *go*—"

DeLacey was stunned. "I see it now. I see it now very clearly . . . he told you this before he left, but *you* decided to deny me—"

Her eyes were fever-bright with anger. "He did no such thing—"

"Or else he sent word." Shock was fading; his mind worked rapidly to assess the circumstances, to repair his broken approach. He understood now. "You must have known for some time what your father wanted . . . and it is your foolish woman's fancies that leads you to this folly—"

"It isn't folly to desire to make my own decision," she declared. Then, furiously, "Will you let *go*—?"

"Yes." And he did, but only briefly, long enough for him to shift his grip to her arms, to spin her in place so the guards were at her back and Tuck stood before her. "Marian, this is Father Tuck. I admit I had intended to act wholly selfishly in this, merely to please my own interests, but now I see there is much more to it than that. Indeed, I see that this is necessary if only to please your father." He nodded at Tuck. "Begin the ceremony."

The monk stared at Marian as if transfixed. Perspiration stippled his upper lip. His mouth trembled minutely.

"Father," deLacey said meaningfully, "pray, begin the ceremony."

Tuck looked at him. "No."

DeLacey was astounded. "By God—you *will*—"

"By God, I will not." Tuck smiled nervously at Marian. "Be at ease, lady—I am monk, not priest. Nothing here is binding."

Marian tore free. DeLacey looked only at Tuck. "Fool," he said softly. "O corpulent, fatuous fool, who once was a monk but shall end his days as nothing."

Tuck's eyes filled with tears, but his gaze held steady. "Indeed," he said unevenly. "I should have refused you before."

DeLacey turned to the liveried guard. "Escort the Lady Marian to private chambers, and leave one of your number outside the door at all times." He cast her a pitying glance. "Your behavior merely proves that you require a man's guidance. Your father would be appalled."

Marian was furious. "By *your* behavior, yes—"

"Take her," he told the guard. "Lodge her most comfortably." He waved fingers in Tuck's direction, as if flicking off a distasteful substance. "Go," he said softly. "Be assured Abbot Martin will be informed."

A glint of rebellion flashed briefly in the monk's bovine eyes. "Have you anyone here who can *write?*"

DeLacey laughed. "There is always Gisbourne. There will always *be* a Gisbourne."

The earl paused silently in the open doorway, watching his son. That Robert was as yet unaware of his presence was obvious, or surely he would have instantly stopped the haphazard excavation of his trunks. Lids were raised on several, leaning against brick walls; contents spilled over the sides and out onto the floor; a pile of personal items was left in the center of the bed, heaped in disarray.

The untidiness offended the earl. *Did the boy learn nothing of neatness while on Crusade?*

"Robert." His lips thinned; he had come to speak of something else, but this was a beginning. It had never been easy to talk with his son as a boy; it was less easy now. "What are you doing?"

Startled, Robert stopped digging at once and jerked his head upright, swinging on his knees to stare blankly at his father. The earl marked all over again the bruises on his son's face, and the alteration of his expression from annoyed concentration to a rigid, frozen mask in which only the eyes were alive.

"Looking for something," Robert answered. Then, with infinite clarity, "Something of mine is missing."

"Nothing is missing," the earl retorted, irritated by the disarray that did not appear to disturb his son. "All was moved here from Huntington Hall. If you have lost something, it is due more to your habitual sloppiness than any inefficiency on the part of the servants."

Robert cast the open trunks a shuttered glance, and spared another for the pile of clothing in the center of his bed. Then his gaze returned to his father. "My mother's jewels are missing."

The earl blinked. He had not thought of the jewels in some time, nor the woman who had worn them. "Certainly not," he said crisply. "Do not lay blame where none is due; it is not appropriate behavior for men of rank." A gentle rebuke only. "I disposed of the jewels some time ago. Two years, in fact."

"Disposed—" Robert blanched very pale. The scar along his jaw stood out plainly. "By what right did you do that?"

The earl impatiently reminded his son of the ordering of their lives. "By the right of a husband, to whom all possessions pass upon the marriage sacrament."

Robert's hands gripped the trunk tightly. "She left her jewelry to me, to be bestowed upon the woman *I* marry."

Huntington permitted himself the luxury of faint contempt in order to make a point. "Do you believe Prince John will not provide better for his daughter than a handful of trumpery jewels?"

For a long moment Robert did not respond. Then he said in a deadly tone, "They were *hers.*" The bruises showed uglier against the pallor of anger. "When she died, they became mine; she told me so, my lord. She told me before she died."

Probably she had; it was very like her to impetuously give away something that belonged to her husband. "She was always too tender-hearted." The earl shook his head, smoothing the drape of his robe. "What does it matter, Robert? If you require money, you need only ask."

"Very well." The tone was dry. "Give me the loan of one hundred thousand marks."

"One hundred thousand!" The earl nearly gaped, but recovered himself in time to gaze sternly at his recalcitrant heir. "What is this babble, Robert? Have you gone mad?"

"Not for me, my lord. To buy back the King of England."

It was utterly preposterous. *Did the boy learn nothing at all of reality while in the Holy Land?* "A flight of fancy, Robert," he said heavily, intending to squash it flat. "Do you think I have given nothing toward the ransom? Do you think the Huntington coffers are bottomless?"

"Indeed, no. That is obvious, if you are moved to sell off what is not yours." Robert slammed down the trunk lid and got to his feet. "My lord, if you will excuse me—it will take some time to put order to my chamber."

The dismissal was obvious. *He's learned that of me, at least,* the earl reflected. "Robert, the Jews are not always the most patient of men—"

"So you gave them my mother's jewels as partial payment."

He had permitted the boy much latitude since his return. *It is time Robert recalls who the master is.* "I do as I see fit, with no seed of my loins rearing up to say me nay."

The contempt was brief, but plain. "No, my lord."

Anger flared dully within Huntington's narrow chest. "By God—do you question me yet? What I do, I do for England!"

"If your quarrel is with Prince John, would it not be more prudent to spend money on the king's return instead of on useless symbols?" Robert gestured with a hand. "The cost of this castle might have paid more than half the ransom."

The earl was truly annoyed. "This castle was begun before Richard was captured," he retorted. "It was begun before you left on Crusade, which you well know. These things take time."

Robert's face was tense. "Marrying me to John's bastard will not aid England."

"Is *that* it?" The earl's laugh was harsh. "Are we to that? By God, Robert, you are but a mummer in this play." He shook his head and sighed. "You assume the worst and respond without considering all the facts."

"My lord—"

"If John believes you the best match for his bastard, we would be a fool to say him nay. There is every chance the king may not return, leaving his brother to rule in his stead—"

"Why do you say the king may not return?"

"Because, given the opportunity—which he will concoct himself!—John will buy Henry's willingness to keep King Richard imprisoned." The earl was truly exasperated. *How can a son of my loins be so naive?* "By *God*, Robert—use your wits . . . John is a ruthless, ambitious man who wants to rule England! He will destroy whomever he must to win the throne, but he knows very well that while Richard lives he cannot . . . and since the king is now married, John must move very quickly to usurp the throne before an heir is born. It should be no surprise to you that he seeks to ingratiate himself with the finest families in England—he *needs* us! If enough of us moved to thwart him, we could bring him down."

"Then it is a true conspiracy."

"John would see it as such. Richard would applaud it; it is designed to keep his realm whole." The earl shook his head. "Much has happened while you were gone."

"Indeed, so it would seem." Bleakness replaced Robert's anger. "England is in greater danger than you believe. If there is no male heir, Richard will have to leave England to his brother."

"Naturally the king will see to it there is a son," the earl declared. "Undoubtedly it will be one of the first orders of business."

The answering silence was loud.

The implication infuriated the earl. "By God, Robert, you would have me think—" He broke off, dismay tempered by outrage. "Are you suggesting there is *truth* to that ridiculous rumor?" His face contorted. "That is a scurrilous falsehood put forth by John to discredit the king! You should know that better than anyone, Robert. Did the prince not accuse *you* of basest infamy?"

"He had reason," Robert said tightly. "There are those in the army who would swear I lay with the king."

The subject was highly distasteful. The earl said, "You told John he had mistaken you for the lute-player—"

"He had." Robert was very pale, speaking with precision. "It *was* Blondel, not I—but the king and I were intimate in matters of the spirit. There are those who will say whatever they wish to say."

The earl pressed an age-spotted hand against his chest. "My God, Robert—if the king sires no heir . . ."

"I find it doubtful he could, my lord. He has resided in a prison for nearly a year."

"When he returns—"

"*If* he returns—is that not what you suggested?"

The earl's breath ran short. "Kings understand they must sire heirs. It is imperative. He would not overlook that responsibility, Robert. I am certain of that." He had to be certain of it. He could not deal with the suggestion of perversity.

"He married Berengaria for two reasons only, my lord." Robert's voice was unrelenting. "To stop his mother's nagging—*Ya Allah,* can she nag!—and to gain allies for the Crusade from King Sancho of Navarre. Sancho would have done nothing until his daughter was safely wed . . . so Richard married her, my lord. In Cyprus, after he conquered it. Had Berengaria escaped the storm that drove her ship to Cyprus . . ." He shrugged implication. "Had Isaac Comnenus not insulted Richard by repeated discourtesies toward the future Queen of England, I doubt the wedding would have happened at all." He shook his head deliberately. "England would be far better off if she ransomed her king at once."

"There is no money," Huntington insisted. "The taxes have bled us dry." He saw his son's eloquent glance around the chamber. Testily he declared, "The castle is built, Robert. I cannot tear it down again merely to please your outraged sensibilities."

Robert's smile was slight. "Blame not John for your vanity. You built this castle for *you.*"

"And who shall inherit it, then? You blame me for taking jewels you claim your mother left to you—is *this* not enough?" A trembling hand stabbed out in a sharp gesture encompassing the chamber. "Which of us shall live more years inside these walls?"

It hit home, he saw, in the blaze of shame and anger. *"I* never wanted these walls!"

"Robert. *Robert—*" The earl spread his hands. "Look at me. I am old. All of my children save you are dust in the ground. And you also, I feared, when word came of your capture—" He swallowed painfully. "I had no one left. No wife, no sons, no daughters . . . the only thing I had was the shell of this castle. It was my duty to fill it."

The mask began to crack. "You began it *before* I left!"

Huntington nodded. "And I finished it in your name. It was all I had left, Robin." The use of the nickname was deliberate. "Stone in place of flesh. Memories in place of reality—"

"But I never was *here*," Robert cried. "If memories are what you desired, you should have stayed in Huntington Hall!"

The earl felt older yet. He had failed to make a man of his youngest, most fanciful son, who managed somehow to survive when none of the other boys did; it was God's most telling irony that wondrous Huntington Castle be left to an utter fool.

Even the Crusade had not proved beneficial. *Too soft,* the earl reflected. *Knighted or not, there is too much of his mother in him.*

Fifty-Five

Tuck methodically gathered together his few belongings, trying to think of nothing but each individual motion as a ritual of blessedly simple requirements: first this, then this, then this. Once the ritual was completed he paid his final addresses to God in the tiny castle chapel. The prayers were difficult: a part of him felt vindicated that he had at last refused to follow the orders of a man obviously damned, and had saved a woman's soul—and virtue—in the doing of it; but the other part of him quailed beneath the knowledge his religious vocation was doomed. A single letter to Abbot Martin would destroy his career, and he had no doubt the sheriff would send that letter.

Ponderously Tuck made his way through the hall to the keep door. It was there a woman met him: the sheriff's daughter,

Eleanor, who gave him a basket containing wrapped parcels. Food, she told him, and then directed him to wait outside the southern gatehouse after he had passed through.

Curiosity dissipated the dullness of his despair. He would never again accept anything at face value. "Why?"

Eleanor cast a brief glance over her shoulder, clearly irritated by the delay his question caused. "Do as I say," she snapped, as autocratic as her father, with less subtlety. "There is good reason, I promise you . . . after what you have already done, this won't prove a worthless task." Her mouth was a grim, fixed line in the sallow sullenness of her expression. "I do this for myself, but it will reflect well upon me regardless . . . remind God of that tonight, in your prayers."

He was confused. "Lady—"

"Just *go*," she hissed. "Wait beyond the gate, as I told you." Then, acidly, "Have you anything better to do?"

He had not, of course. Tuck nodded glumly and exited the keep.

DeLacey assumed an appropriately concerned expression as he faced Marian's attendant, the woman named Joan, behind the screen dividing hall from kitchen passageway. "So you see, I think it best she remain here until she is fully recovered. A slight fever only, but these things can prove dangerous if left untended."

Joan's frown betokened a difficulty. "She felt well enough earlier."

"I have known fevers to come on very quickly," he said calmly, as yet unruffled; he had dealt with worse than she. "It really is best if you go back."

"But shouldn't you let *me* tend her? She knows me, and would be more comfortable with me beside her."

DeLacey shook his head. He lied very well, because he took care to tell as much of the truth as possible, phrasing it in such a way as to put the woman at ease. "The Lady Marian is more concerned that Ravenskeep be put into proper order after the storm. She had not intended to remain here, of course . . . now she must, and she fears the villeins might succumb to idleness while she is away." He knew her villeins *were* idle, judging by the condition of the manor; he knew also Marian had not intended to stay after delivering her message.

All was confirmed in the woman's eyes. "Roger," she muttered grimly. "With so much work facing him, he'll likely run away again."

Inwardly he rejoiced. "There now, do you see? It will set her mind at ease if she knows you are there to oversee matters."

Twin lines knitted Joan's brows. "She caught it from him, I'll wager."

DeLacey frowned. "From whom?" A genuine fever, then, and probably a villein's; possibly even difficult Roger. Marian was one of those who took too personal an interest in how her peasants fared. *Another reason why she will do better married to me.*

"Sir Robert," the woman answered. "He stayed the night with fever after he brought her back from the boar hunt." Blue eyes were guileless; the woman spoke a version of the truth with no hint of special knowledge.

"Sir Robert of Locksley?"

"Aye, my lord. He left only this morning—she decided not long after to come here."

The timing was exquisite, too definitive for coincidence. He had never anticipated convincing Marian to marry him would be easy, but now he understood completely the newfound conviction that gave her the strength to oppose him even against her father's wishes.

She fancies herself in love.

He had known it from the first, from the moment he learned from Archaumbault that it was Locksley who had effected her rescue, Locksley who escorted her back to Ravenskeep. Had it not been for John's poorly timed arrival at Nottingham Castle, *he* might have been able to assume the role of the rescuer, supplanting the heroic Sir Robert.

Cold fury abraded his soul, but deLacey showed none of it to Joan. "I thank you for your concern; I will see to it your lady is told how reluctant you were to leave her. But I think it best. It may rain at any moment. She would be very foolish to court danger by riding home in poor weather."

Troubled, Joan nodded. "They'll have need of me there."

"To put—Roger—?" she nodded, "in his place, no doubt."
His tone was dry. "Some villeins are fools not to accept their
place."

"He's a troublemaker," she conceded. "I've no use for a man
like him; I told my lady many times she should send him off, but
she refuses."

"She is tender-hearted." A light touch on the woman's arm
turned her toward the kitchens. "Please, have a meal packed so
you may sup on the road. Your horse is being readied. I'll send
a man with you."

Joan's eyes were avid. "You'll send for me if she worsens?"

"At once," he assured her warmly.

Abraham the Jew was a kind man of infinite patience who
bore ill will toward no man because he believed it reflected
poorly on his faith. Why give a Christian the satisfaction of
claiming his belief in Jewish perfidy was proved by bad behavior? It was a far more telling blow, Abraham felt, to show
kindness to his tormentors, because the resultant frustration was
in its way a subtle sort of retribution.

Most galling, he knew, was that so very many Christian
nobles were required to borrow money, and to pay the loan
back with interest that benefited Jews. They were willing
enough to go into debt over this petty trifle or that, but utterly
*un*willing to understand that usury was a business, not a personal affront. And certainly not the sort of heinous transgression
punishable by insults and physical harm. Abraham himself was
known as a fair man—for a Jew—who did not unnecessarily
trouble a man for payment even when it was past due. He even
forgave some debts; he saw no sense, for instance, in asking a
poor widow to pay for her dead husband's folly.

Sir Robert of Locksley—*Robin*, he had said quietly—poked
the leather pouch on the table between them with a rigid finger.
His mouth was a thin, grim line. "Not enough, then."

In an attempt to mask much, the tone betrayed all. Abraham,
who understood more of empathy and sympathy than most
because his business bared a man's soul, felt sincere compassion. Gently he said, "I pray you, my young lord, consider it not

as a matter of amount, but a matter of business. The jewels were not given to me as surety against later payment in coin, but as partial payment of themselves."

The fair face blanched paler. "You sold them."

Abraham made a practiced gesture of helplessness that was, in this case, genuine. "There are circumstances when all a client may offer is something of the family—silver plate, jewelry—which serves me only as a means of discharging a debt, not as a personal item. Therefore if someone expresses an interest in purchasing the item, I accept the transaction."

Robin nodded tightly. "I understand."

Without question, Abraham knew; some of them did. "I am sorry, my lord." He truly was. There were those who came to him with glib falsehoods designed to win his trust or his compassion, but he had trained himself very young to distinguish between truth and falsehood. Huntington's heir told the truth, but expected no largesse. He intended to buy back his legacy. "There is nothing I can do."

Robin nodded again. "They were not for me," he said quietly. "Yes, originally—she meant them for my wife, when I married—but not now. I intended to send them to Chancellor Longchamp, for the king's ransom."

"Ah." First a start of surprise, then Abraham suppressed the accompanying twinge of dismay that threatened to alter the professional neutrality of his tone. Mildly he said, "Then you would do better to give your money to the sheriff."

"Then one might suppose William deLacey has replaced Longchamp as chancellor."

The response surprised the Jew. He had not heard cynicism in the young man's tone before. "No, my lord," Abraham demurred politely, "but one might suggest the sheriff has of late become overzealous on Longchamp's behalf." Exasperation showed a little; he squashed it without compunction. "Were you to give me that purse in exchange for the jewelry, the sheriff would soon have both." He gazed steadily at Robin, making no excuses; offering no apology for his unprofessional candor. "In three days' time, I am told; he put it to me quite plainly."

Robin had no reluctance to state what he believed; but then he was Christian, and could, and his station gave him full blessing. "I would not wager a penny that this collection would go to London. More likely into *deLacey's* coffers . . ." He frowned, eyes narrowing. "Or perhaps into John's." His gaze sharpened. "We spoke of this before."

"Indeed." Abraham was determined to remain noncommital. It served no Jew to publicly state an opinion on matters of policy. Christian sensibilities took offense so easily.

The young knight—*so young! War is indeed harsh*—sighed wearily and rubbed his brow, baring the knurled gouge that bespoke a head injury of some seriousness. But at least he had survived, Abraham reflected; many Crusaders had not.

Robin reached for the purse. "Then I will take it back and keep it for myself—" But he broke off, staring fixedly at Abraham. "You have collected coin for the king's ransom before . . ." the Jew nodded "—what if you were to send your money to London, to Longchamp himself, instead of to the sheriff?"

Abraham shrugged. "We would be punished, my lord. And Longchamp would never know."

"Then pay only part of what is due. Set part aside, and send that to London." Robin picked up the purse, moved his hand closer to Abraham, then smacked the leather pouch back down with a metallic clink of finality. "The *sheriff* need never know."

Abraham smiled sadly. "We can be searched at any time, and our property seized."

Robin shook his head. "You must do business with your brother Jews in London . . . *that* is where Longchamp rules in Richard's stead."

"Of course, my lord. Regularly."

"Does the sheriff interfere with those shipments?"

"Not so long as we pay the taxes in good time."

"Then pay them." Robin pushed back his stool and rose. The rush-light was kind to his coloring; a Michael, Abraham reflected, or perhaps a Gabriel, fair hair shining. With a single outstretched finger, Robin indicated the purse. "Set that aside, Abraham. When I have brought you more, you must send it to William Longchamp."

Abraham gestured helplessness. "All well and good, my lord—but how are you to get more?"

Robin's expression was hard. "My father stole from me. I shall do him the same favor."

Gisbourne started out of his doze when someone—or some-*thing*—knocked sharply on his door. He thrust a hand through the disarray of his hair, pushed himself up against the bolsters and resettled his leg, then called for whoever it was to enter.

Eleanor came in with crude crutches in her hands.

He understood instantly. "No."

"You must." She swung the door closed with a foot. "He put her under guard."

He eyed the crutches with dismay. He recalled all too clearly how the cart ride had hurt, and the transfer from cart to bed. "The guards won't listen to me."

"One man," she said. "Before God, are you that incompetent? You are seneschal, Gisbourne . . . you may not be a man to inspire much personal devotion, but you have some authority here." She held out the crutches, thumping the knobbed ends of the sticks against the floor. "If you concoct a plausible falsehood, the man will believe you. You should realize that. Have you learned nothing from my father?"

He chewed at a thumbnail.

Eleanor thumped the crutches again. "The monk did his part. Now you must do yours."

He wiped his sweating face. "I am hardly dressed properly to convince anyone of anything."

Eleanor propped the crutches against the door and strode to his single trunk, from which she pulled a fresh bliaut. She threw it at him. "There," she said venomously. "Do you wish me to put it on you?"

His face flamed. "No."

"Good. I prefer to *un*dress men." She snatched up the crutches and leaned them against his bed. "Don't delay, Gisbourne. The monk is waiting for her. I want Marian FitzWalter gone from here immediately." Her eyes were angry, he saw; she hated her that much. "If it convinces you, Gisbourne, this service will most assuredly commend you to her. What imprisoned woman would not look with favor upon the man who helped her escape?"

He had not thought of it that way. Hastily he reached out for the bliaut even as Eleanor laughed.

Nottingham was still a quagmire. Robin, watching where he allowed the horse to step as he traded the Jewish Quarter for Market Square, reined in sharply as a slight figure darted from an alley directly into his path. A deft hand caught at the reins.

"Much!" Robin leaned forward urgently. "Don't show yourself like this!"

The boy grinned, displaying residual grease left over from a meat pasty. He stepped around the horse and caught at the stirrup, holding up a bunched fist. "Ro-bin."

Robin reached down. A purse with leather thongs sliced through was put into his hand. *"Much—"*

But the boy merely grinned more broadly. "Lionheart."

"Much, *wait* . . ." He swung down from the horse. "Here— come with me." He led his mount into the alley with Much following. There he stood against a building with the horse serving as a shield for them both. Robin held out the purse. "How often do you do this?"

Much shrugged guileless ignorance.

Robin hid a smile. "And if I told you not to, you would do it anyway?"

The boy's dark eyes glinted. A sullen look altered his face from bright alertness to withdrawal. Thin shoulders hunched.

Robin, who knew a mask when he saw one, shook his head. "No, Much—I am not your father. I will not tell you what to do—or what *not* to do." He smiled crookedly as the boy's expression relaxed. "If you want to serve the Lionheart, who am I to say you nay? And Richard needs the money; I doubt he will object." He glanced out at Market Square, taking care they were not seen. "Much." He was serious now, and saw that the boy knew it. "There is a man, a Jew, called Abraham. He's a moneylender. Do you know him?"

Much nodded at once; probably the boy knew everyone.

554

Robin showed him the purse. "Take this to him. Tell him I sent you; that it's for the Lionheart."

Much bent his head toward a hunched shoulder: eloquent reluctance.

"He won't hurt you, Much. I promise. He'll send the money to London, to buy back the Lionheart."

The boy remained uncertain. He stared sidelong at the purse, then edged toward the square.

I need something to convince him. Robin chewed at a lip a moment, then smiled. Without regard for his hosen he went down on his knees and rested both hands on Much's narrow shoulders. Solemnly he decreed, "I swear to you by my oath as a Crusader and a knight, sworn before King Richard himself, that what you do to serve him can never be used against you. That if any man harms you, he also strikes at me." He saw the worship in the boy's eyes and made his tone stern. "But you must be wary, Much. You must take no unnecessary risks."

Much nodded. He snatched the purse from Robin's hand and darted away.

The duly sworn knight watched him go, then got up and regarded his hosen soberly. The knees were caked with a thick, malodorous muck that had worked its way through the nubby weave to drip slime down each of his shins.

"For God and King Richard," he murmured. Then Robin grinned. "And Much."

Fifty-Six

Marian's pride kept her from shouting through the door at the guard. He would refuse to heed her furious demand to be let out no matter what she said or how explicitly she phrased it, and she preferred not to demean herself to no good purpose. If he entered, she would hit him with whatever loose object was close at hand. Until then, there was nothing for it but to sit quietly and patiently, which she could not do, or to pace rapidly from one side of the room to the other.

The first moment of realization had nearly driven her mad. The soldiers had taken her unceremoniously to the chamber and locked her in before she could fashion a properly coherent protest. The instant the door closed she had broken every nail trying to claw it open again, trying to lift the latch, because the high-handed treatment reminded her all too clearly of Will Scarlet, and in that moment of panicked disbelief she reacted accordingly.

Now she had time to think. She no longer asked herself how or why, as she had the first few outraged moments of her imprisonment. She knew why; William deLacey had told her. She knew *how* because she had come to believe him incapable of denying himself anything, regardless of the seemingly insurmountable obstacles lying in his path.

This meant the sheriff was doubly dangerous, because he saw no impediment to marrying her even without her consent. Had the mock priest not refused to carry out the sham ceremony, she would now be in bed with William deLacey believing herself legally married as he took her against her will.

Marian shuddered. Legality had nothing to do with it. What she felt for him was not hatred, not even rage, for that had passed. What deLacey engendered now was a sick apprehension augmented by futility: short of killing the man, there was nothing she could undertake to stop him from doing whatever he liked with her, or *to* her, from torture to brutal rape. His power was absolute.

A royal ward is protected by the King's grace. Marian laughed bitterly. *Only we both of us are imprisoned. King Richard in Germany, and his ward in Nottingham Castle!*

She froze as the latch was rattled. For a tiny moment of renewed panic she was unable to move or think. Then it passed, and she reached as planned for the first loose object at hand: a wooden candlestick. The candle on it fell over and was extinguished as she snatched up the fat stick, but light poured in from corridor torches as the door swung open.

Sir Guy of Gisbourne, on crutches, stood—no, *tilted*—in the narrow doorway. He wore a knee-length cambric bliaut; his saturnine Norman face was stubbled and hollowed. "Lady Marian," he said gravely, "there is little time to waste."

Lady Marian set down the candlestick and went by him into the corridor, wasting none of the little time.

Well-pleased with matters on the whole, considering their delicate and very nearly tragic nature, William deLacey walked leisurely out of doors to the guardhouse tucked against the bailey wall, and had a liveried man brought forth. "Your name?"

He was young, of russet hair and dark brown eyes, with a wide mouth and firm chin. "Philip de la Barre."

DeLacey smiled briefly. "A good French name, de la Barre."

In view of the cordial comment, the soldier permitted himself the familiarity of an answering smile. "Yes, my lord . . . my family is quite old."

DeLacey's was not. He forbore to pursue the topic, lest it become apparent to de la Barre that he took orders from a more recent addition to the lengthy roll of proud names. In fact, much of his heritage was not even French. "You are to ride escort to Ravenskeep, the FitzWalter manor." He put a small pouch into de la Barre's hand. "There is a villein there called Roger. After you have seen the serving-woman safely delivered, find this Roger and question him. I want to know how disaffected he is, and if he has wit enough to be of use. Give him the coin, but tell him nothing. We must whet his appetite first."

"Yes, my lord."

"Good. I'll expect you back before sundown."

Robin lingered in Nottingham briefly, seriously considering riding on to Ravenskeep. He owed no time to his father in view of the circumstances, and did not particularly care what the earl's guests might think of his behavior. He supported the king in all things, but it was hardly politic to contemplate overthrowing a man who merely *desired* to be crowned king before the present monarch's unhappy situation had been resolved. His father, he felt, was premature, and following the wrong scent. If the noblemen of England looked to freeing Richard instead of fighting John, the civil difficulties might be resolved without shedding a drop of blood.

He squinted thoughtfully as he mounted his horse, settling into the saddle gingerly in deference to sodden, muck-weighted hosen. *But there is Geoffrey de Mandeville.*

It was worth consideration. The Earl of Essex was not an alarmist and was unlikely to commit himself to anything as significant as a plot against John unless he truly believed there was need. As Justiciar, de Mandeville was privy to the kind of information few other men were given leave to know. It did nothing to support Robin's contention that John's threat to his brother was as yet undefined. If de Mandeville had involved himself, the implications were far more serious.

He gazed longingly in the direction of Ravenskeep. *It would not take so much time* . . . But he had promised Marian he would speak to his father first. He owed her that much.

Gisbourne regretted intensely his haggard appearance and lack of proper attire. The bliaut was clean and certainly decent enough, but was hardly the apparel he would select to wear before *her*, were the circumstances different.

Marian halted in the dim corridor outside the chamber in which she had been imprisoned, turning sharply to face him. Her face was bruised, he saw, and deeply scratched in places, which prompted a response of nearly overwhelming proportions: he wanted very badly to make certain no one ever abused her again.

I want— Gisbourne swallowed heavily, denying body and mind the admission both longed to make. "You had best not tarry."

"What about you?" she asked. "He knows nothing about this, of course."

He wanted to laugh. The "of course" gave her away; she had learned the truth of the sheriff. "No. I will see to it he remains ignorant of the truth."

"Sir Guy—" Marian smiled tightly, poised to flee; clearly she did not underestimate deLacey. "Your aid is much appreciated."

He wanted more than that, but it was all she could give him now. "Go to the southern gatehouse," he told her. "The monk is waiting for you."

She nodded, yet hesitated. "I came here with a woman."

"The sheriff dismissed her without raising her suspicions; he is expert at that, so expect no alarm from her." He glanced beyond her urgently. The guard would return soon. "You had better go, Lady Marian." He hitched his crutches more tightly beneath his arms. "Think kindly of me tonight when you give your thanks to God."

"And tomorrow," she declared fervently. "For all the days of my life!"

"Go," he said curtly, unable to bear the look in her eye while knowing what he did was for his sake, not for hers.

Marian went. Gisbourne waited, then swung around on his crutches and hobbled his way back into the chamber. With care he swung the door shut halfway, then gritted his teeth on a curse as he levered himself to the ground. He tossed the crutches away from his body, then doubled up his fist and smacked himself squarely on wounded thigh. Fresh blood stained his bandage and soaked through to bliaut. Sweat broke out anew. He collapsed against the floor in an unfeigned half-swoon of weakness, gasping audibly.

Raggedly he muttered, "You owe me more than prayers."

Much made his way into the Jewish Quarter, darting from alley to alley with the purse tucked inside the sleeve of his soiled tunic. He found Abraham's dwelling and slouched against a wall nearby, making himself small, less than nothing—"not much," as his mother had called him—and watched those in the street laboring to clean away the stormwrack. He let his presence be marked, commented upon, then forgotten in the press of duties: he was a boy, nothing more, *not much;* a stranger to them all.

When certain of their disinterest, Much made his way idly across the street and kicked at a loose stone. Twice more he kicked, until the stone skittered against Abraham's door. Much approached, bent down as if to study the stone, then snatched open the door and darted inside.

The old Jew was startled as the purse was plopped onto the table in front of his twisted hands. "Lionheart," Much declared purposefully, consumed with righteous fire. Then, as the old man gazed at him in wonder, he explained with more diffidence. "From *Robin.*"

After careful consideration, Abraham slowly upended the purse and dumped out the coins in chiming clumps.

He looked at Much and smiled as his fingers counted coin. "And why not?" he asked. "He is sovereign to us all, Christian and Jew alike, nobleman or serf. England's interests will be served *despite* Prince John and the sheriff." He nodded at Much. "Tell Robin I agree."

"More," Much suggested.

"More," the Jew agreed; this contract, unlike most, was implicit.

After attiring himself in a new tunic of rich blue samite trimmed with Eastern-style golden braid—a touch of clove to sweeten his breath—deLacey went to the tiny castle chapel. It was empty, of course; Brother Tuck had been dismissed.

He genuflected out of habit, not conviction, then slid onto a bench at the back of the small chamber. It was damp and cool, redolent of mice; he supposed he should set someone to cleaning it. Marian might prove devout.

DeLacey smiled, schooling himself into a quietude at odds with his inner self. Anticipation was sweet, with the slightest undertaste of illicit perversity adding a fillip. She would protest, of course, because Marian had proved only too willing of late to challenge him in every conversation, but he was in general unconcerned.

She has only herself to blame.

He did not intend rape, of course; he was a man who had bedded many women, including cold ones such as his wives, and knew precisely what it took to rouse a woman's ardor. Marian was passionate—that was proved already by her sudden infatuation with Robert of Locksley—and would warm to his attentions even as others had without recourse to force. In fact, he required it to be so. His tastes lay not in physical domination, but in manipulation. Physical gratification satisfied a simple animal urge, but a well-laid strategy was an aphrodisiac for the mind.

He gazed upon the alter, regarding the crucifix. "Hugh, old friend," he said, "we would neither of us desire this, but what is left to do? She has proved a willful and disobedient daughter, much too headstrong to be left to rule herself. The manor is a travesty, and her deportment highly suspect . . . if there is to remain any honor attached to your name, I must tend to it myself."

The chapel was full of silence.

The sheriff nodded. "Eleanor to Gisbourne, Marian for me. Both women redeemed from defilement and dishonor, so that no one may suffer for it. Not I, for Eleanor's; not you for Marian's." He touched the high collar of his tunic, liking the texture of the braid. "A father's task is difficult, but this will ease my mind, and your memory."

Sir Hugh of course made no comment. For the moment transfixed by memories, deLacey stared hard at the crucifix and conjured before him his old friend's face. There was nothing of Marian in it, save a stubborn set to the chin.

"If I lie with her," he said, "she will have to marry me."

Guilt was unexpected. DeLacey stood up swiftly, upsetting the wooden bench, and strode out of the tiny chapel.

Marian, who had not dared breathe as she walked steadily and without haste from the keep to the southern gate, at last sucked in a much-needed breath as she passed through into the city. There was no difficulty with the soldiers. She hid all of her hair and most of her face in the draped hood, but did not allow herself to behave furtively for fear the guards would suspect.

She walked through in silence. The gate was shut behind her; Marian looked urgently for the monk, and saw him with two horses waiting not far from the gate. She walked quickly to him and peeled back the hood. "Brother?"

"Tuck," he supplied morosely. His heavy face was strained. "Lady Marian, I pray you forgive me."

She touched his arm briefly. "Whatever you have done— and whatever you may do in the future—is forgiven ten times over." She cast a sharp glance over her shoulder, then assessed the horses attached to Tuck by virtue of reins. "Are you coming with me?"

He nodded. "It is best, Sir Guy said . . . but—I've never ridden a horse. Only a mule—and now I am too fat for that. I walked here from Croxden."

Marian pitied the monk—she knew it cost him to admit that—but they could not afford to walk. "I'm sorry, Brother . . . perhaps when we are away from Nottingham, but until then we must ride. The horses are much faster, and I promise you we have no time to waste. A good man has put himself into difficult circumstances." She thought of Gisbourne as she took from Tuck one set of reins and looped them over the bay mare's head, kilting up kirtle and mantle as she stretched a foot toward the stirrup. "Brother Tuck, I beg you—give me the loan of your hands!"

He did, if clumsily, aiding her to clamber up into the saddle.

Marian arranged kirtle skirts as best she could and depended upon the mantle to provide a measure of modesty.

Tuck stood square on the ground, legs planted widely, his face a study of despair.

"Please," she said urgently, "you know what he means to do; would you have me taken now after all you've done to prevent it?"

Distressed, he shook his head. "No, Lady—"

"A horse is not so different from a mule." Though inwardly she rebuked herself for lying to a monk. "I'll lead, Brother—but I beg you, please make haste. I want to get to Huntington as soon as possible."

Tuck paused in the act of lifting the reins over the chestnut's head. "Huntington? I thought we were bound for Ravenskeep. Sir Guy told me so."

"Sir Guy was mistaken." Marian looked again at the gate. "Ravenskeep is the first place the sheriff will go."

With effort, Tuck stuffed a sandaled foot into the stirrup, caught great handfuls of mane and rein, and dragged himself upward as the gelding first staggered, then spread his legs and grunted. "Lady—"

"Hurry, Brother Tuck." She did not feel it wise to tell him she feared if he lingered longer between the saddle and the ground, he would pull the chestnut over.

"Aye—" He heaved himself up into the saddle, grasping uncertainly at a cassock that, stretched across saddle, bared an alarming expanse of thick ankles and thicker, hairier legs. His face burned red from exertion or embarrassment; she could not predict which. Perhaps it was both. In a muffled tone he asked, "How far is Huntington, Lady Marian?"

"Not so far." Yet another lie; to him, it would take forever and cause much discomfort. "Come," she said guiltily, "Huntington is this way."

Gisbourne roused as hands clasped his shoulders and levered him into a sitting position. The pain was excruciating. He opened his mouth to yell, but forbore as he focused upon the sheriff's rigid face.

"Well?" deLacey asked. He stood in the doorway while the guard knelt on the floor and hoisted Sir Guy upright.

Gisbourne knew that tone: ice-cold and oddly flat, curiously lifeless, as if the only emotion in the man was utter indifference. It was a deadly assumption Gisbourne knew better than to make. Such miscalculation had cost other men their lives.

In a pain-drugged bewilderment not entirely feigned, he passed a trembling hand across his face. "My lord—"

"*Well,* Gisbourne?"

"My lord—I—" He licked his lips. "She *tripped* me, my lord . . . she knocked my crutches aside!"

DeLacey did not spare the crutches so much as a glance. "I see that, Gisbourne. I have no doubt it was incredibly painful. What I *do* doubt is your reason for being here at all."

Gisbourne breathed heavily. His wound was afire. "I came to thank her, my lord—"

"*Thank* her!"

"—and to pay my respects . . . she was kind to me at Huntington after the boar hunt."

DeLacey's face was taut as a drumhead, the bones of his nose cutting flesh. White indentations bracketed the corners of his mouth. "Surely it might have waited, Gisbourne . . . until your wound was less painful, certainly. It distresses me to see you in so much discomfort."

Gisbourne clamped shut his mouth on the retort he longed to make. Instead, he ventured a sickly smile. "As always, you have my best interests at heart . . . my lord, the truth is I heard she was ill—"

DeLacey's tone sharpened. "What?"

"Ill, my lord." He blinked guilelessly. "Servants' gossip, of course . . . I know I should not listen, but when I heard it was the Lady Marian . . ." He coughed weakly and reached a hand toward his wound, as if to soothe it by touch. "All I meant—all I *wished*—was to thank her for her kindness, and tell her I hoped her own discomfort would pass." He swallowed painfully, then opened his eyes very wide. "She wasn't ill at all! She must have *feigned* it . . . but why would she do such a thing?"

DeLacey's eyes glittered. "Women are capricious." He

glanced at the guard. "Assist Sir Guy back to his room. He has been ill-used."

Gisbourne slumped back in relief as the sheriff departed, the better to hide the smile that threatened to betray the truth. *I have beaten him at last.*

The guard's grip was painful. "A pretty piece," he murmured. "I don't blame you, Sir Guy."

His eyes popped open. *"What—?"*

"The woman, Sir Guy; I don't doubt she'll thank you in your bed for keeping her out of the sheriff's. I knew what you meant to do when you sent me off to relieve myself." He hoisted Gisbourne up. "But don't worry yourself—if you keep my purse well-filled, I'll say naught of it to the sheriff."

Robin reined in on the hillock overlooking Huntington Castle. He was no more fond of it at this moment than he had been the very first, when he had come home to a strange keep after two years in the Holy Land. England was alien then, soft and cool and wet, while the blood burning in his veins was thinned by heat and sun.

England was no longer alien, but Huntington Castle was. The lord within it, unfortunately, was exactly as expected; exactly as he had been for all of Robin's life.

"An English winter," he murmured. "Cold and unforgiving, with a bitter wind in his mouth." His mother had been much different, too kind a soul for the earl. She had dwindled and wasted away in the frigidity of his spirit.

A frieze of pewter clouds was hung against the sky as backdrop to the castle, with a smudgy tree line for a border. Rain began to fall: a misty spring drizzle that turned the world opaque. Robin resettled his mantle, then spurred his horse into a gallop. His angle was oblique: instead of riding to the castle he skirted the curtain-wall and continued on around it. Just over the hill behind, flanked by oak and elder, lay the hall that was his home. It was there he would go, to pay his respects to his mother before returning to his father.

* * *

The Earl of Huntington sat at table with powerful friends, supping on sweet red deer that was, within the bounds of vert and venison granted decades before, legal for him to serve. It was a privilege of which he was most proud, and was keenly aware of how the others viewed it.

He lifted his silver goblet. "Now then, we have drunk to the king's health numerous times . . . shall we drink to a healthy heir?"

De Vesci snickered. Henry Bohun raised an eyebrow slightly, while Geoffrey de Mandeville's color deepened. Nonetheless the aging Earl of Essex caught up his goblet. "Say you so, Robert! To a fine and healthy heir, God willing!"

"And to the queen's fertility." Bohun's tone was dryly circumspect.

De Vesci snickered again. "*If* the king is so moved—"

"Eustace!" Huntington snapped. "I will not countenance sly innuendo and unfounded rumor in my hall."

"*Unfounded*—" de Vesci began in disbelief. "Methinks—"

"Eustace." Bohun lifted a warning finger. "We are guests in this man's hall."

De Vesci subsided in sour humor as Ralph glided into the hall and came to stand at the earl's side. "My lord. A visitor has arrived, much harried from wind and rain."

Huntington glanced at the others as they stiffened. "One of us, Ralph?"

"No, my lord."

Relaxing, the earl flicked eloquent fingers. "Send him to the kitchens, then. I'll see him later, if it concerns me."

"It may concern you, my lord. But only one of them is a man; a monk. The other is a woman."

De Vesci grinned. "Have her in, Ralph. A woman's company sweetens a meal."

Delicately, Ralph ignored Alnwick. "My lord, it is the Lady Marian FitzWalter."

The earl frowned. "Marian Fitz—" He lurched upright. "Marian *FitzWalter!* By God . . ." But he broke it off, stiffly resuming his seat before the astonished countenances of his companions. "And a monk, you say?"

"A Benedictine, my lord. Brother Tuck."

"Well." Huntington chewed a morsel of venison. "At least she has the good sense to admit she requires absolution." He glanced the length of the table and took note of three attentive faces. With grave deliberation, he looked back at Ralph. "Have them in, then. He may have a bench in here later; she may sleep with the kitchen girls."

De Vesci blurted his shock. "A knight's daughter, my lord? Surely she deserves better!"

The earl faced him down with a cold stare. "The woman is despoiled. An escaped murderer carried her off to Sherwood Forest . . . would you care to wager how many outlaws made use of her?"

De Vesci guffawed crudely. "Who would have the courage to *ask* her?"

Geoffrey de Mandeville frowned disapproval. "Surely this is a most unfortunate circumstance, Robert . . . I met her father once, when old King Henry knighted him. He was a good and gentle man—I find it appalling that she is relegated to such disparagement through no fault of her own."

"Perhaps so," Huntington conceded acidly. "But would you have her at table now, as we plot to bring down a royal prince?"

De Vesci grinned. "Not at table, perhaps—but later, in my bed—?"

Bohun shook his head. "Crudity has no place here."

"No," de Mandeville agreed with pronounced asperity.

Huntington looked at Ralph. "Send them to the chapel, as I assume both are in need of it. I'll see the woman later; she must have come for some reason."

Ralph bowed. "Yes, my lord."

The earl nodded dismissal. "Tell the kitchens to send them food."

Fifty-Seven

Eleanor opened the chamber door without bothering to knock because she did not particularly care if Gisbourne desired to see her or not; she had business with him and intended to settle it. She thumped the door closed with finality and crossed swiftly to the narrow bed on which he slept, her slippered feet scraping on beaten earth. He was asleep, twitching like a dog, mouth open slackly so that labored breathing issued forth.

He was gray of face and stubbled, with hollows in his cheeks. No doubt the leg hurt, but that was beside the point. There were matters to discuss. "Gisbourne."

He awoke at once, all stiff and flailing and awkward, much like a startled dog. Dark eyes were briefly white-rimmed, then his breathing settled again and he slumped back against the pillows. He shoved a trembling hand through lank hair. "What do you want?"

"We must take steps to make certain the guard is dealt with."

His bleary expression turned sullen. "I have no money to buy his silence."

Eleanor shrugged elegant disdain. "Then kill him."

His face went white, then red. He bared his teeth like a cornered hound. *"You* kill him. You've spent much of your life intriguing to get whatever you want without regard to the harm you do. If you think he should be killed, *you* arrange the deed!" It was his turn to show contempt. "You are your father's daughter, after all; he will admire your handiwork."

Eleanor sighed, folding her mouth up small. "Very well, Gisbourne." She walked quietly to the door, then paused with her hand on the latch. "You believe yourself a good man, do you not? A man unlike my father?" He offered no answer, of course; but then, she did not expect it. "You both want the woman. You both connive for the woman. You both intend to have her regardless of what is required, to the point of betraying your king—and yourselves—to satisfy your loins." Eleanor shook her head and tugged open the door. "The devil does not distinguish the *degree* of the sin, Gisbourne. He merely profits from what is done in the taking of your soul."

The chapel at Huntington Castle was larger than Nottingham's, with more inherent elegance. The walls were plastered and whitewashed, which brightened the chapel considerably. It smelled damp from rain, but fresh, scented by beeswax candles and herb-strewn rushes. Soaring stone arches and vaults and molded ribs replaced thick, ungraceful columns, so that the roof was high and spacious; one entire wall was filled with a wide stone bench, divided into individual seats: the sedilia, for the priest, his deacon, and others, each seat framed by delicate, elaborate arches.

"A wealthy man," Tuck murmured.

Marian, who held the tray of food brought to them by one of the kitchen servants, was less impressed by the chapel. She knew the earl was wealthy. She suspected *he* knew all about her abduction and subsequent—if hypothetical—defilement; being sent off to wait in the chapel until his pleasure permitted them to come out was a succinct and eloquent comment upon her status, and did not commend him to her.

"Yes," she said dryly. "And generous, one may say, if one is inclined to speak." She was not. She set the tray down on the nearest bench, then put up her hands to her wind-lashed hair. Strands had come loose in the ride, and rain had crept inside her hood. She was damp, mussed, self-conscious, and embarrassed; she had been certain Robin would receive them. She had not once considered what the earl himself might do.

Marian shut her eyes, feeling heat steal up to her hairline. *This is not a man who will allow his son to dirty his thoughts with me, let alone his body.* Tears stung as she opened her eyes, glaring balefully at the food to keep them from spilling over. She had not cried before William deLacey; why would she cry now? *I will tell him everything, from Sherwood to the sheriff. But I will not lay a wager that it will do any good.*

Tuck genuflected, then approached the altar. Marian watched despondently as he lowered himself to his broad knees, his shoulders collapsing inwardly as he bowed his head and clasped his hands. He murmured inaudible prayers.

He is sore from the ride, poor man. Marian sat down next to the tray, slipping out of her damp mantle. Anxiety gnawed at her. If Robin was not at Huntington, what were they to do? And where *was* he? *He said he was bound for home.*

"Lady Marian?" Tuck was done with his prayers. "What will you tell the earl?"

She had expected the question eventually. Marian sighed. "I had intended to tell him little. It isn't *his* help I sought . . . I came here for his son."

Tuck's baffled gaze betrayed incomprehension.

Why not tell him all? "Sir Robert of Locksley. Robin." She smiled, still ducking the whole truth. "He is just home from Crusade."

The monk brightened. "Did he see Jerusalem? Did he pray at the Holy Sepulchre?" His face was alight. "Oh Lady, what joy that would be . . . to *see* the tomb from which our Lord Jesus rose . . ." His face relaxed, smoothing into tranquility, and she realized the sheriff's actions were as disturbing to him as they had been to her, and somehow as threatening.

"What did he mean?" she asked, recalling deLacey's words. "The sheriff, when he said he would write to the abbot—that was more than merely babble. What did he mean, Brother? What threat did he make you?"

Tuck's eyes opened. The transfiguring light died from his face. "He will see me turned out of the abbey. He will have me dismissed from the order."

Marian was appalled. "Can he do that? He is a *secular* authority—he cannot, can he? His office is temporal, not spiritual."

Tuck sighed heavily, face sagging. "I have been but recently convinced that a man such as the sheriff may accomplish many things I once believed impossible. As he reminded me, there is intrigue even in the Church. . . ." He sat down heavily on the bench beside hers, clasping in spatulate hands the crucifix depending from his rope belt. "Lady Marian, I must trust to God. What I did was right. If I am dismissed from orders, my vocation will be ended—but certainly not God's knowledge that what I did was proper." He shook his head decisively. "I should have defied him sooner."

He meant the sheriff, she realized, not God. She could not imagine Tuck defying God in anything. "You are a good man," she told him, distressed that the words did not adequately convey what she felt. "Few people are able to defy William deLacey; if they do, it is at their peril. He will take his retribution."

Tuck's dark eyes were worried. "Lady—what could he do to you?"

"Little, now." Her conviction offered an unanticipated relief. It buoyed her spirits. "He could not discredit me; that is already done. He can't take Ravenskeep, because it is part of me and I am the king's ward. He can't surprise me again with a forced wedding, because he knows I am forewarned. He cannot go to my father and simply demand my hand, because my father is dead." She smiled wanly. "I am safe, Brother Tuck. Certainly safer than you."

His gaze was steady. "Then why are we here instead of at Ravenskeep?"

She had not believed him so astute. "Because I am a coward," she admitted hollowly. "And because I am in love."

"Love?" Tuck echoed. His entire demeanor changed. He smiled beatifically, a smile like those on the carvings of saints' effigies in one of the great cathedrals. For the first time she believed him a man appropriate to his office. He sketched the sign of the cross. "God keep you, Lady Marian. Love is a wondrous thing."

Her mouth crimped tightly. "Love is a *frightening* thing."

He was astounded. "Why? I have heard the songs, Lady Marian—isn't love what people crave?"

"Indeed, when one can afford to love." She did not like the cynical tone of her voice. "I am not so certain I can."

"Why not?" He gestured expansively, encompassing the chapel. "Love is pure, Lady Marian. *God* is love."

Marian laughed softly. "But the Earl of Huntington, despite what he may believe, is not God."

"No, of course not." Tuck took it literally and answered in kind. "But surely a man who causes a chapel such as this to be built understands true devotion."

"Perhaps." *But probably not.* She picked at the weave of her mantle. "A man who rules his son understands only himself. Certainly not the wishes—or needs—of others, most especially not those of despoiled women."

Illumination lighted his face, then died away. "Oh," Tuck said glumly.

Marian nodded agreement.

DeLacey chewed vigorously as his daughter approached the table. He was grateful his appetite was sound, for surely a woman of such sallow coloring and sullen demeanor would put another off his feed.

He drank wine to wash down the partridge, eyeing her over the rim of the cup. She waited demurely enough, hands folded into her kirtle. *Yellow again,* he reflected. *My birds have better taste.*

"My lord." She held her head very still on the column of her neck. "My lord, there is a matter we should address."

"One among many, no doubt." He bit off another chunk of thyme-stuffed fowl. "Which one is this?"

Only the briefest tic of a muscle in her jaw betrayed her irritation. "It has to do with a man's willingness to neglect his duty, my lord, merely to please a physical need."

He laughed. "You refer to me?"

Color splotched her face. "Certainly not, my lord. I would never criticize you."

He snickered rudely. "The faeries are out, I see—surely they have put a changeling tongue into my daughter's mouth."

She took a lurching step forward, then stopped short, a contrivance of subtle unspoken language that might have fooled another man, but he was well-versed in such things. "My lord,

I beg you . . . this is serious. It has to do with the man who left Marian FitzWalter's door unguarded."

Laughing softly, deLacey tossed a bone down on the trencher and sat back in his chair, flicking fingers free of debris. "Yes, Eleanor. Pray tell me all."

Color climbed higher in her face. "He came to me, my lord. He made lewd suggestions."

"Which you accepted with alacrity, no doubt."

Brown eyes glittered briefly, but she was not provoked. "No, of course not." In a rush, she said, "I am ashamed—"

"Eleanor." He cut her off succinctly. "Eleanor, you have been ashamed of nothing since the day your mother whelped you. Say what you have to say, and discard embellishments." He uncrossed his legs and leaned forward. "Did you lure the guard away?"

"Give me credit for taste," she snapped. "He is a *soldier,* nothing more . . . I take my men from better."

"Ah. Forgive me." He grinned. "So, you are accusing this mere soldier of improper behavior."

"He made lewd suggestions to me."

"And why not? Your reputation is entrenched." He sighed, weary of the wordplay. "I assume you want him punished."

Her lips parted in surprise. "You were quick enough to sentence the minstrel to maiming! Why not this man?"

"Because you *want* him to be punished. That leads me to wonder why." He tapped fingertips upon the chair arm. "Shall I have him in, Eleanor? Let you accuse him to his face, to judge the truth of the matter?"

Eleanor's glare was deadly. "Do have him in, my lord. I enjoy listening to lies."

"The better to improve your own." He smiled thinly. "Very well, we'll have the man in." DeLacey raised his voice. *"Walter!* Bring in the unfortunate wretch!"

Eleanor's teeth clenched. "You've questioned him already."

"Yes, of course, immediately after he put Gisbourne to bed." He was indulgence personified. "But we'll try him once again just to content you."

His daughter made no comment. DeLacey consumed more

partridge, drank more wine, and sat back, sated, as Walter and two other soldiers brought in the unfortunate man.

DeLacey watched Eleanor as she deigned to cast the man a condescending glance, then stiffened into immobility. "There," he murmured, "you see? Already maimed for you."

And he was. Shortly after determining the man had deserted his post—the reason was unimportant—the sheriff had ordered both hands cut off.

A somber soldier on either side held up the former guard. The stumps had been cauterized, but the linen wraps were bloody. Without the aid of the others the guard would have swooned.

DeLacey looked at his daughter. "He tried to blame Gisbourne. He did not mention you." He waved the soldiers out, along with white-faced Walter and their incoherent burden. "You see, Eleanor—" he paused thoughtfully, to make certain he had her full attention; what he intended to tell her was an important lesson, "for all of Gisbourne's faults, he is a competent seneschal. A man in my position cannot blithely dismiss someone who offers good value for his keep. But someone had to be punished. Someone must always be punished." He thrust himself up from the chair. "And now I am away. The lady has had long enough—I am bound for Ravenskeep." He paused beside his daughter, then leaned very close to speak into her ear. "I will have her, Eleanor. One way or another." His voice dropped to a whisper that ruffled the hair over her ear. "And Gisbourne will have *you*."

The rain slanted obliquely as Robin rode over the swell of a hill into the pocket below, where Huntington Hall stood.

He drew up sharply.

Had stood.

The horse snorted wetly, shaking rain out of its ears. Its mane straggled down its neck in horsehair rivulets, dripping onto the soaked grass.

A shudder wracked Robin. Transfixed, he stared mutely, deaf to the world, unperturbed by somber drizzle because he felt none of it.

He bestirred himself at last to slip both stirrups, then slid off awkwardly, slithering against leather and horsehair. He clung to the saddle a moment, holding himself upright, then lurched away and began to run in graceless disbelief down the hill into the pocket, where Huntington Hall had stood.

All of it torn down.

Save the remnants of shattered brick and splintered timber rendered useless by time or miscalculation to masons who wanted whole brick, and peasants who needed wood.

Fifty-Eight

Robin walked among the ruins of his boyhood, ignorant of the rain. He kicked over broken brickwork, tossed aside cracked wood panels, and cursed the cold-blooded monster who could destroy one hall merely to build another to honor his vanity, so that all men might call him great.

He uncovered no treasures, save a single colored stone he had found in the brook down the hill, when he was six years old. A wine-tinted rock with a splash of white in the center, like a drop of blood, except the color was backward. He had decided the faeries bled white when humans pierced their flesh with magical arrows blessed by the nearest priest. It was a tale that amused his mother.

He had showed his father the stone, eager to repeat his tale. The earl, upon the hearing, had taken the rock from his grimy palm, boxed his ear for impugning the morals of a priest, then sent him to his room without a single bite of bread. Later had come the strap, when small Robin had hoped aloud the faeries would shoot his father with *their* magical arrows, so that he bled red.

Robin had never regretted his wish. He had regretted speaking it. After that he merely thought it.

He squatted in the rain, rolling the stone in a hand grown to manhood. The faeries were dead because his father had killed them. His mother was dead because his father had killed her by destroying her dreams of faeries; by leeching the life from her spirit like lye from bloody linens—*the bandages of the field, the ragged shreds of cloth wrapped around a gaping stump where a Saracen sword had cut through flesh and shattered bone, until the men who called themselves surgeons merely finished the job the Turks began—*

Robin swore. He shut his eyes tightly. In the gentle spring rain of England he lived again in the Holy Land.

"Curse him," he muttered raggedly. "He builds himself taller out of the wreckage of those whom he squashes."

Even me, his inner self said. *Even his son, if that son permits it.*

Robin rose abruptly. Clutching the wine-tinted stone with the white blood of faeries on it, the sole living child of Alice and Robert walked out of his mother's plundered hall toward his father's rain-washed castle, unheeding of the horse who followed dispiritedly.

Servants, directed by Ralph, cleared away the detritus of the huge meal in the great hall at Huntington Castle. Hard bread trenchers were fed to the dogs, while the remains of fowl and venison were wrapped in bundles to be distributed once a week to the poor who gathered at the gate. Only then did English peasantry know the taste of deer without fear of retribution.

Business concluded, the earl and his guests relaxed, drank, and discussed all manner of political and casual matters bearing no relation whatsoever upon the king, his traitorous brother, or whether it was worth the money and effort to wager if the king would—or could—get himself an heir.

Eustace de Vesci drank deeply, as always, and his face showed the effects in heightened color, glittering eyes, and effusive—if crude—good humor. He leaned both elbows on the table and fixed Huntington with a sly, provocative stare. "Have her in," he suggested. "Let us see the despoiled woman."

Henry Bohun's tone was dry. "Eustace, I think the wine overrides your good sense."

"I want to *see* the girl, not bed her!" de Vesci cried. "By God, Henry, d'ye think I want what every outlaw in Sherwood's had?"

"Perhaps," Bohun commented. "There are men whose tastes are piqued by things out of the common."

"Well, not *mine*." De Vesci reached for his goblet and thrust it into the air in eloquent invitation: a servant scurried to fill it from a pitcher. "I like my women clean, pretty, and willing. If Adam Bell and his ilk have had her, she'll be none of those things, now."

Ralph answered Huntington's beckoning finger. "Bring the girl in, Ralph. We'll have this travesty finished before the night grows older."

"Yes, my lord." Ralph bowed himself away.

"Well," de Vesci murmured, "here's sport for a moment." He drank deeply, then nodded at his host. "To your hospitality, Robert—not every man would take in a woman such as she."

"A man should." De Mandeville frowned. "I knew her father, I tell you—Hugh FitzWalter's daughter is not a common whore."

De Vesci scowled. "I say it does him credit. The Earl of Huntington is not known as a warm-hearted soul, yet now he disproves it."

Unoffended, the earl arched a brow. "Warm hearts are filled with passion, which can lead a man astray. A cooler head is preferable."

Bohun exchanged a glance with de Mandeville. "If there are wits in it, I agree."

Ralph returned. "My lords. The Lady Marian FitzWalter."

De Vesci turned eagerly, poised to extend jocular welcome. None was offered. His tongue fell into stillness as she walked slowly into the light. "By Christ," de Vesci breathed. " 'Tis a sin to despoil such as she."

If she heard, she made no sign. Geoffrey de Mandeville, Earl of Essex and Justiciar of England, set back his bench and rose. "Lady Marian," he said warmly, "your presence honors us."

Hereford, too, found his feet. "Indeed," Bohun murmured. De Vesci said nothing at all.

She looked at Huntington and raised her chin slightly, as a warrior might a shield. "My lord, I thank you. Were it not for your hospitality, we would have spent the night in a byre."

Seeing her, the earl believed the byre preferable to his castle. The woman was dangerous. If she affected such experienced lords so, what could she do to his son?

A door boomed open from near the front of the hall. Robert of Locksley strode into the hall, shedding rain from his ash-hued mantle as he stripped the hood from his head. "You cold-blooded, cold-hearted bastard—"

The earl was on his feet. "Robert!"

The rage was abruptly extinguished by the swirled folds of kirtle and cloak. *"Marian?"*

A trembling Earl of Huntington read the truth in his son's body before his heir even touched the woman.

Gisbourne, dropping gravy-soaked bread onto his tray, gazed at Eleanor in alarm. "He *knew?*"

"From the beginning." Her former contempt was banished, replaced by tense displeasure. "There was no need for me to go to him at all."

Gisbourne smiled at that, and was further contented to see the slow flush burn her cheeks. It lent her sallowness some color. But he did not remind her he had protested; Eleanor was no lackwit. If he slighted her intentionally she would look for retribution. He had learned his lesson well.

"Well," he said meditatively, "it is pleasing to learn I am of some value after all."

"Be not so proud," she retorted. "While you are useful, he will use you; prove difficult, he will discard you." She looked meaningfully at his leg. "He might just cut *that* off."

He dismissed her pettiness absently. He had escaped danger for the moment, and he had no intention of permitting himself to be used against his will in another of Eleanor's schemes. If he stayed free of her, he could be the kind of seneschal the sheriff desired him to be, while drawing no suspicion that he courted Prince John's approval.

Gisbourne recovered his crust of bread and bit off a dripping piece. "You must be pleased nonetheless. The Lady Marian is gone."

Eleanor's eyes glittered balefully. "For now. He's left to fetch her back."

The bite was suddenly tasteless. *"Now?"*

"He's ridden out to Ravenskeep." She shrugged. "Now, tomorrow, next week—does precisely when matter? He intends to bring her here and install her as his wife." Her tone turned venomous. "We shall have to think of something else to rid ourselves of her."

"We," he reflected. *"We" could be dangerous.*

And as dangerous to tell her.

Gisbourne merely nodded, chewing hard bread again.

Ravenskeep's gate was not yet repaired, so the bailey welcomed William deLacey even if Marian did not. She could not, apparently; Joan, clearly shocked by the sheriff's appearance, said her lady was not at home.

"She stayed with *you*," Joan declared. "Because of the fever, you said."

The sheriff found it intensely annoying to be required to explain himself to a woman with whom he had been so purposeful in an earlier contrivance. Lying, if one were not careful, could lay insidious traps.

He stood just inside the hall, dripping rain, while his equally soaked troop of Normans lingered out-of-doors in the bailey. He supposed he should bring them in, but he had expected Marian to offer the usual amenities. She was lax in authority, but never in courtesy.

When offered to others. He glanced briefly around the hall, frowning disapproval. "It is wet."

"Indeed, my lord," Joan agreed readily. "Roger didn't finish the shutters, and the roof's leaking again."

"Ah. Roger." He wondered if Philip de la Barre had found

disaffected Roger sufficiently suitable for future use. "If you like, I will send workmen from Nottingham to help you in your repairs." His gaze was penetrating. "We cannot permit your lady to live below her station."

Joan flushed crimson. "No, my lord," she muttered. "But—if she isn't at the castle, where *is* she? You said she was in bed."

"She was." He had intended for her to be in *his* bed; the truth made him surly. "Apparently she felt herself sufficiently recovered to leave." He shook his head, sighing. "She is of an independent mind. I would have sent an escort with her, of course—"

"Where *is* she?" Joan was now alarmed enough to interrupt. "My lord, 'tis raining, and near sundown—if there were a sun to go down—we can't have the Lady Marian on the road by herself!"

Retreat was necessary before he floundered more obviously. "No indeed, Joan. I shall set my men to searching immediately." DeLacey turned on his heel and strode swiftly out of the hall, shutting his ears to the woman's distressed murmuring.

Where, then? he mused. *Someone in Nottingham? One of the neighboring manors?* He checked just outside the hall as the rain renewed its assault. "No," he said tautly. "She'll have gone to Huntington."

The troop formed up in answer to his sharply imperative gesture. One man brought his horse. "My lord?"

"Nottingham, for now." He mounted quickly, swinging the cloak out of the way with a deft, practiced motion. "In the morning we ride again."

In shock, Marian gazed at Robin. Water ran from his cloak to splash onto the floor where it beaded briefly in the rushes, then ran off to the beaten earth. She searched his expression raptly, looking for repudiation now that they stood before the earl and three lords of England in the castle that was *his* home—not hers where she was comfortable, where she knew herself well loved by people who mattered. *Can he love me now? Will his father permit it?*

Pale hair curled damply where the wet had found a way in

beyond the edge of the hood. He was white and tense and angry, though the anger died as he saw her, altered by an astonishment that transmuted itself to joy.

Her body roused to him in that oddly intimate moment in front of five other men: flustered servant, outraged earl, three stunned lords.

It was loud in the silent hall, the mute tension that sprang between them, ringing a pale echo off a tight-wound lute string stretched very near to breaking.

Then he touched her shoulder, threading his fingers through her loosened hair, and the lute string abruptly snapped.

"Have you had her?" the earl rasped. "Have *you* had this woman, also—like every outlaw in Sherwood Forest?"

From the tail of her eye, Marian saw the motion of Robin's hand toward a sword that did not hang at his side, and for that she loved him the more. But she required no blood shed in the name of a petty truth.

"Yes," she said clearly, speaking to the earl. "But not *also,* my lord . . . it was your son who made me a woman. Last night, in fact—at Ravenskeep, not in Sherwood. In my mother's oratory." She lifted her chin in answer to the challenge she saw building in his eyes. "But I think God didn't mind. He allowed us to please one another without defilement."

She felt rather than saw the stunned recoil of the others as Robin tensed beside her. Marian herself was strangely detached, completely divorced from the emotions that imprisoned everyone else. *It is because I am too angry; in a moment I will burst.*

The Earl of Huntington pointed a trembling hand toward the screened door of the hall. "Leave at once. I will not have such language spoken in my hall."

"English," she said plainly. "Not Norman French, my lord Earl, but common Saxon English. Is that not what all of us are?"

"*Leave* here!" he cried.

"No," Robin said.

The earl shook with fury. "I will not have her in this hall."

"Why not?" Robin released her shoulder and took a single step forward, linking his hands behind his back. She knew him well enough now to hear the subtle undertone that warned her

581

of his mood; if his father had sense at all, he would comprehend the danger.

But his father has no sense. He believes I am the cause of this. Marian knew better.

"Why not?" the earl echoed. "By God, Robert, you heard her—"

"She told you the truth, nothing more, as you have often required of me. That truth may distress you, it may even offend you, but it is what it is. If you accuse her of dishonor for that act which we both committed, then you must send me from your hall also."

De Mandeville sat down quietly. Bohun lingered a moment longer, then also resumed his seat. Marian saw the opacity of their eyes, the studied negligence of their movements as they took up cups of wine. They were powerful noblemen accustomed to subterfuge, to turning away attention so as to guard another's pride.

Mine? Marian smiled. *No—I think the earl's.*

"Robert." The earl pressed hands against the table as if to steady himself. "Robert, I will not have this played out here before my friends—"

"Why not?" Robin took another step forward, hitching a single shoulder. "They have heard much of it already, have they not? I doubt you could convince my Lord of Alnwick to leave; he is much entertained, I believe."

Marian glanced at the man. Indeed, the other looked on with a bright-eyed fascination.

The earl's voice was crisp. "This is not suitable business to be aired before others."

"Then air more suitable business." Robin's spine was rigid. "Perhaps you might explain what has become of Huntington Hall."

It was not at all what the earl might have expected. "I had it torn down," he replied simply. "Only a fool would have overlooked the brick and timber. Why buy more when the old can be reused?"

She could not see Robin's face, but she marked the sudden

surge of interest in Alnwick's avid eyes, and the utter stillness of the others.

"You shame me," Robin breathed. *"Ya Allah,* but you shame me."

"I shame *you!"* The earl was infuriated. "By God, boy, I should disinherit you on the spot for speaking to me this way. Shame you, indeed! I am of a mind to have you flogged for such impertinence!"

Very softly Robin said, "You will never flog me again."

The earl's mouth tightened to a grim, flat line. He turned from his son and stared harshly at Marian. "You are to leave this hall."

Say nothing—don't give him the satisfaction. Marian gathered her kirtle and cloak and curtseyed very slowly. "As you wish, my lord."

"No." Robin half turned toward her, staying her with a hand. "No, Marian . . ." He turned again to his father. She saw the line of level shoulders, the rigidity of his spine. "There are few things in life I cherish, my lord. One of them was my mother. The other was that hall. Both of them you destroyed."

"Robert—"

He raised his voice. "There is the regard of my king, of course, which was earned on the battlefield . . . and the regard of this woman, which was never earned, but given." Robin paused thoughtfully. "No—nothing more. Disinheritance would strip me of nothing I do not willingly forsake."

The earl clutched the table. "Before *God,* Robert—"

"Before God, certainly. Before your peers as well." Robin spread both hands. "Shall this be *attendre,* then—to employ the language of our sovereign . . . or, in good Saxon English, do you declare me attainted?"

Geoffrey de Mandeville set back his bench and rose. "I am Justiciar of England, so declared by Richard, King of the English," he said quietly. "If you so desire, my Lord of Huntington, I will officiate over this disinheritance."

"I desire no such thing!" the earl snapped. "You know that,

Geoffrey . . . this is a boy speaking, no more, offering hard language and idle threats merely to provoke me."

De Mandeville looked at Robin, then turned toward the earl. "If you would for one moment cease behaving very much as you have accused your son, you would see that neither of you desires this. But I am convinced that both of you are eminently capable of seeing this travesty through merely to outface one another." His blue eyes glittered. "You have no other son. Will you so easily forfeit this one?"

"Geoffrey." The earl's tone was raw. "Geoffrey—you heard the things he said."

"Harsh words, old friend"—de Mandeville's expression was sad—"but if you would have him be a man you must let him declare himself." He shook his head slightly. "Put away the strap, Robert, even in your thoughts . . . the time for that is done."

The earl's face crumpled. He sat down hard upon his bench and stared blindly into his wine as Robin reached for Marian's hand.

DeLacey sat in the castle chapel. He profaned it with drunkenness, drinking from a pitcher without recourse to a cup, so he need not leave the chapel before he desired to. He did not, just at present, desire anything but recompense, and relief from bitter conviction.

"He's had her," he said. "Locksley. He's *had* her." DeLacey drank wine. "Tupped FitzWalter's daughter." He stared hot-eyed at the altar. "*Last night*, I'll wager—"

God, but it hurt. It hammered in his head.

"She sends *me* away, then spreads her thighs for him." Wine ran down his throat until he took the pitcher away. "Earl's heir or no, I'll have the whoreson's balls."

In the darkness he called her name. Marian awoke, twisting, and put her hand on his chest. "What is it?" He was damp with sweat, breathing raggedly. She smelled the tang of fear. *"Robin—"*

"No," he said, "no . . ." And then moved almost frenziedly, gathering her to his chest. She felt the lean, hard length of his body as he wrapped her in his arms, hooking a leg over hers. "Let me feel you breathe. Let me feel your warmth—I need to know it is real—"

Her head was cupped in the hard hollow between his jaw and collarbone. Her breath touched his face. "It is real," she whispered. "And *I* am real—I promise."

Pale hair mixed with dark. "I need you," he said unevenly, "for more reasons than I can count . . . but also for the dreams. To drive away the *nightmares*—."

"I know," Marian whispered. He lay very still against her as her naked flesh warmed his. "I know," she said again, thinking of his demons. She hoped it would be enough; that *she* would be enough.

Fifty-Nine

The dawn was wet, but drying. Marian stood at the narrow splayed window and folded the shutter back, admitting infant daylight. Behind her Robin dressed, pulling boots on over hosen.

The subtle sound of his movements and the knowledge of his presence filled her with fierce joy, but also a poignant awareness of a division she felt too keenly: love, but also anger, that joy could be usurped by the presence of other realities she had no desire to acknowledge.

She glared fiercely out at the dawn. *It isn't supposed to be like this.* Certainly it hadn't been in any of her dreams, in the discussions with her mother, in the comments of her father. Love simply *was,* a purity of passion, without the impedimenta of men like William deLacey and fathers like the earl.

Cynically, she reflected, *This is not what the minstrels sing about.*

He said something then, a murmured inquiry, and she knew reality had shattered the fragile illusory web spun in dream-filled sleep. *Dreams are childish things . . . I cannot afford them now.*

"Marian," he said, and she turned to tell him finally what had brought her to Huntington. His face was very still as the cock in the castle bailey crowed the day duly come.

She had awakened early, thinking of how to say it. So now she spoke with little inflection, merely reciting facts, to strip the words of weight so he would not react as another man might: in fury and foolish vows.

Robin listened quietly, then resurrected the mask she had wrongly believed discarded. It closed him off to her.

"Don't," Marian said. The mask was not for her, she knew, but she disliked the omen of it. It conjured Robert of Locksley before her, not the kinder Robin; she wanted very much to vanquish the former forever. "It is done, Robin. Finished. Surely the sheriff knows that."

"No." He shook his head. "You know that as well as I, or surely you would not have come here last night." Marian bit her lip; he read her too easily. "He is not the kind of man to accept defeat meekly, or even to tolerate it." The scar writhed briefly. "Nor are you the kind of woman a man would be willing to lose."

It was something men like the minstrel said, to flatter vain or plain women. But she did not view it in the same light; it was not what they discussed. What might please other women, women like Eleanor, served only to underscore her rising desperation.

The child in her cried out, "It isn't supposed to *be* like this!"

Robin smiled faintly with no hint of condescension; perhaps he had believed it also, before he went to war. "No doubt Helen said the same when Menelaus attacked Troy." He rose, gathering mantles and brooches.

In the aftermath of pleasure, knowing what lay before them, she was hollow and spiritless. "Troy was destroyed. It was impregnable, like this castle . . . but the Achaeans burned it down."

Robin stood before her, smiling into her eyes. "The Trojans believed too implicitly in false gods and their own abilities." He draped the mantle over her shoulder, touched her cheek with intimate fingers, then pinned the brooch deftly. "I have learned better than that. If my father is to be Priam, I will not stay here to see it."

"Ravenskeep will be a poorer Troy," she said dryly, wishing he might touch her again so she could forget William deLacey and the father who was an earl. "We have no gate anymore."

He grinned, swinging on and pinning his own mantle. "No. We'll go somewhere else . . . somewhere my father will never think of, so I am left in peace, and somewhere the sheriff will not think of either, so *you* are left in peace."

"Ah." Marian nodded. "We are leaving England, then."

It amused him, as she meant it to; anything to crack the tragedian's mask. "No," he said, laughing, "we'll go to Locksley. It's mine, after all—I should have gone before."

Marian blinked in surprise; she had not considered it. "Where *is* Locksley?"

He turned his face to the open window. Beyond the curtain-wall lay lush and undulant fields; farther yet the encroaching tree line, slate-gray against pewter-pink sky. "Out there, beyond the trees."

She looked. "But that's Sherwood Forest!"

"The hem of the skirts," he said. "Not the blacker soul." His breath was on her cheek as he turned his mouth to hers. "And if he strips *that* from me, I'll simply be Robin of Sherwood."

When she could speak, when he allowed her mouth respite to frame words instead of kisses, Marian asked, "Could you do so much? Could you give up so much?"

So close to her, he was warm. His eyes were not. "I count it little, Marian—he threatens disinheritance when I want nothing he means to withhold."

She would not let it go. "An earldom, Robin—"

"I care little enough for that." He put fingers to her lips, smiling faintly. "Do not name me a saint for it . . . I admit to some advantages for being heir to Huntington, and such things as my father's power are craved by many men. I use it myself, now, to serve the king"—his eyes glinted oddly—"but not in my father's way. Nor ever would. I have learned my own way—have *made* my own way—and it is patently not his."

If he would not look at all facets, Marian would. "You are his only son. Is it fair to an old man to deny him a fleshly legacy?"

He stroked her cheek. "Is it fair to ask me to live in my father's image, when I am not he?"

She smiled; he was nothing like his father. "No."

"Then do not." He kissed her briefly again. "And I am no longer precisely the honorable son he would have me be." Deftly he displayed the purse tied to his belt, peeling back the thong-snugged lip. A shake of his hand spilled the contents into his palm.

"Robin!"

His tone was peculiar. "I am turned thief, Marian: I crept into his treasury early this morning to see if there were truth to his claim of penury, and found there was little. He kept back his own jewels, while he sold my mother's." Robin turned over a cloak brooch of heavy-worked gold. "He stole from my mother what would have been yours, to build this stone monstrosity rearing over our heads . . . now I steal from him to buy a king his freedom."

What would have been yours . . . He meant more, then, than this; or had. Before. Her fingers trembled as she touched the gem-weighted rings. "When he learns what you have done—"

"Who but a fool would question an action done in the name of the king?" He smiled, pouring his father's wealth back into the purse. "Arrangements have been made. . . . I will send this to a man in Nottingham, who will send it to another. And then on to Germany, to ransom the Lionheart."

Her protest was immediate. "You cannot be expected to assume so much of the burden—"

He cut her off. "And I do not. The Jews have already done much, and everyone else in England; are the taxes not ruinous, and more frequent than usual?" He nodded even as she did. "I assume no more than I am willing to carry. Others carry more.

588

This is a token merely, but perhaps it will help. When added to everything else, it may prove enough to satisfy German Henry."

She would not ignore the truth, not even for a king. "*Thievery*, Robin. Such men are executed."

"Many of them are not. Many of them live *there*, not so far from Locksley."

Marian followed his finger as he indicated the vistas lying beyond the window. "Sherwood Forest."

"It is something," he told her. "And worth it, for a king."

DeLacey did not permit himself the luxury another man might require after a night of too much wine. He dressed, broke his fast, called for a horse to be saddled, and summoned Philip de la Barre to attend him in the great hall.

"Tell me of Roger," he invited.

De la Barre drew himself up, helm clasped in the crook of his elbow. "An ignorant man, my lord, but not altogether lacking in wit. He is sullen and much given to complaint, so much so that other serfs dislike him heartily, which adds to his sorry state. He is most unhappy with his lot, and believes without doubt that if he could go elsewhere that lot would be improved."

"To another manor?" The sheriff shook his head. "Anyone other than Lady Marian would have flogged him to the bone."

De la Barre allowed the faintest hint of contempt to sully his otherwise correct tone. "Saxons always believe what they cannot have is better."

"Indeed." DeLacey hid a smile; he knew of few men, Saxon or otherwise, who did not want more than what they had. But he forbore to mention it to de la Barre; a young Norman that close-minded would make an excellent aide. "What do you think of Jews, de la Barre?"

The soldier blinked. "Jews?"

"Do you admire them?"

De la Barre was at a loss. "*No*, my lord—they are Jews!"

It was enough for now. DeLacey returned to Roger. "Does the villein's discontent have to do with Normans, or with his present lot?"

"My lord, I believe nothing would satisfy him. He is a man who resents others no matter who they are."

"But he accepted Norman coin from the hand of a Norman soldier."

De la Barre's tone was dry. "With excessive haste."

DeLacey smiled coolly. "Have a troop assembled, de la Barre. I have a duty for you in the city."

No longer was Much a stranger in the Jewish Quarter, but a frequent visitor to the house of Abraham. He had learned the routine of the family so as not to disturb their privacy, and never stayed longer than required to deliver a purse to the aged moneylender. Abraham once suggested he wait and bring his findings all together, instead of one at a time, but Much remained unconvinced. He knew better than to be caught, *if* he were caught, with more then one purse in his possession; maiming he could survive, but they hanged habitual thieves.

At midday, in Market Square, he cut a third purse, and went immediately to the Jewish Quarter to deliver it to Abraham. There he found the streets entirely empty of Jews, and Abraham's house full of Normans.

He ducked back swiftly into a deep-cut doorway, sliding down to squat in the shadow, and watched in wary alertness. One man held the horses to keep them from being stolen—too many for him, Much knew; he would surely be caught and hanged—even though no Jew would touch a Norman possession for fear of retribution far greater than ordinary. One by one he chewed off his broken fingernails.

When the soldiers were done they filled the street once again, laughing and trading jests in Norman French as they sorted out their horses, put things into saddle wallets, then mounted and rode away. From the open doorway of Abraham's house came the sound of a woman's keening.

Much waited to see if the Normans would come back; they did that sometimes, to discover if the one they wanted was being brought out of hiding. But these Normans did not return, and Much at last rose and hurried to Abraham's house, where he found the front door shattered and the common room filled with wreckage. A young woman mourned broken things while an older one tended Abraham, who bled from a cut on his head.

Much stood in the doorway watching mutely. When the old man at last saw him, he knew the hope was gone. "Ah Much, here you are . . . *this* coin they will not have." He beckoned the boy in, fussing testily at the woman who pressed a damp cloth against his head. "Woman, I will heal—let me speak to the boy." When she made no reply but remained stolidly in her place, he sighed and beckoned again. "Here, Much—you must take a message to Robin."

"Robin," the woman muttered. "Why is *he* not here? He lets an old man risk himself, while he remains unknown."

"Silence, woman . . . what's done is done. Esther! Stop your wailing, girl . . . broken crockery can be replaced, and other things repaired."

The girl collecting bits and pieces shut her mouth on her mourning, but her face was unrepentant. Tears ran down her cheeks.

Much stood before the old man and took the purse from his tunic. "Lionheart," he said.

The older woman clucked her tongue in contempt. "Lionheart, indeed! What has he done for us? He goes to take Jerusalem while Jews suffer here in England."

"Sarah, hold your tongue." Abraham accepted the purse. "I thank you, Much. With this we begin again. But you must carry word to Robin that the sheriff's men took it *all.*" His dark eyes were dull with pain. "Do you understand? Not just the tax money, but the king's money as well; as you see, we could not stop them." Abraham sighed. "They thought we merely cheated the sheriff, nothing more, so our intent remains safe. But there is nothing left save this." He held up the leather purse.

Sarah stroked his blood-matted hair. "And what will this Robin *do?* Go to the sheriff himself and demand the money back?" Her face was strained; Much sensed fear for what might become of an old, ailing man. "Better he keeps his own coin. Better he keeps his own counsel."

"Go, Much," Abraham said wearily. "His father is the Earl of Huntington; he'll likely be found there."

Sarah inhaled sharply. *"Huntington's* son? This thief who steals for a king?"

"Go," Abraham said.

Much turned and ran out of the house.

They found him in the chapel concluding morning prayers. Tuck smiled at them tremulously, hideously self-conscious. He had spent the night in the hall on two benches shoved together, but he knew she had not. It was a sin they committed, carnal love with no sacrament, and yet he could not damn them for it. Better for her the man she loved than a man who would trick her to bed. *And that very thought is a sin. I require a priest myself.*

He slipped hands into wide sleeves. They were dressed for weather, and riding. Tuck was not surprised; the hall was full of gossip regarding the earl and his rebellious son, and the woman with whom he had passed the night. Tuck knew without asking that Marian would not stay beneath the earl's roof, and that Robin would see her to safety.

He drew in a deep breath. "I have nowhere else to go. If you will permit me, I'll come with you."

"To Locksley?" Robin smiled faintly. "It isn't a castle, Brother."

He lifted a fleshy chin. "I am from a very small village. I do not require a castle."

"But what about your abbey?" Robin asked. "What would your abbot say?"

Tuck's face flamed, but he would not look away. They deserved the truth from him. "My abbot will dismiss me."

Robin's mouth thinned. "For refusing to do the bidding of a perverse, selfish fool?"

"Yes." Inwardly he cringed. "Yes, my lord, he will—because my abbot is that and worse." He heaved a massive sigh. "I disbelieved the sheriff—I *wanted* to disbelieve him . . . but I am not so great a fool as all that. I see what I want to see and justify it later . . ." He shrugged again. "I am a weak man. Surely you can see that."

"There is nothing weak about you." Robin's voice was

steady. "She told me what you did. Few others would have done it."

Tuck smiled sadly, less innocent than before. "The sheriff is a powerful man. He will inform my abbot, to whom he will know just what to say, and I will be dismissed. Better I come with you now." He glanced sidelong at Marian, hoping not to offend them. "I will provide the proper escort so no false assumptions are made."

After a stunned moment, Marian laughed. Robin, eyes bright, managed a grave word of thanks.

Tuck's spirits lightened. *God hears*, he reflected buoyantly. *God hears everything. How can one question it? It is proved again and again.*

Much stood at the roadside waiting for the carter. He reckoned as best he could when the man might actually see him, then turned his back on the approaching cart and limped along the road. As the cart drew nearer yet, he essayed a profound misstep and sprawled face-first into the mud.

"Here, now!" The carter drew rein. "Here, now, boy—are ye hurt?" The man jumped down as Much struggled to get up. "By our sweet lady, you've made a mess of things . . ." The man squished through the mud. "Here—come up from there." The carter clutched at a hand and hauled Much upright. "Are ye hurt?"

Much smeared the back of his hand against his dirty face. He shook his head mutely, squared his narrow shoulders, and turned to limp away.

"Here, now." A hand closed on his shoulder. "Where are you bound for, boy?"

Much gazed longingly at the cart. "Castle," he whispered.

"Huntington Castle?" The carter brightened. "Hop up, boy—'tis where I'm bound." Then, more seriously, "Here—I'll set you up there myself. *Here*, boy—wait—"

Much suffered himself to be lifted into the cart. He slumped against the side and examined one muddy bare foot.

The carter was concerned. "Not hurt bad, is it?"

Much shook his head, gazing forlornly from under a mud-freighted forelock.

The man's relief was obvious. "Well, then, that's all right. We'll go on, then, won't we?" The carter climbed up onto his seat, grasped the lines, and clucked to the horse. "Hold on, boy—mud's bogging the wheels."

Sly grin blossoming, Much held on tightly as the cart jerked into motion.

As he did every morning, the Earl of Huntington went out to walk the wall surrounding his massive keep. He paused at every fifth crenel to gaze across the vista, assessing weather and wind, then continued on his way.

But half of the way around there was life stirring in the bailey; he glanced down curiously and saw first the woman, then the monk with her.

The earl clutched the crenel. *Let her go back to Ravenskeep and entertain other lovers.* He looked more eagerly, marking provisioned horses. He nodded, intensely pleased. *My son will soon forget her.*

But his self-satisfaction was extinguished as Robert crossed the bailey leading a third horse. On the saddle was hooked a common yeoman's longbow and a quiver of white-fletched arrows, as well as bulging wallets; in his left hand he carried a sheathed Norman sword, its massive pommel winking briefly an eye of purest steel.

No. He took a single step toward the closest stairs but four paces away. Aloud he announced, "I will not permit this. No," though no one could hear him. The earl descended swiftly. "Robert! Wait!"

Three faces turned to him: the woman's, the monk's, his son's. His son's was all that mattered.

By God, show no haste . . . give her no chance to gloat. He slowed perceptibly as he reached the bailey cobbles, moving with a solemn dignity that would not, he was convinced, betray the burgeoning fear so alien to him.

"Robert." He halted before his son and linked hands behind his back in seeming idleness. The earl forced a smile, though it barely crimped his mouth. "The chase is lush with game. Which are you hunting today?"

Robert shook his head.

Desperation augmented fear. "Robert—Robert wait—" *No, not like that.* He intensely disliked his tone and schooled it accordingly into the crispness he favored. "When may I expect you back?"

Robert turned and hooked the sheathed sword by its belt over the saddle, then led his horse to Marian, whom he assisted to mount. "When I am back, my lord."

"Robert—" The earl lowered his hand quickly so as not to betray too much. "Robert, you *will* return."

He watched as his heir tugged free Marian's tangled mantle and murmured something quietly, letting a hand linger on her knee in an intimacy the earl found as infuriating as embarrassing. Robert glanced toward his father as he turned to mount his horse. "There are things I must attend."

"But you *will* return!"

Adroitly avoiding longbow, quiver, and sword, Robert tossed his mantle clear and mounted easily with the fluid grace of youth, swinging a hosen-clad leg across the horse's broad rump. "I will return, yes. When I have settled my business."

"*Ro*bert." He moved the two steps and grasped at the tightened reins. "By God, *listen* to me—"

"No." The tone was the earl's own; he saw what Ralph meant, now. "I listened to you last night. I have no desire to hear more of the same now."

"You've only just come back!" It was a cry from the heart which he regretted instantly. And yet it served his purpose.

His son's expression altered. "Father," he said quietly, "I will come back again."

It was the first time in many years, too many years to count, that his son had called him anything less formal than "my lord."

The earl loosed the rein. "Then go," he said harshly, so as not to sound too soft.

He watched them ride through the gate, then swung and strode to the steps to remount the castle wall. The day he altered his habits would be the day he died.

Sixty

Marian understood why Robin had said Locksley was the hem of Sherwood's skirts, rather than its heart. In fact, Locksley was not so much a part of Sherwood as Sherwood was its wind-break; from Huntington Castle one saw only trees, but as Robin led them beyond the wood she discovered its density was sparse and its depth negligible. The ragged hem of Sherwood's skirts hung down in a sweeping curve, and in the hollow of the curve was cradled the village and manor of Locksley.

The village was neither large nor small, but somewhere in between. Spring crops were being sowed: peas and beans in the furrows, oats and barley on the ridges between, so standing water would not drown the grain. Each team of oxen required two men: one to drive the oxen by voice and goad, the other on the plow handles, the stilts, to make certain the coulter, share, and moldboard dug the furrows properly, piling up even ridges. Behind came the women and elders who performed the actual sowing.

She stared again at the tree line, at the edge of infamous Sherwood. Earlier that morning, as they rode from Huntington Castle, Robin had committed himself to the future that lay before them. His father's jewels, duly stolen, were sent with a trusted yeoman to someone known as Abraham—a Jew, then, surely—who would dispatch them to another, who would in turn send them along again, until at last they arrived in Germany. A matter of days, Robin promised.

Is it enough? Marian wondered. *How much to buy a king?*

Robin dropped back to ride abreast of her horse, so closely

their knees touched. He reached out once to stroke back a strand of hair that troubled her eyes, let his knuckle linger at her cheek as they smiled at one another, then lowered his arm reluctantly. His expression was more relaxed than Marian had seen since she'd told him of deLacey's unsuccessful trick to lure her into marriage.

She grinned. "Locksley agrees with Locksley."

It was a poor jest, but he laughed anyway. "I've always preferred the forest to halls and castles. This part of Sherwood was mine long before my father gave it to me."

A sprig of hope blossomed. "Then perhaps you should stay *here,* rather than at Huntington."

He shrugged, smile fading. "I may have no choice."

The intensity of her response was unexpected and overwhelming. It had nothing to do with his comment, merely with the comprehension of what they now shared. Their world had been remade in a reflection of their desire, yet others still attempted to shape it to fit their own designs.

In that instant Marian was swept up by the need to touch him, to reach out and press flesh to flesh, finger to finger; to close her hand on his arm so she could feel the warmth and vigor beneath the tunic sleeve. She wanted to know without question he was living, breathing, and hers.

But Tuck was just behind them, miserable on his horse; she did not consider it seemly or necessary to increase his concern by behaving inappropriately. Such behavior would reflect on him in his self-imposed role of chaperone.

Unevenly she said, "You must make peace with your father." *For yourself, if not for me; I want your world set right again, so there need be no more nightmares.*

But he was not thinking of the nightmare that had visited him the night before, frightening her half to death as he called out desperately in a foreign language. He was thinking of a man who dominated his life as powerfully as his memories of the Crusade. "No one may make peace with my father, because he will not permit a war. One does as he expects, or one is discarded." He shrugged dismissively; she knew it meant more than that. "He gave in last night because of Geoffrey de

Mandeville, not because he truly desired to admit he could be wrong—"

"You cannot know that," she protested. "I was present, Robin . . . he was truly distraught at the thought of losing you."

"No." He blocked a low-hanging limb, then twisted to warn Tuck of it. "No, not at the thought of losing *me*—the 'me' I truly am, whom he cannot fully acknowledge—but the thought of having no one of his blood to whom he could leave that castle."

Inwardly she sighed, knowing he was wrong; knowing also he was as stubborn as his father, and would never admit it. *Dealing with a man's pride is as difficult as planting a crop in rocky ground: everywhere you dig, another stone appears.*

He glanced at her sidelong. "The hall is just ahead, through the trees. There—do you see it?"

She did. It was a daub-and-wattle rectangular hall of willow- and oak-wand walls mixed with clay and chopped straw, supported by oak cruck trusses and beams, so that the thatched roof stood high and peaked.

No stone, no chimney . . . it will be an open hearth. Marian gazed up at the thatched roof. Chimneys were easier, venting smoke out one exit. Open hearths fanned smoke mostly into the hall, though some escaped through the roof vent cut in the thatching for that purpose.

Marian smiled wryly. Part of her longed for Ravenskeep and the luxuries she was used to, such as a chimney, stone walls, and courtyard. The other part of her longed to stay and make Locksley hers and Robin's. But she was not a knight's daughter for nothing. She understood the aristocracy, the demands of nobility, the requirements of rank. He was heir to vast estates and an ancient English title. If a woman's future was too often prescribed merely by gender and dowry, Robin's was by blood.

Much roused as the carter called a greeting to the guards at Huntington Castle's main gatehouse, and scrabbled up to peer over the side. He saw the stables, the vegetable garden, the guardhouse, then the carter was down from his seat and offering to lift *him* down, so he could be on his way. Much scrambled out of the cart himself, then stood with one foot cocked up so the man wouldn't tumble to his trick.

"Shall I fetch someone for you?" the carter asked. "Spit-boy, are you? Or horseboy?"

Much shook his head; there was no one to fetch.

The carter scratched his head, mussing wiry red hair. "Well, then, you're here. Don't put too much weight on that foot."

Much shook his head again.

The carter squeezed Much's slender shoulder and walked back around to his horse. "Off with you, then; I've work."

Much hobbled off until the carter had gone around to the other side of the keep, then walked normally, if swiftly, toward the stable block. First he would look at the horses to see if Robin's was present.

If not, he'd think of something.

"Lionheart," he muttered.

Tuck sent thanks to God as the horses were halted at last. It mattered little to him that they had reached Locksley Hall; he wanted to reach anywhere at all so long as he could get off his horse.

What is wrong with two good feet? he wondered forlornly. *They carry me well enough at a pace I much prefer, and they do not require feeding.*

Tuck sighed heavily, grateful at last to dismount, and clambered down clumsily as he dragged at voluminous cassock. A questioning glance at Marian and her skirts underscored the problem with excess material as purely his own. Marian's face was radiant, her expression exalted; she did not appear to notice any difficulty with skirts, but then she was noticing nothing but the man who lifted her down from the saddle into his arms, where she remained without protest.

Tuck smiled ruefully, no longer quite so embarrassed. *They can look at nothing else save one another. I doubt they would notice rain if it fell right on their heads.*

With infinite care he pulled his cassock into good order, fussed with his belt and rosary, then cleared his throat loudly; he could not condone too many such displays—or an inordinate length in *this* one—or he would be a failure in his role as chaperone. It was one thing to presume they had shared a bed; quite another to see the prelude.

He cleared his throat again. His tone was a little more strident than he intended. "Is there water to drink in your hall?"

Robin's single outstretched arm indicated the nearby well while his mouth made use of hers without recourse to speech.

Ah well, Tuck sighed as he walked somewhat stiffly toward the well, *it is theirs to confess, not mine.*

Robin's horse was not present. Much chewed at a ragged thumbnail, slipping back out of the stable into the bailey. He needed to ask someone, but who was he to ask? A mud-caked Nottingham cutpurse with no business at the castle—

Hooves rang on cobbles and someone shouted out that the sheriff was coming in. For an instant Much froze, then skittered back inside the stable to duck down in the nearest shadow.

More horses. More shouting. Norman French, and English. He peered through a crack between two timbers and saw the sheriff himself swinging down from his horse. He was cloaked and booted for the road, with thunder in his eyes.

Much bit into his thumb. How could he find Robin while the sheriff was in the castle?

He couldn't be a horseboy; he might give himself away.

Much removed his thumb. The word was in his mind. Spitboy, then, just as the carter had asked.

Robin paused in the doorway, then proceeded two more steps before halting again to watch her. Marian stood in the bleak, empty hall and surveyed its disrepair. Spiders had spun thick webs, generations of mice lived in the walls, and old rushes were mildewed and rank.

She knew he was there, already tuned to his step. She did not bother to look back. "How long has it been since you came?"

Hair had come loose of its coif and cloak hood to tumble down over her shoulders. *The shadows are kind to her.* . . . Robin, distracted, did not answer at once. He was less concerned with the hall than with the woman in it, whom he could not put out of his mind for more than a single moment until he thought of William deLacey, who wanted her as well.

She glanced back across a shoulder. "Well? Has it been *that* long?"

He recalled her question at last. "Here?" Robin shrugged. "Never *here*. I came for the woods, not the hall." He felt a little embarrassed; he had not considered the condition of a hall too many years left empty. "I've spoken to the reeve just now. He'll bring villeins in at once to help you. I'll be back as soon as I can."

"Back?" She swung sharply to face him. "Where are you going?"

"I promised you once before I would speak to my father."

"Yes, but . . ." Marian's mouth tightened. "He will never consider it. Not now. I shamed him, Robin. I shamed him before his peers."

It stung him to quick retort. "You shamed no one! *Ya Allah*, Marian, he is a stubborn old fool with no blood left in his veins. You heard Geoffrey de Mandeville and Henry Bohun—they were more than prepared to pay you respect and honor—"

"But *he* wasn't," she said. "Nor will he ever be." Marian swallowed tightly, pressing the flat of her hands hard against her kirtle skirts. "Robin, go if you must—I will never hinder you—but go to make peace. I can wait. Let him come to know his son without the impediment of a woman who offends his sense of morals."

It infuriated him. "I care little enough *what* part of him is offended—"

"Robin." She smiled and put up her chin. "You sound very like your father."

It silenced him at once, as he knew she intended. But he could not help wondering if there were truth in her statement. He disliked the idea there might be. "Marian—"

She cut him off. "You intended this all along. I see it now . . . you meant to bring me here, then leave me."

He nodded; he could not lie to her. "I knew you would not stay beneath my father's roof another moment, after what he had said. I resolved last night to bring you here even before I knew of deLacey's plot. . . ." He shrugged self-consciously. "I wanted you to myself. At Ravenskeep, there are servants—"

Marian laughed. "There is *Tuck* here," she said dryly. "Did you intend to make him sleep with the livestock?"

"No, of course not." He had not considered Tuck at all.

"And there is Tuck *now,*" she said as someone beyond the door cleared his throat very loudly. "Go, then, if you must—I will keep myself occupied with the cleaning of your hall. I won't even notice you're gone."

He clapped a hand to his chest. "Clean through the bull's-eye, Lady!"

"Go," Marian said, laughing, "you know I will be here."

First my father. He strode from the hall past Tuck to the horse outside the door, bearing longbow and quiver and sword, *and then William deLacey. I will settle this once and for all.* He gathered rein and looped it up, preparing to mount.

"Wait," Marian said from the doorway.

Robin turned and she was there, stepping in hard against his body. "Let him *see,*" she said fiercely, catching handfuls of his hair as she dragged his mouth down to hers.

Ralph came quietly into the solar and extended a folded and sealed parchment to the earl. "The messenger waits below, in the hall."

The earl grunted as he broke the wax seal and withdrew the letter. De Vesci, Bohun, and de Mandeville looked on, waiting curiously. The earl ignored them, then forgot about them entirely as he read the letter. *My God . . . could the man be serious?* He scanned the letter again as well as the heavy seal impressed at the bottom, then glanced without urgency to Ralph. "Please give the messenger my gratitude for his haste—feed him, of course—but say he is not to wait upon my pleasure. I am sure his master does not expect an immediate answer."

"Yes, my lord." Ralph bowed his way out.

"Well?" de Vesci barked. "A man would be blind not to see the look in your eye."

The earl permitted himself a slight smile. He displayed the parchment briefly, pleased to see his hand did not shake. He could not afford to tell them everything in the letter, but part of it, yes. "Prince John sends his regards. He thanks me for the entertainment provided at the boar hunt. He discusses the need for more money to pay German Henry his ransom for the king."

"And?" de Vesci prodded.

And? the earl echoed inwardly. *More than you could imagine.* "He sends his affections for my son, whom he would like to see at Lincoln as soon as possible."

De Vesci swore softly.

Bohun grunted. "So it comes."

"The daughter," de Mandeville said. "He dangles her yet again." The older man nodded. "He wants to bring the barons in line. By acquiring your loyalty, he seeks to convince others of the wisdom in supporting him."

"What will you do?" Bohun asked.

"Send him to Lincoln," the earl replied. "If for no other reason than learning John's mind, he should go. I doubt anything will come of the marriage, but why not test John's sincerity?"

De Vesci grinned. "The same son who departed this morning with the FitzWalter girl?" The Lord of Alnwick laughed. "It will be days, possibly weeks, before he gets out of bed. And you want to send him to John?" He paused. "Were you ever young, Robert? Do you recall what it was to tup a lovely woman?"

In view of what the letter contained, the question bore particular weight. "There is no place for that sort of language here," the earl said. "Eustace, you devalue my son by suggesting such a thing."

"I suggest only that he may be less inclined to go to Lincoln than to stay wherever he is." De Vesci paused. "Where *is* he, Robert?"

"Never mind," de Mandeville chided. "This is but a small part in our play. There are other matters to be discussed."

Huntington opened his mouth to speak again, but broke off as Ralph appeared once more. "My lord, forgive me—there is another visitor: the Sheriff of Nottingham."

"In John's pocket," Bohun said promptly. "Sent to flush us out, do you think?"

De Mandeville shrugged; de Vesci, impatiently, threw himself down in a chair. "What now, Robert? On John's business, or his own?"

The earl considered it. "God knows the man is ambitious," he said, thinking rapidly. *This could be fortunate.* "He believed it possible to wed his daughter to my son. His common slut of a daughter, already despoiled!"

De Vesci laughed. "It would begin to seem as if your son has an affinity for women of loose morals."

Huntington glared at him. "My son will do as he is told." He turned to Ralph. "Is he alone?"

"He brought an escort with him, my lord, but he waits alone in the hall. He seems—subdued."

"Subdued? William deLacey? He must want something." The earl waved a hand. "Tell the sheriff I will be with him presently."

"Yes, my lord."

"Have him up here," de Vesci suggested with a sly grin. "Let us see what he would say then."

"No." The earl folded small the letter from Prince John and tucked it into his sleeve. "No, I think not. DeLacey serves himself before serving other men. Better I see him alone."

Below, left to his own devices, deLacey waited impatiently. He would have preferred to conduct the meeting in his own hall, but one did not summon the Earl of Huntington to Nottingham Castle, one went to the earl. It placed him at a disadvantage, but he would have to find a way to make it work for him.

He linked hands and tipped back his head, assessing the quality of the earl's architecture. DeLacey was much impressed. Techniques of construction had improved since the building of Nottingham Castle.

The earl came in at last, adjusting the fit of his robe. His expression was slightly impatient, which gave deLacey his cue.

"My lord." The sheriff bowed briefly. "My lord, I apologize for disturbing you without invitation, but I believe there may be a matter of business to be settled." He hesitated pointedly. "If I may be candid, my lord—?"

"Please." The earl seated himself and waved to the bench at the end of the trestle table. When the sheriff had seated himself he lifted a beckoning hand and a servant came up at once, bearing a fresh cup.

DeLacey accepted it and waited for the servant to pour it full. Then he turned his attention to the earl. "My lord, if you will excuse an aging man for his folly"—his smile was ingratiating—"I have come on an errand for which there may be no sane explanation. That is, I have come to retrieve the Lady Marian FitzWalter."

The earl of Huntington smiled. "I would be most grateful."

Sixty-One

The reeve's name was James. He was a tall, thin man with a stoop to his back, and yet Marian knew he had to be a sound husbandman or he would not have gained the position. Reeves were elected from the best farmers in the village, those who were quicker of wit than others, but still worked with them.

She glanced sidelong at Tuck, who stood with his hands hidden in wide sleeves, then met James's curious stare evenly. *Pretend this is Ravenskeep.* "Sir Robert told me he spoke with you."

"Aye, Lady Marian. I've brought some villeins in from the fields, and women for the hall."

He would suggest nothing, she knew. It was her place to give the orders, his to see they were carried out. "First, the rushes," she said. "I want the old ones taken out and burned, the floor swept clean, then new cut and brought in."

"Aye, Lady." James paused. "We've none of us seen the earl's son for a long time—are you his wife, then?"

Marian's smile faded. It would make a difference, she knew. A very great difference.

Astonished, she heard Tuck's voice from beside her. "This is God's work," he said quietly. "He has sent us here to put Locksley Hall to rights." He moved forward, clapping a fleshy hand to James's shoulder. "There are those among you in need of instruction . . . I am not a priest, James, but I can teach the need for humility as God has revealed." He urged the man out of the door. "Tell the others to start their work, while I begin mine."

"Aye, Brother." And James was gone, removed painlessly from her sight.

Marian sighed as Tuck turned back to her. "Thank you, Brother. But it won't put them off for long."

"God willing, Lady Marian—" Tuck kissed his crucifix, "we'll not *need* long. Has he not gone to see his father to have this matter settled?"

He meant well, Marian knew. But she was not convinced that anything would be settled.

The earl contemplated the sheriff. *Can I use this man? Can I lure this man into serving my needs while he thinks to serve his own?* He broke off a grape and consumed it. "When can you retrieve this woman?"

"Permit me to express my profound embarrassment." De-Lacey shifted his weight on the bench. "As you know, her father was killed on Crusade." He waited for the earl's acknowledging nod. "As you may *not* know, Sir Hugh and I were friends, *good* friends, my lord—I was deeply sorrowed at news of his death."

"Of course," the earl murmured. *Get on with this, you fool. Give me what I need.*

"Many people were unaware that his daughter and I were to be married. Out of deference to her mourning, I did not speak of the betrothal; I'm sure you understand."

The earl's interest increased tenfold, though he divulged none of it. *If he wants her for himself, he will be easy to use.* "Indeed,

I understand. One does not always speak of such personal matters."

"My lord." DeLacey set down his cup. "My lord, it grieves me to say the Lady Marian has asked to be granted release from the betrothal."

Has she indeed? The earl drank wine. "It is a request you might do well to grant," he remarked lightly. He let deLacey consider that a moment, then added casually, "I think she must be a witch."

"A—witch?" Clearly deLacey was startled.

"She must be. She's bewitched my son." Again he waited. "Why else would he take to bed a woman despoiled by outlaws?"

Two spots of color burned high in deLacey's cheeks. He was moved to drink most of his wine before saying anything further. "Then naturally you will have no objection if I remove her from your protection at once."

"I would grant you leave to drag her shrieking from my hall, were you so moved to try." In silence the earl ate more grapes, while he let deLacey think. He spat pips into the rushes with neat economy of motion. "I am grieved she has proved a burden to you, William . . . she is a difficult young woman. I, too, have suffered—and *will* suffer, if this matter is not resolved very quickly." He ate another grape. "I am certain your office is capable of rendering me relief. It lies well within your power to aid me; in aiding me, you aid yourself."

DeLacey's expression was thoughtful. "By all means, my lord, I would wish to relieve you of any suffering."

"And your own portion of it, of course."

The sheriff's smile was odd. "My own is of a different nature."

"Indeed," the earl said dryly.

DeLacey hesitated. "May I speak frankly, my lord?"

"Do."

"She has dishonored her father's memory—"

"*Frankly*, William; this is prevarication."

DeLacey's mouth flattened almost imperceptibly. "Times are difficult, my lord. England's king is imprisoned, while her prince squanders her wealth on personal desires."

Huntington said coolly, "You bore me, William." He ate another grape. "I want the FitzWalter girl managed." He lifted his cup and drank, then set it down again. "It matters little to me if you desire to marry the girl"—he freighted his words with disdain and was pleased to see answering color in deLacey's cheeks—"or merely to bed her. Do whatever you like with her; a man's tastes are his own concern." He tore free four more grapes, ridding his mouth of pips before inserting new fruit. "I suppose even witches are redeemable when given the chance to recant."

DeLacey's expression was odd. "Indeed, my lord. We must see she is given that chance."

"And I suppose if a man of my position should suggest to the king—or to his heir—that a recanted witch be given in marriage to a man such as yourself, there would be no objections from anyone if it were celebrated under duress." He spat out pips, anticipating the next question. "She is not presently here. Nor is my son."

"Ah." DeLacey smiled faintly. "It seems we are both embarrassed by their temerity—"

Huntington's tone was crisp. "My son is not, has never been, and *will* not be an embarrassment to me." He smiled coolly. "I believe I have made my desires quite clear to you."

"Indeed, my lord. Very clear." DeLacey's tone was circumspect, but his eyes glittered intently. "I will attend to the matter at once."

"Good." Huntington rose. "I believe this discussion ends the matter for now. Have you any other business?"

"No, my lord. No, of course not." DeLacey stood up quickly. "My lord, I thank you for your time. I am sorry to have troubled you on so personal a matter."

The earl nodded coolly. "So long as this difficulty is resolved very soon, the trouble was negligible." He made a practiced gesture. "Ralph will see you out."

Much made his way with care across the castle bailey, walking with assurance so as not to look out of place, but not so much cockiness that he did not fit the part. He meant to find

608

one of the kitchen entrances at the back of the keep. It shouldn't be difficult; usually spit-boys came and went on various errands for the cooks.

He grinned to himself. This was *truly* a castle, not a figment of his dreams. A fitting one, Much decided, for the prince and his princess.

Someone shouted in French. Much spun sharply, staring, then darted against the keep wall.

No, it wasn't for him. The Normans were mounting horses again as the sheriff came out of the hall.

Much knelt against the cobbles, making himself small. He recalled very clearly the strength of deLacey's grip when he had closed it on his wrist.

"Won't cut it off," he whispered, tucking his right hand under his left. "Robin won't *let* you."

Robin rode up the curve of the road to the front of his father's castle, and found the gate wide open. Someone was leaving the castle—Alnwick, Hereford, or Essex, or perhaps all three at once—or someone was arriving.

More of John's enemies? Robin smiled faintly as he rode up to the gatehouse. *Is even Huntington large enough?*

One of the guards saluted him with a welcoming greeting. "No luck on the hunt, my lord?"

Robin acknowledged him, admitting he'd had no luck without explaining himself. He drew rein briefly, letting the horse sidle. "Is someone coming, or going?"

"Going, my lord; he's come! The Sheriff of Nottingham."

Robin twisted in the saddle as the horse circled noisily, hooves ringing off cobbles. He stared hard at the entrance to the inner bailey some thirty paces away. "Then I'll wait here to wish him farewell." He stationed his mount to block the gate, held him in place with his heels, then quietly bided his time.

By the time William deLacey strode out into the bailey to grasp the reins of his horse, he knew what he would do. It would be complex in execution, but for Marian it was worth it.

And the earl himself supports me. He did not care why, though he supposed it was because Huntington looked much higher than Marian for his son's wife. Prince John had a bastard girl; perhaps she was being dangled.

"Gisbourne," he murmured intently. "I'll need Gisbourne to write the letter, since I've dismissed that gluttonous monk." He swung up into his saddle, swinging aside his mantle, and lifted his voice to the waiting Normans. "To Nottingham."

He led them out of the bailey. *I'll need Abbot Martin, and a witness . . . someone from Ravenskeep.* DeLacey smiled. *I'll use the unhappy Roger—*

The cool voice cut through his thoughts. "My lord Sheriff, greetings. We have business, you and I; a small matter to be settled."

DeLacey pulled up short. Before him, blocking the gate, waited a lone man on horseback. He was green and gold in the sunlight, pale hair falling over broad shoulders. The eyes and the tone were steady, displaying neither reluctance nor the headlong anger that marked a fool.

DeLacey nodded slightly. *Not a boy any longer.* Behind him his escort gathered, murmuring in Norman French. He heard swords being loosened in sheaths.

He thrust out an imperative hand to check them instantly. Then, with excess civility, "Robert! What business is that?"

"The Lady Marian."

Nothing more than that. DeLacey nodded again. Too much lay between them now for diplomacy or subterfuge. Besides, he had a weapon: knowledge. Robert did not know that the earl supported him.

It made deLacey most lighthearted, though he maintained an even tone. "It was her father's wish. Do you blame me for seeking to fulfill it?"

To his surprise, Locksley laughed. "And I who brought her the message. Do you blame me for regretting that I ever told her at all?"

"You brought it . . ." He let it go with a tongue-cluck of irritation; none of it was important now that he had begun to devise his plan. "What's done, is done," he said simply. "Let her father's soul deal with it." *And you will deal with me.*

Locksley said nothing at first. Then, with cool disdain, "I fail to see how her father could have believed you would protect her. You are her greatest danger."

He is the earl come again; you can hear it in his tone. The sheriff smiled. "There was a time when Marian was naught but a girl, and I but a friend to her father. She was an enchanting child, but nothing more than that . . . until her father died, and I went to offer my aid. The child-Marian was banished. In her place was a glorious woman whom no man might ignore, nor put out of his thoughts at night; you should know well enough what I mean." He was rewarded by the brief flash of anger in Locksley's eyes. "To Hugh, she was his daughter. He would never see the woman who usurped the little girl's place. It would never occur to him that he could get an earl's son for a knight's daughter."

Locksley reined in his restive horse. "She is the king's ward, not yours."

Which king is that? The one in prison, or the one in Lincoln? DeLacey smiled. "But kings die in battle. Hugh had to be certain someone he trusted would see to his daughter's welfare. That was what I intended: to ward her welfare utterly." He shrugged. "But what is a simple sheriff when compared to Huntington's son?" He let that sink in; it would mean something to Locksley, who would know very well that high rank was an elegant bait even when it tasted bad. *His own father strikes at it.* "In my desire and ambition, I overstepped my bounds." He softened his tone. "But I did not reckon on falling in love with her."

Locksley's horse pawed noisily, ringing shod hoof against cobblestone. He checked it with reins and a single murmured word. He said nothing at all to deLacey, though his eyes burned bright as coals.

He's learned to hide himself . . . the earl—or the Crusade—has taught him well. DeLacey inclined his head in a graceful admission of defeat. "I wish you well of her." *For as long as you may have her.*

Locksley drew aside. He sat easily in his saddle as deLacey rode by with his Normans.

Longbow? deLacey wondered. But he was through the gatehouse. None of it mattered now; there was the plan to be put into motion.

"Insh'Allah," Robin muttered, reining his horse toward the inner bailey, "the day I believe that man is the day I am dead—*Ya Allah,* boy, watch out!"

But it was Much. He knew it at once without knowing why; he recognized the swift dart beneath the horse's head, the deft grasp of the reins, the pert face peering around the muzzle.

"Much?" He swung down off the horse. The boy hadn't known his rank, merely his nickname. *Someone told him.* "Much, what is it?"

"Lionheart," Much said.

Robin cupped the horse's muzzle and guided him back from the boy's bare feet. The thought was inconsequential: *Marian has his shoes.* "Is it Abraham? Something about the money?"

Much nodded urgently. He pointed out of the gate. "Took it."

"Who took—*he* took? The sheriff?" Robin bit out a curse.

Much nodded. "Abraham said, 'tell Robin *all* the money.' "

"That whoreson bastard . . ." Robin considered it rapidly. They would have to retrieve it, of course, one way or another. But there was one consolation—"—at least the jewels were sent; Abraham said so. And a little money." Robin glanced past Much to the keep, then scrubbed a hand over his face. "Too much to do . . ." He let it go, dropping the hand to Much's shoulder. "My oath to you," he said. "We serve the Lionheart."

Much nodded vigorously.

"But there is another promise I made, and it also must be honored. Do you understand?"

Yet another nod.

Robin smiled. "We've a journey ahead of us, and a difficult task to do. I'll need your help, Much. Will you aid the Lionheart?"

Much plucked a thin purse from his tunic sleeve and pushed it into Robin's hand.

Robin sighed. "Before God, Richard will owe you his kingdom." He grinned. "Hold on to it for me." The purse disappeared. "Much. Can you find me the Hathersage Giant? Will Scarlet? Adam Bell?"

Much nodded at once. "Sherwood."

Robin laughed; oddly, he felt lighthearted. *Because I have made my decision. Because I will be what I must, regardless of my father.* "Do you know *where* in Sherwood?"

Much nodded again.

"Good. I want you to go there and find them, tell them I desire to speak with them—tell them, too, there is money in it"—he grinned as Much's face brightened—"and that I will ride out to the place where Adam Bell and I practiced archery."

"Abraham?" Much asked worriedly.

Robin nodded. "After I meet the others. We need them, Much. I cannot do this alone." Then, at the boy's anguished expression, he amended it instantly. *"We* cannot do this alone."

Much was satisfied.

Sixty-Two

Gisbourne wrote his name laboriously at the bottom of the page, blew at the ink to dry it—the boy had brought no sand—then carefully folded up the letter and squeezed the creases tightly. He wanted to seal it closed, but the boy had also brought no wax.

I should be grateful he brought me this much. Besides, few in the castle could read; he was in no real danger of discovery. Gisbourne motioned the boy over. He disliked having to depend on him for this, but his leg still was not able to support him for long periods of time. It was improving, but he knew better than to press himself too hard. "Take this out to the guardhouse and find one of the off-duty soldiers to deliver it for me. He is to ride to Lincoln, to Prince John. This is royal business."

He waited for the boy's big-eyed nod of acknowledgment, then dismissed him and slumped back against the pillows. "There," he murmured. "So he knows I have not forgotten."

Eleanor waited until the door to Gisbourne's chamber was shut, then called the boy to her at the end of the corridor. "Give it to me."

After a moment's hesitation, the boy complied.

"What did Sir Guy say to you?"

He stood stiffly, arms at his sides. "That I was to take it to a soldier."

"And?"

"That *he* was to take it to Prince John, at Lincoln."

"Ah. Good. Here." Knowing a shrewd boy would return at once to Gisbourne with news of the interception, she gave him a penny bearing old King Henry's countenance. "You have the day free. Go spend that in the city."

The boy's face lighted. He stammered his thanks, then hurried off down the corridor to the hall beyond.

Eleanor looked at the writing on the outside of the parchment. It meant nothing to her, just marks upon the page. But she had seen the boy, clutching parchment, quill, and ink, go running to Gisbourne's chamber, and knew Sir Guy planned something. "To Lincoln," she murmured thoughtfully. "What have *you* to say to Prince John?"

For that matter, what did she? John had said he expected reports. Perhaps it was time she told him what her father had attempted to do with Marian FitzWalter before *Gisbourne* could, since Gisbourne wanted her for himself.

"No doubt he explains it all in his favor, in this letter." She tapped the folded parchment against one palm. "I need to hire a clerk." She could not afford for Prince John to decide that Gisbourne could have the FitzWalter woman. The whole point was to be rid of Marian entirely.

"A royal ward," Eleanor mused. "She's meant for better than Gisbourne . . . for someone who can afford to pay the king for her hand." It was done all the time. Ambitious men bought rich heiresses to increase their own holdings, which in turn increased their power. "I need to remind John that she's worth more than Gisbourne can pay."

There were clerks for hire in Nottingham. All she need do was find one who knew how to keep his tongue still.

"Money," she muttered tightly. "All it requires is money."

As deLacey dismounted in the bailey of Nottingham Castle, Philip de la Barre appeared with alacrity. He held himself very stiffly upright with the helm at rest in the crook of his elbow, but the glint in his eyes was pronounced. "My lord. I have come to report success."

"Good." DeLacey handed off his mount. "Come report it in my chamber; I want to change my clothing." And as soon as possible, since much of what he wore was covered with mud. "Come, de la Barre . . ." He turned swiftly and strode off, unpinning his cloak and tossing it off to a waiting servant as he moved. "Have it brushed clean," he ordered, then went on his way with de la Barre hastening in his wake. "The road is disgustingly foul after the storm . . . one forgets the misery of rain when spring first appears." DeLacey unlatched the chamber door and swung it open one-handed. "Precede me, de la Barre." He followed the young Norman in after shouting for a body servant to attend him. "Now, if you please."

De la Barre sighed a little and gave his report. "There was more than you expected, my lord. Much more. The Jew had hidden some in another room, locked away in a wooden casket."

"Ah?" DeLacey sat down on his bed as the servant entered and thrust out his foot so the man might divest him of his boots. "Pray do not twist my ankles."

"He would have said nothing about it. He was willing enough for us to take the money for taxes, but he protested when my men found the casket."

"Coin is precious to Jews. They prefer it to food." DeLacey hung on to the bed as the servant tugged off his boot. "What did the old man say?"

"That it was not for you, my lord. That it was no part of the new tax."

"That is to be expected." One foot bared, he extended the other boot. "You have brought it all back."

"Yes, my lord. Under lock and key."

"Good." DeLacey swore as his ankle twinged. "Not so hard, villein!" He clapped a hand against the man's ears. "Did the Jew speak of anything more? If he hoards coin apart from others, it may be for some greater purpose."

"He said little, my lord."

DeLacey nodded thoughtfully. "But one cannot trust them. They lie to protect their own, and they worship coin." He frowned. *What purpose do they serve? The king's? Could the money be meant for Richard?*

De la Barre shifted. "My lord—"

The sheriff cut him off. "I have another task for you. Do you recall Roger, the villein at Ravenskeep?"

"Indeed, my lord."

"You recall also his willingness to aid us."

"Yes, my lord."

The other boot came off. DeLacey bent and massaged his ankle, then gestured for the servant to begin undoing his hosen wrappings. "Philip." He used the Christian name purposely, and saw the answering fire in de la Barre's eyes. "Over time, a sheriff has occasion to collect certain things gathered from miscreants."

"One would think so, my lord; yes."

Such an eager soul, my Philip. "We have had occasion to do part of the Church's work here as well . . . those suspected of witchcraft are brought to *me*, of course, for examination and, if necessary, execution. We have acquired any number of strange oddments since I came to Nottingham." He glanced sidelong at earnest de la Barre. "You are ambitious, yes?"

"My lord—"

"It is not a sin, Philip. I prefer ambitious men. They serve better than those too satisfied." He removed his own tunic and dropped it to the floor, then extended his arms so the servant could untie his sherte sleeves. "How does Archaumbault fare?"

De la Barre was taken off-stride by the change in topic. "He fares much better, my lord. In fact, he has resumed some minor duties."

"Good." DeLacey stood and stripped out of sherte and hosen, motioning impatiently for fresh clothing. "If you desire to prosper here, you will do me the following service."

De la Barre nodded eagerly. "As you will, my lord."

DeLacey smiled satisfaction as he was handed fresh sherte and hosen. *So accommodating, Philip. You may indeed rise—or fall, as it suits me.*

Something unseen and unheard alerted him. Robin glanced up sharply with a hand to his meat-knife, and found no more than his father in the doorway, watching him pack his things. "So," the earl said, "she has won after all."

"It wasn't a battle, my lord. This is the natural order of things."

The earl entered slowly, moving like an old man. He sat down wearily on the bench next to the door. "Indeed, it *is* the natural order of things . . . as it is natural for a father to desire the best for his son."

The earl's ascetic face was stretched too tightly over sharp bones. *How much do I resemble him? And will I look like this when I age?* Robin sat down on the edge of his bed, packing forgotten. "A father may desire things for his son, but he must also admit that son has a mind of his own."

"Do you?" Huntington smiled wearily. "Yes, perhaps you do—and perhaps I have not been cognizant of it for too long." He set his spine against the wall, stretching fallen shoulders. Frowning vaguely, he asked, "Why are you wearing such clothing? You look like a yeoman instead of an earl's son."

Robin smiled wryly. He *was* wearing yeoman's clothing: plain brown hosen, cross-wrapped to his knees; a simple dark green tunic with sleeves cut off at elbows; a collared leather hood slipped to lie flat across shoulders and spine; and dark leather bracers over wrists and half of his forearms. In his saddle wallets there was also a plain leather jerkin for cooler days. All of it was borrowed, save boots, belt, and meat-knife, from his father's finest archer, who had trained the earl's son without the earl's knowledge.

Robin shrugged, offering no answer; in a moment his father,

attention distracted, returned again to the topic that occupied his mind. "I admit freely, Robert, that Sir Hugh FitzWalter was a decent man, a good knight—"

"Then why—"

The earl lifted a hand and his son fell silent. "A moment, pray you—then I will listen to your side." He smiled faintly. "Had the other boys lived, you would have been a third son. Even the Earl of Huntington might find it sufficiently difficult to parcel out his holdings among three sons, although I daresay at least one of you—*you*, perhaps?—would have gone into the Church."

His eyes creased in faint amusement, puckering fragile flesh into a netting of silken wrinkles as his son looked skeptical. "You doubt me? Well, perhaps not you—no man can predict where a religious vocation might grow." He sighed. "Had the others lived, I would have no objection to you marrying Hugh FitzWalter's daughter"—and now the tone altered—"had she not been despoiled by outlaws." His eyes were steady, unflinching, intolerant of protest. "Do you understand? I could not have countenanced it that way; do you believe I can permit it *now*, when you are the only living seed of my loins?"

Fascinated in spite of himself, Robin stared at the man. It was the first real conversation they had ever had, although as yet he had not had his say. It moved him to hear the man speak simply about how he felt instead of merely announcing orders.

"My lord—" he checked himself. "Father." He appealed to flesh and blood in hopes the earl would weigh things by a different measure. "Permit me to say very frankly that I find your feelings old-fashioned."

"Old-fashioned?" White eyebrows shot up. "I have said nothing at all of your behavior, Robert, which was reprehensible. In my day decent men did not bed unmarried women—"

"Perhaps *you* did not—"

"Of course I did not!" some of the earl's ascetic querulousness returned.

He laughed. "Did you bed married ones?"

"Robert!"

Robin sighed, laughter checked. *It was an aberration, the reasonable tone. I should have known what to expect.*

"What I am trying to tell you," the earl said on a note of immense patience, "is that I understand the nature of her appeal. She is surpassing beautiful—but I cannot allow you to marry a woman who has been publicly despoiled."

Ya Allah, what a refrain. "She has not been despoiled, my lord . . . unless you name me as the despoiler." He shook his head. "Will Scarlet did not violate her, nor did anyone else. She was a maiden when I took her." He did not allow emotion to enter his tone; that more than anything would slam shut his father's mind. "I will swear it before any altar you desire, my lord, on any Bible, on any relic—"

"No." The earl sat rigidly on the bench. "It doesn't matter, Robert—don't you see? You may swear before the king himself, but they will always wonder. It is the woman's lot to be blamed when a man steals her virtue."

"Why?"

"Because women seduce men," the earl declared simply. "Eve seduced Adam—"

"The Serpent had something to do with that," Robin said dryly. "And if Eve *hadn't*, we would not be here."

"That is beside the point." The earl did not appreciate levity or irony. "The point is, Robert, that people will *believe* she is despoiled."

Just as Marian said herself. Robin sighed and hung on to waning patience. If he lost his temper, nothing would be accomplished. "A more generous man might say I would remove the taint from her if I married her."

"The taint would extend to you. If a child were born to you within nine months of the wedding, there would be questions of its parentage." The earl shook his head. "Robert, I speak of your future. You are my heir. I cannot permit you to destroy your life with this."

Anger flickered. It took effort to remain civil. "You destroy my life by denying me the right to marry."

"You may *marry*," the earl said tightly, "and very well indeed! One need only be patient."

"Insh'Allah, not John's daughter again!"

"Robert! I do wish you would forbear to use the Infidel's language! This is a Christian land."

He opened his mouth to protest, then shut it tightly. It was habit, nothing more, formed by an eye toward self-preservation while among the Saracens. He had not realized it was so prevalent in his speech. "I have no intention of marrying John's bastard."

"Then perhaps you should go to Lincoln and tell the prince himself." The earl produced the folded letter from his sleeve and held it up. "This arrived today. He expects you in Lincoln no later than the day after tomorrow."

Robin did not hesitate. "Then he will be disappointed."

"Robert. You will go." The earl leaned forward. "It isn't a certainty, this marriage—and even if it is—"

"No."

"Before God, Robert . . ." The earl sat back against the wall again, as if his strength had run out. "This man may be King of England."

"Not if you undermine him with de Vesci and the others."

"They leave at midday tomorrow. For now our discussions are done." The earl closed his hand around the letter. The parchment collapsed from the pressure of his grip. "Robert—if you must have her, then you may . . . but do not marry her. Take to wife a woman who will give you the latitude to love another, if you will—but reserve the name for one of more proper aspect."

Ya Allah—He broke that off laggardly as a chill washed his flesh. *He cannot mean* . . . Robin stared at the earl in disbelief. "Latitude . . ." he echoed, understanding too well. *The latitude to love another.* "Is that what my mother did?"

The earl's pale face stiffened into immobility. "We will not discuss your mother."

Everything else, of a sudden, was insignificant. "By God, we *will*—"

"No." The earl rose, stuffing the letter back into his sleeve. "Your mother was—and is—my concern, Robert. We will not speak of her again."

"Why not?" Robin lurched up from the bed. "Why not? Is it too painful for you?" He stared at the old man, seeing utter inflexibility and a cold arrogance that surpassed even the king's. "Or is it that there is no pain at all, my lord . . . no pain because you are incapable of feeling any emotion beyond that pleasure taken in controlling the lives of others?"

"Enough, Robert." The earl made a slashing gesture demanding silence. "I have given you the means by which you might be happy in company with this woman—"

He shouted with laughter. "You tell me to make her my leman! What means are those, my lord? I want to *marry* her. I want her to bear my children, and to raise up an heir in my place one day."

The earl's face congested. "By God, Robert—don't you see? If you marry that woman, no son of yours can ever *be* heir to my title!"

The silence was loud. It filled up his ears and set his head to ringing. He was tired, so very tired. There was no anger at all, no heat or fury, no contempt. Merely a certainty of ending. "So." He shivered with cold. "Geoffrey de Mandeville's words bear no weight after all." He nodded. His lips felt numb. "Have it as you will. This will be a mutual forfeiture—"

"Robert!"

"—because I will not claim as father a man who cannot see beyond the ignorance of his own bias."

"Robert—"

"I will take nothing from this hall—this *castle*—that is not mine to take."

"Don't do this!" the earl cried. "Can you not see my side?"

Robin took from his bed the packed saddle wallets. He felt sluggish and painfully slow, as if some perverse part of him wanted to make the moment last. "All I have ever been made to see is your side, my lord. But never once have you tried to see mine." He slung the wallets over one shoulder and took two steps toward the door, which brought him very close to his father. He looked into the aging face, marking sags and lines and old bones, and saw nothing of himself there. "Tell me the truth, as a parting gift: did I ever even approach being the son you wanted?"

The earl stood perfectly straight. His face was a mask of indifferent civility. "Not once."

Robin nodded; it did not hurt. It was merely confirmation.

"It was your mother's doing," the earl declared bitterly. "She ruined you with softness. *I* tried to put you to rights, but she had already filled your head up with too much fey nonsense."

"Yes, my lord. So she had." Robin walked out of the chamber in which he had slept but six nights of his life.

When his son was gone, the earl sat down again. He felt sick and old and weary, weary enough to die. He took from his sleeve the folded parchment again, and stared at it bitterly. "John offers the FitzWalter girl to *me* . . . has he no sense of what he is doing?" No, of course not; John did whatever he liked for reasons of his own. He meant her as a reward, as a favor, to curry the earl's approval, to add to a proud house the honor of Ravenskeep—"Save there is little enough of it left!" Anger seethed briefly. "To expect me to be persuaded to support John in exchange for a pittance and a dishonored woman . . ."

Although, to be fair, it was possible John did not know of Marian's abduction. It was probable, in fact; John believed what he offered whole and worth consideration.

Once, it might have been. Ravenskeep and Huntington, with Nottingham in between.

But now, it was insult. Unless one looked at it another way, seeking another value.

The earl's mouth crimped. He saw his son's face before him, stark and bleak and white. "Should I marry her myself, just to keep her from marrying you? I could send her away, lock her away, make everyone forget her . . ." The words died quickly, replaced by surging hope. *If the sheriff is successful* . . . But the thought also died. He was too weary even to think.

"Damn you." The Earl of Huntington crumpled the letter in palsied, age-spotted hands. "Damn you for being a stubborn fool."

But he was not certain, even then, if he damned John, or himself, or his son.

Sixty-Three

Marian sighed wearily as she raked out of the hall the last pile of old rushes. *I just did this, every bit of it, at Ravenskeep.* She sidestepped her way toward the door, yanking rushes along with vigorous exasperation. Tines scratched beaten earth floor, leaving shallow scars behind.

She paused a moment, scrubbing her damp forehead against a forearm. Sweat trickled stickily down her ribs and the sides of her neck; she had kilted up kirtle *and* hair in an attempt to reduce her discomfort, but the hall admitted little air through its few narrow windows. The day was bright after the storm, and close, warmed by a spring sun.

Marian was not alone. The reeve, James, had sent her the promised village women, and they had shyly come in with rakes and brooms to help her clear the hall. They spoke quietly among themselves, snatching glances at her as she worked, but only rarely did any of them speak directly to her. It was for Marian to give them orders, which they executed with care.

She knew they believed her Sir Robert's wife. They were subservient and respectful, never failing to call her Lady Marian, never suggesting by word or action they believed her other than legal wife. It would not cross their minds that the daughter of a knight might cohabit with an earl's son without benefit of marriage, because that was an aspect of peasant life when priests were hard to come by. They often handfasted for a year while waiting for a mendicant priest to come to their village, and the children born from such bonds were as legitimate as others. But the nobility did not lack for priests, and so of course the Lady Marian and Sir Robert had married quietly. Lords did not tell villeins private, personal matters such as the dates of weddings.

Marian raked her rush pile out of the door, where another woman took it up to carry off to the refuse pile as directed. She knew some of the peasants might prefer to take it for their own dwellings, but she did not desire to add any more vermin to the homes of villagers than were already present, and insisted it be burned.

Now the women came with armloads of fresh-cut rushes and baskets of herbs. One of them brought a cat as Marian had requested, a half-grown young gray tom, to begin work on the mice in the walls.

"There's more kittens," the woman said.

Marian grinned. "One will do for now. Besides, he'll find a lady soon enough to bring home to the hall."

The young woman colored. "Aye, Lady. Like Sir Robert did." She thrust the cat into Marian's arms and hastened away to help with the laying of rushes.

Marian sighed, tucking the tom into her elbow. She did not know what to tell them. No one but Tuck could quibble if she let them assume what they would, but that was too close to lying for her to feel comfortable.

The thought was sudden and unbidden. *What will they say when I go back to Ravenskeep?*

A hollowness cramped her stomach. She had not come to live, she had come to escape first the sheriff and then the earl's displeasure. There had been no word of her staying, any more than there had been word of *Robin* staying; he had gone to make peace with the earl. She could not expect him to live at Locksley when he would inherit a castle, any more than she could expect to live there herself as a leman. She had her own manor and attendant responsibilities. Rents were due her, but she also owed her own share to the king. She could not let Ravenskeep go for the sake of wanting to share Robin's company.

A part of her asked, *Why not? I want to be with him. I want it so much it hurts.* And it did, with a strange, discomfiting pain that lingered on the threshold between joy and futility. The pleasure she took in his presence was full and unobstructed, but now that he was gone she could look at things more clearly, she could see the truth of the moment. *If I were a man, I could do my own choosing. Make my own life. Decide where I would live, and with whom.* And yet Marian knew better. Even Robin could not choose.

The cat squirmed in her arms. Marian bent and set him down and watched him inspect the nearest rush before bounding off to look for mice. "I can't just stay," she murmured, "no matter how much I want to."

"Lady Marian?" It was James in the doorway. "We've thatching cut for the roof."

"Good." It was something else to distract her. "Cut out any old thatching that seems too thin, or too brittle, and replace it with new. And make certain the vent is clear of debris. I want the smoke to be drawn out instead of floating throughout the hall."

"Aye, Lady Marian."

She nodded absently, thinking about screening. Locksley Hall boasted no separate rooms, no second storey. It was a simple rectangular building without refinement or adornment. *I'll have a reed screen woven to block off part of the hall, just a corner, for us . . . and one of the other corners for a kitchen . . . I abhor outdoor kitchens in the winter.* She looked up at the peaked roof. *I should have more windows cut, and shutters.* Marian took up the longest broom she could find and began to tear down the webs. *I will make this hall bearable yet.*

DeLacey leaned forward in his chair as the castellan made his way forward. "Archaumbault! It pleases me well you have recovered so quickly." He smiled warmly and sat back again, relaxing. "I have need of your expertise."

"My lord?" The older man, in mail again after several days of rest, carried his left arm gingerly but did not otherwise appear to be much hindered by his wound.

"Yes." DeLacey nodded, frowning slightly. "I find myself involved in a delicate situation, Archaumbault. It calls for extreme care. It is not at all the sort of thing I can trust to any man, especially"—here he smiled indulgently—"especially one as young and eager as Philip de la Barre."

Archaumbault's eyes did not flinch, but there was a flexing of muscle in his jaws. "No, my lord. De la Barre is often overeager. But there is promise in him."

Too much, to your way of thinking; you see your position threatened. "Therefore I would request that you attend to it personally, Archaumbault—we can afford no whisper of this getting out. It would be most distressing to me, and could certainly damage someone I care about a great deal." He waited.

Archaumbault stood erect, as always. "My lord, you know I will do my best."

As you did in rescuing Marian? But deLacey did not speak of that. There would be time for censure later. "There has come to my ears a whisper of witchcraft, Archaumbault. A rumor only, but these things must be dealt with carefully, as you know, lest we cause a panic among the peasants."

"Indeed, my lord." Archaumbault's tone, as always, was a bland neutrality that occasionally irked the sheriff, who preferred to goad his men into displaying something more. It was how he learned to control them.

"It is peasant superstition, of course . . . but it must be investigated. I want you to ride to Ravenskeep and bring the villein here, so I may question him." DeLacey tapped his fingertips against the arm of his chair. "His name is Roger, I'm told. He says he has proofs of devil worship at Ravenskeep."

Archaumbault nodded, seemingly oblivious to the possibility. "Do you want the hall searched, my lord?"

He considered it thoughtfully, cradling jaw in hand as he propped an elbow against the chair. "For now there is only suspicion . . . I would dislike suggesting there is truth in it by searching the hall yet—" He sighed. "Then again, we dare not let this go on if there *is* truth in it." He pulled himself upright. "A cursory search only. Do not upset the villeins any more than is necessary."

"Yes, my lord."

"Archaumbault—" It cut off the man's withdrawal sharply. "Do bring me word if the Lady Marian is present. If she is not, you might ask where she is."

The castellan bowed his head. "Of course, my lord."

DeLacey watched him depart. *With the earl's own blessing, I will do what I have to do.*

Robin reined in his horse precisely at the place he had been stopped before by Adam Bell's men. He waited mutely, at ease in the saddle, keeping his horse to the center of the road with an occasional heel tap or twitch of reins. He did not doubt the others were there, watching from the foliage, and when he heard the low-toned bird call he answered in kind.

"Here, now." It was Adam Bell, leaving behind the leafy screen. "What use is the whistle to us if you can mimic it?"

Robin grinned. "Of great use, perhaps. It may be necessary for you to answer to mine."

Bell stopped at the roadside as the others came out of the trees. "Answer to yours? What for?"

Clym of the Clough nodded. "So you can lure us to the sheriff?"

Robin laughed, reining in his restive horse, who pawed at the muddy track. "So I can lure you to profit, more like." Then he dropped the bantering tone. "I've business to discuss. Will you listen?"

Adam Bell considered it. "No knight has business with us."

Clym's tone was belligerent. "The boy says nothing but 'Lionheart.' What's the king to do with us?"

Robin studied them in silence. He blamed none of them for wariness or disbelief, nor did he think they would all welcome his words. He was hindered by his knighthood, though he could not say if they knew more of him; it would be difficult to convince them to look beyond his rank.

"What the king has to do with you," he began, "is better explained in comfort."

Will Scarlet murmured a derisive oath. Adam Bell arched an eyebrow. "Then come into my hall, Sir Knight. Come sit upon my throne."

"King of Sherwood?" Robin smiled. "Then let me bestow proper gifts." He pulled his right foot free of the stirrup and bent his knee upward, sliding three curved staffs free of their fastenings. One by one he tossed them out: to Will Scarlet,

Little John, and Alan. "Gifts," Robin repeated, digging coiled bowstrings out of a wallet. "Can you shoot?"

Will Scarlet scowled. "Not like you."

"Nor I!" agreed Little John. "The staff's my weapon, when one's needed."

Robin nodded. "My head remembers that." He tossed out the bowstrings. "But there are times when a man prefers to be at distance from the enemy—a bow's the thing for that."

Alan of the Dales laughed. "Gift or no, I'm useless for this. I've shot a bow before, but my hands are too valuable—"

"Your hands are already strong and callused," Robin interposed. "I need you to shoot a bow."

"Here," growled Clym. "What's this for?"

But Robin looked at Much, seeing the boy's tensed alertness, the keen desire for a bow. He smiled and shook his head. "Quickness is your weapon, Much. I need that, and your deftness. Will you give me both?"

The tenseness faded. Smile growing, Much nodded.

"Good." Robin looked down at the others, then hooked a leg over the saddle and dropped off his horse. "If you'll do me the honor, my lord"—he gestured at Adam Bell—"I will be pleased to share with you a certain knowledge that will be of great value."

Clym swore. "He's mad. What's a knight want with us?"

Robin, pulling quivers and bundled arrows from the saddle, cast a sidelong glance at the minstrel. Alan of the Dales merely smiled and shrugged slightly: it remained for Robin to tell them, *if* he chose to do so, that he was far more than a knight.

Adam Bell remained where he was. "Let me see the arrows, Sir Knight."

Robin tossed him a quiver. Bell drew one of the arrows and studied it, marking the preciseness of the fletching, the fit of the arrowhead, the straightness of the shaft. He pulled another and examined it as carefully, then pursed his lips and slid both back into the quiver. He passed it to Alan. "A man who knows his fletching made those."

Robin tossed the other two quivers at Little John and Will Scarlet. "You've seen his handiwork. The man who taught me to shoot is the man who made those arrows, as well as the bows."

Bell's eyes narrowed. "I have a professional interest, Sir Knight."

"Edward Fuller," Robin said.

"Ned!" Bell very nearly gaped. "Old Ned Fuller makes the finest bows in England . . . or he *did*, before he stopped shooting at fairs and took service with the Earl of Huntington. By God, boy, how did *you* come by them? He doesn't sell one cheaply, and you've got three—"

"Four." Robin smiled inoffensively. "I've one of my own, as well."

Bell's gaze was steady. "Four," he said quietly. "Four Ned Fuller bows . . . even a knight might find it hard to afford so many."

"I didn't buy them," Robin said. "He wouldn't take my money. Ned told me if they were meant to help bring King Richard home, he'd give them *and* the arrows."

Clym swore. "Old Ned Fuller *gives* nothing—"

"Wait." Bell cut him off with a raised hand. "He does if he believes the man will do as he says." Slowly he lowered the hand. "Come say what there is to say."

Sixty-Four

Alan found himself a stump on which to sit and settled himself comfortably, hooking the belly of his lute against his right thigh as the neck nestled into his left hand. He found the tableau inspiring and longed to make a song of it, wondering in the back of his mind if he could create a legend merely by singing the truth.

An earl's son hunting coin with the vilest outlaws in Sherwood Forest. Alan pursed his lips. *There might be something in it . . . something to lure the ear . . . God knows he's fodder enough: a noble, a knight, king's confidant, Crusader.* He grinned to himself, thanking his Muse, and bent his head over the lute as he toyed with a verse. He did nothing aloud, merely play acted the minstrel's part to help himself think.

> *In summer, when the woods be bright,*
> *And leaves be large and long,*
> *It is full merry in fair forest*
> *To hear the small birds' song.*

"Now," Adam Bell said quietly, "let's hear what you have to say."

In various postures the others sat, or hunched, or leaned; in the dull colors of their clothing they blended into the foliage and trees, melding into shadows. Only Robin stood, at ease, one hand wrapped around his bow. In the light of a late afternoon, brass-bright after three gloomy days, his hair glowed like need-fire.

"I have a plan," he said quietly, "to help you, and me, and all England."

Alan's smile grew. The verse begat another:

> *Come listen to me, you gallants so free,*
> *All you that love mirth for to hear,*
> *And I will tell you of a bold outlaw*
> *That lived in Nottinghamshire.*

Robin's tone was pitched conversationally, but with a casual note of camaraderie, as if he counted himself among them. "You know as well as I the Forest Laws are too binding, robbing all but the king and nobility of the chance to eat venison."

"You want to change the law?" Will Scarlet was clearly contemptuous. "D'ye mean to make yourself king, then?"

Robin grinned. "No. I mean to bring *home* the king, so he may do something about it."

Clym swore. "D'ye mean to march us to Germany then— maybe walk across the water!—and beg King Henry oh so prettily to give us our Richard back?"

"I mean to pay the ransom," Robin told him. "And you can help me do it."

Ah, Alan thought, *what a ballad there is in this!*

"We've no money," Scarlet declared. "How are *we* to pay?"

Robin arched a quizzical eyebrow. "Then what do you do with the coin you steal? Eat it in place of deer?"

Clym laughed. Cloudisley smiled. Bell merely looked thoughtful.

"Here," Little John said. "You mean to steal it, then? For the king?"

Robin nodded. "The chancellor, William Longchamp, has taxed everything in England. Men like the Sheriff of Nottingham see that all of us pay the tax. But it's never enough, is it? More and more is demanded, until even the Jews claim poverty—"

"Jews," Clym muttered. "They eat Christian babies."

"No," Robin said patiently. "It is true they eat no pork, but they do not eat babies in its place."

Clym was unconvinced. He swore softly, then spat. *"That* for your Jews."

The minstrel marked how Robin weighed expressions, looking at each of the outlaws. *He's been in the army—with his name, he likely commanded. He knows how to win men.*

Alan's smile widened again as Robin continued easily, showing no impatience with Clym's foul temper, or contempt for the man. "There are those who escape paying as much as they should—"

"Rich men," Scarlet said sourly. "Rich men like Normans."

"Rich men like *nobles,*" said Wat One-Hand.

"And bishops, and abbots, and archbishops." Robin nodded. "There are those men who speak of God while robbing the poor to adorn themselves with jewels and cloth of gold, and altars with silver plate."

Alan laughed to himself, exulting inwardly:

These bishops and these archbishops,
Ye shall them beat and bind;
The High Sheriff of Nottingham,
Him hold ye in your mind.

"And knights," Clym said pointedly. "What do *knights* pay?"

"Knights pay what they can in service, if not in coin," Robin answered patiently, unoffended by the implication. "It isn't the rich on Crusade, because the Crusade has made all men poor."

Fascinated, Alan watched him in silence, offering no comment or question. Robin's words made sense, but his matter-of-fact approach misdirected the others into believing what he suggested was a perfectly normal thing for a man such as himself.

An earl's son telling outlaws they should rob the clergy? Even in the king's name, it is not so simple a thing. His fingers twitched. *My God, what fodder he is! All it wants is a woman.*

Adam Bell nodded, pulling idly at his bottom lip. "So, you want us to rob rich men and give the coin to you, so you can ransom the king." He nodded again. "We're not mad, Sir Knight. Nor are we simpletons—except the boy, there."

Much's face colored. He glared blackly at Bell.

"No," Robin said, "not simple. Much has a special gift. There is no boy—*or* man!—who is quicker with his hands or more loyal to a cause."

"Lionheart," Much said stoutly.

"Agh, God—d'ye think we're so foolish as all that?" Clym asked. "You come here to Sherwood and tell us we're to rob priests and noblemen, then give it all to you—"

"Not to me." The camaraderie faded. Robin's tone was level, with no hint of amusement in it. He was deadly serious, with the look of a man who would not tolerate obstruction if there were no grounds for it. "We will set it all aside, then send it to Longchamp in London."

"Longchamp!" Bell shook his head. "You said it yourself: he's taxing England to death."

Robin tapped the foot of his bow into the earth, watching intently as leaf mold was ground into motes of fine powder. "There is a difference," he said quietly, "between a tax levied to buy back the king"——he looked at them now, and Alan caught his breath at the fixed determination that transfigured the hazel eyes—"and one levied to have him killed."

"What?" Little John's tone was sharp. *"Who* wants him killed?"

Robin stopped tapping. "Prince John desires the throne. He will do whatever he must to make certain his brother remains imprisoned forever—which is impractical, because the threat of escape is too great—or that he dies unexpectedly of means no one quite understands." He stood very still, looking at each man. The fading bruises on his face underscored his intensity.

'Tis the eyes, Alan decided. *He knows how to master his face, but the eyes give him away. When they're cold and dead and steady is when he's most intent on his quarry.*

"And I suppose you know all this because you're a knight." Cloudisley was less belligerent than Clym, and less deliberate than Bell, but his skepticism was plain.

Coolly, Robin said, "Among other things."

Alan grinned. *Here it is . . . will he tell them now, or wait?*

"This latest 'tax,' " Robin went on, divulging nothing more, "is nothing but Prince John's vanity demanding coin for his debts. It is not Longchamp's doing."

"But—" Cloudisley was astonished. It was preposterous even to outlaws that a prince would do such a thing. "Then the money isn't going for the king at all."

"No."

Adam Bell nodded musingly. "Into Prince John's coffers."

Robin nodded. "I'd rather send it to German Henry than put it in John's hands."

Bell glanced at Clym, then at Cloudisley. His smile ran crooked. "Tell me," he said, "why we should aid the king."

It startled even Clym. "But he's the *king—*"

Bell thrust out a silencing hand, staring hard at Robin. "I want *him* to answer. I want a pretty knight—and more than that, perhaps?—to tell us why we should steal to buy back a king who's as Norman as any of them."

They had none of them thought of it. Not even Alan, whose fingers stilled the strings. *Norman as any of them—aye, so he is*

. . . but Richard was born *to be king*—He looked at Robin. *Let him answer the riddle.*

Robin nodded. "A fair question, Adam—but one for *him* to answer."

Bell scoffed. "So I thought. So, then, why should *you* aid him? He's a Norman. You're Saxon." His eyes were veiled behind lashes. "Or so you'd have us think."

"We've lost England," Robin said. "We lost her long ago when the Conqueror took her from us. And certainly we have suffered, all of us, though some more than others—"

"Some *less,*" Clym muttered.

"And some less." He did not shirk the admission. "They are here, Adam. We cannot send them home again. But we can reclaim our country by teaching the invaders how to live as Englishmen."

Adam grunted. "And King Richard can do that?"

"I believe he is a man who trusts another man regardless of his birth, so long as that man puts his faith in the king."

Cloudisley stirred. "And what does that gain *us?*"

"Consideration," Robin declared. "He will treat you as men, not beasts. He understands the wealth of a land lies in what folk produce, not in crushing them down."

Clym was troubled. "He's a warrior, they say—"

"So he is. I have seen him in battle."

"A strong man, then?"

"The strongest I have met, in all the ways a man is measured." Robin slanted a smile at Little John. "He might subdue the Hathersage Giant."

Alan struck a chord. "Robin has the right of it. We'll not rid our shores of the Normans . . . what serves us now is to retain as much of England in the rearing up of her kings."

"Bring Richard home," Robin said, "and I promise you better days. Far better than John does; would you rather have *him* as king?"

The silence was loud. Then Scarlet stirred. "If all of England is so poor, there's no more coin to be had. How can *we* help?"

Robin's answer was flat and measured, empty of emotion. "There are three lords riding out of Huntington tomorrow, at midday. They are wealthy, powerful men. I intend to waylay them on the road and demand their purses of them—and anything else of worth that can be put toward the ransom."

"*Do* you?" Adam Bell grinned. "This is your information?"

"It is."

A subtle, contradictory man. Alan cradled his lute. *And to think I believed him tedious back at Huntington Castle.*

Bell, Clym, and Cloudisley exchanged eloquent glances. Clym grinned hugely, though he directed it at the ground; Cloudisley proved intent on the wrap of his longbow's handgrip; Bell was the one who answered. "And who is to say we will not kill you now and rob them ourselves, without your assistance?"

Robin said merely, "Because none of you *can* kill me."

Gisbourne, who had succeeded in changing from bliaut to tunic, also struggled into baggy hosen. He sat on the edge of his bed and gathered his strength, determined to rejoin the world from which his injury had cut him off. He could do nothing in bed in his chamber, could conduct no affairs nor see to running the castle; and if Prince John *did* send word in response to his letter, he might never receive it. But if he were up and about, taking an interest in his responsibilities, his lot would no doubt improve.

He hooked the crutches beneath his arms and hitched himself up, putting as little weight as possible on the injured leg. It itched abominably as the swelling went down. Laboriously Gisbourne made his way to the door, unlatched it, and crutched out of the way as he tugged it open.

In the corridor, prepared to knock, stood the sheriff. "Gisbourne!" He smiled delighted surprise. "I have come to put you to work."

Taken aback, Gisbourne leaned on his crutches. "Oh?" he inquired weakly. He had hoped to avoid the sheriff for as long as possible.

"Yes." DeLacey waved a hand, shooing Gisbourne back toward the bed. "Go on, go on—this can be done from over there."

"But I wanted—"

"No, Sir Guy. I understand your feelings of unworthiness, but I assure you I have no intention of allowing you to return to work too soon. There are some small tasks which can be done here, such as this letter." He displayed parchment, sand, and wax. "Come, Sir Guy, I have no time to waste." DeLacey's gesture suggested Gisbourne sit down at once. "This is an important letter."

Gisbourne sat down unsteadily, grimacing absently. "But— you have a clerk for this."

"*Had* a clerk for this. He has been dismissed."

Gisbourne opened his mouth to feign ignorance of the reason, saw the expression in deLacey's eyes, and forbore to say anything. Tuck had done his work in freeing Marian from a forced marriage, but he had paid the price. Now both of them were gone, and it was Gisbourne's turn to deal with deLacey.

He took the proffered parchment, wax, and sand, set all aside, then pulled the piece of wood he'd used as a table onto his lap. "Yes, my lord?"

"To Abbot Martin," deLacey directed. "He is commended for his godliness and wisdom in all things, and praised for his attentiveness to ridding the world of evil."

Writing, Gisbourne frowned. He wanted very badly to ask the sheriff what the letter concerned, but he was being used as clerk, not confidant. He began the salutation, which in itself would take up much of the parchment.

DeLacey's tone was relentless. "He is commanded to make his way here to Nottingham as soon as possible, for the examination of a woman suspected of being a witch."

Frowning, Gisbourne sketched out the bare bones of the message. He would flesh it out fully later.

"Say to him I am in great fear for her soul, for she has always led me to believe she is a good and godly woman, conducting herself with decorum in all things. But articles have been found . . . a suspicion has been raised—" deLacey waved a hand. "You know what to write, Gisbourne. You've seen these letters before."

Indeed he had. He had not been required to write them— that had been Brother Hubert's responsibility—but he had seen the letters themselves, and the results. When deLacey sent such letters, people often died. The Church was unforgiving. "My lord—"

"I want it sent without delay."

"Yes, my lord, but—" He glanced up at deLacey, intending to ask something, but the question left his mind. "It's she," he said, understanding. "It's *Marian*—"

"Of course it is," deLacey agreed. "Whom did you think I meant?"

Which one? Robin wondered. *Who will be the first?*

It was Scarlet. "None of us can kill you?" he echoed in disbelief. "None of us *can*, say you?"

But it was Clym who moved, and quickly, lunging up from his rock.

Robin threw the longbow to distract and foul the outlaw, then jerked nearly five hissing feet of Norman steel out of its sheath. As Clym, swearing angrily, knocked aside the bow, his throat was kissed by swordblade.

"Down," Robin said, and walked him back a single step.

Clym went down hard, tripping over the stone, and sprawled on his back. The sword remained at his throat. *"Here, now—"*

"I challenged you once," Robin said, "you forbore to answer. To Huntington, I said, come and I'll give you a sword." He nicked Clym's flesh, letting a thin slit of blood well. "Here I am, Sir Outlaw—have you an answer yet?"

He knew where the others were; he had taken pains to know. The giant would not interfere, nor would Alan. Bell would, he was certain, and Cloudisley as well; Wat One-Hand, probably not; possibly Will Scarlet.

"Yield," Little John said. "Clym—don't be a fool!"

Don't be a fool, Robin echoed, *I need every one of you—but only if you're with me.*

"Let him up," Bell ordered curtly.

Robin loomed over the downed man, watching Clym's eyes. "Are you next, Adam Bell?"

"Let him up, I said."

"Tell me who is next."

"By God!" Bell's anger burst free in a roar ripped from his

637

belly, reflecting years of frustration. "D'ye want us all, then? To grind us into submission like the Normans?"

One step to the right, he is mine—one more, Cloudisley is. "No," he said clearly.

"Then what *do* you want?"

It ran through his head again. *If I lean, Clym is dead—then a pivot to the right and Bell is—Cloudisley would have more to do than time.* "What I want is for you to look at Clym."

Clym lay very still as six men and one boy looked at him. "Here," he said tightly, "what?"

"I want them to know," Robin said.

Clym swallowed heavily, then flinched as the tip drew more blood. "Know *what?*"

"I killed Turks in the Holy Land in the name of God and King Richard. Do you think I will balk at killing a lowborn Saxon dog?"

"Damn you—" Bell began.

"I want you to *know!*" Robin cried. "I want you to know what it is to die for what you believe."

"By Christ," Cloudisley rasped, "what are we to believe? That you're mad?—Aye! We believe!"

"No." Robin shook his head without taking his eyes from Clym's. "No, not that."

"Then what?" Bell asked. "What are we to believe in?"

Robin bared his teeth at Clym in a feral grin. "God and King Richard," he said. "And that I'm a better man with a sword than any of you are with longbows."

Wat One-Hand grunted. "Better with a longbow, too, splitting three arrows."

"But not with a quarterstaff." Little John's tone was lighter. "In that you've met your better."

"So I have. But you're not a man to use it when I've a sword at Clym's throat."

Little John scoffed. "I don't know as I care if you cut open his throat. What's Clym of the Clough to me?"

"What do you want?" Bell asked. "What *else* do you want?"

"I want you to come with me when I rob the three lords." Robin slid him a sideways glance. "I'm new at banditry."

638

"Adam!" Clym shouted. "Will ye have him bleed me to death?"

"Let him up," Bell said gruffly. "We'll help you to rob your lords."

Sixty-Five

It was miraculous, Tuck thought, the way the hall had been changed by a few hours of intense cleaning. *Or is it blasphemous to call it such?* He wasn't sure. He only knew that Locksley Hall was much improved, though more work was yet required.

He moved through the center of the hall slowly, head tipped back to survey the roof. The webs were gone, new rushes sprinkled with aromatic herbs replaced the mildewed filth, and the gaps in daub-and-wattle had been filled in with new. The open hearth was clean and the vent high overhead had been recut and freed of debris. Mice were still a problem, but the cat would soon see to it that fewer and fewer survived.

It was gloomy inside the hall as fading daylight withdrew illumination. They would need to light rush-lights soon, though Marian appeared not to notice. She stood in the doorway with her back to the hall and Tuck, gazing out at the waning day. By her posture he could tell she was thinking of Robin: she hugged herself rigidly, head tilted slightly as if to listen harder for the sound of his horse.

He groped to bring her peace. "The hall is much improved."

She bestirred herself to speak, turning her head slightly so he could hear her. "It is better. It needs much yet. More windows, and I'd plaster the inside walls, then whiten them." She paused;

her mind, he could tell, was not on the hall. "But it is better, yes. Fit for an earl's son."

"He'll come," Tuck said comfortingly. "Did he not send a messenger to say so?"

She swung stiffly, then fell against the doorjamb, pressing her spine to wood. "To say he would be delayed, and I must wait longer yet?—yes, so he did; a small bit of relief. But there was no news other than that, nothing at all of what passed between Robin and his father." She drew in a heavy breath, giving away trepidation. "And when at last he comes himself, what news will he bring? That he has reconciled with his father, and goes home to live in the castle? Or has broken with the earl, and stays here while *I* go home?"

Tuck smiled. "He could marry you, Lady Marian. Then you could live at Ravenskeep and let the reeve and bailiff administer Locksley, or the other way around."

Marian sighed, tucking behind her ear an errant strand of hair. "Methinks you look to the easier side, Brother—the harder side is more likely. He's an earl's only son. What man alive would give up such an inheritance?"

"Do you believe it will come to that? That the earl would make it a choice?"

"Or Robin will." Her mouth twisted. "He is stubborn, Sir Robert of Locksley . . . as stubborn as his father. What one perceives as weakness, the other perceives as strength."

"Then I'll pray for you," he said simply. "I'll pray for you *and* Robin."

Marian sighed. "Let us hope your Father is more understanding than his."

Tuck's round face shone. "Oh, He is. Of that I am certain. And much less concerned with rank and titles and castles, since all men are as one in His eyes." He made his ponderous way across the hall, hands thrust into wide sleeves. "Is there more that I can do? I was useless in the cleaning—is there something else I might do?"

Marian was pensive. "Robin sent word to me—*I* need to send someone to Ravenskeep, to tell them I am safe. Joan will worry, and Sim—I can't let them believe misfortune has befallen me."

"Then let me send someone," Tuck said. "I will find James and ask for a man who can go to Ravenskeep." He was pleased; it was something he could do. "I'll go to him now, Lady Marian. It is not so far—if the man hurries, he could be at Ravenskeep by dark—"

"No, he could not; not by dark. It's nearly thirty miles to Ravenskeep from here."

Tuck relented. "If he found a ride with a carter—"

"But we could not count on that."

"He could reach Nottingham before dark."

Marian laughed. "Yes," she agreed. "Brother Tuck, do you never give up?"

"I pray for patience nightly."

"Ah." Her eyes glinted, but her smile was kind. She pushed the fallen hair from her face. "I will not dissuade you, Tuck. Let the man go, if he will."

Tuck nodded. "Shall I write you the message, then?"

"Write it?" Her expression was baffled. "You can write?"

He nodded vigorously. "Indeed, Lady—it was why I was sent to Nottingham. To be the sheriff's clerk."

"Oh." She smiled distantly. "I had not thought of that. I was just grateful you weren't a priest."

He laughed. "Will you tell me what to write?"

Marian shook her head. "No one there can read. It will have to be remembered, not written down."

"Ah." Tuck nodded. It was not unusual. "Then I'll find James and have him send the best man for it. What would you have him say?"

"That I am safe, and well . . . and that I am protected. That I will return when I can." Marian smiled sadly. "Very much as Robin said to *me.*"

"Aye." Tuck paused as she moved aside, then went out the doorway. " 'Tis a beginning, Lady."

"And perhaps an ending."

They had gone to ground nearer Nottingham, Adam Bell and the others, with Robin in their number. Alan, who was full of words and music, was pleased to have his company, because it gave him more with which to work.

They settled at a campsite Bell said was a regular haunt, though the grimness in his tone suggested it would be no more; there was no certainty, Alan knew, that the outlaw trusted Robin, and would really believe he meant no more than to rob his three rich lords.

Clym of the Clough sat close to Cloudisley and Wat One-Hand, talking quietly, slanting sideways glances in Robin's direction. Adam Bell unaccountably sat alone, inspecting Alan's bow, quiver, and feathers, paying no mind to anyone else. The others sprawled against trees and rocks and stumps: the giant near the boy, who showed him tricks with stones and quick fingers; and Scarlet by himself, fingering his bruises as if the presence of the man who had given them to him made each one ache again.

Robin sat apart, leaning against a tree. *Indolent as a cat,* Alan mused, *but as quick and effortless in his movements. No wasted motion.*

The minstrel went to him and sat down atop an exposed root, cradling his lute. "There are some who would say you are mad."

Robin hitched a shoulder, working idly at a long stem hanging from his mouth. "I am angry, not mad."

"Permit me to say, my lord, that few only sons of powerful earls would consort with lowborn outlaws merely to vex their fathers."

The indolence evaporated. "Is that what you think this is?"

Alan shrugged. "Unless you tell me, I can't know."

"It is not for you to know."

With exaggerated servility, "Yes, my lord."

It annoyed, as Alan intended. "That is over."

"Is it?"

"It does not apply here."

"Here in England? Or here in Sherwood?"

Robin said something concise and clipped in a foreign language. Not French; Alan spoke and sang French. *Spanish?* He thought not. But he understood its intent: he had driven the thorn too deep.

Alan probed delicately. "This is for the king, then."

"I said so."

"Do you think it will change anything?"

"If we bring him home, it will change *something;* I will insist upon it."

Alan nodded to himself; things were falling in place. "My lord—"

"Robin."

"Robin, then." He paused. "Are you quit of all of it, then? The privilege of rank?"

The mouth flattened. "I am quit of my father. If he chooses to strip me of title and heritage, he is free to do so."

"Ah. Few men would be willing to risk it." Alan gestured. "Certainly none of these men."

The dying day gilded pale hair, dappling his face with shadow. "No. None of these men would; I daresay you count yourself among them." He did not wait for Alan's answer. "I make no apology for my birth, minstrel . . . I only offer such to those men inconvenienced by it, as my father would have them be." He shifted against the tree. "England needs her king."

"And you believe this will bring him home."

Robin sighed, jerking the stem from his mouth to discard it with a sharp motion. "Nothing else has."

"What assurances do you have that Longchamp will accept the money?"

"He will."

"Because the earl's son sends it."

Robin's scowl was black. "I will use it as I have to."

"And make yourself into a wolf's-head." Alan dropped the careful probing. "You may do with your life as you wish, of course; who am I to argue? But I daresay any of those men over there—no, perhaps not the giant, and certainly not the boy— would kill to have your place. Is it fair that you ask them to aid you when what you are doing is an insult to them?"

"How is it an insult to them?"

"You give them hope," Alan said. "You couch your desire for banditry in the words that will move them the most: for God and King Richard, you said." Suddenly he was angry. "They are *outlaws,* my lord—what hope have they of pardon?"

"I have mentioned no pardon."

643

"No. But Adam Bell is quick-witted enough to understand it is the unspoken reward . . . it is what you intend, isn't it? To ask the king to pardon those who helped to buy him back?"

Robin's fingers curved around the grip of his Norman sword. "He will assuredly give it."

The worm was on the hook. Alan lowered it into the water. "Because you ask for it."

The fish neither rose nor struck. "What do you want, minstrel?"

Alan grinned. "To be one. A minstrel. To be a *famous* one. To pull myself up from the commoner sort and set myself apart."

Robin's expression was quizzical. "And you think *I* can aid you."

"You have already." Alan ran his fingers down the neck of his lute, bringing a shimmer of subtle sound. "It only requires a hero, and appropriately heroic feats."

Robin laughed aloud, startling the others into a hushed silence. "What do you want of me that might be heroic?"

Alan grinned widely. "To survive long enough that you are worthy of my talent."

Robin laughed again. "Assuredly, I will try."

Alan bent over his lute, keeping his gaze indirect. There was more yet he wished to probe. "You were with the king in the Holy Land."

"I was."

"He knighted you himself."

"After Acre; yes."

"Blondel was with you, then?"

"At Acre? Yes. And—elsewhere."

Alan did not miss the subtle check. He knew the earl's son had been captured and imprisoned, which left a gap of unknown size in Robin's awareness of developments between the time he was taken and the time he was released. *How long?* Alan wondered. *He says nothing of it, and I dare not ask him for it.*

"I know a little of Blondel," he said lightly. "He is well-respected. A troubadour of the old school, harking back to Queen Eleanor's day."

"He is too young for that. His style is older, yes, but he is a young man."

Alan smiled. "As young as you?"

Robin's gaze shifted. He pulled up another stem and began to shred its length.

"I know a little of Blondel," Alan repeated. "And I know the rumors. A fair-haired man, they said; a *white*-haired man, they said . . . was closer to the king than the wife he does not sleep with."

Robin's eyes were shuttered as he stared fixedly at the work his fingers made of the stem. "It is difficult to sleep with a wife when you are imprisoned in Germany."

Alan laughed. "A courtier, to be sure. Ah well, I wondered"—He rose, then checked his step as he finished his sentence—"you seem so certain of the king."

Robin merely smiled a cool, elegant smile divulging nothing at all. "Have no fear, *jongleur*—I will see you have your pardon."

It wasn't what Alan wanted, nor what he had expected. But he was unsurprised. He had come to believe the earl's son might do and say anything to accomplish what he desired. *Even rob his father's friends to buy his king's freedom.*

James, the reeve of Locksley, sent an obliging man to make his way to Ravenskeep with a message from its lady. The man was willing enough—it never hurt to ingratiate yourself with the wife of the manor's lord—and set out in good spirits, watching the end of the day with a practiced eye. Though many were superstitious about traveling after dark, he was not much troubled by it; and anyway, he would stay the night in Nottingham with a friend, then set out again in late or midmorning. He was not particularly concerned about delay; what did it really matter *when* the villeins at Ravenskeep were given their lady's message? She was Locksley's lady now. Her courtesy was admirable, that she wanted to tell her old manor how she fared at the new one, but it wasn't imperative that they be told immediately. The morning would do.

So saying to himself, he was pleased to meet another on a similar errand. The man was a villein from Huntington bound for a manor beyond Nottingham, as pleased as the Locksley man to meet up with company, and they passed the time in friendly talk about respective lords.

It soon came about that the Huntington man knew Locksley's lord, and the new lady as well. "Lady Marian? Of Ravenskeep?"

"Aye. Now of Locksley."

"Ah. Well then, there's no need for you to go on at all. Stay in Nottingham another day; I'll take your message for you."

"You?"

"Aye. I'm for Ravenskeep myself, on the earl's business."

The Locksley man thought it fortuitous and gave the Huntington man the message. At Nottingham they parted; the Locksley man went to his friend, while the Huntington man turned around again to go back to Huntington Castle.

The earl would pay him extra for traveling at night, especially when he learned the lady in question was but two or three miles away instead of twenty-one.

DeLacey heard the report: Archaumbault was in the bailey, on his way to see the sheriff. Quietly deLacey assumed his place in his chair, called for wine, then lost himself in thought as the castellan came in.

Archaumbault was rigidly correct, as always, as he drew up before the sheriff. "My lord, we have brought in the villein."

DeLacey glanced up. "Roger?"

"Yes, my lord. He tells an interesting tale."

Ah, here we are. "In what way 'interesting'?"

The man's eyes glimmered with disgust. "Witchcraft, my lord. You were right to send us there. The woman is involved."

"Which woman? Some serving-woman?"

"No, my lord." Archaumbault pressed his lips together until they nearly disappeared. "The Lady Marian herself."

"Marian!" DeLacey was on his feet. "Are you mad? The Lady Marian would never countenance such a thing, let alone participate herself! Before God, Archaumbault—" But he broke it off. "He must be mad. Marian? Oh—no." He sat down slackly, all

646

the strength leaving his legs. *A nice touch; he believes me implicitly.*
"Let us *pray* he is mistaken."

"My lord, he may be; he is a villein, a Saxon dog." The tone was perfectly level, betraying no suspicion. "But he has accused her, my lord—and we found proof that someone worships the devil."

"What proofs?"

"A broom, my lord."

A broom? What hall hasn't *a broom—did de la Barre think that enough?* "A broom." DeLacey nodded. "What else, Archaumbault?"

"A poppet, my lord."

"Oh?" *Better, de la Barre.* "In whose image?" *Mine? That would be too much . . . but it is too clever for de la Barre to think of.*

Archaumbault shook his head. "It was too crude for it to be recognizable, my lord . . . but there is no doubting its meaning."

"Witchcraft. At *Ravenskeep* . . . oh God, let it not be Marian." DeLacey sighed heavily and bent his head, rubbing at his temples as if in pain. "The devil tempts so many, and we are so helpless against the onslaught."

"Indeed, my lord."

DeLacey sighed. "What of the Lady Marian herself? What did she say, Archaumbault?"

"She was not present, my lord. Her woman is very worried."

The sheriff bit back an oath and contrived to look more sorrowful. "Yet more proof, I wonder? She smells the hunt and bolts?" He shook his head. "What else am I to do? She must be questioned, of course. And the villein, naturally—where have you put him, Archaumbault?"

"Below, my lord. Shall I have him brought up here?"

"No. No, not yet." He drank slowly, thinking it over. "No, we'll leave him until morning. For now, let him be." He shook his head wearily. "Mount a detail at dawn, Archaumbault. We must find the Lady Marian to learn the truth of this."

"Yes, my lord."

DeLacey waved a hand in dismissal. *Good man, Archaumbault. Find the lady for me while I prepare her reception.*

* * *

Marian sat by the door on the bench James had brought, staring out into waning daylight. The fields were green and gold, gilded by lowering sun. Locksley was not Nottingham, nor even Ravenskeep, and offered little of comfort. But the hall itself was improved. She just could not stay inside.

Tuck lingered in the doorway. "Lady, perhaps he'll come yet. There are any number of delays—"

"Tuck." She cut him off crisply. "He is not a patient man, nor close with his tongue when he's angry. He will have told his father by now. What is to be said, is said." *What is to be done, is done.* She picked at her kirtle. "He said not to expect him tonight. I only *hoped* he would be back." *And prayed it, as well.*

Tuck did not answer at once. The early evening was cool, touched with a hint of dampness. The hall smelled of fresh-cut rushes, new thatching, and tangy herbs. Her bed was at the back wall, in a corner, made of matting and borrowed blankets; she could not retreat to that, not while it was empty.

"Lady Marian," he began, "perhaps—"

She didn't let him finish. "This is what my mother did. This is what *all* women do: we wait. We tend the hall, and wait." She twisted her head to look at the monk. "I would rather be a man, I think. Then I would be there also, instead of here. Waiting."

"And in war, too?" He meant it to dissuade her; to point out the folly of bootless wishing.

Marian shrugged. "I would as soon there were no wars—but that is a woman's hope, also . . . a man prays for it." She sighed heavily. "Forgive me—I am sour of spirit tonight. But it seems I grow weary of the tedium of my life."

"Your life is hardly tedious," the monk demurred. "Ravenskeep is your portion, yet you marry no man even though you share a bed." He paused delicately. "But I am sure he will marry you."

Marian laughed. "In all things, there must be decorum. Well, Tuck, perhaps you are right . . . perhaps he *will* marry me, and then I'll tend his hall forever just as I tend it tonight. But I wonder, is there a difference?"

"There must be, Lady Marian, since God blesses a marriage."

She could not argue with that, though she was uncertain God

cared one way or the other if she slept with Robin or not. *Where is he?* she wondered again. *Has his father ordered him thrown in his new dungeon?* Something pinched hard in her stomach. *Or did he go to Nottingham to settle things with the sheriff?*

A cricket chirped beneath the bench. Marian shut her eyes. "Tuck?"

"Yes, Lady?"

"Pray for me tonight. Pray for us both tonight."

"Aye, Lady. Of course."

She found it small comfort, but better than none at all.

Sixty-Six

Robin looked at them all as they gathered after breakfast. Hard-eyed men, all of them, save Much who was a boy, yet even *he* reflected a certain toughness that other boys did not.

The morning was cool, still drugged with mist. It draped layers amidst the trees like a cat across a lap on a cold winter night. Robin nodded at them. "Nearer to Huntington."

Clym protested at once. "Aye, where the *earl* is; d'ye want us caught, then?"

Robin studied the outlaw. He was a sullen, contentious man who questioned the suggestions of anyone save Adam Bell, for whom he had something akin to respect. Robin knew he lacked it, and would undoubtedly never gain it. *He will argue every time. Clym is the kind of man who, as Crusader, robs the dead of dignity and squalls about his own. He will play sapper to my wall, undermining every step.* He smiled grimly. *But I am not Acre.*

Adam Bell was matter-of-fact. "Why not wait for them here?"

649

He's testing me also, to see if I mean what I say. Robin smiled more widely. *Well, he has more right.* "They may ride as far as Nottingham, then split up, which reduces our opportunity. If we wait nearer Nottingham than Huntington, we chance being seen, or that the sheriff might send out a routine patrol."

Bell grunted noncommittally. "Clym's right about the earl— what of him? Huntington's powerful."

Robin quashed a laugh. "He won't expect this."

"Maybe not," Bell agreed, "but if we rob them, and they ride back to Huntington, he'll send out men, won't he?"

Robin considered it. "Possibly," he conceded, because he knew it was true. His father might be so infuriated by thieves daring to rob his former guests that he could very well retaliate almost instantly.

Bell nodded. "Halfway, then," he said. "Between Huntington and Nottingham. Given a choice, most men would go on to the sheriff to complain; 'tis what he's there for, to keep the law." He rose from his squat, catching up his bow. "Come on, then. We'll go. We'll give our fair knight a taste of the outlaw's life."

Scarlet laughed crudely. "He might even find he likes it!"

"Do you?" the minstrel asked. "Do *you* like it, Will Scarlet?"

Scarlet spat, scowling at Robin. "I'd rather be a knight."

Robin did not miss the eloquent glance Alan shot him. It irritated him.

DeLacey summoned Archaumbault to the hall. When the castellan arrived, the sheriff asked a simple straightforward question. "Are you fit enough to ride to Lincoln?"

"Yes, my lord. I'm fit."

DeLacey hesitated. "I could always send de la Barre."

"My lord." The castellan's tone hardened. "If I were not fit, I would declare myself so; the duty is more important than a man's pride." His mouth jerked flat at the corners. "Philip de la Barre will undoubtedly make a fine castellan someday—if you intend to replace *me*, my lord—but he requires seasoning."

DeLacey hid a smile with effort. *I have found your chink, Archaumbault.* "Indeed," he said noncommittally. "You are undoubtedly correct, Archaumbault; he is yet young and too eager. There are duties that require wisdom and experience." He nodded decisively. "Very well. You will choose your best men and see that the shipment is safely delivered to Lincoln, as commanded by Prince John."

"Is that all, my lord?"

"I want to speak to them before you leave." DeLacey waved dismissal. *Just get it there, Archaumbault—or I will make de la Barre castellan before the week is through.*

Adam Bell sent Clym, Cloudisley, and Wat One-Hand to the far side of the road, while he remained in hiding with Robin, Little John, Will Scarlet, the minstrel, and the boy—whom he said should stay out of the business. Much refused.

"Leave him be," Robin said. "He's quicker than any of you."

"You're not so much older yourself."

Robin grinned. "Old enough to learn the butts from Ned Fuller."

Bell scowled. "Will you throw that in my face?"

"Why not? It's an ugly face."

Bell nearly smiled, then managed a dark scowl. "All right, enough. We'd best be quiet." He ordered the others to spread out, then squatted down in the foliage near Robin. "You'll know them when you see them, then?"

"Yes."

"Seen them before?"

"Yes."

"Where?"

Robin grinned. "Huntington, Adam—but that tells you nothing. You already know I've been there, or Ned Fuller wouldn't have taught me what I know of splitting arrows."

Bell grunted. "Your sort doesn't stoop to banditry."

"Your sort didn't, once. A yeoman archer, were you not?"

"Aye." The voice was harsh. "But still not a knight."

"I won't be a knight for long if they catch me playing at this."

Bell glanced at him sharply. "Do *they* know you, then, these lords?"

Robin weighed his answer, then settled for an idle: "They

have seen me before." The three might have seen many men in their lifetimes, but that marked no one out for Bell to fix upon.

From across the road where the others lay in wait, Wat's bird call sounded. "Riders," Bell whispered. "It's for you to say."

Robin nodded. He scooped up a handful of mud, rubbed it along his nose, his chin, and across both cheeks, then slicked his hair back and pulled the hood from his shoulders. He settled it over his head, taking care to tuck in loose hair.

"Aye," Bell muttered, "not many so fair as you."

Three horsemen, followed by lackeys, rode abreast on the Nottingham Road. Their heads were bare in sunlight, leaving little doubt to their identities. The quality of their mounts, the richness of their attire, and the accompanying servants underscored their wealth.

"Yes," Robin said.

Adam cupped his hands around his mouth and whistled a bird call. From the shrubbery across the road, another answered him. Then he grinned at Robin. Quietly, too quietly for Little John or Scarlet to hear him, he said pointedly, "This is for you to do."

The lords and their lackeys came on, too close now for Robin to argue with Bell or discuss it with the others. With an inward curse he did not permit to pass his lips, Robin jerked an arrow out of his quiver, nocked it swiftly, then stepped out of the foliage into the center of the road.

"Hold!" He raised the nocked arrow. As the three men drew up putting hands to swords, he fixed the arrow's point on one: Eustace de Vesci. "Hold," he repeated.

Swords were no match for an arrow loosed by longbow, and none of them rode with shields. De Mandeville at once began to remonstrate, while Henry Bohun attempted to ride forward, to cut off the arrow's angle and protect the other men. Eustace de Vesci, targeted too well, cursed and turned deep red, tensing in the saddle.

The hood hid hair and head, and shadowed a face made purposely obscure by mud. Robin held his place in the hoof-churned road with the bowstring drawn to his chin. "No," he said quietly, altering his accent to something very like Clym's.

"I'd as soon shoot the horses as not—d'ye fancy walking, then?"

Bohun drew rein at once. "This cannot be tolerated. We are peers of the realm."

"I know what you are. Rich men, all three. Lords, are ye not?" Robin looked at de Vesci. "A bullock for the bleeding, from the color of your face."

"By God—" de Vesci burst out. "I'll have the whoreson quartered!"

De Mandeville said dryly, "You must catch him, first. Have you seen what an arrow from an English longbow can do to a man from this range, Eustace? He'll pierce your heart easily, then the one in the man behind you."

The servant behind de Vesci slowly edged his horse aside.

"He'll tire," de Vesci grated. "Wait him out, I say—he can't keep it drawn all day."

"No," Robin agreed, "but if I slip or lose my grip, the arrow flies to you. So you might do as I say a wee bit more quickly."

"Damn you, you churl—"

"Your purses," Robin said. "And your rings. And your chains."

"Chains," de Vesci echoed.

"Chains of *office*," Robin clarified. "That great rope of gold on your chest, my lord . . . 'tisn't a snake, is it? I want it for its gold."

"I am the Lord of Alnwick—"

"*I'm* the King of Sherwood."

Adam Bell's voice rang out. "Here, now! Tell them the truth, Robin! *Who* is King of Sherwood?"

"Here," agreed Clym from the other side of the road. "We can't have us *two* kings!"

"Why not?" called Little John. "We've got us three lords, don't we?"

Bohun's eyes were furious, though his face showed little of it. "Enough of your tricks. We are outnumbered—" He jerked his purse from under his mantle. "Here." He tossed it down, then stripped the heavy chain of office over his head. "And this." It landed near the purse. "There. You have my wealth."

"And your rings," Robin said. "The ones under your gloves."

"By *God!*" de Vesci swore. "What gives you the right to steal from your betters—"

"No man is my better except the King of England." Robin grinned, though he doubted they could see it in the shadow of the hood. "And if he were here, I'd rob him, too."

"Here." Geoffrey de Mandeville removed purse, chain, and gloves, working his rings free. "Take it, then. Everything." The man who had carried in his hands the crown of England before Richard accepted it threw down his wealth. "Everything."

Robin did not like the feeling growing to fill his belly: a cold, viscid emptiness. He was on Crusade again, preparing to kill again, stripping his mind of emotions, of the arguments against dealing death. "You," he said to de Vesci, whom he liked much less.

De Vesci glared back. "Take off that sword," he ordered. "By God, take off that sword! You've stolen it from some poor knight, or nobleman—" He broke off as the arrow wavered minutely, then steadied itself.

So little to do so much—merely loosen the fingers slightly—"No," Robin said tightly, not knowing whom he answered: his impulse, or de Vesci's bluster. "The sword is mine."

"You've no right to it." De Vesci yanked his purse free and threw it to the ground. "You've no right to any of it." Next, his chain of office; lastly his rings. "It is no wonder the Normans took us with Saxons such as you raiding carcasses. Did you feed off the guts of brave men?"

"Ride on," Robin said harshly, "before my fingers slip."

"Eustace," de Mandeville snapped. "Call him what you will when we are free of him, but—by God!—watch your tongue now. He'll have *your* sword, as well."

Bohun nodded. "And I'd much prefer to die in my good lady's bed than here in the muddy road, brought down by an outlaw's arrow." He eyed Robin with cool disdain. "We've not met your like before. I hope we will not again."

"Ride on," Robin said tightly.

De Mandeville glanced briefly at the mounted lackeys, then nodded. "Eustace. Henry." The dignified Earl of Essex did as ordered and rode on steadily as the others filed behind.

Adam Bell and the others came out onto the road as Robin

at last allowed himself to relax, loosening the bowstring. He stared after the lords as they rode into the distance, only half aware that Much and Clym bent to retrieve the purses, chains, and rings from the drying mud of the Nottingham Road.

"By God," Cloudisley said, grinning, "that was well done!"

"Aye." Bell's tone was even, with a hint of dry respect. "Knighthood makes a man after all . . . I've no complaint of you."

Robin rattled his arrow back into the quiver. "I have one of you."

"Of Adam! You?" Clym's expression was malignant. "What complaint of the *real* King of Sherwood?"

"You wanted it known," Robin told Bell, ignoring Clym entirely. "You wanted it made very plain."

Adam Bell laughed. "Aye, so I did! What kind of man is it who hides behind a hood, thinking to keep a secret? No bravery there, now, is there—many a man can call himself an outlaw and steal for a lark, so long as no one knows him . . . but a man who means it, a man who has good reason, will risk his name as well." He bared crooked teeth. "A man in a hood, called Robin. But no one saw your face. You're safe enough, Sir Knight."

Robin nodded as Much came up with a purse and rings. "Did I pass your test?"

"Aye." Bell laughed. "You'd have done the same."

"Oh?" Robin, assured the lords and their lackeys would not attempt a return, slipped the hood at last and shook mud out of his hair. His daubed face itched. "I did do the same. You failed my test."

"Failed?" Clym stepped in close as Robin turned. "What test did we fail?"

"Honesty," Robin said. "I want this wealth for the king, not for myself. Yet you stuff coin away thinking no one is looking."

At once the others stiffened, staring hard at Clym. Robin sensed the tension in the air, the unalloyed contempt, and knew it had not been planned, that Clym had done it for himself. It was something. A little more than something; the test had been less for a man he already distrusted than others he wanted to.

"Clym." Bell's tone was clipped. "You'll have another chance."

"He'll keep it for himself, not the king!"

Little John stepped close, using sheer size to intimidate. "Give it over, Clym."

"By Christ, I'll not listen to *you*—"

"Give it up," Scarlet told him. "He earned it, didn't he?"

"Lionheart," Much announced. *"Lionheart's* money!"

"Christ," Clym muttered, "we're all women and boys, giving in to a man like this."

"More man than you," Little John jeered. "I only saw one of us on the road, and it bloody well wasn't you!"

Clym reached into his hosen and jerked out the purse, then threw it to the ground. *"That* for your king's ransom!" He spat onto the leather.

Robin turned to Bell. "You have a choice," he said. "Come with me to Locksley, where there is food, ale, and a hall. We've more to discuss now."

"Or?" Bell asked.

"Or not." Robin shrugged. "I've another idea."

"Like this one?" Wat One-Hand grinned. "I'm with you, then. This was the easiest job I've seen in a long time."

"Aye." Little John's tone was derisive. *"He* did all the work."

"My favorite kind." Wat's eyes were bright. "Won't hurt to listen, will it?"

"He's a bloody *knight!*" Clym cried. "What does he know of our life?"

"Something now," Bell retorted. "As the giant said, only one of us was on the road, and it bloody well wasn't us." He nodded at Robin. "We'll come, for now. We'll eat your food and drink your ale and hear what you have to say."

Much picked up the purse Clym had thrown down. He handed it to Robin. "Locksley."

DeLacey supervised as Archaumbault ordered the shipment—an ordinary locked chest—placed in the sturdy wagon, then covered with sacking tied down with rough hemp rope. The castellan indicated no particular interest in what it was he

656

intended to escort to Lincoln, merely that the loading be done quickly and properly. DeLacey watched, then motioned for the boy to bring over his own mount.

"My lord?" Archaumbault was surprised. "Do you come, also?"

"I have business with Prince John." He gestured. "Here, de la Barre—"

But the young man, mounted only paces away, put up a delaying hand a bit too imperative for deLacey's liking. "My lord, if it please you—there are riders coming in. And speedily!"

"Who? Can you see them?" *What will delay me now?* "De la Barre—"

"No, my lord." De la Barre cast a glance over his shoulder. "If you permit, I will go see who they are."

"Do," deLacey suggested dryly. He glanced to Archaumbault. "Were we ever that young?"

Archaumbault's eyes glimmered. "Yesterday, my lord."

He was astonished. *Before God, the man's made a jest!*

And then de la Barre was back, taut-faced, stumbling over his words as he reined in his fractious mount. "My lord Sheriff—*they* are lords . . . they speak of robbery, my lord!"

"*What* lords?" But deLacey irritably waved him back. "Never mind—I'll tend it myself." He glanced again at Archaumbault. "Hold the wagon. We'll leave in a moment." Without waiting for the castellan's answer, deLacey motioned for the boy to continue holding his horse and went forward, marking the clatter of hooves against cobbles and the shouts of an angry man. *Who is that?* Then his eyes widened. *Eustace de Vesci? What is he doing here?—My God, Henry Bohun—and Essex!*

"Sheriff!" De Vesci reined in his horse so hard its mouth gaped. "My lord Sheriff—attend to this at once! We have been set upon and robbed—"

Geoffrey de Mandeville, less bombastic, said indeed de Vesci was right: they had been robbed.

DeLacey was astounded. "Where? In the city?"

"No." It was Henry Bohun, Earl of Hereford, younger even than deLacey recalled, but it had been some time since last they had met, and then only briefly. "No, it was but a few miles back—"

657

"Between here and Huntington," de Vesci finished. "Before God, that whoreson—"

DeLacey assumed a suitably disturbed expression, though at that moment he was less concerned with the robbery than he was with their presence at Huntington. *What were they doing there? And then, thinking rapidly, I wonder—does John know?*

"A plainspoken fellow," Bohun agreed. "Most unwilling to be cowed by our rank."

A further astonishment; it overtook the first. "He *knew* you?"

"Not by name," de Mandeville said, "but he knew our rank well enough. He took even our chains of office."

DeLacey spun. "Archaumbault! To me!" He swung back. "I will undertake every effort to have this outlaw caught and hanged, my lords. I am appalled that men of your substance can be set upon so baldly—"

"And *boldly,*" de Mandeville said dryly. "He had companions in the brush, but faced us quite alone."

"Whoreson," de Vesci seethed. "He's stolen a good man's sword."

That stopped deLacey. "An outlaw with a sword?"

"And a longbow." Bohun shook his head. "I wouldn't have tested him."

The sheriff frowned. "No outlaw I know carries a sword. Longbows yes, some of them . . . but they are villeins, usually, peasants who turn to poaching and are outlawed for it"—he shrugged—"the occasional yeoman—"

"He stole a good man's sword," de Vesci repeated, clearly unconcerned by the sheriff's observations. "For that alone he should hang."

"If he can be caught, yes." Bohun sighed. "He wore a hood. His face was obscured. We'd not know him again if he stood here before us even now."

"Robin," de Mandeville said. "Someone called him Robin."

DeLacey frowned. "You are certain?"

"Quite certain," the earl told him gravely. "The voice was perfectly clear, as was the name. As if it were *meant* to be heard."

DeLacey indicated Archaumbault. "This man is my castellan. I will set him and others on the trail . . . is there anything you can tell him about the man's appearance?"

"He was hooded," de Vesci snapped. "We saw nothing of his face."

DeLacey sighed. *A hooded man named Robin. I need only walk out beyond the gates to see ten or twenty hooded men—and as for Robin? As many Robins as hoods.* "Anything else, my lords?"

Bohun, frowning, nodded. "He wore plain clothing, yeoman's clothing, with good boots, and bracers—here." He tapped one forearm. "Green tunic, brown hosen—a belt, and a sword-belt—"

"And the hood," de Mandeville finished. "A collared leather hood, like any yeoman might wear." His expression said he knew well there was little to distinguish the thief from any other man. "A tall man, well-fleshed . . . twenty-five or younger." He shrugged. "Without a face, it is difficult to say."

"Of course. I thank you for trying, my lord." DeLacey glanced at Archaumbault. "I give you the duty."

"Yes, my lord." A glint was in his eye. "Shall I take de la Barre with me?"

"No." DeLacey now was angry. This simple robbery had upset every plan. The three victimized lords had ridden in from Huntington, whose earl was opposed to John. It would not do to say where he was bound, or for whom his shipment was intended. *I'll send it to Lincoln tomorrow.* DeLacey tugged at his robe. "My lords—may I offer you food? Drink?"

De Vesci threw himself out of his saddle, jerking the reins free. "By Christ, *yes!* And perhaps as we wait, your castellan will flush this whoreson free."

"Indeed," DeLacey agreed urbanely, wishing de Vesci to hell.

Sixty-Seven

Marian cast a glance around Locksley Hall. She sighed, scrubbing hair back from her face. *There is nothing more I might do to improve upon the hall save what I have already done . . . and nothing else I can do simply to pass the time—*

"Lady Marian?" The call came from outside: Tuck, who sounded triumphant. "Lady—he's come back!"

She spun to face the still-empty door and could not help but think of her own condition as she had the hall's: hair straggling down, kirtle snagged in girdle, the hem of her shift soiled and ragged. *Not even a coif to cover my head—oh God, could I not at the very least have washed my face?*

Undoubtedly it was filthy, streaked with dust and grime. Marian attempted one-handedly to jerk the snagged kirtle free of girdle while the other rubbed at her face, and then Robin was in the doorway and she forgot all about the snagged skirt and the dirt on her face and the straggling hair stuck to her neck.

With the setting sun behind his back he was mostly in silhouette, but she knew him by a hundred intimate things. He stood within the doorway, filling up the opening.

Her body's response was instant, astonishing her with its clamor. Marian laughed out loud, bursting with emotions she had never thought to feel, because she had not known, then, what it was to live. Inconsequentially, she thought, *Tuck's prayers carry weight.*

Rush-light warmed his features, glinting off sword and knife. *"Ya Allah*, but I need you—" And he was there within the hall, leaving the door behind, crossing the distance swiftly to catch her in his arms, to pull her against his chest, to murmur something into the tousled hair she had foolishly fretted over, something in a language Marian did not know, but full of abiding relief and an intense desperation assuaged now by her presence. "Say nothing—let me hold you . . . let me be human again . . ."

And she let him hold her, let him hug the breath from her lungs, crushing her in his arms; knowing she needed it as badly, the simple power of touch, of possession, that had nothing to do with ownership and everything to do with reestablishing self. *My God—not even Eleanor said it could be like this—*

"Too long," he rasped. "I meant to come sooner, I meant to come straight from my father, but there was something else—"

Marian gulped a laugh, too happy to let him fret. "You did send word, Robin—"

"I meant to come anyway, sooner . . . but I could not leave it, or risk losing the courage—" His mouth was against brow, then cheek, then lips, caressing with warm breath even as he spoke. "I am sorry, Marian—I cannot give what you deserve—"

"It doesn't matter—"

"—and now there is something more that must be done—"

She closed his mouth with fingers. "Hush," she told him, laughing softly. "Do you think I have so little faith in you that you must explain all to me?" She smiled to see the surprise in his eyes. Her own hands were busy as his were, sliding against his tunicked chest as she looped them over his shoulders, then up behind his neck through thick, pale hair. Her skin cried out for his. "I despised being alone, but now that you are here I cannot recall what it was."

He shook his head, twining his fingers into her hair as she twined them into his, smoothing it back from her face. His eyes were dark and avid, his tone abrupt and ragged, but the words spoke of things other than the needs of his body. "You know so little of me . . . of the things I can do, and have done—"

"I said, it doesn't matter—"

"It does." He pulled her more tightly yet into his arms. "Marian—it isn't ended yet. It's only begun. And all of it *does* matter. It must. Or there is no reason to do it."

661

"Rob—" But he cut her off with his mouth, which sealed her own until she was breathless, then broke away with effort. In that instant she no longer cared there was no screen to shield their bed—*surely Tuck will ward the door*—

"Marian—I have brought men with me. They will stay here the night, some of them—I meant us to be alone, but there is something yet to be done, things to be discussed." The tension made his face stark. "Some of these men you know."

She cared about nothing else but Robin, not what he was saying; she wanted to kiss away the starkness of his face, to ease his tension with her body.

But gradually his words dissipated the sharp joy and pleasure of touching him. *"I* know these men?"

"The giant," he said quietly. "The minstrel. The boy, Much—and Will Scarlet."

Desire burned into ash. "You've brought *Scarlet* here? Why?"

"I need him—"

"Him!"

"Marian." The flesh of his face was rigid. "I need him. I need them all. Those—and the others." She saw there was mud in his hairline, and a smudge across one cheek. "Adam Bell, and others."

Marian was astonished. "Adam Bell is an *outlaw.*"

"A wolf's-head." His eyes were bleak. "I know. Marian—I said you knew little of me, of the things I can do—"

"—and have done," she finished. "But—outlaws? Why? They are not your kind. Will Scarlet?" Marian shook her head. "We were well quit of him."

"Not now. He is outside." Robin drew in a deep breath and exhaled noisily. "I have broken with my father."

It was what she had hoped against, rather than for; Marian had no desire to strip a man from his kin. "No," she said sharply. "Robin—no."

"It is done. I took nothing from his castle other than what was due me, or already mine . . ." His gesture encompassed the hall. "This is mine. Nothing more."

She reached up and touched the residue of mud in the angle of one cheekbone. "You are both of you stubborn men. I said so to Tuck . . . and now you have infuriated one another so that nothing can be settled—"

"It *is* settled." He pulled her hand away, kept it trapped in his own. "I have made certain it is. He will never condone what I have become, even for Richard's sake."

She was abruptly furious, angry with his manner and angry with her ignorance. "*Tell* me!" she flared. "Do not hint, do not hide in obscurity—tell me the truth!"

He caught her other hand, clinging to both of them. "I am made thief," he said plainly, "by the vanity of rich men, and the poverty of poor. Not outlaw—*yet*. Not wolf's-head—*yet*. But when they know, it will come. And it must come, because it must be done."

She did not understand. "You said you would send the jewels to help the ransom. But that is done, Robin—what more can you do?"

"More," he said only.

"Adam Bell," she murmured. "And Will Scarlet. Outlaws, all of them." She understood him now. "What have you done?"

He turned away, releasing her hands, and went to the door. A quiet word beckoned the others in, murmuring her name, something more, but she heard none of it.

Marian stood in the dimly lighted hall and watched the men file in. Some of them she knew. Some of them she did not. But *of* them, every one.

"Wolf's-heads," she murmured hollowly. *Oh God—not Robin—*

And then Much stood before her holding purses and chains and rings. He grinned his delight. "Lionheart!"

Marian looked over his head to Robin by the door, who denied none of it by gesture or expression.

"De Vesci's," he said, "and Bohun's. And Geoffrey de Mandeville's. They're the poorer for it—but the king is closer to England."

She did not look at the proofs of thievery filling Much's hands. She looked instead at Robin, knowing now what he was; what he had made himself to bring the King of the English home.

DeLacey sat over the evening meal with his unexpected guests, discomfited by their presence but unable to discharge them. He was intensely relieved when a servant came in with a message, murmuring to him quietly that though unsigned it came from the Earl of Huntington. No answer was expected, merely action.

DeLacey, bemused, accepted it with apologies to his guests, then broke the seal and read it. When he had finished, he apologized once again and made a trifling comment about the responsibilities of a sheriff. The meal continued, and deLacey fretted inwardly until at last the lords excused themselves. No doubt they wished to share his company no more than he did theirs, since he was an avowed prince's man; he wished them good night amidst their courteous assurances that they would depart at dawn, and his own that the matter of the robbery would be tended to with care.

As soon as they were gone, he sent for de la Barre.

Food, Robin had said; all of them were hungry. And so Marian carried out the duties of a proper chatelaine and ordered foodstuffs from the villagers to feed old- and newmade outlaws. Bread, pork, beef; the first fruits of early spring. Butter and cheese and ale. Locksley's inhabitants believed they fed their lord; he had made himself something else.

Marian learned Robin's companions quickly enough as she labored to feed them all: Adam Bell, small, dark and quick; William of Cloudisley was young, sweet-natured, and married; Clym of the Clough lacked a finger and all pretensions to simple courtesy; Wat had lost a hand for poaching. The others she knew already: Little John, Will Scarlet, Alan of the Dales, and Much.

But for Alan, who had good manners from his years of dining in great halls, and the giant, whose movements were measured so as not to overset things with his size, all of them lacked for refinement when it came to eating and drinking. They were rough men in general, unaccustomed to halls, and she found their habits disgusting as they clustered around the open hearth to eat and drink and tell rude jokes and stories. It was smoky there, but better since she had ordered the vent recut. Still, drifts hung in the air, thickening as the evening wore on. The hall was dyed ochrous by weak rush-light and russet coals: gilt and gold and amber.

Marian did not eat with the men but withdrew quietly to a safe distance and sat upon a bench. None noticed, save Robin, who slanted her an enigmatic glance she could not interpret but nonetheless remained with the others; and Tuck, who came with his own share of food and sat down upon the bench.

She smiled at him crookedly. "Pity for the outcast?"

"Ah, but *they* are the outcasts." Tuck's expression was pensive. "But God's children as well . . . we must remember that."

Marian raised her brows. "Surely God would enjoin them to bathe more than once a year, and to eat with less—exuberance."

"No doubt they are accustomed to eating worse fare," he told her quietly, picking at roasted pork, "and often stolen, I'll wager . . . poaching, methinks, gives a man little time for refinement."

It stung more than she expected, because he was correct. "And so I am rightly reproved." Marian smiled to stave off his stricken apology. "No, Brother—who am I to revile them? But when I think what Robin means to do . . ." She shook her head. "He is *wrong*."

Tuck's expression was troubled. "Aye, Lady Marian—God does not condone men who steal from other men."

"Regardless of his birth."

Tuck gazed at Robin. The pale head was bent, the face obscured by hair. "He explained it well enough, and with surpassing eloquence—"

"But a thief is still a thief." Marian's jaw tightened. "Every single one of these men—even Much!—would be hanged if caught. And yet Robin swears to me it is the only way."

"It is the only way *he* sees," Tuck said. "There must be others, surely . . . but this is the path he chooses." He chewed thoroughly, digesting meat and thoughts. "He risks much for his king."

"Too much. I wish—" But Marian let it go. Robin had risen from his place near the hearth.

The loud jesting died, the ribald boasting replaced with curiosity as he stood before them all. "I swore an oath," he said quietly, so quietly Marian had to strain to hear him, "when I went on Crusade, to free Jerusalem from the Infidel and pray at the Holy Sepulchre. All Crusaders did." He looked at each of them, weighing them in their silence. "I swore an oath to my king that I would serve him before myself, to do what was required. At Acre, I killed men and women—"

"Saracens," Clym muttered.

"—and served my God and king. And I was knighted for it." His smile was grim. "Yet another oath."

Cloudisley lifted his cup. "Here's to the valiant knight!"

Robin did not even look at him. "And when I was captured by the Turks on the field near Arsuf, I swore yet a third oath: that I would win my freedom and return home to England."

The silence was suddenly loud. Marian was acutely aware of small sounds made large: the fire in the hearth, the cricket outside the door, the rustling of bodies in rushes. "What is he doing?" she breathed. "What is Robin *doing?*"

Tuck's voice was as quiet. "Telling you what happened."

"He's telling *them,* not me!"

"Perhaps because he knows they require convincing." Tuck's brown eyes were filled with a great compassion. "Lady, this is confession. We are all of us his priests."

"Here, now," Wat said. "Captured?"

"I spent one year and one month in the company of the Turks," Robin said. "They made me do many things, among them pray to Allah in place of my own God." His face was a pale mask. *"Ya Allah. Insh'Allah. La ilaha il' Mohammad rasul Allah."*

Tuck crossed himself.

"Had the king not ransomed me, I would be there still."

Marian's food was tasteless. She had no interest in it, or in anything beyond the words Robin spoke. Comprehension was painful. "This is why," she murmured. "Honor, duty, respect—the oaths he swore . . . and the king who ransomed *him.*"

"I will bring him home," Robin said. "I will pillage even the coffers of the highest in the land to bring Richard home."

Clym swore. "By God, you *won't!* Who are you to say so? Who are you to dare? Robbing three lords today doesn't mean you'd dare again—"

"Tomorrow," Robin said, "or the day after, if it is then. That depends on the sheriff."

"The sheriff!" Adam Bell's voice was sharp. "What has this to do with him?"

"I mean to rob him," Robin said. "In Prince John's name, he has stolen from each of you, from every villein in this village and all the other villages, and the Jews—"

"Jews!" Clym spat into the rushes.

"—and the Christians and the lords—"

"You can't rob the sheriff." Bell's tone was deadly. "D'ye know what he'd do to us?"

"What he would do to us anyway, if he caught us," Robin answered. "We will take pains to see he does not."

"No." Bell shook his head. "Not him."

"Why not?" Robin asked softly. "Why not *him,* Adam?"

"Because he's the sheriff, damn you! 'Tis one thing to rob a merchant—or a *lord!*—but I'll not risk the sheriff. He lets us mostly alone."

" 'Mostly alone'?" Robin echoed.

"Aye. We've enough trouble keeping clear of him—if we rob the sheriff, he'll send every Norman in the castle after us." Bell shook his head. "I'm not a fool. We can't hide from that many."

"In Sherwood? Of course you can. You *do.*"

"No. Not me." Bell cast a glance at Clym, Wat, and Cloudisley. "Nor any of mine, I'll wager."

Don't do it, Marian pleaded in the confines of her mind. *Oh Robin—don't.*

Clym's voice was thick. " 'Tis a trap," he announced. "A trap—don't you see? Ned Fuller himself taught you archery. You're a bloody knight. A king *ransoms* you. D'ye think we're blind? The sheriff *himself* has sent you!" He cast a wild glance at the others. "Don't you see? He's to lure us against the sheriff, and then we'll all be taken."

"No," Robin said.

667

Adam Bell nodded. "He's not known for his wits, but Clym may have grasped the truth. You are all of those things, Sir Robin of Locksley. And perhaps a lapdog, too, serving Norman lords and sheriffs—"

"No." In rush- and firelight, Robin's eyes were black. "I am no friend to Normans."

Wat laughed. "And why not? Enough English lords line their coffers with Norman gold. Why not you?"

Robin looked at Marian. In his face she saw contempt, but none if it was for them. *For himself—* And she knew what he meant to do. "No," she blurted, though only Tuck heard.

Deftly Robin undid the sword-belt and let the sheathed weapon drop. Then the plain leather belt with meat-knife attached. He stripped off his tunic, shook hair forward over his shoulders, and turned his back to them all.

Marian bit into her lip. Humiliation bathed her, that he would show so much to men who could not understand; who would revile him for it. He was *hers* now, by his own volition; what hurt him also hurt her. She understood what he intended, and why, but knowledge did not mitigate the intensity of her emotion. *Give them no opportunity—* Because they would laugh, or jest, or revile.

On fair skin, old weals were livid. In stark, diagonal relief— purple on white—they cut his back into sections like a newly plowed field, with furrows of clean flesh between the heavy ridges.

Tuck's voice was ragged as he began to whisper a prayer. Marian's tears were silent.

Robin turned again. "Crusaders," he said. "Normans."

"No!" Clym declared.

"Normans," Robin repeated. "Because the fair-haired Saxon dog dared to usurp the place they believed was *their* right: at the side of the Lionheart. And some said, in his bed." His face was expressionless. "The king had sailed for home. I was ill after harsh captivity. I was left behind to recover. A few of them thought it amusing to play physician to the patient . . . if he died, what was the loss? The Saracens had weakened him—who was to know the difference?" His smile was thin and edged. "In the name of *any* god, I have no love for Normans."

Alan sat in the shadows and let the others drink. For him, that was finished; he knew a stronger lure than the mists induced by ale. His Muse was a jealous woman.

He had thought to sing earlier, to command them with his gift, but they were none of them interested in a minstrel's songs. They argued among themselves over whether it was wise to rob the sheriff.

It mattered little to Alan. He was lost already, trapped by the promise of more verses. Adam Bell's time was done. He had showed himself small-minded and unambitious, a thief merely to live, which, Alan believed, was understandable on one hand, but on the other surpassingly tedious. Hand-to-mouth existence was not the stuff of legend.

He laughed. Legend stood before him. Legend spoke of kings and oaths, of Crusade and captivity, of wrongs done to poorer men in the name of richer princes.

Legend's name was Robin.

Alan shivered. The Muse had cold fingers. "Robin," he whispered. "Robin in the wood. Robin in the hood."

He laughed to himself. He saw legend walk to the woman—*I could not have asked for a better one!*—and put out his hand for hers, then guide her into shadow beyond the blackened door leading into the temperate night.

A verse suggested itself:

> *A bonny fine maid of noble degree,*
> *Maid Marian called by name,*
> *Did live in the North, of excellent worth,*
> *For she was a gallant dame.*

Alan of the Dales sighed complete contentment. All of it lay before him. He need only find verse and music.

Sixty-Eight

In the thickets and trees behind the hall, Robin made a bed of piled mantles. More promising, Marian reflected, than the bed of boughs and leaves he had made for her before.

She watched as he moved, marking lithe grace and concise purpose, the single-mindedness of a man not so much commanded by need as by preference. He was more reserved than in the oratory, where he had been unmanned by self-control left too long in command, then made man again in her body; less fierce than in the bed beneath the roof of his father's castle. This was *Robin:* the man he had made himself to answer what he interpreted as the need of a realm for her king.

She loved him no less for it. She thought she loved him more.

In the distance, a dog barked. In darkness, rush-lights glimmered. Tuck remained with the others in Locksley Hall, while the villeins of the village blew out wan lamps to sleep. The moon stood high overhead, lingering on hair and hands as Robin settled the makeshift bedding. He had left off sword and knife.

Now, she told herself. *Before he lures me from my senses.* "When do you leave?" she asked quietly.

He was wary. "I will not be dissuaded, Marian."

"I know that, Robin. It's in your eyes, your mouth; in every line and motion of your body." She swallowed tightly. "You have remade me. I am two women now: the one who wants you to remain here safe from danger, regardless of provocation . . . and the woman who would detest you for doing precisely that, because you are made for more." She smiled to see his expression; wariness was replaced by muted puzzlement. "I know you mean to go. I want to know *when,* so I may go with you."

He knelt at the edge of the bedding, stilled by her words. His face was a mask of hollows, blackened by the darkness where the moon could not touch. "I can't let you come with me."

It was not unexpected. Calmly, she refuted. "You can't deny me," she pointed out. "We owe nothing to one another save what we choose to give. There is no question of obedience, or the right of a wedded husband to command his wife in all things . . . there is only what you want, and what I want; we will make the best of that."

He shook his head. "What I want is for you to remain here."

"And what *I* want is to come." Marian smiled. "I don't mean to turn thief, Robin . . . I only mean I weary of waiting here for you. You have no idea how taxing such duty is; men don't." She shrugged, dissipating the sting because it wasn't his fault, and she meant to point out truths, not weaknesses. She felt there was a difference. "Men go, and men *do;* women wait. Women wait, and worry—"

As a man, he answered, "There is no need to worry."

She pointed to the moon. "Tell it not to rise."

He sighed. "Marian—"

"I have no intention of robbing the sheriff," she said dryly. "I mean only to accompany you, to be close enough to *know* instead of left behind to imagine."

His hands were still on his knees as he knelt beside the bedding. Deliberately he said, "I value you too much."

She laughed. "Value? An interesting word." Marian knelt down also, so that the bedding of piled mantles formed an acre of cloth between them. *So far yet to cross.* "I value *you.* I would sooner see you killed in front of me than to wait, wondering, for someone to bring me the news. And who *would,* here? The sheriff? Your father? Adam Bell?" Marian shook her head. "I will dress myself in the colors of the forest, and hide myself nearby."

"I value you," he repeated. "If you came, *I* would be left to wonder what might become of you. Do you want my attention diminished? Do you want my concentration divided? It would be. I would be but half a man facing the sheriff's Normans, because I could not forget that you were there, too." His voice was soft. "You would be the death of me."

She struggled with self-control, wanting to show him nothing of mounting desperation. "Who suffers more, then? The woman, here, waiting? Or the man there, fighting?"

"Dependent upon the results," Robin said gravely, "the man might suffer more in the wounds bestowed upon him." He moved then, reaching out to her with an outstretched hand. "I know, Marian . . . as much as a man can; as much as *I* can. But I saw women killed at Acre, and I killed women"—his voice was stark and tight—"and I refuse to risk you. Stay here at Locksley. Stay here where you are safe, so I may come back to you."

She had lost, and knew it. She was her mother reborn, and every woman before and since who had lived to send a man into a danger that he would not share with her.

Not fair, she thought bitterly. *In the name of preservation, men deny us the chance to live.*

But her hand reached out to his, fingers touching, then locking, and she knew the best she could hope for was to take what he gave her now, in the shadows beneath the moon.

At Nottingham, just after dawn, deLacey saw off the Lords of Alnwick, Hereford, and Essex, then summoned Archaumbault into the bailey as the men and lackeys rode out. "Well?"

The castellan shook his head. "There were no traces, my lord. I do not doubt there was such a man, but our usual sources know nothing. There are two facts only: he wore a hood, and his name was Robin. The hood is of no moment—how many men *desire* to be recognized as they rob passersby?—and the name means nothing also. I have sent men into the city to learn what there is to learn, but until we know more there is little we can do."

The sheriff grunted. "So I thought. He vanishes into Sherwood like all of the others." He sighed. "It is time we undertook a thorough housecleaning—but today I haven't the time." He glanced past Archaumbault to the gatehouse, making certain the lords were gone. "Extra men, then, for the journey to Lincoln."

"Today, my lord?"

"Why not? Why give Hooded Robin more time to plan for us?"

Archaumbault was skeptical. "No thief alive would dare to attack a full complement of Normans."

"Perhaps not. Perhaps the precautions are a waste of time." He smiled coolly. "But it is my time to waste—and yours is subordinate to mine."

Not long after dawn, they stirred. They ate a little, drank more, gathered bows and quivers. Then went out into the day, where Robin waited for them.

Adam Bell shook his head. "You know my reasons," he said. "Good reasons all . . . I intend to abide by them."

Robin nodded. It was a bright, unadorned morning, hinting at early summer. "Do as you will," he said.

They had divided themselves already: Bell's men in a knot; Marian and Tuck on the bench beside the door; the others strewn loosely in front of the hall like a broken necklace, divulging no loyalties.

"You're a fool," Bell told him. "A brave man, but a fool. Why steal for a king when there is yourself to please?"

"I will please myself when the king is home again." Robin wore sword and meat-knife, as well as a full quiver. The bow was in his hand.

Clym laughed harshly. "You stood off the lords by yourself. You'll not stand off the sheriff."

"He won't be alone," rasped Little John.

Cloudisley glanced at him. "You, giant?"

Little John's face reddened. "Aye."

Clym scoffed. "What of the sheep you love so well. D'ye desert *them*, then?"

"There's my cousin for the sheep," Little John answered. "Tom'll tend them well enough." Red hair and beard blazed in the sun. " 'Twasn't my choice, now, was it? But I was there when Scarlet escaped, and the sheriff saw me. I was there when the soldiers died, and the Norman saw me. What chance have I?" No one offered an answer. The giant nodded. "You've made an outlaw of me—if I'm to live the name, I may as well do it for a reason I can stomach." He jerked his bearded jaw toward Robin. "He says we'll bring home the king."

"King's man," Clym jeered. "King's *fool*, more like."

"The giant, and the boy." Bell shook his head. "Bad odds for attacking the sheriff."

Alan spoke clearly, as only a minstrel can. *"And* me." He grinned as they turned to stare. "The sheriff has a bounty on my tongue—and perhaps something more, now." A vulgar gesture prompted faint smiles. "I'll fill our victims' ears with such noise they'll never hear us coming."

Amusement faded. Wat One-Hand shook his head. "I've listened. But I'm with Adam. 'Tis safer to avoid the sheriff."

Clym looked at Scarlet. *"You'll* not stay."

Will Scarlet's bruises were tinted yellow-green in a dark, stubbled face. He stared hard at Robin from near-black eyes fierce and predatory as a raptor's. "Meggie," he rasped, and cast a hard glance at Clym. *"Normans.* That's what I get of this."

"So." Adam Bell nodded. "You've got the giant, the boy, the minstrel, and Will Scarlet. And a fat priest—and a woman." He grinned faint contempt. "A right merry band, I'd say."

Clym spat disparagement. "Robin in the hood."

Much glared fiercely. "Robin *'ood,"* he slurred.

"Robin dead, more like." Adam Bell shook his head. " 'Tis yours to do, Robin." He hitched a shoulder to the others and started on his way, heading back into the wood. With him went Clym of the Clough, William of Cloudisley, and Wat One-Hand.

Robin sighed inwardly as he glanced to the others. *A right merry band, indeed.*

"Robin Hood," Much declared, making an end to it.

DeLacey called de la Barre to his private solar. He sat as the other stood. "Tonight," he said clearly. "You will take the others with you, and you will do as I have said. I will be in Lincoln, so as not to be linked with this. You and the others will put off your mail and helms, and dress as peasants. I do not wish to forewarn the woman."

De la Barre nodded. "I understand, my lord. But—if the earl's son is with her?"

"The earl will see to it his son is not present. You may act without hindrance."

"Yes, my lord." De la Barre risked a smile. "When you return from Lincoln the witch will be waiting."

"And perhaps the Abbot of Croxden." DeLacey sipped wine. "A convenience not to be ignored."

The earl's messenger arrived at Locksley Hall well before midday, but after Bell and his men had left. Robin, squatting in the dirt with the others to talk of plans, saw him, knew him, saw the others looking at him, though they could not know who he was, and took the man inside to listen in privacy. He was grateful the young man had worn unremarkable clothing so as to give nothing away; it would not do *yet*, Robin thought, to tell the others another thing they could not—or *would* not—comprehend: that the Earl of Huntington's son stooped to banditry. Later, perhaps, when the thing was done; but he could not count forever on the minstrel's silence.

Marian was in the hall seeing to baking bread, but from her Robin hid nothing. He simply put out his hand, waited for her to take it, then looked at the messenger.

The Huntington man was Thomas: young, sandy-haired, diffident. He spoke almost as if reciting the words. "You are asked to come home, my lord. For tonight, at least. The earl desires to speak with you."

Robin felt Marian's hand stiffen in his. "And the lady?"

Thomas reddened. "No, my lord." He flicked a glance at Marian, then looked away quickly. "I'm sorry, my lord . . . the earl is most anxious to speak with you in private. It is a personal matter."

Robin sliced a little more deeply. "Does it concern the Lady Marian?"

Thomas's face grew brighter. "My lord, I beg you—please . . . the earl confides nothing in me. He sent me to tell you, no

675

more. He said"—he moistened dry lips—"he said it has to do with your mother."

It astonished Robin completely. "My mother!"

Marian squeezed his hand. "Go," she said. "Go to Huntington. If there is peace to be made, swallow your pride and go."

He considered it. His father had volunteered nothing of his mother before, hiding much behind the unyielding wall of cold impersonality that refused every inquiry. No matter how often his son had asked. *Not now. Not tonight. Not even for my mother.* "No," Robin said finally.

The red in Thomas's face was replaced by pallor and something akin to desperation. "My lord, I was charged—he said you must come!"

Still he thinks to rule my world with this order and that. Robin smiled grimly. "Tell him I cannot. You need give him no reason—merely say to the earl that I confide nothing in you."

Thomas had wit enough to recognize the irony in the reference. He nodded, then inclined his head. "As you wish, my lord."

"Let this wait," Marian said when they were alone. "You don't know when the sheriff intends to send the money—it could be a week from now. There is time to see your father."

"It may not wait even an hour," he said grimly. "If the sheriff sends the shipment today, there is no time to waste."

"Robin." She clung more tightly as he made to withdraw his hand. "Do not be so obstinate. You are very like him in that."

It stung, but he had no time to explain all to her. "He will not wait, Marian. John wants his money as soon as possible, while I—"

"—want it for Richard, I *know;* you have made it abundantly clear. But do you even know which way they will go? Or where?"

He did. "By the shortest route, to Lincoln. That is where John is." He let go of her hand and touched her cheek gently. "I do not guess, Marian. I know because I was sent for. John summons me to Lincoln to speak of his bastard daughter."

It shocked her. *"That again!"*

"I have no doubt that is what my father desires to speak with me about. He uses my mother as bait." He bent and kissed her lingeringly, then took his hands from her as if afraid he would lose himself. "I must go, Marian. The others are ready—it is time we took the forest tracks to the other side of Nottingham."

She said nothing immediately. Then, "Robin." He turned at the door, pausing. Light from narrow windows was kind to her face and hair, as the moonlight had been to her nakedness the night before. "The shipment will be well-guarded. How can you think to defeat so many soldiers with only a handful of men?"

"Men—and arrows." He felt cold, distant, strangely detached, as if he fought already. It took effort to speak to a woman who could not know what it was to match oneself against another in an effort to end his life. "Have you ever seen what longbows do to Norman mail?"

Marian shook her head.

"The arrow goes through," he said quietly. "Through cloth, through leather, through mail—and certainly through flesh." Brutally, he added, "A single man with an English longbow need never fear a Norman . . . and we have *four* archers."

Gisbourne, newly shaved and in fresh clothing, crutched out to the hall for the first time since the boar had sliced open his leg. It brought him much satisfaction to again be mobile.

He stopped short in the hall, squinting disapproval. "I said to *reduce* the candles . . ." He leaned on crutches in the center of the hall, looking at rack after rack of stumpy wax candles. "Before God, they've put *more* out! Do they think we're made of money?"

"Sir Guy?" It was Walter, coming in with a parchment in his hand. "Sir Guy—this just arrived."

Gisbourne scowled. His mind was on money, not messages. "Who is responsible for all these candles? I said to reduce the number, Walter . . . I said too much money was being spent on unnecessary things. This many candles are *unnecessary*."

Walter nodded. "But it was the sheriff himself who ordered more put out. Sir Guy—here." He extended his hand. "The message."

"The sheriff ordered more?" The message was unimportant

when compared to a waste of coin. "But he agreed to allow me the latitude to make my own assessments."

"Aye. Sir Guy—the message—"

"Not *mine*," Gisbourne snapped. "Who would write to me? It's for the sheriff, is it not?"

"It bears no seal, merely the sheriff's office." Walter shrugged. "I thought it might be important."

"It doesn't matter," he told Walter irritably. "The sheriff is on his way to Lincoln. Whatever this is will have to wait."

Walter was plainly troubled. "The messenger was quite out of breath, Sir Guy, and his horse near broken down. He spent himself to get here. It must be important."

Impatiently, Gisbourne beckoned. "I'll read it, then . . . I'll judge if it's important enough to act immediately."

Walter was much relieved. He handed the parchment over.

Frowning, Gisbourne broke the blob of wax that bore no seal. There was no salutation, no intricate honorifics, merely a cryptic message in a hand unknown to Gisbourne:

> *Of France comes word to England:*
> *"Look to yourself for the devil is loosed."*

And beneath it a single letter: *J.*

Gisbourne read it twice. Then he looked at Walter. "From where did the messenger ride?"

"From Lincoln. He said he even risked Sherwood Forest to get the message here quickly." Walter smiled. " 'Tis important, isn't it?"

"From Lincoln," Gisbourne echoed. *Through Sherwood—then he missed the sheriff altogether.* He read the message a third time. He had learned much of the sheriff since he had come to Nottingham, so obliqueness and intrigue were no longer alien to him. His mind knit it together quickly. Gisbourne *knew.*

Walter now was worried. "Sir Guy? Is it bad news?"

*I sent a message to Prince John avowing my loyalty. He has it in writing—he has written proof—he can use it against me if he believes it could help his cause—*And he would, of course. John would use anything in any way to force others to assume his guilt. And now that the king was free—

678

—the devil indeed is loosed—Gisbourne laughed at Walter, though what he wanted was to cry. "Yes," he said, "and no. Depending on your plans."

"Sir Guy?"

Gisbourne laughed again, in bitter apprehension. Walter no longer mattered. Nothing of import mattered, if one had supported the wrong side.

"Sir Guy—do we need to send word to the sheriff?"

Gisbourne's smile was ghastly. "I think he'll find out in Lincoln."

Sixty-Nine

Alan was irritated: he had left behind his lute because Robin had said it was dangerous to bring it. He had initially protested, then given in. Robin was right. They went to rob the sheriff, not fill his ears with music; it was entirely possible the lute might get in the way. So he had left it behind with Marian at Locksley, and now suffered for it. He felt naked without the instrument close by where he could reach it in answer to a capricious Muse who did not understand such things as stealing tax money from the sheriff.

They took the shortest route through Sherwood Forest, as described by Much, who knew it better than anyone had suspected. Their object was to cut straight across to the Lincoln Road, find the place most favorable to their intentions—a narrowing of the road that would squeeze the Normans close and foul a laden wagon—then wait. A day, two, perhaps even three; Robin did not believe it would take longer, for deLacey would want very badly to transport the money to Prince John as quickly as possible.

They struck a pace that was part trot, part lope, a ground-eating gait that would bring them to the Lincoln Road before the Normans could arrive at the predetermined place even if they had left today. Much went first, slipping under low-hanging limbs that threatened everyone else, particularly the giant; Little John muttered impatiently from time to time, and once had stopped long enough to rip an offending branch clean of its trunk.

Scarlet said nothing at all, which surprised Alan a little. He had expected the man to complain about this or that, or make it plain he thought little of their knightly leader—Scarlet had never made a secret of his contempt for Robin—but he held his tongue. He simply clutched the bow tightly and went on behind Robin as Clym had gone behind Adam Bell.

Alan dismissed it. He brought up the rear, because when his mind was so full of verse and music it was hard to think of other things such as keeping up with others.

A fragment drifted in:

> In summer time, when leaves grow green,
> When they do grow both green and long,
> Of a bold outlaw, called Robin Hood,
> It is of him I sing this song.

Robin might not appreciate being called an outlaw—he wasn't one, yet—but by intending to steal the tax shipment from the sheriff himself, he undertook the sort of thievery that would result in a hanging. Once the sheriff discovered who it was, Robin would be speedily *un*hooded—and his rank declared forfeit, his inheritance stripped from him, the capture of his person worth money. It would undoubtedly be more than the seven pennies' bounty on a wolf's-head, but they would call him that anyway, just as they did the others.

He gives up more than any of us, but his faith is stronger regardless. Alan shook his head. So much done in Richard's name, with so few certainties. *If* they succeeded; *if* the money arrived safely;

if German Henry accepted it and *if* he freed the king—then perhaps this would be worth it.

Meanwhile, the verse continued.

> *As Robin Hood in the greenwood stood,*
> *All under the greenwood tree,*
> *There he was aware of a brave young man,*
> *As fine as he might be.*

It was a conceit, Alan knew, to enter himself in the lyrics, but he saw no reason not to. Did he not also accompany Robin Hood on a foray against the sheriff?

Alan sighed in frustration. Without his lute his music was crippled, and so was he.

Tuck laughed at Marian, which infuriated her. "Why *not?*" she asked. "Women have done it before, I daresay. All I need do is borrow the clothing, stuff my hair into a hood, and off I go."

She faced him within the hall, hands resting on hips. She was straight, slim, and fiercely lovely: a Celtic warrior-queen. Tuck groped for the kindest way to explain, though he himself was not certain she would fail to accomplish whatever she set out to do. He had learned Marian FitzWalter was no helpless maiden, but a woman with a strength of will to rival any man's.

Still, he was quite certain in *this* instance she was wrong. "No," he said gently. "Lady Marian—you would fool no one."

"I just told you how I could . . . if required, I could cut my hair short—"

"No," he said again, forestalling her argument. She was not serious, he knew; or not as serious as she believed. She was lonely and intensely helpless. She grasped at straws because there was nothing else to do. "Lady—no one would *ever* mistake you for a boy."

The line of her mouth was mutinous. "There are ways of disguising oneself. I could darken my features, puff out my cheeks, walk like a boy—"

Tuck made himself stern, which went against his nature, but

he saw nothing else that might aid him in this particular battle. "You are too well-grown to portray a boy, too settled in your features—young boys are like unshaped clay, lacking character in their faces. Your face has *much* character—"

"I'll distort it. I said so."

"—and far too much beauty." He smiled self-consciously, aware of his reddened face; monks were not supposed to notice such things, but of course they did. "If you were a brawny, plain Saxon maid, perhaps you might accomplish it. But you are fine-boned and delicate, and—" Tuck broke off. How was he to tell her—even he, a *monk,* who might be expected to speak of such things with detachment—that the very lushness of her body would preclude a masquerade. Lamely, he finished, "No man alive would take you for a boy."

"Delicate?" she echoed incredulously. "Let me tell you what has become of my life recently, and we'll see if *that* applies—"

"Lady Marian," he said firmly, "you were asked to wait. Only a fool would go against his wishes, which are for your safety, and put on a poor disguise to join him in an enterprise from which no one may return."

At last he reached her, if with brutal frankness instead of pious platitudes. She was white-faced and still. The fading bruises on her face stood out in stark relief against the pallor of her flesh. Unshed tears made her eyes bright in the midday dimness of the hall. "Perhaps," she began unevenly, "perhaps I wish so much to be a fool because I would rather die *with* him there, than learn of his death here."

It was poignant, and painful. "I will pray," he told her, not knowing what else to offer. "I will pray for his safety."

With a hint of her former acerbity, Marian suggested, "And pray for my *sanity.*"

Tuck smiled. "I will."

When Much came darting back through trees and foliage, Robin knew the wait was ended before it was truly begun. He had been correct, then; the sheriff wanted to deliver the money to John before the day was finished, rather than wait two or three more, a delay sure to infuriate the prince.

They squatted in the bracken, shielded by hip-high fern, and spoke softly of the plans laid at Locksley Hall, adapted now to the circumstances of road, of trees, of Normans.

Carefully he questioned Much, whom he knew to be limited in speech but shrewd in observation, and learned there was a driver on the seat with a mailed Norman next to him, plus ten outriders spaced around the wagon. They wore swords, knives, and carried crossbows, as was expected.

"Sheriff," Much said.

Robin, thinking ahead rapidly, fixed his attention again. "The sheriff is with them?" Much nodded even as Scarlet swore. Robin put up a hand. "It makes no difference. He is only one more man . . . we will treat him as the others." He looked into serious faces: a red-bearded giant wrestler who preferred to tend sheep; a hard-faced Saxon murderer who had more reason than most to hate Normans; a pretty troubadour who had, of late, grown to look more like the others than the silk-clad seducer who had nearly lost his tongue.

And Much. Robin sighed.

"Well?" Scarlet asked curtly.

Robin marked the dilation in Scarlet's eyes, turning them from brown to black. "Will—" For the first time he used the man's Christian name, and saw it register. "I will have you with me."

Brief surprise lighted the darkening eyes; then Scarlet jerked his head in a single nod of acknowledgment.

"Little John, you and Alan will take the other side. And Much"—he smiled at the boy's poised eagerness—"you are to do as I said before. Have you the knife?" It appeared in Much's hand. Robin nodded. "Good. Stay clear of crossbows and swords—there is no need to go so close when we have long-bows. We can do most of our work from a distance. If this goes as it should, we will not risk ourselves."

"*If,*" Alan said lightly.

Robin smiled. "The only man who countenances no '*if*' is Richard, King of the English—and he is not here."

"He will be," Little John murmured, "if this works . . ."

"*If,* again." But Robin's amusement faded. "There is no

more time. We must take up our places, and wait. I will loose the first arrow—after that do as you will."

"We're not you," Alan said quietly. "We are apprentices, not masters. We each of us will miss more than once or twice."

Robin nodded. "Use every arrow in your quiver. Each of us has thirty—if we cannot find thirteen targets with so many shafts apiece, we had better go back to Locksley and begin plowing fields." He put his hand on Much's thin shoulder. "You have the most dangerous role—do what you have to *quickly,* and take no more risks than you must. A dead boy serves no king."

Much nodded intently, then ran ahead to give them warning when the Normans approached the curve.

"Wait—" Little John blurted.

Scarlet swore. "No *time—"*

The giant's face was pale. " 'Tis murder to kill all of them outright. You've killed Normans, Will, but I haven't."

"You agreed!"

"I agreed to help steal the money—"

"Enough." Robin cut them off sharply, aware of dispassion rising in his soul. This was as much a war as Acre, if different in size and design. He required dispassion. "They have crossbows, Little John. If we give them the chance, they will use them."

The giant's expression was anguished. "We can't just *kill* them!"

Scarlet growled. "By God, you've spent too much time with sheep—"

"All right," Robin said curtly. "We'll give them the chance to surrender the money. But remember, John—they'll kill the boy first."

"Then *I'll* do Much's job—"

"You can't!" Alan hissed. "Before God, giant, can't you see? If they caught any of us now, they'd hang us within the week."

Little John's face was corpse-white in the frame of brilliant hair and beard. "I can't just *kill* a man."

"Then don't," Robin told him. "Shoot *near* them—let them be wary of you. It will keep them distracted."

The giant nodded eventually. Robin jerked his head at Little

John and Alan. They moved through bracken and dropped down to the road where it narrowed and swept left, then disappeared again into fern.

"Why?" Scarlet challenged. "Why d'ye want *me?*"

Robin hitched a shoulder. "You have no love for Normans."

"You'd want the giant, or the minstrel."

"I prefer a man unafraid to kill as many Normans as we must." Robin spared him no kindness, but the truth was kind enough to a man like William Scathlocke. "Scathlocke, to Scarlet. How did you come by it?"

Scarlet grimaced. "They found me with the last man, the one whose throat I bit out." He did not duck the brutality of fact; he had seen it as necessary. "I was bloody all over by then, from the other three I killed—this one was the worst. He nearly killed *me*—I had to do something." He shrugged a little. "I was blood up to my elbows . . . they called me Scarlet for it." His dark eyes were steady. "If you can do *this*, you'd have done what I did."

Robin nodded. "But I've done more than this . . . and you will do more than that."

"You do it for a king."

"You did it for a wife."

Scarlet's face stiffened. "God, but I'd kill them *all*—"

From ahead, Much whistled a birdcall. Robin slapped a hand to Scarlet's shoulder. "Now you will have your chance."

Scarlet rose to assume his own position, but lingered a moment. He touched his swollen nose. "A right smart blow, it was."

Robin laughed softly, reflecting on his fading bruises. "And I've only now begun to chew on both sides of my mouth."

Gisbourne sat in the sheriff's chair, nearly paralyzed from the multitude of thoughts filling his head. He feared it might burst, so packed was it with anxiety.

" 'The devil is loosed,' " he murmured, quoting the message once again and knowing how true it was; the king would be furious. Richard was not John, they said—he did not foam at the mouth in his rage—but he was a large, physically strong man of incredible warrior skills in addition to temporal power.

"He'll come home and find out what his brother has been doing . . . he'll learn what we've *all* been doing . . ." Gisbourne smeared his hands against his face, stretching it out of shape. "All I wanted was the woman, and the manor . . . I only did this for her."

He fixed on it instantly, comprehending the explanation, the motivation that justified a man in his circumstances. "For *her*, to make my way in the world . . . and I've nearly lost a leg, and now I may lose my place—" Gisbourne nearly squirmed, except it was too painful. "I know—*I* know—and the sheriff does not . . . *nobody* knows, here, save for me . . . is there anything in that I can use for myself?" And then he laughed into the hall. "Think like the sheriff—is there a way I may salvage myself? Is there a way I can profit from this?" Laughter died. He gazed speculatively at the parchment in his hand. *No one here knows . . . if no alarm is given, I may yet profit from it while the sheriff drowns in spite*—Gisbourne smiled realization—*and the woman may yet be mine, along with her manor, and I will be a knight in truth instead of in ledger books.*

When the first arrow flew, deLacey did not fully realize what it portended. From his place near the back of the wagon he saw only that the driver abruptly reeled in rein, jerking the cart horses up short. In the center of the road loomed a white-fletched arrow.

"Hold!" someone shouted. "Leave us the wagon!"

"Crossbows," deLacey ordered crisply.

"Climb down from the wagon and go!"

DeLacey rode up toward the driver. "Leave now."

The driver lifted his whip. A small, quick figure darted in to catch and halt the horses, then sliced at and severed the reins. Control was lost instantly.

"Kill him!" deLacey roared as the wagon lurched to a halt. The figure—*a boy?*—darted away again even as a crossbow bolt flew past.

The wagon driver abruptly slumped forward—and then the soldier beside the driver was clutching at his chest and falling sideways off the wagon. DeLacey heard the harrowing hum of clothyard arrows loosed from English longbows, and knew what was to come.

No—He saw a few arrows miss their human targets, while others drove through cloth, mail, and flesh. All around him men died instantly, transfixed by white-fletched shafts, or fell wounded until killed by other arrows. Horses also died, struck by wayward shots.

John's money—"By God, I say *no*"—He grasped first at his sword, meaning to unsheath it; then realized what folly lay in that. The attackers used longbows from dense cover, effectively stripping the sheriff and his Normans of the chance to retaliate. Already too many were dead. DeLacey's only hope of survival was simply to get away.

But the sheriff, dragging his own mount aside to distance himself from the wagon, saw an arrow slice across the shoulder of his horse, leaving behind a crimson furrow.

He gathered rein but the animal reared, then crumpled forward as another arrow took it. DeLacey scrambled, trying desperately to wrench boots out of stirrups and throw himself free of the falling horse, but it went down too quickly, too awkwardly; an arrow plucked at his sleeve, another teased at his helm, and then the horse was down, collapsing, with one of the sheriff's legs caught beneath the body, squashed between heavy flesh and the soft give of the still-damp road, which saved his leg from breaking.

Alive— While all around him the others died, struck down from unseen archers armed with deadly longbows. His leg ached from pressure, but he knew the bone was whole. *Must get free*—

But another horse fell nearby, kicking out in its death throes. One of the hooves glanced off the sheriff's helm, snatching it from his head. Mail coif was knocked askew.

DeLacey was abruptly vulnerable as air cooled his dampened hair, and acknowledged in laggardly fashion that his senses were fading from him, decreasing incrementally as his brain realized the truth: the hoof, smacking steel, had also jarred the skull, driving mail links into flesh.

Who—? But the thread of thought was lost as blood ran into his eyes. The day turned black around him.

Seventy

Christians lay sprawled in the sun, intermingled with Saracens; in death opposing viewpoints dwindled to insignificance, except to the unbodied souls seeking heaven or paradise, dependent on belief.

It was hot in the desert sun, too hot to live in mail, yet they did to preserve their lives. No one dared doff hauberks save in the safety of field pavilions when hostilities were ended. Even now the king wore mail, striding back through Acre's streets—

"No—" Robin squinted, then shook his head to clear it. He scrubbed a forearm across his face, ridding himself of dampness born of a foreign land, though the body was in England.

He squinted again. The dead remained, tumbled from panicked horses like dice from a gambler's hand. Despite mail hauberks, Norman chests sprouted shafts adorned with white feathers.

Will Scarlet ventured out first, armed with a meat-knife, to learn the truth of the bodies sprawled across the tree-fringed road. He was, Robin thought, prepared to kill the survivors, if any had survived. But even that was dangerous; a spanned crossbow was discharged with little effort, and a bolt from a dying man could strike Scarlet before anyone could prevent it.

"To the wagon!" Robin called. "Someone catch the horses— everyone else watch for living men." He himself pulled up his hood to shield his face from all but the most discerning of wounded men, then made his way down through bracken to the trampled road beyond.

From four directions they approached, converging on the bodies. Much went at once to the horses, catching a severed rein and looping it deftly through the snaffle ring to hold the wheel-horse in position, while the other men—bows drawn—approached cautiously.

Scarlet moved among them, checking every body. He stopped at deLacey's. "My lord Sheriff," he mocked, "brought down beneath a horse." He bent, knife in hand, as if to cut his throat.

—Christian looters walked through Acre's dead, cutting throats for no reason at all—and Richard would behead the garrison—"No," Robin said sharply, then grasped at another truth easier to explain to those who had not been there. "Men dead of arrows mark us merely as outlaws—dead men with cut throats mark us as something else. You've a reputation already—shall you worsen it with this?"

Scarlet spat onto the sheriff's unhelmed head. "Dead already, it seems," he said. "But no arrow that I see."

Little John's face was solemn. "Mine," he said. "I shot his horse, not him."

Scarlet laughed. "Aye, well . . . a smashed head is as good as an arrow."

"Be certain," Robin said sharply. "We can leave no one alive, or risk them learning who was responsible."

Laughing, Scarlet moved away to another body. The giant approached reluctantly, bent briefly to assess the bloody head, then straightened quickly. "He's dead."

Alan laughed briefly, though it had a strained sound. "With *him* dead, I'm free. I can sing for my living again."

Robin unnocked his arrow, slid it home into the quiver, then hooked an arm through his bow to settle it across his shoulders. "Gather up what horses are left . . . we've money to carry with us." He mounted the wheel, climbed up into the wagon, then squatted next to the chest. "Key," he muttered, then glanced at Much. "You've the deftest fingers—the sheriff will have the key."

"Here." Little John stood at the team's head. "I'll fashion new reins so we can drive them back."

"No wagon—it will mark us too easily." Annoyed by the hood, which muffled his hearing, Robin slid it off his head to lie across his shoulders. *Everyone is dead—*"Cut the horses loose;

we'll use them for riding, since so many others are dead, or heading back to Nottingham." He was curt, but there was little time for kindness. *No time at all, in Acre.* "We'll take every horse we can—ride back to Locksley with the money, then arrange with the Jews to send it to Longchamp . . . Much? Ah." Robin caught the key one-handed, inserted it in the lock and broke it open. Inside were sacks he tested for contents, cutting cord away.

The others gathered around as he reached into the bag. "Well?" Scarlet asked.

Robin looked at Much. "Lionheart," he said, flipping the boy a shilling.

Much caught it easily. *"Lionheart."*

Marian sat outside on the bench beside the hall door. Her kirtle-swathed lap was weighted with gold and gems aglint in the light of midday, and three wash-leather purses: the spoils from Robin's first theft.

Fingers turned over heavy rings so that gemstones glowed. Coin, gold, and jewels. Enough, she wondered, to ransom a king?

Robin believed it wasn't. He had gone to do it again.

The thought was unexpected: *What can I do?*

Little enough, she feared. He had left her behind to keep her out of danger because a woman was no match for the sheriff and his soldiers. *Physically, no—but there must be something. If not thievery, something else . . . something different, but just as effective.*

Marian considered it, using deLacey himself as her model. Although he was a man experienced with weapons, he specialized in words: sly innuendo, straightforward information timed for the best effect, things left unsaid with all the keenness of a swordblade cutting into a man's bowels. *Selective manipulation—couldn't I do the same?*

"Yes," she said aloud. "If I can determine his greatest weakness . . . decide what might hurt him most, even indirectly . . ."

Surely this sort of battle might prove as effective—and less physically dangerous—than what Robin attempted.

Marian worked through repercussions, discarding ideas she considered difficult to execute, or too weak to be effective. *I cannot count solely on myself . . . I need someone to help, to make it realistic.* But who was there in position to pose the greatest danger to William deLacey?

Marian laughed sharply. "The king, of course . . . or perhaps John, but the sheriff is his man . . ." She frowned, carrying the idea through with variations. And then the answer sprang forth.

The enormity of it astonished her. It was audacious, and rife with possibilities if simplistic in execution. The problem lay in predicting a man's reaction to what she had to propose.

"But why *not?*" she said aloud. "Nothing would be lost. He would most likely disbelieve me and do nothing about it; if he *did* believe me—" Marian's laugh was replete with irony. "He wouldn't, but if he *did*—"

She heard wheezing and glanced up; Tuck approached from the village. Despite the film of sweat glistening on his reddened face, his expression was one of contentment. He made his way to the well and pulled up the wooden bucket attached to the hemp, drank without pause until his thirst was sated, then dropped the bucket back down. He scrubbed a thick forearm across his brow. "Thirsty work, teaching of God."

Marian barely nodded, intent upon her new goal. "Do you think we can trust the reeve?"

Tuck frowned. "James seems an honest man. He is a hard worker and takes his position seriously."

She looked again into the treasure in her lap, stirring the gold. "I think we should send this on to Abraham. If there should be trouble from what Robin and the others do, it would be best to provide as little proof as possible."

"Why not simply hide it?"

Marian looked at him. "Adam Bell and the others did not join Robin. They owe us no loyalty. What is to keep them from coming back for this?"

Tuck nodded slowly. His fleshy face was troubled. "I could ask James to go."

"We'll wrap it in such a way he doesn't know what it is."

Tuck nodded again. His bovine eyes were wiser than they had been the day before. "Is there anything else?"

"You read me too well." Marian smiled. "You said you can write. I would like you to deliver a message to the earl."

"The *earl?*"

"Yes." Carefully she put all of the stolen wealth into the rough sacking used to contain it. "A very particular message. It may prove as devastating to the sheriff as an arrow loosed from an English longbow." She smiled at Tuck. "With less risk to the archer."

William deLacey roused when a small, deft hand searched in the folds of his tunic, his mail hauberk, and the quilted gambeson beneath. Had he not been trapped by the fallen horse and dizzied by the head wound, he might have protested, or caught hold of the wrist. But a muzzy head did not preclude wit; he recalled almost immediately that outlaws had killed everyone else, and that if he expected to live he had better behave as if he were dead.

He lay slackly. His right leg was trapped beneath the bulk of the dead horse, the left still hooked to stirrup by virtue of his spur. His right arm was bent under his ribs, but his left was free, slack weight across his abdomen. The small hand reached beneath the arm, shifting it without squeamishness, then searched in folds and hollows. DeLacey's unhelmed head rested against churned-up, half-dried mud. He felt blood matting the roots of his hair and seeping into his face, which tickled annoyingly, but he dared not so much as twitch in an effort to escape it.

Better to itch, than to die for want of a scratch. His head ached profoundly, which did not surprise him, and his right leg was numb. He maintained a slackness of expression even as the hand approached his groin, searching for the purse. He nearly tensed when he realized the hand had found the key to the chest, and then understood that was what the hand had wanted all along. Not his purse, the *key*—

Which meant the attack was planned specifically for the shipment, not a routine assault on whoever happened by. *Too well planned, too organized*— Someone who knew. Someone who had waited purposely to steal Prince John's money.

The key was pulled away. The hand deserted. DeLacey lay

still and listened, hearing through the pain in his head the bits of conversation that might, if understood, tell him who the robbers were. He dared not open his eyes, not even a smidgen, or risk divulging his condition to someone who might be watching.

Then one sentence cut through the fog of his head: "—ride back to Locksley with the money, then arrange with the Jews to send it to Longchamp."

Locksley. Jews. Longchamp. *Very* well organized.

"Lionheart," someone said, and was answered by a boy's soft whisper echoing the name.

For Richard? DeLacey was incredulous. *They rob John to pay Richard's ransom?* And then nearly laughed: it made a bizarre sort of sense. John diverted money intended for Richard's ransom to pay debts and block the king's release, while someone *else* stole money bound for John to send to the chancellor, who would in turn send it to Germany. *But who?*

The sheriff could not wait. If money were being distributed in the name of Richard the Lionheart, no one would look at dead men.

He opened his eyes the merest crack, peering fuzzily through gummy lashes. He saw first the dark bulk of his dead horse, closer than anything else; beyond it the rear wheel of a wagon, the wagon atop the wheel, the lid of the chest thrown back— and a man squatting by it, flipping a coin to a boy.

A man who had slipped his hood to bare his head and face, and the glare of white-blond hair cascading over shoulders.

Robert. Robin. *Robin Hood.*

William deLacey rejoiced.

Robin surveyed his party with some trepidation. Of horses not dead or missing, only four remained; as the sole expert horseman among them—Alan rode well enough, but peasants were too poor for mounts and rarely learned to ride—he took one of the saddleless cart horses. He gave the other to Little John simply because of his size, and told him sternly to stay on however he could; they could not afford to waste time gathering up fallen riders all the way back to Locksley.

Alan and Will Scarlet inherited the Norman mounts with saddles, and also the bags of money: two to each horse, tied across the withers. Robin swung Much up behind him, then heaved the cart horse around with a signal effort. Trained primarily to pull, the horse responded sluggishly to the touch of snaffle in mouth and the prodding of a bootheel.

He glanced at Little John, hugging his horse with his prodigious legs, and knew it would not be an easy ride. It was midafternoon, but they would be fortunate to reach Locksley by sundown. Alan was easier in the saddle, but Will Scarlet was heavy-handed, understanding only that the horse was to go forward, not that other signals might result in different responses.

We cannot walk instead—the money is too heavy—Robin shook his head. *Nor can we split up . . . we would make too tempting a target for others who do likewise.* "Follow me," he said finally. "Stay on as best you can."

Tuck retrieved creased, blank parchment from his things, as well as ink and quill. He sat with them clutched in his hands on the bench beside Marian, flushed face slowly whitening. "Are you certain?"

"Yes." She scraped dampened palms against the fabric of her kirtle. "Very certain, Brother Tuck. The sheriff has been fighting this kind of battle for many years, now—what is to prevent me from doing likewise?"

"There is danger attached," he said. "Perhaps not physical—"

"It doesn't matter," she said quietly. "I will do this, Tuck. I may not fully approve of Robin's methods, but I *do* approve his intent . . . I think we all of us should do what we can to bring King Richard home."

Troubled, he nodded. "Aye, of course—but the earl? Why should he pay heed to your words?"

"He is, above all, loyal to the king. He wants no part of Prince John. It seems to me the earl would also oppose the sheriff, as William deLacey is John's man."

Tuck smoothed crumpled parchment across cassock and thigh. "Perhaps so, Lady Marian."

She smiled. "You think he will be indisposed to put much stock in what *I* have to say."

He nodded, reddening again.

"Therefore I must be circumspect in my language—and offer him something he desires very much, so he *must* pay heed."

Tuck's mouth opened. "You don't mean to tell him you will give up his son!"

Marian's teeth clicked shut. "Not in so many words. *Imply* it, yes—because this sort of warfare lives on implication. That much I have learned from the sheriff." Her mouth tightened into a grim line. "I want you to put into writing that the sheriff has stolen money intended to ransom the king, and intends to take it himself to John in Lincoln. If the earl requires an additional weapon against the Count of Mortain, he shall have this one. Once the king is home—"

"*If* he comes home."

Marian looked at Tuck. "He must come home. Otherwise what Robin does is naught but outlawry."

Tuck's upper lip was stippled with perspiration. He blotted it, then once again smoothed the dog-eared parchment. "But it is," he said quietly. "It *is* outlawry."

"And in my own way, I do my share. If this fails and John becomes king, I too could be named a wolf's-head." Marian gestured slightly. "Write it, Brother Tuck. Let us give the earl his weapon." *And let me gain mine as well.*

DeLacey waited until the sounds of ill-ridden horses crashing through foliage faded, replaced with a heavy stillness that made him all too aware of fragile mortality. He was the only man of thirteen still alive, and only because of a head wound that spilled so much blood the others believed him dead. He was grateful the squeamish giant had been the one to assess his condition; Will Scarlet would have cut his throat outright, and he did not doubt Robert of Locksley—*Robin Hood!* he exulted—would have loosed another arrow.

When the stillness was replaced by the sounds of the forest, he at last struggled to lever himself up on his right elbow so he could view the scene. It was much as expected: mailed bodies scattered here and there, dead mounts; the wagon bearing its weight of empty chest, bereft now of horses.

"Twelve men," he muttered. "They'll hang even an *earl's* son for work such as this!"

With effort, he untangled his spur from stirrup and freed his left leg, though he could do little with it. But the cramp was gone, and the feeling of helplessness abated. He tried tugging himself free of the downed horse, but was unsuccessful. The weight was too much, though the ground was soft enough to have kept the leg whole. He needed help to lift the horse, but since there was none to be had he would rely on something else.

Twisting, he pulled the Norman sword free of its sheath. At close quarters it was unwieldy, but there was no other help for it. With effort and tenacity, he set himself to the task of scraping away the mud that cradled his trapped leg. If he dug enough of it aside, he could pull himself free. It would take time, of course, but he was going nowhere. He had all the time in the world.

"Marian," deLacey muttered. He was aware peripherally of a curious indifference, as if mind and body were numb to the promise of the woman he had desired for so long.

Then numbness disappeared. Indifference dissipated. *She spread her legs for Robert of Locksley.*

Aware of fury and thwarted desire, he appended a new name to Hugh FitzWalter's daughter with deliberate clarity. "Robin. Hood's. *Whore.*"

James the reeve had been dispatched to deliver the message to Huntington, then was to go on to Nottingham and Abraham. Marian lingered outside the hall as the sun went down, watching again for Robin.

Go inside, she told herself. *This offers nothing.* But she could not make herself turn and go. A moment longer only, and then another moment, until the moments became an hour.

From the tree line behind the hall came a crackle of underbrush. Hope stilled her completely a moment, then gave her the freedom to dart toward the rear of the hall, to see if it were Robin coming back with the others.

Strangers, all of them. One man carried a torch.

Marian knew at once none of them were peasants, though their clothing was simple enough. They were too intent, too organized, fixed on a single goal. "The earl—" Foreboding sprang up, hollowing her belly. "This is his answer."

The man in the lead was young and suspiciously pleased with himself. She saw the slight smile, the glint in his brown eyes, the arrogant manner at odds with his dress. For only an instant she lingered, thinking to attempt conversation, to explain what the message was for. But something in the man's eyes persuaded her otherwise. *Why come out of Sherwood if all they mean is to talk?*

"Tuck—" She spun, yanking her kirtle skirts out of the way. "Brother Tuck!" *If I can reach the hall—reach a rake—*It wasn't a quarterstaff, but she thought it might do.

Near the bench they caught her. Marian felt the hands grasping at arms, the fingers digging in—*Will Scarlet all over again—*

She shouted a denial, recalling the degradation of Scarlet's possession of her. That he had not raped her meant nothing now—he had put rough hands on her and hurt her, forcing her to do things she did not wish to do. It was no different now.

She fought viciously, biting and kicking, jamming elbows at ribs and bellies, grinding heels into toes. In shock they slackened their hold.

Marian twisted, tearing from their grasps. The bench—and the rake—right *there*—

She reached for it, clawed for it, felt a fingertip touch wood. *"Yes—"* But they grabbed her again, knocking aside the rake.

"Hold her!" one man snapped in pure Norman French. "By God, if you can't, *I* will—" And he was there in front of her even as she twisted,-reaching out to sink his hand into her hair, to catch the thick braid and wind it around his palm.

Marian kicked, trying to jam stiffened toes into vulnerable flesh. A raised knee set to slam between the man's legs was turned aside with a kick of his own that nearly hooked her off her feet. He jerked her head up tight, snubbed like an unbroken colt. "No spells," he said curtly. "No spells on *us,* witch—"

He looked nothing like Will Scarlet, but that is whom she

saw. She smelled him again, heard him again. Marian thrust herself against the man and tried to slam her head up under his chin.

He swore a string of Norman oaths. The cuff from a broad-palmed hand landed athwart ear and jaw, shutting her teeth together slantwise. Blood broke inside her mouth even as her twisted jaw protested with a sharp bolt of pain. The intensity silenced Marian and recalled her to herself. *Not Will Scarlet.*

Other men also, gathering near: ten of them, she thought; ten of the earl's men sent to dismiss the woman. Sluggishly she remembered. *He called me witch.*

She struggled briefly and suffered for it. Hands tightened on her, twisting her arms; the Norman took another wrap of braid so tight it pulled her head to the side, jarring her jaw again. "I'm not a witch—"

"Shut your mouth," he said, "or I will stuff it full of excrement and let you choke on it."

She was dazed now, and aching, but understood all too well the danger she was in. The earl had reacted in a way she had not anticipated. "He's lying," she gasped through the ache in ear and jaw. "The earl's *lying*—"

The man's free hand closed on her face, squeezing it out of shape. Pain lanced through her jaw. "We have proof," he declared, "and a man who will swear to your witchcraft. A man from Ravenskeep."

Ravenskeep—? "But it's not *true,*" she protested. "Witchcraft has nothing to do with this . . . this is a petty lord's revenge—"

He bent quickly, scooped up loose, powdery dirt, forced it between her teeth and clamped her mouth shut. "If you do not hold your tongue, I will cut it out and feed it to you."

She shut her throat to keep herself from choking even as tears of effort ran from her eyes. When he took her trembling silence for surrender, he removed his hand. "What we're—"

Marian spat into his face the dirt he had stuffed in her mouth. *"Tuck!"* she shouted. "Tuck—*to me*—"

Her captor did not bother to wipe the sludge from his face. He turned to the man with the torch. "Burn it," he said quietly. "Burn the entire village." He swung back to Marian, pressing a hand across her mouth before she could protest. With grave deliberation he scrubbed dirt- and blood-laden spittle from his young face. "The deaths will be on your soul—if a witch *has* a soul."

Seventy-One

DeLacey at last tossed aside the sword and dug gloved fingers deep into half-dried mud, dragging his body forward even as he braced the other foot against the firmer saddle. The numb leg moved sluggishly until the trapped foot was in the rough-hewn channel he had so tenaciously cut, and then he lurched again, straining, dragging his leg free of the slack, heavy body.

He sprawled facedown in the road newly muddied by blood, while pain beat in his head. Sweating, he gasped, "Is *no one* bound for Lincoln?" The road had been deserted since the attack.

He lay limply for some time, trying to still the pounding of his head. Gingerly he fingered stiff, matted hair bare of coif and helm, the crusted wound itself, and the blood dried on his face. At last, he could scratch it.

"He'll hang," deLacey murmured. "By God—I'll see he hangs . . . and I'll have his whore *watch*."

Robin reined in his horse as Scarlet shouted behind him. It took an extra moment, since the cart horse was unresponsive, and by the time Robin got him turned fully he found Scarlet and Alan laughing as Little John picked himself up from the ground. The other cart horse wandered his way up the track until Robin turned him back, then reached and caught loose rein.

Little John's face was as fiery as his hair. "I'll walk from here."

Robin rode slowly back along the track, grimly leading a horse who pulled against his shoulder. He stopped as he reached the giant. "The first time you sheared a sheep, did you know how?"

Little John shook his head, frowning.

"The first time you wrestled a man, did you know how?"

The giant muttered denial.

"But you sheared a second sheep, and you wrestled a second man." Robin held out the rein. Glumly, Little John took it.

Locksley Hall was ablaze even as Marian was jerked from the ground and slammed down across a horse's withers. She smelled pungent woodsmoke. *Not the hall.* She lost her breath as the saddle jammed into her abdomen, so that even as she drew breath to shout it was driven out of her. Noisily she sucked air back in again, but a man was in the saddle with one hand wrapped in her braid, mashing her face against the horse's shoulder.

Not the hall. She heard the crackle and snap of flame consuming the straw and grass used in the daub-and-wattle as fire made its way up the cruck-beamed timber supports to the fresh thatching James and others had labored to repair. *So much work.*

She shifted, trying to slide off. He caught handfuls of braid and kirtle bodice and pressed her down again. Marian tasted salt, blood, horsehair, and sweat, as well as the residue of dirt left from the leader's attempt to gag her.

"If you struggle," he said simply, "I will hang you by your hair and drag you beside me."

Her jaw and ear ached with unremitting pain. She wanted to struggle again for no other reason than to hold herself upright so the pounding in her head lessened, but he refused her that. She dared not press him too much. Her position was precarious as well as uncomfortable. If she fell, she could easily have a leg broken—or both of them—by the misstep of a galloping horse, or be trampled entirely.

She thought of Tuck again, who had gone out of the hall to visit the villagers. *If he can carry word to Robin . . .*

If Robin lived to hear it.

She heard the startled outcries of Locksley's inhabitants as they discovered the hall afire, and the promise of an inferno as a galloping rider swung by to toss his torch into thatching within the village proper. *Burn it,* the leader had said. *Burn the entire village.*

Marian twisted her head to pitch her voice upward. "Not the village," she begged. "They've done nothing—it was I who sent the message!"

Her wrists were bound behind her by the strength of one large hand. With the other he swung the horse around, then set it to a lope. The saddle ground into her midriff. She banged nose and chin on the flexing shoulder. Marian craned up her head, but the leader jammed her down again with a murmured imprecation against Saxon witches.

The shouting and crackle faded as Locksley fell behind. Numbly Marian thought, *They burn witches, too.*

DeLacey tested his leg. It was whole, if sore; he doubted there would be any lasting ill effects. He recovered his sword, cleaned and sheathed it, went from body to body to see if anyone lived.

Only one man did, if barely: Archaumbault, the castellan, lay half beneath the wagon. A crossbow lay close at hand with the trigger discharged; Archaumbault was the man, then, who had aimed for and missed the boy.

Unfortunate . . . I would have preferred my castellan—or anyone—had accounted for someone. Now we look like fools, bested by Saxon wolf's-heads.

Colorless, the dying veteran breathed shallowly and unevenly. His eyelids were cracked, but deLacey doubted Archaumbault saw anything.

Acknowledgment was bitter. *I need more men like him, yet he is taken from me.*

Archaumbault was beyond help. I remained then to use the

701

man's loss to further the sheriff's ambitions; if a man had to die, deLacey thought, the least he could do was serve his lord by that death.

He drew his knife, hesitated only briefly, then methodically slit Archaumbault's throat. Blood welled, bubbled briefly, then flowed. It slowed after a moment: sluggish tears from a dry eye.

DeLacey went to each man and cut his throat likewise. He was taking no chances that the earl might contrive to bribe his son free of banditry and murder charges, depending on title and influence to mitigate the sentence; this kind of atrocity assured Locksley—*no, Robin Hood*—would be executed.

As for me? DeLacey smiled grimly. He nicked the side of his throat, then cleaned and resheathed the weapon. *Someone happened along before Sir Robert of Locksley could finish cutting me.*

Marian nearly fell when she was dragged off the horse. She ached from the pounding ride, her feet and hands were numb, her jaw and ear hurt badly, and she wanted very much to sit down normally, simply to sort out her wits. But the man merely caught both her wrists at her spine, sealed them again in his grasp, then marched her toward the castle.

She expected Huntington's castle. What she saw was Nottingham's.

"But—" She bit it off. She would give him no chance to misuse her further. And it made as much sense as anything else: the earl would not desire her in his castle. Perhaps this worked in her favor; if she were at Nottingham, the sheriff would come to see her. Perhaps he would explain.

They cannot just lock me away. They want something from me. The earl wants me gone—the sheriff wants me in bed. It flushed her with angry humiliation. *If he thinks this will do it, he is mad.*

The man took her in by a side door, banging her shoulder into the stone jamb—Marian winced; she would be a mass of scrapes and bruises by the time he was done—then pushed her down the corridor she found more reminiscent of a tunnel. Hair pulled free of braid straggled around her shoulders as she shook it back from her face; she felt the cool, damp air—and smelled the stench—of Nottingham's dungeon.

He took her out of the corridor into a dark, low-vaulted chamber, where mail-clad soldiers gathered. "Open," he said, and one of the Normans unlocked the grate in the floor and flipped it back to reveal a rectangular hole. "No," her captor said, when someone dragged over the crude ladder. "She's a witch; let her fly. If she can't, then she'll fall."

And Marian fell as he tipped her over. She landed hard on ancient straw loosely strewn over packed floor.

Gisbourne was in the sheriff's solar when Walter found him to say the Abbot of Croxden had arrived. "He says he's come to investigate a charge of witchcraft laid against the Lady Marian FitzWalter."

Gisbourne recalled the letter he had written at deLacey's order. He had not expected it to be answered so quickly, and just now he had other matters far more important to attend, such as how to incriminate the sheriff with something even more dangerous than the letter Prince John had from *him*.

Gisbourne sighed, annoyed. "The sheriff isn't here; he's in Lincoln. And *she* isn't here, either, so the abbot can't very well do anything yet. He'll just have to wait."

"But she *is* here," Walter said. "Philip de la Barre brought her in not long ago. He put her in the dungeon."

"In the *dungeon*?" Gisbourne was appalled. "Is he mad?"

Walter shrugged. "He said she's a witch."

Gisbourne dropped the papers to the sheriff's table. "She isn't a witch, you fool . . . can't you see the sheriff is using that against her to force her to marry him? There is no truth to the suspicion."

Walter was bewildered. "Sir Guy, all I know is Philip de la Barre put her in the dungeon. He said she is a witch. That the sheriff *told* him so."

Of course he did, Gisbourne thought. *He'd lie to anyone to serve his own purposes.* "Well," he said briskly, hoping to douse any newly raised suspicions Walter might have, "perhaps she is; perhaps she is not. That is to be settled between Abbot Martin and the sheriff." He paused. "And the king, of course—she *is* a royal ward." He straightened his disordered papers. "Walter, de la

Barre made a mistake. Have the Lady Marian brought out of the dungeon and installed in a chamber."

"But de la Barre—"

"—is not castellan; Archaumbault is, and he's gone to Lincoln with the sheriff." *And all the money.* "I am seneschal; the castle currently is in my charge."

In a way it was true, though he trod dangerous ground. He simply could not be certain which way the sheriff might prefer to have the woman held. In his uncertainty, he might as well act and attempt to profit from it. It was what deLacey would do.

Gisbourne carefully pushed himself away from the table and rose, catching up crutches. Idly he said, "If the king were free *right now*, Walter, and on his way to England, do you think he would like to learn a ward of the Crown has been put into a dungeon?"

"No," Walter conceded, "but the king *isn't* free—"

"Pretend," Gisbourne suggested succinctly. "Now go and have the abbot shown to a chamber, then order the Lady Marian brought out of the dungeon."

Marian thrust herself from the floor as the grate was lowered and locked. She could see very little, merely a crosshatched rectangle of wan light, and the indistinct face of the soldier who snapped the bolt home. Then the face went away and she saw no one at all, not even the man who had said she was a witch.

Inane laughter bubbled up, accompanied by despair. "Fly," she said unevenly. "Doesn't a witch require a broom?"

She bit down into her lip, fighting back tears. God, but she *hurt.* "No," she said aloud.

But she could not ignore it. Now that he was gone, now that she was still, now that she was alone—

Marian hugged her ribs, biting more firmly into her lip. The ear and jaw still ached. The inside of her mouth was cut, though it no longer bled. Somehow she had twisted an ankle—*when he pulled me off the horse?*—and her wrists felt bruised from the pressure of his grasp. She was as battered as before, when Will Scarlet had taken her. *At least then I was out-of-doors where I could breathe clean air without the stink of ordure and—rats?*

Yes, rats. She heard them near the walls. Marian stood in the faded patch of crosshatched light and looked at her hole. She was alone at least, but hardly the first inhabitant. The straw was thickly fouled, and an unemptied bucket of slops was set into a corner. There was no bench, no stool, not even a pallet.

But for the moment such knowledge palled. She thought instead of the flames she had seen, the shouting she had heard, the screams but barely begun.

Burn the entire village.

Marian shivered. "Don't let them die for *me*—" Tears stung her eyes. She felt sick to her stomach, wanting to spew up vileness in response to recognition: a man had done this thing because she dared to love his son. "No," Marian murmured, "because the son dares to love *me.*"

She swallowed heavily, fighting the urge to vomit. Her abused belly contracted. Anger-tempered courage wavered, until she fixed her mind on the man's cold-blooded order to burn everything. She did not avoid it. It gave her the strength to overcome the fear, to live on determination to see him answer for it.

She dared not sit, or tempt the rats. So she paced in a small pattern, rubbing a sore elbow, favoring an aching ankle, picking straw from her tangled hair. Around and around she went, crossing the patch of light. She fixed her mind on Robin, wishing him to the castle where he would set her free.

"Childhood dreams," she muttered.

For now, they were all she had.

They had smelled it for some time, but now they could see it. In moonlight the smoke was eerie, lacelike layers snagging on tree branches, then shredding to drift away. Much leaned close to Robin, pressing against his back. "Fire."

Robin nodded. They were very close to Locksley, but the sun had gone down. Only the moon offered illumination. Robin used it to find his way along the track he knew existed, because he had used it earlier. "A bonfire, perhaps—" They broke free of the perimeter fringe into the meadowlands, and saw without obstruction the ruin of Locksley Hall.

"Jesu," Alan whispered. "The whole *village* is gone—"

Avoiding Much, Robin slid awkwardly from the still-moving cart horse and ran toward the charred, blackened timbers, which were still smoking, still glowing, still listlessly burning, like a handful of stubborn coals. "Marian—"

The stench of smoke was thick, intermixed with the tang of burned flesh; some of it was animal, some of it human. Beyond the ruins of the hall lay the village itself. Most of it was burned, but flames were slow to die.

He was aware as he ran of a body making its way toward him, heavy through the shoulders, wide through the hips, thick of ankle and calf. It registered that the body was male, not female, swathed in black wool that was burned through in dozens of places. The face was fleshy and stunned, smeared with ash and soot; the cowlike brown eyes expressed little but naked horror.

"Tuck!" Robin caught at the monk's shoulders and saw the wince in his eyes. "Tuck—*where is she?*"

"Gone—" the monk whispered. "All of it—*gone*—"

"Tuck." He doubled up handfuls of spark-riddled cassock. "Where is Marian?"

"I went in—I went in to see . . . to see if she was there—" Tuck smeared a soot-covered hand across his face. "The whole hall was burning—"

Robin's voice cracked. "*Insh'Allah*, Tuck—where is Marian?"

The monk began to cough, bringing up viscid black spittle. He spat it onto the ground, still coughing, then gathered up his rosary and began to pray.

Robin closed his hand over the crucifix and ripped it from Tuck's grasp. His voice now was deadly. "Is Marian dead?"

Fleshy hands groped. "Let me—I must—"

"*Tuck!*" Others were there now; Robin felt them, saw them, heard them: Much and Will Scarlet, Alan and Little John, and people coming up from the burning village. "Is she dead? Is Marian dead?"

Sense returned to Tuck's eyes. He coughed weakly again, then grasped Robin's shoulder. "No—no . . . someone took her away. I heard her shouting . . . by the time I reached the hall, they were riding away—and the hall was burning, and the village, too—"

"Someone *took* her?" Robin caught handfuls of cassock again. "In the name of God, Tuck—*tell me what you know*—"

"They took her," Tuck repeated. "Mounted men."

"Normans," Scarlet said.

"No mail—I saw no shine, no glint—" Tuck shook his head. "They wore plain clothing, like peasants—"

"But they *rode*," Robin said. He cast a glance at the others, seeing nods of comprehension, the bleakness of acknowledgment. "Tuck—" But the question died before it was asked. He recalled all too clearly Thomas, sent from his father, garbed in plain clothing and begging in desperation that he go home. *"Ya Allah—"* He stared at Tuck. "My father—? Would my father—?" He looked beyond to the burning village. *"This—?"*

"Robin." It was the giant, red hair glinting in fireglow. "What do you want us to do?"

"I want—" He tried again. "I want—" But the words kept dying. He was cold, very cold, and the world felt far away. *I told her to stay here because she would be safe. Because she would be SAFE.* With effort he found his tongue, and the wit to form the words. "I want you to come with me. Now." He looked at them. "Will you?" He looked at Tuck. "Will you?"

"Which way?" Scarlet asked.

"Huntington," he murmured; it sounded like someone else. Much was there with the cart horse, handing rein to Robin.

Seventy-Two

Marian heard footsteps, mutterings, and at last the metallic snap of the bolt being unlocked. She stood beneath the cross-hatched trapdoor and watched as it was pulled open. Dim light crept into the hole into which she had been dropped, illuminating its closeness and the fetid conditions, lessening more than ever her taste for captivity. Already she itched.

Someone else? Then, cynically, *Or someone sent to test me?*

The ladder scraped over the edge and was dropped down as she dodged it. "Come up," a voice invited.

Marian hesitated. She trusted no one now.

"Come *up*," the voice insisted. "D'ye like it down there? We're to put you somewhere else."

Hastily she climbed, kicking aside her kirtle and shift. Nothing could be worse than the filthy, choking hole; even if it were, she was willing to risk finding out.

The man had not lied. She was taken to an ordinary chamber housing one bed and a stool and was left there. The door was latched from the outside; she assumed there was a guard.

Marian smiled wryly. *Perhaps two, this time; last time one proved not enough.*

The splayed windows were no more wide than she was, the slits for admitting light little more than arrow-loops. There was no light to admit; it was dark without and within. A single fat candle on a stand near the door shed fickle illumination, but was better than nothing, certainly far better than she had known in the hole.

Marian sighed and ran both hands through her tangled hair,

scraping it back from her face. She was filthy, she knew, her dishevelled hair still littered with straw, her kirtle stained from a sweating horse, her face smudged with dirt and possibly blood. She scrubbed at it absently, recalling with distaste the leader of the Normans and his attempt to silence her.

She had barely turned to assess her room when the latch rattled again and the door was swung open. She spun stiffly, backing up two steps, until she saw Sir Guy of Gisbourne crutching his way into the chamber. Beyond him stood the guards, who this time shut and locked the door behind him.

Marian was much relieved to see a sympathetic face. He had aided her before, perhaps he would again. She smiled, relaxing. "Do they distrust you now?"

His expression was rueful. "As one might expect. But *I* gave the order—I want no one suspecting me." He actually smiled back. It was the first time she had seen him so at ease. The smile smoothed the intensity from his face and softened the hardness of the dark eyes she had once likened to a boar's. "I am sorry you were put into the dungeon," he said, hiding nothing of his displeasure. "De la Barre was told only that you were a witch, and were to be brought to the castle. He believed the nonsense, of course—the sheriff can be convincing—and so he put you down there, thinking to please the sheriff."

He was different. She heard it in his tone, saw it in his eyes. The awkward intensity was banished, replaced with a hint of pride and a trace of self-satisfaction. But the change in Sir Guy of Gisbourne was not what concerned her. "The *sheriff* ordered this?"

Gisbourne nodded. "He thinks it will force your hand. That you will agree to marry him to escape a witchcraft trial."

Marian found it preposterous. "*No* man would go to so much trouble merely to win a woman! A village—even lives?" She stared at him. "Would he? Even William deLacey?"

Gisbourne's mouth twisted. The glint in his dark eyes was bittersweet. "Men do. The sheriff has. He wants you that badly."

This was at odds with everything she had suspected. "I thought it was the *earl.*"

"Huntington?" He nodded. "He has a part in this—I am told the sheriff received a message yesterday from the earl."

She was cold, so very cold. *Then my message will have failed . . . he is using the sheriff to further his own aims.* She looked at Gisbourne. "One hand holds the other, while both men profit?"

He shrugged uncomfortably, avoiding her gaze.

Laggardly, she recalled her manners as she was struck again by the awkwardness of his posture, draped across two crude crutches. She gestured. "Sir Guy—seat yourself. The stool, there—or would you prefer the bed?"

He shook his head. "I will stand. If it please you, Lady Marian, I would have you sit. There is much for you to hear."

She sought common ground as she perched on the edge of the bed. She had never been comfortable in his presence; she felt guilty now that he seemed at ease and her awkwardness still remained. He had done so much for her. "Have you come again to release me?" She smiled crookedly. "Or is there no help for me at all?"

"I have come to *give* you release, if you are willing to take it." The wording was oblique, but Gisbourne offered no better. He hitched a shoulder slightly, as if to resettle a crutch. "He means to follow through with the trial, unless you agree to marry him. He's summoned Abbot Martin here from Croxden."

Added to everything else, it shook her badly. "He is *here?*"

Gisbourne nodded.

Marian stared at him, putting together the pieces even though she wanted very badly to disbelieve the result. "Both men, united—and the abbot, as well . . ." It hurt to swallow. "What is there to do? How do I fight them both?"

Gisbourne's saturnine face was freshly shaved, and he wore clean clothing. "Lady . . . there is much to do. You may listen—and give me your kindness and consideration, if you would be so generous." He drew in a deep breath. "I tried once before to say this—there, in the forest—but the boar interrupted."

Marian suppressed her impatience; she was more concerned with the abbot's presence and the sheriff's intentions. She recalled the boar, of course, and Gisbourne's injury. She recalled vaguely that he had been trying to say something to her then, before the boar broke into their clearing. He had never said it at all because the boar had intervened. *And then Robin, killing it.* "I am sorry, Sir Guy—"

He cut her off with a shake of his head. "No, do not apologize. I have often been a fool in my life, especially with women. They—you—often frighten me." He managed a self-conscious smile. Then its edges crumbled away, baring nakedness, betraying desperation. "So many times I have tried to speak to women, only to make a fool of myself—to blunder into incoherency."

Marian focused her attention, essaying a smile. She wanted to give him heart; it wasn't his fault there was so much more to think about. "You are not incoherent now."

"No. I am—changed." He swallowed heavily. His dark face was a little gray, but his eyes did not avoid hers. "Lady Marian, I overstep my bounds, but I must say it. I—" He moistened dry lips. "I desire to marry you."

She was empty of emotion. For a long moment all she could do was stare. How could he think of marriage when she might well burn at the stake?

And yet perhaps she wouldn't. Hadn't he come to aid her?

Marian swallowed carefully; her ear and jaw still ached. "Is this what you meant to say? Then?"

"I meant to say then that I would do anything for you," he told her earnestly, hiding nothing from her. "To declare my intentions . . . and to say I would die for you." His voice steadied. "I very nearly did."

So he had. "Sir Guy—" Her mouth felt numb. *This is too much . . . all of this, too much.* But she had no desire to hurt him. Reluctantly she began, "Sir Guy, I am sorry—"

"You don't understand," he said desperately, cutting her off abruptly. "I love you, Lady Marian."

It silenced her completely. Three simple words bearing the weight of a man's soul—and she was required to crush it. Marian thought it might almost be better to inhabit the hole again, to withstand rats instead of dealing with this man's heart. "Sir Guy—"

The earnestness faded, replaced with intensity. "I am devoted to you," he insisted. "I will be what I must be, do what I must do, to make you happy." He crutched closer. His expression transformed itself from desperation to something akin to torment, as if he knew she would not be easily swayed and required a sacrifice. "I have never said that to a woman . . . I thought I never could . . . I thought I would never *care*—" His knuckles were white on the crutches. "Forgive me—I meant to say it differently . . . Lady Marian, please—I meant once to better myself, to improve myself with marriage, but that is past. I want *you,* not Ravenskeep . . . and that is more than the sheriff can claim!"

She wanted to stare at her hands, clasped so tightly in her lap. She wanted to stare at the floor. She wanted to look anywhere save into Gisbourne's face. But she owed him that much. "Sir Guy . . . forgive me, Sir Guy—but I cannot marry you."

"I know," he said raggedly, "I *know* I am only a knight, and a poor one—one whose knighthood was bought . . . I know your father was a real one, a man who deserved the knighthood, but I promise you, I *promise*—I will do whatever I must . . . Lady Marian, I beg you—"

"No," she said. "Don't beg."

Awkwardly, he lowered himself to one knee, clinging to the crutches. "Lady Marian—*please*—"

She wanted desperately to find the words to make him go away before she had to hurt him. "Sir Guy—"

His eyes were avid and determined. "I saw you to your freedom. I brought you from the dungeon. I risked my *life* for you—"

"Sir Guy, I beg you—"

"Consider me," he told her. "Look upon a man who is in an agony of need. I worship you, Lady Marian—"

She was intensely embarrassed. "Sir Guy, get up—get *up!* This is nonsense—"

"Look at what I have done for you, Lady. I have even warned you of the sheriff."

"I don't want to marry him, *either*," she declared, now as desperate as he. "And I won't. Trial or no, I will not marry him. No matter what he does, no matter what he says. I can't."

712

He hung there, staring at her. Clutching his crutches. "Then marry me."

"I *can't*."

"Why not?"

"Sir Guy—" The only way to end this was to give him the truth. "Sir Guy—I love someone else."

"I am here on my knees before you—"

"No." She shook her head. "I am sorry. I cannot."

The boar's eyes were too bright, burning now like Locksley Hall, like the eyes of the man who had ordered the village destroyed. "I *lied* for you!" he cried. "I nearly died for you! I have jeopardized my place, I have betrayed my lord, I have served a traitorous prince—" He wavered on his knees. "I have done all manner of things to bring me to this point." Tears gathered in his eyes, extinguishing the flame. "I pray you, Lady Marian—don't fail me now! I have risked too much for you."

Her mind was utterly empty. She stared at the face that transformed itself out of shape, into a blanched blob of flesh lacking in character. She could see no features in it because she stared so hard.

Words reformed in her mind. *He thinks he can buy me with this.* His face took on features again as she forced herself to think. *He believes I owe him this.* She studied the man, seeing the soul within. *Gisbourne is no different from the sheriff or the earl.*

Trembling, Marian stood up with slow deliberation. The silence seemed very loud, the air between them heavy. It was difficult to speak, to put into words the outrage that she felt. "What you do," she began in cold, deadly anger, "what you choose to do, for or against your lord, for or against a prince, is yours *to* do. I will have naught of it. I will have no *part* of it. You will not drag me down into the madness of your jealousy, Sir Guy . . . I am not part of your obsession. And if I am its object, I say to end it now. End it *now*. I will have none of it. I will have none of you."

"Lady Marian—"

She overrode him easily, pitching her voice above his protest. "And if it means you will put me down into that filthy hole, then do it. Let it be done. Let me stay there until I grow old and ugly enough that no man wants me . . . *I will have no part of you.*"

Gisbourne wept. "You have to," he whispered. "You *have* to, Lady Marian . . . how else am I to save myself from the king's wrath?"

"The *king's* wrath!"

"He will learn I offered to serve Prince John . . . he will learn I have perjured myself to improve my lot, so I could rise in a prince's service, so I could better myself for you—"

"Not for me!" she cried furiously. "You want it for yourself!"

"For you." He put out a pleading hand. "Don't you see? He's free. The devil is loosed. 'Look to yourself,' it said, 'the devil is loosed.' " Gisbourne's hand shook. "I am the youngest son of a wool merchant, Lady Marian, who had no aptitude; whose knighthood was bought; who cannot wield a sword or even ride very well . . . don't you see? I want to be those things. I want to *do* those things." Bitterness crept in. "But I am used to count candles, to keep the accounts in order, to carry out such duties as would sicken an honest man in the name of the sheriff's greed—"

"So you compound your own guilt by serving him." Marian's voice was rusty. She did not enjoy seeing a man grovel before her, or throw into her face the crimes he justified by his need to win her regard. It humiliated her that he had done those things, but not so much as it did to watch him now, begging before her. "You said the king is *free?*"

" 'The devil is loosed,' " he quoted. "The devil will destroy us all."

Her joy was overwhelming. *The king is FREE.* Marian laughed aloud. "Not me," she countered. "Look to yourself, Sir Guy—I am free of you. I am free of the sheriff."

His hand dropped. He clung to his crutches, then heaved himself upright again, balancing carefully. "You don't understand," he said. "You have no comprehension how meticulous is the sheriff—how *very* careful he is when it comes to laying plans." Gisbourne shook his head. "Lady Marian, I promise you: if you don't marry *me* you will be made to marry the sheriff. Or you will surely burn."

Marian laughed at him. "The king is *free*, Sir Guy! You said it yourself. I think I am in no danger."

Gisbourne did not even smile. "How is he to prevent that which he does not know?"

Huntington Castle bulked before them in the darkness, looming up from undulant hills into the argent moonlight. Torches in the bailey lent only superficial illumination beyond the curtain-wall, to paint dimly the hoof-churned earth before the portcullis where Robin and the others gathered.

Will Scarlet scowled at the gatehouse, misliking the idea of going beyond castle walls. The last time it had happened he had been thrown into a cell in Nottingham.

He slid a glance at the giant. "He'll not get us in *there*."

Little John shrugged. "None of us thought he'd take on the sheriff, either."

Robin, with Much clinging to him, reined in his horse before the gatehouse. "Open!" he shouted. "By God—*open* this gate!"

"This is Huntington," Scarlet hissed. "Is he mad to roar at them?"

"He's a knight," the giant hissed back.

"And the earl is an *earl*—he'll not be swayed by a knight!"

Pale faces appeared atop the wall, mail coifs glinting. The features were indistinct, voices inaudible.

"Open!" Robin shouted, thrusting up an outspread hand as if he commanded an army.

After a brief consultation, the portcullis grated once and began to rise.

"You see?" said Little John.

Scarlet glowered. "Likely they'll catch us all and throw us into the dungeon. Or hang us."

"Robin's not so foolhardy as that."

Scarlet stared past the giant. "No—I think he's *mad*."

As the portcullis rose to a negotiable height, Robin twisted to look back at them. Pale hair glowed in torchlight as he shook it back from a face that was a mask of grim, unrelenting determination. "Are you with me now as you were today? Will you trust me tonight as you did this afternoon?" He gazed at each of them, rigid atop his cart horse, but undiminished by its

715

clumsiness. "I promise you all—on my honor as a knight—no one will harm you here."

Alan, smiling, rode toward him with Tuck guiding his horse behind, but Will Scarlet and Little John hung back on their new mounts. Scarlet said it first. "He's the *earl*, damn you! Honor or no, *knight* or no—what chance have we against him?"

Robin laughed. "As much chance as we had against the sheriff and his Normans!"

Scarlet shook his head. "This is different. This is Huntington."

Robin lost his smile. "Is that what you said when the Normans killed your wife?"

Scarlet swore. Then he jammed his heels into his horse's flanks and rode at a clumsy canter past Robin into the outer bailey of England's newest castle.

Little John sighed. " 'Tis done, then, isn't it?"

"Not yet," Robin replied. "Now there is the earl."

Seventy-Three

It was small revenge, but Gisbourne didn't care. He knocked the candle off its stand, plunging the room into darkness, then crutched his way into the corridor. There he ordered the door slammed closed and locked again, aware of his voice only as a distant incoherency, and slowly made his way down the corridor to his room. The crutches were oddly heavy, unexpectedly unwieldy, as if he had grown clumsy in the brief length of time between entering and exiting her chamber.

He wobbled, recovered himself, then moved ahead again, leaning heavily on the supports beneath his arms.

She refused. The air seemed heavier. The silence in the corridor was filled with a sibilant hiss. *She refused.* Repeating it altered nothing, but he seemed incapable of framing other words. *I told her everything.* He had not considered that, only that he would offer her escape from the sheriff, which surely she would take. *I told her everything in my heart, everything I hoped for, everything I dreamed—and she refused.*

Another man, she said. Surely not the sheriff. She said it wasn't the sheriff.

I might as well have cut my heart from my chest and handed it to her . . . she would have respected that as much as anything else. Heat coursed through his body. He felt his loins tighten, the muscles in his belly contract. Humiliation was painful, lifting the flesh on his bones and bathing it in a thin sheen of sweat. *I offered everything, and she refused.*

Another man.

Gisbourne stopped before his door. Horrified, he said, "I told her *everything—*"

He rarely spoke to women beyond what was necessary. But to her he had spoken freely, sharing more of himself than he had shared with anyone. And she had ridiculed him.

Worse, he had told her of the king. She knew his secret, now. She had the weapon, too. The only difference was, he had the freedom to use it.

Self-contempt writhed in his belly, squeezing his bowels. He had told her everything, and she reviled him for it.

Gisbourne put out a hand to lift the latch and saw that it shook. He was weak, weak and foolish, no match for a man like the sheriff, who understood how to turn setbacks into victories. All *he* understood was how to put into writing his support for a treacherous prince, whose position now was threatened by the very brother he had tried to replace.

"The devil is loosed," Gisbourne whispered, and pushed open the narrow door.

Beyond, in his chamber, waited Eleanor deLacey.

Horseboys came running as Robin and the others rode into the bailey. Much slid off at once, then Robin, who thrust out reins to the first boy who reached him. "Hold him here."

A quick glance showed him the others dismounting nearly as hastily. Alan was off his horse, mimicking Robin by handing off the reins; Tuck was slow and ungainly, murmuring prayers, but he, too, was on the ground; Will Scarlet and Little John moved more deliberately, as if not entirely certain of their welcome.

Nor am I, of mine. A flicker of movement in the corner of his eye caught Robin's attention. He turned quickly, hand dropping to his sword, and saw the figure of his father coming forward into the torchlight.

He held his ground, though the palm of his hand sweated against the grip. Part of him was detached and methodical, thoroughly assessing the play of light and shadow, the footing in the bailey, the positioning of his companions. Another part of him longed to cry out to his father to stop so they could begin again; that he had never wanted this; that the earl had brought them to this. But Robin said nothing. It was time to convince his father the boy had become a man.

Behind the earl ranged six men-at-arms, helmed and at the ready. The earl held himself very erect, superficially a younger man, until one looked farther and saw he was old. Tension had diminished some of the inflexible strength in his features, altering them to the brittle sharpness of the aged.

His mouth was set in a tight, repressive line. "I will not have rabble in my castle," he declared. "Take yourselves from here at once. This is not Sherwood Forest; outlaws are not welcome."

He doesn't see me. His father's view of him was blocked by the horse. As the others exchanged uneasy glances, Robin moved quietly around his mount's broad rump into the torchlight.

The earl's start was visible. The inflexibility cracked. "Robert? By God—*Robert?*" His shock was unmistakable; the earl took a single step forward before recalling himself. He flicked a hard glance at Robin's companions, then looked again at his son. Despite his rigidity, his eyes were oddly bright. "Come in," he said simply.

Robin heard a stirring behind him: Will Scarlet and Little John, murmuring something to Alan. But that did not concern him as he stared at his father. *He knows why I have come.* Some of Robin's tension eased. *At least she is safe. I'll take her from here, then go elsewhere.* Ravenskeep, perhaps. *He must know he's beaten.* Robin glanced at the others, jerking his head toward the keep. "Come in."

But the earl's tone hardened. "Not them, Robert. I'll not have such in my hall."

Robin stopped short. "My lord—"

The earl cut him off. "This is not a haven to outlaws." Another glance repudiated them. "I know who these men are, every one of them: a murderer, a rapist, a half-witted cut-purse—"

"No." Robin looked beyond the earl to the men-at-arms. He knew all of *them:* toughened, loyal veterans who served the earl, not him. He was heir, not earl; the old man held precedence. "If you will keep them out, then I stay out as well."

"Robert." The earl's eyes were momentarily hurt, his expression baffled; then he dismissed the emotions and replaced them with cold disdain, relying on the hauteur Robin knew so well. "This business between us is private. We will not share it before such men as these."

Robin gave up his attempt to win entrance. His hopes of a reconciliation were extinguished utterly. "Bring her out," he said plainly, "or I will go in after her without a word to you, and I will use my sword on any man who interferes."

"Robert—"

"Bring her *out,* my lord."

The hauteur slipped. Anger replaced it. "She isn't here," the earl declared. "By God, Robert—do you think me so foolish as to have that woman brought here?" He made a sharp, dismissive gesture that negated his own implication. "DeLacey has her at Nottingham, where she'll be tried as a witch."

"A *witch*—"

"There were proofs," the earl told him. "Also a witness. Abbot Martin has been summoned. They will question her most closely."

Robin wanted to laugh, but he knew better. His father was a careful man, too careful to be dismissed as a blusterer, or a fool telling lies merely for the moment. *"Ya Allah,* are you mad? Marian is no witch! This is nothing more than a ploy to force my hand—"

"Then surely they will discover that she is innocent, and no harm will be done." For a moment the earl's expression softened. "Robert, come in. If you must have these men in also, then I will not keep them out—but come *in*. There are things we must discuss."

He is in his own way as bad as deLacey, using and discarding people as he requires them, manipulating truths to serve his own purposes. Robin shook his head. "Not while Marian is in Nottingham Castle."

"He won't harm her," the earl snapped impatiently. "He'll have her installed in his finest bedchamber, not a cell—he wants to *marry* her, not burn her at the stake." His eyebrows formed a level bar, as if he were deeply annoyed by his son's inability to see the necessity of intrigue. "Surely you understand by now how these things are handled, Robert. You have been in war, as well as being privy to a king's confidences." His expression softened slightly, as if the reprimand no longer were needed, since the point was made. "Come *in*—there are better places for privacy then the bailey of my castle."

Robin did not move. "*You* gave her to deLacey. You found out where she was, and you gave her to deLacey."

"DeLacey took her himself—or, if he was wise, he sent men to do it. Robert—"

The four simple words were difficult to form. "They burned Locksley down."

The earl gestured. "Come in—" Then he broke off as color spilled out of his face. Matched against his hair, it turned his head into a sheer white skull. "Burned—?"

"They burned Locksley down." It was easier this time. "The hall. The village. And nearly Brother Tuck."

"And my lute," Alan murmured.

The earl did not spare so much as a glance at Tuck or Alan. "*Burned*—?" he repeated. "But I said nothing of that . . . that was never suggested—I sent word where she *was*, not that he was to have the village burned!"

"It was done. Locksley is destroyed." Robin smiled grimly. "Smoking me out, my lord? But what good is that if the hive is destroyed?"

"Robin." It was Alan, moving into the torchlight. "Robin, go

720

in. We can wait for you here. If she is at Nottingham, she is safe."

Robin turned on him. "Before God, Alan—"

"Robin—no." With distinct deliberation, Alan shook his head. "The *sheriff* will never harm her."

It was enough to bring home the truth: Marian *was* safe, because deLacey was dead. There would be no trial. There would be no questioning. All the sheriff's plans lay sprawled across the Lincoln road along with deLacey's body.

For the first time since he had left his father's hall, intent on redressing wrongs done to Jews and kings, Robert of Locksley acknowledged what he had done.

He looked at the others: at Alan, Much, Tuck, Will Scarlet, Little John. *This is what I am.*

His voice felt long unused as he turned again to his father. "You sent Thomas to fetch me home."

"Of course I did. I knew you would fight for her. I wanted you unharmed."

Robin shook his head. "Did it tell you nothing? Did it mean nothing to you that I would have risked my life for her?"

"Robert—"

"What kind of son would I be if I turned my back on a woman merely to save myself? What sort of *earl* would I be if I shut my eyes to such things?" He felt old and empty and fragile, too used up to debate the issue. "What sort of man would I be if I concocted a travesty, then took pains to see my son was not present while others burned to death?"

The earl's tone frayed. "You are my *heir*, Robert! A man takes pains to preserve his heir."

" 'A man takes pains,' " Robin quoted. *"Ya Allah,* but I am weary . . ." He looked at his companions. "This man was my father. This man *was* my father."

"Robert."

"My father, the Earl of Huntington, who felt it appropriate to have a woman abducted merely to rid an impediment from his heir's future." He nodded faintly. "The impediment is removed. But now there is no future, because there is no heir."

"Robert, *wait*—"

He swung back to the earl. "Did you have any intention of speaking to me of my mother?"

The earl's mouth compressed itself into a thin, flat line. "Your mother has nothing to do with this."

Robin nodded. "So I thought." He turned toward the boy who held his horse and retrieved the reins, looping them up over the horse's neck. To the others, he said, "We will camp outside the walls; what there is to be done at Nottingham is better done in daylight."

He wanted very badly to ride directly to the castle, but it was possible no one yet knew of the sheriff's death. If they believed deLacey in Lincoln, no one would release Marian without proper permission. Tomorrow the truth would be known, and no one at the castle would be in a position to refuse a request for her release.

"Robert—?" the earl blurted. "Robert—*wait*—"

The earl's son swung up into the saddle, then reached a hand down to Much. "Robin," he said clearly. "Robin—in the hood."

"Robin *Hood*," Much declared, settling behind the saddle.

Alan mourned softly. "Ah, but it wants my lute."

Well after dark, William deLacey walked through the castle gatehouse into the outer bailey. The questions began at once— *My lord, are you well? My lord, what has happened? My lord, are you harmed?*—but he answered none of them. He walked on blistered feet through the outer and inner baileys, refusing to limp, then up the front stairs. It was as he reached the door that Philip de la Barre came striding rapidly from the guardhouse.

"My *lord!*" De la Barre broke into a run and caught him just inside the door, where the torchlight was most distinct. His brown eyes were wide and shocked. "My lord Sheriff—what has happened?"

"Outlaws," deLacey said succinctly, briefly touching his neck where the blood had dried. "Have you done as I asked?"

"The woman?" De la Barre's eyes cleared and acquired a self-satisfied glow. "Indeed, my lord. She awaits the sheriff's pleasure."

DeLacey might once have appreciated the unintended innu-endo. Just now he did not; his head ached, his feet stung, and he wanted very badly to take a bath to rid himself of crusted blood. He nodded briefly, then turned away from the young Norman and walked toward the hall.

"My lord?" De la Barre sounded afraid; perhaps the sheriff's casual dismissal denoted displeasure. "Lord Sheriff—is there anything else I might do?"

Anything else? DeLacey swung around. "Yes. You may take a detail with a wagon to the Lincoln Road and gather up the bodies. The money, I fear, is gone."

De la Barre nearly gaped in shock. "Bodies?"

"Twelve of them. One is Archaumbault's." DeLacey turned back and walked into the hall with only a slight limp. *For every blister I count, I will cut off a piece of his flesh before I see him hanged.*

Marian sat in darkness on the narrow bed, leaning against the wall. She stared hard into darkness, examining the strength of her will and the contents of her spirit.

Her anger had died. Its initial intensity had waned as the darkness waxed, muting itself after a brief sharp brilliance to a deep-seated smolder. She needed her wits now. Anger blunted wits. There was no one she could rely on save herself.

She had stopped asking herself how Sir Guy of Gisbourne could have imagined her so foolish as to exchange the undesired sheriff for an undesired knight. It had filled up her head and mouth for too long after the candle died, when she first stood in darkness in the center of the chamber, until she acknowl-edged her own folly and shut her mouth on it so as not to waste what wit she had on fruitless questions. There was no answer. Gisbourne had done as he had done because he believed it necessary. Because he believed it the only way.

Marian laughed softly. *Just like the sheriff.*

Darkness. Silence. The weight of *solitude.* Each was a weapon meant to break her, to drive her into humiliation out of defiant self-possession; to goad her into surrender, into pleas for mercy, for compassion, for understanding.

Grimly she reflected, *But mostly into compliance, in bed and out of it.*

A sound destroyed the silence even as light banished darkness. The heavy door scraped open. "Marian."

She wanted to laugh. *Such a soft, seductive whisper.* But with the edge of a blade in the sound, issuing from a man long accustomed to being heard no matter how loudly he spoke. No matter how softly he whispered.

He brought the torch with him, unattended by liveried soldiers; what he wanted from her he wanted given—*or taken*—in the privacy of the chamber. *Capitulation?* she wondered. *Perhaps even retribution.* Or merely the opportunity to have what another man had.

Marian smiled grimly. *I will not be broken. I will not be humiliated. You will get no surrender from me.*

They sat in a knotted circle beyond the castle walls: Alan of the Dales, Little John, Brother Tuck, Much, and Will Scarlet, beneath the full spring moon. Its light was kind to them, smoothing away gaunt hollows, the etched fretwork of constant tension, the stubble of unshaven faces—save for the giant, who was bearded, and the boy, who could not yet grow one.

Will Scarlet's gaze followed Robin, who tended the horses some distance away. In the moonlight Locksley was patchwork: dark, unremarkable clothing; the glint of sword and knife; the pallor of hands and face; the lucent fall of hair. "Earl's son," Scarlet muttered. "By Christ, the earl's *son.*"

"Does it matter?" Alan asked irritably, naked without his lute.

"Aye, it matters! He's a bloody nobleman—"

"And a knight, and a Crusader," Little John said slowly, "as well as an outlaw." He cast Scarlet a hard glance. "He's given up more than you."

"I gave up a *wife*—"

"Aye," Alan agreed, "who was unfairly taken from you; we're not arguing that. We're arguing that you killed those men in a fit of rage, of revenge; *he* gave up everything after thinking very carefully about what needed doing." He yanked a thistle from the earth, then tossed it aside. "He's no better than any of us now, nor worse. Let him be, Will."

"I know what you'd have done," the giant accused. "You'd have left us in the bailey and skittled in to see the earl, turning your back on outlaws to save your inheritance——"

"So would *you*."

"Aye. Probably," said Little John. "Probably so would the minstrel. But *he* didn't, did he?"

Scarlet scowled. "Because of the woman."

"More than that," Alan countered. "He's the makings of a hero, with what he's done. Just like Charlemagne. Just like Roland."

Scarlet's laugh was a sharp bark of sound. "Hero! Him? What did he do but help us kill Normans and steal the sheriff's money?"

"It's in the doing," Alan replied carelessly, "as any jongleur knows. *You'll* steal to stay alive. He stole to buy back a king."

Scarlet scoffed. "Because he knew he never had to steal again. He had an earldom to keep him warm."

"He repudiated it. You heard him, Will: 'This man *was* my father.' "

"Aye," the giant rumbled, digging through his beard to scratch his face. "With his father calling after him even as we rode out of the castle. He never looked around."

Tuck rattled beads, wide face shiny in moonlight as he mouthed prayers. Much hunched big-eyed in silence, staring avidly after Robin.

"Let him be," Alan said. "We can no more pretend to know what he is inside his heart than to know what you are in yours."

Scarlet's mouth warped briefly. "Wolf's-head," he muttered.

Little John nodded. "So is he."

"Lonely," Much murmured into the top of one knee.

Seventy-Four

Some time after cockcrow Marian was brought before the dais of Nottingham Castle. The hall was arranged differently. The massive trestle table had been broken down and set aside against a wall, leaving much of the hall floor clear. Two chairs sat upon the dais in place of one, side by side. Both were empty.

Her armed and mailed escort put her in the center of the huge expanse of floor. She was dwarfed by massive columns. The soldiers left her there, then ranged themselves nearby.

Marian drew in a steadying breath. She had been allowed nothing: no food, no water, no time to tend her hair or mussed clothing; or even to wash her face. She had managed to use the chamber pot just prior to being brought out, but she was exhausted from tension and very little sleep. *If I swoon, it won't be from fear.* She took some comfort in that. It was important that she display to William deLacey a calm, unruffled spirit capable of withstanding him no matter what he attempted.

She knew the sheriff by the scrape of boot on stone and the faint metallic clicks as his soldiers drew themselves up into perfect immobility. She waited quietly, her fingers tautly clasping her kirtle folds, and counseled herself to show him only calmness.

The resolution required more effort than she anticipated: he wore mail, a massive sword, a thick gold chain of office, and carried a shining helm in the crook of his elbow. The mail coif was pushed to his shoulders, freeing head and hair.

He halted upon the dais just before his chair. His brown eyes were impassive. Marian saw no anger there, no passion, no ambition. She saw the Sheriff of Nottingham in full command of his power.

In skirt folds she fisted her hands, trying to summon courage. It was time to implement the course she had determined during the night. *Think as he thinks. Anticipate him. Do not permit provocation. His strength is in finding weakness.*

"Marian FitzWalter."

She did not answer.

"You are called here before us—"

"*'Us'?*" she said clearly, purposely cutting him off. "I see no king present."

He continued relentlessly, seemingly unperturbed. "—to answer a charge of witchcraft."

"Yes," she agreed, "so I was given to understand when I was brought here against my will. Surely if I were a witch I could have prevented *that*, and then you would be here alone holding court as if you were king."

The impassiveness faded. Dark eyebrows hooked upward. "Marian," he said curiously, "for whose benefit are you speaking? For mine?—but it makes no difference; I will do what I will do. For my men?—surely not; they have little interest in what becomes of you."

She bit back an angry retort, conscious of heat in her face. Quietly she inquired, "For whose benefit do *you* speak? Mine?—but it matters little; you will do what you will do. For your men?—surely not; they have heard such talk before and are likely weary of it. You do often border on tedium."

DeLacey sighed. "This is serious, Marian."

"Is it?" She glanced around, then turned her eyes wide back to him. "But where is the abbot? Surely you are not the only authority in matters of the soul; it requires a more forgiving spirit than the one you possess, as you proved to me last night."

"I am the only authority in the matter of your disposal."

"But I believed that decided last night. You said then you intended to burn me at the stake. Why this travesty? Burn me." She managed a smile more tranquil than she felt. "Though it is no doubt somewhat discomfiting to take a charred corpse to bed."

* * *

Robin roused them at dawn, calling out each of their names. In either hand he held two linked sacks of tax money, brought first to Locksley, then to Huntington. "Tuck," he said quietly, "we have need of your cassock."

The monk, wiping blearily at his face, gazed up at Robin blankly. "My cassock?"

"I want it to look natural." Robin hauled the sacks upward as he stepped to Tuck's saddled horse. He swung the first linked pair up across the horse's withers in front of the saddle, then placed the other linked pair athwart the horse's loins. He slapped the saddle. "Here, Tuck . . . there should be enough of your 'skirts' to hide the money."

Tuck brightened. "So there should."

"Brother," Little John warned, "is this what you want to do? You've done naught wrong by falling in with wolf's-heads to protect the woman . . . this will bespeak your willingness to help us."

Tuck smiled. "The money belongs neither to the sheriff, nor to Prince John. It belongs to the people, Jews and Christians alike, who have raised it for their king. I doubt God will look harshly on me for this."

"Did He say so?" Scarlet asked acidly.

Tuck's smile widened. "I will ask him later—*after* we have reclaimed the Lady Marian."

"Then let us ride," Robin suggested, flipping reins over the head of Tuck's mount. "Brother?"

Alan hummed a tune as he strolled to his horse.

Scarlet tugged his filthy tunic into place. "You want to ride into Nottingham Castle carrying all that money?"

Robin went to his own horse, arranging sword, bow, and mantle as he swung up into the saddle. "No. I intend to give it to Abraham the Jew, from whom it was stolen. He'll see that it is taken to William Longchamp in London."

"Who'll then get it to the king?" Little John asked.

"To the *German* king; we'll have to hope Henry is in the frame of mind to count it enough." Robin gathered rein, then freed

728

a stirrup so Much could clamber up. "Waste no more time, if you please . . . I think Marian might admire haste."

Marian raised her chin as the Abbot of Croxden made his way into the hall, face downcast as if in pious meditation. Delicate hands were clasped at his abdomen, mostly hidden by full sleeves. His tonsured hair was graying from brown to silver.

The abbot quietly assumed his seat next to the sheriff. He looked at Marian briefly, then turned his head toward deLacey. "Nuns must be contrite. Has she proved contrite?"

Strike now. As deLacey opened his mouth, Marian forestalled him. "I am contrite," she said, "in my congress with God, who hears my prayers nightly."

The abbot ignored her. "Nuns must repent sin. Has she repented?"

"She—"

"I repent of allowing myself to be misled by the man now seated beside you," she interposed swiftly, "and I have no intention of becoming a nun so you may have my lands." She saw the flicker in his dark eyes. "Isn't that what he told you to bring you here? That if adjudged a witch, I might repent and become a nun?" She shook her head. "Do not be fooled by him."

DeLacey waited until she was concluded, then said quietly to the abbot, "We have proofs of her witchcraft, and a witness."

"Who?" Marian demanded. "No one would denounce me— except the Earl of Huntington, perhaps . . ." She looked hard at the abbot, who did not favor her with a glance. "But his denouncement has nothing to do with witchcraft, Abbot—he denounces me so his son will forsake me."

At last he looked up. His eyes were small and black, betraying no humanity.

Courage wavered briefly, until she reclaimed it. "I confess this much: I am an adulteress. I lay in carnal congress with Sir Robert of Locksley, the earl's son. *That* is my crime, Abbot. That is why I am here."

The abbot addressed her in a soft, gentle tone, much at odds with his expression. "And do you repent of it?"

"No," she declared. "What is conducted between men and women is their concern, and God's . . . it is the responsibility of no man, neither sheriff nor earl, to dictate the actions of a man and a woman who consent to the bedding—"

"Adultery is a sin," the abbot rebuked mildly.

"So is attempting to force a woman into marriage against her will." She slanted a glance at deLacey. "Ask him about Brother Tuck, whom he required to lie. Whom he required to play the part of a priest."

DeLacey smiled. "Witches are very clever. Their lies are most astute, bordering on the truth. It makes them dangerous."

"Gluttony is also a sin, which requires harsh discipline." Abbot Martin sighed softly. "What proofs have you found, Sheriff?"

"A broom—"

"A *broom!*" Marian laughed. "How many halls haven't a broom?"

"—and a poppet."

"In whose image?" the abbot inquired.

DeLacey looked at Marian. "She must have feared discovery—the poppet's face was obscured."

"I feared no discovery," Marian declared, "because it isn't mine. Everyone at Ravenskeep will bear out my innocence."

"No," the sheriff said lightly, "I fear one won't. A villein known as Roger."

It stunned her. "Roger?"

"He is our witness. I have questioned him already, and am quite satisfied that he tells the truth as he knows it."

"'As he knows it,'" she echoed in disbelief, then turned quickly to the abbot. "Do you see what he's done? He twists a peasant's words into falsehoods he can use against me."

The sheriff merely smiled.

Marian wiped damp palms against her kirtle, regaining self-control. "Abbot Martin, I beg you—end this travesty. This has been contrived to force my hand. He desires to marry me—"

"No," deLacey said lightly, "I think not, now."

She meant to retort, to say he fooled no one, least of all her, but as she opened her mouth to say so something in his eyes prevented her. "You mean it," she blurted.

"Yes, I mean it. Do you count me less fastidious than the earl? Once I offered you escape from dishonor, as a decent man would, but you repudiated me. You went from me into carnal congress with Robert of Locksley, as you yourself have admitted, who is himself as guilty as you are in things far worse than making poppets." He rested his hand lightly on his sword. "I have no desire to lie with Robin Hood's whore, and less to marry her."

Marian swallowed back the shout she longed to make, replacing it with an edged courtesy modeled after his own. "Then what *do* you desire?"

"Robin Hood," he said gravely. "If I must burn you to get him, be certain I shall."

Dust floured the air as Robin and the others approached the split in the Nottingham Road. One branching led into the city itself, the other out beyond Ravenskeep and on toward distant Lincoln. A large mounted party clogged the split, blocking anyone else who might desire to approach the city. Sunlight glinted off mail and the equipage of fine horses.

Robin drew rein abruptly, signaling the others to do the same. "Normans?" Alan fell in beside him. "Or a Saxon lord?"

Will Scarlet muttered imprecations; Little John growled at him to hold his tongue until they knew better what was worth swearing at. Tuck, like Much, was silent, carefully rearranging the 'skirts' that hid the sacks.

"It's a vanguard," Robin said softly. "But no pennons are flying—*wait*—" He stared harder. *"Ya Allah*—John?"

Little John gaped. *"Prince* John?"

Robin nodded, frowning. "But John is a man whose vanity requires everyone to know who he is . . . yet he flies no pennons, has no one crying his approach."

Alan edged closer, squinting through the dust. "Are you certain that is the Count of Mortain?"

Robin glanced at him. "You've seen him. Aren't you?"

The minstrel squinted harder, then blew out a breath. "Yes."

Scarlet swore again. " 'Tis over, then, isn't it? You're selling us to Prince John—"

"He's doing no such thing," Alan retorted. "Are you forgetting who it was ordered all those Normans killed?"

It silenced everyone save Tuck, who murmured a desperate prayer.

"Well." Robin chewed briefly at a lip. "It may serve us. John's presence breeds confusion and distraction—he'll keep the attention focused on himself while we seek out Marian."

Little John was worried. "D'ye think they've found the bodies?"

Robin shrugged. "With John at Nottingham Castle, no one will notice if we prop up the sheriff's body itself in the great hall."

Abbot Martin's eyebrows arched in delicate inquiry as he turned to William deLacey. "Who is Robin Hood?"

DeLacey did not remove his gaze from Marian. "A murderer," he replied. "An animal, Abbot—not only did he kill twelve of my men, but he cut their throats as well to show his contempt for my authority."

"That is a lie!" Marian cried. "He would never do such a thing!"

The abbot did not react in the slightest to her shout. He turned instead to the sheriff. "Is this true?" The question was posed with very little inflection, as if the abbot were quite bored.

"Perfectly true," deLacey answered readily with unshakable confidence. "I myself escaped death only because one of the outlaws—a red-haired man known as the Hathersage Giant—believed I was already dead."

"Then why wasn't your throat cut?" Marian asked acidly.

DeLacey pulled awry the mail hauberk, displaying his neck. "It was my good fortune—and God's intervention"—he nodded at the abbot—"that a party approached as the giant bent to me. I was left for dead as they escaped; my men already were."

From where she stood Marian could see no mark upon the sheriff's throat, but clearly the abbot did. His face paled markedly. Small eyes glittered as he turned to Marian again. "You lay with this man? This 'Robin Hood'?"

"Not *that* man," she said flatly. "Not the man the sheriff portrays him to be . . . Abbot Martin, he has concocted false truths: first to force my hand, now to catch a man who is innocent of this crime——"

"Innocent?" deLacey asked softly. "Be assured, my men were killed. Be assured of their murderers: Robin Hood and others, among them Will Scarlet, already guilty of murder; John Naylor, the Hathersage Giant, who was unmistakably present at an earlier attempt to kill my castellan, so sworn by him; a pretty troubadour, who raped my daughter——*my daughter*, if you please!——and a boy cutpurse whom you yourself aided to escape when he tried to take my purse." His voice was suspiciously silky, presaging what she now recognized as true danger. "Tell me I lie, Marian. Tell me again I lie about the men who abet Robin Hood."

For the first time since she entered the hall, Marian cut free her hold on defiance. What was required now was practicality, and the sort of inflexibility deLacey had once counseled. She must adopt his own methods if she were to survive.

And Robin also. She took a single step toward the dais, looking only at the abbot, and softened the arrogant posture that had so irritated the sheriff. "Abbot Martin," she said quietly, "I realize he has made it quite impossible for you to believe me. He is a clever, eloquent, persuasive man, a man who once swore an oath to my father as he left for Crusade that he would guard my welfare with his life." She raised her head slightly and met the abbot's opaque eyes. "You see how he keeps his oaths."

DeLacey hooked his hands over the arms of his chair and thrust himself to his feet. "De la Barre!" he shouted. "Philip de la Barre!"

A man came into the hall, doffing his helm. He uncovered thick brown hair; a young, earnest face; the russet-brown eyes that had held no mercy as he ordered Locksley burned. His face was peculiarly white. "My lord?"

DeLacey frowned as he slowly resumed his seat. "De la Barre——what manner of attire is this? You appear before Abbot Martin in crusted mail and soiled leggings——"

"My lord." De la Barre's voice wavered, then he recovered himself. "My lord, I apologize for the state of my attire. But this is blood, my lord . . . the blood of twelve men found murdered on the road."

"So *much* blood?" DeLacey marveled. "After so much time?"

"My lord, I could not avoid it. Their throats had been cut."

"No," Marian said sharply. "He is lying. This man himself is a murderer. He ordered——"

De la Barre turned on her. "If you like, Lady Marian, I will be most pleased to show you the bodies." He flicked a glance at deLacey. "With the sheriff's permission."

DeLacey turned to the avid-eyed man beside him. "Is it necessary, Abbot? She says de la Barre lies; shall we see if he does?"

"Stop it," Marian said. Her self-control frayed. The colors of the hall bled one into another, blurring the outlines of chairs, benches, and men. *I am tired, only that—and hungry.*

"Very well; for now I shall stop it." The sheriff relaxed into the chair. "As to the charge of witchcraft, I'm afraid it remains to be dealt with. Do you intend to refute the charge?"

"Of course," she replied promptly, snatching by force of will at an argument that would provide her with a focus. "You have only the proof you yourself have manufactured."

DeLacey looked thoughtful. "What of your handiwork?"

"Mine?" Marian shook her head. "There is no such thing. A broom? I think not. A poppet? If you truly have one, undoubtedly someone bribed Roger to produce it."

"No." DeLacey fingered his chin. "No, I meant something else. Something more incriminating."

"There *is* nothing," she retorted. "This nonsense is meant merely to mislead the abbot."

DeLacey looked past her. "Sir Guy, will you come forward?"

Startled, Marian turned. Sir Guy of Gisbourne crutched slowly into the hall from the distant door. His hair was freshly combed, his face newly shaven. His eyes, as they met hers, were perfectly opaque.

Marian shivered. *Just like Abbot Martin's.*

DeLacey's tone was serene. "Sir Guy, I understand you have your own charge to lay against Lady Marian."

"I do, my lord." Gisbourne halted near her, balancing carefully on crutches. "She cast a spell on me."

"What—?"

Abbot Martin cut her off with a sharp gesture and leaned forward. "What manner of spell?"

Gisbourne colored. His voice was low. "She seduced me. She put witch-marks on my body."

"In the name of God," Marian cried, "how far must this travesty go? Witch-marks? This is madness! Abbot Martin—"

"Show me," the abbot said, and his small eyes glittered.

In silence, eyes averted, Gisbourne stripped down his bliaut. On the flesh of his chest, from throat to abdomen, were the deep empurpled marks of a passionate woman's mouth.

Seventy-five

Scarlet stared hard at Robin as dust slowly settled. "What do we do, then, Robin in the Hood? Ride up to the hall itself and walk in behind Prince John?"

"I think—yes." Robin smiled, gathering rein. "I think that is precisely what we shall do."

Scarlet blanched. "Wait—I wasn't meaning it like *that*—"

"But why not? We will be lost in the crowd, and even if we are not"—Robin laughed mirthlessly—"I am known to Prince John as the Earl of Huntington's son, to whom he wished to marry his daughter."

"His *daughter!*" Now Little John stared. "You're to marry John's daughter?"

"Bastard daughter," Robin clarified. "And now I think not. I think my actions this day have rendered me entirely unsuitable." He tapped Much's knee. "Ready, Sir Cutpurse?"

Much leaned forward alertly, murmuring assent.

* * *

Marian gazed in horror at the livid bruises on Gisbourne's flesh. She understood instantly what such "proofs" implied. *Don't give in now.* She swung back quickly, beseeching the abbot. "Listen to none of these lies—"

"Lies?" deLacey interrupted. "Look again at his flesh."

She ignored him, knowing instinctively her only chance now lay in convincing the abbot to wait and make no judgment. To force that delay she had to find something that could divert his attention. "Before you judge me, judge the man at your side. He has connived and intrigued to win Prince John's favor, so much so that he takes money intended for the king's ransom and sends it to Prince John instead of to the chancellor." She went on swiftly as deLacey opened his mouth to refute her. "Ask him why his men were robbed on the road to *Lincoln* instead of the road to London." She flicked a glance at deLacey. "There is something of a difference between north and south, I think . . . surely a man so astute as the sheriff would not confuse the two."

DeLacey's eyes glittered. "Only a fool would send so much money by the ordinary route. I chose to send it toward Lincoln, later diverting it to London. It was to confuse any possible attack; sadly, it failed."

Marian plucked another arrow from her quiver. "Ask him why he had his man—*that* man, Abbot!"—she pointed at de la Barre—"set fire to Locksley Hall and burn the village down."

"Witch-fire," deLacey murmured. "A spell gone awry."

She had no time to debate it. "Ask him why he tried to force me into a false marriage using a clerk in place of a true priest."

DeLacey was unruffled. "Your father desired us to marry, which you yourself admitted. The sham was to protect your questionable honor until a real priest could be brought."

The quiver now was empty, save for a final arrow. Marian loosed it with careful deliberation. "Ask him why he contrives to destroy a woman who is a ward of the Crown, and is therefore answerable only to the King of England, by whose mercy and wisdom you yourself hold office." She weighted the last purposefully and was pleased to see the abbot take notice at last.

She slanted a glance at deLacey. "The sheriff purchased his position, Abbot. How much integrity has a man who *buys* his office, when your abbacy is purchased by a divinely inspired vocation and obedience to the king?"

Color burned in deLacey's face. "A clever woman," he rasped, "with a clever tongue in her head. The Serpent's, perhaps? Surely she must be guided by the devil."

"If that is so," she said, "it must be for the king to pursue."

Abbot Martin shifted in pettish annoyance. "The king is imprisoned, as you well know. I suspect you intend to rely on your wardship merely to hide the truth, since you are aware the king can have no influence in the matter."

Marian looked straight at Gisbourne. "I pray you, then, Abbot Martin . . . why did this man here—the sheriff's own seneschal—see fit to tell a witch the king has been released?"

She had expected some manner of reply from the abbot or the sheriff; some accusation of falsehood; a derisive comment on her perfidious witch's tongue. But there was only silence.

As Marian glanced back at deLacey she found him rising from his chair. His face was tight and pale. *Did I strike true at last?*

But deLacey looked beyond her. "My lord," he said evenly, though the expression in his eyes was one of grim futility. Then Abbot Martin rose, small hands clutching chair arms, and Gisbourne blurted something she did not understand.

Marian spun in place. Standing two paces behind her was Prince John shaking road dust from his mantle as much of his retinue gathered in the hall. "Sheriff," he said lightly, "I seem to require your castle . . . and any soldiers you have to spare. I may have need of them."

In the bailey, the last stragglers from the royal retinue hastened into the hall to join their lord. Robin dropped off his horse even as Much slid down the slick rump; as Will Scarlet and Little John clambered off and Alan swung down with something approaching his old elegance, though he was stubbled and soiled. Only Tuck remained ahorse, hiding money sacks beneath his cassock.

Robin nodded, glancing around the bailey to see if anyone

watched. Then he swept off his mantle and approached Tuck's horse, signaling for the monk to dismount. As Tuck climbed down, Robin draped the mantle over saddle and sacks, tucking folds in. "Much." The boy was there, waiting expectantly. Robin gave him the reins. "You are now a horseboy at Nottingham Castle. Conduct yourself as the others do, but let no one lift the mantle."

"Won't work," Scarlet muttered. "They'll know he's not one of them. We should have left it with the Jew."

"Look around," Robin suggested. "John has brought horseboys and pages aplenty. Mixed with the Nottingham boys, no one knows who belongs to whom." He touched Much on the shoulder. "We will be back soon."

"This is madness," Scarlet insisted. "Walking right into the great hall?"

Robin nodded. "All of John's people are in there. As with the boys, no one knows where anyone belongs. You will lose yourselves in the crowd."

"*I* won't," Little John muttered.

"No," Robin agreed, "but neither will I. Marian deserves to see me."

In the hall before the sheriff and abbot, Marian swung to face Prince John. *This the best chance I will have.* "My lord Count," she said quietly, "I beg your leave to speak."

DeLacey's response was immediate. "No."

With a quelling glance in the sheriff's direction, John indulged her. "Speak."

She was hideously conscious of her dishevelled state, as aware now of his avid gaze as she had been in Huntington Castle the night of Robin's feast. But now it did not matter. "The sheriff accuses me of witchcraft. This is a lie, my lord, and a blatant one, contrived by a desperate man who cannot reconcile my desire for another—"

"This is nonsense," deLacey declared.

John lifted an admonishing hand without looking away from Marian. "Be silent."

She went on as quietly as before, conscious now that she

never need be afraid of John again, or of the connivance of deLacey, because she had learned to believe in herself. "My lord, this man has contrived all manner of false proofs and innuendo to force my hand, believing I would be desperate enough to accept him. I am not and never was, despite his best efforts, desperate enough to accept such a man as he." She lifted her chin in quiet defiance. "I am a ward of the Crown, my lord. I believe that still bears some weight."

"Indeed," John agreed dryly, "more now than ever before." He looked beyond her to deLacey. "I will have the truth of you. Now. Here. This moment. I have very little time."

DeLacey inclined his head.

John's eyes narrowed. "This woman is not a witch."

A tiny bubble of laughter broke within Marian. *He does not ask, he tells!*

DeLacey's face was stretched taut. He did not look at the abbot. "There was evidence that someone at Ravenskeep—"

"Say it, deLacey."

The sheriff's jaw muscles flexed. "I think perhaps the serf was mistaken."

"Indeed," Marian muttered.

John's eyes glittered. "My lord Sheriff, you have overstepped your bounds in this matter. It is not for you to decide the disposition of the lady's hand, but to guard its welfare. If you desire her so badly, you must petition the king for her in marriage . . . you may buy her, if you like, should you have the money; I am quite certain Richard will sell her as quickly as not, provided he requires more money to fund another Crusade"— he hitched a negligent shoulder—"or whatever whim he may next fix his mind upon."

Marian heard a litany within the confines of her head: *It is done, it is done, it is over.* She wavered as she stood, so swept with relief and the residue of tension released that hunger and exhaustion nearly prevailed. *Surely the king will see that it is Robin I want.*

"Petition the king?" deLacey echoed. "But that is impossible. He is in Germany."

"No," John said thoughtfully, "he is in France by now, unless he has already sailed. In which case he may well be in Dover already." His eyes were pupilless, completely opaque. "He is on my trail, do you see? I have become my brother's prey." His smile was a travesty. "Do you understand *now* why I require your castle?"

Will Scarlet's face was ashen as he pressed himself into the stone wall just inside the outer door. "They'll know me," he hissed. "The soldiers know who I am. They'll throw me back into the dungeon."

Robin and the others clustered around Scarlet. Little John dropped a hand to the smaller man's shoulder. "They'll know *me,*" he said.

"But they don't want to *hang* you!"

Little John's tone was somber. "They do now—or will soon enough. Recall what we've done this day."

Scarlet rubbed violently at his bruised face. "This is mad—"

Robin's tone was cold. "They killed your wife," he said. "Would you have them kill yet another woman?"

Scarlet was unconvinced. "But if the sheriff's not here—"

"What is to stop the guardsmen from abusing Marian as they abused your wife?"

Scarlet opened his mouth, then closed it. His lips clamped together tightly. Dark eyes glittered. "Go on, then, all of you."

"And you?" Alan asked.

William Scathlocke, known as Scarlet, nodded his assent.

"Good." Robin touched his shoulder briefly. "I need every man."

DeLacey thought rapidly. *Richard is free—and John has just solicited from me a vow of loyalty.* He glared wrathfully at Gisbourne, hanging miserably on his crutches. "Why was I not told?" he asked. "You told *her* quickly enough—wasn't this message for me?"

"You were gone," Gisbourne countered. "You'd gone to Lincoln with the money."

"Money?" John's voice was hawk stooping. "You sent my money to Lincoln?"

Gisbourne, I will have your tongue cut out. "I escorted it personally, as far as I was able." He steeled his nerves. "It was stolen, my lord. Outlaws from Sherwood Forest."

"Stolen?" John took three large steps forward, passing Marian and Gisbourne to halt again before the dais. "Is it gone? All that money?"

"My lord—"

"All of it, deLacey?" John's face was corpse-white.

There was no help for it. "Yes, my lord. We attempted to prevent it—"

"Did you?"

"—but we were overcome. Twelve men died, my lord."

"I do not care if twelve *hundred* men died, Sheriff!" John shouted. "I need that money! With Richard back soon, I need every mark, shilling, and silver penny I can find to support myself, should I have to go into exile!"

DeLacey no longer cared what might become of John. He had his own future to think about. He had bought his office from the king; perhaps Richard would allow him to retain it, if he reassured the king of his complete loyalty. "I did try," he told John coldly, satisfied to see the trace of condescension strike home. John was out of favor and in serious trouble. What deLacey said now was with impunity—if Richard returned soon. "There was nothing to be done. I was fortunate to have survived."

"Indeed," John declared. Even his lips were white.

DeLacey felt much better. He would find a way through this. "In fact, the attack was one of the things—" He broke it off abruptly. By virtue of the dais he saw the hall more fully than others, and stared in disbelief as the side door admitted the very outlaws he intended to describe. There was the giant, Will Scarlet, Eleanor's minstrel, the traitorous monk— and Locksley himself.

DeLacey rejoiced. *Here, here in my hall.*

"Yes?" John's tone was ominous.

DeLacey instantly discarded his surprise, letting his face assume its most serenely urbane expression. *This must be handled carefully.* He continued speaking effortlessly, adopting a less challenging tone. "This attack was one of the matters I discussed with the Lady Marian." *Get off the dais—he will see you over their heads.* Idly he stepped down to the lower level. There was John to get past first, then Gisbourne and Marian, then any number of John's retinue. *He won't see me in the crowd.* Quietly, he said, "It seems the man with whom the Lady Marian prefers to sleep is the outlaws' leader."

"No," Marian said sharply.

DeLacey nodded. "His name is known to you, my lord, although he has adopted another." He moved beyond John and a handful of John's soldiers, then Gisbourne, gesturing to others to move aside. "In fact, if you will permit, I will introduce you—" He threw one man aside hard, shouldered away another, then jerked his sword from the sheath.

"No!" Marian cried. Then, in shock, *"Robin!"*

Even as John's men drew weapons and their lord shouted to hold, deLacey thrust himself through the remaining human impediment and brought the point of his blade to within an inch of the throat he longed most to cut. "Sir Robert," he acknowledged politely, inwardly jubilant.

Will Scarlet turned on the giant, who stood just behind him. "You said the sheriff was *dead!*"

In the stunned silence of the hall, the accusation was condemnation. DeLacey laughed aloud. "My lord Count, I beg your forgiveness for drawing steel in your presence—but *this man* is the reason your money was stolen. *This man*, my lord, is the very thief who stole it."

"This man?" John echoed. *"This* man, deLacey?"

"This man." The sheriff smiled. "Robin Hood," he said, "I'll see you hanged before sundown."

Seventy-Six

Robin did not so much as glance at the swordtip that lingered so close to his throat. He looked straight into the piercing eyes of deLacey, full of self-satisfaction and a barely restrained exultation, and summoned the voice and manner he had so detested in his father. "Who are you to lift hand, blade, or voice against a peer of the realm?"

The imperious condescension infuriated deLacey. "By Christ," he choked, "I lift what I must against an animal such as you—"

Robin pitched his voice to carry to John, whom he needed; John would understand the division between peerage and purchased service. "This 'animal,'" he said coldly, "can name his ancestors more than ten generations back; we are an old, *old* family—older by far than your office."

The blade trembled minutely. "Tell me," deLacey said, "on whose side did your ancestors fight at the Battle of Hastings?" His smile was barbed. "Lineage means less than nothing when another has conquered you."

"Ah," Robin said, "then that explains why Prince John desired to marry his daughter to me."

"Enough," John snapped. "I want to know about my money. Explain, if you please."

DeLacey's smile broadened. "This man has it, my lord—or *had* it, if it is elsewhere. He and the others—these men here: the giant, the minstrel; infamous Will Scarlet, who killed four of your men—attacked the shipment on its way to Lincoln." The blade was steady now. "This man here, this confidant of kings, also robbed the Lords of Alnwick, Hereford, and Essex. If you believe nothing of what I say, summon them here. They were most explicit in description: hosen, they said, green tunic, leather bracers on his forearms, and a collared hood." The swordtip dipped down to tease at the collapsed hood lying loosely across Robin's shoulders. "Not the attire of a nobleman, is it? But the attire of Robin Hood?" DeLacey nodded. "He'll have your coin, my lord."

"Well, then." John approached. "Well then, Sheriff, if this is true, you may indeed find yourself hanging this man before sundown." He paused, affecting a puzzled tone that fooled no one, especially not Robin. "But how do you explain the presence of Will Scarlet *here* when you yourself hanged him before my very eyes?"

DeLacey's face sagged minutely.

"With lies," Marian said clearly. "The way he always does."

John shrugged slightly. "Lies are useful," he said. "Lies serve certain purposes. But their value is diminished when someone uncovers them."

"I *saw* him!" deLacey declared. "I was there with the shipment when he and his men attacked. Will Scarlet admitted he thought I was dead; how could that happen if he wasn't there to see it? This is no lie, my lord—Robert of Locksley, in his guise as Robin Hood, did willfully and viciously attack and kill twelve men, cutting open their throats for spite after the men were dead."

"No!" Little John cried in horror. "*No*, we cut no throats—"

John's eyes narrowed. "Perhaps I should let you settle this between you—a decision made in trial by combat." He glanced around the hall, marking avid eyes. "Would it serve, do you think? If he is indeed this Robin Hood, I have no qualms about permitting such a fight."

DeLacey laughed in vindication. "You see—?" But the rest was cut off as Robin brought up his bracer-guarded left arm against the flat of the sheriff's sword, knocking the blade aside. His own sword he jerked free of sheath to kiss the sheriff's blade, coyly placing distance between them.

Robin smiled grimly. "What say you, my lord Count—*shall* we determine the truth in a trial by combat? Surely we are well matched—he is the sheriff, so closely concerned with the daily administration of the shire, while I am a knight but recently returned from Crusade . . . indeed, a well-made match!"

"No," deLacey said coldly. "I am sheriff of this shire. It is my responsibility to determine the truth by the questioning of witnesses—"

John's voice intruded. "Do you expect me to wait until you have produced de Vesci, Bohun, and de Mandeville?" he asked incredulously. "Do you think I dare? They are my brother's men, you fool . . . as is Sir Robert, and his father. What you propose is ludicrous, Sheriff—do you expect me to condone such folly?" John's brief laugh was loaded with contempt. "If given a choice between you, whom would I select? Although you have certain useful administrative skills, the Earl of Huntington's son offers many more advantages to a man in my position. I have no doubt as to the outcome of this battle. I think I shall let it continue."

Robin saw the comprehension in deLacey's eyes, the angry acknowledgment. He was devalued and therefore discarded, no longer necessary to any of John's plans. *John has deserted him, and he knows it.* Robin's blade scraped deLacey's, emitting a metallic sibilance as steel kissed steel. *He will be more dangerous now than at any time. Desperation hones even the bluntest of blades.*

The sheriff half turned toward John, as if to plead. "My lord—" But he swung back, slashing, to level his sword at Robin.

"No!" Marian cried. The crowd surged back, lurching out of the way. She heard John shout something as he moved aside hastily, but neither Robin nor the sheriff heeded it. They were thoroughly engaged in battering at one another with swords.

No— She was knocked off balance by a man hastening away from the immediacy of the fight. No one left the hall, they simply moved as one to the walls to watch from relative safety. Marian staggered, regained her balance, saw Gisbourne crutching aside.

Blades clashed, locked briefly, then scraped apart, filling the hall with clangor. Steel glinted in candlelight, striking slashes of light into the eyes of the crowd. She saw Robin's face, masked as she had seen it before, and the sheriff's, grimly angry.

They moved like dancers, weighing one another by small things such as posture: the tilt of a head, the slant of a shoulder, the position of the free arm, the subtle sliding of a foot. She saw how they watched one another's *chests*, not eyes, not blades; how they judged their own movements as well as the opponent's. It was a dance of steel and flesh, a savage seduction of deadly seriousness.

"Christ," Scarlet blurted, shouldering someone aside so he could see more clearly, "he *is* a bloody knight!"

Little John, next to him—looking *over* heads—snorted inelegantly. "Did you think he lied, then? He's an earl's son, Will—"

"But *look* at him," Scarlet blurted. "He bloody well knows how to fight!"

"Mmmm," Alan agreed. "He did say he was better with a sword than Adam Bell—or anyone else—with a longbow." He sighed. "I wish I had my lute."

"By Christ, *I'd* say so." Scarlet's eyes were avid as he followed the fight. "Had I coin, I'd lay a wager on him."

Tuck winced. "I pray you, Will Scarlet, not to take the Lord's name in vain."

Little John glanced around. "A wager, is it? Then let's see what we can scare up—" But even as he bent to suggest a wager to the nearest man, one of Prince John's soldiers cut him off with a sword.

"You," the Norman said. The blade's tip was at Little John's belly. "*And* you." He stared hard at Scarlet as another soldier appeared. "You'll hold where you are."

"Normans," Scarlet said tightly. "I hope he *spits* the sheriff!"

Marian knew nothing of sword fighting, save that her father and her brother had learned the uses of a blade. She recalled practice in childhood when Sir Hugh had honed himself, but he had not seen fit to explain to his daughter the things he told his son. Marian watched in ignorance of skill and of technique, knowing only that neither man gave way to the other.

Steel chimed, then screeched as blades were wrenched apart. There seemed no grace in the fight, no elaborate preparations; they simply smashed at one another, clanging blade off blade in repeated efforts to break through the other's guard to reach the flesh beyond steel.

She was distantly aware of an inequality: *The sheriff is mailed.* Robin wore nothing but tunic and hosen. If deLacey got through, his task was easier. *He will carve him into quarters.*

They moved the length of the hall, battering back and forth, catching edges, then snatching them free. Pale hair flew, hiding much of Robin's face; deLacey's darker expression was avid, seeking weaknesses, breath hissing through clenched teeth.

They cut at legs and arms, slashed toward throats, stabbed toward midriffs. And always the blades caught, screeching awkward protest, until they broke apart again to begin another attack.

It was subtle at first, but the tenor of the fight altered. Marian was aware of the difference before she could name it; when she saw it at last, she wondered if Robin did.

He's moving—he's moving back. DeLacey gave way again and again, allowing Robin the advantage, while turning his blade away. *He is moving back on purpose.*

She edged the length of the hall with them, wrenched arms free of hands that would stay her, pushed in front of those blocking her view. She would stay even with Robin so she could see every movement, every expression, every subtlety. Her entire concentration was fixed on him. As they stopped and held ground, Marian stopped also, only dimly aware that Gisbourne was beside her, propped up awkwardly on his crutches.

Then deLacey moved again, beaten back by Robin. He backed the length of the hall, working toward the dais. She wondered if he would recall there were two steps, and if he knew where they were. They could trip a man easily and prove his undoing.

"Fall," she said tautly, and heard Gisbourne's derisive comment that she was no proper woman to wish for a man's death. "Proper?" Marian laughed. "Not so proper as *you,* using Eleanor to put 'witch-marks' on your body." She did not look at him, but only at the fighters. "Or was it her idea?"

Gisbourne forbore to reply, and she didn't care enough to prod him for an answer. She cared only that Robin defeat the sheriff so all of them were freed.

He was tireless. His movements remained fluid, his power undiminished. In the midst of savagery, she began to see the inherent grace and eerie seduction in a swordfight well fought.

He is younger than the sheriff . . . honed in the Crusade. Surely he would be better. Surely he could endure, while the sheriff's strength waned.

DeLacey's foot found the dais steps. He went up them swiftly, lurching aside even as Robin struck, then lunged behind the chair he had once inhabited. He set a shoulder against it and shoved, knocking it awry; it was enough, Marian saw, to afford the sheriff both respite and advantage.

Robin brought his sword around just as the chair was shoved awry. The blade came down, glinting white in candlelight. It bit into heavy wood and was caught.

"There," Gisbourne said.

Robin's hand slipped as he jerked at his sword, trying to snap the steel free of wood. Just as the blade came free of the chair, deLacey, shouting exultantly, thrust himself from the floor with sword fully extended, intending to sheath it in Robin's flesh.

"Hold!" bellowed a voice. "By God, I say *hold!*"

The roar caused a stirring, but she spared no time to look. She expected deLacey to hold because the authority in the voice was undeniable—*is it John? No*—but the sheriff appeared perfectly willing to ignore the order.

"Hold, damn you! HOLD!"

William deLacey laughed.

"Robin!" Marian cried. But he read the sheriff as she did and lurched aside, sucking in belly, off balance from the steps. His blade, freed at last from wood, was twisted out of his hand in the last awkward tug; sword clattered to the floor as Robin went down. He landed hard on his back, arms and legs asprawl.

"No!" Marian shouted, hoping to distract deLacey.

He was not distracted. The sheriff kicked aside Robin's

sword, then placed the tip of his blade against pale, sweat-sheened flesh. "Shall I cut your throat for you?"

"Yes," Gisbourne breathed.

"You bastard whoreson—" Marian wrenched a crutch from beneath Gisbourne's arm, ignoring his startled bleat as he toppled to the floor, and ran toward Robin.

As the sheriff bent over the downed man, she slashed with all her strength at the back of deLacey's knees.

Legs buckled. Robin rolled aside as the blade lurched up. DeLacey collapsed to his knees, roaring his surprise; Marian, with methodical precision, smashed the crutch down across his sword arm. The blade clattered free.

"No," she said fiercely. "The trial is *over.*"

DeLacey clutched his arm, swearing furiously. "By Christ, you bitch, it's *broken*—"

"Good." His sword lay within reach. Marian kicked it aside, sending it chiming away to clatter against the dais. "My lord," she said to Robin, "will you recover your sword?"

He did with alacrity, moving to deLacey. Marian stepped away, now that she knew he was safe. Her hands on the crutch shook as the fury waned abruptly, leaving her weak and shaken. *Not now, you fool—show no weakness now.*

She looked at Robin. He smiled the kind of warm, private smile she had seen shared between her parents. Exultant, she grinned back.

There was a stirring in the hall. Men fell to their knees and blades were sheathed abruptly. "My compliments," boomed a voice, "to the lady with the crutch. A well-placed blow—*two* of them, by God . . . the sheriff should be grateful she did not have a sword to hand."

My God—is it the king? Marian looked quickly at Robin. She heard his muttered prayer, gratitude extended to God and Allah. His smile now was peculiar, a lopsided, tight-cornered smile, as if he were afraid to show too much of his thoughts. But his hazel eyes shone.

The king's joviality waned. "Where is my brother?"

Had John wanted to hide or to slip away, his plans now were thwarted as the crowd flowed away from him, leaving him alone and unattended near the center of the hall. In his fine blue tunic and fur-trimmed surcoat, with gemstones on each finger, he struck an incongruous and supremely vain figure before the warrior-king of England, who wore plain soldier's garb. Only the rich crimson of Richard's surcoat, emblazoned with the triple lions of England, hinted at royalty—that and the arrogant posture, the powerful *presence* of the man whom others called Lionheart.

John lifted his head. His eyes were unrepentant, though his expression was curiously blank. "Here," he said. "Here I am, Brother."

"Here," Richard said pointedly. As John approached, he said lightly, "See you the sheriff, John?" A gesture indicated white-faced deLacey kneeling upon the floor. The king's tone hardened. "Do you likewise."

John's face reddened, but he knelt. "I pray you, Brother, for mercy."

"Indeed." Richard kept him there on the floor, the dark-haired head bowed in submission rather than homage. "Do you know I have followed you from city to city? Like a dog hunting its master—only I am convinced it is the other way around, and you should follow *me.*" He displayed large teeth in a mirthless smile. "In London, they sent me to Lincoln. In Lincoln, they sent me here. I am so very glad I've found you, if only to rest my buttocks."

"Indeed," John murmured.

The king cast a quick glance around the hall, taking note of those present. Marian, who had heard her father describe the Lionheart, marked his height and wide-set stature, the powerful shoulders, the understated aggression in his posture. His blue eyes were large and slightly protruding, and exceptionally piercing.

I would not want to be his enemy. Marian looked at the kneeling prince. *I would not want to be his brother.*

"There, now, John . . ." The king placed one cupped hand on his brother's bowed head, as if comforting a boy. With perfect clarity—and quiet condescension—he forgave his brother so all in attendance might hear. "Think no more of it, John; you are only a child who has had evil counselors."

Seventy-Seven

Robin smiled crookedly, scraping sweat-stiffened hair from his face with a bracer-warded forearm. *He looks well for his captivity . . . better by far than I did—but then I am not a king. And no one else is Richard.*

In the sheriff's private solar, the king poured wine himself and handed the cup to Robin. The royal eyes were intent. "DeLacey did not harm you?"

Robin shook his head. "Only my pride, when he forced me off the dais." He laughed self-consciously, recalling his startled chagrin when the strategy succeeded. "That will heal, I think."

Richard grunted. "So will his arm, but his pride may require more time. Being beaten by a *woman*—" Teeth glinted briefly. He poured wine for himself absently, then prowled the chamber as Robin waited quietly. He was not a man who suffered stillness gladly; imprisonment must have taxed him. "Sit down—sit down, Robin; we have shared too much to wait on ceremony." Teeth flashed again in his ruddy beard. "By *Christ*, but what a battle Acre was!"

Robin agreed, amused by the king's high good humor. He was a man who thrived on adversity, at home or on campaign.

Richard nodded, prowling again. "It is good to be free, though I should lop off Henry's head for making me swear homage and agree to England's becoming Germany's fief, but what else was I to do?" He shook his head, swearing softly. "There are things yet to be done . . . I had spent too much time in Germany to wait another day."

"The ransom—?" Robin suggested.

751

"Part of it paid, part of it promised." Richard grinned. "I think Henry knows he will never see the balance. But what does he expect? He extorted unlawful promises from me that I could not possibly keep. I have duties to attend, and all of them require money." He sighed. "It is always money, Robin. There never is enough."

"No," Robin murmured, thinking about the ransom and his method of adding to it. *No need, now.*

"But as you've sent what you stole to Longchamp, there will be more to support the campaign." The king swung toward him, clearly unconcerned that anyone might steal *his* money. "That girl," he said abruptly. "What did you say was her name?"

Robin smiled. "Marian FitzWalter. Sir Hugh's daughter."

"Hugh's!" The king laughed. "Then I know from where her courage comes . . . those were two frightful blows she struck deLacey! He is fortunate to survive."

"Yes," Robin agreed dryly. "Marian has a habit of snatching up the closest length of wood to level the enemy."

"I should have had her on Crusade." But the humor waned quickly. "I wish . . ." His face colored. He turned abruptly away, speaking to the wall. "I wish I might love a woman the way you love her."

Robin sat very still. He could find no answer, nor manufacture one, to ease the king's discomfiture. "Yes," he said finally.

It seemed to be enough, or else Richard chose to make it so; he was bluff again, and jovial, speaking of his plans. "I'm to France, as soon as may be," he explained. "Philip is chewing at the corners of my empire again . . . it is time I put him to rout forever. I'll sail for Normandy almost immediately."

It was entirely unexpected. *He's just come home.* He could not imagine a king newly freed sailing away again; but then he recalled this was Richard. "My lord." His homage was deliberate; it would gain the king's attention, who asked informality of his Robin. "My lord, do you think it might be better if you remained in England? She has been hard-pressed by your absence."

"You mean my brother." Richard laughed harshly. "He is a fool, Robin; a greedy fool and an ambitious lackwit, to stir up

752

so much trouble. But he has learned his lesson. I'm stripping him of his lands and allowances; I need the money from them. He can swallow his pride and serve my interests . . . he will be most concerned to do it, if he thinks himself my heir."

"Will he *be* your heir?"

"Perhaps." Richard frowned. "There is Arthur still . . . Geoffrey was next after me, and I would like to see his son gain something of this. John was never meant to be king." He sighed gustily and drank wine. "But what does it matter? I'm but thirty-six; there are years left to me yet." He prowled again briefly, then paused and looked at Robin. "Will you come with me?"

"To France?" Robin drew in a noiseless breath and released it carefully. In this instance, before this man, there was only one answer. "I am yours to command, as always."

"No." Richard was serious. "No, Robin—friend to friend, I ask, not king to subject. Will you sail with me to France?"

Robin shook his head. "I have been too long away. I have, as you do, duties to attend—"

"And a woman?" Richard smiled, eyes briefly shuttered, as if he retreated. "A comely and valiant woman, very like my mother. I wish you joy of her." He assessed Robin again. "You think I am wrong to go."

Robin didn't hesitate. "Yes."

"Blunt as ever. Ah, well, so I ordered you to be." The king swallowed wine, then scrubbed dampness from his beard. "I can't stay here. There is Philip in France. We must settle things."

"Because he deserted you?"

"That, and other things. He will have my French holdings, if I take no steps to prevent him." His voice now was harsh. "England is not France."

"No." Robin agreed. "But England has need of her king."

"I could be King of France."

Robin gazed at him. *Do we mean so little, then, when weighed against France?* After a moment he nodded. "So you could, my lord."

Richard was abruptly brusque, as if afraid he had divulged too much to the man who would no longer share his confidences. "Now. I must ask you to leave me. I must speak also to deLacey, and to my brother."

Robin did not immediately move to go. He had his own questions. "What do you mean to do about the sheriff?"

"Provided he has enough money with which to apologize, I will let him keep his office." Richard laughed softly. "He, too, has learned his lesson. John led him astray, but he is an able man. While I am in France I will require such men."

"Such men may ruin England."

Richard's tone was sharp. "Then I shall charge you to prevent it! Hear me, Robin—look after my realm . . . what you can of it." His expression softened. "Do what must be done."

Robin rose, setting the wine down. "About my companions—"

"The outlaws?" The king laughed, in high good humor once more. "A shepherd, you said, and a minstrel, and a gluttonous monk?"

"And a murderer also—Will Scarlet killed your brother's men."

"After they raped his wife, you said."

"Yes."

It seemed enough for Richard. "I have no quarrel with them. Nor does England, now; tell them they are pardoned." He waved him toward the door. "Go, Robin . . . no—*wait*—"

Robin turned at the door.

Richard approached, pulling something from his belt-purse. Candlelight glittered off a faceted gemstone, and another. The king gestured as he reached Robin. "Your hand, if you please."

Robin put out his hand. The king set into it two of the earl's rings. Softly, he said, "Did you think I would not recognize the device of Huntington?"

For a moment Robin could say nothing. Then he smiled faintly. "I did not think you would see anything I sent to recognize it or no. But I am grateful it arrived, to serve the Lionheart."

"Sweet Jesu, Robin—" But Richard checked it. His face was expressionless. "Did you do as deLacey accuses?"

Robin's hand tightened on the latch. "We killed twelve men. We did not cut their throats."

"I thought not. You are not the man for butchery." The king was unsmiling. "I recall how you railed against the executions at Acre."

"Yes, my lord."

The king's mouth tightened. "Acre was necessary. If you argue it was not, think again what *you* have done."

"I did it for you, my lord. We all did it for you."

"Yes," Richard said, "and that is why the Crown will overlook what occurred."

They stood very close, but a pace apart, and yet Robin was very aware of the distance between them. He nodded, then lifted the latch. "In God's name, not Allah's, I welcome you home to England."

"Robin—" The tone was peculiar. "One more thing. Send your lady to me."

Marian sat on a bench in Nottingham's great hall. Confusion still was paramount; seneschals for the prince and king discussed with a tense Gisbourne and haggard Walter how to feed so many people, while others discussed the miraculous return of the king, and still others laid wagers as to how much punishment the king's brother might receive. She was interested in none of it. She waited only for Robin.

A woman crossed the hall, weaving her way through the throng. She wore an unflattering yellow kirtle. Dull brown hair straggled from her coif.

Marian waited. Eleanor at last arrived. Her sallow face was mottled with color. "I would do it again," she declared. "Given the chance, I would again . . . but this time I would do it better."

"Yes," Marian said. "You are very like your father."

Some of the hostility faded. Eleanor clenched fists in her kirtle. "Will he lose his place? Do you know?"

Marian felt an amazing serenity she did not know she possessed. She had expected to be angry with Eleanor, but anger dissipated beneath the acknowledgment that nothing now could hurt her. Robin was safe. So was she. "I am not privy to the king's mind."

"Privy to Robin Hood's *bed.*"

Marian laughed. "And grateful for the honor."

Tears shone briefly in Eleanor's eyes. "All I ever wanted was to be free. When I took that freedom and was discovered, dishonor accompanied it. But *you* escape it all. *You* sleep with Robin Hood, and yet regain the honor I can never have again." Eleanor's chin trembled. "It isn't fair."

"No," Marian agreed softly. "Nor was it fair when your father declared me a witch, and you tried your best to have me burned at the stake."

Eleanor opened her mouth, then clamped it shut. With a great show of hauteur—enough to rival Prince John's—she walked back into the throng still milling in the hall.

"Marian?"

At last. Robin looked drawn, and weary, and young. She tensed instantly, wanting to reach out to him, to comfort him somehow, but she let him dictate the moment. *His life as well as mine has been changed by all of this.*

Quietly he said, "The king would like to see you."

"Me?"

His smile was odd. "I think he wants to thank you."

It was incomprehensible. "I don't understand."

"Go and find out."

She pointed. "Just—in there?"

"In there." He reached down and caught her hand, drawing her to her feet. "I will wait for you here."

"Robin—" She touched his chin, tracing the scar. "I thought deLacey meant to kill you."

"So did I. He would have, too, had you not prevented him." Teeth glinted briefly. "No more tarrying—go and see the king."

"Like *this?*" She could not help herself. "I can't let him see me like this!"

"Marian," he said sternly.

She went to see the king.

Richard Plantagenet, King of the English, seemed ill at ease as Marian entered the chamber. She shut the door and stood with her back against it, hands folded primly in skirts. She was hideously aware of her tangled hair, grimy face, black-rimmed fingernails, and the odors of cell and smoke that clung to her.

When he looked at her she recalled she was to curtsey. She attempted to do a proper one and nearly fell, blurting an unladylike oath as her knees and ankles protested.

He was there at once, helping her up. His hand was huge and calloused, hard as horn; he released hers at once. He assessed her condition swiftly. "You have been sorely misused."

It popped out of her mouth before she could prevent it. "So has England, my lord."

His eyes widened slightly. "Yes," he said finally, "so Robin tells me."

She was red-faced and mortified that she had spoken so rudely. "My lord, forgive me—"

"No." The king smiled. "Yes, I forgive you—what I meant to say was, I should ask your forgiveness."

"Mine?"

"For being so laggard a soldier as to force *you* to act." He grinned. "In the hall, Lady Marian, when you broke the sheriff's arm."

"Oh." Heat flushed her anew. "I was afraid he would kill Robin."

"He meant to. I mistakenly believed he might listen to his king, but deLacey had other ideas." He turned the wine cup repeatedly in his hands, as if he were nervous. "You have done England a service by preserving Sir Robert's life."

He was much more casual than she had expected, using "I" and "me" in place of "we" and "us." There was no question of his authority, but he did not wield it like a sword above her head. "My lord, I would do anything possible to preserve his life."

"Yes. So would I." Blue eyes darkened perceptibly. He stood but a pace from her. Harshly, he said, "I wish you joy of your marriage."

There was something in his expression she could not interpret. "Thank you, my lord, but there has been no discussion—"

He cut her off with a brief gesture. "There will be. Be sure of it." His smile was slight. "I care very deeply what becomes of my Robin."

She understood him then. "Yes, my lord. I know."

"Do you?" He arched ruddy brows. "How *much* do you know?"

Steadily, she answered, "That he worships Coeur de Lion as a son worships a father; his own is not easily loved."

"A father." Richard's mouth twisted briefly. "A father—and a son." His eyes bored into hers. "Perhaps it is time I sired my own."

She said, "All England would rejoice."

The Lionheart laughed. "Yes, I imagine she would." He raised his cup. "To your health, Lady Marian. To *his* health also—and to England's as well."

This time when she curtseyed she did not require his help.

Robin sat on the bench as she had, slumped against the wall. He looked up as she came forward and put out a hand to her, drawing her down beside him.

Marian sighed, leaning hard against him. "He is—impressive."

"Yes. And persuasive. And many other things."

She smiled. "But not an unkind man."

"Not if it suits his purpose." Robin opened one hand. "A gift from Coeur de Lion."

"Robin—those are your father's rings—"

"Yes."

"Then part of the ransom arrived."

"Enough. Henry trusts him for the rest, but Richard says he will not pay it." Robin's eyes were bleak. "He has forgiven John. He will forgive deLacey also, provided the price is met. He even permits him to keep his office." He rolled his head from side to side. "Nothing is changed. I expected—more. I thought he would stay here and administer England, instead of sailing for Normandy to harry Philip again. I thought—" He cut it off abruptly, thrusting the rings into his belt-purse. "Does it matter what I thought?"

Marian shifted closer. "You said nothing is changed; it is. We are. You, and I, and all of us."

He laughed tightly in self-contempt. "We are pardoned out-laws."

"But alive, not spitted on a sword, or hanged on Nottingham gallows." *Or burned at the stake.*

"I wanted things to be *different.* I wanted him to stay. I wanted him to make England right again. Instead, he tells *me*——" He broke it off bitterly. "None of it matters."

"He told you—what? To tend England?" Marian smiled. "I cannot think of a better man."

He grunted disagreement.

She prodded him with an elbow. "Come, Robin—the others are outside. Let us not add to their worries by keeping news of the pardon from them."

"No." He allowed her to pull him up, then caught her shoul-ders in his hands. "Marian——"

He was visibly upset. "Robin, what is it?"

"This . . . just *this*——" He trapped her head in his hands and drew her face to his, then took her mouth with his own.

For a brief moment Marian thought of Eleanor and the others, of Gisbourne and de Pisan, perhaps even the king, who loved Robin also. And then awareness of them faded, concern for them dispersed; she gave herself to the man rather than the moment. She took back her own fiercely, impressing upon Robin that she as much as he comprehended the needs of a body once threatened by assault.

"I wanted to kill him," he breathed against her mouth. "I wanted to cut his throat, cut out his heart, cut to pieces his tongue . . . but how was I to know you would take a *crutch* to him?"

Marian laughed huskily. "Spine," she said softly. "I think I have finally grown one."

He kissed her again hard, then gently, then took her hand into his again and led her outside to the bailey, where Little John, Will Scarlet, Alan, Tuck, and Much waited with the mantle-draped horse.

Scarlet's face was white and tense. "Are we dead men, then?"

"No," Robin replied, "nor wolf's-heads, either. While the Lionheart stays in England, we are safe from the sheriff's jus-tice."

"Safe?" Little John echoed. "I can go back to my sheep?"

Alan's face was mournful. "I have no lute."

"Buy another," Robin said.

"I have no money, either."

"Steal it," Scarlet said, jubilant in forgiveness.

"Stealing's a *sin*," Tuck declared. "And we are past that, now. The king is home at last."

"For a while," Robin said in dry disgust, kicking aside a broken cobble. "Until he leaves for France to make war with Philip Augustus. Then it will all be the same again. *Exactly* the same." He glanced around, mouth knotting up into a grim, unforgiving line. "Let us go elsewhere. I weary of Nottingham."

Marian's throat felt tight. Here at last was the future. "To Huntington?"

"No." He was annoyed that she even asked it. "That is finished, Marian; whatever I become, it will not be the Earl of Huntington." Irritation faded, replaced by the warm, private smile she had seen inside. "My hall has burned, Lady—may I share yours a while?"

Relief blossomed painfully, filling up her spirit. "Then Ravenskeep. All of you. And if you want to stay, there is work for each of you."

"I'm a jongleur—" Alan began, and then a thoughtful look replaced his affrontedness. "It will take time to write my ballads."

"D'ye have sheep?" Little John asked.

"I have sheep. And I have a manor that needs men." She slanted a glance at Scarlet. "Even you." She looked away quickly so as not to embarrass him, or herself, and smiled at Tuck. "The oratory is small, but there is room for a monk. Perhaps we might even build a chapel." Lastly she looked at Much. "And I need you most," she said. "Who else will see to the running of the manor?"

Much frowned fiercely. "Robin *Hood*."

She looked across his head at Robin. "Robin Hood is no more."

"Here," Scarlet said. "What about the money? Doesn't the king need it?"

Robin looked at Tuck's horse, muffled in cloak and coin. His eyes were speculative.

No, Marian thought. *He wouldn't—*

Robin glanced back at the keep, then looked again at the cloak-swathed saddle. "No," he said lightly, "the king doesn't need it—not as much as others do. We'll give some of it back to the Jews, who raised most of it; and some of it to the people of Locksley, so they can rebuild the village; and the rest to poorer folk who need it much more than the king."

Alan's eyes narrowed. "That doesn't sound like Richard Plantagenet."

"No," Marian said, sighing, "it sounds like Robin Hood."

"Lionheart," Much murmured.

Robin caught him under the arms and swung him up into the saddle, leaving him perched atop the mantle. "The Lionheart," he said, "is a very busy man. There are still wars to be fought." He looped up the reins and gave them to Much. "Ravenskeep," he directed, "hard by Sherwood Forest."

Alan laughed softly, slanting a bright glance at Marian as his eloquent voice rang out:

> *And I shall think my labor well*
> *Bestowed to purpose good,*
> *When it shall be said that I did tell*
> *True tales of Robin Hood.*

Robin swore. "I am not the man for *that.*"

Marian looked at Alan. In perfect accord they grinned at one another as, with grave deliberation, Robin Hood robbed the king for whom he had learned to steal.

AUTHOR'S NOTE

The reconstruction of popular myth carries with it the burden of preconception and expectation; no reader, touched in some fashion by the Robin Hood legend, can escape certain preferences in the manner of retelling.

Lady of the Forest is not a recounting of the classic story, because there *is* none; the ballads that introduced Robin Hood to English folklore (initially mentioned in 1377 via *Piers Plowman*) consistently contradict one another throughout the several centuries of their creation. This novel therefore is purely my own concoction, a fictional interpretation of imaginary events leading to the more familiar adventures depicted in novels, TV productions, and films.

Lady of the Forest is more properly a "prequel"—the story of how the Robin Hood legend was born. The major emphasis is on Marian's contribution, but I also desired to create a logical underpinning to the otherwise unwieldy version of the disinherited earl's son forming a band of outlaws. The social stratification of the times would not permit the admixture of such distinctly delineated social classes; the events in *Lady of the Forest* are my attempt to explain in believable fashion how such an unlikely admixture might occur.

Many scholars have investigated Robin Hood with an eye toward proving or disproving his existence. Evidence appears to support the theory that no single outlaw existed to fill the role we know, but that "Robin Hood" was a composite of several outlaws, including Adam Bell. Adding to the confusion are the conflicting opinions regarding the actual time frame; different versions of the ballads present Robin as active during the reigns of three separate kings: Richard I, Edward I, and Henry III. As entire books have been written on the subject, among them Professor J.C. Holt's excellent *Robin Hood,* and Maurice Keen's *The Outlaws of Medieval Legend,* I will not attempt here to outline proofs and theories, but urge readers to investigate on their own.

Authors who care deeply about historical accuracy are often faced with a dilemma: to relate documented facts in a cut-and-dried fashion that quite often harms a story's dramatic potential, or to use history like a crazy quilt, stitching together the truthful patches with the fictional ones. I have employed the latter method.

Historians disagree with regard to Richard I's apparent homosexuality. I adhere to the conventional opinion for the purposes of this story. Supposition aside, it must be noted that while Richard married Berengaria of Navarre solely to gain her father's financial and military support for the Third Crusade, this sort of political alliance occurred frequently. That he sired no children also is no infallible indication of sexual preference— Richard was too busy crusading and making war to spend much time with his wife, though one might argue a king would acknowledge the distinct need for an heir.

Although the Lionheart as hero has indelibly stamped history with his charismatic presence, he too suffered documented bouts of the family temper tantrums. His facility for brutality and selfishness is evidenced by his execution of 2,600 captive Saracens following the Siege of Acre, and his apparent indifference to his English realm—during the ten years of his reign, Richard spent only four months in England. He died of gangrene in France in 1199 while besieging a castle erroneously reported to contain great treasure. For those interested in historical trivia, it should be noted that Richard's quote regarding Prince John and "evil counselors" is a documented one, as was the note Philip of France sent to John upon Richard's release.

Any linkage of Prince (or King) John to the Robin Hood legend conjures the term "evil." While John indeed tried to steal his absent brother's throne, kidnapped an affianced bride from a powerful baron (he later married her), and murdered his nephew, Arthur of Brittany, he was neither a stupid man nor a complete fool. As king he proved a far more able administrator than his brother, but had an unfailing knack for infuriating and alienating powerful barons. Americans in particular may look to this latter trait with approval; John's actions led to a revolt of the barons, among them the Earls of Alnwick, Hereford, and Essex, who created and forced John to sign the Magna Carta in 1215, thereby laying the foundations for the U.S. Constitution.

One of the most difficult aspects of writing a historical novel is how to accurately portray female characters. Contemporary authors are often taken to task for imbuing medieval women with anachronistic independence of thought and feminist leanings. In Eleanor deLacey, a character entirely of my own invention, I tread close to the boundaries; nonetheless, there were women of "loose morals" even in 1194—I choose to believe an Eleanor might well have looked to sexual dalliance as a means of seeking freedom of choice in an age when women had very little.

Marian is a truer product of her times, shaped by the ordinary responsibilities and expectations of a medieval woman. That she was freed to become something more (or less, depending on point of view) is attributable to the destruction of her reputation. In losing that, she gained the freedom to love where and when she most desired to, and the strength to make her own way.

Although Marian's small part in the ballads does not appear until the seventeenth century May-games, I hope I have done justice in bringing to life a woman who has, throughout distant and recent history, remained little more than a cipher.

I am indebted to a multiplicity of resource materials, foremost among them Holt's *Robin Hood* and Keen's *The Outlaws of Medieval Legend; The Ballads of Robin Hood,* circa fourteenth, fifteenth and sixteenth centuries, edited by Jim Lees; Elizabeth Hallam's *The Plantagenet Chronicles;* W.L. Warren's *King John;* and several books by Joseph and Frances Gies, including *Women in the Middle Ages, Life in a Medieval Castle,* and *Life in a Medieval City.*

J.R.
Chandler, Arizona
1992

DISCOVER DEANA JAMES!